AFTERLIFE

THE AFTERLIFE SAGA
BOOK 1

STEPHANIE HUDSON

Afterlife
The Afterlife Saga #1
Copyright © 2020 Stephanie Hudson
Published by Hudson Indie Ink
www.hudsonindieink.com

Afterlife/Stephanie Hudson – 6th ed.
ISBN-13 - 978-1-913769-18-5

*Afterlife is dedicated to my very dear friend Faith Cottrell,
whose unique humour and extreme kindness in life would have
the Gods both laughing with joy and being thankful for such a
pure soul. And as I like to say...
"We all need a bit of Faith in our lives."
What it means to have Faith.
All at once the world seems so small, lost in a vast space of
endless doubts,
But beyond the sky full of clouds and dust is the light we see and
the Faith in which we trust.
Friends' tears will fall and crash and burn,
And rain to our feet with an unspeakable yearn,
Heavy hearts and unrelenting hope we hold on tight,
Not giving an inch, not with Faith's strength and might.
Laughter, love and never fading warmth,
Is what your body sings,
To our lives every damn day,
Is what a Faith's soul brings.
To say we love you is just words on a page,
But to know we love you,
Is in Faith's way to gauge,
And you know to your very core,
That we want nothing more,
Than that love to shine through, because Faith,
We will always have you.*

*By an everlasting friend
Stephanie Hudson*

WARNING!

This book contains explicit sexual content, some graphic language and a highly addictive Alpha Male.

This book has been written by a UK Author with a mad sense of humour. Which means the following story contains a mixture of Northern English slang, dialect, regional colloquialisms and other quirky spellings that have been intentionally included to make the story and dialogue more realistic for modern-day characters.

Please note that for your convenience language translations have been added to optimise the readers enjoyment throughout the story.

Also meaning…

No Googling is required ;)

Also, please remember that this is the 1st book in a 12 book saga, which means you are in for a long and rocky ride. So, put the kettle on, brew a cup, grab a stash of snacks and enjoy!

Thanks for reading x

PROLOGUE

"Why are we afraid of the darkness when the light shows us more of the land of nightmares?"

I listened overhead as the footsteps grew nearer. My body convulsed as a natural reflex took over. Every fibre in my being was screaming as every sense told me danger was near. The smell of the damp space was flooding my nostrils as though a rotting corpse was sat in the corner. The palms of my hands bled from the nails I was embedding into them, knuckles bone-white until every finger ached.

I heard him now. The boots he always wore were like the drums of Hell, dragging him closer to me, and the sound was my very own personal mental torture. They were thick-soled like biker's boots, only every time he came to me, I never heard the heavy roar of a bike's engine. I knew I didn't have long now until the foul breath of a true monster was breathing down my ear, explaining to me how the things Hell created could feel… *Could love.*

I didn't believe his lies, for who could?

My breath caught in my chest as I counted the time in heartbeats I had left. Was this the end? My end? Was this the time, my final time, in which the darkness would drag me under?

The black space flooded with unnatural light and a figure

emerged like death's silhouette. No matter how many times he had come to me, I still couldn't prevent the gasp that escaped my bitten lips, already swollen and bloody. Fear gripped at them, making them quiver uncontrollably, the way they always did every time I saw something I couldn't explain. I wanted to be strong enough. I needed to be, or I would never be freed from this curse.

The time was now.

His time was at an end.

The sharp edges I wouldn't let go of dug into my hands, making them slick with blood. I heard that first footstep descend the stairs, but I wouldn't turn my head again. Turning away from the face of my death, I did what I had to do.

"Goodbye," I said with my last breath before my vision filled with blood.

I opened my eyes with a start, alert and ready. It took me a moment to understand my surroundings and take in all the other passengers who were staring at my sudden movements. I guess on a long-haul flight everyone was a little twitchy and the sight of me bolting upright gifted me with a few startled looks. It was fine; I was so used to those looks that it was second nature to me now. I was a master at feeling numb and I stared ahead as if no one else was around.

I scratched my arms out of sheer habit as the details of my recurring dream came back to me with a nauseating churn in my stomach. I tasted the familiar flavour of bile in my mouth. The dark aftertaste my dreams always provided. I looked down at my arms and I released a sigh when I saw the long sleeves of cotton that covered them. The dream wasn't how it had happened, but it was always the same way my mind played it back to me, no matter how wrong the details were.

"Did you have a nightmare, dearie?" I almost jumped as the first person in hours spoke to me. A plump, grey-haired lady with a flower print top that looked like it had once been curtains smiled at me, as she waited for the only words I could say.

"Something like that."

CHAPTER 1

NEW WORLD

New sights. New smells. New life.

This was New England.

And this was my last-ditch attempt at making something of my life, something that would be better than my past. So, I hitched up my shoulder bag and bent my knees to pick up the two suitcases that held everything I wanted to bring with me into this new life venture. I felt brave and slightly empowered with the knowledge that I had actually done it. I had boarded that plane and let it bring me here to start over. Yes, this was going to be a good thing.

I looked up, nodded to myself and started to walk with confidence that lasted all of half a second. I made it two steps when one of the other herded passengers bumped into me from behind, knocking my bag from my shoulder and making me stumble a step.

"Good start, Keira," I muttered to myself. Of course, now instead of walking through to the arrivals gate at Portland's International airport looking ready to take on the world, I was dragging a bag along the floor and walking along being pushed and shoved like the rest of the cattle. But none of this mattered, not when I saw her waiting for me.

"Libs!" I shouted as I jumped up and down, taking my bags

with me and looking like an overweight bird struggling to take off.

"Kaz?" My sister said trying to look over the tops of heads, and as soon as I saw an opening, I went for it. I ran with my cases rocking behind me as though they couldn't keep up on their pathetic little wheels. 'Sod it' I thought dropping them not far from my sister and her husband who were both waiting for me. I ran into my sister's arms as she ran into mine. We embraced as though we hadn't seen each other for years when, in actual fact, it had been about nine months.

"Kazzy!" She shouted in my ear, making me smile at hearing my nickname once again. I looked over her shoulder at her husband Frank to see him wink at me before going to save my bags from the human stampede. He was a good man and one, luckily for me, who was built to handle the masses. I smiled as I saw everyone getting out of his way.

"Hey Libs, I guess you missed me then," I said laughing as I felt the air being squeezed from my lungs.

"Oh, I don't know, maybe a little." I laughed and nudged her on the arm after she finally let me breathe freely.

"Yeah right," I commented, making her smile.

"Hey kiddo, you do know we don't have a shortage of rocks in this country, right?" He asked and then pretended someone with those heavy weightlifting arms was struggling to lift my measly cases.

"Ha, ha, whatever tough guy!" I said, leaving my sister's side to hug my big bear of a brother-in-law. He hugged me like he meant it, which was something he always did, and then lifted me up, causing me to do the whole girly thing and squeal in surprise. I had been lucky to get on very well with who my older sister had decided to marry, but the only downside had been where he hailed from. I didn't mind him being from the US, for starters, his accent was fun to have around, but what had sucked was that Libby had moved away and that had been like saying goodbye to my best friend.

It had been hard at the time; I realised that, especially after certain things happened in my own life, things we don't speak of for obvious reasons. But we all knew it was what she wanted and for the most part, other than missing her family, she loved it here. And now I was about to discover why for myself.

"So how did Mum and Dad take the big send-off... did poor Mum do that sniffing thing?" She referred to our mother and her sweet attempt at trying to keep the tears at bay. This, however, only ended in this endearing snuffling noise and I hated to say it, which reminded me and Libs of a pig sniffing out truffles, a very cute pig mind you.

"Oh yeah, there was truffle finding by the plenty," I said making Libby laugh as we had both discussed this habit before, ever since we were kids and Libby went off to camp with school. Anyone would have thought she had been called off to war with the way my mum tried not to cry.

We both laughed as we walked out of the airport, and I continued to tell my sister all the news from back home. It was a strange feeling to know that pretty soon I would be pulling up to a new house and calling that my new home. But in truth, I was more than ready for it as there were just some things you just couldn't get over, not unless you left the country.

The decision had been hard for my mum and dad as they had been torn between what was right for me and what was best for them. They had already lost one daughter to the States, and the idea of losing another hadn't been very high up on their bucket list. I felt bad, but I knew sticking around was only making it worse. I was an adult after all, and according to my passport twenty-one years old, so it wasn't as if I needed my parents' consent. In the end, it was simply my own decision to make and I made it... truffle finding or not.

I wanted to do something with my life, but like many, at my age, I was still at a loss as to what it was. I knew that I wanted to go back to college and start afresh, giving myself once again that reason to get up in the mornings. It had been so easy to lose myself into that dark place; now I was out of it, I never wanted a trip back there.

I found out from Libs that Mum had already called her to inform them I got on the flight okay and when to expect me, which made me smile. I knew my parents would worry; it was natural for any parents but mine had even more reason to worry, and I hated knowing that. I shook the dark thoughts from my mind before they had chance to develop further. 'You are not going there today' I told myself firmly.

"Man, it's freezing!" Libby complained, and I suppressed a giggle. My sister hated the cold, and if she'd had her way, I would have been arriving at Los Angeles International airport if Frank hadn't been born and bred here. His family all hailed from these parts, and this was where he wanted to start a family more than anything else in the world. It was sweet really and I knew my sister felt the same way, although it never stopped her from complaining about the cold.

"Still not acclimatised to the weather then?" I asked, looking to Frank and seeing him roll his eyes behind my sister's back. This time I really had to suppress a laugh, or I would've got him in trouble. We found the car in the sea of metal and Frank popped open the boot, which I knew was referred to here as the trunk. He put in my bags just as Libby said,

"No, and neither will you, just wait until you see it snow! We actually have to put snow chains on the wheels of our car." On hearing this, Frank actually snorted a laugh after slamming the door and then bravely said,

"We?" Libby shot him a look and said,

"What? I'm a girl, and I like heels…can you see me putting on snow chains when I am dressed for the office?" Frank smirked as he walked round to the driver's side of the car and said,

"Oh yeah, now I can…mmm." I burst out laughing at Libby's scowl that was only halfway there due to her also trying not to laugh. It was nice to see how well suited they were to each other. They bickered like any married couple did, but most of the time it was all in good fun, as there had been plenty of times they had been caught acting like teenagers.

We all got in the car, and I smiled when I saw Libby playing with the controls in an attempt to make this car the warmest place on earth. I saw Frank's secret smile as he checked out his wife's antics before pulling out of the space. I had always wondered what it must be like to find that kind of love. The type that brought on those secret smiles, insight of your loved one's quirks, or the way their stories were always told in parts with the other filling in the gaps.

I always thought that the unique 'true love' couples could make everyday mundane things, like cooking or cleaning, look like a well-synchronized dance. Or they knew what the other one was thinking with just a look or a single touch. And secretly, I had longed to discover what it must be like but never having been in love myself; I was left only to wonder. But in the end, I was just happy my sister had found it and in doing so, set so many futures spiralling down different roads, which now included mine.

The rest of the drive to my new home was filled with Libby playing catch up on gossip on subjects I was at a loss to understand, but I had to say, one car journey and I now knew by name all of the people that pissed her off at work. Libby worked as an interior designer for a company in Portland, and she lived for it. Whereas Frank originally worked as a bodyguard and now owned his own business recruiting other bodyguards for his security firm.

That's how they'd met, Libby and Frank. She was at a concert at the time, and he was contracted to provide the security. She had been stood in the wrong place when a fight broke out, and she had been knocked out in the process. She would have been trampled on if Frank hadn't been doing his rounds and seen the whole thing happen.

So, like a knight in a black T-shirt and jeans, he jumped from the stands and over the barrier to take my sister in his arms, shielding her from the angry mob that had started to join the fight. This quick action surely saved her from serious injury, as they needed three ambulances on the scene after the mob finally broke up. It was like a big halo hung around his floppy, honey-coloured hair that no matter how many times it was pushed back, always managed to make its way back in front of his kind, chocolate coloured eyes.

9

It was sweet the way she always told the story, and when he first got introduced to the family, you could almost see my father rubbing his hands with glee. As if a fine suitor for one of his daughters had just walked in and was soon to claim her hand in marriage. Okay, so it hadn't been that far off the mark as it was only six months later, and they were getting hitched… I think my father silently wept with joy that day.

As we pulled up the gravel driveway, my mouth dropped open at first sight of the house. I had of course seen pictures of the house via that beautiful thing we all called 'A way of life' better known as the internet. But now seeing it in person and I quickly realised my little laptop screen really didn't do it justice at all. I was amazed and just sat there wide-eyed and speechless. My mouth was still hanging open and a wide grin lit up Libby's beautiful face.

"So, I take it you like it?" It wasn't really a question as she already knew the answer.

"It's… it's so BIG!" I said without needing to exaggerate.

"Welcome home kiddo!" Frank said, twisting in his seat to look at me before cutting the engine and exiting the car. Libby and I both did the same and I was shamefully left standing there all wide-eyed and staring at the house whilst we let Frank do all the work. I was definitely overwhelmed.

"She likes it," Libby said as Frank retrieved all my bags in one hand, slammed the boot and grinned at his wife's statement.

"Of course, I like it, what's not to like…? But I bet you guys rattle around in a place that big or at least you must lose each other," I said, looking up and up.

"Nah, she just needs a few rugrats running 'bout the place!" He said beaming at the idea of producing a family for his worthy home, one I had to smile at since he called it a 'she' like you would a car or a boat. I looked back to the house and saw Frank with key in hand already with my bags at the door. At this rate he would be inside with a cold beer in his hand, TV on and sat in his favourite chair before me and Libs had finished staring at the place.

As I said, the house was huge and very timeworn but in the

best way possible giving it that ancient fairy tale touch. It had so much character I didn't know where to look first. The charming building was a large wooden structure with faded white paint that just added to the magic the place held.

Clusters of little nooks and windows of different shapes and sizes and slate-coloured roof tiles came down at different points on the unconventionally shaped house. The front of the house was framed with a large deck, which even had a swinging chair that looked as ancient as the building itself. Faded green shutters framed most windows, which were now nailed open after being retired during the installation of triple glazing. Still, the effect was enchanting and the whole aura left no doubt, this was one well-loved home.

What astonished me more was not just the house itself. No, it was more the grounds it sat in. Positioned on the very edge of the White Mountain National Park, we were surrounded by deep forest, and everywhere you looked were oceans of green. In fact, I think I was now looking at every shade of green on the spectrum.

The landscape was an endless tide of mountains overflowing with enormous trees that wound around the house like a barrier, encasing it in living, breathing safety. It was only when I followed them one by one did I notice a clearing to one side.

It drew me closer like a magnet as I walked forward to discover its treasure. Then there, in front of me, stood the most fantastic view I think I had ever seen in all my years on this beautiful planet. The vista exploded into a sea of even more mountains made from a lush green carpet of thousands of trees. Hell, it looked like millions!

The beauty before my eyes held me captive like a rabbit caught in headlights, taking my breath away. If I could cry, which I didn't do much these days as my tears had long run dry, I would have now. I wanted to show my pleasure in what I was seeing, but I was rendered speechless.

"As you know it was inherited from Frank's uncle." Libby's voice brought me back, and I turned around to see that she had followed me to the clearing.

11

"How old is it?" I asked, hoping for a background story on the place.

It definitely looked like the type to have a few horrors in its past. It wouldn't have looked out of place in one of Stephen King's novels or even the family home in Hitchcock's Psycho.

"Not really sure, everyone in Frank's family we have asked can't really give us a date. But it's been in his family for generations." She made a strange face as she said this, which made me think there was more to the story.

"What is it?" I asked, as light-heartedly as I could but from her face, I knew this was it, any minute now she would spill the house's deepest, darkest secrets and then I would never sleep again. Not that I slept great anyway, but I didn't care. I still wanted to know, no matter how horrible it was.

"It's nothing really, just a bit creepy, that's all." She leant around me to get a good view of where Frank was. When she was happy enough that he was out of sight, she continued,

"Well as I said before, Frank inherited this place from his Uncle..." she said whispering in my ear.

"Yeah, so what happened to him?" I asked, whispering back.

"Well, he...he committed suicide." She uttered this last part like a naughty word, waiting for my response with that usual sad look in her eye. Worried I suppose that she might have said something that could 'set me off'.

"Where?" Was all I managed, praying it wasn't in what was to be my new room.

"Oh no, no... not in the house, don't worry." I think she understood my mortified look of dread.

"Oh well, at least that makes me feel better, I was about to think I was going to have to share my room."

"Share your room?" She looked confused about my answer as we made our way back to the house.

"Yeah, with a ghost or I'd have to move in with you and Frank, 'cause I think I'd be too terrified to sleep on my own." We both laughed at the thought.

"Nah, don't worry, if that ever happened, I'd make Frank sleep in your room with his uncle. They would have something

12

to talk about at least... being family and all." This just made us giggle some more but more from a way to shake off the eerie vibe the thought left us both with.

"So, where did he do it then?" I asked, getting back to the morbid story.

"Oh... well that doesn't matter." Was all she said and then quickened her pace back towards the house. This clearly wasn't the end of the story, so I knew I would have to get it out of her later when Frank was out.

I followed after her, catching her up and said,

"Okay, show me this gorgeous house of yours!" Then I linked my arm with hers as we walked up to my new home.

I soon found myself sat on my new bed, in my new room, feeling so touched at all the effort my sister had gone to in making me feel at home. It was like leaving your childhood home a teenager and walking into this one as an adult. Obviously being my age, I didn't feel like a teenager anymore, and hadn't for some time due to past experiences we won't get into. But my room back home was filled with all things from my childhood you never seem to be able to part with. It still had old posters of cheesy bands I liked and Trolls and beanie babies on the shelf gathering age-old dust.

So, getting settled in this room took all of the four seconds it required getting to my new bed and sitting down. My new bedroom was at the very top of the house on the third floor, in the attic room which had been converted. There were other bedrooms in the house, but this one definitely had the best view.

I was fortunate that the window was on the side of the house with the amazing clearing. So, this meant I had my very own personal view, which was the serene vista of the national park. One that was laid out in front of me like a blanket of green ready to engulf the artist in me. This was why she picked it; she told me as we had climbed the second staircase. Frank had already carried my bags up and was now happily watching a game on the telly.

I surveyed my room and looked at all the effort my sister had gone to. It was amazing how well she knew me. There was a pine double bed with deep purple covers and a mountain of pillows to match. A bright purple lamp lay on the bedside table, which even had a copy of my favourite book on it waiting to be read.

It had been a while since I had picked up Jane Eyre, but I just loved the idea of dear plain Jane getting the rich and broody Mr. Rochester, above the beautiful and wealthy Blanch. I was now looking forward to reading it again, only this time with a view like that to sit in front of.

I smiled at the pictures on the walls which represented our lives so far. There were ones by the sea whilst staying at my grandparents' house in Cornwall, done in sepia. And then family pictures printed in black and white, from holidays abroad to Christmases and Birthdays. It was nice knowing how treasured you were, and it warmed my heart, seeing the proof of just how much my sister wanted me here.

Unpacking my measly cases didn't take me long as there hadn't been much I had needed to bring over with me. My parents had been more than willing to send things over, but deep down I knew there was nothing I wanted. This move was all about starting a fresh and moving forward, which meant not dwelling on the past. Of course, this was easier said than done but I was here to give it my best shot. Besides when I had mentioned the magic words to my sister that we would need to go shopping it was almost worth coming with just hand luggage for her happiness alone.

After this I couldn't wait any longer to go exploring. So, I grabbed my jacket, kicked my feet back into my shoes and made my way downstairs.

"Hey, it didn't take you long, wanna cup of tea before you go exploring?" Libby said as she straightened up from the freezer compartment after retrieving tonight's gourmet meal.

"Nah, I'm good thanks, I won't be long, I'm sure to be jet-lagged soon."

"Okay, pizzas will be done in thirty minutes." With that she went back to preparing the pizza, which consisted of opening a packet and turning the oven on to full heat.

Pizza, was about as much cooking as Libby did. If you couldn't just rip open a packet and bung it in a modern appliance, then it didn't make the grade with Libby. I was actually surprised Frank hadn't revolted or called mutiny by now the poor guy. Thankfully though cooking was one of the things I enjoyed doing, so was quite happy to do my bit and take over this side of things. Plus, I liked my stomach lining where it was and didn't fancy trying the food poisoning diet any time soon.

As soon as I opened the front door two things hit me. First, it was so cold that it literally took my breath away, turning it into a visible cloud of misty white and second was how fantastic everything smelled, helped by the lack of a polluting population.

I inhaled the heavenly scent of wet wood, damp grass and clear mountain air. I had spent so much of my childhood in the woods, that this smell brought back a flood of memories. Happy times camping with friends, nervous times, like when Johnny Carlson, my first boyfriend kissed me on that camping trip.

Then there were the sad times, like when I would argue with my parents (mostly about that boyfriend) and go running to the woods to be alone with my thoughts. But no matter what the emotion was, being there always made me feel better. Like an old friend giving me a big hug and telling me that everything would be just fine. It was as if somehow the elements of the earth knew what I was feeling and worked to ease every crying breath.

I would just lose myself in the smells and sounds of the forest, sitting there for hours, knowing it was the one place on earth I could truly be alone... somewhere not even my curse could find me. I tried to shake off the darker thoughts and focus back on the reasons I had come here.

I didn't want to be that whiny girl anymore. I didn't want to look up and find I had been sitting in the corner of a dark room holding myself and getting lost in what I had become…

I didn't want to feel *broken*.

I swallowed the hard lump that my body expelled at the bad memories and tried to inhale my new life. It seemed ironic that I was now living in a place that held 'New' in its title. Maybe it was a good omen and maybe that's why Libby had insisted to our parents that this move would be the best thing for me. After all she did know me better than anyone. A genuine smile curved my lips and it felt good it being there again. No, this time I was going to do it, and nothing was going to get in the way of that.

I followed the stone path that led from the house and took note of the old wooden fence that ran on one side. It looked to be patched up so many times I almost felt sorry for Frank considering it looked more like a lost cause. It led into the woods and only finished when nature had started to win. Years of shifting earth and wild growth had broken up the stone flags until eventually it was swallowed up, creating its own trail.

I wandered further along the beaten path made now from man's constant footsteps, walking further away from the house towards the thick wilderness. The ground was making squelching sounds under my impractical shoes as the earth was muddy from the fine rain that had started whilst I had been unpacking. Another thing I loved was the rain. It just enhanced the feel of the place, the mossy floor sparkled as the sunlight touched it and the trees swayed in the wind that had now picked up.

Then the majestic forest suddenly took on a very different look as the clouds darkened angrily, hiding the sun. The fine rain turned to heavy raindrops that fell to the earth like little water bombs, drenching my hair flat and curling it around my face. I decided to turn back before I got too wet and in truth, the dark forest had somewhat lost its appeal. Also, I didn't want to get lost. After all, I lived here now and there would be plenty of time for exploring. Also seeing as I didn't know anyone in this town, I doubted my social calendar would be fully booked for quite some time.

With wandering thoughts clouding my senses, it took me a moment to realise why the skin on the back of my neck tingled. You know that feeling you get when you're sure somewhere close by eyes are drinking in the sight of you. Well it starts with the creeping sensation at the base of your skull and then quickly has you spinning round in unsure circles.

I scanned the earth's natural maze for any other sign of life and tried to listen out for any other sound than that of my heart pounding a frantic beat. The gentle tapping song of water hitting leaves was suddenly disrupted as a branch snapped close by. My head shot around without thought and then I saw it.

A hooded figure stood in the shadows...

Watching me.

CHAPTER 2
VISITOR

My heart pounded an unnatural beat in my chest as my greatest fear flashed up in my mind.

"Not happening, Keira, get a grip." I whispered to myself without taking my eyes off the figure before me. However, the person just tilted their head as if they could hear me from thirty feet away but other than that, they remained motionless. It was nothing short of creepy that was for sure.

"Uh… hey there… are you okay?" I asked thinking one of us had to say something first, as we couldn't just continue to stare at each other until the sun went down. Or God forbid, creepy over there decided to speak with their hatchet and write their reply in my flesh… Okay, new rule, no more horror movies now I lived in the middle of nowhere. Not in a place where hiding a body would be as easy as finding a swing in a playground.

"It's you…?" A female voice penetrated the still forest and I instantly relaxed at the discovery. Now I looked more closely you could make out the smaller frame wearing a woman's fitted jacket. It was black with a big wide hood that covered her face and flared out around her knees. Whoever she was, she even looked small from the distance between us and I myself was only five foot three.

"I'm sorry?" I asked in confusion just now letting what she had said filter through.

"It really is you... she said the time was now and here you are." The musical voice seemed to draw me in, and I took a step closer.

"Do...do I know you?" I asked both trying to sound calm as if I might frighten her but also looking down, trying not to trip and break my neck on the uneven ground.

"Not yet, Electus, but you will... and so shall *He.*" She said, and I shuddered at the silent promise in the way she said *'He'*. I shook my head and fiddled with the edge of my jacket sleeve.

"I think you have the wrong person, lady," I said, and this inspired her to laugh gently... at what exactly I had no clue.

"Oh, I don't think so. You will learn who you are soon enough, don't you worry." I frowned before a humourless smile touched my lips.

"This is crazy, you don't even know me! Look, do you need to use the phone or something..." I looked back in the direction of the house and carried on speaking.

"...'cause if you're lost then my house is just... wait! Where'd you go?" I shouted as when I turned back the hooded woman was gone. I took a few steps closer to where she had been, my head whipping back and forth trying to find her. But she was nowhere to be seen.

"Did that really just happen?" I asked out loud. I walked over to the same spot she had been stood and looked around in all directions but there was nothing. It was strange and hard to explain but I felt drawn to her in some weird way. Almost as if she held the answers, but what the Hell were the questions?

"You're not making sense," I said to myself, shaking my head and in doing so caught a small flash of light on the ground. Right at that second the sun was reflecting its rays through the tiniest of gaps in the thick tree canopy above and shining it down directly on a small white card. I bent down to pick it up and as soon as I touched it the magic that was lighting it up vanished. I looked up to see the sunbeam gone and the forest around me grew darker from where it must have hidden behind a cloud.

"Um, this must have fallen out of her pocket," I said still crouched down and now looking at the stark white business card in my hand. It was blank, and I turned it over to check the other side to find nothing but a black glossy side that also held no words. I was frowning down at it trying to make some sense of why it would be blank when I turned it back over. It was only on doing this that I saw it. Two words that were slightly raised and only when held in a certain way did it become clear enough to read…

'Club Afterlife'

"Club After…Ahhhh!" I started to read it out when I screamed in fear at the same time falling backwards and landing hard on my backside. A massive black creature flew out from the forest floor coming straight at me. It snatched the card out of my hand, barely missing my fingers.

I still had my hands protecting the top of my head in case it came back when I finally braved a look. My head whipped from side to side, looking at all angles ready to protect myself once more.

"Jesus! What the Hell was that?!" I shouted with my hand going to my still pounding heart. Whatever it had been it was huge! I got up on shaky legs and brushed off the wet leaves and mud from my jeans and jacket once I was sure it was gone. Then my mind started to race. Was I seeing things again, was that it? Did this mean more pills for the crazy little Kazzy? God, I hoped not! I wanted to run back to the house and tell Libby and Frank about the girl but wasn't sure exactly what to tell them.

I closed my eyes and rubbed my forehead hoping this wasn't a sign of things to come. It was only my first day here!

"Great start Keira," I said scolding myself for seeing things. Well it was either that or admitting something weird was going on around here and I really didn't want to go down that route. Not when I hadn't even seen the town yet or had my first cup of tea.

But more than anything I hated the idea that there might have been a lost girl out there somewhere. And one with a few screws loose or still drunk from the night before, either way it wasn't a good thought. But then deep down I knew she was neither lost or crazy… or even drunk for that matter. For a start it wasn't as though I had walked far from the house. And let's face it, someone who is truly lost doesn't come across the first person they see and then sprout off a load of cryptic mumbo before doing a disappearing act.

But I couldn't chance it either so decided to try and reach out to her just in case. I mean she couldn't have gone that far.

"If you're still out there and lost, then keep walking north and you will reach my house!" I shouted feeling like an idiot talking to what appeared to be myself. So, with a shrug of my shoulders I turned around and left.

I could still see the end of the path through the trees but if I had walked any further it would have disappeared, replaced by a green wall of forest. I quickened my pace as the sky started to turn black and I wondered if there would be a storm tonight. I also worried that the girl could have been left lost out there to battle the raging elements. I shuddered at the thought.

When I finally got back in the house, I kicked off my shoes by the door and went straight in search of Frank, who was watching a game.

"Uh… Frank?"

"Yeah honey? You enjoy your walk?" he asked not taking his eyes from the screen.

"Umm, yeah, it was great but… well can I ask you something?" I was still trying to figure out how to word this without sounding crazy.

"Shoot."

"When I was out there I thought I saw someone, do people often go walking out there?"

"Oh yeah, we get loads of hikers and kids knocking around out there. It's not that far from the house where there's a trail, and further along is a clearing where they park their cars and stuff. If you saw someone then that's just the norm, although it looks like a storm is coming in," he said taking a brief look outside the sitting room window.

"So, if I saw someone, you don't think I should worry?"

"Nah, not unless they said they were lost. That trail is as clear as taking a walk in the park. So, don't worry your little head over it, Kazzy. Now if you wanna worry over something serious, then I would worry about what your taste buds are about to endure," he said nodding his head back towards the kitchen. I laughed once and then said,

"I guess I'd better go check the kitchen isn't in flames, wanna beer whilst I'm in there?" I asked nodding down to his near empty bottle.

"That be a good call there, Kazzy," he said smiling, and I left him to his game to go assess the damage.

The smell of burnt pizza and oregano came from the kitchen as I walked in, only to see my sister wafting the smoke from the oven with a tea towel. This made me giggle and laughter soon followed as she started to blame the oven. One look at my face though was all it took for her to join in. It wasn't long before the sound of her grunting laugh had me in hysterics and my own unfortunate piggy laugh started making me snort until it almost hurt.

"At least I can assume the kitchen's not on fire... that or you're high on fumes!" Frank shouted from the sitting room.

"Well, I hope you like your pepperoni crispy and well... your crusts extra crunchy," Lib said ignoring Frank's comment and trying to slice into what looked like a charred concrete slab.

"You forgot black and cremated," I cracked and walked over to her to kiss her on the cheek.

"It will be just fine, I don't much like the crusts anyway," I reassured her, only silently thanking the Lord that I didn't yet have any fillings in my teeth.

The pizza could have been made from drywall for all I cared, I was starving. She automatically poured me a glass of milk and handed me the plate. I headed back into the sitting room, with a beer under my armpit and noted that Frank hadn't moved from what I assumed was his regular seat. It was perfectly positioned in front of a huge flat-screen TV with what looked like an American football game still in full swing. I was used to a different type of football, and this reminded me more of rugby only with a lot more padding.

"Cheers Kaz," Frank said not caring one bit his beer had been nestled under my armpit due to having no free hands.

Libby followed me into the room and was about to tell him to turn it over, when I shot her a look to say that it was fine. I didn't really mind what was on. Plus, he looked like a man possessed, shouting players' names I didn't know and calling them very different names instead.

I smirked when he first realised he had been caught by his wife and Libby didn't like swearing at all. His face now looked like a little boy who had been caught drawing on the walls with a marker or cutting his own hair with toenail clippers. I had to swallow my amusement and bite my smile.

So, there was one person in this world he did fear then. My small-framed sister stood waiting for the 'sorry', arms folded and pouting lips. Of course, she didn't have long to wait.

"Sorry babe, it's just this guy's a joker, let one right by and well…" He was cut off with just a look and a head tilt in my direction.

"Uh… sorry Kaz." The sheepish look on his face made me smile.

"It's okay. I've heard a lot worse." And that wasn't an overstatement, as when I worked as a barmaid, I'd had to learn to tune it out. Libby huffed and walked back into the kitchen to get her own gourmet meal as I looked down at my own, mentally cursing myself for not eating much on the plane.

I waited for my sister to come back into the room before asking the question that seemed to be bursting to get out of me. She was just sitting down when I spoke.

"So, have you guys heard of a Club Afterlife?" I said knowing even without the card as proof I would never forget the name. Both of their responses were equally telling. My sister dropped her fork with a clatter and Frank coughed.

"The more important question is how *you* heard of Club Afterlife?" my sister asked frowning at me like I was the one now swearing.

"Lighten up, Libs," Frank said bravely, to which his efforts were only rewarded with a 'Humph' sound from Libby.

"Uh... I thought I heard some girls talking about it when walking in the woods, why... what's so bad about the place?" I asked after some quick thinking. I hated lying and one of the reasons was I sucked at it but what else could I say, I found a card and then some freaky bird stole it... nope.

"Ha! What's right about the place more like, it would be a shorter list!" my sister said before taking an angry bite out of her pizza, but then that probably wasn't a bad thing considering she would need the extra power an angry bite gave you just to get it down. Me, I just picked at a solid piece of pepperoni trying to think of a way to get the information I wanted.

"It's just a nightclub in town Libs, stop overreacting," Frank said rolling his eyes at my sister's dramatics.

"Oh yeah, you would say that, being that you're the one who supplies them with the security."

"Yeah, and do you think I would do that if I thought there was anything suspicious going on there?" At this she just huffed then ignored him to say to me,

"He hasn't even met the boss. I mean who arranges security for their club and never meets their staff, and then there are all the rumours..."

"Private people do that, Libs, and as for the rumours, that's all they are... *rumours,*" Frank said interrupting her and emphasising the word. I almost asked about these 'rumours' but stopped myself in time, not wanting to rock the marriage boat.

"Well either way, you won't catch me going there." At this Frank burst out laughing making Libby frown. I smiled even though I was trying to figure out the joke and when Frank caught my look, he elaborated,

"It's one of those Goth places. Lots of heavy metal screaming and black makeup... not really your sister's scene." I smiled looking at my sister's pink fluffy slippers. She was as far from a Goth as you could get, and this wasn't just down to the footwear.

She had naturally curly, fiery red hair that was always

perfectly styled. Instead of the normal fair skin she was tanned with a lightly freckled nose, this she got from our father. She had the most beautiful green eyes that looked more like jade stones or some deep lagoon you wanted to jump into on a hot day. They gave a lot of insight into her character and her feelings, which at the moment was utter distaste and that wasn't for the pizza.

"Sounds more up my street," I said knowing Libby would cut me a look... the place definitely had my attention now. Libby was about to comment when Frank beat her to it,

"Yeah, you're into all that headbanging stuff, aren't you?" I had to smile at this, as Libby rolled her eyes at her husband.

"I like my rock, yes, actually it would be pretty cool to get a bar job like I had before, if you know of anywhere that's hiring?" I asked thinking this was a great time to bring up the subject of a job.

"Don't you think it's a bit soon, you haven't even settled in yet and you know we're not expecting rent or anything?" At this I wanted to get up and hug my sister, but I also needed to reassure her that this was something I wanted to do. I hated being out of work but what I hated more was having free time to think too much into things, and thinking about the past was a dangerous place for me to go. Plus, bar jobs were easy to get so it shouldn't be any different here.

"I know, Libs, but honestly I am ready to get back to work, it will be good for me. New start and all that." To this Libby nodded reluctantly before getting up to put her half-eaten pizza in the bin. I knew where she was coming from and she was just worried about me overdoing it, but what she didn't realise was that it was more important for me to keep busy and my mind moving forward

"Actually, I have a friend who owes me a favour and if you want, I can put a good word in to see if he's been looking for extra staff," Frank said leaning forward as soon as Libby had left the room.

"Yeah, that would be great, is it like a bar in town or something?" I asked getting excited.

"Well put this way, you already said you'd like the music,"

Frank said with a wink and my heart started pounding. I wasn't sure why, considering I knew nothing of the place other than Libby didn't approve.

"Do you mean...?" I waited with bated breath to be sure I had it right, not even fully understanding why I wanted to work there so badly.

"Yeah, my friend Jerry manages the place, should be no problem, like I said, he owes me one."

"Wow, that would be great, thanks Frank."

"Thanks Frank what?" my sister asked, making her way through the arched doorway.

"Frank thinks he knows a place," I said enthusiastically, knowing that Libby wouldn't see the good side to this.

"Then it's sorted, I'll have a word with Jerry tomorrow," Frank said looking pleased with himself on saying this last statement, as if he had won some epic battle. Libby on the other hand still looked sceptical but refrained from saying anything more on the subject. However, I doubted Frank had heard the last of it.

By the end of the game, I was fighting a losing battle with my eyes to stay open. Libby had noticed how tired I was so had gone to my room and got the bed ready for me, which was sweet of her.

I made my way towards the bed like a zombie not really thinking about my feet and where they were going. It was as if they knew where to find the bed, so they didn't need me to think for them. This was good, as my head felt like my brain had been replaced with pink foam. I think I fell asleep before my head turned horizontal.

That night my dreams were strange and hard to decipher. I was back in the forest, but I was panicking because now I was the one lost. The weather was stormy and wild, producing a downpour that drenched my skin and the cold stung with invisible shards making my face numb. I kept slipping on the muddy ground where twigs and branches tore at my clothes from all angles. I was frightened as I heard the night's creatures come alive, but one sound cut through the storm and caused my blood to freeze.

It was the sound of a large bird calling out what sounded like a warning cry. I automatically ducked and cowered with my arms above my head as it was directly above my shaking body. I couldn't tell whether or not I was still crying, as my cheeks were both soaked from the storm and from fear. With quivering lips, I pleaded,

"I want to go home," in a whisper to myself but it was as if someone else heard my frightened plea. I looked up to see a bright glow light the angry sky and only when I blinked fresh tears back, could I make out the purple orb that started to pulsate and grow bigger.

It lit the forest life around where I knelt as it descended and all the black shadows of Demons that had surrounded me backed away and began to retreat from the kill they had engaged. My fear doubled at the sight of hundreds of creatures all scuttling backwards like crabs in a desperate attempt to get away, leaving me with no chance of an escape. Some snapped jaws full of bladed teeth at me as though it was my fault they were being ordered to retreat.

By the time the last creature had disappeared from sight, I got up from my knees and studied the source of the light more closely. It now looked like a huge ball of gas that was effervescent. I could feel the power it emanated like a small sun, warming my face, creating little beads of sweat to replace my dried tears.

At first, I was locked into place as my mind generated a mixture of possibilities, but in the end, sheer impulse took over and I started to move my feet. It seemed to feed from this, as with every step I took the more it grew. When I stopped moving closer it spoke to me.

"Come to me." The voice was purely hypnotic and hummed in my mind making me move my stumbling feet again.

"Yes, come to me... you belong to me." I felt my fear melt

27

away with every syllable that flowed from it and into me. As if the energy was surrounding me in a heat source so comforting, I could do little but obey. I took the last steps before reaching out to touch it. My fingertips were so close I could feel the tingle of my blood beneath the skin that covered them.

"Yes... be mine... Electus... The chosen girl... My Chosen One," it uttered before a man's hand emerged suddenly from the purple mist and encircled his strong fingers around my arm, encasing my limb in flesh and bone. His effortless strength pulled me forward and off my feet into the fiery heat of darkness. The solid band of his arms captured me, securing me in an embrace, holding me locked to a concrete chest of muscle.

I wanted to scream out in fright as my vision came up empty in the black darkness, relying solely on the strong touch of a male to keep me safe. Why was I trusting this, I didn't know, but for some reason I had never felt safer.

I tried to move to see what would happen, when the arms around me tightened possessively, pulling me even closer as the words of a very authoritative male spoke out his dominance,

"Mine!" he shouted as I felt my restraint slipping away into an endless abyss and my body collapsed into the arms of my dark possessor.

One word escaped my lips on a whisper...

"Yes."

CHAPTER 3
HOODED FIGURE

I woke up, my eyes opening reluctantly to the sight of a red glow slowly coming into focus. The clock by my bedside told me it was six-thirty in the morning and that I had slept for a good twelve hours. I decided it was best to get up as I doubted I would be able to sleep anymore no matter how tempting it was to stay in bed, if only to keep warm. I saw a blanket at the end of my bed and grabbed it to wrap around myself before braving the cold.

I looked around my new room and saw the perfect place to perch myself until the rest of the house woke. I grabbed the copy of Jane Eyre and I went to sit at the window seat of my quaint little attic room. As I walked over to the window, I noticed the ice that had formed around the edges, like tiny white spiders trying to make their way to the centre.

Wrapping the blanket around myself I curled up to keep the warmth in like a cocoon and looked out at the eerie view in front of me. Rolling thick mist invaded the scenery looking as if it belonged in some horror film. I imagined werewolves or some crazed beast eating tourists. The headlines 'Campers Missing' came to mind.

Of course, this brought back flashes of what happened yesterday, and my thoughts not only went to the girl but also the creature that flew at me. I shuddered and pulled the blanket tighter before opening my book. I didn't want to think about it or other dark things that usually followed that line of thinking. I came here to get away from my past, not relive it on a daily basis.

I had read this book a million times before, but I just loved the story; the forbidden love of master and governess. The thought of nothing but this unstoppable force they held for each other, a love so strong that it could call out to one another between space and time. Okay so I admit, a crazy wife held up in the tower did get in the way a bit but show me a love story that didn't have its ups and downs. I always skipped to the part of the story where they met for the first time and missed out the depressing childhood bit.

But something wasn't quite right. I couldn't seem to focus on the words as I sat there flicking through the pages. It was as though something was playing on my mind, and that's when the dream started to filter through. My eyes started to close as I replayed the dream, pulling it back from my deep subconscious.

"Mine!" The growl of a man's deep voice echoed in my head causing delicious chills to wrap around my body. This place felt safe and secure. His arms holding me as though they could protect me from the usual nightmares my mind had to face alone. But here… well let's just say…

Here, in his arms, I was untouchable.

"Good morning!" I woke suddenly to the sound of Libby's cheery voice entering my room. I peeled my face from the frozen glass and shamefully wiped away the cold drool from my cheek. I had to thank my lucky stars I wasn't stuck there, like that one kid we all knew growing up who was always caught licking ice from a frozen lamp post.

Libby was always happy in the morning. This was another trait we didn't share. I was not a morning person and I groaned as I unfolded myself from the window seat and the blanket I had been curled up in.

"Hey, what you doing over there? Surely the bed wasn't that bad?" she teased.

"Nah, the bed was great, but over here is a better view." I smiled then noticed what was in her hand.

"Oh God, you're an angel!" I said jumping up, forgetting about my tired limbs at the sight of a cup of tea. I eagerly took the cup from her hands and that first sip was like meeting an Angel in heaven. It felt good, warming me up from the inside as it slid down to my stomach.

"Mmmm nectar." This had been my only request before moving here. My mum was going to keep sending me a good supply of real English tea. I already knew from my sister's complaints that this was hard to come by as most Americans drank coffee, so this rule suited her just fine.

"So, what do you want to do today?" Libby said this with hope in her eyes. I think she had been starved of a good shopping partner for far too long.

"I'm easy, if you want to drag me around the shops, then that's cool with me," I said trying to sound as if I meant it. I didn't take as much pleasure in shopping any more, but it made my sister happy.

Her blissful face stared back at me and then glanced to my long sleeves. I instantly knew what she wanted to ask but she stopped herself at once, not wanting to upset me by bringing up the past.

Ever since the incident I hadn't shown any skin on my arms. I just couldn't bear the questions that would follow, and pity was not what I needed. So, I kept my scars concealed at all times, it was bad enough for my eyes to have to see them as a constant reminder. At least in this cold place I could get away with it with no questions asked. It was quite normal for everyone here to be wearing lots of layers to protect them from the bitter temperatures, so I told myself I would fit right in.

"It's fine, people won't notice," Libby said after reading my thoughts.

"Thanks," I said with a sad sort of smile that no doubt matched my pale complexion.

31

"Right, what's for breakfast?" I said with loads more enthusiasm than was needed.

"Umm… cereal. Sorry I really do need to go food shopping." I giggled thinking that my sister's idea of food shopping consisted of a quick nip down the frozen food section. At least if I went with her then I could get some actual ingredients.

"Cereal is fine, and I wouldn't say no to another cuppa," I said giving her a cheeky grin.

~

We had finally made it out of the house and were on our way to Evergreen Falls' mall before lunchtime. Libby took quite a bit longer to get ready than me. Of course, thanks to my new views on my appearance, I hadn't needed to apply make-up and my long hair was always pulled back and tied up in a secure clip. I used to dress and look quite different, making the same effort as Libby did. But now I just wanted to fade away into the crowd and not draw any attention to myself. Depressing I know but it worked well for me.

"So, do you know what you're looking for as there is this cool shop I know you're gonna love." I looked down at my ripped faded jeans and my scuffed-up old skull converse knowing she wasn't talking about a Nike megastore.

"Let me guess, it sells fashion gym wear?" I joked with a smirk.

"Ha! You in a gym, you're more likely to grow wings Miss Piggy snort." Libby sniggered then grunted a laugh which set me off.

"Oh yeah, you can talk, you sound like a…" The sight of a sleek black car coming the other way cut me off mid tease. Especially with its unmistakable grill and winged hood ornament you could tell instantly it was a Rolls Royce. The closer it got, the more imposing and intimidating it became with its jet-black paintwork and tinted windows. Libby saw me looking in awe as the shiny beast cruised effortlessly past us and I watched it until out of sight.

"Since when are you into cars?" Libby asked dragging me back from what had kept me so captivated.

"I'm not," I said still looking behind me, almost sure it would turn back around and start following us... but where I had got that thought from, I had no clue.

"Oh really? Then why is your jaw on the floor?" I didn't answer but just stuck my tongue out at her like back when we were kids. We were both silent a moment before Libby said,

"It looks like they're back in town then."

"Who's back in town?" I asked becoming even more intrigued with the soulful look on my sister's face.

"It doesn't matter, look we're here... let's park up and get shopping!" my sister said changing her mood now we'd arrived.

"Does it fit?!" my sister shouted through to my cubicle. I looked in the mirror at the long-sleeved top I had picked out and was currently trying on. It was one of those you could find in every colour, but the only one I was interested in was black. I didn't really do bright colours which was why my wardrobe was made up of various shades of grey. I pulled down on the bottom after rolling it down my curvy top half and was happy at least it didn't show my belly button. That was one of the many downsides of having an ample bra size, shorter tops and a bad back later on in life... or so my mother tells me.

"Yeah!" I shouted back before whipping it over my head, making sure my hair didn't come loose. I liked having long hair but rarely wore it down. So it spent every day knotted up into a big thick twist, instead of how it used to look, long and thick golden blonde waves down my back. Libby used to say I looked like a surfer chick when I wore it down, even though I had never been surfing in my life.

I grabbed the stuff on the hangers I wanted in one hand and the ones I didn't in the other before turning around.

"Ahhh!" I shouted falling back on the chair as a hand coming through the curtain made me jump. It immediately transported me back into my dream last night and the man's hand that had grabbed me.

"What do you think?" my sister asked shoving through a chiffon dress that was exactly her style. My hand went to my heart in aid of slowing it down and I answered,

"Yeah, it's nice."

"Okay great, I am gonna try it on then. If you're finished, wait for me by the shoes." I nodded to her hand as her face hadn't yet come into view and then realised, I would have to make my response audible.

"Okay, will do."

I grabbed my stuff that I had dropped on the floor and tried to get back to being organised before handing my unwanted items back to the assistant. The shoes were right outside the changing rooms along with the accessories, so I wandered over to check out if they had any fingerless gloves. I noticed the sunglasses and almost laughed when I saw they were on sale. Of course they were, as I thought it would be a while before anyone would be needing a pair, not when snow loomed just around the corner.

I was just picking up a pair that I knew my mum might like for their usual trip to Spain when something caught my eye in the mirror on the stand. It was a dark figure that moved across the shop and was looking at me. I turned around quickly but only in time to see them raise the hood of their jacket and leave the store. I took a few steps to follow but then my sister's voice startled me.

"Ooh, Mum would like those," she said looking over my shoulder at the sunglasses I still held.

"Yeah, that's what I thought," I said distractedly, thinking to myself did I just see that?

We paid for our stuff and walked back into the main part of the Mall. It wasn't as small as it had looked from the outside, having all the usual shops from shoes, sportswear, formal wear and a funky looking alternative shop that Libby had mentioned in the car.

The shop named 'Rebel Rose' had all the usual stuff you would see in a shop like this, Goth, Rock, Punk and Emo. But the reason I liked these types of shops weren't for the clothes, although they were cool. No, it was for the fingerless gloves that Goths seemed to love so much.

I walked straight over to the accessories and looked at my options. Libby didn't look comfortable in a shop like this, but that was because she was a complete girlie girl. We had always been different that way. I liked the alternative look, never really following a fashion, just wearing what I liked whether it was 'in' or not. My favourite look had always been my pair of faded jeans and a fitted T-shirt. But now I was looking for a way to wear some of my short sleeve T-shirts without having to keep my jacket on.

I picked up a pair of black and grey striped long gloves that could be classed as sleeves. They didn't have holes for your fingers to go through but just a hole for your thumb, the rest of the material came down past the knuckles. This suited me just fine, the longer the better. I already had a few tops with sleeves like this. The thumbhole had always been a kind of comfort to me. Sort of like knowing that with my thumb securely in place, no one would ever be able to see my scars.

With this in mind I grabbed another couple of pairs, one in plain black and the other in dark grey, and made my way to the counter.

The girl behind the counter was tiny and almost elf-like. She wore all black, which made her bright pink hair stand out like a loud beacon, screaming for attention. The dark make-up around her eyes didn't make her look as fierce as she had intended. She looked at me with curiosity, yet it was still friendly as she smiled at me. The girl took my items with spotty black covered nails and rang them through the till.

"You're new here, aren't you?" she asked in a bouncy, friendly voice which didn't match her 'I don't take any shit' appearance.

"Yeah, I just moved here, yesterday in fact," I said trying to sound casual.

"Wow and you're English!" she replied excitedly.

"Yeah, my sister lives here too." I indicated towards the door where Libby was stood waiting for me.

She looked at Libby and did a double take, not ever imagining us as sisters considering we looked quite different, and not just in style. We were very different, like chalk and cheese. The only thing we had in common were our figures. We were both five three with small frames and slim builds, which we had inherited from our mother along with our curvy top half.

Libby looked more ready for the office in her dark brown pencil skirt with tights and boots that made her legs look great. The fitted red sweater that showed off her beautiful hourglass figure finished off the look, complimenting her red hair.

When she had come downstairs, she had looked ready for a catalogue shoot not just a shopping trip at the local mall. I could see now why it had taken her an hour longer than me to get ready. I didn't wear makeup but thankfully I had lucked out on the skin department, only briefly going through the spotty phase in school. However, as punishment this then meant I was as pale as they came, and I always looked as if I had just woken from my crypt in the mornings.

"My name's Rachel Jane, but everyone calls me RJ." She held her hand out waiting for my response.

"I'm Keira…Umm Johnson, but everyone calls me Kaz." We smiled at each other as we shook hands. I hated telling people my full name, always holding my breath until it came out right.

"Are you at the college here?" I asked hopefully, as it would be nice to know at least one person before I started.

"Yeah, I'm going to be a freshman in a couple of weeks." Result, I thought enthusiastically. Okay, I'd better keep this going, just keep talking, maybe she would give me her number.

"Great me too, just wish I knew the area better," I said hoping she would get my hint.

"Well, let me give you my number and we could meet up

some time. Hey, have you heard of Club Afterlife yet?" My interest spiked on high alert when hearing the name.

"Yeah but I haven't seen it yet. I would love to check it out though." Hint, hint, I thought again.

"Cool, a group of us usually go, let me give you my number." She was already writing down her number on my receipt as she said this. She handed me my bag after ringing through the things on the till and taking my money.

"Give me a ring tomorrow and I'll let you know which night we're going there, that way I can introduce you to my friends."

"Okay great, talk to you tomorrow then," I said almost buzzing with excitement, and that wasn't just from the prospect of gaining new friends.

"Cool, nice meeting you, Kaz."

"Yeah, you too, RJ." I made my way to the door and turned to wave only to find her already on her phone chatting away. I could have sworn I heard her mention my name.

"Well done you, Kazzy," my sister said putting her arm around my shoulder and pulling me side-on.

"You got a date, I am so proud!" I rolled my eyes at my sister but couldn't help laughing at the same time.

"Oh my God, look at these shoes!" Libby shouted looking over my shoulder at the shop next to me. I looked but it wasn't shoes I saw. I squinted my eyes to see the dark figure stood watching me in the background which was being reflected off the store's window.

"I have to get them! And look 20% off everything in store… you coming?" Libby asked when she noticed I hadn't followed her inside.

"Uh… you go, I just want to check something out." She shrugged her shoulders and said,

"Okay, I'll meet you out front in ten," nodding to the front of the store. But my mind was elsewhere as I turned to find the dark figure was on the move. I decided to follow who I suspected was the girl from the woods as it was a similar jacket to what she was wearing. She had turned as soon as she saw me looking at her and her pace picked up, walking in the opposite direction. I, in turn, stepped up my pace as I didn't want to lose her but also didn't want to be seen running after someone in such a public place.

She took the escalators down to the lower level and I almost panicked as she went out of sight for a few seconds. I followed her, looking down momentarily as I chose my step but when I looked up, she had already reached the bottom. I ducked, looking to see which direction she was headed until I was off the descending steps myself and found her easily in the crowd.

I excused myself through some people and quickened my pace. I didn't really understand what was compelling me to follow this girl, maybe it was the feeling I got that I was being followed myself and this was the question I needed answering.

I saw her disappear around a corner by a stand selling cookies and as soon as she went out of sight I jogged to catch up. I ignored the funny looks from shoppers and almost skidded around the corner in my haste to catch up.

"What the Hell?" I said out loud as I was met with nothing. It was a dead-end, and other than having some cash machines there was nothing. No shops, no toilets but more importantly no exits. She had vanished.

After standing there looking around in bewilderment for a few minutes I left feeling disheartened to go back to the shop where no doubt Libby was waiting for me.

"Where did you get to?" Libby said loaded with bags. I had to smile at the sight... Libby was a sucker for a sale.

"Found more than one pair then?" I asked trying to mask my confusion at not finding the girl. She lifted them up and said,

"They needed friends." Making me laugh before helping her with her bags.

We had lunch and walked around nearly every shop the Mall had before deciding to call it a day. Finding the car was easy as the Mall wasn't that busy and most of the spaces were empty, which was surprising as when we found our car it wasn't parked alone.

"That's a bit weird," I said looking at the same sleek black Rolls Royce that had passed us earlier.

"Let's go," Libby said, quickly stuffing her bags in the back seat and getting in the driver's side as though we were being chased by the Devil. I followed suit as she had already started the engine, and as we backed out of the space I looked to see if I could make out anything through the tinted windows.

To my surprise there was someone in there already as the window started to descend and I gasped as the hooded girl came into view. But this wasn't the only thing that had me freaked. No, it was the sight of the figure sat next to her, still hidden in the shadows, but his silhouette was clear. I say 'his' as there was no doubt it was a male but now I knew I was losing the plot as I could have sworn his eyes had flashed purple as we drove past.

"Did you see that?!" I asked looking back at the car, but Libby had been too focused on getting out of there like a bat out of Hell.

The drive back gave me time to convince myself it had all been my imagination, one fuelled by a combination of jetlag and worrying about that girl in the woods. We got back after deciding to pick up takeout, much to Frank's delight, and after eating some crispy noodles, I was done for the day. I said goodnight and carried all my bags upstairs.

I had done well today. Okay, so everything I had bought was a shade rather than an actual colour, but I'd picked up some warm clothes. I had bought a new pair of jeans, two sweaters and most importantly a warm black jacket. It was a long coat ending below the knees with a warm interlining. It had long sleeves that were more like gloves as they had a hole you could put your thumb through. It had a big hood that hung nicely when down and above all, it looked waterproof, which was a must as Libby had told me how much it rained here.

It was fully dark outside my cosy window by the time I got out of the shower and dried my hair. I pulled on some warm sweat pants and an old T-shirt that I was using for pyjamas and a chunky woollen throw to put over my shoulders. I had put my long fingerless gloves on as soon as my arms were dry.

By the time I was ready for bed, I had already heard Libby and Frank make their way up the stairs, calling it a night themselves. I decided to tiptoe downstairs to get a drink before I turned in, and not remembering where the light switch was, I braved doing so in the dark. I was just about to knock into the cupboard at the bottom of the stairs, when a sudden flash of lightning lit up every window in the massive hall, illuminating my way.

Of course, it also scared the life from my bones and I froze, too terrified to move, with my hands clamped around my mouth so as not to scream. Then it came five seconds after the light, the loudest bang and crack of thunder I had ever heard. I put this down to the location, as it must have echoed off the mountains because it seemed to go on for what seemed like minutes.

I remembered something vague from my childhood that for each second after the lightning strikes the waiting for thunder represents a mile. So, therefore, the storm was five miles away. This was somewhat comforting.

It wasn't that I was scared of storms normally, but being in an unfamiliar house in the middle of what seemed like nowhere didn't appeal to me. In fact, storms kind of fascinated me. The power of them was so immense. I used to like to think of them being created in anger by the almighty Zeus, forged by his own hand to be sent to the Underworld ruled by his brother Hades. This was to be a warning of his impending wrath towards his treacherous brother living in the pits of Hell.

I nearly ran into the kitchen and turned on the light before the next angry blast of light could erupt. I grabbed a bottle of water from the fridge as I noticed that a heavy downpour of rain had now added to the night's stormy weather, and left quickly, now changing a light foot for a heavy one. I took two steps at a time desperate to be in my bed for when the next one hit. Amazingly, I only stumbled once, and considering the steep, uneven steps to the attic that were consumed by darkness; I thought that I did pretty well not breaking something.

Once inside the comfort of my own room and seeing the warm glow of my bed lamp, I felt as if I could finally breathe. I got my cold body into bed just in time before the next eruption. The explosion of light and noise indicated to me that the storm was now right above us and Zeus was most definitely pissed off tonight! This was by far the worst storm I had heard in years. It seemed to last forever.

I didn't know whether it had finished or not by the time I finally fell asleep, but I awoke suddenly to the strangest sound. I lay wide-eyed and breathing heavily as I waited for the sound again.

It reminded me of something trying to scratch their way out of my window. When I had been halfway in between sleep and consciousness, I tried to make sense of the noise, coming up with explanations in my mind as to what could be the cause of this irritating sound. My mind led me to a more familiar sound that our family cat used to make when she jumped up to my window ledge. Puddy, our big grey pet cat, used to scratch at the frame to get my attention hoping I would share my warm bed with her.

This thought quickly had me sitting in an upright position, frozen and staring out into the darkness. The noise hadn't been something trying to get out, but more importantly, something was trying to get in!

I sat waiting for the noise again hoping to God that it had only been part of my dreamy state and that I had imagined the whole thing. But then I heard it again and nearly jumped out of my skin. The clawing had become more erratic, sounding more frantic to enter my room and get to me.

My heart raced; it felt as if it would burst through my chest like the thing in the Alien movie. I still couldn't see what it was and knew that if I put my lamp on it wouldn't help. So, the only thing left for me to do was to get out of bed and walk over to my window to get a better look. The problem with this plan... I wasn't sure that I wanted a better look.

It was getting louder now, and I did think briefly about waking up Libby and Frank but then what if it had been nothing or was gone by the time I got back to the room. I would feel like one of those kids waking their parents up from a nightmare about monsters under my bed.

I decided that I had been through worse things and that I

would brave it. It was just harder to get my legs to agree with my decision, as my body and mind refused to co-operate with each other.

Finally, I got to my feet and stood very still waiting for the noise to begin again, wondering if I would ever be able to get back to sleep not knowing what it was. I had to find out even though I was terrified.

I crept forward taking a deep breath with every step I took until the vision started to get clearer. The clawing was so violent that the glass sounded near to shattering at any second. Suddenly, I was beyond all fear and ran over to the window as fast as I could, tripping over the clothes I had left on the floor and falling into a heap on the window seat. This put me face to face with the creature trying to get inside.

Two huge black wings battered against the window in frustration as the thick set of claws on each foot looked deadly enough to rip through skin like a hot knife through ice cream. I sat staring at this enormous bird trying to destroy my window. I was fixated as I couldn't move.

It looked like a raven only more the size of a giant eagle. Its scruffy feathers all looked as if they had been pushed backwards. Not at all like the usual majestic birds I'd seen on TV. Oh no, this one looked bloody possessed! What had come over this creature to want to behave this way? It looked almost Demonic with eyes bulging with a fierce hatred that glowed in the darkness. It was the look of a killer that had finally found its prey.

Just then a great scream rang through the dark sky... no, not a scream but more like a roaring howl. I had never heard anything like it before. It sounded part animal, part man, part... *something else.*

The bird heard it too, pushing from the window frame and launching itself into the night and towards the direction the noise had seemed to come from.

My mind raced as I still sat at the window, looking for any explanation as to what just happened. Had it even really happened or was I still asleep? Was this another dream and if so, where were my solid arms keeping me safe this time?

When I had been taking my medication, I would often hallucinate, seeing strange things but even then, I was sort of aware that the reason at the time was due to the drugs in my system. This was not the same at all. Whatever had happened, one thing I knew for sure was that it had been real.

My mind wandered through any explanation I could think of, none of which made any sense. I finally crossed the room towards my bed when I stopped dead as something important hit me. The memory of the look on the creature when it too had heard the same blood-curdling sound that ripped through the forest.

The same forest where something black had flown upwards scaring me that day. And that howl wasn't just some random sound the forest produced at this time of night.

No, this was something more, this was…

Its master calling.

CHAPTER 4
NEW FRIEND & DARK STRANGER

T he rest of the week went relatively quickly and well,
more importantly, without any more crazed bird
incidents. However, it didn't keep me from wondering
what the hell had happened that night or with the hooded girl.

I had been for numerous walks and hiked as far as I could
until I was sure I knew the area in hopes of seeing her again so
that I might demand answers, but there had been no sign of her. I
soon moved on and tried to forget about it ever happening,
which helped when I arranged to meet up with RJ for coffee at
the Mall.

The week hadn't completely gone without some progress
towards this new life I was trying to create. I had landed myself
a job as a waitress at Club Afterlife, thanks to Frank's
connections. Better still, this all happened without even needing
an interview. All I had to do was show up for my first shift the
following week. Libby didn't take this news well and acted as if
working there was the equivalent to signing myself up to a death
cult. I heard her and Frank arguing about it that night, and I felt
bad for him. But I was impressed to hear him standing up for
himself, and in doing so letting Libby know that this was not
only what I wanted but also what I *needed.*

I really did need a job, besides, from what I had heard from
Frank, it was where most of the… and I quote "kids your age"

hang out. Although trying to explain to someone in their thirties that being in your twenties no longer qualified as 'being a kid' was met with deaf ears.

At least there I would meet other people if the RJ thing didn't pan out. Luckily, I wouldn't have long to wait to find out as I was due to meet her in about twenty minutes.

Libby had been kind enough to offer to drop me off as she wasn't due back in work for another week. She had booked time off to help me settle in and show me around.

This included taking the time for us to sisterly bond on a hiking trip, which I quickly discovered to be a passion for her and Frank. She showed me the best spot to find on a clear day. Unfortunately, it had been cloudy and raining at the time, but it was still an amazing view. A brilliant place for a date, she told me with a wink, to which I groaned. It had been nice spending time together, almost like we were making up for lost time. In fact, the more time I spent here, the more at home I felt and the more convinced I became that I had made the right decision... that was if I didn't die on the way to the Mall.

"Slow down; I'm not late, Libs!"

"What? I'm doing the speed limit," she said, oblivious of the other angry drivers around her giving her the one-finger salute.

"Yeah right, around the bends maybe. See that thing there, next to the accelerator? It's called the brake. Maybe you should think about using it once in a while." I only half-joked.

"You just chill out about my driving and worry about meeting the Goth."

"What... I'm not worried!" I didn't even convince myself with this statement seeing as my voice went high pitched at the end.

"Okay, then why did it take you longer than me to get ready this morning? Plus, your room looked like a bomb went off and the clothes were the shrapnel." This was true; it was a complete disaster zone.

It wasn't that I was worried, but more apprehensive. It had been years since I had to do anything like this, and it felt like high school all over again. The panic was more down to not knowing what questions were going to be asked. It felt like a test that I hadn't studied for... Hell, I didn't even know the subject. It was the 'where are you from?' and 'why did you move here?' questions that I was dreading. All seemed perfectly normal things to ask, but for me, these were the times that my answers needed to be constructed from lies...And I was a really bad liar.

In the end, I chucked on a pair of old jeans that had seen better days, a pair of trainers that had the same problem, and of course a long-sleeved top that was grey with thin black stripes. My hair was wrapped up tightly into a twist which was held securely by a large metal clip. This had a butterfly on one side and a rather large point on the other.

I had bought this from a Christmas market the previous year thinking it would serve two purposes. One, with being made of metal it would be strong enough to hold up all my long thick hair, and secondly, it would also make a useful weapon. And going off my track record the second was a comfort.

We pulled up in the parking lot right outside the main doors as it had started to pour down with rain.

"Well, good luck. I have some stuff to do, but I'll be back here in about an hour...okay?"

"Yeah okay, no problem, I'll meet you here."

I got out of the car and ran towards the swinging doors, and as I turned to wave, I just caught a glimpse of Libby making a speedy getaway. I would have to talk to Frank about her driving to see if he couldn't talk some sense into her. Thanks to her speeding, she had dropped me off with ten minutes to spare. I walked over to the escalators and up to the food court. I remembered my way from last week's shopping trip and knew exactly which coffee house I was meeting RJ at, so I had time to find a seat before she got there, or so I thought.

I walked through the door to find a bright pink-haired girl sat in the corner. She wore all black like the last time I had seen her, except for a very long multi-coloured scarf. It was wrapped around her neck a few times but still managed to make its way to her feet. Her hair was cut short and spiked into pink points at the back, a style that suited her look. She waved and stood up just in case the erratic waving hadn't caught my attention. I couldn't help smiling as I walked over to the booth she occupied.

"Hey Keira, how's things?"

"Yeah, good thanks, but you can call me Kaz, everyone else does," I said sitting down.

"Cool, so what have you been up to? Have you settled in yet?"

"Yeah, just about, I didn't really have that much stuff to unpack as most of it is still in England with my parents." I smiled at her look of horror.

"That sucks, are they going to send the rest of your stuff over?" If she had seen what most of it was then she wouldn't have thought this. Unlike most girls, I didn't collect shoes or have handbags galore. Nor did I wear jewellery or really have anything of much value.

"Nah, but my mum said she would send anything I needed over to me. This was the main reason behind the shopping trip last week; I was in dire need of a warm jacket." She smiled at this last statement.

"Yeah, it gets pretty cold out here, just wait until winter, and you'll be sleeping in that jacket!" We both laughed. She was so easy to talk to I didn't know what I had been worrying about.

A waitress came over to take our order but didn't look so happy at the task. She was quite old and haggard looking with white hair with some patches of grey. There were deep, dark circles that lined her eyes along with the most wrinkled skin I think I had ever seen. The uniform didn't help her appearance as it was a pasty green shirt that looked to be the same colour they painted hospital walls. She looked ill and the colour brought out the green tinge in her skin.

"What do you want?" A rude, harsh voice came from a pair of thin tight lips that looked like she was more used to sucking a lemon than chewing gum! RJ's bubbly voice answered first.

"Cappuccino, please." She turned to me but didn't meet my eyes.

"And you?" Was all she said, which sounded more like an order than a question.

"Hot chocolate, please." I always felt like a child ordering this, but I didn't like coffee, and I doubted that they had English tea.

"Oh, and can I have a double chip muffin?" RJ's voice was the complete opposite to the waitress' whose name tag revealed her to be called Meg. She just gave a vague nod and walked away towards the counter to start the order.

"Wow, she was happy, must love her job," I said with a sarcastic tone.

"Yeah," RJ agreed and giggled,

"Don't mind her, she's never happy, and she's been working here for years. I think she used to go to school with my mom but dropped out. She's been working as a waitress ever since."

I now understood why Meg wasn't the happiest person in Evergreen Falls.

"Ah, I see," was all I could think to say.

"So how come you moved to little old Evergreen, if you don't mind me asking?" And there it was. The dreaded question I knew was going to be asked and the one I didn't yet know how to answer. Oh, I knew the truth. I was running from my past, and it had brought me here, but I couldn't come out with that for an answer. It always made me laugh the way people added 'if you don't mind' to the end of a question they really wanted to know. What was I going to say in reply, 'Hell yeah, I do mind!'

Just then, the waitress brought us our drinks, which gave me a bit more time to think of an answer that seemed logical. She dumped them down and walked off.

RJ blew on her cappuccino and looked up at me with big eyes that were caked with thick black make-up.

"You were saying," she said as she studied my face for an answer.

"Umm… well I decided to move here because…" think Kaz, think!

"…because of Libby, my sister," I finished, mentally slapping myself upside the head combined with that inner voice, hand on hip, giving me attitude saying, 'smooth Kazzy, real smooth'.

"Your sister?"

"Uh...Yeah... she was kinda missing her family and stuff, so I decided to move here and start college in the new term." This was partly true as she did miss us in the beginning.

"Wow that was really good of you, you two must be real tight."

"We are, she's not just a sister she's a friend too."

"That's cool, I have a sister, but she's younger than me and is going through her bratty teen years, driving my Mom crazy, along with us all for that matter!" We both laughed, and I couldn't help wondering if they were as different as Libby and I was.

"Yeah, I get on better with my brother Jack, he's two years older than me, but we spend a lot of time together as we hang with the same crowd. He's into rock music like me... Hey, speaking of which, what type of music are you into, 'cause there's this great live band playing at this club called Afterlife. I think I mentioned it before in the store, but a bunch of us are going tomorrow night and it would be great if you could come." That word 'Afterlife' started to have a magical pull to it, one I didn't fully understand, but I knew this was the perfect opportunity to learn more about it.

"Sounds great, I love live music and pretty much like most of the ones on your bag," I said nodding to her canvas bag that was covered in pin badges. She looked down herself and then smiled proudly at what I could imagine was her prize collection.

"Cool, so you're in?" she asked me, again referring back to the holy grail of subjects.

"Club Afterlife? Yeah, I know the place... I've actually kinda got a job there."

"SHUT UP! No way...*really?*" She had sat bolt upright, spilling frothy coffee over the edge of her cup as she looked ecstatic at this new discovery.

"Yeah, I start next week for my trial day, but I should be fine. I think so anyway, I mean I've worked in a bar before."

"Oh my God, oh my God! I can't believe it. You are so lucky. Everyone I know would kill for a job there... how the

Hell did you manage that?" she said obviously getting more excited by the second.

"Well, my brother-in-law Frank knows the owner or something and well... he just asked him, I think he must owe him a favour." At this, her jaw dropped.

"Wait, hold on a sec...so let me get this straight. Does your brother-in-law know...*The Dravens?*" She whispered the name as though it was the town's biggest secret, and my reaction felt like spiders dancing down my spine.

"Who?" As soon as the name was said, she had my full attention. It was weird, as if some bulb just flipped on in my head. Why did that name suddenly have an effect on me, as though I had heard it before in a memory or a dream I couldn't fully remember?

"The Dravens are a family who come here once a year. They are stinking rich, millionaires or even billionaires who knows. But they own the club and half the town for that matter and like I said, they come here for a couple of weeks every year to this tiny town. Nobody really knows why. They bring in loads of really crazy looking people; I mean *really* weird looking!"

"That's strange. I wonder what brings them here," I said out loud while this same question played on repeat in my mind.

"Like I said, no one really gets to the bottom of it, but we get a lot of these 'visitors' while they're here and they all stay at the club." She said this making quotation marks in the air with her hands for a more dramatic effect. It worked.

"What do you mean... they like, live there or something?" She could see my confusion and smiled.

"It will make more sense when you see the place, trust me. Which reminds me, are you up for it? Tomorrow night that is? The band's called the Acid Criminals. They do quite a heavy set, but it's worth it just for the dreamy drummer." She was getting carried away with herself and went on talking about the drummer for fifteen more minutes before we arranged a time to meet.

I really wanted to ask her more about the Dravens but chickened out, plus Libby was due to pick me up any minute.

RJ's easy-going nature and friendliness had made the time fly by, and I found myself looking forward to tomorrow night. I had a feeling that we were going to make an odd pair of good friends.

She walked down with me to the front entrance of the mall and waited with me until Libby's car was in sight. She continued to tell me about tomorrow night and who I was likely to meet there. The group included her older brother, who apparently was dying to meet me. I couldn't understand why, but I figured she had said this to put me at ease about meeting everyone or maybe it was because in a town this small a new girl was probably a talking point. Especially one from England, well hopefully the novelty would soon wear off.

Libby waited while we said our goodbyes.

"Okay, see you tomorrow, oh, and don't forget your ID, they're really strict…wait what am I saying? You will be working there, durr, I forgot that!"

"See you then RJ," and with that, I made my way to Libby's car and noticed she had the window cranked down despite the weather.

"What's on tomorrow night?" She asked, and I smiled as I got in the passenger side and waited for my interrogation.

"She's invited me to see this band tomorrow night."

"You must have made a good impression then, where's the band playing?"

"Club Afterlife." This was when her face dropped.

"What? I am going to be working there; I think it's a good idea if I go and check it out before my first shift." I said first trying for logic.

"Yeah look, about that." Here it was, I knew what was coming, the big sister 'Talk'.

"I was thinking maybe a quieter job would be more suitable to your situation. I mean you don't want to rush into things do you and you know if you're desperate for a job then I could see what I could do, maybe office junior?"

"Oh great, making coffee for thirty people and a whole load of photocopying." She looked hurt, so I quickly changed tactics.

"Look, I appreciate your concern, but I have done bar and waitress work for years, and you know what I'm like around machines, they blow up if I just look at one wrong. I can't even get my mobile phone to work without calling Zimbabwe!" She laughed and with that the ache I got when I had hurt someone's feelings faded.

"Libby, I will be fine and anyway, what is it about this club you don't like?"

She made a face like she had just smelled some bad cheese and I knew this to be one of those 'things she shouldn't say' faces. So, I pressed harder.

"Come on, Libs, what are you not telling me?" She hesitated.

"It's just…just you hear some really weird things about what goes on there."

"Like what?" I looked at her with a sceptic eye, which she refused to acknowledge.

"You hear some crazy stuff that goes on there, and with the Dravens coming I'm not sure you should be there, that's all." Okay, hearing this name now was like waving a red rag to a bull.

"What do you know about the Dravens?" I asked, and she frowned before shooting me a questioning glare.

"More like, what do you know about the Dravens?" She snapped back. Well, she had me there. I mean I had only been here a week, and I seemed to know about the town's favourite gossip.

"RJ told me that they're a rich family who come here once a year and nobody really knows why," I answered shrugging my shoulders like it was no big deal. She just stared ahead, and for once concentrated on the road which was so unusual for Libs, it was scary.

"Libs!" I shouted when I couldn't take the suspense any longer.

"Sorry but I…well I don't want to sound like some gossip queen, but I just don't like the stories I've heard about them. And no, I'm not just being dramatic like Frank thinks, but it just doesn't fit, the reason they come here. Why not some big city to do their business? Why this little country town?" She sounded a bit crazy herself as if she believed they were some secret murdering cartel.

"You think its drugs?" Although it didn't seem likely as that would be more fitting to a big city environment, not little Evergreen Falls, New Hampshire.

"No, I mean… oh, I don't know. It just doesn't feel right; they bring all their own staff including bodyguards, which even Frank thinks is really strange. I mean why would they need them?" I had to agree with that one. This town didn't exactly scream badass, so what they would need protecting from I didn't know. But still, this was not really a valid reason behind thinking the worst of a couple of rich bigwigs coming to the area.

"They bring their own staff? I mean that's a little strange, but I guess they must entertain really important people and just want things to be right."

"Yeah, I guess," was all she said but didn't look convinced and this didn't seem like the only thing that bothered her about the Dravens. But knowing she didn't want to say anymore made me all the more determined not to give up.

"Come on. I can see there is more to this story." I insisted.

"It's just one story I heard, and before you ask a million questions, I don't know much about the details!" She was getting touchy now as the truth unfolded.

"So, what was it?"

"A girl… she went missing." She said in a low voice, and I couldn't help the shiver that went through my body when she said it. I could see I wasn't going to get more than that out of her, so I dropped the subject, not really knowing if I wanted to know more anyway. Not if I was going to be working there.

When we got back to the house, there was an urgent message for Libby on the answerphone asking her to call the office.

"Are you okay if I pop into the office, this client is driving me crazy, he's always changing the design spec and…"

"I'll be fine, Libs. Honestly, I could do with a wind-down anyway. A good book and a cup of tea, and I'll be set," I said interrupting her mid-rant and finished this with a hug I knew she needed. She was out of the door and running to her car before I barely had time to shout…

"Not too fast, Libby, take it easier with your right, I mean left foot!" She pulled a face laughing and just waved as she sped off down the driveway. I was still shaking my head as I closed the door.

To be honest, a bit of quiet time wasn't a bad thing, and since I was feeling more positive these days, I wasn't as worried about where my mind would wander to.

I decided to go for a walk instead of the book and tea idea, so I grabbed my new coat and my keys. I followed the footpath Frank had mentioned was like a walk in the park, and he was right, that was until I went too far, and the undergrowth got thicker.

I was starting to love walking out here. It's the only time that I felt free, the only time when you can truly be yourself, with no one judging you. No one to have to act in front of, and most importantly, I could let my emotions flow through my body with ease. To cry when I wanted and not feel guilty about who it may be affecting.

But today's walk was different, not the overwhelming sadness and depression that used to sweep over me. Instead, it had been replaced by a wave of unanswered questions and a sea of curiosity. I kept finding myself thinking about the Dravens. Who were they? Why did they even come to this tiny town? And more importantly, when would I finally get a glimpse of them for myself?

I would have to restrain myself tomorrow night so as not to bombard RJ with loads of questions. I was hoping she would have been more forthcoming on the subject, but once she had mentioned the drummer, he had become the main topic of conversation. The one thing she did say, which I found to be very disappointing, was that no one hardly ever saw any of them. As soon as they arrived, they spent all of their time upstairs in the VIP lounge and of course, they had their own private party guest list, one that no one who lived in the town was ever included on.

I didn't really understand why I was so fascinated. Why I was obsessing over them? But at heart, I knew it wasn't 'them' I was dying to find out about.

No, it was *him.*

As soon as RJ had mentioned the name Dominic Draven, I had latched onto it like a good murder mystery book you couldn't put down. She only mentioned his name briefly, but it was enough to spark my imagination. Who was he, and what did he look like?

By the time my brain had calmed itself down and started to get some real-life perspective, I had arrived at the spot I had been looking for, or so I thought.

I frowned as I saw a natural-looking archway framed by the trees. I didn't remember this being here the other day and I was sure I had taken the exact same route with Libby. Maybe we came at it from a different angle. Yes, that must have been it. I convinced myself of this long enough to pass through the entwined branch arch but not before looking back over my shoulder one last time.

Once my doubts left me, they were quickly replaced by awe. The place was incredible. It didn't look like part of the forest. No, it was more like someone's secret garden I had stumbled into. Only instead of being surrounded by a stone wall to keep it hidden, the stone had been replaced by a wall of life. The forest enclosed the open space like a protective barrier with trees hundreds of years old all standing guard.

It was obvious standing here now that it wasn't the place Libby had brought me to, but it mustn't have been far away as it seemed to have the same view. This place looked like someone's property, and I had just stumbled across their own private Garden of Eden. It was almost too astounding to be real.

Upon closer inspection, the trees were different and more

exotic looking. They had huge palms and vines growing on them with bright red flowers that looked very similar to hibiscus.

But this couldn't be right, it would be far too cold here for them, and there were even more plants that would definitely not survive in this climate. How was this possible without a greenhouse or tropical climate? Yet here, in front of me, was the colourful proof. The blues, oranges and yellows of the Birds of Paradise and the bright pink bell shapes of Angel Wing Begonia. There was also sun bursting Dahlias and the beautiful purple and red Blue Dawns, which all lay around basking in the winter sun as evidence to this incredible place.

I walked into the middle, trying not to make a sound, only I wasn't sure why. It was so breathtakingly beautiful that it was like walking straight into a dream world.

There was not one murmur or movement for that matter, which I didn't understand. How could there be no wind in this big open space when there were clouds above me that were moving? There wasn't even the slightest breeze. I could feel my nerves kicking in, and I started to tremble. I wanted to turn back, feeling something not right under my skin but I couldn't see where I had come in. Where was the archway?

In the stillness, I heard a sound and knew I wasn't alone. My instincts kicked in and I pulled the metal clip from my hair, releasing long blonde waves down my back. My eyes darted from one space to another as I held onto the cold metal. I spun round on one foot, my jacket flaring out along with my hair, only there was nothing but the beautiful cocoon of colour, radiant in the high sun.

Then suddenly, I heard another noise from behind me and as I spun back around, I tripped on some uneven ground. I lost my footing and found myself falling to the forest floor. Letting out a yelp, I automatically put my hands out to break my fall, losing my unconventional weapon in the process.

"Ah!" I shouted breaking the silence and feeling the wet moss across my skin, causing my hands to slide. With my grip lost, I tried in vain to hold my body upwards. Instead, my hands flew out in front of me again coming into contact with something hard and smooth like leather. I swear I could now hear someone breathing, momentarily forgetting the noise I had heard before.

That was when I realised they were directly in front of me.

I lifted my head towards the objects my hands were touching, but my hair had fallen forwards like a yellow blanket. I shook my head trying to part the sea of hair that was obstructing my view. I moved my hands quickly when I saw a pair of black men's leather boots I had been touching and I gasped in shock.

I tried to get up quickly, but the earth under me had other ideas and I slid around as if on an ice rink. Then just as I was about to fall again, a large, strong hand circled the top of my arm bringing back a wash of memories I couldn't explain. However, before I had time to think, another hand grabbed my waist, pulling me upright and preventing me from hitting the ground.

My eyes followed the figure from the ground upwards to find boots, jeans, a heavy belt buckle and a long black jacket that started at his knees. I worked my way up his muscular frame, feeling the heat generated from his body as he still held me tight.

He wore a dark T-shirt that showed the indents of a muscled washboard stomach and an incredibly wide solid chest with strong shoulders to match. Expecting to see a harsh, hard face to match this warrior body, I reluctantly raised my head to look. I had to keep looking up at him as he was exceptionally tall, being well over six feet, making my eyes level with his hard chest. The face, however, wasn't harsh but extremely handsome. No, no, that wasn't merely enough, he wasn't just handsome...

He was breath-taking!

He was Mediterranean looking with very dark features and olive, sun-kissed skin. His jet-black hair was down to his shoulders but looked as if it had grown naturally into this style. He was very well groomed but still had a roughness about him with deep-set eyes that burned right through me. They were incredible as if they were trying to see into my very soul, searching deep and finding what hidden secrets lay there. They were endless, dark pools of hard emotion framed by thick, long lashes. Not quite brown, more like onyx black, but they had a slight purplish edge to them, one I had never seen before.

He was truly startling to look at, so much so, that I couldn't stop staring at him. His hand finally released me, and my body was left feeling cold as if his touch had been sending a warm pulse coursing through my veins heating me up from the inside. My skin tingled as though it begged for his touch again. What was wrong with me? This guy could be anyone.

I took a cautious step back. He watched me in what seemed to be amazement as if he was trying to distinguish if I were real or not. The heat rushed to my cheeks with being stared at and I tugged down at my sleeves nervously. I could swear after doing this I heard him groan but then he spoke, cutting off that thought.

"Are you alright?" His voice sounded like velvet with a cutting edge. Smooth and soft, but most of all, a strong, comforting essence encased every word. I was speechless and was just staring at him, finding it hard to turn away from his intense gaze.

What he saw in me, I didn't know as his features were unreadable. His face was just so familiar to me, but I couldn't understand how I knew him. That was impossible, as I would have definitely remembered a man like this. I needed to make my lips work before he thought me a simple, staring mute.

"I'm... fi...fine... thank you." My voice didn't sound as cool and calm as I had hoped. His lips curved slightly, as though amused by my obvious shyness, and this made my heart skip a beat. My face blushed even more than normal, so much so it felt like my flesh was seconds away from melting away from my cheekbones. I had always disliked the fact that I blushed so easily, giving away my embarrassment for anyone to see, but at times like this, I downright hated it!

"What is your name?" He seemed to be getting closer to me and for some reason, I was backing away. I don't know why, but he really intimidated me. After all, we were here all alone in the forest and I knew nothing about him. For some reason, I felt both at ease, as if I knew he wasn't going to do me any harm, and scared, as though there was something not quite right about him.

It was conflicting, so I didn't know whether or not to tell him my name. He looked shocked that I hadn't yet given him a response.

"It's alright, little one, you can tell me," he said looking down at me, speaking in that soft voice, making me trust him even more but instead of giving him my name, I confessed my fears.

"I don't think I should be here," I said while looking down at my feet and trying to escape his dark penetrating gaze. It didn't help with the sheer size of the guy. I mean I was used to being around big guys with having Frank for a brother-in-law but this guy…well, let's just say there are very few words needed to describe how I felt right about now and those would be 'Prey and Predator'. And it was easy to guess which part I would play in this little scenario.

"Oh really… then pray tell me, why are you?" I looked up, meeting a confident smile, which was the complete opposite to my own.

"I guess I got lost." He was shaking his head to tell me I was wrong.

"Oh, you're not lost, you're found at last and right where you need to be I think… Now for your name?" This sounded like an order, all velvet now removed, and I gulped down the hard, frightened lump in my throat before answering him.

"Keira… It's… Keira Johnson." His hand extended to mine offering it to me and reluctantly I did the same. But as he took my hand in his large grasp, his grip tightened suddenly, and he pulled my body closer to his. This instantly took me back to my dream and I almost tripped into his body.

Warmth coursed through my blood once again making me lightheaded. He was looking down at me, but I refused to meet his lust-filled eyes. Instead, I focused on my surroundings trying in vain not to be affected by the intoxicating scent of raw Alpha male, leather and a spicy musk, all combined into one indestructible looking man.

"What's…what's happening?" I stuttered in a whisper when I realised the lush Garden of Eden that surrounded us had started to fade away into a forest of demise. The exotic flowers began to wither and turn to ashes of grey. The trees blew in tornado winds that didn't reach us, uprooting them into splinters. The world began to spin with darkness and die as though in the presence of Death himself.

I choked back a scream and tried to pull away from this dark stranger's vice-like grip. The movement caught his attention enough to pull me back and one arm snaked its way around my back putting an end to my plans of escape.

"Do not be afraid, for I will not hurt you." His face looked down and came closer towards mine. For a moment, I thought he was going to kiss me as our lips were mere inches apart. I knew I would not have stopped him, even as the world around us had started to crumble away. Then he moved his free hand to my face, pushing my hair back from my neck to whisper something in my ear. Every touch sent a shooting desire down to my very core as I could feel his breath on my skin. At first, it just lingered there before the words were released from his perfect lips.

His voice was light and soft as if trying to lure me into a trance as he spoke the words…

"Somnus, my Keira."
("Sleep" in Latin)

CHAPTER 5

ALONE

I woke up on the couch with a blanket around me, and I was alone. I felt strange as if I'd had a dream I couldn't quite remember, and when did I fall asleep anyway? I'm pretty sure I went out for a walk or did I dream that too? My head felt all fuzzy as though I had a hangover or something.

The house was empty, and it was dark but most of all, it was unnerving. I got up and went into the kitchen as my throat felt like a new place to store woodchips. On the way, I grabbed the phone to see if Libby had left a message. Just as I turned on the lights, I felt a cold chill run up my body. I turned to where it was coming from and noticed the front door was wide open.

My heart froze as a million thoughts went crashing through my head at once. The first being…was I actually alone? I ran into the kitchen and grabbed a knife from the counter and started to ring 911 but decided to hang up before I heard the first ring. What was I going to tell them? "I thought I went for a walk, found a Garden of Eden, and met the most amazing looking man I'd ever seen before, before waking up in a blanket with the front door open." Yeah, I don't think so. For starters other than the front door being open, it all sounded pretty nice to me.

Unless… no it couldn't be! I would have been warned.

I got that idea out of my head like shaking off cobwebs from my body and walked to the front door. There was no porch light on, and it was quite wild outside. The trees were blowing angrily, and the swing chair's chains creaked. No wonder I was spooked. I closed the door and locked it. It could've just blown open. I tried to convince myself, but knowing I would have to search the house didn't make me feel any better.

With all the lights on, I checked the downstairs which, no surprise, was all clear. However, when I got to the last door, I realised what was behind it. It swung open and I stared down into the darkness unable to step one foot down into the basement. My mind froze in fear and I slammed the door quickly as though fire from the pits of Hell was coming up at me.

"Shake it off, Kaz. You had to unlock the door to open it; nobody is going to be down there," I said, reassuring myself for not going down there and instead deciding to check the rest of the house.

I then checked the first floor, again turning on all the lights as I went. I swapped my knife for a baseball bat I grabbed from the cupboard under the stairs. I used that to open the doors as I braced myself for anything that might be there. Plus, I figured the bat had better swinging range.

The first floor was like the last, all clear, so by the time I got to the attic, I was feeling pretty foolish. I opened my bedroom door and turned on the last light in the house. It all looked as I had left it that morning. Clothes were everywhere from getting ready to see RJ and not knowing what to wear.

I put the bat down, and I started to pick stuff up, piling it up on my bed when I noticed something was wrong with the way I had left it. My copy of Jane Eyre, which I had left on my bedside table, was now gone. I was sure I had left it there. I was reading it last night and always put it there. This was strange, maybe Libby had taken it to read but then on reflection, I couldn't see it being a likely reason. Libby was more of a gossip girl and loved all the celebrity and fashion magazines. I don't think I had ever seen her read an actual book before.

I tried to look for it, but gave up when I heard a car door shutting and knew that Libby or Frank must be back. I got up from looking under my bed and was just about to make my way downstairs when I noticed my window was open. How had I missed that? It wasn't even cold in here, why hadn't I noticed?

I walked up to it, and the wind blew my hair around my face. But how did my hair get loose? It brought me back to my dream and I wondered where my metal clip was? I twisted it back up and knotted it, before trying to reach out to close the window.

"Hey, Kaz, sorry I've been so long, work was insane. Hey, are you alright? You look really pale... you feeling okay?" Libby said, looking concerned.

"Yeah, I'm fine, I just woke up actually. I must have crashed out on the couch." She gave me one of those worried head tilts.

"Maybe you should get an early night, you still look beat, and I wouldn't leave your window open, you'll freeze up here. Talking about that, do you have enough blankets and stuff?" she asked, and started fussing about the bed and folding up clothes, doing the whole mother-hen thing.

"Yeah, I must have forgotten to close it this morning. Say, did you borrow my book?" Her blank look said it all.

"What, Jane Eyre? Not unless there's a new one out that includes Orlando Bloom and George Clooney!" She gave me a cheeky smile, and I tried to smile back but it was hard when my thoughts were all over the place.

"So... are you thinking about taking up baseball or joining a club?" Libby said spying my weapon propped against the wall.

"Oh, that...well...umm..."

"No, it's cool, no need to explain... I think I will just take this downstairs with me," Libby said, picking it up by the end like a dirty stick a muddy child had brought into the house.

"Cuppa?" she asked, going out of sight, not needing to wait for my obvious reply.

I slumped on the bed and in doing so knocked over the folded clothes tower Libby had made. I let out a sigh looking at it, but my mind was elsewhere. It was back in the forest and now searching my memory for another glimpse of *him*.

I could still remember the smell of the flowers and taste the damp air. And the feel of his touch that seemed to sear my skin couldn't be forgotten. Marking him there for all time…that… well that, I just could not get out of my head.

But what could I do about it? Nothing about what happened or didn't happen made any sense. Even if that place had been real, the part when it crumbled into dust should be enough to convince me otherwise. And there was my dark mystery man. Could my mind really conjure up such powerful perfection? I was so confused.

Had it been real?

I decided to have a shower to try and relax before bed. I let my bathrobe drop to the floor and stepped into the cubicle, instantly feeling better as the hot water rained down over my body. I could feel my muscles slowly relax and the tension in my neck ease. I loved the water; I loved everything about it, when it rained, the sound of a stream or a river, even the sound of droplets lashing against my window in a storm. But most of all, I loved the way it felt on my skin. As if it not only cleansed your body from everyday life but could also wash away any bad thoughts or memories, making you feel brand new.

Now, if it could only bring back old beautiful memories, then I would stay in here until I became 'Prune Woman' defender of the bathroom! I let my long hair fall down my back, and held my face under the rushing water of the power shower, wishing it could be more like a waterfall in some exotic rainforest far away, somewhere hot and full of mystery. This immediately brought me back to my dream as I closed my eyes and let my mind wander in and out of blissful remembrance.

I had washed my hair and body with Libby's extensive supply of bathroom products, wondering if she wasn't a little bit consumer mad. There were six different types of shower gels, and bottles of all shapes and sizes, holding God only knows what. I used what I needed and came out of the shower smelling like a mixture of jasmine, honey and a touch of coconut. I would have to read the bottles more carefully next time; otherwise, I could come out of there smelling like a Piña Colada.

I hadn't realised how long I had been until the water had started to go colder, and the signs of Prune Woman were starting to appear. I looked in the mirror at my face and frowned. I looked so pale, even though I had just come out of a hot shower and the bathroom was still steamy. I wiped the mirror again with my arm and studied what the world saw when looking at me. My eyes were a boring greyish blue colour that looked more like the sky when there was a storm coming. They were big, but the only thing blessed about them was that they were framed with thick eyelashes that Libby would have given her right arm for.

I rolled my eyes at myself and gave up trying to find fault with everything. It seemed to be a theme with some women when faced with a gorgeous man that immediately you wanted to pick away the parts you didn't like about how you looked. I wish I could be more like one of those 'burn your bra' types as I thought that all women were beautiful creatures, if only we weren't our own worst enemy. But of course, I also believed beauty started within your soul as you could often find a beautiful woman made ugly through their actions.

I dried myself and changed into my sweat pants, and a vest top with an old hooded zip up my dad had given me years ago. One he used to fit into until a beer belly had gotten to him. He knew it was one of my favourites. It had his old University football team logo on the front and it was lined with fleece inside. Most of all, it reminded me of home and kept me warm in more ways than one.

I scanned my room before getting into bed, mainly wanting to find my book. It was strange; my room looked as though someone else had been here. Had I taken it with me this morning? I would have to check my bag. I shook off the feeling and put it down to the stress.

I was like this when I first started taking the drugs the doctor had prescribed me. I didn't know whether I was coming or going. I would do something completely random and then wouldn't remember why or what I had done. It was one of the reasons I had stopped taking my medication. It made me numb and, in my opinion, not a nice person to be around. The only thing I did still take occasionally was sleeping pills. Now they *did* work for me, but I still would be a bit hazy on the details before I slept as they made me a little incoherent should we say.

This made me wonder, could I have taken some after Libby had rushed out to work? It was possible. Was that it? My dream man was a drug-induced fantasy? God, I hoped not! I couldn't think of anything crueller. Forget dangling a bloody carrot, that was more like dangling a death by chocolate cake in front of a diabetic!

I decided it didn't matter. I'd done enough thinking about it. I got into bed and started reading some course material. It was about time as I was starting college in a week, and they had sent me a reading list. I had an advantage though as I had already done the first year in England but as my plans had to change, I decided that it was best to start over from scratch. Towards the end, I had missed a lot of work and found it impossible to catch up, not that I wanted to at that point. At least here, I might be ahead of the game.

I was looking forward to History the most. I loved History. I used to watch all the documentaries on the History Channel with my dad since I was a child, only now understanding them better.

My grandparents had a huge library in their house in Cornwall, and it was full of historical books of all eras. I used to sit for hours on an old worn rug and look at all the pictures, imagining that one day I would go to all these old temples, tombs and monuments to see them for myself. I used to pretend I was an archaeologist and I would uncover all their mysteries and secrets.

But my favourite kind of history had to be mythological. I loved where the stories originated from. The fantasy behind them fascinated me. Ancient Greek, Egyptian, Aztec, I just couldn't get enough. I loved the drama of it all, the scandal of Gods, Kings and Pharaohs; it was my version of a gossip magazine. So naturally, it was what I really wanted to study. The other classes I had just picked to fill the void. Art had been the only other passion of mine but not anymore. No, that had all changed for me now.

That incident had changed everything.

There was a light tapping at my door, and I knew it to be a Libby type knock. She cautiously peeped around the door in case I had been asleep,

"Hey, how was your shower?"

"Great but I think I now smell like I work at a cocktail bar." She laughed as she plonked herself down on the end of my bed. This reminded me of so many moments in my childhood.

"You know me; I do love my bath stuff. So how are you finding it all? I'm sorry I had to leave you today."

"No, no, I was fine." My sister gave me a head tilted look, and the disbelief was written all over her face. I mean I couldn't really blame her considering she had found me upstairs with a baseball bat.

"Come on, Kazzy; you can talk to me you know." My heart melted. I didn't want her thinking I was losing the plot, or this move hadn't been the right thing.

"I'm just trying to find my feet a bit…don't get me wrong I love it here, and you were right, it's the best thing for me. I'm just worried about work and college and stuff, but you don't need to worry too." I smiled trying to reassure her, but I could see what was coming.

"Why don't you hold off for a bit with working. You could do with a rest, and it's not the quietest of places." She pulled a face like she had just had her upper lip waxed. I couldn't help the laugh that escaped my lips and it felt good. Only once I started, I couldn't stop. Libby saw the funny side and joined in. I could feel the tension lifting from my shoulders and gave Libby a big hug.

She flicked her red hair back off her face and looked more closely at me. She then reached out and pushed back a strand of my hair behind my ears.

"Wow, your hair is so long, I didn't realise, why don't you…?" She cut herself off knowing the answer. She understood I wasn't the same girl now.

"Never mind, but it's still a lovely colour," she said as she fiddled with the ends through her fingers.

"And you've still got Dad's old hoodie, well I don't suppose it has fit him in a while." She grunted a laugh. She touched the sleeves and instinct kicked in, so I tugged down the material hiding my already hidden scars. This made her wince, and she got up off the bed and made her way towards the door as if a memory had hit her and she didn't want me to see the emotion building up.

"Libs...I..." I started, but she interrupted me.

"Get some rest, honey." Then she left without looking at me. She was gone before I even finished a good night. I felt bad about this, but understood that it wasn't only me that had been affected by what had happened.

~

I brushed my hair ready to plait it for bed, and it squeaked as my hands split it into three parts. It was overly clean due to the amount of time I had spent in the shower. I hoped no one else was planning on having one as they would be in for a chilly shock.

I gave up on reading after only ten minutes. I just couldn't concentrate on college stuff with my mind now on other things. I had been so frustrated most of the evening that trying to forget about it seemed impossible. However, there was one aspect I desperately *didn't* want to forget.

Why couldn't men like that really exist in the world? Men just weren't that perfect, were they? Well okay, I hadn't really had an extensive knowledge of the other sex, but from what I saw (or can remember) he was just staggeringly beautiful. More like a God than a human. Maybe I had read too many mythological stories.

I took my dad's sweater off and finally started to relax as I settled down my wired mind. I turned off my lamp and pulled the covers around my body like a cocoon. I could feel my heavy lids falling and knew it wouldn't be long until I found sleep.

~

Stirring from my sleep, I woke frowning. Something was irritating me, and I turned my head looking to see how much time had passed. I had only been asleep for an hour and I groaned in frustration. Then I heard it. The noise that must have woke me. I shot up fast…

It was back!

My head spun around the dark room, looking for any movement in the shadows. The moon was out and there was a faint glow behind a cloud that would soon come into view. I held my breath not wanting to move. My body froze, and my hands were curled into balls, gripping so hard on the quilt that I was sure I would tear it.

I wanted to switch the light on but knew that it wouldn't help me see outside as I would only see my own pale reflection looking back at me. I waited for the moon as the tapping continued, only this time it wasn't as erratic. It made me too curious, so I bravely got up and walked over to the window seat. I strained my eyes in a desperate attempt to see the creature once more, but I was at a loss to understand why.

The moon was coming out now, and it started to create more shadows in my room. Both relief and disappointment washed over me as there was nothing there. My eyes searched everywhere but still no bird, and also no trace of anything that could have been making that noise. I was about to give up but decided to open the window. I didn't know why or what difference this would make but my hand still reached for the window latch. It was a bit tough, but I didn't need to worry about waking anyone as nothing could be heard from up here in my attic room.

The paint flaked and the hinges squeaked as I pushed on its frame. The cold air hit me and went straight down my spine, continuing all the way down my body. I held my arms around my ribs wishing I was back in my warm bed. Instead, I was stood here feeling like an idiot, freezing my butt off.

I poked my head out and looked down at the yard, but there was nothing that had changed. Still, just a shed with some car parts dotted here and there. But no bird… nothing. What did I expect, my mystery dream man to be stood there with a handful of stones he had been throwing at the window?

I laughed at myself and pulled the window back to slam it shut. The noise startled me even though I was expecting it. What I wasn't expecting however, was the floorboards behind me to creak. I turned around too quickly and almost stumbled over the cushion from the window seat which had fallen to the floor.

"You have trouble staying on your feet, don't you?" That perfect voice. The one I had been trying so hard to remember. It was hypnotic. I didn't know what to do or to say. I just wished that I could see him as well as I had heard him.

The room was still black because the moon had disappeared again behind the safety of its clouds. I could just make out the tall, dark silhouette standing at the bottom of my bed, no more than four feet away from me. My heart rate must have tripled in seconds, yet I was still too scared to breathe. Speak Keira! I mentally yelled at myself.

"I umm... I mean... what are you doing here?" Was all I could think to say. What a moron I sounded! Wait... forget that, there's a strange man in my room and I was the one worrying about what I sounded like. Way to go Keira on getting your priorities right.

I couldn't see, but I was sure he had a smirk on his face. I could hear it in his voice when he said,

"Yes, well apart from it being my right to see you, I also wanted to bring you something. You dropped this." He held out his hand to give me something, but I didn't move. And what did he mean by 'his right to see me'?

"There is no need to fear me. I would *never* hurt you." He emphasised the word 'never' as if it would cause him physical pain to go back on his words. His voice also did that hypnotic thing again and made my brain turn to mush. Even with all the mush, or maybe because of it, there was no way I could get my legs to work.

"Come here." That was until he *ordered* my legs to work.

I stepped forward cautiously, and reached out as far as I could to take what it was he was holding. I was just about to get it when he moved so quickly. His movements were a blurry wave, and I felt the hairs on the back of my neck stand up as I realised how close he now came to me. My hand had dropped to my side as I struggled to breathe again. He must have noticed my reaction because he whispered in the softest voice,

"Don't be afraid, little one."

I wish I could have found words to speak, but I was numb, and not all of it down to fear. Everything about him held me in some kind of spell; his smell, his body heat and most of all, the secret lure of that voice. I think I would have done anything he asked of me.

"I...I'm not afraid," I whispered in a cracked voice that sounded anything but convincing. He was so close; I could hear him smiling.

"Here," was all he said as he took my hand very slowly into his own. The heat that coursed through me almost blew me over. It was as if I had been struck by thousands of red-hot pins of pleasure. My body literally ignited as I had never felt so alive. He turned my hand over ever so slowly as if not wanting to frighten me with any sudden movements, all the while, his eyes never left me.

He held my hand in his with my palm raised upwards and with his other hand, he placed something there. His weight shifted towards my body as he leaned down towards my ear once more as he had done in the woods. The words flowed from his lips in such perfection I couldn't breathe at the sound.

"I shouldn't be here yet, but I was curious about you, little one." This made me notice something else in his voice. He had an authoritative edge that made me shudder under his hands. Hands that dwarfed my own, making me feel every bit of the nickname he had given me. Hell, the hand that held my own could have crushed my skull with ease. I tried to swallow down a frightened lump as if I had a plum stuck there.

"About... *me?*" I asked, barely speaking the words. I was in shock. Why on earth would he be curious about me? He raised his hand up to my face, and I froze. I could barely take a small breath. Meanwhile, the moon had come out, but he was still in the dark, unlike me. My pale face was now on show as he had his back to the window. The back of two of his fingers touched my cheek making me quiver at the warm path they left on my skin. I closed my eyes as the silent moments went by and his fingers continued to explore my heated face.

"Exquisite," his lips whispered against my forehead after he leaned in closer, cutting all space between us to nothing. My breath hitched at the word he used, and this time instead of turning my insides to mush, he set them on fire. I was suddenly worried he could feel the points of my desire pressing into him thanks to my hardened nipples.

I looked up at him, and I inhaled sharply when I saw for the first time his stunning features bathed in moonlight. I was right. He was Godly. And more incredible was that this Godly figure was smiling down at me. Of all the people in the world... he picked damaged little me to smile at.

"You will sleep, my girl, and you will sleep well this night, understand?" It wasn't a question but a command, one I was almost positive I would not be obeying. I mean, who could sleep after meeting such a man in their room. No, sleeping would not be on the menu but fantasising... oh most definitely!

Then he broke the spell,

"Until next time, *my Keira,"* he whispered, and I loved the sound my name made on his lips. His whispered promise stayed in my mind like a drug working over my body. I could feel myself getting weaker until finally, I couldn't fight off the urge to close my eyes.

My last thought, swimming happily through the current of bliss...

He called me his.

CHAPTER 6
GETTING READY

When I woke, the window still held the last few shreds of night. I rubbed my eyes and wondered what it was that I had been dreaming about. I sat upright and stretched out my arms yawning, when I heard the thud of something hitting the wooden floor. I leaned over and picked up my copy of Jane Eyre. I must have fallen asleep reading it last night. How strange, I couldn't remember anything.

I looked at the clock and saw it was 6:30am. Rubbing my eyes, I pulled back the warm covers before I got up, and regretted it immediately as the cold air hit me. I quickly rushed into the bathroom, wishing I owned slippers as I dragged my frozen feet across the hard-wooden floor. I decided to get back into bed when I had finished as it was much warmer there. The house was still quiet, and I was in no rush to start the day in this weather.

I grabbed my book and noticed something attached to one of the pages. I shook my head at the unbelievable sight as I removed my metal hair clip. How it got there, I didn't know, but I had a vague memory that I had lost it. I opened the book and my first thought was it had been placed there for a reason. The point was positioned as though to draw my attention to a part in the book I knew well.

It read...

"An impulse held me fast—a force turned me round. I said—or something in me said for me, and in spite of me— "Thank you, Mr. Rochester, for your great kindness. I am strangely glad to get back again to you; and wherever you are, is my home—my only home."

I held the book open on the page staring at it for a long time, trying to comprehend why it should be marked on this page. My mind didn't feel like my own. It felt as though I had dreamt the last couple of days. I tried to recall what I had done yesterday but my mind came up empty. The last thing I remembered was meeting RJ at the mall and talking to Libby on the way home. But it finished there. What on Earth?

My train of thought was interrupted by the noises my stomach was making. I realised I was starving. Did I even eat anything yesterday? Jesus, I couldn't remember that either! How strange, but more than anything else it was utterly frustrating.

I grabbed some thick socks from one of the drawers and put them on my feet as quickly as I could before they turned to blocks of ice again. I tried to be as quiet as I could when I crossed the landing and went down the stairs. The steps creaked under the weight of my body, making them sound as though they were moaning at me for waking them too.

Once in the kitchen, I flicked on the light switch and headed for the huge double door fridge. My eyes hadn't quite adjusted to the light as it was still dark outside and as always, raining. I grabbed the carton of milk and put it on the table, got a bowl, spoon and hunted for some cereal. I found one called Captain Crunch and thought I would give it a try. I clicked the kettle on and put a teabag in a mug, thus completing my breakfast.

Libby walked in the kitchen dressed in a fluffy robe with

slippers to match. She looked like a pink marshmallow but hell, at least it looked warm.

"Nice," I said waving my hand up and down motioning to her ensemble. She gave me a smarmy smile before saying,

"Frank bought these for me last Christmas and trust me, you'll be wanting some in winter."

"Why, does it come in black?" I replied with a cocky smile of my own.

"So, how did you sleep?" she asked as she sat opposite me with her own bowl and spoon in hand.

"On my side mainly." I giggled.

"Ha, ha, very funny, you know what they say about sarcasm, don't you?"

"Highest form of wit, oh, and I don't recall the rest," I said as I put my bowl and spoon in the sink after finishing my breakfast in record time.

"Yes, and the lowest form of intelligence! Also, we do have a dishwasher," she said nodding to one of the cupboard doors it was no doubt hidden behind.

It felt so normal to be talking like this with my sister. The way we were before my shit hit the fan.

"What?" she asked, looking at me as if she wanted in on the joke. She was so beautiful, even now when her hair was loose and suffering a funky case of bed head, it just gave her a more natural beauty, unkempt and wild. Like some Amazonian princess.

"Nothing really, just reminiscing. You in work today?" I asked, trying to change the subject.

"Umm… well no but…" she paused, and I clocked the guilty look right away.

"It's okay, you gotta work. I'll be fine, Libs. Plus, I've got my big night clubbing to plan for." I winked.

"Ah yes, the Acid… umm… something or others. Yeah, good luck with that," she said, now being the sarcastic one.

"Acid Criminals actually, and they sound rather cultured," I said this last part in a posh English accent and Libby couldn't keep a straight face. We both laughed.

"Well, like I said, good luck with that! Hey, but didn't you say RJ has a brother?" Her cheesy wink said it all.

"Yes, but you know that won't mean much to me. I don't date, remember?" I said firm enough to get it through.

"Okay, okay, I was just saying. You know they go crazy here for the English accent right." She winked again at me, which had me quickly rolling my eyes.

"Umm… well, in that case, I'm just gonna have to practice my American accent then." I couldn't keep the smirk from my face. I got up to take the second mug of tea that Libby had poured me back upstairs when I heard Libby ask about my book. I stopped in the hallway and backed up a few steps.

"What did you say?"

"Did you find your book?" she asked, her mouth still full of cereal.

"Umm, when did I lose it?" I was confused, did she take it and was she the one that attached my hair clip to it?

She looked even more confused.

"Yeah yesterday, you were asking me if I had seen it, remember?" She looked curiously at my non-responsive face. I honestly didn't remember even speaking to Libby after she had dropped me off after the mall. My mind was a blank, and Libby was shifting slightly in her seat and had put her spoon down waiting for me to answer her. Her face was about to quickly shift to worried, so I decided to lie.

"Oh yeah that, sorry. I found it under the bed, must have forgotten. I've slept since then, Libs." I smiled, trying to play the dumb blonde act. Only my acting skills weren't my finest attribute.

She answered me with a nod and picked up her spoon again, which indicated that she was at least satisfied with my response.

Once upstairs in my room, I examined the book again and read the entire page over and over, trying to make sense of the significance.

It was the part in the book where Jane had returned from her aunt's house after she had died, and Jane was returning to Mr. Rochester. She felt like she was home, or more like wherever he was, was her home. The thought lingered there in my mind like a lost memory trying to find its way back through the fog. I gave up making sense of it all and put it down to coincidence.

I got into my baggy jeans and double layered top, which had long grey sleeves and a plum coloured outer T-shirt. I also put on a thick knitted cardigan that was far too big for me. I decided to do some housework and take the burden off Libby. I started in the bathroom, which was really my own personal en-suite. It was the only other room on the top floor, so naturally, I was the only one who used it.

It only had a shower, sink and a toilet in it but it was big enough to house a bath. It was decorated in a whitewashed style that reminded me of a beach hut. There was a corner cupboard that housed extra towels and lots of empty shelves waiting for me to fill them with everyday things.

I cleaned the beautiful arched, wooden mirror that hung over the sink and around the little shelf at the bottom which had a candle on it.

Libby walked in just as I had finished the sink. She was dressed in a black suit that looked fantastic on her. It was tight-fitting and had a thick belt under the chest. A bright white shirt showed underneath at the collar and cuffs. She wore heels that looked far too high to be comfortable, the type that I would most definitely fall down in.

"You look nice." She smiled and tried to twist a stray curl back into her bun.

"Thanks. And you're sure that you'll be…"

"It's okay; you don't have to worry. I told you I will be fine." I would have hugged her but my rubber-gloved hands that smelled of bleach wouldn't have mixed well with the power suit.

"I'm just going to do some housework and maybe try and get some reading done ready for next week."

"Okay, well I'm off now. Frank's already gone so you've got the whole house to yourself. What time are you meeting up with the 'Goth Gang'?" This was no doubt her new nickname for my hopefully soon to be friends.

"Umm, I'm not actually sure on that one, RJ said she'd ring, but I will ring you on your mobile to let you know the details."

"Don't you mean 'cell' phone?" she said in her best American accent, which was about as good as mine, and that was pretty weak.

"Oh yeah, don't want the locals getting all rallied up 'cause there's a stranger in town." God, my red-neck accent sounded more German. I laughed at myself.

"Nope, but I think the town will be more pre-occupied with the other newcomers, the scarier ones." She said this bit in a dire tone, and she wasn't laughing. Why did she dislike them so much? Had she even seen them? 'Cause from the sound of things, not many people had.

Libby looked at her watch and soon rushed off saying she would be late if she didn't leave now. I shouted my goodbye and combined it with telling her to watch her speed but was met with the sound of the front door slamming.

I went back to cleaning, shaking my head. I couldn't wait to start work and college as I was getting seriously bored. But thinking about tonight I was both excited and nervous. I didn't really know what to expect, but at least from what RJ had said I had high hopes for the band being good, or at least the drummer being hot.

I spent the rest of the day trying to find things to do as unfortunately my list of jobs didn't take as long as I thought they would have. RJ had called to confirm I was still 'up for it'. I think she was excited about being the one to introduce me into the 'Goth Rock' society. To be fair, though, any would do at this point. I just needed to get out and would have joined the chess club if I had to.

It made me miss my little Ford Fiesta. What I wouldn't do now just to be able to get in a car and drive around and explore the place. After ringing Libby on her 'cell' and informing her of the plan, I finished getting dinner ready.

I had made a casserole, so all they would need to do was heat it up. I'm sure even Libby could handle that without burning it. Or maybe I should put it into bowls ready to just shove in the microwave. That way, she wouldn't have to light anything. I chuckled to myself as I remembered the pizza on my first night here. It was time to get ready for the big night, so a shower was first on the agenda. I had done the girlie thing and asked what RJ was going to wear, not wanting to stand out. Not that I ever really wore anything to stand out, but still, I had to check.

I had been quite relieved to find out that the place wasn't the dress code type. I was just going to stick to my old faithful blue jeans that weren't as baggy as my usual ones and a long-sleeved black top with a v neck. This one at least had black embroidery across the neck, giving it a bit more of a layered look. It had a bit of a gypsy vibe to it giving it a retro feel. I thought it would pass for the alternative look that I was aiming for.

It clung quite tight to my skin, which showed off a little too much of my figure than I liked, so I added a hooded top which was also black with red piping around the edges. It had a huge hood that would give me lots of protection from the weather should we have to queue to get into this place. It also had long sleeves that went right down past my knuckles.

I dried my hair, which had taken me the longest part to get ready, as it always did. It was just so long and thick; it looked more like a shaggy rug hanging down to my waist. My hair had always been a head-turner. I used to enjoy the compliments I received, but now I just wanted to hide it away, with tonight being no exception.

I tied it into a knot and secured it up at the back with my strong metal clip, and I had this down to a fine art. The shorter bits at the front fell down framing my face, with one side thicker than the other. I examined myself in the long mirror in my room, and I was satisfied that I didn't stand out yet hopefully didn't look too much like the newbie I was.

Libby was already downstairs finishing her dinner off and was mopping up the juice with the baguette I had asked her to get when I called. She looked as if she had enjoyed it.

"A bit of a change from fast food?" I said as I joined her at the table. She would have replied with some sarcastic response, I could see it in her eyes, but she was too engrossed in her food to bother.

I loved watching people enjoy my food. I had always enjoyed cooking, ever since my dad had shown me how to make potato cakes with leftover mashed potatoes from Sunday dinner.

"Yum…mmmy, that was delicious, thanks. Frank is going to love that when he comes in. Hey, can't I say that I made it and win some brownie points?" I smiled gratefully at her.

"Since when do you need brownie points? Frank adores you." I removed her plate before she started to try and eat the pattern on the bowl.

"Umm, is there…" I changed direction from the sink to the stove before I had chance to get the bowl wet. I dug the big spoon in the mixture and poured her another bowlful.

"Only if there's enough." But this last statement was said while she was digging into the hot mixture of meat, gravy and vegetables.

"It's fine. I made enough for leftovers. I know how much Frank eats and anyway, you didn't answer my question."

"About?" she said with her mouthful.

"Brownie points," I said reminding her.

"Yeah, well he may adore me, but not my feet, and I could kill for a foot rub. Those shoes were crippling me by the end of the day, and well, you see he's got these really big, strong hands that…"

"Okay, okay, I get it! Please, spare me the details," I said making a gagging motion, but getting it all wrong as I laughed.

"You look nice by the way, didn't want to wear your hair down? No, I don't blame you, not in this weather," she said, answering her own question.

"You not eating before you go?" she added.

"I had some earlier," I said, lying as it was easier than saying I couldn't eat because of my nerves.

Libby nodded her head toward the clock on the wall, and I followed it dreading what it might show.

But it only confirmed my time had run out...

Afterlife here I come.

CHAPTER 7

AFTERLIFE

Not one thing was what I had expected.

We had driven further out of town than I would have thought necessary and when Libby had reminded me that it was on the outskirts of town, she hadn't been exaggerating. It was more like in the middle of nowhere!

We drove along the main road for what seemed like forever, and then turned down a small one-lane road which was covered either side by thick forest. It almost looked like a dark green tunnel, which didn't help my nerves. The angry tunnel, more like the mouth of Hell, opened up into a big clearing that looked like a car park. Libby drove round to the front, but I couldn't get out.

I was stunned.

The place was enormous and astonishing. I hadn't expected it to look anything like the picture of beauty that was before me. Libby noticed my surprise and just nodded saying,

"I know, nice, isn't it?" Nice! Nice wasn't a word I would have used. Out of this world, stunningly beautiful, truly amazing, breath-taking, anything other than just plain old nice! Surely her being an interior designer would have evoked a better response from those red glossy lips of hers.

"It's more than nice, Libs, it's incredible!" I said gobsmacked.

It looked so out of place, and yet it didn't somehow, as

though it had always been there. It looked hundreds of years old but surely it couldn't be. It wasn't like any club I had in mind, or any that I had ever seen for that matter.

In England, a lot of nightclubs just looked like pubs or normal buildings. One I used to go to was an old cinema, but this was like a bloody manor house.

I couldn't see the entire house (house, what an understatement!). It looked as if it went further back but was surrounded by thick forest, so only the front was exposed. It was made from thick stone blocks that were once, I suspected, a lighter shade than they were now. This was due to weathering I guessed, and it reminded me of Bath, a city in England, which was famous for its old Roman baths and sandstone buildings.

One side was covered in a thick blanket of rich green ivy that curled its way around the windows, looking as though it was trying to overtake the building but only reaching so far. This certainly gave it a creepy vibe. The entrance was as grand as the rest of the building with its impressive stone archway jutting out. Big thick black gates stood open on either side that looked strong enough to keep out an army when closed.

They had been secured back to allow access into the club where people were now entering. However, there were no lines outside with rope barriers as I had expected. In fact, the only thing that made it resemble a club was the two huge monster security guards who stood on either side of the gates. I looked at Libby.

"Frank's?"

"Yeah, that's Cameron and Jo, they're nice guys. I met them at last year's Christmas party." She laughed as if remembering something, and as it turned out, I didn't have long to wait for her to fill me in.

"Jo got so drunk, doing too many vodka shots with Frank that in the end, his mum had to come and get him." She gave a smug laugh.

"Well, have a good night, just give me a ring, and I will get Frank to come and pick you up… it's fine," she said before I had chance to say I would get a taxi. "He's working late anyway and said he wanted to pick you up."

"Okay," I said, not believing her for a second and knowing this was more likely down to Libby worrying about me.

"You'll be fine, go get 'em, kiddo," she said, trying to sound positive.

I got out of the car reluctantly and turned to shout bye.

"Have fun and relax. You look as though you are going to pass out!" she said through a small gap in the passenger side window. I was being ridiculous; the place wasn't that creepy. I watched as Libby's Ford disappeared into the fog before I turned and made my way towards the imposing entrance.

My eyes took in every raw edge, every stone block and every arched window. I noticed how the forest to the right side looked thicker and wilder in some way. When I narrowed my eyes, I thought I saw a massive balcony on the right side of the building. I wanted to take a better look, but when I started off in that direction, I caught a quick glimpse of a large figure standing there. I chickened out and turned my attention back to the main entrance.

I walked slowly, barely hearing the gravel crunching under my old purple Doc Martens, due to the loud pounding of my heart. I caught sight of the two men standing there by the entrance waiting for me to come closer. They eyed each other as if amused with the look of dread on my face. They could no doubt tell I was a newbie.

"Evening," was all the shorter one said. He had a kind face which didn't match his coarse, hard voice. Both were wearing thick black jackets that made them look even bigger. The smaller one didn't look as fit as the taller one did, but he stood looking at me now as though he was about to speak. I looked at the taller one as he was looking at me impatiently for something. Had he asked me a question?

"I said ID!" he snapped impatiently. Oops, come on Keira don't piss off the big men.

"Yeah, sure," I replied, swallowing hard as I reached in my pocket and grabbed my new licence. They eyed it carefully and then all of a sudden, their features transformed. Well, at least now, they were smiling at me instead of scowling.

"You're Frank's sister-in-law?" the taller one asked me enthusiastically (the one with the intolerance for vodka shots).

"Uh, yeah," I said warily, not knowing if Frank would want them to know that.

"Ah Hell, him and Libby have been waiting for you to come for months! It's damn good to finally meet you, I'm Jo, and this is Cameron." He held out a big bear-like hand for me to shake, and I was touched that Frank had mentioned me. His hand swallowed mine up as I placed it in his and he shook it gently as though eyeing my little breakable body.

I nodded hello to the other guy while Jo still had hold of my hand. He was turning it around, and I looked at him curiously to see what he was doing. He stamped it and I examined the red word 'legal' across my skin.

"We allow a lot of age groups in here, but they need ID to drink, and you fit the bill," he said with a big infectious grin on his face.

"Do you want me to come in with you and make sure you get to your table?" Jo asked, and I almost visibly cringed at the idea. I mustn't have done too good a job at hiding this as he laughed.

"I take that as a no," he said in good humour.

"You're just not cool to be seen with, buddy." Cameron laughed hitting his friend on the back. I chuckled nervously hoping I hadn't offended him when a more pressing matter came to mind.

"Wait... did you say table?"

"Yeah, one was reserved for you and your friends. They're already in there. Go on in, honey." Cameron winked at me, just as a couple of young, dark dressed youths were coming up behind me. They turned to them and said "ID" in a less friendly manner than I had received.

I smiled to myself and thought bless Frank for doing this. It was a nice perk being related to my big brother-in-law, and I didn't feel as nervous as I had before. I would have to remember to thank him later and also for giving me a lift home.

After walking past the imposing gated entrance, I found myself staring at a massive set of wooden doors that looked as if they once belonged to a castle. The deep oak was encrusted with black iron studs, and both doors were left open for guests. I couldn't help but touch them as I walked over the threshold.

They were warm, which I found odd. I studied them for a few seconds before I entered. There appeared to be a symbol carved deep into the middle of each door. I think it was some kind of family crest, but it was hard to make it out, as some people behind me were trying to get past. I walked through them, getting the strangest feeling, one that made the hairs on the back of my neck stand to attention. But it wasn't through fear.

No, if anything it felt like...

I was coming home.

～

"Hey Kaz, you made it!" RJ said, sounding shocked. Had she really thought that I would have stood her up? Maybe she could sense my reservations on the phone.

"Yeah, of course, wouldn't have missed it," I said trying to sound enthusiastic, which wasn't hard, as now that I was here, I was really looking forward to the night. It was as though something had made its way inside my body giving me the most amazing rush of confidence. As if something wanted me here and knew that to get me through those doors, I needed some help. Well, whatever it was, it had worked.

"Follow me. You need a drink!" she said with a huge smile on her face, which didn't match the Gothic vamp look she was going for. She was in a tiny black mini skirt with chains hanging from it everywhere. I wondered how it didn't fall down with all the extra weight. She teamed this with a black top with rips slashed across the chest revealing bright pink netting underneath. It matched her hair, which was as pink as ever but was pinned into twists at the front, and when she turned, she had a chaos of spikes at the back. To complete the outfit, she had on a long black jacket that went to the floor. It looked military style with lots of big round metal buttons going down in a V shape either side.

We made our way through the crowd towards what I assumed was the bar. It was sweet the way she kept turning around every now and again to check I was still following. I could understand why she did this as it looked as if the whole town was here and the place was so big, it could easily have been done and with room to spare. I had to keep my eye on RJ's bright pink points so as not to get lost in the mass of bodies. This was proving difficult as I couldn't help but stare everywhere.

I had never seen anything like it. Inside didn't really match the outside, a bit like old battling new. On the outside, it looked like a stately home from the sixteen hundreds, but on the inside, well that's where it started to look more like a club. One with a definite twist. The massive open space could have been built around some ruined church. The shell remained, with its really high ceilings and massive stone arches everywhere. The whole ceiling was a series of them that all mingled together, interlocking and then going off in different directions like the type you see in a grand cathedral.

The room was separated into different levels with seating around the outside in booths. The interior was lush and rich looking with crimson reds and deep purples. There were great wrought iron chandeliers that hung down from where the bigger arches met in the ceiling. All were lit with candle bulbs which flickered for effect. The same style lamps were along the walls in a random fashion. The walls were of the same stone as the outside, but they weren't weathered, so still had their natural softer colour. This gave the room a warming glow as the light reflected from the pale stone.

I was amazed by my surroundings as if I had been transported back in time to a medieval age. Only I don't think there would have been quite so many scary looking people here back then. Words like witch hunt, devil worshipper and burned at the stake came to mind. There were so many people dressed in black; it almost looked like a cult gathering. Some of them stared at me as I made my way past, trying my best to keep up with RJ. We were nearly at the bar as the crowd began to get thicker. She stopped in front and turned to face me with a huge grin across her black lips.

"You okay?" she said with a little bit of concern in her eyes.

"Yeah, I'm fine. I just didn't expect it to be so busy." She laughed as though I had missed something... something very important.

"Well, it's not normally this busy until the Dravens come here, and the Acid Criminals aren't that popular, so it's great for your first night that they're here early," she said and clapped her hands together like a child.

"What, the Acid Criminals?" I was confused, still not understanding the reason behind the mass of people who looked more like they were attending a Gothic comic convention than a nightclub.

"No, no... not the band..." I was about to ask when she suddenly shouted the reason with pure unrestrained excitement,

"The Dravens!"

After receiving this bombshell, we finally got served after about twenty minutes of trying to push our way to the front. Well, RJ pushed, and I followed. Now, once again, I was following RJ back to where her friends were waiting for us. My mind was now elsewhere, and instead of being nervous about meeting new people, I was consumed by seeing *them*. I looked around and I knew I wasn't the only one as people seemed to be buzzing with excitement.

RJ grabbed my hand, as it was obvious she knew where we were going.

"Come on! The table's just over near the stairs and we will have the best, sweeeet ass view ever!" RJ said, dragging out the sweet part and giving me a satisfied smile.

They were situated near to the mezzanine level and one of the immense staircases that led up to it. There was another one that mirrored it on the opposite side. Both of which created a perfect frame for the centre stage. It was a raised platform high enough for everyone lower than it to have a clear view of the band playing.

The layout of the place was perfect for the purpose it served. It was the classiest nightclub I had ever seen, one that you would have expected to find in a big cosmopolitan city, not a remote little town in the middle of the wilderness.

"What's up there?" I asked as we passed the staircase on the left that had two enormous men guarding it as if it held the crown jewels up there. I thought that Jo and Cameron were big, but these guys put them to shame. The story of David and Goliath popped into my head.

"Ah, now that's a good question, my dear Kazzy, as that up there is the one and only VIP area," she said dramatically as she eyed the giants.

"That's where the Dravens spend all their time; it goes further back than you can see," she elaborated motioning her hand backwards.

"Not that I have ever been up there myself," she continued with a slightly bitter tone.

"But my dad has his own building company, and one of his guys went there last year to do a job, which is strange 'cause they usually get their own people in to do stuff like that. I guess they got desperate or something... Anyway, I got my dad to describe it in every little detail to me and then, of course, passed that important information on like any good town gossip." She smiled proudly. I laughed back, not being in the least bit surprised, and also making a mental note never to tell her anything that I didn't want ending up on the town's bulletin board.

By this time we had managed to make it through the alternative looking crowd to the booth that housed all of RJ's 'Goth Gang'... that wasn't actually that Goth at all.

There were three of them in total. Two guys and one more girl all sat round a massive half-oval seat covered in red velvet. There was a table in the middle already filling with empty glasses and bottles waiting to be collected. As soon as they saw us, they budged round to make room for two more bodies.

"That was a nightmare, and I think next time I would rather

die of thirst!" RJ complained as she sat down putting her bottle of Bud on the table, ready to make the introductions.

"Everyone, this is Keira!" she announced to the gang, and I suddenly felt like I was being introduced to one of those 'self-help' groups.

"Uh... Kaz is fine," I said, trying not to sound shy. Of course, it didn't help when I had all eight eyes studying me. I sat down and rested my freezing cold bottle on the table as my hand had started to go numb with holding it so long.

"Hi Kaz, I'm Lanie." I smiled in reply to a pretty girl with short, bobbed hair. She had a kind face and small oval glasses that sat upon a tiny delicate nose. She got up to shake my hand and I leaned forward to reciprocate.

One by one, they all introduced themselves, and I started to relax once I wasn't the main topic of conversation any more. I was relieved to be chatting about starting college. They all lived locally apart from one, Charles, or Chaz as he liked to be called, who had also just moved here.

Chaz was cute looking with a baby face that looked like it still hadn't fully matured. He paid a lot of attention to RJ, but she didn't seem to notice. Every now and again, he would stare at her and smile to himself, one he thought was hidden. The other guy was Andrew, or Drew as he also preferred. He confessed himself to be a bit of a geek. He was studying computer engineering and loved to play World of Warcraft. He started to go into detail about the game or 'community' but he could have been speaking Japanese for all I knew.

"Leave it out, Drew Cap!" RJ said, throwing a piece of the beer label she had been playing with. She was a good shot as it landed on his head and rolled down only to rest on his glasses. Everyone laughed, including Drew.

I learned that he and RJ had grown up together as neighbours and had been best friends for an age. The nickname Drew Cap continued throughout the night. Drew was tall and very thin with a face to match, but he had the most amazing deep brown eyes with hints of toffee in them. They were big, very expressive, and they seemed to like what they saw in Lanie as they kept glancing towards her general direction.

They all made me feel very welcome, and I felt at ease telling them about myself (well, to a point) but they all had a laugh with the different things that I said and started with all the "say this…say that" malarkey.

Libby was right; my English accent had gone down well with them all. I didn't think it would be long before they had me doing impressions of the Royal family! But I took it all in good fun and was having so much of a good time that I didn't realise when RJ's brother turned up. It was very embarrassing to find that he was behind me the whole time I had been slightly snorting like a pig with laughter. I didn't realise until RJ looked up.

"Hey, there you are, I thought you were going to miss the band starting, but they're not on for another ten." My face went bright red with embarrassment as I could feel his eyes on the back of my head. I turned around sheepishly to see a very handsome face smiling down at me.

"Well hello there, giggles, I'm Jack. You must be our English rose, Keira," he said in a very confident, smooth textured voice. I blushed again like a nun in a nudist colony. I hated receiving compliments. I never knew how to react, not wanting to be rude but most of all not wanting to be the centre of anyone's attention.

"Jack, don't be a freak, you're embarrassing her!" RJ said coming to my rescue… well, sort of.

"I apologise for my brother. He was dropped on his head a lot as a child." I lowered my head to hide my grin.

"Don't you mean hit on the head by you!" Drew said, now joining in the debate.

Jack leaned down to my face with a cheeky grin that would make any heart melt and said,

"Sorry about these two, there's no stopping them when they get going. Let's start over, I'm Jack, and I don't have any problems with my head." He smiled at the end of this speech, replacing the cheekiness with a charming wink.

There was something so likeable about him; it was hard to

keep from smiling to myself. He looked a bit like a rough catwalk model. One you would see in an advert for a Gillette shaving product, as he had the stubble and messy hair for it.

His hair was brown but with streaks of gold cast lightly through it. It flopped around in every direction as he moved, his streaks getting caught in the warm glow of the club's lighting. His eyes were a warm hazel that matched his hair, and they were framed with long lashes. But none of these were his best features, oh no, it was his very heart-warming smile; the kind of smile, that when it appeared would light up his face, transforming it entirely.

He sat down next to me as we all budged up once more. Drew and Chaz seemed happy about the close proximity that Jack had created. But now we all looked more like couples, there being three girls and three guys. This thought made me nervous. The last thing I needed when moving here was any complications, and guys always bring complications. Especially when they looked like Jack.

"So, we have you to thank for the table?" Jack asked, and I smiled thinking about Frank.

"My brother-in-law supplies the security here," I said clarifying when RJ jumped in,

"Yeah, and the lucky cow also got a job here too!" I grinned when she winked at me, no doubt assuring me she was joking with the 'Cow' comment. I looked back to Jack to see him looking slightly concerned, but then he hid it almost immediately as RJ cut him a look. It was strange.

"So how do you like our cold little town?" Jack asked with a crooked grin as his arm rested slightly on the back of the velvet seat behind me.

"Umm, to be honest, I haven't really seen much of it, but what I have seen I like. My sister and I went hiking the other day, which I loved." This made his eyes react as though I had said something to spark his interest.

"Oh, you like to hike. I do too, well growing up here, there's not much more to do. Until this place opened, that is." I wondered how long this place had been open. RJ had said the Dravens came here every year.

"I know all the best spots if you would ever like an expert guide," he continued nudging me at this last part.

"Best spots of what?" RJ said with an abrupt manner.

But before she could get her answer, the crowd started to shift and people that were sitting were starting to rise to try and get a better view of something. I found myself thinking that considering the band wasn't that well known they sure were getting a lot of attention. I thought out loud and said,

"So, I'm guessing the band's here." I directed more at RJ as she was now stood like the rest of them. Jack and I were the only ones still sitting.

"You guessed wrong," she said through a wide black-lipped grin, now nearly standing on the seat to get a better view. I noticed Lanie was doing the same, only with her height she didn't have the same problem as RJ.

"This is going to be awesome!" And with that, her hands went to her face in what looked like pure joy!

"Is she like this at Christmas?" I asked Jack who wasn't looking as thrilled as he rolled his eyes at his sister's behaviour.

"Sadly no, nothing gets her this excited. I really don't understand what it is about them," he said in a bored tone, shaking his head slightly.

"Them?" Was I missing something? And that's when my mind kicked into gear and realised what all the fuss was about. RJ's excited squeal just confirmed things for me.

"The Dravens!" She went so high pitched I could just imagine all dogs within a ten miles radius howling in pain.

"Ah," was all I could mutter as I was trying to sink further down in my seat and angle myself away from where everyone was straining their necks to see. Jack seemed to notice my movement.

"Well, it's nice to see not everyone here has Draven fever," he said, smiling down at me but receiving RJ's middle finger in retaliation.

"Nice, and very ladylike, sis," he said, laced with sarcasm.

Then the whispers started, which indicated they were here. I don't think that anyone had even noticed that the band was already on the stage and ready to start their first song.

Heads turned towards the front entrance where I had not long since walked through. Then it was strange, like something from a Godfather movie when the Don walked in. Everyone who had been staring was now trying not to look directly at them. From what I could make out, they were now passing through the crowd, and it looked a lot easier than when we did it. People were now parting as if Moses was leading the way.

The music had started right on cue, as though trying to divert some of the attention. If anything, it just enhanced their entrance making it more dramatic. I tried not to look but found myself glancing up every now and again, wishing the commotion would soon be over. I don't know why, but I was embarrassed for them. I would have hated to have all those eyes watching me... so I didn't look, as if it would help having one less pair of eyes watching them.

But there was also another set of feelings that were coursing through my body and mind. Ones I couldn't understand. I felt nervous again, and my arms began to itch, as though the well-concealed scars beneath my sleeves were burning.

I sat on my hands, trying not to fidget too much. My heart raced uncontrollably, and I was thankful the music had started, as I was sure you could hear my body's erratic behaviour. I tried to concentrate on my breathing, slowing my inhaling down the way the doctor had shown me to control my panic attacks.

What was wrong with me? Why was I acting so crazy? So, it was just some rich family that had a bit of mystery to them; they probably just wanted to be left alone. I started to relax my thoughts. Yes, this was good, keep this up Keira, I commanded myself. But then something RJ had said to me earlier struck me.

The stairs!

The bloody stairs that led them up to the VIP area. The very stairs that we were all sat right next to. That's why RJ had been so happy about our positioning. She had known that they would have to walk right by us to get there. Okay, I wasn't so calm now. Then, as if to make matters worse, Jack was having his own rebellious feelings towards them and got up swiftly, declaring,

"I think I've had enough of the theatrics, I'm getting a drink," and left, leaving me fully exposed in view of anyone who walked by. With the crowd parting in front of us, we would now have a clear view of the Dravens, almost like being in front of the stage at a concert. RJ gasped in delight and Lanie sighed with contentment.

I, on the other hand, had stopped breathing.

Because there, in front of me was…

Dominic Draven.

CHAPTER 8

THE DRAVENS

I was like a small, helpless woodland animal caught in the sight of wild prey. I knew it was dangerous, but still, I had to look. I tried to tear my eyes away from the most perfect being I had ever seen. And Holy shit! This man was incredible. He was just too perfect, like a Greek god sent to torture me for my sins. I think if Air Force One had crashed through the building, I still wouldn't have noticed and would have died still staring.

I was aware that I was staring and hoped that no one else noticed. Not that I thought this was an issue, not with Dominic Draven around as I could now understand what all the fuss was about. He had a sort of magnetic pull to him, something unnatural, almost haunting but utterly mesmerising at the same time.

He was ahead of all the rest, so I knew he was the one in charge. A little further back, there were two men that caught my eye, one of which was gargantuan. The crowd didn't stare at him, and it was no wonder as his face was just as intimidating as his size. He had deep coloured skin like leather that had seen too much sun over the years, and it was full of what looked like potholes. Maybe from a severe case of smallpox, I wondered. Of course, being the size of a seven-foot wrestler, I doubted many people questioned his looks.

The man on his other side was tall and athletic looking, with very white blonde, straight hair that you could just see under his large black hood which concealed most of his face. I could have sworn that I noticed what looked like tattoos down one cheek. Then he came closer and it soon became hard to miss the startling difference between the whitest skin of an albino and the ink that featured down one side. I don't know why, but he reminded me of the white knight on a chessboard being taken over by the opposing dark side.

Behind these two, who looked like guards, were two other men, one dressed in a Japanese robe and had kind Asian features. His raven black hair was slicked back, and he had a distinct sharp point to his chin. High cheekbones matched oriental features that spoke of a nobility lacing his bloodline. He stood next to another man who was all light next to his dark.

He was angelic looking, and in stark contrast to the others, but had eyes that suggested otherwise. They were like black ice with a cruel, harsh glint to them. His skin was almost luminescent, even in this low lighting it glowed as if he had just spent the day basking in the sun's rays. His hair was cut short creating a halo of tight golden curls, reminding me of a handsome antique doll. His face, however, was set in firm lines, screaming out in both arrogance and pride.

But all these were insignificant factors, shadows in the background, behind the God that stood in front of them. They moved according to the way their master moved, scanning the crowd for anything unexpected.

He was slowly approaching now and looked straight on as if oblivious to everyone. All the girls (and some guys) had the same look imprinted on their eager faces. They all wanted to be seen by those seductive eyes of his, to be noticed... Well, everyone except me.

I looked down at the table, now trying to resist the urge to look again, but I knew he was getting closer as I could feel my heart rate going through the roof. It was RJ that made me fail my objective.

"Oh my God, he's looking this way!" she whispered through

97

half-closed lips. Then I did the unthinkable. I looked up, meeting a pair of intense eyes that amazingly, were also staring back at me.

Arctic. Black. Consuming.

He had paused in front of our table, and the bodyguards behind him looked just as confused as the rest of the spectators did. We had both frozen and were using precious time to drink each other in. It was as if we were now the only two people in the room.

The feelings he invoked attacked my system, flooding me with too many new sensations to deal with. Like lightning had struck, and now all I felt was electricity coursing through my body. If I thought my heart rate was going crazy before, now I thought I was going to go into cardiac arrest! He wouldn't move his intense stare from my face, and I blushed every shade of red in the spectrum. However, something inside of me would not yield. I sat up a little straighter as a mere slice of bravery gave me the strength to match his gaze. I thought I saw a small glimpse of a smile, but it was gone as quickly as it came.

I could almost hear RJ hyperventilating. He looked the pinnacle of dominance, standing there with all the club's eyes behind him watching his every move. Like waiting for a mythological warrior to issue his first command to his armies. Although with his massive body dressed in a black designer suit, he looked more like a modern version of a warrior. Maybe 'Commander of the Night' would be more fitting.

There was just something so unnerving about him... no not only unnerving, but almost unearthly. The whole club seemed to be at a standstill, my heart included. It was as if he was searching for something in my eyes, but then he frowned, breaking the spell and obviously coming up empty. Then his expression turned harsh and his frown deepened, pulling his eyebrows tighter together. This released his hold on me, and I finally lowered my face and turned my back to him to hide my shame.

I could still feel his presence as though he had somehow buried his essence under my skin. I couldn't help but scratch at my scars that started to burn under layers of clothing. I don't know how I knew, but I could feel his eyes taking in my movements. Then something snapped. A link shattered. I noticed RJ's eyes following him, and then they turned to me indicating that they were no longer in sight. I could finally breathe.

"Oh My God, what the fuck! What just happened? Did everyone else just see the Prince of Darkness himself just stop to look at our table... do you two know each other?" RJ asked me, now on a mission. She eyed me curiously and then looked back at Lanie for back up.

"Yeah, what was that? Did he know you? Did you recognise him?" Lanie said now joining in the Spanish Inquisition.

"No!" I said a bit too abruptly as if it had hit a nerve. But then my mind went into overload when she had asked 'Did I recognise him?' That was the nerve that had hit the bullseye... and holy mother did it hit me hard!

I did recognise him.

That's the reason I had the reaction when I saw him. He was the man from my dreams. The dreams that were now starting to flood back to me like a crashing wave. Yes, they were all so clear now, so clear in fact that it was hard to think of them as just dreams. They had seemed so real, but why did I forget about them. And more importantly, why was a man, who I had never seen before tonight, the exact same man that I had been so vividly dreaming about the last couple of days? None of it made any sense!

The girls didn't look convinced, and neither did the guys for that matter.

"Well, the way he was staring at you, maybe he knows you." RJ shot Drew a look for saying this, and he shrugged his shoulders replying 'what?' to her dirty look.

"What did I miss?" Jack said as he came back holding a tray full of drinks.

"You will never guess what happened," Chaz said in a high-pitched voice trying to mimic one of the girls.

"Oh, please tell me this was finally the year that he tripped and fell on his rich, pompous ass!" he said, raising his hand and dramatically slapping his forehead with the back of it. I moved closer around to give him room as he resumed his place back next to me.

"Sorry dude, guess again."

"Oh, I don't know, some girl flashed him to get his attention and even then, I doubt he would have looked, he's probably gay, you know," he said with a wicked smile. I just stayed quiet, still embarrassed from the memory. My thoughts were doing a pretty good interpretation of Formula 1.

"No flashing needed, he took a fancy to Kaz though, couldn't stop staring at her." Okay, I was going purple now. I had to get away from everyone staring at me, and it wasn't just my table, it was the entire club!

"I…I gotta go to the bathroom!" was all I could manage to get out. I felt like I was going to be sick. I know it was a silly reaction to have, but I couldn't help it. I just needed to get out of there. I pushed my way through the Gothic Draven fans over to the bathrooms. I knew the direction as Jack had pointed to them in reply to my rude exit. I saw the neon sign glowing like a beacon as it was near the bar on the same side of the wall as the entrance.

Once inside, I could feel myself calming down like the air in here was clearer. There was no one in there apart from the reflection of myself staring back at me horror-struck. I looked terrible! No, worse than terrible, I looked ill. I was so pale, and my eyes looked almost black. I felt so ashamed, no wonder he was staring at me. He probably thought of me as riffraff, wondering what a plain, fragile little thing was doing in his club!

I ran into the cubicle not being able to stop what was coming next as I threw up the one bottle of Corona that I had consumed. Thankfully, I only heard the door open after I had finished. It sounded like two girls, and no guessing needed as to who they were chatting about.

"And oh my god did you see his body, he gets finer every year. What I wouldn't do to have a night alone with that man!"

"Tell me about it. Now there's a man that I bet has good equipment, if you know what I mean!" A girl's giggle followed.

"Yeah, and I bet he knows how to use it!"

"Yeah baby!" They both giggled again, stupidly like superficial teenagers. I found myself angry at them being so vulgar towards him. I was just about to leave when I heard more.

"Yeah, but did you see that girl he was staring at… urgh." The silly cow then made a gagging noise. I was furious even though I was in the same frame of mind just a moment ago, but still, it wasn't the nicest thing to hear.

"I know, right! She wasn't at all pretty, nice skin; I suppose, but way too pale."

"It was just make-up, I bet my life on it." Well, I sure hoped that this girl didn't get into any unforeseen accidents on the way home on account of my skin type, I thought to myself angrily.

"Well, I bet he was only staring because he couldn't believe she got in his club and if we would have been sitting there, we probably would be in the VIP area now!" Oh god, it was getting worse. Now they were clearly deranged!

"We are going to have to come earlier next time and try for those seats."

"Yeah, then he won't have to be put through that sight again!" They giggled again, only this time making high-pitched squeals. My blood boiled as I walked out of the cubicle, head held high. I knew that they were young from the sound of their undeveloped conversation, but they were practically kids. They were applying lip gloss when they saw me, and their faces dropped.

I washed my hands that were slightly shaking in anger and dried them. Once I had finished, I made my way to the door but just before I left, I turned to say my piece.

"Oh, and by the way, he might not be into pale and plain, but I'm pretty sure he's definitely not into kids, so why don't you two run off home before you miss Hannah Montana!" I walked out with the biggest smile on my face, leaving them with their mouths still hanging open. As I walked back still grinning, I looked up to stifle a laugh and noticed a pair of eyes that were watching me in amusement themselves.

I could see the VIP area from back here and it looked full of people, which was strange, as not one person had gone up the stairs after them. Maybe there was another entrance to it for the 'special guests'. These little factors were irrelevant compared to the statue of a man staring back at me now, just as he had before. He wasn't as clear up there in the low light, but I could have sworn I had seen the flash of white brought out by a smile. He was so damn enigmatic. I stopped smiling and put my head down determined not to look again as I hurried back to my seat.

~

The rest of the night went quickly and without any more incidents. Jack insisted on staying with me while I waited for Frank. The others were going on to Drew's house, but as I was getting picked up I didn't want Frank having to wait up for me any longer, so I declined the offer.

"Are you sure? I could drive you home. I've only had one beer," Jack said with a hopeful look in his eye. "I'll behave," he added with a mischievous wink.

"Thanks, but Frank's probably on his way now... rain check?" I said hoping he wouldn't take it the wrong way. I mean, maybe before at a different time, I would have really gone for someone like Jack. He was really warm and sweet to be around, with a happy-go-lucky nature that was infectious. You couldn't help but smile around him.

But I didn't want him to get the wrong idea. How could I get it across that I didn't date? Maybe I could hint to RJ about the whole 'not dating' rule. But what was I saying, I was being conceited enough to believe he wanted to be more than just friends. He was just a nice guy, plain and simple.

"Okay, okay I give in, but how would you like to meet up and I will show the big bright lights of our small town?" I raised one eyebrow and said,

"Bright lights?"

"Oh yeah, there's one really bright street lamp on 5th, no really, you should see it, Vegas has nothing on us baby!" I laughed, and he smiled down at me sweetly, his hair flopping over his eyes. He was really tall. I hadn't really noticed in the club. He had long legs and a wide chest that went out in a v shape from his waist. He wore jeans that were ripped at the knee and a T-shirt with an Iron Maiden picture on it, underneath a combat style jacket.

"I will have to get your number off RJ, so next time we can arrange for me to pick you up and take you home again, that way you don't have to wait here in the cold." He paused and touched a single finger to my chilled cheek. "We don't want that pretty skin of yours to get any paler." I blushed as always and smiled not knowing how to respond.

"Or I could just keep embarrassing you, that seems to put some colour in those cheeks," he said laughing and then nudged me, trying to get me to smile again.

"I can wait on my own if you're cold, I feel bad you waiting with me like this," I said trying not to offend him. "Plus, they're going to be waiting for you at Drew's," I added trying to sound light hearted.

"Are you kidding? I don't mind waiting with you, besides RJ and Drew are probably just brawling around on the floor, which I've seen a hundred and one times before, and trust me when I say it gets old. Nah, I would much prefer being here with you." I blushed again, hoping he didn't notice.

"Brawling?" I said trying to imagine the two of them, 'The Goth and the Geek' going at each other.

"Yeah, and I would put my money on RJ any day, she fights dirty, at least that's the way I taught her." He gave me a wink as the penny finally dropped. He'd been teasing me.

"You shouldn't tease gullible people, it's against the nice guy law," I teased back.

"Oh, but where's the fun in that?" Then he rubbed his hands together and blew into them. I couldn't help but feel guilty but then he stopped suddenly.

"Wait... you think I am a nice guy?" he asked beaming at me. The only reply he got from me was a laugh. He joined in and went back to rubbing his hands.

"Are you sure you don't want to go. I'll be fine, the club's not even closed yet and the doormen are only over there," I said pointing over my shoulder.

"I think I'll survive, plus if I get frostbite you can nurse me back to health. I would be expecting first-class health care though, sponge baths, back rubs, dangled grapes… you know, all the extras included." He was in front of me now and he poked me gently in the ribs. I, of course, being very ticklish, giggled, and to my embarrassment snorted a little as well. I stepped back as a wicked grin spread across his face and he held out his finger threatening to do it again.

"What an adorable sound you just made," he said mocking me but trying very hard not to laugh. Just then Frank's car came into view and Jack nodded as if to ask, 'if that was him'.

"Yeah, that's Frank. Thank you for waiting with me, Jack, it's been… amusing," I said smirking back at him. I went to turn but before I could go, he said,

"Oh, come here," and then wrapped his big arms around me in a bear hug. He whispered down into my ear,

"It was very nice meeting you, Keira," and then let go and walked away, waving over his shoulder. I composed myself and got in the car a bit red-faced. Frank turned to me and said,

"Boy, you sure do make friends quick, kid." The fact that he called me kid made me smile.

"So how was it?" he said as he pulled away nodding briefly towards the doormen. I looked back at first at the doormen to find them waving, but then something else caught my eye. A lone figure on the balcony to the side of the club stood there motionless and watching. I had to wonder… was it him?

"It was good, everyone was really nice," I said realising Frank was still waiting for my answer. I noticed his lips curve into a mocking smile.

"Yeah, I noticed that, he seemed *real* friendly," he teased aiming a thumb over his shoulder back at where Jack and I had stood.

"It's not like that," I said getting defensive.

"Sure, sure, I'll say no more but I'm warning you, your sister might grill you when you get home."

"What, she stayed up?" This was bad. She would want every minor detail about the whole evening, and unless I could convince Frank not to mention 'the Jack thing', I was screwed! She would push it and push it until I repeated every word he'd ever said to me and then never let me forget it.

"Umm... Fr-a-a-a-n-k?" I said in my sweetest voice dragging out his name.

"Y-y-e-e-s-s?" he said doing the same.

"Could we kind of not mention the whole Jack thing to Libby?" He raised his eyebrows and a cunning smile crept across his lips.

"Oh, it's Jack is it?" Damn! I tried the puppy dog eyed thing and then... score! I knew it would work. His features turned to putty in defeat.

"Okay, okay, I promise, not a word." This was why I loved Frank.

"Thanks, only I would never hear the end of it." He was on the main road now and I knew there wasn't much further to go.

"No, neither would I. She's still having a go at me for getting you that job. Speaking of which, did you see Jerry?" I smiled thinking back to it. Frank had rung him to let him know I was going to be there and must have given him a description of me because at the end of the night Jerry the Manager had come over to introduce himself.

He also asked if I could start earlier due to the Dravens' unexpected arrival. The place had been packed tonight and there didn't seem to be enough bar staff. I told him that wasn't a problem and he looked thrilled. Added to that, he also looked tired and worn down. I wasn't surprised with the night he must have had.

"Yeah, I did, thanks for that. He asked if I could do a small shift, starting tomorrow."

"That's great but..." he shifted slightly in his seat, looking uncomfortable.

"But?"

"But Libby is going to shit kittens! I try and tell her that she worries too much about you, but she can't be reasoned with," he said looking sympathetic to my cause.

"I know but I can handle it. Her heart's in the right place." I didn't like where the conversation was leading so I quickly changed it. "Oh, and by the way, whilst it's in my head, thanks for sorting out that booth for us tonight, it was manic busy."

"What you talkin' about, kid?"

"You know, the table you had reserved for us." Frank gave me a vacant look and then shook his head.

"Sorry honey, that's nice but it wasn't me." I frowned thinking back to who could have reserved us a table but more importantly, why would they?

"It must have been your friend, Jerry."

"I doubt it, as he's a great guy but as tight as they come and those seats are normally bought for the night."

"Really?" I asked, now even more confused. He nodded, and we didn't speak of it again. However, my mind went into overload trying to figure it out, and of course my thoughts led me back to the sight of that lone figure stood on the balcony.

How long had they been watching?

And more importantly…

Was it him?

CHAPTER 9
FIRST NIGHT

"*W*hy can't I control you?*"
I woke up suddenly with his voice still echoing in my mind. But then I heard the phone ringing and knew it wasn't just the sound of his voice that had dragged me from sleep. I left it to ring as there was no way I was making it downstairs in time. It wasn't long before RJ's excited voice could be heard leaving a message.

I looked at the clock thinking it was way too early for phone calls, but to my utter shock I had slept in. I never slept in this late so was surprised to see it was almost lunchtime, which meant I only had hours until my first shift.

I got up, rushed through a shower and called RJ back after listening to her message with a towel still wrapped around my head.

"Yeah, he wouldn't shut up about you last night at Drew's. I think my big bro has a bit of a crush!" RJ said after telling me I was a big hit with everyone.

"Oh, I think he was just being nice." I tried in vain, but this didn't sway her efforts.

"Trust me, there is being nice and then *there's being nice!*" Thankfully she soon forgot about this subject, however her next wasn't any easier to hear.

"Hey, speaking of being nice, what was up last night with tall, dark and dreamy staring at your ass?"

"I was sat down, RJ, there was no ass looking," I said going red just thinking about it.

"Yeah, yeah, you know what I mean. He couldn't take his eyes off you!" I bit my lip just thinking back to it, and even more so to the dream I'd just woken up from.

"RJ, he was frowning at me. If anything, I thought he was going to have me kicked out of his club!" At this she started laughing.

"What?" I asked frowning now myself.

"Oh, come on, did you not see him first playing all Mr. Lusty, he only frowned when he realised you weren't dropping to your knees and begging him to take you… which by the way, officially makes you the coolest person I know." I laughed and cringed at the same time.

RJ ended the conversation by making me swear to tell her everything about my first shift at Afterlife. We also arranged to meet up for our first day of college, Jack had offered to show us around as he was in his third year already. I had to admit, knowing I wasn't starting college on my own was comforting. And now with having a new job, things had really started to fall into place more quickly than I ever imagined.

I was feeling so good that I decided to call my mum and let her know how things were going. The conversation didn't last long as she had a spinning class to get to, but she was obviously thrilled to hear I was doing so well with the move. We promised a time to speak for longer, only next time on Skype so Libby could also be there.

Pretty soon I found myself getting ready for my first shift, and this was where the nerves kicked in. The thought of going back there made my palms sweaty again. I didn't know why… well okay, that wasn't entirely true as I was pretty sure I would be more at ease if the Dravens weren't there.

What was it about that man that had my body in knots? And the word intimidating didn't even begin to cover it. Of course, now there were the dreams to explain. I mean, how can one man

I had never laid eyes on before, end up being so real? I had tossed and turned over these very questions all last night.

It was a strange mixture of nerves and excitement as the clock ran down. Every time I thought about last night I tried to put it down to nothing, but that one look just kept creeping its way back into my mind like a little bug munching away at my brain.

~

By the time Libby got home and walked in through the front door, she was greeted by the sight of me sat at the foot of the stairs facing her. I had my jacket on and bag next to me all ready to go, which she obviously hadn't been expecting.

"Oookay..." Libby said dragging out the word like she was worried as she slowed her motions down from hanging up her jacket.

"I was kinda wondering..." Libby cut me off when she took back her jacket knowing what I was asking.

"Let's go then," she said turning back around and out of the front door. I got up, and only then realised I had been sat there way too long as my butt felt numb. I grabbed my bag and followed Libby to find she was in the car with the engine running.

"Okay, so where to?" Libby asked as I sat down but before I could answer her, she got the wrong idea.

"You look nice, you have a date don't you! It's with that Jack guy isn't it?"

"No, it's not but wait... how did you know about Jack?" I asked, already having my suspicions.

"Do you really think I don't know when my own husband is keeping something from me, besides he does this thing with his lips that looks like he's sucking a lemon. Oh, that, and he's ticklish, so he was easy to break," she said smirking at me, and now I knew what all the raucous laughter was last night.

"Well he obviously wasn't that easily broken," I said cringing at what was coming next.

"What do you mean?" she asked looking sideways at me.

"My date isn't a date at all. I'm actually starting work tonight... and technically this isn't being dressed up... I just thought I would make a bit of an effort, being my first shift and all..." I said, rambling in hopes of skipping the lecture. She closed her eyes briefly as if trying to find the right words when I beat her to it.

"I know you don't think I should work there, but honestly it's fine. In fact, I'm really looking forward to getting back into work, and besides, I can't have you and Frank driving me around forever. I need a car, and with that comes the need for money." Libby let go of a big sigh at this, and instead of the argument I was expecting, she shocked me by saying,

"Okay. I get it. I might not like it, but I understand you wanting your independence and after what happened, well it makes sense." I felt my muscles tighten when she brought up the past, but it was gone as quickly as it came. Libby wasn't going there, which meant I didn't need to go there either.

"Thanks Libs. You know I love you, right?"

"Yeah, yeah, I love you too, which is why I had Frank promise me that his guys will be watching out for you and if you get any trouble, then ass will be kicked."

"Alright, kinda scaring me now, Libs," I said laughing, but she still made me promise before I got out of the car to let Cameron and Jo know if I had any problems.

It was a clear night but still cold and crisp. I pulled my long jacket collar closer up to my face, keeping my neck warm. At least it would be warm inside. I was about twenty minutes too early, but I was sure that wouldn't matter. I knew tonight would be mainly showing me around, but that part excited me. It was just such an amazing place. I could imagine some Lord or Lady owning the town and this was where they resided.

But that thought sobered me pretty quickly considering which 'Lord' did in fact live here... well for the time being at least. And from the sound of things, that *Lord* did own most of this town. A man I was going to be working for. Now this thought got my pulse racing. I got a hold of myself and made my feet move forward.

The same doormen greeted me as I approached the door which made my nerves calm slightly. The place was empty at this time and looked three times as big as it had done last night. You could now see much more detail that had previously been lost in the mass of bodies concealing it.

The bar area was made from a glass front with metal entwined through it. The metal was made to look like a thorny vine that was piercing the glass and at each point it did, it was surrounded in a blood-red tint. It looked like a piece of art.

The rest of the bar followed on with the theme, housing big glass shelves with vine metal supports, holding a variety of different bottles of liquor upon them. Some of which I recognised and some that looked imported from God only knows where.

"Hey, you're early, that's good!" Jerry was coming towards me not looking quite as flustered as last time. He was tall and very thin, and he reminded me a bit of Nosferatu, as he was bald and had the palest skin I had ever seen, even paler than mine. He held a constant fear in his eyes and he moved nervously from side to side. He didn't strike me as a club Manager, and I couldn't see the kindness in his eyes that I had last night.

"I hope that's okay," I whispered, not knowing what else to say. He nodded as though distracted by something. His eyes seemed locked and he stared behind me with a frightening gaze. I was just about to turn and look but he blinked twice and turned back to me abruptly.

"Okay then, let's get you started." I turned to follow him but not before looking in the direction he had been fixated on. He had been staring at the VIP level, but whatever he had been staring at was now gone and you could only make out faint shadows that didn't seem to be moving.

"Now there's only one thing to warn you about, we only have one rule… but it's very important you understand." He was speaking in hushed tones but then he stopped and looked around as though he was about to tell me a deadly secret. He leaned in close and I could smell a sour tinge to his breath, which made me gag slightly.

"Nobody goes upstairs… EVER!" he said, shouting this last part louder than the rest. I couldn't help taking a startled step backwards. This place didn't seem real, like this guy was an actor and I was on some weird 'caught on camera' show. The ones where they trick some poor unsuspecting fool that it's all real and they get a big kick out of their scared witless reactions.

"Oookaay," I said drawing out the word.

"Yes… I mean no, *no one* goes up there unless instructed. They have their own staff, and the VIP area never closes whilst the Draven family and guests are here… I mean there, up there!" It was like deciphering a conflicted code talking to this man!

"No problem, got it," I said a little too over enthusiastically. Thankfully this seemed to throw a spanner in his babbling.

"This is Mike, and over there is Hannah. Mike will be showing you the ropes, but don't worry we will just have you collecting glasses tonight until you get… uhh… *a feel for the place.*" It was odd the way he said this last part, as if there was something amiss. He scratched his head with a violent rub that made me jump slightly. I was sure I saw him twitch before he did this. Then abruptly, he turned and almost hovered away.

He was odd to say the least. I would have to ask Frank about him later when he picked me up, that was if I was brave enough to find out.

"Hi, sorry what did he say your name was?" A voice talking to me brought me back to earth.

"I don't think he did, but it's Keira or Kaz for short."

"Don't worry about him, he's a bit of a weirdo, but you will get used to it. Of course, it's worse now the Dravens are here, he won't relax until they're gone again." He stood with his arms folded looking very defensive, which made me think that he'd had a few problems with the manager, ones he'd like to share.

"His brother Jerry is the more relaxed one." Ah! That explained a lot. It wasn't even the right guy.

"Twins?" Although it was obvious, I said it anyway.

"Yeah, that was Gary, but they are nothing alike, that one's a bit… how can I say… a bit special." Oh, okay that explained it I thought, feeling a bit guilty.

～

Mike stayed with me all night and he turned out to be a fun guy. He reminded me of Frank's younger brother Justin.

Justin was around my age and I had met him once at their wedding. He was a lot like Frank, easy going and sweet-natured but his looks were the opposite. They were both very handsome but in different ways. Frank was more like a cute cuddly bear, big and burly. Justin was a baby-faced beauty, but boy did he know it. I would be the first to admit that when I first saw him I had a bit of a crush, and if he hadn't brought a girlfriend with him to Libby's very English church wedding, then I'd have hoped for more.

The bar started to get busier as the time got on. I didn't even realise that a band had started to play until it was finally time for me to collect some empties. Mike begrudgingly left my side to go and help serve at the bar. I weaved in and out of all sorts of people, who looked like they were trying to belong to something greater in life. Wasn't that what we were all doing in some way, trying to belong to something better than ourselves? Trying to evolve our thoughts and expand our minds to different exciting new possibilities. Wasn't that what escapism was all about?

Sometimes reality just doesn't seem enough. In my mind I held so much faith in fantasy. It was safer for me that way, because in my fantasies the things that happened to me in my real life, those were the dreams… No, not dreams but nightmares. It was as if they hadn't happened and that's how I coped. I decided that the hurt could be numbed, that I could lose myself in a perfect state of ignorance. After all, 'Ignorance is bliss'. However, this didn't make the cloud disappear completely, but it helped me get from one day to the next without bringing anyone else down with me. It was my curse, no one else's.

So, as I walked or more like ducked, squeezed and pushed my way through all these troubled looking souls, I found it was a bit comforting too, well... 'fit in'.

The night went very quickly, and I hadn't realised that my two-hour trial night had turned into my six-hour trial. Now I was outside taking out the trash and it was fully dark. Luckily, I had rung Frank and arranged for him to pick me up later. I smiled when I heard Libby in the background asking, 'is she alright, does she need me to go and pick her up now?'

Mike had shown me where the bins were and the number to get back through the security doors that had a four-digit code. He told me to just remember a square, 1452. His fingers touched the keys in the order that made that square and I nodded saying "got it" not wanting to give blondes a bad name. But now I stood here alone behind a closed door, not getting that fuzzy lift that the club's music and atmosphere gave off. No, now I was looking behind me at the looming forest, that looked too close for comfort, and wishing I had taken Mike's offer to do the bins.

Now I was alone. Of course, the fact that this side of the building was completely surrounded by an eerie black wall of forest didn't help with my jellified backbone. I automatically started to look around but when my eyes scanned the side wall they found a black abyss that didn't seem to end. How big was this freakin' place?

I shook off the feeling that someone was watching me, getting that tingling feeling at the base of my skull again. I started to walk to the place Mike had shown me where the bins were hidden. Great... hidden! But of course, they were I thought, rolling my eyes to no one.

I struggled down the steps with my heavy load and nearly slipped as the temperature had dropped significantly, covering the earth's surface with an icy blanket. My gloved hand caught the metal supports and I steadied myself letting out a nervous giggle. I picked up the sacks I had dropped and walked slowly around the corner to where I had been directed. My feet crunched the icy gravel making my heart quicken. It was so stupid to be scared.

"Man up, Keira, it's only bin duty," I said reassuring myself.

I could see the 'dumpsters' as Mike had called them. I wondered if I shouldn't go back and ask for his help, they were so big I didn't know if I could even lift the lid. I paused and turned back to the door where a faint glow of the security light could be seen around the corner of the imposing stone wall. It cast shadows across the ground, making my mind wild with images that weren't there. The light caught the icy gravel making it look like glass or mirrors, sparkling in millions of directions.

I tried to focus on the job at hand. The quicker I got this done, the sooner I could be inside safe and warm. I pushed the lid and it opened, only to come crashing back down again missing my fingers by mere centimetres.

Okay, it was going to play hardball. Then bring it on, stupid pain in my ass plastic top! I bent my knees down, planning to launch myself upwards, hopefully giving it enough momentum to keep going until it was back on itself. Okay, here goes. I took a deep breath, flung my body upwards and pushed the lid's lip as hard as my little frame could manage. But it wasn't enough.

My hands were gripped on the inside where the lid had been and was now crashing back down angrily. I didn't have time to move, just had time to wait for the pain to hit.

But the pain didn't come. Instead, the wind did. A gust that was so strong and powerful, it pushed the lid back with an almighty thunderous crash. The plastic bounced back and forth until it cracked under the strain. It made me jump backwards, landing on my backside with a thud of my own. That was going to bruise, but hell, it was better than eight broken fingers. I got up and wiped down my jeans and rubbed my sore bottom. I picked up the stupid black sacks and threw them with shaky hands into the dark pit.

"What was that!?" My voice shook in response to the noise that had just cut through the dark silence. Okay, definitely time to leave. But hey, why was it so dark? Shit! I hadn't noticed before but where did the light go? There was no longer any glistening floor or shapeless shadows. Oh God, the security light had gone out!

There had been a noise; I was sure of it. The sounds of trees rustling, then a branch snapping had me frozen in pure dread. It must just be an animal. But what if it wasn't? Okay, breathe. Just breathe.

I stared into the surrounding trees, but there was nothing to see. Just tall black shapes that entwined themselves closer to me, like a wooden cage I couldn't escape from. I could feel my chest getting tighter as it was getting harder to breathe. I tried to tell myself not to panic and to get back to the door, but my feet were rooted to the spot. Fear had me trapped in time and I felt my scars almost burn their way through the material that concealed them. My blood froze, and my eyes filled with tears.

Memories came rotating back at me over and over, hitting me hard like a bloody sledgehammer to the chest. Repressed memories assaulted me and flooded my brain. It had been a night like this, cold and hauntingly beautiful. Only then I had never been afraid; I had seen its beauty and not the living nightmares it could bring; the evil lurking in wait amongst its flawless setting.

I had stood waiting unaware of the danger that night held in store for me. And after expecting something sweet to come along in reality, the only thing waiting for me was horrifyingly evil and sour. Then I heard a noise I would never forget but wished more than anything in the world that I would... *That I could.* Had it been a warning? It was the last noise I ever heard before Hell had truly found me.

Before I changed... *before he had changed me.*

A single tear escaped my eye and ran down my cheek towards my quivering lips. But something happened before it got there, it stopped... no it didn't just stop... *it froze.* I could now move. It pulled my focus out of its mental confinement, and I raised my hand to my cheek. There, my fingers peeled away a single frozen teardrop.

My eyes then started to focus on a familiar sight. For there in front of me was an image getting closer, flying through the trees so gracefully as if there wasn't any forest in its path. It glided through the black evening air, tilting its wings as if to catch the cool breeze.

The bird from my dream was back.

But more importantly…

Where was its master?

CHAPTER 10

WHISPERED LIPS

One look at the bird coming at me again and I ran back towards the door, which wasn't easy in the dark. I fumbled my way along with my hands sliding off the wet stone wall. Of course, the Heavens had decided to open, and with the rain beating down hard, it made everything slick.

But thankfully the moon had come out from behind the trees and was leading the way. I didn't know whether or not the creature was still out there. I had not waited long enough to find out as now I didn't have the safety of glass from my window to protect me.

I could feel something watching, but it didn't make me feel as scared as I had been before. It made me feel warm and safe. I couldn't explain it, but whatever it was, it was comforting. However, it still didn't change my need to get back inside.

"If only I had more light." I hadn't realised that I said the words out loud instead of just thinking them until, to my great surprise, the security light flicked twice before illuminating fully. It lit up my pathway to the door, which wasn't as far as I had thought it had been. But wait, oh damn! I had forgotten the bloody password! Oh, God, what was it?

I almost fell on the steps in my haste to get to the keypad. I fumbled with the keys pressing them too fast to even register.

Oh, come on, think. Think damn it! A square that was it! 3256. No, that wasn't it, 1254 again no.

"Oh, come on, please work!" I said in a panic, whipping my head back and forth in case anything was behind me. The feeling that I was being watched still hadn't left me. Then something different started to happen. A calming wave overtook my body, travelling its way down from my neck to my hand like some soothing touch I couldn't see. Then the feeling of a larger hand taking my own and gently forcing it to move, took hold. Almost like a lover coming up behind me and taking matters into their own hands.

My mouth dropped open, but there were no words. I just gasped, taking in more cold air. The hairs on the back of my neck stood on end as if a much bigger body was getting even closer to my trembling frame. My head even tilted to one side as I felt the hidden breath there before it travelled down my body as though I was waiting for the kiss that never came. My finger moved gracefully over the digits in perfect order as though they weren't attached to the rest of me.

1…4…5…2. and the door clicked. My hand gripped the cold metal handle and pulled it down. When the door opened easily letting the warm air and light seep through the gap, I finally took a much-needed breath. My hand was quickly released, and I was once again capable of moving of my own accord. I spun around quickly trying to capture a glimpse of I don't know what. My eyes came up empty, just as my mind did. I could not explain any of it. Only that whatever it had been, had been truly…

Magical.

The rest of my shift came and went in a bit of a blur. Mike had given Gary a glowing review of my first night, so I now officially had the job if I wanted it. I knew in a town like this getting this job was like winning the lottery considering how many people would kill to work here. So, I accepted gratefully, and was now stood outside waiting for Frank, with a smile on my face.

Jo and Cameron were kindly giving me their congratulations on getting the job before I even told them. I took note of their earpieces and gathered news travelled fast around here. Speaking of which, Jo put his hand to his ear and after listening for a few seconds, they both hurried inside. I knew something must have been kicking off back in the club for them to have rushed inside like that as you rarely saw them leave the entrance.

I started walking slightly away from the club, so it was easier for Frank to pull in and pick me up. I looked back to Afterlife, and my eyes wandered over to the side of the building where the bins were situated. I rubbed my hands thinking of the warm sensation that overtook my body earlier. My hand hadn't been my own, and the feeling hadn't completely left me. No, it had stayed with me in a more delicate form, but it sure felt good. It made all the fear go away, and was replaced by a warming bliss so intense it had me struggling to keep my secret smile hidden.

"Hey, Blondie!" a guy shouted over to me, and in my reminiscing state, I hadn't noticed the two guys now approaching me.

"Do you need a lift somewhere?" the other guy asked, and both were carrying beer bottles.

"Uh… no thanks, I'm waiting for someone," I said taking a few steps back the closer they got.

"Aww honey, don't be like that. Why wait when we are right here." The guy sniggered to his friend nudging him on the shoulder.

"Yeah, why don't you come with us? We know a little place where we can all get to know each other a little better." I rolled my eyes at the jerks that obviously had issues with a girl saying no, so I decided to make it clearer for them.

"Look, I don't mean to be rude, but I am not interested, so just move along." They both laughed holding up their hands and mocking me,

"Whoa, you know, bud, I think she's trying to blow us off."

"Yeah, and after we have been so nice to her," the other butthead said. I turned back to face Beavis when he walked up closer to me and said,

"I think you just like being a cock tease and playing hard to get, so stop being a little bitch and play nice." Then he grabbed my forearm, and I freaked. I hated being touched on my scars, so I yanked my arm free and stepped in to face him.

"Listen, tosser. I said, no! And you ever touch me again it will be the last thing you ever do, as my boyfriend is on his way and will kick your dodgy, gormless, ugly ass, face!" I said, wishing that swearing came more natural to me. I had to admit when their faces dropped, and they started backing away, I felt good.

"Okay, okay, we're sorry! We didn't mean anything by it… we don't want any trouble now."

"Yeah, yeah… no…no trouble, we're just leaving," they both stuttered out in their haste to leave.

"Yeah! You'd better run!" I said, rolling my shoulders and puffing out my chest. I turned around still watching them over my shoulder when I walked straight into what felt like a wall. I bounced backwards, only to be caught before I fell on my bum. Unyielding arms secured me not only upright but also pulled me a step closer to his body. I had that dreaded feeling of who I would find when I finally looked.

I blew some of the loose hair that had fallen in front of my face as I raised my eyes to his, only to find the one man I had been obsessing over. Like in the club we had a silent moment pass between us, one that was shattered with the sounds of the two guys freaking out in the distance. His head shot over mine, which wasn't hard given our height difference. His frown put mine to shame and was scary enough in its own right.

"See they don't come back," he ordered over to one of the men with him in a voice I had not yet heard, and I shuddered at the authority in it. The massive guy I had seen him entering the club with last night looked like a battle-scarred Viking. He was possibly the biggest guy I had ever seen, and one that would have me quaking in my boots if he merely said 'boo' to me. He grunted in response before following orders and leaving the two of us alone.

Meanwhile, I was still trying to think of something to say when he beat me to it.

"It is not wise standing alone in the dark," he told me, and it almost sounded like a threat. I went to take a step back, and the arm he still held around me tightened possessively before letting me go. The feeling it created being so close to him was intoxicating, and the spell was only broken once we had some space between us.

"Uhh… Okay, well, thanks. I guess I needed to add a few inches to my threats eh," I said raising up on my tiptoes and looking him up and down, knowing I would need bloody stilts to match his height. However, I knew this was the wrong thing to say when his frown deepened.

"This is not a joke. If you have a boyfriend, then I suggest informing him of the dangers that can occur when leaving a beautiful girl waiting alone at night." My breathing hitched when he called me beautiful, and I exhaled in a puff, not knowing what to say. It came out as a wheezing noise, and one perfectly shaped eyebrow arched at the sight of my strange behaviour. What, had he never seen a girl flustered before? Being as handsome as he was, I very much doubted it.

"Uhh… I would say that to him… but there is no him… boyfriend, I mean… just me." He didn't say anything to this but looked over my head once more, and I followed his gaze to see headlights illuminating the trees. Just then, Frank's car came into view.

"Your ride?" I nodded, too scared of what else to say as everything that I'd said so far had made me sound simple.

"Don't let this happen again, *Keira,"* he whispered in my ear, and my body froze with the feel of his lips so close to my skin. I still had my eyes to Frank's car coming closer but all I wanted to do was close them and sink back into the strong body behind me.

"I promise I won't…" I said, turning back round to face him to find he was gone.

"What the…?" I muttered in sight of his disappearing act, and I looked everywhere to see if I could spot him.

"You ready, kid?" Frank asked through the window, and I nodded my head even though I was in no way ready to leave yet... and after what just happened, I didn't think I ever would be.

∾

It didn't take a genius to know my mind was elsewhere, and Frank gave up after his third attempt at a conversation. At least with the smile on my face, he knew from the power of elimination that my shift had gone well.

The same thing happened once we were back at home when Libby tried to ask me how it went. I saw Frank shaking his head at her as if to say, 'don't ask'. I walked over to where she was curled up in the armchair, kissed her on the forehead and said,

"I am beat, gonna sleep, it was a good night, loved working there, night, night."

"Uh... night," she said, shocked when I just turned around and left for my room after kissing Frank on the cheek and thanking him for the lift home. I walked away to the sound of Libby asking,

"Is she pissed?"

I was definitely drunk, but not from alcohol. I ran up the stairs taking two at a time. Once inside my room, I stripped off my work clothes and draped them over a chair by my desk. I then pulled out some clean baggy clothes I used for pyjamas. I let my hair down, running my fingers close to my scalp. I couldn't help moaning out loud at how good it felt after a day of weight twisted at the back of my head. I brushed it, plaited it, and then finished getting ready for bed.

While brushing my teeth, I thought about how my shift had gone and how much I had enjoyed getting back in the swing of working again. But this was a fleeting thought quickly replaced by what happened after work. For starters, he knew my name! And what had he been doing out there in the first place? Did he usually take midnight strolls in case there were damsels in distress? This thought didn't make me happy and the jealousy was irrational.

I decided to think back to nicer thoughts, like how it had felt to have his arms wrapped securely around me, almost as if he hadn't wanted to let me go. This was a nice thought to be having when about to get into bed being, as it was one of the main places I wanted a certain someone to join me. After all, I was only human! But not only that, but I was also woman enough to know that when a man like him is around, then, that affects you in places you normally have to touch to be affected. Well, that meant something in my book. So, with this in mind, my hand wandered down under the covers and did the next best thing a girl could do when having a devastatingly handsome man on the brain.

For the act to play out to its fullest, I transported myself back to that first night in the club. I was now sat there in that booth wearing a black, barely-there dress of silk. I was also alone, and this time when the doors opened only one man walked in. My breath caught as my pleasure increased at just the sight my mind created. He was utter perfection, and that perfection was once again walking right up to my table.

I bit my bottom lip, both in the realms of fantasy and bland reality. He homed in on me and stormed through the mass of people with only one thing on his mind... *me*. This time, the world didn't part for the powerful-looking man getting to me. No, in my mind I wanted him to work for it and as his long legs ate up the space, he most certainly worked it good. Damn good in fact, thanks to the way his muscular frame looked in a black suit.

Once he got to me, he looked almost wild, and the intense gaze told me one thing was on his mind. Before I even got a word out, that look of restrained lust snapped and he hauled me up against him. I think my knees would have given out if one of his arms hadn't banded itself around my torso.

The other hand travelled excruciatingly slowly up my side, brushing my breast as he went, extracting a moan from my parted lips. His hand continued its exquisite journey upwards until the whole of his hand was stretched along the column of my neck. I had closed my eyes, hiding myself from the intensity of his soul-searching eyes. This was allowed to happen for less than a second before I heard the possessive growl coming from deep within him.

"Look at me!" he commanded. At the same time, his hand fisted in my loose hair, forcing my head back to look up at him. I gasped when I saw the purple fire burning in his eyes. Eyes that looked as though they wanted to devour me whole. I was caught in some mental web he intended to keep me sealed in, and at this point, I never wanted to escape. Even when his head lowered fully, welding my personal space to join his own.

"You *never* hide from me." His intimidating order was enhanced by the growl on the word 'never', and I shuddered in his arms.

"Say it!" he added, and when I hesitated, his grip tightened in my hair but holding back from developing it into too much pain.

"I…" I tried to get my brain to work harder and somewhere along the line; this fantasy was slipping out of my control. But how?

"Say it. Now!" His voice broke not only the argument but also any hesitation. So, I gave him not just what he wanted but what we both wanted…

A small forever.

"I will never hide from you," I whispered, and I heard the breath leave him quickly. Then, before I knew what was happening to this runaway fantasy, I clearly no longer controlled, my head was forced into another angle. Where now his perfect lips descended and just before the connection was made, he whispered above me,

"Good girl," in the softest voice I didn't know could come from such obvious strength. His arms pulled me tighter at the same time my world exploded. He took control of my lips in a way that caused a need in my toes to curl. On a gasp, he took his opportunity to drive the connection home, and home is how I felt when Dominic Draven was kissing me. It was completely soul consuming, and I felt myself break into pieces as I came apart under my own touch. The orgasm tore from me with such force I could only hope I hadn't screamed the name I felt leave my lips.

"Draven!" And with that one name coming from deep inside my core, I felt that at that moment, all was right in my world.

"Keira." That was until I heard my own name being spoken aloud, breaking through the euphoric fog. My eyes snapped open, and I shot up, seeing my room in darkness but more importantly, without a moving shadow.

"It couldn't be," I whispered but even as my mind was grasping back reality, my hand raised. My fingers touched the tender lips that felt slightly swollen from receiving a commanding kiss like no other. But that wasn't the only thing I felt there, or the most important. No, in the end, it wasn't just the kiss itself that was the only thing to stay rooted deep inside me; it was the word spoken afterwards. A name whispered.

My name whispered…

Over my kissed lips.

CHAPTER 11

FRIENDS & DRUNKS

he rest of the week came and went without any more incidents. I had worked three more nights at the club and was getting the hang of it. I was now at the stage where I could serve behind the bar. Mike had become my little protector for the week. Bailing me out when I got the complicated fancy card machine wrong, sticking up for me when customers were rude and most importantly taking out the trash. This I was most grateful for.

I tried to ask about the Dravens, as my curiosity got too much for me one night, but everyone was always so vague. No one would reveal any useful information about them. It was always the same story, as though rehearsed.

There were two brothers and a sister. The head of the family was the older brother, Dominic Draven. I wasn't sure if I had seen the other brother. When they first arrived there were only men, so I knew I hadn't yet seen the sister. Dominic, I had seen twice in the flesh and the rest in my dreams, but that had been enough to start my obsession.

My thoughts always seemed to be about him. I didn't really understand why. It was as if he had a power over me that just wouldn't fade. There were the obvious reasons, of course. Like he was the most remarkable human being I had ever seen. He was stunning, like a transcendental Godlike creature making him completely heavenly. But on the darker side, he looked intensely strong, almost invincible, as if he could have been a Spartan or Trojan in a past life… even dressed in Armani.

I found my eyes wandering up towards the first floor more times than I could count but then my head would look away quickly before I got there. My cheeks would flush just thinking about him, and when I had been waiting for Frank. Thinking about the way he'd looked at me that night, with those consuming eyes piercing through me, ablaze with a fiery passion, devout and excruciating.

I had to convince myself on a daily basis; it was nothing, just to function. My daydreams about him were getting ridiculous and were ever constant. Being at work was the worst and also the best. That was when I felt it most, like a magnetic pull drawing me towards him. But it was my embarrassment that kept me reined in and stopped me from looking.

I was the only one with this restraint; however, as everyone else in the club seemed to stare in his direction. Of course, you couldn't really see him, just shadows of people up there. But no one ever went up or down the staircase. And considering there were always people up there, I had to wonder where they all went, did they stay there? Like some luxury 5-star hotel? Well if that was the case, then hell, where did I check-in!

In fact, the only time I had ever seen anyone walk those steps was with Draven himself a week ago. It was all very strange, especially when not one person seemed to know anything about them, yet they had been coming here for years and owned half of the town. It was as if the whole of Evergreen was part of some weird conspiracy with the Dravens at the head of it all. And needless to say, I was the little outsider in this X files episode.

Getting back to reality, I grabbed some clothes before I was late for 'Fresher's day' at my new college. With something black and grey in my hand, I put it over my head not really knowing what it was, but it had sleeves, which was all that mattered.

It was joined by a pair of faded jeans, which had seen better days. They were a bit too long for me, so they were badly ripped around the bottom. Every now and again I would have to pull a bit off as they got caught around my trainers, or 'sneakers' as they were called here, which was funny 'cause you never really got much chance for sneaking in everyday life.

"You ready, because I think RJ is here?" Libby shouted from at the bottom of the stairs. I had found her in the kitchen at an ungodly hour trying to make me a full English breakfast. Of course, it looked like it had been cooked with Plutonium. I had eaten as much as I could with my teeth screaming in pain as I crunched my way through what could have been lava rock. Pity we didn't have a dog, having said that, I don't think even a dog could have digested this and animal rescue would have been on our case.

"Yeah, I'll be there in a minute." I grabbed my bag, putting the strap around my head and my jacket on top. I didn't need gloves today as the sleeves I wore had a thumb hole. I ran down the stairs and slipped on the step, landing on my already bruised bottom.

"Ouch!" I complained.

"You okay?" Libby shouted up, and I grumbled out my reply,

"Yes." It didn't venture a guess that it was going to be one of those days.

It took what seemed like an age to get away from Libby doing the whole mothering thing.

"I have done this before, Libs; it will be fine. I'm not going off to war." I gave a little salute and made for the door. Poor RJ had been waiting for so long she had cut the engine.

"Sorry about that, my sister can be a little... neurotic at times." I gave her an apologetic smile, but she didn't seem fazed, just as happy as always. Extremely happy, in fact, she couldn't keep still.

"So, come on tell me everything, and don't leave a thing out, even if it seems insignificant, I still want to know." She clapped her hands and started the engine. She had a comical little car that sounded angry as she pulled forward. It looked like an old VW, but the badge had fallen off the front, so I couldn't tell.

The conversation about the nightclub had continued all the

way to the college, and she hadn't been joking about the small details. So, by the time we got there, RJ had been filled in on all the details... well, all except one. I never mentioned about Draven in the carpark. No, that one I wanted to keep for myself. It was as if it was sacred to me.

"We will never get a space nearer to the campus, plus Jack said he would meet us here." She gave me a wink which I ignored. 'Here' was a car park surrounded by trees that were turning different shades of reds and oranges. It was a little further away from the main campus, which was fine with me as it had finally stopped raining.

In fact, the sun had come out from behind its clouds, transforming the once dreary day into a utopia of sun bursting colour. It made me want to pick up a paintbrush for the first time in a long while. I shuddered at the thought.

I grabbed my bag from the back seat as RJ did the same. I slammed the door too hard, and little flecks of rust started to snow from the door. Oops!

"Sorry about that," I said with a sheepish grin.

"Oh, it's fine, I get a shiny new one when I graduate, but to be honest, I don't think it will last till then, so you go ahead and bang it all you want!" We both started laughing and didn't notice when Jack had come up behind us.

"What's so funny? What did I miss?" He instinctively came towards me, grabbing my canvas bag off my shoulder and giving me a wink. RJ didn't miss it and put her finger in her mouth, accompanying it with a gagging noise.

"What about my bag?" RJ demanded as she flicked Jack on the ear. He winced and dodged her punch on the arm that followed.

"You're fine with your own bag. You have a strong, sturdy back, like a camel." He patted her on the back, which sounded more like a slap. They were a typical brother and sister. Full of banter and fooling around, but deep down at heart you could tell they adored each other.

We all walked towards the campus, which looked more like a town of its own. There were huge red brick buildings all situated in their own little woodland, matching the colour of the trees that surrounded them.

RJ and Jack were obviously used to the place, as they didn't look half as impressed as I did. I didn't say a word all the way to the main building. I just stared wide-eyed at my beautiful surroundings, thrilled I would be seeing them daily. It was like something from a movie. It looked far too posh to be a college, well okay maybe Oxford or Cambridge I could understand but here? No wonder my parents hadn't wanted to disclose the amount they must have coughed up. A small fortune!

I had tried to contribute, having saved up a small amount during the summer, and I also had my inheritance. My grandfather had left us all a substantial amount of money when he passed away. I was too young to understand at the time, as he passed away when I was only two years old. My amount was still gathering dust in the form of interest in a savings account and I still hadn't touched it, even though it was legally mine once I'd turned eighteen.

My father's father had been a kind man who had a number of businesses in Liverpool. He had only one son, my father, who he brought up on his own after his wife had died during childbirth. His father adored him, telling him daily how he reminded him of his mother. They were very close, but due to hard times, my grandfather spent most of his time working and building up his small empire. He, therefore, enlisted the help of his sister Olivia, whom my sister was so proudly named after.

She was a widow and childless and as a result, a very lonely and depressed woman. After a series of failed suicide attempts, she finally found happiness being a surrogate mother to my dad. She also adored him and spent the rest of her days tending to his every need. They were inseparable, like two peas in a pod as my dad had described. So, when she had died, it had been like losing a mother all over again, only this time one that he knew.

My grandfather, however, had sold his businesses for a small fortune, knowing that my dad wasn't really interested in running them. He then retired and moved abroad, living out the rest of his days in the sunshine. My father hadn't realised how much money he had saved over the years until the reading of the Will. Of course, it had all gone to my dad as there was no other family left. My mother had told me that he'd nearly had a heart attack when he found out the amount.

He split it three ways, putting mine and Libby's into a savings account. My parents bought a bigger house with their share, where they still lived today. And the house my grandfather had in Spain they kept as a holiday home.

Libby had already used some of her money emigrating here and remodelling the house Frank had inherited. Our parents had paid for their wedding, being only too eager to get her hitched and "on her way" as my dad had joked. He also told Frank there were no refunds available, in other words 'Best of luck and no bringing her back!' We had all laughed at this part of my father's speech at the wedding.

"Earth to Kaz, is anyone reading me?" What, oh RJ was staring at me with a confused look in her eyes. I had been daydreaming again.

"Sorry, I was in my own little world, this place is amazing." She shrugged as if she was used to eating breakfast at the Taj Mahal.

We walked up the mass of steps towards the main building, which was swarming with students. There were tables everywhere topped with banners all advertising different clubs and sororities. People buzzed around like clones in matching T-shirts and sweaters. There were so many people shouting, all the voices seemed to merge into one. The odd "Try out" and "Wildcats" could be separated from the rest.

Not surprisingly, no one flagged us down, as one look at RJ sporting her usual Gothic attire and they quickly looked away. I grinned to myself realizing what a perfect match we were. She dressed this way to be noticed and to stand out. I did the complete opposite, shying away from any form of attention. What was funny, however, was that we both did each other a favour. I didn't draw any attention away from her and she was scary enough that she didn't bring any attention my way.

Granted, it was more in my favour than hers, but I was still happy about it.

Now Jack, however, was a different story. He stood out from the crowd and for all the right reasons. With every step his long legs took he was admired... or envied. Girls winked and giggled in silly girl fashion and guys nodded in respect, some even used coded hand gestures which were all foreign to me.

He was extremely popular, but he had been here for two years. He also seemed perfectly at ease showing us around, despite the funny looks RJ was getting. I suppose he was used to it with RJ being a heavy Goth, but it didn't stop him introducing us to his friends when they stopped him. He even put his arm around my shoulders in a playful manner when introducing me to a group of them. I received plenty of evil looks from the girls but wicked smiles from the boys.

I couldn't quite understand it. It was as if he was proud, but I was at a loss to know why. I must have looked even plainer and boring compared to the living billboard model that stood next to me. My cheeks would flame every time he introduced me while RJ just nodded looking bored. She played ice queen very well... I, on the other hand, was not so down with the cool, calm and collected act.

The rest of the day was filled with tours of the campus, a lot of which I didn't need to go on as I wasn't living there, and little lectures of groups we might join. Also subjects we were taking and charity events etc... but by the end of the day I felt mentally exhausted.

Jack decided we needed a drink after such a hectic day, so we all went to a local bar near the campus. We met up with Drew and Lanie and it soon became apparent things had progressed between them as they were more than a little friendly with each other.

We all walked the short distance to the bar, and 'Willy's One-Eyed Joe' was no Club Afterlife that was for sure, in other words, it was a complete dive. We all walked through the decrepit doors to find the inside very much like the outside...

dilapidated. It was in desperate need of a makeover... hell, the place needed re-building!

The walls looked as though they were melting, with a mixture of paint and paper that was trying desperately to get to the floor. There was a strong smell of disinfectant in the air and I looked down to see the tiles had also seen better days. With patches of broken and new that didn't match the originals, in fact nothing matched in the whole place. Chairs and tables were all odd and scruffy, making me wonder if they had ever been new.

We sat at one of the big booths in the corner and it creaked in pain as we all sat down. I noticed I was the only one who didn't look completely at ease. The rest looked very relaxed and used to this place, seeming oblivious to the state that surrounded them.

"Joe... hey Joe!" Jack shouted towards the bar, which had also seen better days. A big fat man with a jolly-looking face turned in surprise. There were only two other people in the whole place and they were sat at the bar. Must be regulars, I thought. I could spot them a mile away.

"Oh, hey guys." The guy looked more like a Father Christmas lookalike than the jolly owner of this place. He came over and met Jack halfway.

"Hey Joe... uh, how's business?" I almost choked. Was that a joke? But Jolly Joe just smiled and replied, shaking his hand.

"Not too bad, could be better though. The bikers rally is passing through next week, which always brings business in." Jack nodded his head, looking as if he didn't quite know what else to say.

"Say how's your ma?" The conversation turned a different course about family and other stuff I didn't quite catch.

"Yo Joe, could we get a round in, I'm spitting feathers here!" I had to hand it to RJ, she sure had a way with words. Joe waved in acknowledgement and walked back behind the bar. Jack resumed his place next to me and got cosy. We all started chatting about college stuff when I couldn't help noticing one of the guys staring at us all from the bar. Actually no, he wasn't staring at us all he was just staring at Jack. I frowned finding this odd, and when Jack noticed he too followed my gaze. He found the guy scowling at him, so Jack just shrugged his shoulders and put his back to the guy.

"Didn't I tell you that this place had it all... *even crazy drunks.*" He winked at me putting his arm around my shoulders and giving me a squeeze. I laughed but it didn't sound right as the guy's intense stare was creeping me out. He looked like he wanted to rip Jack's arm off and beat the crap out of him with it.

"Yeah I know, but seriously that guy is acting like you scratched his car or something." Jack smiled down at me and then raised his hand to push back a stray bit of hair behind my ear and I tried not to flinch so as not to offend him.

"Don't worry your pretty little head over it, that guy doesn't know me."

"BARTENDER! Another drink!" The drunk shouted, startling us all as he pounded his fist on the bar.

"Ahh!" Jack shouted, standing up as his drink tipped all over him, soaking his pants.

"Way to go, Bro, real smooth now you look like you've wet yourself!" RJ said giggling to herself and Jack sent a fake angry scowl her way and then gave her the bird.

"Bite me!" Jack said over his shoulder as he walked to the restroom. I felt bad for him as I didn't even see him move so had no clue how it even happened. But I guess my attention, like us all, had been on the aggressive behaviour coming from the drunk.

"Alright Billy, keep your hair on, geez...what's with you today, man?" Joe said coming to refill the guy's pint, and the one called Billy, just shook his head as though just waking up from a dream.

"What?! What'd I do?" he asked as though the last ten minutes hadn't happened. Looking at him now he looked completely different. I would even go as far to say he was dopey looking with no aggression whatsoever.

RJ got from her side of the booth and came to sit closer to me, taking Jack's seat.

"He's got it bad for you, Kazzy girl," she said nudging me

talking about her brother. I bit my lip as I didn't want to be having this conversation. It was strange, like I needed to be cautious for some reason. I looked towards the bar once more and saw Billy still shaking his head as if he didn't know what had happened. But it was no longer Billy that took my interest, no, now it was the other guy who seemed fixated on me and RJ. It was almost as if he could hear what we were saying. He saw me looking and met my gaze head-on, then something flashed in his eyes; a purple glimmer that must have been a trick of light.

"So?" RJ said, nudging me and breaking the connection.

"So?"

"Yeah so, as in, sooo... are you interested?" This was a tough question to answer, so when the mobile phone I borrowed from Libby started singing Abba, I sent up a prayer of thankyous. I answered it before it could ring off, getting Jerry on the other end asking me if I could work tonight.

"Yeah, no problem I just have to see if I can get a lift in with my sister or..."

"No, no, that won't be a problem. I have already sent a car for you. It's on its way and will be out front soon." I frowned as he hung up, so I didn't have time to question anything.

For starters, how did he know I was going to say yes?

But the biggest question of all...

How did he know where I was?

CHAPTER 12
PROTECTING BEAUTY

I ntroduction to Historical Thinking was my next class. I grabbed my map out of my bag and found a quiet corner to read it. All my classes had names of buildings and room numbers next to them to make it easier. But easier, it was not. The place was as large as a town. It would take me half an hour to walk from one class to the next. Luckily, I had a few free periods between classes so I made it on time, but there was nothing free about them.

Starting college had been hectic, but to be honest I had loved every minute of it. History, Spanish and English Literature had been whirling around my head for days, leaving no room for anything else. The only time that didn't belong to my own mind was in my dreams.

My dreams still held that one face, as though scorched inside my mind for all time. It was as if something else controlled me, planting images and fantasies that seemed so real I would wake to find myself asking if he was still there. I would also find myself going to bed early in the hope of dreaming of him and then when I did, I would wake in a blissful state of euphoria.

Although, this didn't make it very easy when at work, I would fixate on the staircase using every ounce of self-control I had to not going running up there and making a fool of myself. I hadn't seen him since that first night I had worked, but in my dreams he had not faded. If anything, his image was getting clearer with him dominating my nights.

The dreams varied slightly, but the one concept remained. He would always come to me in my bedroom. I would wake (in my dream) to find him there at a distance watching me. I was never scared but I was always wary. After all there was a strange man, whom I hardly knew anything about, sat at my window seat or standing by my desk staring at me.

He was always so perfect. Like a living statue you would have found at the Trevi Fountain in Rome. I would find myself staring back trying to make out every detail, but the moonlight was never enough. I would start to sit up to get a better look at him, which was when he would make his move. He just seemed to be beside me in a blink of eye, and I was always left wondering how he had gotten to me so quickly.

I would freeze, locked in his penetrating gaze. He would smile down at me, causing my heart and lungs to work erratically. I held my breath waiting for the next part I knew was coming. He would raise his hand and touch my cheek with the backs of his fingers. The way he touched me was always so soft, as if he was handling something so breakable and delicate.

But I didn't understand how, as when I could finally focus on his hands, they looked too strong to be so gentle. He'd trace the line of my blushed cheek all the way to my chin, lifting it slightly when he got there, leaving a warm trail on my skin. He'd tilt my head closer to his face, and I could feel his breath. It was cool like the fresh air when it snows, and the scent was like nothing I had ever encountered before. It was hypnotic, and I'd feel my head spin with every breath I would take.

His face would be very close, yet I still couldn't move, not that I would have wanted to. He would trace his finger across my lips, and I would feel every touch with tiny little electric pulses, as though my lips were having an emotional attack, mirroring my own mind. I just hoped he didn't notice how they quivered at the very sight of him. That confident smile again. He knew what he did to me, and he enjoyed it.

I would try to speak but his velvet voice would intervene

saying only "Ssshh, be still," which would blow more mind-numbing venom my way, infecting my brain's functions, making me do nothing but obey.

I knew that soon the dream would be ending but hoping that this was one of those nights it would last a little bit longer. Every so often he would stay, if only seconds more but it would always end the same way. It was when I was starting to focus that this would normally happen. The time when I would try desperately to grasp onto whatever was feeding this delusional fantasy, driving it to its most pleasurable peak.

And that peak would most certainly be worth waiting for, although cruel in its own right as it also signified the end. One look in the reflection of his dark depths became evidence enough that we both knew what was happening. My eyes became pleading for him to stay and let the dream continue on, taking us to the next level of intimacy but his look never mirrored my own that way. No, it was like something inside him was holding back, whereas I was trying to hold on.

His hand would find its way to the back of my neck and it would send ripples of desire down my spine. My body would arch upwards slightly in response. His big, strong hand would hold all the back of my head and entwine his fingers through my hair. I was glad I was unable to speak as every fibre in my body wanted to let out a moan. He would then lean his face to mine as though we were one and his lips would gently touch mine, but he did not kiss me. He just held them there slightly making contact. Then he would whisper…

"Sleep, my Electus, sleep for me."

And once more I would obey.

Then that would be the end. I would wake suddenly to find it was morning and I was most definitely alone. That still wouldn't detract from the contentment I felt. It was as if I had taken happy pills, and most of the time it would last all day.

"Hey, heads up!" Pink hair flashed in my peripheral vision, along with something hurtling its way towards my head. I turned in time to catch a soda that I wouldn't be able to open for a while.

"Hey, good reflexes. So, you got a free period?"

"Yeah, but I'm probably going to spend that looking for my next class." She smiled.

"What, no chauffeur-driven car to take you to class, *my Lady?*" RJ joked, but I blushed all the same. That night had been strange to say the least as I had never had a job where you received transport to work before, especially in a car that was worth more than some houses.

"Uh, no," I answered RJ, smiling.

"So, come on, what was that all about? I mean it's not exactly the norm." I had to agree with her there.

"I asked Jerry about it when I got there but he just gave me some management spiel about how any girl working there who doesn't have their own transport now gets it provided so they get home safe." RJ whistled before saying,

"Wow, are they going for workplace of the year or something? I mean, how many girls even work there?" I frowned as I thought about this before answering her,

"Well I have no clue up in the VIP as you don't meet any of the staff…" RJ gave me a weird look, but I carried on,

"…but downstairs, it's just me and Hannah… oh and some other girl I haven't met yet who collects glasses on busy nights."

"So, they must be pretty happy with the new rule then." I thought on this for a second.

"No not really as they both have cars." RJ smirked and nudged my arm playfully.

"So just you then, Miss Special Treatment." This made me blush even more. Thankfully though she dropped the conversation making her point and went back to helping me find my next class.

"Well lucky for you I know my way around this joint… where we off to?"

"Wakewood Hall, and I would sell my soul right now for a clue as to where it is." She laughed,

"Aww, come on now, Kazzy, wouldn't you want to save your soul selling for the right buyer? I know who mine would be…

mmm, oh yes." Okay, well she had me there, and I was pretty sure we were both thinking of the same person. If only she knew just how deep my little fantasies about Dominic Draven really went.

"Come on, I'll walk you there, and on the way, I'll also tell you about the most amazing bit of gossip I have ever heard, better than the time Mrs. Waterman got high and tried to stab her husband over their last Ding Dong."

We walked towards the building I needed, and RJ didn't take one breath the whole time, I was sure of it. The girl was a machine! She told me of when poor Mr. Waterman nearly lost his life due to half a bottle of wine and some badly prescribed meds. From that day on there had always been a more than ample amount of Ding Dongs in the Waterman household. Oh, and just to clarify, a Ding Dong is a chocolate cake product not a door bell like I first thought!

"Okay, now for the real juicy stuff, did you hear who is going to be enrolling here?" She was red-faced and bouncing as though she couldn't contain her excitement any longer, but this still didn't stop her from prolonging it.

"Enrolling...? I thought it was too late to enrol." She grinned, enjoying the fact I was out of the gossip loop.

"Well, I don't think that would ever stop this person, seeing as her family puts a hell of a lot of dough into this place each year." She pointed to the building in front of us that looked old and imposing. It was a huge brick building that could have been a school on its own.

"Welcome to the newest edition, Wakewood hall." I couldn't help but smile, knowing that I had most of my history lessons in this gorgeous place.

"This was the latest gift, last year it was a new sports complex." She waved her hand as though this had been a donated bench for the gardens. So that's how the college had been so grand for such a remote place, it must have a multi-millionaire for a benefactor, and I didn't need to guess as to who that was.

"That's one hell of a gift!" I replied still in shock, but she hadn't finished telling me the gossip of the year. So, I pressed for it.

"You were telling me…"

"Oh yeah, and anyway that's why she can get in any time. I doubt she would even have to pass a single class! They wouldn't dare fail her, that's for sure." Okay, now I was lost, was she ever going to tell me who this bloody girl was?

"And… she's?" She rolled her eyes, clearly loving every minute of my blondness.

"Well isn't it obvious, it's Dominic Draven's sister!" Okay now she had said it, then yeah it had been obvious. But Draven's sister studying here, did that mean they were staying? RJ was talking to me now doing her usual overload of information about the girl's name, subjects and full timetable, she was like some confessed stalker, but I wasn't taking any of it in.

I just kept on seeing his perfect face in the dim moonlight, feeling the essence of him as more of a myth than human. Now it was just such a normal thing for him to have a sister who was enrolling here. My imagination had run wild and I was going to have to get it under control. It was getting ridiculous! What did I expect? He was, after all, just some normal rich guy that happened to be the most handsome man that I had ever seen. I just needed to get a grip!

But deep down I knew what I had been feeling and there was some truth behind it.

There was just something different about him, something… *unnatural*.

"You're so lucky, but hey, you're going to be late." So instead of asking her why I was so lucky as I had missed most of the conversation, I said goodbye and went to try and find my next class.

I got there with only minutes to spare but the class was nearly full. There were a few seats left but they were dotted around like holes in an old sweater. I found one in the middle in a cluster of empty spaces.

The room filled even more with only the space left next to me and the obvious lack of a tutor. There was a hum of whispers and a continuous nervous tapping of a foot from the girl behind me. Any other day it would have driven me over the edge of my already fragile sanity, but today my mind was too busy being filled with thoughts of Draven.

Then silence descended as a man walked towards the desk at the front. He slammed his bag down, followed by a pounding from his books. He did *not* look happy. You could feel the room instantly tense as everyone seemed to straighten up at the same time, causing a wave of creaking chairs.

He cleared his throat and began.

"This is not a class for easy credit, so if you don't want to work hard then I suggest you take up the creative arts for those easy A's and stop wasting my time." He paused and looked about the room. One guy got up but kept his head down, hiding his shame.

"Ah, we have a taker, try woodwork, I hear it's a slam-dunk." The class let out a series of nervous noises. The lad left, taking with him the tension in the tutor, which seemed to please him as if the initiation process was over and he could now continue.

"I am Mr. Reed, Head of History. I will be taking many of your classes, and believe me when I say I do not accept excuses for any reason as I don't care for them. So, unless you are on your death bed in excruciating pain and expelling every liquid from your body, I do not accept absence, just as I don't accept tardiness." This was directed towards the door as a face had appeared in the little porthole. She knocked and we all held our breath, instantly feeling a mutual sorrow for what was about to occur. We could feel the humiliation ready to erupt as the handle pulled downwards, letting the unsuspecting girl into a pit of misery.

She walked in with such grace I think even Reed was taken aback. The classroom actually gasped. She was just so stunningly beautiful. In fact, you could almost hear all the breaking of hearts from the boys and the envious mental screams from the girls. She glided through the door in a way that would put any ballerina to shame.

Reed composed himself ready for the kill and stared at the girl who just smiled sweetly in return.

"I do not accept anyone late to my class, but as it is the first day, then I will make an exception. However, if this were to happen again then you will be removed from my lessons and failed on any paper which is due, do you understand?"

"Of course, and please accept my most sincere apologies." Her voice sang out reminding me of one very similar. She was small and elf-like, with beautiful black hair that resembled silk as it hung down in curls to her shoulders and bounced as she moved. Her skin was almost translucent with a rosy tint to her cheeks. She looked like a china doll, as though her face had been painted in some way. It was an ancient-looking beauty, like one you would find on the Sistine Chapel ceiling or the works of Bouguereau.

She looked around for a space and you could see guys standing ready to give up their seats for this lovely creature. I put up my gloved hand and the tutor nodded in my direction. You could hear the groans of disappointment. She walked up the steps and people rose out of their seats to let her through to the middle, I moved the bag that I had put on the other seat and moved one of my books off the now occupied table.

"My name is Sophia and…"

"Excuse me, Miss 'I want to disrupt the class', I have had about enough of you today." I don't know what came over me, but I felt compelled to stand up for this poor innocent girl. After all, I was the cause of her now being punished. So, I did the unthinkable. I broke my one rule and drew attention to myself.

I stood up only to get a better view of the students gasping at my madness, some even held their breaths.

"Uh…" I had to clear my throat as the words would not form.

"It was not her fault, I asked her a question and she was answering me." I managed to say, not as forceful as I had hoped but at least it made sense.

"And pray tell, what exactly was that most essential question, as now you have all the class' full attention, we're all just dying to know what is more important than my lecture?" His words burned as I started to realize his full meaning. Every head in the room had now turned to look at me and I was in my own personal Hell. I could feel my palms start to sweat and I rubbed them together as I tried to continue.

"I just asked her if she had a book or if not, would she like to share mine," I said trying to sound confident.

"What a Good Samaritan you are, and your name would be?" Oh shit, how long was he going to keep this going? I could imagine it from now on. I was going to be a target for every question, the butt of every joke and the bullseye for every sarcastic comment that would escape those small, chewed lips.

"Keira," I stammered as I sat back down, trying to indicate the end of my humiliation.

"Well, Keira, I assume I can continue and would hope you are going to show the same dedication in my class as you have done with your unprepared friend there."

I just nodded in response and tried to ignore the stares I received from every eye in the room.

"Well, now that little drama is over, open your books to page 68, for those of you that have them that is." His tone was cutting, and I knew that my chances of this blowing over and being forgotten were not going to happen any time soon.

"During this lesson you will see that reading and analysing text is central to understanding and knowing history. In this class you will understand the importance of facts. You will live and breathe the intensive study of books and documents from varying historical fields and periods." He continued like this for the rest of the hour, loving the sound of his own voice. Well at least someone in the room did.

The girl next to me and I didn't say another word to each other throughout the class. She did, however, keep smiling at me as if I was some kind of saviour. She wrote the words *'thank you'* in her notebook in the most amazing ornate handwriting I had ever seen. She pushed it my way for me to read, never taking her eyes off the Himmler lookalike down at the front. It was the large forehead and the shifty eyes peering from behind small round glasses that gave him the appearance of the Head of the Gestapo. Hitler would have been proud to see his lieutenant's reincarnation dictating history.

I scribbled in my not so neat handwriting *'no problem'*. My handwriting looked as though it had been written by a toddler compared to her flowing calligraphy. The lecture continued and made History sound excruciatingly boring. Something I love so much could easily be destroyed by this man's voice alone.

He continued on just like all the first lectures I'd had. The introduction to History was a little wasted on me as I had been studying it all my life. So, as his boring voice droned on, I let my mind drift to other thoughts. Like the fact I was working at the club tonight, and the possibility of seeing Draven again created a buzz of anticipation within me.

The class finally drew to an end and I realized that I had missed most of it due to my daydreaming. I would have to pay more attention in future, or I would definitely be caught out in the firing line. I was already an easy target in Reed's mind.

I got up, grabbing my books, and as I was putting them in my bag I noticed a pair of doll-like eyes examining me. I met them with a curious look of my own.

"You have lovely hair, why do you wear it back?" Her question had caught me off guard and I started to stammer my answer out.

"Uhh well… it…it gets in the way. But thanks." I couldn't believe that this enchanting looking creature was complimenting me when her hair looked like it had been styled ready for a photoshoot for Vogue.

We both walked down following the mass of numbed students trying to escape before another word leaked from Reed's mouth, when something caught my eye. Reed was talking with a student and they were both looking our way, but it was Reed's expression that held my interest. He looked as though he was in shock. It was as if something the boy had told him was about us but wait, it wasn't *us* it was *her.* He was staring at Sophia but now he looked troubled.

She didn't seem to catch the same horror in Reed's eyes that I had or if she did, she didn't hold much consequence to it. I shuddered as we walked out of sight and I realised she was still smiling at me. I felt as though she was studying me more than just being friendly. Was there something more behind her smile or was there just something in my teeth? Either way I felt my tongue run over them just to be sure.

"Thanks again for bailing me out back there, he's a real piece of work, right?" she said as she followed me, and people were staring at us in a curious manner.

"Yeah, he's a bit scary but I think we handled it okay, though I bet next time we will get bombarded with questions," I said, making her laugh at this and she held out her hand ready to receive mine.

"It was nice to meet you, Keira." I placed my hand in hers and the warmth I found from her soft skin was comforting. She seemed to read my thoughts and smiled once more before she left, saying over her shoulder,

"See you soon." My hand tingled slightly then went very cold along with the rest of my body… *Strange.*

"Who was that?" RJ asked as we both watched the back of my new friend disappear out of sight.

"No one… how was class?"

RJ went on about her day and I happily listened, not really wanting to tell her about my little run-in with Dictator Reed. And I didn't really know why I didn't tell her about Sophia. I guess I just felt a weird connection with her at the end of class. I couldn't explain it, but I'm pretty sure she felt something as well, and in a strange way it felt like kinship. Maybe that's why I had felt so compelled to defend her to Reed. In the same way when RJ asked me about her, I wanted to keep her friendship to myself in some selfish way and protect her from RJ's personal prying.

We were nearly home when RJ's word by word account of her day had finished and my mind hadn't retained any of it, luckily though she hadn't noticed.

"So, what you up to tonight? 'Cause a couple of us are going to Afterlife, there's this great group playing and…" I stopped her mid-sentence before I forgot what she'd asked, and we were nearly at my house.

"I can't, but I will see you there anyway as I'm working. Maybe I can join you if I get off early."

"Oh my God, you are so lucky you work there, I would have to keep sneaking a peek upstairs." She giggled at the vision. If only it was that easy, I thought bitterly.

"Yeah right, have you seen the security they have, those guys give new meaning to steroid abuse... breakfast, lunch and dinner." I said this last part getting out of the car turning to add,

"See you later."

"Yeah laters, you lucky Biatch!" RJ was still laughing as she turned her little car around and I watched her go out of sight. Only laughter wasn't on my mind. No, there was only one thing to occupy my thoughts, and it included 'lady luck' putting me in the same room with a certain someone...

One Dominic Draven.

CHAPTER 13

VIP

I had grabbed my usual black top and jeans, only this time swapping long sleeves for a vest top as it got quite hot in the club, especially with lots of enthusiastic Goths swarming the bar. But that was the bonus working at a place like this, the gloves didn't stand out.

I wore my hair in its usual knot, tied up by its clip. There was nothing to suggest that this wouldn't be just like any other night at the club, but I had a strange feeling that was gnawing at my stomach. Maybe it was just after the weird effect meeting Sophia had on me, or maybe I was just hoping something might happen. Either way I just couldn't shake off the feeling.

"Oh Kazzy!" Frank shouted up to me as he must have been ready to go. I had told Jerry on the phone that I didn't need a lift for my shift tonight as Frank had already offered. In truth I had been relieved when Frank had offered this. I didn't want to sound ungrateful, but it was getting a bit embarrassing now as I was the only one being chauffeured around in a flash new car. The last thing I needed was for people to think I was getting special treatment and if anything RJ said was to go by, then rumours spread like wildfire in this town.

I grabbed my bag and rushed down the stairs not wanting to keep him waiting. However, on the last few steps I faltered to a stop as I was met with Frank holding the front door open. He had a big grin on his face as I took in the sight, yet again, of a big shiny black car waiting for me.

"Did you win employee of the month or something, 'cause I gotta tell ya, that's a nice perk?" he said with a wink, and I closed my eyes and sighed before descending the last three steps.

"I thought you were a barmaid, not a stockbroker?" Frank asked laughing at his own joke.

"Ha, ha, not a word of this to Libby." To which he burst out into raucous laughter... my response was an unimpressed look which only fuelled his amusement.

Great... just great.

The club was quiet when I first walked in and the band had only just arrived. I recognised the drummer to be the same guy RJ had given her number to on my first night here. No wonder she was coming again tonight. What was their name again... Acid um... Acid Criminals. Actually, they weren't half bad.

Mike and Hannah were both working tonight and another girl I hadn't seen before, but I knew her to be Cassie Jones. Hannah hadn't kept it a secret of her dislike towards the girl.

"You watch, she will be all over Mike like a fly on shit. Not calling Mike shit of course, but you know what I'm getting at. She will hang around him all night like a lost kitten digging her claws in ready for the attack! That girl is poison." Of course, she hadn't been the first to warn me about her. RJ, the 'town crier', had filled me in with knowing everyone in Evergreen. Of course, she had told me every sordid little detail. Was there anyone in this town she didn't know? Well, I immediately thought of one, and couldn't help looking up.

RJ had used some choice words when describing Cassie, which had surprised me seeing as they were both Goths. But there was no comparison, RJ informed me. Cassie wasn't a real Goth. She was now just the flavour of the month being Emo.

She was one of those who changed with whatever was 'in' at

the time. Apparently, the number of alternative looking people increased this time of year due to the new arrivals, most hoping to get noticed and make their way into the VIP. Cassie was no exception, and she wanted it bad. Her father knew some important people in high places and had wrangled her the job here. But she was still only seventeen and couldn't serve behind the bar, so she collected bottles and glasses as I had done on my first night.

RJ had said the difference between herself and Cassie was that unlike most, RJ was a Goth with style and didn't dress that way just to have an excuse to look like a slut, like Cassie. At this point, Lanie had also jumped on the bandwagon, adding her own story that included an older married man, who also happened to be one of her teachers. This was a lethal cocktail destined for trouble. Luckily no one seemed to find out about the sordid little affair but the whole town still knew about it, which I found a little confusing. I really didn't understand how that worked, but Lanie carried on telling me more about the little hellcat.

I stood talking to Hannah at the other end of the bar, watching as Cassie did everything but fling herself into Mike's arms. She flicked her hair and bent across him trying to show him more than just her cleavage. He clearly wasn't interested, trying everything apart from smacking the hormonal girl to one side. Poor Mike shifted awkwardly trying to avoid her advances, when he saw me. He winked and walked over, leaving her midsentence, which had her almost shaking with anger. She saw me and looked like a bulldog chewing wasps.

"Hey Kaz, how's college? You had the dreaded Reed yet?" Mike had kindly forewarned me about Reed, but to be honest, I thought he was exaggerating with his description of him. Of course, now I knew that if anything, he hadn't said enough.

"Yeah, it's going okay and wow, you weren't kiddin', he really does put the Grim Reaper to shame, doesn't he?" He let out a hearty laugh that reminded me a bit like a pirate. Hannah had left us to talk about college with a smug smile on her face as she was enjoying the evil glares I was receiving from Cassie.

She finally strutted her way over to us on impractical looking heels with her face like thunder.

"Who's your friend, Mikey?" He cringed at the sound of his name. He mouthed the word "sorry" before turning to face her.

"This is Keira, Keira this is Cassie." He clearly wasn't enjoying the introductions.

"Hey," was all her two brain cells could muster, and I just nodded in response. She was clearly happy with herself that plain old me wasn't any competition. She turned her back to me rudely and carried on.

"So, Mikey, do you think you could sneak me up there tonight?" she asked as she flicked her bleached hair for the millionth time and popped her gum. I couldn't help the laugh that escaped my lips, and she shot round giving me daggers.

"Yes… is something funny?" She had her hands on her hips like the spoilt teenager she was, and it made it harder for me to keep a straight face.

"Nope," was all I said before turning to help Hannah with the cleaning. I felt sorry for the girl. I mean, the very idea of her trying to sneak upstairs and not getting caught by the massive security guards was almost too funny… she was clearly delusional.

The night got busy, and I wasn't surprised that both Jerry and Gary were managing the club tonight. Luckily, Gary was manning his station from somewhere else and Jerry was behind the bar with us. Although the bar was manic, we kept on top of it and it reminded me of old times. Jerry kept coming up to me and telling me what a good job I was doing and how impressed he was that I had picked it up so quickly. I reminded him that I had worked in a bar for years, and that's why I could juggle serving customers and remembering large orders. After that he just kept coming out with comments like 'Keep it up kid' and 'She's a trooper this one' which was sweet and endearing.

The large orders were mainly from the groups that occupied the many booths surrounding the club. Jack had come up to the bar with such an order. He had wanted to get someone else to serve him so as not to bombard me with remembering eight drinks, but I had impressed him with my multi-tasking skills. I wasn't surprised that the barracuda Cassie had helped him take the drinks to his table. Jack would be her next target, but I could understand why. Excluding the VIP area, he was the most attractive person in the room, and it didn't go unnoticed.

The bar area quietened down for a brief moment and I made my move to the ladies, but when I returned, I found Jerry stood waiting for me with a crate in his hands looking impatient. I took a look in the crate to find bottles of green liquid with old foreign labels on them. He didn't look his usual calm self.

That was when my night started to get very weird...

"I need you to do me a favour. You need to take these up to the other bar."

"Uhh... other bar?" I looked blankly at him, feeling like an idiot.

"You know, up there." He motioned with his head to the balcony and my mind went into panic mode. Was this a joke or a test? The one rule I was told, hell, the whole town knew the one rule of Afterlife, and now after less than two weeks of working here he was asking me to break it. Was this man insane?

"Why me?" I said this last part out loud and then repeated it when he stared blankly back at me.

"Why me, why not someone else? Maybe someone who's been here longer, I know Cassie would want to..." What was I saying? Was I really going to give up my one chance to finally go up there, especially to the Emo Barbie herself? I was torn as the Mr. Hyde in me was screaming YES! YES! But the reserved Dr Jekyll was terrified at what a bad cocktail of events this could turn out to be.

"That's why it has to be you, you're the only one who doesn't go on about it..." No, I just fantasise about Draven everywhere I go and dream about him almost kissing me in my bedroom every night. Oh no, that wasn't worse, I thought sarcastically.

"I need someone that won't do anything stupid and will be quick, in and out without... umm... well without getting noticed." He said this last part as if it had offended me, but it had been the truth. I was the only one who didn't stand out. I played my last card in the hopes he would fold.

"What about you or Gary? I could watch the bar and…" He cut me off, no doubt already anticipating that was what I was going to say.

"I can't leave the bar unsupervised and Gary starts to go into meltdown whenever you mention the VIP, so that's a no go," he said, thrusting the crate into my hands and left, taking my silence for a yes. I stood motionless for a moment contemplating what to do. I looked down slowly and was surprised when I saw nine green faces looking back at me. The old bottle labels were all the same, no name, but all held a beautiful green-winged fairy laying naked, sipping a green cocktail.

At first, I had wanted to call Jerry back and tell him no, but I chickened out. I also thought about just dropping the box and making a run for it, but that wasn't a practical solution either. I liked this job and didn't want to lose it. I started towards the staircase wondering how I was actually going to make my feet move up each step. I was nearly there when Gary came out from nowhere, scaring the life out of me.

"Not those stairs, there is a door around the other side of the stage, that's what they use." He said this as though they were some alien life force that didn't belong here.

"Ooookaaay," I said dragging out the letters as if I wasn't freaked out enough. He looked as nervous as I was. What the hell did he have to be nervous about? I was the one who was being thrown to the bloody rich wolves.

I walked in the direction he had nodded to when his hand reached out and grabbed my arm. His grip tightened as his face went whiter.

"Be as quick as you can for your own sake!" Oh great, that was a confidence builder!

I carried on towards the stage, and I could see the door he had been talking about. No wonder I had never seen it before, as it was well hidden. I was just about to put my crate down to open the door when two huge guys came out from nowhere making me jump. My nerves doubled. I kept my direct gaze on theirs and tried to think of what I could say. I half hoped they wouldn't let me up. But of course, they just opened the door for me without saying a word. I walked through, jumping again as the door slammed behind me, sealing my fate.

There was no going back from this 'oh shit' moment.

Once inside, I took a few seconds to try and calm myself as I was pretty close to hyperventilating. It was like something you would have found in a castle. The staircase was huge! So big you could have pushed a grand piano up it and still had room either side. It was all made out of the same stone as the rest of the building, only instead of blocks, it looked as though carved from one big piece. It was incredible.

I put the crate down and straightened my arms and fingers. There were red marks and deep impressions across each finger. They then made cracking noises as I moved them in and out of a fist. My thin, puny arms weren't up for the task as they ached and I had only made my way across the club. There was a door the same as the one I had walked through opposite to where I stood. I was tempted to try it, but the fear of being caught was greater than my curiosity.

My feet moved up the ancient-looking steps as if they had a mind of their own. The walls were bare but for the wrought iron candle holders, only this time they didn't hold flickering light bulbs for effect. The light from the flames didn't seem as if it would be enough, but there was an ample amount of light to take in my surroundings. There was also a matching bannister with twisted iron making its way up the staircase alongside me. There were two doors at the top of a small landing mirroring the downstairs. I knew which door it would be but as before, I still had the same urge to try the other one.

I could still hear the rhythmic hum of the Acid Criminals getting louder as my heartbeat was matching the bass. I stopped behind the carved wooden door and wondered 'what next'? Should I knock or just walk in? I decided to just walk in. After all, would anyone hear my knock? I held my breath, put down the crate and turned the ornate handle. Here goes, I thought with my bottom lip firmly between my teeth.

I walked into what seemed like the dressing room for some Gothic production and everyone's eyes were on me. I pretended not to notice, happy that the lighting was an ambient glow which hid my bright red face nicely. I could see the bar clearly on the other side of the room and a path through the chairs and tables full of the strangest looking people I had ever seen in my life.

I looked around, taking in as much as I could as I struggled my way to the bar. The room was breath-taking. It was like something from a different era. Maybe more like something you would have found in a stately home hundreds of years ago. But there were also new, modern aspects to the place. The mix of old and new worked well together. There were the same twisted wrought iron fixtures that ran throughout the entire club, but they were lit by candles instead of electricity. I doubted that this was to do with the electricity bill and more to do with the authentic setting.

The furniture was a mix of antique carved chairs and modern metal tables with lush fabrics that covered them in luxury. There were dark red rugs that were scattered on the floor over black slate tiles. The walls held nothing but light fixtures and twisted iron artwork. These were beautiful pieces, all entwined metal flowing in and out of each other. Some held metal roses attached to vines. Others were in the shape of the moon and the sun but were being attacked with metal claws. It was by far the strangest room I had ever seen.

But stranger still wasn't the room itself. No, it was the groups of people occupying it. I tried to keep my head down but that proved difficult. Like taking a child to Disneyland and asking them not to look at the parade. I was so engrossed, I momentarily forgot what it was I was doing here. I stepped around the pathway that led to the bar on the other side, trying not to meet all the eyes that were staring at me.

Some were kind-looking, others harsh and nasty, like those made more intimidating by the blood-red contact lenses they wore. Their clothing was something else entirely. Some wore normal everyday outfits, but others were dressed very differently. One group all wore what looked like eighteenth-century costumes that seemed as though they had just stepped out of a classic period drama.

Another group looked as though they could have been extras from a Vampire movie, with long black coats and long black hair to match. Eyes like red pools of hate, and lips curved into sadistic grins. I shivered as I walked past.

I would say my mind was playing tricks on me with my imagination to match. But there was so much fuel in here for my overactive brain, that I couldn't tell what was real and what was in my head. I could have sworn that at one table I passed, they all snarled at me. And this particular group all had halos of tight curls of white hair and gleaming silver fingernails that looked like sharp metal spikes. No wonder I gasped.

I was coming to the middle now, walking in front nearest to the balcony. I could see quite clearly all the people below which seemed so normal in comparison. They were all dancing and busy socialising, completely unaware of the horrors that resided in the VIP. It was weird to think that where we couldn't see anything, they were all looking down on us and could see everything. I could now understand why no one else was allowed up here. People would be terrified and rumours would spiral out of control.

It had me wondering what type of business this was. What could warrant all these different kinds of people to meet like this? It was like something from a horror film convention and they were all dressed up as their favourite characters. I had expected business suits and fancy looking models hanging over them as paid pleasure, but not this.

I tried to concentrate on the job at hand and shake off the creepy vibe that licked at my skin. I was directly in the middle, where the balcony widened into a semi-circle and jutted out from the rest of the club. It also didn't take me long to realise why it had been designed this way as it clearly offered the best view of the whole club below, and this of course meant that there was nowhere really to hide other than the small space directly below.

However, knowing who owned this place, then I shouldn't

have been surprised. Speaking of which, I tried so hard not to look but it was as if I was going against the Gods of nature by not turning my head. My eyes burned as I was fighting a losing battle. I knew he was there, I could feel him. It felt bizarre, like the sensation I got when I dreamed of him. I would seem to be awake, but also not. I couldn't really explain any of it, not into words that would make sense anyway.

I turned to see a large oval table that mirrored the shape of the balcony. It was on a raised dais so anyone on the table could look down at the unsuspecting fools who thought this place held rich suits. This was clearly to show the importance of the people who sat around it, as if this was even necessary as it was evident enough without all the theatrics.

The table was the biggest one in the room with everyone sat on a high-backed wrought iron chair. However, there were no chairs at the front of the table to obstruct the view from the head of the group. The head of the table being of course, where Dominic Draven himself sat.

He was the most breath-taking person in this marvellous room. He seemed higher than everyone else, and the chair he sat upon looked more like a throne. It was twice the size and looked even more amazing with him sat upon it. The back which twisted up from the legs was ornately carved from wood, like the spindles you would have found on a staircase. They met at the top in an arch, which was intertwined with iron. The middle had the same crest carved into it that I had noticed on the entrance door. There was a centre section covered in purple velvet for his back and I guessed this was also the same on the seat. The arm rests were made from what looked like stone or maybe marble. But these small factors of where he sat were unimportant compared to the living masterpiece that was sat upon it.

He didn't seem to notice me, so my eyes didn't move from his perfect face. I was so enthralled that I didn't even take in the other people around the table. He was the only one my eyes could see. I followed his body up from the waist, as I had done that first time in the forest clearing in my dream, but I had remembered every detail correctly.

He wore a black pin-stripe suit, waistcoat, and black shirt and tie. My eyes followed the material as it widened for his powerful looking shoulders until I paused at the neck. My heart fluttered, and my stomach ached in knots, knowing I had reached my favourite part... *his face.* But I chickened out. I couldn't bear to look into his eyes, scared to see what I might find there.

After all,

I was breaking all the rules.

Quickly pulling myself back to reality, I walked with my head down towards the bar. It wasn't far from the central table, so I didn't have much further to go. The bar was a match to the one downstairs, only on a slightly smaller scale. It was the only thing in the room that reminded me that I was still in the same club and not some European castle. There was one man behind the bar, and now I was suddenly nervous for a new reason. Confrontation.

I walked up to it, placing the crate down on the bar's counter when the man turned towards me. Having had my entire mind concentrated on everything in the room, it had made me forget the aching pain in my arms and hands. They were now burning. I straightened them out again as I had done before but now the imprints the crate had made wouldn't go away.

"Are you alright?" A silky, accented voice had asked me; I looked up to see a man smiling sweetly at me. He looked from Moroccan descent with a soft dark tint to his skin, deep dark eyes and long black hair past his shoulders. His eyes were kind which was comforting compared to the wave of scrutinising looks I had received crossing the room.

"Sorry?" I said, feeling stupid, as the first person to talk to me up here must think me a simpleton.

"I was just asking if you were alright my dear, you must have carried that a long way and no offence, but you don't look built for hard labour." He chuckled to himself at this last part.

"Yeah, I'm fine thanks. I was told you needed this crate, and so they sent me... well Jerry sent me... I mean not sent me... asked me." I needed to stop talking. I was babbling on like a lost child. He couldn't keep the smile from his face as he must have known my reason for being nervous.

"Okay, well thank you very much, we did need it quite badly as we were down to our last bottle, and we are extremely short-staffed... due to umm... well let's just say compromising circumstances." I didn't really understand this last part, and couldn't imagine anyone using the term 'compromising circumstances' as a way of saying someone either quit or got sacked!

"I'm Karmun, and you are?" He held his hand out for me to shake, and I leaned over to offer mine in return when someone shouted my name.

"Keira, is that you?!" The same familiar voice that I'd heard today in history was now speaking my name behind me. I moved my hand from hovering towards Karmun and turned to face her. Only a combination of surprise and fear that the girl had followed me up here, not knowing the rules had my body rebelling against my orders. I lost my footing and fell sideways into someone. It wasn't Sophia as I had hoped, as she was opposite me now, grinning. The person I fell into was still holding me upright and I was about to turn to face them with a chorus of apologies, when Sophia giggled and spoke the name with which I was only too familiar.

"Nice catch! Keira, I would like to introduce you to Dominic Draven." I lifted my head and saw his perfect face staring down at my scarlet cheeks, and I hung my head in shame. I straightened myself up and instinctively stepped away from him. I was still warm and branded from his touch on my skin.

His eyes followed mine, and I managed to say a quiet 'Sorry' that anyone would barely hear. He looked me up and down with hard unimpressed eyes and my knees weren't up to the task of keeping me up straight. I tried to regain some control to prevent any further embarrassment.

I couldn't understand how Sophia knew him, and then it hit me. Maybe she was his girlfriend. She certainly fit the bill. She was beyond beauty and perfection. She was the very meaning of desire and the reason artists and writers had a muse. I suddenly felt a sickening feeling in my stomach. I would never, in a million lifetimes, be good enough. Not for a man like this.

But then she said something that answered my unspoken thoughts, and it all made sense.

"Brother, this is Keira, the girl I was telling you about."

CHAPTER 14
OFFER I CAN'T REFUSE

Brother!

She'd called him brother, of course, it all made sense now. Even down to why RJ was calling me lucky before class. She had known that I had the same class as Sophia. I would have to start paying more attention to people and less time daydreaming.

Now I knew, I could see the resemblance in them both. They had a way about them that drew you in and held you captivated as though under some secret spell. I could imagine that her effect had worked on guys as well as her brother's had worked on me. It was obsession, plain and simple.

I stood silent as she was recreating the events of this afternoon, but her brother looked more than unimpressed, he just looked bored and most of all, rude. He stared at me as though I was an intruder, just some outsider that needed to be removed. Maybe the shit on his shoe would be the right analogy.

His eyes were the only thing different from the way he was in my dreams, but they had just the same, if not more of an impact. He didn't even look away when my eyes met his. He just kept on with the malevolent glare as though his sister's words had meant nothing.

"I didn't realise you worked here, what a small world."

Sophia smiled. At this, she received a harsh look from her brother, as though someone had clicked their fingers to get his attention away from me. One she ignored as she carried on.

"Actually, we don't usually have people from around here working up in the VIP. You can understand we don't like the gossip that a small town generates, but seeing that you haven't been here long then maybe you could help us out."

"What?!" This was the first word from Draven's lips, and for once, it wasn't worth waiting for.

"That is not a good idea, Sophia." He paused to look down at me, which wasn't hard given his immense height, and then continued,

"She does *not* belong here." It was like being punched in my chest with a battering ram. I squeezed my fingers into fists until they hurt just to stop the pain in my head and my heart. I couldn't believe how different he was from my dreams. There he remained soft and kind, but here was a different matter entirely... he was unnecessarily cruel.

"I don't agree. We need staff up here, and I think she deserves a chance, or do you no longer trust my judgement?" She was fearless as she now stood facing him, looking up into his deep black eyes. He didn't look at me again, but only ended the discussion by adding his own dark judgement on the idea.

"Sophia, you know my thoughts on the matter, so let it be on your head when this goes wrong. Do not forget our ways, sister," he said with a terrifying glint in his eyes and a deadly flex in his strong jawline, before leaving Sophia and me alone. I watched as he walked away, not taking my eyes off his impressive figure. I knew Sophia was watching me, but I couldn't help it. I still couldn't believe that he was just speaking about me as though I wasn't there.

I wanted to hate him! I mean, what was the worst that could happen? I would break a glass or get an order wrong. It wasn't astrophysics! I was just serving drinks. And yes, it was a little bit different, mainly down to the weirdo people that I would be serving. But come on, who did he think I was... a bloody axe-wielding psychopath? Did he think I was going to serve them drinks with a severed hand?

"Don't mind him, he's... well, he's always cranky around new people. But he will get used to you." If this was supposed to comfort me, it didn't!

"Maybe it's not a good idea, and I don't mind working down there." She didn't look convinced.

"No, really," I added.

"Well you get better money up here, and I want you to, it's the least I can do, and we're friends, right?" It wasn't so much a question, more of a statement. She had known, as I did, that we would be instant friends. I decided to deal with this tomorrow as the mental whiplash where Draven's words had attacked at my soul, still seared deep. I would just explain tomorrow after class how I appreciated the sentiment but would have to refuse.

"Okay, when would you like me to start?" She gave me a smug grin and said,

"Tomorrow night would be great. I'd better go, but I'll see you in class." She gave my arm an affectionate squeeze and left in the same direction as her brother had. I needed a minute to take everything in, but a voice interrupted my thoughts.

"Well, it looks like I will be seeing a lot more of you now you're going to be working with us up here." Karmun smiled and winked at me before continuing on with his duties. Well, at least two people seemed happy about having me up here. I was so confused I couldn't think straight. I knew I had to move, but my brain was too busy trying to process all the information. I was just standing there like the fool I felt. I wanted to run from the room, anything to get away from the essence of him still lingering in the air around me.

A waitress pushed into me hard enough for it not to be an accident, and I turned in time to see a blonde-bombshell beauty scowl at me. This was enough to bring me to my senses and I looked for a way out that wasn't past his table, but I couldn't see one. So, I decided to ask Karmun. I leaned over the bar and watched as he was pouring a green liquid into what looked like a fountain, like the ones you would find at a cocktail party.

However, this one was different. It had a tube in the middle, which was where the liquid was being poured. It was moving around the glass container like a twister tornado, and as a result, the liquid had a reaction. It was changing colours from greens to blues to black and then back again. I was fixated. Then a button was released, and the liquid would start to flow out of four taps into goblets below, stopping automatically when filled. These he placed on a tray for the blonde to take away. The whole process was fascinating, so when he noticed me and came over, I was taken aback.

"Are you alright?" he said, looking at me with concern in his expression.

"Oh sorry, but I was intrigued by what you were doing. I've never seen anything like that," I commented, nodding to the liquid still swirling round in the glass cylinder.

"It's absinthe, and it's a favourite around here, but you will soon get used to it tomorrow night as it's what most of them drink." He nodded towards the tables of people as he said this. He must have mixed something with it when I wasn't looking, as there was no way anyone could drink a cup full of that stuff straight! I had heard about it and knew it had been illegal for a long time due to its strange effects and its ridiculously high volume of alcohol content.

"I was wondering if there's a more discrete way of getting out of here?" I cringed as I said it, feeling weak and pathetic for asking, but he smiled taking the feeling away and replied,

"Sure, I understand, it's over there near the entrance to the outside balcony. There's a staircase before the double doors; you won't miss it. Just look for the big gangster looking guys."

"Thanks, and I guess I will be seeing you tomorrow then." I shook his hand as I didn't get chance to before, and he looked touched that I had remembered.

"Sure thing, and don't be worried, you will be fine, I will look out for you." He gave me another trademark wink and left again to carry on with his cocktail making. I felt a bit guilty, knowing I would be turning down the job tomorrow and yet knowing this, I had still repaid his kindness to me with lies.

165

I headed in the direction he had shown me, happy in the knowledge that I wouldn't have to walk past those judging eyes of Draven's again. I rounded a pillar, and the stairs came into view as they were slightly hidden from the rest of the room, out of the way which was perfect for me. I noticed as I got closer, not only the usual Hercules standing guard, but the frosted glass double doors that must have led outside to the balcony Karmun spoke of. I had a sudden urge to open them and take a peek, but realised I had spent way too much time up here already and Gary and Jerry must be having kitten human hybrids by now! I wondered what they would say when I told them of Sophia's request.

As I walked downstairs, I could see Jerry pacing up and down the bar like a hungry cougar. But that wasn't the only thing I noticed, as I was now walking down the stairs where everyone could see me. All eyes stared in amazement, and the embarrassment level reached new highs. I could see RJ nearly jumping out of her seat to get to me. I tried to play it cool and not notice but that was proving impossible, as now there weren't just stares to contend with, they had now been joined with whispers.

I could hear 'Who is that girl?' and 'Why's she so special?' But this time I just raised my head up and hid my shame, because all these facts were insignificant in comparison to the feelings that were heating up inside me. I didn't know what hurt the most, the fact that he had been so mean and disgusted towards me, or the fact I'd finally realised what an utter bastard he could be.

After all, what did I expect? It wasn't like he was the man from my dreams. No, he was just the empty shell. The image to put with the kindness and warmth he had shown me in my dreams. I knew it was too good to be true, and I couldn't have it both ways. No one that gorgeous was ever going to have a personality to match.

These thoughts brought me all the way to the bar without even thinking about it. Thank God for autopilot, that's all I could say. Jerry spotted me then came stomping over to me with a hard, red face. I had guessed that this wasn't going to be easy but man, did he look pissed!

"What the Hell took you so long?!" He pulled me to one side, and not in a friendly manner.

"I sent you up there because I knew you were the only one who didn't want to go, so I knew you would be quick, so what…? You thought that you'd have a good look around, take a tour, 'cause it's my ass on the line!"

Oh yeah, he was definitely pissed. I couldn't deal with this now, not after the cold backhanded slap of pain that Draven's words had inflicted. I was about to turn, not say a word but just leave and never look back. Then I heard his phone ring, and frustrated, he fumbled for it in his jeans pocket.

His eyes looked down at the screen and then froze in what looked like fear.

"What did you do?" he questioned me, and I frowned, shaking my head to indicate I had done nothing. He didn't look convinced as he cautiously put the phone to his ear as though it might explode.

"Uh… yes, can I help you?" His voice was shaky, and his eyes were everywhere.

"Oh, I see… no, no, of course, that won't be a problem. No, I'll take care of that personally. Yes, I understand, and it won't happen again… please allow me to apol…" It was clear he was cut off and I felt bad for him. He turned to face me but smiled instead of the evil glare I was expecting.

"So, you have been promoted upstairs. Well done, you must have made quite an impression for me to have received that call." I didn't know what to say, so I didn't respond.

"Well, you start tomorrow night and don't worry, you won't have any problems from anyone. I've been instructed to take care of any gossip." He said this with controlled bitterness.

"Look, I'm sorry, I didn't know. See, I met Sophia in my History class and…" He tilted his head before interrupting me.

"Sophia?" He stared blankly at me, and I continued,

"Yeah, Sophia… Mr Draven's sister. Didn't you just speak to her on the phone?"

"No, but I guess that makes sense now… anyway, you start at eight, and wear all black." He started to walk off, but my curiosity wouldn't let him leave without giving me the information I needed to know.

"Then who was that on the phone?" My pulse quickened waiting for the answer that I hoped for. I didn't think he was even going to answer me at first as he didn't stop, but then he just looked over his shoulder and said the name I wanted so badly to hear.

"It was my boss, Mr. Dominic Draven."

My shift had finished soon after the call, and now I had to explain things to RJ. This wasn't going to be easy. All I wanted to do was go home and try and make sense of what had happened. I couldn't get my head around it. Why would a man who obviously didn't want me anywhere near him be ringing Jerry to make sure I didn't get any trouble from anyone? The only explanation I could fathom was that his sister had put him up to it.

I felt angry at myself for even thinking… no not just thinking, but hoping that it could be just an inch of what I only wished for. Of course, he didn't care. I mean, why would he? I was nothing to him, a thorn amongst the roses that surrounded him.

"OH MY GOD! Tell me everything!" RJ nearly bounced into my arms as I walked over to their table. It was situated on one of the lower levels, not like the booth we'd had reserved for us before.

Everyone was there except for Jack, but they all watched me as if I had just met the president. I just wanted to scream by this point and run all the way home. Why did things have to get complicated so quickly? I felt like a bloody magnetic force that attracted trouble. I just wanted to be normal, but I guess you had to know what normal was to begin with. I had never been 'just normal'. I knew that much.

Ever since that day at the fairground, my life had changed. Hell, who knows, maybe even before then. She had seen it, something in me that had scared her. She had looked into my eyes and feared what she had seen there. So, she had changed me.

RJ thankfully interrupted my thoughts as the real-life nightmares of my past started to invade my conscious state. Not here, not now. It wasn't the place for my Demons.

"Sooo… come on, don't hold out on me, what was it like?" She looked like a child who had just found the golden ticket to Willy Wonka's. I sat down, and they all waited for me to speak. I was now wishing that I hadn't agreed to meet up with them after work.

"It really wasn't that big a deal, just some weird looking people who drink a lot of absinthe. But honestly, that was it." I tried to sound casual, but I didn't even convince myself, so I had no hope.

"Aww come on, you have to give me something! All these years everyone has been waiting to go up there, and they pick you. No offence." Everyone kept saying that to me, but I was so far past caring, I couldn't even see the insulting line that people kept crossing. I mean I agreed with them, which was even more pathetic. Did I have even an ounce of self-confidence left in me or had the monsters destroyed me completely?

"Look I hate to burst the fantasy bubble, but it was nothing, no cult, no blood-sucking, not even a voodoo doll. Nada!" I think this was the most animated they had all seen me get, so I guess it got the right message across. Basically, I wasn't in the mood.

"Not even Dominic Draven?" she asked in a deflated voice with her grin gone from her Gothic black lips. It pained me to hear anyone speak his full name as if I had the right to be the only one. Who was I kidding? I thought about the question and answered it with a half-truth.

"No, Draven wasn't there." It was true. The Draven that I had

169

constructed in my dreams didn't even exist. I had just used the thought of him, and combined it with his good looks and my need for a kind, comforting stranger. Someone who knew nothing of my past and wouldn't judge me, but love me in some small way for who I used to be and not the broken counterpart I had become.

I decided it best not to mention the job offer I had received, seeing that I would only be turning it down anyway. So, there was no point in prolonging the painful, scrutinising looks I was receiving from everyone in the room. And that was just from taking some bottles up there for Pete's sake. What would they do if they knew I had turned to the dark side and joined the VIPs? Grab their pitchforks and hoes… I think I'll pass.

I looked around the table, and all faces dropped with disappointment, all except one. Chaz looked amused and concerned at the same time. I didn't want to stare, like he was doing back at me, but his eyes were fascinating. They flashed a different colour ever so slightly, but I was sure it was in my mind, so I tried to blank it out. This was harder than I would have liked as he was now grinning at me and it was only when Lanie started to talk to him that he seemed to snap out of it. It was as if he had momentarily been taken over by pod people.

"Hey there pretty lady, how you doing?" I hadn't even noticed that Jack had turned up after the Spanish Inquisition. He said this putting on a half Texas accent and half Joey from Friends. It was the first time I had smiled all night. Then it burst, spoiled by RJ's reconstruction of the evening's events.

"Oh my God, Jack, you'll never guess!" She didn't wait to hear a reply or to take a breath.

"Our little Kazzy here only got singled out and sent upstairs to the V…I…P." She mouthed the letters, dragging each one out for more effect. Jack didn't look shocked, and like a gentleman, he didn't make as big a deal out of it as RJ had, or still was for that matter.

"So how was the Master of the Universe and his disciples, just thrilling I bet?" RJ scowled at her brother's sarcastic remark.

"Shut up, Jack, what do you know?" He laughed in response.

"Oh, come on, sis, it's all bullshit, smoke and mirrors. Anything gets this place rallied up, and everyone loves a good rumour," he said trying to sound more light-hearted, as he could see RJ's explosive side coming through.

"Well, that's the thing... it's not always just rumours though is it, Jack?" She stared at him with a knowing look, as though this would jog some memory of his.

"Leave it out, Rachel!" It was the first time I had heard anyone say her full name. At Jack's outburst, she backed down as though he had shouted at her for the first time in his life. Which had me wondering, what had I missed? It must have been something bad. For two reasons, the first being if the town's biggest gossip hadn't told me about it, and secondly, it would have to be something pretty big to get her to back down so quickly.

I felt even more awkward now, and I needed some air, so I decided to make my excuses and go outside.

"Hey guys, sorry, I'm going to bail. RJ I'll see you tomorrow, okay?" I got up and started to put my jacket on when Jack grabbed one side and helped me with the other arm. I froze as he was so close to my scars but thankfully it was over quickly, and he didn't realise my hesitation.

But then I noticed Chaz had resumed his glaring at me, only this time his stare was no longer one of amusement and had been replaced by one of abhorrence, but this wasn't only directed at me. No one else seemed to notice, and just before I lowered my eyes, I saw the deepest colour of purple flash in them before once again, Lanie spoke to him, breaking the spell.

"I think I'll join you outside for some air. It's a little crowded in here tonight," Jack said, clearly still angry with RJ and it was strange to see his face in this new light. His soft features turned hard and made him look more like a man, taking away his boyish charm. However, it had been replaced by something else. He now looked insanely sexy instead of cute.

We both walked outside, and I couldn't help but look back at the balcony one last time before I left through the huge, carved oak doors. There my eyes played tricks on me as I could swear that I saw a dark figure staring back. But I looked away quickly, knowing I was only seeing the things that my mind wanted to.

I let the cool air sweep over my body and cleanse my exposed skin. It felt good to be outside. Even the smell of that place did strange things to me. I couldn't think in there as it played with my emotions. But out here I could think clearly, and more importantly, rationally.

"You okay?" I had almost forgotten Jack was with me and felt embarrassed when he noticed me with my eyes closed.

"Yeah… sorry. I just really needed some air and to get away from all the stares." I don't know why I chose to add that bit, but I felt like Jack was becoming a good friend and one that wouldn't judge me.

"I know what you mean. I just hate it when they come here, and the whole town hypes up all this crap about them. I just wish they wouldn't, ever, bother coming back." He sounded different, like something about the Dravens hurt him personally, but I couldn't think for the life of me what it could be, seeing as the Dravens didn't have anything to do with the locals.

My phone suddenly started singing 'Gimme, Gimme, Gimme' by ABBA and I fished around in my pocket frantically before it started to get louder. I would have to remember to change the ring tone once I got home.

"Nice, hey if you wanted to boogie, then all you need to do is ask." He laughed, giving him back that warm glow I was used to. I smirked back before answering the phone.

"Hello, oh Frank… is everything alright?"

"Hi honey, bad news, I'm sorry, but I'm going to be late, things got a bit crazy here, but I'll ring Libs and ask her to come and pick you up." At that very moment as if on cue, the usual black car rolled up.

"Well, it looks like that won't be a problem anymore," I said conveying across my frustration in my tone.

"The car's there again, isn't it?" He laughed when I groaned in response.

"Man, he must have it bad."

"What do you mean?" I asked, thinking this was a strange comment.

"Never mind, kid, I won't ring Libs. Catch you later." I said goodbye and flipped the phone shut. Jack was still smiling at me with a huge grin on his face.

"It was my sister's phone and what can I say, she loves ABBA." We both laughed, and it felt good in spite of the car. I had already told Jerry that I no longer needed the special treatment, but someone clearly wasn't listening.

"Come on. I'll drive you home if you want. Warning you now though, it's nowhere near as fancy." He was walking towards the car park before I could object. I looked back to the black car to see the chauffeur looking back at me, so I did the only thing I could think to do. I gave him the thumbs up and then pointed to where Jack was walking to his blue pickup truck.

I could just see the look of disapproval from the chauffeur who never said a word to me, but I didn't care. They needed to get the hint, so with that in mind, I ran after Jack.

"Hey, wait up!" He turned to me and smiled, putting his arm around my shoulders.

"I told you it wasn't as fancy."

"Looks great to me," I said taking in the slightly battered pickup. Just at that moment, the sounds of an engine revving and wheels spinning made us both look back as we caught the car driving out of sight. We both looked at each other confused and Jack shrugged his shoulders.

"He must have really wanted to drive you home."

"Bored, I guess," I said as I got in the truck.

Once inside, Jack cranked up the heater and switched stations from the death metal to something softer. Then he turned to me and said,

"Sorry sweetness, no ABBA." I couldn't keep the smile from my face when I replied,

"Ha, ha, I told you it was my sister's phone." He leaned over and nudged my arm saying,

"Yeah, sure it was." He was such a tease. But this was one

kind of attention I wasn't minding as much. I really wanted to ask him what RJ had meant, but I didn't want to spoil his good mood as I had witnessed the change in him earlier. It must be something of a delicate nature. Maybe I would subtly ask RJ tomorrow on our way to college.

We were just chatting about friends and college stuff when he asked me outright about something of a delicate nature himself.

"So, how come I always see you wearing gloves?" I don't think he expected my reaction, so he couldn't have been thinking the obvious. I sunk down into my seat and looked out of the window before thinking of what to say, when I noticed something moving with us...no, not moving but more like following. It was quick, whatever it was, and very dark with a bluish tinge when the moonlight hit it. Like a fast-moving black cloud.

"What's that?" I said, pointing to my passenger side window. Jack looked but by the time he turned his head; it had gone. Great, now he just thinks I see things. Well, it wouldn't be the first time and no hope of it being the last.

"I don't see anything. I suppose the effect of the VIP is playing tricks on your mind." That smile again, if Helen of Troy had the face that could launch a thousand ships, then Jack's smile held the male equivalent.

"So, what did happen up there? You didn't seem yourself when you came down, and you were up there a long time?"

"How do you know... I mean, you only just arrived when I..." He shook his head, hiding a smile while he was pulling into the dirt road leading to my house.

"I got there earlier but was sat at the bar with some other friends. I asked if you were working and Mike told me where you were, so I waited."

"So that's why you weren't shocked when RJ told you, you already knew." He nodded as though embarrassed about something, but I couldn't tell what. He had pulled in front of the house and cut the engine. The lights were on, and I saw a curtain move. It must have been Libby.

"The ABBA fan?" he asked, chuckling to himself.

"Yep, she's also taken on the role of my mother, warden and caretaker seeing as my real one is in England. She's sweet though but a little paranoid. She doesn't like me working at the club and also doesn't trust the Dravens." I said this last part to try and prompt something out of him.

"She's a smart girl," he said with a distant look, as though the thought of a bad memory had re-entered his mind. I decided to call it a night, feeling bad for him. I didn't like seeing him all serious; it was just like a puzzle piece that fit but was the wrong shade.

"Well, thanks for the ride." I opened my door and noticed Jack also getting out. He walked round to meet me and said,

"Please allow me to walk a lady to the door." He put on a southern accent and tilted an imaginary hat taking my hand adding "Ma'am" for effect. He made me chuckle, and the dreaded snort showed itself. He laughed as he walked me up the porch steps to the front door. He still had hold of my hand and I was going red with embarrassment. He then stopped in front of me and leant down to my ear, which shamefully reminded me of someone else. I felt guilty for even thinking it, but I couldn't help the way I felt about Draven.

Jack whispered in my ear.

"Did I mention it's the cutest thing, that little snort of yours." I held my breath, knowing what was coming next. Maybe if I had never had this weird obsession thing with Draven going on, then this would have been what I wanted. But that fact remained, I did still feel the same and I didn't want to hurt Jack's feelings in the process.

He was turning his head towards my lips; his arms were moving their way around my upper body. I hadn't yet decided what to do. If I stopped it, it would hurt his feelings but if I didn't, then I was leading him on.

My mind was reeling off excuse after excuse in the seconds it took for his lips to close the distance but then something happened. He paused suddenly, and his arms that were around me went rigid. I lifted my head but saw his eyes were elsewhere.

His arms dropped, and he moved to stand with his back to me facing something I couldn't yet see.

"What the hell is that thing!?" I looked around his shoulders and saw a familiar sight.

My stalker bird was back...

And it looked enraged.

CHAPTER 15
DREAMING OF MY DRAVEN

As soon as I had laid eyes on the bird, it took flight, pushing from the porch bannister where it was perched. Jack had been freaked.

"What the hell was that thing doing? Not like any crazy-ass bird I have ever seen! Shit me, was that an eagle?!" I didn't even know if he was talking to me or himself, but he hurried a short,

"Goodnight," and went back to his car still muttering.

It was the one time I was thrilled the bird had reappeared, and it also confirmed that it wasn't just my imagination. It had been real all this time.

Libby was trying to act casual when I got in, sat on the couch watching TV. Well, if she wanted to put on a convincing show, then she shouldn't have put the TV channel to Football highlights. She hated most sports. I pulled her up on the bluff.

"Who's winning?" I said, trying to hide my smile.

"What, oh uh... Liverpool." I very much doubted that, seeing as she was watching an American football game.

"Umm, strange that as I didn't know Liverpool were playing the Broncos this week... that should be an interesting game." I laughed as I watched her realise her mistake.

"Okay, so I wasn't watching the stupid TV."

"No, really? I would never have guessed, but you were

177

watching something." I was making my way to the kitchen when she followed me.

"There's some pasta still left in the fridge." I opened it up to reveal a car crash of a meal left in a bowl. I couldn't understand how you could burn pasta. I would have to think of something quick to cook tomorrow before work.

"It's okay; I just fancy some toast." I put two slices of bread in the toaster and filled up the kettle.

"You want one?" She nodded in response, and I grabbed two mugs out of the cupboard.

"So, he seemed nice, was that Jack?" I knew it wouldn't take long, so I sat down and joined her.

"Yes, that was Jack, and we're just friends." I knew she just wanted me to be happy like she was with Frank. In her way, she thought that if I could just meet someone nice, then everything would work out. Well, what she didn't know was that I *had* met someone, but tonight just confirmed he was *far* from nice.

"Oh… do your friends always kiss you?" I knew it! She'd been spying on me.

"Libby! What were you…?" She cut me off.

"Toast." She pointed towards the smoke coming from the bread inside, and I reacted with waving a tea towel about trying to get rid of the smoke. I removed the charred bread and changed the setting down from five to two. No wonder it had burnt.

"See, I'm not the only one who burns things," she said in a smug tone.

"Well, maybe if it wasn't on the highest setting then I would get toast instead of charcoal, and anyway, don't change the subject. Why were you spying on me?" I put the black squares in the bin and decided to give up on the toast idea and just settle for the tea. I poured the boiling water into the two mugs and let the teabags brew.

"I wasn't spying, jeez you're so dramatic. I was just checking to see who it was and I saw him about to kiss you, so I stopped. But man, he's cute and tall. Didn't think you went for blondes though? I always thought it was tall, dark and handsome you liked?" I passed her tea and sat down, giving her one of those looks.

"Libby, it's not like that, he's a friend."

"Does *he* know that?" Okay, so she had me there, but I really didn't want to talk about it, so I changed the subject.

"Anyway, how's that new client going?" I knew this would work. She loved to talk about her job, and when she got going, it was as if she had entered a different world.

Libby chatted until Frank walked in, and then I made my excuses and went upstairs to my room. It was finally nice to be alone. I got ready for bed, hoping that I would dream of him. Not the asshole version I had met tonight but *my Draven.*

"NO!" I shouted at myself. It was getting out of hand, and I needed to stop it all! I knew what Draven was and he was out of my reach. It was pointless to dream of something that wasn't real. I went back into the bathroom and filled a glass and grabbed my sleeping pills off the shelf. This was one night that I needed to myself.

$\sim$

Back in the club, the band played but it was surprisingly empty for this time of night. Jerry came over to me with a tray in his hand, looking flushed, and his brother followed behind. It was the first time I had seen them both together, but it was only Jerry that spoke.

"You're needed upstairs again, but you need to be quick." He handed me the tray, but I shook my head at him.

"No, I turned down the job. I'm not working up there, and you can't make me." I finally said it and it felt good. Unfortunately, it was short-lived.

"No, but Draven can. So, hurry up!" Now, this did scare me. I didn't want Draven to speak to me again, so I gave in. I took the tray and headed for the back staircase, when Gary spoke in that disturbing voice of his.

"Be careful not to bleed." What the hell! Why did he say that? I turned to demand what he meant, but neither of them were there. What was with that dude? Did they teach 'creepy' at his school, or was he just born weird? I mean, I know that Mike had called him 'Special' but come on.

I went to the doors that led to the staircase I had used last time, but something was different. There wasn't the usual muscle standing guard, so I shrugged my shoulders, and I pushed the doors open. It was strange without the hum of people busy enjoying themselves down in the club. It made it more eerie.

The door at the top was open, unlike last time, and I walked through after a moment of hesitation. Once I was inside, the door slammed shut, sealing me in along with my fate. I dropped the tray and tried opening it but it seemed stuck, or worse… *locked.* I turned to the room, which was the same as I left it the night before. There were the same groups all sat at exactly the same tables and I walked the same steps I had done the night before. Thinking of the one friendly face I could find, I walked towards the bar in hopes of seeing Karmun.

I was getting close to the centre table, and my hands started to shake. I really wished there was a different way to the bar, but it had been cleverly positioned. I took a deep breath, letting my lungs fill with air so that I didn't have to breathe while I walked past. I wasn't sure why I did this, but I was almost convinced that the very scent of him had me feeling strange. I wouldn't look. I wasn't going to look. I promised myself not to look.

I looked.

Of course, I did. I was weak. However, he didn't look back. I tried to move my eyes, but they wouldn't listen to my silent pleas. He wasn't wearing a full suit tonight. He wore a tight-fitted T-shirt instead of a shirt and tie but had kept on the jacket. My God, he looked sexy. I started to mentally undress him and stopped before it got too much to handle.

I found myself thinking what his skin looked like in the glow of candlelight. More than ever, I wanted to touch it. Would it be soft or hard under the strength of his muscles? He leaned over to the Goddess next to him and listened to what his sister was whispering to him. Then my cover was blown as his head snapped up too quick for me to react. I almost ran the rest of the way to the bar.

I bumped into people on the way but what I saw in them wasn't the same as last night. My curse! It had come back to haunt me, and I screamed. But no one looked at me, even when they pushed around me. I dropped the tray, and bottles smashed around me in slow motion… but wait, hadn't I already dropped the tray? This thought was soon lost in sight of their faces… they were monstrous! I was terrified, and I wanted to run. NO, no, no, this couldn't be happening. Not now… not again!

I began to run, but it felt as though my legs were made of metal. I could hear the crunching of glass beneath my feet and the heavy thunder of my own heartbeat. I was looking for the way out of this Hell but as I passed each table, the horrors kept showing themselves in wave after wave of Demons.

There was one whose skin looked as though it was melting from the bone, but it just smiled as though what I was seeing was normal. I gagged at the dripping skin and lipless grin. I ran past another table of men who didn't have faces but teeth. That was all, just teeth that locked together like prehistoric sabre-toothed tigers. Their lips started from their foreheads and went down to their chins with just deadly teeth, but their faces kept twisting and contorting into their normal faces, the ones I had seen last night.

I couldn't get a grip. I turned around looking to hide from them only to see more monsters. The table I thought looked like Vampires were actually a table full of broken skulls that bled through the cracks. They turned to look at me and pointed to me with broken fingers that kept fading into the air like they were made from the ash of cremated corpses.

I grabbed my head and sank to my knees, wanting to curl up into a tight ball saying, 'There's no place like home,' over and over.

I could see from the corner of my eye a figure coming over to me before I made my secure ball. Everything was blurring, like when I was a child. I couldn't make out what was real and what was my madness. The figure was getting closer, and every instinct told me to run but I was paralysed with fear. I hung my head and let my hair cover my face, and the tears started to erupt from eyes that couldn't take any more.

"Please make it go away," I whispered like a frightened child.

"I will, little one. Don't worry; you're safe now." When a voice answered me, I realised that I had begged for this out loud. I recognised the voice, but I no longer cared.

"You can open your eyes now, don't be scared, little one." A hand touched the top of my head before it flowed down to my chin and lifted it slightly. I opened my eyes as he had instructed and saw that I was back in my familiar bedroom.

Oh, thank you God!

I was in my bed, and it had all been a dream. I saw the room just the way I had left it and I started to relax my tense muscles from the ball I was still in, but then I froze mid-stretch. If this was a dream, then why was there a figure stood over me now? I shot up out of bed before I could think and dragged the covers with me, nearly tripping over them.

"Whoa, easy there… you're alright, I won't hurt you." He walked towards me with his hands up as though I was holding a gun. He looked as he did in the dream, only he wasn't wearing a jacket, just a T-shirt and black trousers. I instantly looked down to make sure I had gloves on, which he noticed. Thankfully I did.

"I didn't touch you," he said in a soft tone taking my fears about exposing my scars the wrong way.

"I know you didn't but…but what are you doing here?" I tried to keep my voice steady, but it was proving difficult with my heart going so fast it felt like a jet engine firing up.

"I should go." That wasn't the answer I was hoping for, and I said the first thing that came to mind,

"Please don't!"

"You want me to stay?" He seemed surprised, and I wondered if he'd looked in the mirror lately?

"I don't understand. Was…was I dreaming… *am I still dreaming?"* I added in a whisper.

"No and yes, it was a nightmare, but now, well that's a different matter." He had slowly been making his way towards me and I shivered with the breeze that flowed through my open window. Was that how he had entered my room? And what was with the cryptic messages?

"What about now?" I asked as he bent down, not taking his eyes from mine for a second. I could see him smile in the dark when I asked this. I knew what was coming. This was the time that he would leave. It was the same smile I would always get when I didn't want it to end. But what was I saying, there was no way this was a dream, it felt too real.

Far too real.

He held something in his hand as he came so close to me now that I had to arch my neck back to see his face. He looked down at me.

"Are you cold?" He raised his free hand to my face and touched my skin with the back of his hand, running it down my neck. This had to be real! I closed my eyes as my nerves became tense, hoping his next move was the one I had waited what felt like an eternity for.

He answered his own question.

"Yes, you are." Then with one swift motion, my covers were around me like a cloak. He pulled me closer, gripping the quilt like a collar on a jacket. I could feel him breathing as he got closer still to my face. I, on the other hand, had stopped breathing altogether, afraid that he would leave me as always. I needed to speak. I needed answers even if they were just in my dreams. There were things I simply needed to know.

"Thank you. But please… I need to know." There was just enough light from the moon for me to see one of his eyebrows rise. I carried on before I lost track of what I was saying.

"Is this real, are you real, or am I still asleep?" He gave me what seemed like a sad smile and answered me,

"Yes, you are, but you won't have another nightmare. Not tonight." His voice sounded harder and somewhat possessive.

"But why, I mean… you…" I didn't know how to word it, and he picked up on it.

"Why do you keep dreaming of me, you mean?" I nodded, half knowing why. I was sick. I was obsessed, and my dreams were only one of the symptoms of my sickness.

"I don't know why, but I will tell you one thing…" His hands moved up from the makeshift collar until his fingertips caressed the cool skin along the column of my neck. I couldn't help the deep quiver coming straight from my spine. Then he made it worse and added to the spell he had over me by speaking the words I longed to hear.

"I like it." He lowered his head, so he could see my eyes when he said this, and I could feel my skin burn under the hand that still held my neck. He smiled again as though feeling the evidence for himself.

"But why?" I finally asked. The reaction I got made me shiver as his fingers on my neck tensed and held me there, tightening his grip. His thumbs applied pressure under my chin, forcing me to look up. My breathing hitched when I saw the intensity directed down at me. I tried to move back when I saw the flash of purple create a ring of fire around his black eyes. However, this move wasn't permitted as not only wouldn't his hands release me, but he slowly shook his head.

"You asked me why," he reminded me, but I couldn't concentrate. Not when one of his hands moved so that he could caress my bottom lip with the pad of his thumb. I only managed to nod, and even this was made more difficult as his fingers had now started to explore my T-shirt's low neckline.

"Please," I pleaded for anything more. His hand fisted in the material, and for a moment he looked close to tearing it from my body in response to that one barely uttered word.

"The reasons why will be known in time, but for now…" he said quickly letting go of my clothes, and I made a small sound of protest before it could be stopped. Although there was no need for it as he framed my face with both his hands and pulled me closer so that his lips could whisper the rest over my skin.

"…never doubt yourself, Keira, you are so beautiful." I couldn't help but allow my eyes to close as his words washed over me. He thought I was beautiful?

"I…" A noise faintly heard in the distance interrupted me and caught his attention. He looked at the window as though something was calling.

"Time's up, my little one." But before he could do his usual disappearing act, I stepped away from his hold. He looked shocked as though this wasn't what he was expecting. Well, if this was my dream, then I was in control, wasn't I? Although it sure never felt like it.

It pained me to be far from his body, but I needed something different to happen. I wasn't ready to let go of this yet. I moved to the corner of my room, putting distance between us, which he didn't seem to like at all. I could even make out the hard lines of his displeasure from the other side of the room.

"Why do you have to go if it's my dream?" I bravely stated the obvious but was still retreating, backing into a corner. I looked down for a split second to make sure I wasn't going to do my usual tripping over act.

"That's a good question, but unfortunately one I cannot answer." The breath of his words hit me across my lips, as he was once again so close to my face. I couldn't understand it. How had he reached me so quickly?

Before I could react, his hands gripped my hips roughly and tugged me into his body. He grinned as though he found my startled breath amusing and then slowly leant down to my ear. I held onto his biceps just for something to anchor myself to in the flood of sensations he was causing to my body. Then it came. The whispered words that would end one of the nicest dreams I had ever experienced. And as always, his last words lingered in my mind, making it impossible to ignore such a commanding voice.

"Sweet dreams my Keira, for this time I promise…" he paused, which mirrored my breathing, and then I felt him inhale deeply the scent at my neck before he vowed against my beating pulse,

"…to protect those dreams."

CHAPTER 16

CHILDHOOD

As soon as those words had been uttered, my mind instantly found sleep, but with the words echoing round and round in my head, it felt like no time at all before I quickly awoke. It was still dark outside my window, but it was closed as though it had never been touched. My heart sank instead of the usual rush of pleasure I would normally feel. I tried to piece together the nightmare, which had then erupted into the second-best fantasy yet; the first being the one that included a kiss.

It had seemed so real I could barely believe it was just constructed from stunning visual memories and sweet fictional ideas. Mainly ideas of what I longed to do to Mr. Arrogant himself. In fact, the only reason I still believed they were all just dreams, was because any other explanation was impossible. The man despised me, that much was clear. To him, I was an intruder who didn't belong, not only in his world but most definitely not in his club. So, what did my mind do to rectify this? I conjured up a sweet centre to go with his delicious hard candy casing, instead of the bitter aftertaste spending time with Draven really produced.

I got up, wrapping a knitted throw around my shoulders, as I was about to do something I hadn't done for a very long time. I walked over to my whitewashed wooden desk and took out the supplies I needed from one of the drawers. Libby had put a load of art stuff in one drawer in the hopes that one day I would start up my passion again. As it turned out, she had been right. I held the pencil in my hand as though I had been Harry Potter finding the right wand.

Libby and I had both shown a passion for art from a young age. But Libby then went on to develop a taste for interior design, begging our parents to let her decorate their lounge at the age of sixteen. Ever since then, she had known what her calling in life had been, and she was a master at it. I, on the other hand, had developed mine in a very different way.

You see, I had a secret. The deepest and darkest of secrets. I was different from the rest. I had always known that one day it would catch up with me. Like a personal realm of Demons, I just couldn't hide from, and no matter how much I closed my eyes, they were there… they were always there.

Waiting in the shadows of what was left of my mental control. Waiting until the day I finally broke and gave in for the very last time. The scariest thing was it really didn't feel like that far away. It started when I was younger, one year when we all went on vacation down to Cornwall to spend the summer with my mother's parents.

My grandparents lived by the sea, which would attract various types of tourists. The summers would be buzzing with people from all walks of life and was a breeding ground for all types of entertainment. Everyone would wait with excitement for the famous travelling circus and fairground to come to town.

Only this particular year would end up being a life-changer I would never forget.

∽

My sister and I went skipping through the crowds with giggles and smiles, taking in all the wonders our eyes could see. Fire eaters, acrobats, men that would eat swords, stilt walkers, and

STEPHANIE HUDSON

clowns with sad faces that squirted each other with water-filled flowers. The rides with happy screams of excitement and the smells of sugar treats and hot dogs filled the field, transforming it into a child's blissful playground.

It had been my first time at a fair, well one that I could remember anyway. I was nearly seven, so I couldn't go on every ride like Libby, but I didn't care, I was just so happy to be there that I could barely contain my excitement. Libby and my dad had just come off a roller-coaster called the 'Inferno Twister' when I started to ask about the candy stand over near the 'House of Fun'. My mother had waited with me and bribed me with the chance of candy-floss if I waited like a good girl. Given my love for all things sweet, this wasn't a hard task to comply with. But as soon as they came in sight, it was all my mind could think of.

"Libby, take your sister to get some teeth rotting sweets before she gnaws my hand off." My sister laughed and took my hand in search of the red and white stand.

"What's gnaws mean?" I had asked innocently enough when the crowd started to get thicker due to the end of a show in the big top. My sister's hand squeezed mine in vain just before I broke away. I couldn't see for bodies all moving in different directions. I was pushed along with a family who weren't speaking English and I couldn't hear the sound of my sister's voice calling my name over a language that I didn't understand.

Finally, after following them, I was left standing in a quieter part of the fairground where there were no rides or stalls. I was on the outskirts of the park. I stood with a wet face from tears of panic when a woman with a kind voice approached me. She was dressed strange, with a number of red and purple scarves around her head like a turban. I remembered seeing people dressed like this in some of the books in my grandparents' library, and I recognised her to be a gypsy.

She wore a white shirt with big sleeves and a red dress on top that tied under the bust with ribbons crossing over. Her arms were covered in bangles and gold bracelets with what looked like coins hanging from them.

She wore multiple sets of matching hooped earrings. And her

hands were covered in so many rings that you could hardly see the skin on her fingers. One caught my eye as it was shaped like a silver dragon's head and its mouth opened up as though it had swallowed her entire finger. The teeth on the end looked sharp as the spikes interlocked and clamped together.

"Are you lost, young lady?" I remember thinking it was nice to be called young lady instead of my usual "Little squirt" Libby called me.

"Yes, I can't find my sister, she was taking me for some sweets." She smiled, showing a full set of yellow teeth, like ones you would find on an elderly person after a lifetime of heavy smoking. Her tanned skin was awash with lines of age and I noticed a small red star close to her right eye, nearly lost in the wrinkled folds.

She looked at me strangely, staring deep into my eyes. Even as a child, I had known that something wasn't right about this woman, and remembering the golden rule of childhood, I took a step back saying,

"I should go and find my parents, and I shouldn't be talking to you, you're a stranger." I turned to leave but somehow, she stood facing me once more.

"How did you do that?" Her red lips curled up on one side, revealing a yellow fang and she bent down to the level of my young face.

"Magic!" she said, and with a movement of her hand, she produced a pretty pink flower. She gave it to me and then straightened up revealing a less creepy smile.

"My name is Nesteemia, but my friends call me Ness. I'm a palm reader."

"What's a palm reader?" I was at my questioning phase, wanting to know absolutely everything there was to know about anything.

"I can tell you your future, my dear, by touching your hand."

"How? I hold my sister's hand all the time, and I don't see anything." She bit her lip trying to hide a smile that would no doubt turn into a laugh.

"You have to know the magic to be able to see." I nodded my

head in understanding, thinking she could be a witch. I held out my hand with a firm mind and said,

"Show me please." This would turn out to be the biggest mistake of my life because when she took my hand in hers, what I saw next truly terrified me... and the gypsy.

She closed her eyes as she ran her heavy metal covered fingers across the palm of my cold small hand, and she started to chant words I didn't understand. I got scared and tried to pull away, but she held on tighter, stopping me from removing my now quivering hand. She opened her lids, but her eyes were somewhere else. Rolling back into their sockets, so all you could see were the cloudy whites of them. She started to shake her head, and her eyes that had turned blood red in colour were now flickering back and forth as though trying to read the lines in a book a million words a second.

I looked around searching for anyone who might be able to help me, but I hadn't realised she had pulled me further from the fair. We were now completely out of sight. I tried to speak and scream, but when I opened my mouth, no sound came from it. It was as if she had put some sort of spell on me, forcing my silence. I was helpless, wishing I had never even wanted candy-floss in the first place.

She started to slow down her breathing, and her eye movement was less erratic. She looked at me but now she was the one who looked scared. Fear caught up with her body making it vibrate as mine once did, as though what she had seen in my future had been so disturbing she couldn't contain the terror. I stopped struggling now as a new fear had gripped me.

What had she seen?

"What is it? Tell me... what did you see?" I asked in a panicked voice. She just stared at me, not speaking a word, but she wouldn't let go of my hand.

"TELL ME!" I managed to scream, bringing her out of her comatose state.

"It's all true, but it can't be... you can't be real... what trickery is this?" I didn't understand her babbling, so I struggled once more to break free of her fierce grasp.

"Let me go!" I said over and over, but she wasn't listening to me. She just kept saying the same words over and over.

"It has come, it has come." Finally, I could see someone coming this way and tried to make another run for it. She caught sight of them before I managed to draw attention to us both, and she clamped her other hand around my mouth, pulling me back behind a work shed, out of sight.

"I will make you see ready for your master, young mistress." I didn't understand, and I shook my head under her grasp.

"Be still," she ordered as she grabbed my arm and held it out with my palm facing upwards. I was losing the strength to struggle anymore and was giving up. The tears streamed down my face and on to the hand of my captor. She held the dragon finger out, pointing it at my palm.

She said something that sounded like a command, only it was in a different language.

"укусить!" ("Bite" In Russian) Then my eyes saw something impossible. The dragon's head moved, opening its mouth wide, releasing its teeth into a biting position. I mouthed the words *'Don't!'* and *'No!'* But the sound was muffled by her hand. The dragon bit down hard on my palm, making small puncture marks with its teeth. I cried out in pain wanting this nightmare to be over, wondering if I was ever going to see my family again. She whispered in my ear yet more words I couldn't understand.

"Θα τελειώσουν σύντομα ένας γενναίος." ("It will soon be over, be brave." In Greek)

She pulled her hand away from my lips, and I was in too much pain to say anything apart from cry. Then she repeated the same words once more to the dragon ring and placed it to her own palm letting it once again taste blood. At least this time it was hers. Unlike me, she smiled at the pain as though welcoming it and pressed it tightly to my own bleeding hand.

"It has been a pleasure, Electus. Until next time."

. . .

These were the last words I heard until my mother's voice woke me up. I opened my eyes to the room my sister and I shared in my grandparent's guest house. I first thought it was all a dream as I looked down at my hand for a cut in my skin, but it wasn't there. I later found out that my parents, along with a number of fairground staff, had found me curled up asleep near the tool shed. There was no sign of a gypsy woman and nor had there been one working the fair that year. I tried to tell my parents, but without proof, they put it all down to a traumatic nightmare.

I, too, had been convinced until the day I saw her again.

It was on my seventh birthday, we had all gone out to an American themed diner where they served burgers and chips (Or fries as it was on the menu), which was a favourite of mine. Afterwards, we all walked along the shore to get some ice cream, spotting one made with traditional Cornish clotted cream. I pointed it out as though the colourful ice cream van was a beacon drawing me in.

I walked right up to the open window already knowing the flavour I wanted when I noticed something familiar. The man who served me had the same deadly red tint in his eyes as the gypsy in my dream. I tried to shake it off, but the red kept getting deeper and deeper until it soon looked as though his eyes would overflow with blood. I stepped back before giving him my order when my father's voice came up behind me making me jump.

"Whoa, hey kiddo, what flavour are you getting?" I didn't answer as my dad walked past me, giving the man three orders for himself, my sister and my mum.

"Honey, what you having…? Come on, make your mind up." My dad was getting impatient as he could see a line forming behind me. I still couldn't speak. Why couldn't he see what I was seeing? He turned to give me a look that translated to 'if I don't pick soon, I wouldn't be getting one' so I mouthed a silent 'chocolate' and he frowned at my strange behaviour. He passed me mine with his hands full and walked towards my family who had sat down on a nearby bench. I was about to follow when the man from the van shouted,

"Hey Guv, you forgot your change," in a thick Essex accent.

"Oh honey, could you grab that for me?" I froze knowing I would have to explain myself if I refused. Maybe I was just seeing things. That had to be it. No one else in the line looked freaked. People moved out of my way to let me pass as I reached up my hand to receive the money, but the man grabbed my hand forcefully, and my eyes met the gypsy woman's face, the one that had haunted my dreams for weeks.

Her eyes were bleeding, and the blood dripped down her face. There it gathered into thicker drops until finally onto people's ice creams that lay in the holders. Customers still took them and licked away as though they were consuming the blood of a witch-like Demonic strawberry sauce. And nobody seemed to notice this mad looking woman as she was pulling me closer to the window. They were just going around me as though I was merely a traffic cone in the road.

"Now you will see...7...7...7, and I will see you again at 7...7...7." She kept repeating the number over and over as she let go of my hand. I fell back, and an elderly couple helped me off the floor, picking up the change that the crazy gypsy had dropped around me. I looked back and the ice cream man's face smiled, saying,

"Are you alright, love?"

I couldn't understand what had just happened, and my parents just thought my tears were from when I had fallen and lost my ice cream. But from that day on I would see things that made people's nightmares seem like happy cartoons. My nightmares started to come to life when I wasn't even asleep. I would be on a bus or in a car and one minute I would see just a normal person, and then I would see them change into something utterly terrifying.

Sometimes I would see them with scales where skin should be, or their hair would move as though they were floating underwater. Then there were the very scary ones, the ones that had black empty holes where their eyes should be. Sometimes these holes would glow red, and the cracks in their skin would light up in reaction. It would move under the cracks as though thousands of tiny little creatures were trying to claw and scratch their way out from under what looked like a dry riverbed.

Others would flicker back and forth like the top of their heads kept screaming. As if the other side of them was trying to escape. These would let out a screeching sound so high pitched that I would have to put my hands over my ears, and they would always ache afterwards, leaving me with a ringing in my fragile mind.

I now lived in fear of when I would next see one, soon becoming withdrawn and nervous. I tried to tell my parents about my fears, but they put it down to everything and anything. They would tell me off, sending me to my room, and then my mum would get so upset about what she was hearing. I would cry to Libby, pleading with her to believe me, but as the months went on, she did less and less. I had no answers to any of her questions, so why would she?

"Why can no one else see them?" She would often ask, but I just hung my head feeling helpless in a secret world no one else could see. Occasionally, I would see a kind looking one but even these were disturbing. They would glow with eyes bright, and their veins would move as though you could see the blood flowing through their bodies. But it was normally a bluish light that would follow through into their backs to what looked like wings. These too would sometimes differ in shape and size and also type of material.

I remember one woman looked as though hers were made from clear plastic bags stretched out onto long thin twig-like fingers that curled at the ends. But the images would flash in and out so quickly that sometimes they would change. It got to a point where I didn't know what was real anymore.

One day at school it was getting too much for me when a new teacher had asked why I was crying and why wouldn't I go outside to play with the others? When I had replied, "'Cause there's a boy in my class that's a monster," she had rung my parents to come into the school. The meeting had lasted the rest of the day with different teachers and staff being involved. No one spoke to me, but my father came out and barely looked at me. My mother just placed her hand on my back and said,

"Come on, we're going home."

Nobody said a word in the car.

Later that night, I had heard my mum and dad having an argument and I had tiptoed to the landing to hear. I found my sister there already with her face full of sorrow. Marks down her cheeks revealed she had been crying. The voices downstairs grew louder and I could make out that my mother too was crying.

"But she's not sick, and I won't send her to that place!" my mother said between sobs.

"You know I don't want to send her there either, but what else can we do?" Tears filled my eyes at all the trouble I had caused. I wished I could erase it all. I wished I could go back to the happy kid I once was, and then none of this would be happening. My sister turned to me and wiped away my tears.

"I don't understand why this is happening to you, but I know you're not faking it. However, Mum and Dad will send you away if you don't do something." She looked at me with pleading eyes and her face blurred through my watery vision.

"Send me where?" I tried to control my sobs so as not to alert my parents that we were listening.

"The school thinks you should be sent to a special hospital, so you can be monitored by doctors and therapists." She lowered her head in shame to be the one to tell me this.

"They think I'm crazy, don't they?" She nodded, and a single tear rolled down her pink cheek.

"What am I going to do? I don't want to go, I'm scared, Libby." She held me close to her, hugging me tight, not wanting me to be taken away. She leaned into my ear and said one word.

"Lie." My head popped up and looked at her. She was serious.

"What?"

"Lie. Tell them it was all a lie to get attention, tell them a girl

at school put you up to it, tell them it's scary films you have been sneaking downstairs to watch, I don't know, but tell them anything so they won't send you away!" She was almost as desperate as I was, but she'd clearly had time to think about this.

I nodded saying,

"Okay, I will but, Libby, what do I do about keeping the monsters away?" She looked worried at my response and sadly said,

"I don't know but let's deal with this problem first."

It felt so comforting to hear my sister's semi-belief, so it gave me the confidence I needed to do what I did next. After telling my parents one of the excuses Libby had come up with, everything went back to normal pretty quickly. Apart from my seeing things I could not explain, my life went back to the usual young girl's life I had originally had.

Only now I had to fake a lot of things. Why, for example, I would jump at nothing and look shocked at some random person walking past. But my parents were more than happy to believe that I was fine. If only for just one day they saw the same things I did. I would sometimes dream that this would happen but then felt guilty about it instantly. I would never wish this curse on anyone. Even at such a young age, I still knew the consequences such a life-altering event had on one human mind.

However, it all changed again six months later when Libby came running into my room with an idea. She had recently seen a documentary about a man who travelled around the world, talking about different cultures. My dad was watching it as he did every week, when my sister took notice of one part in particular. It was when he tried to take a picture of the Aborigines, they held up their hands in protest. The guide then explained why this was.

Spiritualists would claim that the human image on the mirrored surface was akin to looking into one's soul. The spiritualists also believed that it would open their souls and let Demons in. Aborigines believed that taking one's picture took part of one's soul. It somehow kept it locked away.

Locked... that was the key.

AFTERLIFE

This was how her idea was born. She thought that if taking a picture of someone let Demons in then maybe taking the picture of a Demon would somehow contain them. But it didn't quite make sense, and I could hardly go around taking everyone's picture just in case. So, she came up with another way. She told me to try and draw them whenever I saw one. Maybe this would act as a sort of prison for them to be locked out of my mind. It was something I had never thought of, so I did as she asked and started sketching them every time I saw one.

I found that every time I did this, it would lock the image from my head and I wouldn't see it any more. The effects didn't stop there. Because after years of seeing these living nightmares, they grew less and less, until one day I realised I hadn't seen one in over a month.

However, they didn't go completely. They were now only coming to me when I was asleep. I would playback part of the day and somewhere there would be one changing into something horrible but as long as it remained in my dream, I could cope with it. I would then get up and draw what I had seen and keep it in a hidden folder, locking it out of my head forever.

The next time I saw the same person, they would be just like everyone else and I wouldn't dream of them again. By the time I hit my teens, the dreams had also stopped, only coming back to me a few times a year. I owed it all to Libby, and she would never know the full extent of what she had done for me. She had saved me from my curse.

Now, of course, I was back to my own unusual therapy, drawing the visions that had come to me in last night's horror. Of course, the difference now was that I had a knight in not so shiny trousers and T-shirt, but man what a knight he was! It was worth being so scared in the mists of Hell to see the Heaven there waiting to pull me out. It was just a pity that he too was just a fragmented version of the truth.

Draven at the club and Draven, my knight, were miles apart. It was just a shame that the only one of those who was real actually disliked me. I sat back staring at the pictures of faces made up of teeth and shuddered at the thought. But this time I didn't have a book I could add it to. This time I would have to start a new one, for new nightmares.

And I had a feeling this was only the beginning of my recurring past...

My Curse was back.

CHAPTER 17

FALLING FOR DRAVEN...
LITERALLY

I went downstairs just before the morning light filled the kitchen. No one was up yet, and I was thankful for it. I still felt strange from the night's events, and Libby would no doubt pick up on it. Hopefully, I could get away with not seeing her until later today before I started work.

The thought of work gave way to new worries. It would be even harder now, knowing that everyone would soon find out I was about to turn down a once in a lifetime opportunity. For them maybe but for me, more like a recipe for disaster.

I sat and wondered as I played around with my breakfast, one I couldn't eat. I let my mind go over every detail of the dream. Had he awakened me from a nightmare in a dream? How was that even possible? I'd searched my room before coming down here for any evidence of the possibility that it could have been real. But I was living in hope of an impossible reality. What had me so fixated? He had completely seduced my mind, but more importantly…

Was there any way of going back?

But did I want to, even if I could? I knew the answer. There was no turning back now. He had ruined all chances for me feeling like this about anyone else. Jack had made it perfectly clear about his feelings last night, but I had shied away from his attentions, yet before I would have relished it. I would have really gone for someone like Jack. He was funny, handsome, charming and above all, a perfect gentleman. But Jack wasn't the problem… *I was.*

And I knew what my problem was, I was attracted to the one guy who didn't care and never would… or was that true? His actions contradicted his behaviour at every turn, even from the very first time he saw me in the club he went from hot to cold in seconds. Then there were the jerks outside the club when he came nobly to my aid. Not to mention the chauffeur driven car and the phone call to Jerry. To say I was confused was an understatement.

I carried on fighting with my own thoughts like this until I got out of the shower and I had to finally concentrate on something else, like getting ready. I realised I was running late when I heard RJ's little car beep it's pathetic horn. It sounded more like Road Runner. I ran downstairs with half-wet hair trying to put it up into its usual twist, but it wasn't co-operating. The sides hung down wet and wavy. I got in the car after a quick goodbye to Libby and Frank, and must have looked as if I'd been dragged backwards through a car wash.

"Hey, you okay? Just woken up by any chance?" She laughed and started the engine into semi life. She rubbed the dash saying,

"Come on old girl, you're warm now." I laughed, and the car spluttered into motion.

"Believe it or not, I woke up at 4:30 this morning." She shot me a look in disbelief.

"Tell me you weren't getting ready this whole time?" She eyed me up and down, already knowing that I obviously hadn't.

I sat fiddling with my seat belt waiting for her to start back up the interrogation.

"So… good night?" She smiled, half biting her lip to contain herself. But now with that look on her face, I wasn't sure what she meant. Was it about the VIP or Jack?

"It was okay. Look I'm sorry I got all weird last night, but you know I just hated all the attention, that's all." She nodded, still smiling like I was missing the joke.

"But you must have liked the attention from someone… *right?"* Ah-ha, so she was talking about Jack. I was now wondering what he had said as I would have to be careful.

"I don't know what you mean." Okay, she wasn't stupid, and she shot me a look to prove it. God, it was like having CSI Grisham on the case. I'm surprised she didn't have a lie detector strapped to my ass.

"Oh, come on, we all know Jack likes you, and he drove you home and…"

"And…and what?" I decided the best way to play this out was good old faithful 'playing dumb'.

"And what happened next?" Well, at least this was confirmation that Jack hadn't said anything, which meant that I could get away with also not saying anything.

"Okay… so what did Jack say?" Another smirk, she had taken my asking the wrong way.

"He didn't say anything, that's my point, which is how I know something happened. He's only secretive when something's going on." Now I was starting to feel really bad. I was going to have to make it clear to Jack as I didn't want to hurt his feelings.

"Nothing happened. Jeez, you're like a pit bull with a lamb chop!" She laughed and seemed pleased with the analogy. I carried on talking in a more serious tone.

"Honestly, nothing happened, he's a good friend, we chatted, and he was the perfect gentleman, but that's it," I said making her sigh in defeat.

"That's a shame. I really think he likes you and it's been so long since his last girlfriend." Her cheerful tone dropped, but I couldn't understand why. I mean, it's unusual for a sister to really care who her brother dates unless she was a friend.

"Why, what happened?" Now it was *me* being nosy. RJ must be rubbing off on me.

"I shouldn't have mentioned it, forget I said anything." What! This coming from RJ, gossip queen extraordinaire, now how could I let it go?

"Can I just ask, does it have anything to do with the

Dravens?" She whipped her head round to stare at me in amazement, but come on, it really wasn't that hard to put two and two together.

"Who told you!?" She looked upset as she raised her voice and gripped the steering wheel as though she was going around a circuit.

"Was it Lanie? That little…"

"No! No, sorry but I just guessed, and after what you said at the club last night about some stories not being just gossip and something that Jack said, I just kinda put it all together." She relaxed her muscles a little and slowed her speed, not that the little car went much faster, if anything it just made more noise.

"I shouldn't have said that last night, I hope he's forgiven me." It was horrible seeing RJ sad, it looked wrong in the same way when Jack looked angry last night. It didn't suit either of them.

"I'm sorry I said anything, let's just forget about it," I said trying to be a good friend, even though I really wanted to know.

"Okay I would tell you, but this really is the one thing that isn't my place. But I'm sure he will tell you soon, he does really like you… you know that, right?" I did, and I wished I could do something about it but I couldn't. I wasn't that girl any more. So, I said the only thing I could think of, without giving away too much information.

"I like Jack, I really do, but I just don't date anymore… call it a bad experience." She rolled her lips back into her mouth and nodded getting the idea.

"Boy, somebody must have done a real number on you." I just nodded, holding back the tears.

She really had no idea.

～

The rest of the day flew by without any more talk from RJ about last night. We spent lunch outside as the sun was out for a change, and most of the students were taking advantage of the freak weather. There was still a chill but nothing a hooded sweater couldn't handle. The rest of the gang met us, as RJ had sent a mass text inviting everyone. There was the usual lot and four others I didn't know. They seemed like Jack's friends, as they kept nudging him as soon as they saw me. Jack came over to sit by me and asked sweetly if I was cold. I said I was fine and we continued to talk about our day's classes.

I wished, at this moment, I felt that tingle that you get when you're sat next to someone you fancy. I mean, what was wrong with me? He was gorgeous, and today was no exception as he wore a faded Led Zeppelin T-shirt with a leather jacket and hooded zip-up underneath that looked warm. Oh, and his usual faded jeans with rips at the knees. His hair was untamed and floppy, but it could have been styled by Toni and Guy, as he looked once more as if he had just come from a photoshoot for Men's Health magazine. His big shoulders leaned in towards mine as he sat with his body turned into me. He wanted to be close, that much was clear.

"Wow, now why won't Mum and Dad buy me one of those?" RJ's eyes nearly bulged out as she stared at a huge brand new, shiny black Range Rover that had just pulled up less than twenty feet away.

"Because Mum and Dad don't have ten grand to spend on anything, let alone over a hundred grand for a car." Jack turned his head back round in disgust as if knowing who was in it.

"Is that a Range Rover Project Kahn?" one of Jack's friends said, as though he wanted to go up there and start licking the bodywork. Another answered his question with amazement himself.

"I thought they were only available in Europe, man that's a sweet ride." Every student was now staring at it as they went by. Some even took pictures with their mobile phones. Jack had leant into me as if to try and draw my attention away from who it was.

"So, I was kind of wondering if maybe you'd like to catch a movie one night?" Oh no, was he asking me out on a date? I was starting to think of how to form the words when RJ saved me.

"Oh my God, Kaz, there's a stunning looking girl waving to

you." I turned my head around and saw Sophia's perfect figure standing there in a designer dress, waving one manicured hand at me. I got up and went bright red as everyone, but Jack was staring at me with their mouths wide open.

"I'd better go and see what she wants." I walked over to her and the big black beast of a car that was still burbling behind her. I heard RJ say as I walked off,

"Is that who I think it is?" And then a murmur of whispers continued about the mystery girl.

"Hi Keira, I thought we could walk to history together." She embraced me as if she hadn't seen me in years. The scent of her perfume nearly knocked me out. She smelled like a luxury flower garden, and I imagined the Hanging Gardens of Babylon to have the same effect. She was about to link my arm but then stopped.

"Silly me, forgot my bag. Do me a favour and just grab it from the back seat, would you? I need to tell the driver when to pick me up." I shrugged and said,

"Sure." Then, as if I had just been programmed to do so, I opened the car door. It was slightly high for my 5ft 3 inches to get into without heaving myself in using the sidestep. So, after I opened the door, I looked down to get my footing and pushed myself up. This turned out to be a colossal mistake as I overdid it and fell forward into the back seat. I would have been fine if it didn't turn out that the back seat wasn't empty as I would have hoped... or prayed. No, because instead of face planting into a leather seat, I did so into a man's lap.

"Oh God, please no," I whispered into a suit pant leg.

"Keira?" And with that one name said, I knew no amount of wishing would make the man I'd fallen into turn into someone I wasn't obsessed with.

"Unfortunately," I muttered, too low for him to hear. I held my eyes tightly closed for a second, knowing I not only had to apologise, but also had to move off his lap considering I was pretty certain I had outstayed my welcome... that and my shameful encounter with a certain part of his anatomy.

"I...I... am...am so, so sorry, Mr... Draven." His last name came out strangled as though it physically hurt me, knowing this was the first time I was saying his name to his face. Or more like his crotch... oh shit, God, damn, bugger, shit, shitty, shit, shit! I cursed in my mind holding in the much-needed F word.

"Keira it's..." he started as his hands curled around my arms to help pull me up. The strength in this move practically dragged me the rest of the way in the car, and now I found myself facing him, with the shorter parts of my hair covering most of my scorched cheeks. Then my heart must have stopped beating for a whole minute as disbelief struck. Draven raised his hand and with one gentle sweep, he pushed the hair from my face and tucked it back to rest behind my ear.

"Keira," he whispered my name, and my reaction couldn't be helped.

"I'm dreaming." My first thought flew out of my mouth, not just skipping the 'saying stupid shit' filter, but blowing the damn thing to smithereens!

"Am I interrupting something?" Sophia asked, her voice so full of mischief that I started to wonder if she hadn't orchestrated this little 'accident'. Upon hearing her voice, mine and Draven's reactions were the same and sudden. We both separated, only Draven's hand lingered where my cheek had once been for a few seconds before it made a fist and then dropped to his side. I bit my lip and braved a look up at the man's face, which made me ache with wanting. His dark eyes cut to me, and I saw a flicker of gentleness before they morphed into harsh black ice. Now all I saw there was cruel indifference.

His fisted hand uncurled then tensed again before he leant down to pull out a Gucci bag to match the dress and shoes and everything else about Sophia's outfit. This prompted me to move back as though I had been stung by that same hand. Draven's eyes never left me, and I didn't think it possible, but his look went from furious to glacial.

"I...I am so sorry, Sir," I said again as I got all the way out of the car, and before I could see his reaction to my mumbled apology, I fled from sight. I was leaning with my back up against the car trying to find my breath, when I heard Sophia speak.

"Thank you, Dom, see you later," she said sweetly and then started laughing at the growl she received in return. I wanted to run. Instead, I just turned around to face the other direction and held my head down. She came back to where I stood and linked my arm.

"Come on then, let's get the dreaded Reed over and done with." I plastered on a smile and waved goodbye to my friends who were starting to disperse themselves. They stared in amazement, but only Jack looked hurt. Sophia noticed as he was now glaring at her, full of hatred in his eyes.

"Who's that, your boyfriend?" I choked back a nervous laugh, and she looked at me with a strange expression.

"No, why would you think that?" She smiled and looked back in front as we walked towards the entrance of our building.

"Well, it was actually my brother who noticed you... umm... seemed cosy sat there, deep in conversation. I guess he just assumed." I couldn't speak. I just made that strange little grunting noise I had done earlier. Like trying to swallow a big pill that was stuck halfway down. Why on earth would he even mention me, let alone notice me?

"Nah, that's just Jack, my friend RJ's brother... I... uh... I don't date," I said as it felt like this was the theme of the day. I felt like a quiz show contestant where the presenter introduces you in a dramatic, loud voice saying your name and something about your personal life only mine would read:

'I'd like to introduce our next contestant, Keira Johnson. Keira enjoys obsessing about her boss, who barely knows she's alive. She's come over from England due to being cast out, likes drawing the monsters she sees in her head, and most importantly enjoys explaining on a daily basis how she never dates... COME ON DOWN!'

I could have added a lot more, but I did want to make it through the day without feeling like a complete loser. After all, it was bad enough that I had Reed for my next lesson, not to mention the news I had yet to tell Sophia about me turning the job down. With her cute little doll-like face, it was going to be like telling an entire Kindergarten, there was no Santa.

We both found our seats, which so happened to be the same as last time. I got the same old stares as we took our places, but with one look from Sophia, they stopped, along with the whispering. Everyone knew who she was now, and from the look of things they were all just as intimidated as I was. I decided to wait until the end of class to mention the job. It would at least give me another hour to think of what to say. It was amazing to think that last night I had thought this would be easy, now I wasn't so sure.

"So tonight, are you okay to start at seven instead of eight?" Worst luck in the world, and trust this to be a day when Reed was late. She noticed me looking towards the door, searching in vain.

"Reed's having car trouble, he will be late." She snickered like a naughty child, but I didn't know why.

"How do you know that?" I asked as she smiled a wicked grin, but it was still cute on her.

"I overheard one of the other tutors… so, tonight?" Well here goes, I was going to have to get it over and done with at any rate.

"Well about that, I was thinking that maybe it wasn't such a good idea." I tried not to look at her, but she turned fully facing me with her arms folded. I looked into her eyes, and she looked confused and hurt. I felt like the child catcher out of Chitty Chitty Bang Bang!

"Why, I don't understand… is it me?" What! How had she come up with that reason?

"No, no, of course not, it's just I think that it would be easier if I just stayed downstairs, your brother looked really hacked off about the idea of it and well…" She smiled and cut me off mid-sentence.

"Don't worry about him, he's already warmed to the idea. Our family is very private, and he doesn't trust new people. But it's no reason not to take the job, he just needs to get used to you being around." She relaxed as though this had convinced me.

It hadn't.

"Still, I think that it would be best…" Again, she jumped in.

"It will be fine. Look, we really are desperate for some new staff, and you haven't been tainted by all the lies and gossip of this small town, plus it's a lot more money."

"It is?" I didn't want to sound shallow, but I really did need a car soon, and if I could do it without dipping into my life savings that would be a plus.

"Oh yes, it's over thirty bucks an hour." Wow, now that was a lot more than I was expecting. I wondered why it was so much. Did you have to donate blood at the end of each shift or something?

"Okay, that is something to think about," I said, and she smiled at her near triumph.

"Are you saving up for anything?" What, was she reading my mind now?

"Yeah, I really need my own car. I can't keep relying on my sister and her husband or chauffeur driven cars for that matter." I gave her a look, but it was one she ignored.

"And on friends?"

"Yeah sometimes, I mean me and RJ ride together here most days, but it would be nice to be able to drive as well, so it isn't always her that does it." I was kind of getting the feeling that she was digging for information, but I couldn't for the life of me figure out why?

"And from work, will Jack be driving you home from now on?" For a minute, I was considering if she could be a spy for Libby. What was it with all the questions?

"Uh…"

"We were told you passed on being driven home last night." Sophia smiled as my face must have blushed.

"I don't want to sound ungrateful, as I think it's great you provide that… it's just, well it's kind of… see the thing is…"

"It's okay, I did tell Dom it could be embarrassing singling you out like that."

"What do you mean?" I asked feeling my chest getting tight.

"Sometimes he just rattles off his orders and doesn't really think about the little things." At this, my mind was in turmoil. I didn't know what to make of it but now one thing was confirmed. Draven had given the order for my safety.

Just then, Reed came racing in all red-faced and panting. He had what looked like oil down his shirt in little spots and his trousers had marks at the knees as if he had been changing a tyre. I smiled to myself as I thought of a little thing I like to call…

Karma.

CHAPTER 18
FIRST NIGHT TAKE TWO

When the class finished, RJ was standing waiting, ready to walk me to my next class. It was so sweet the way she did this, but whenever I thanked her, she just waved it off as no trouble and said that she had a free period. When the truth was, she was worried that I would still get lost.

Sophia was still behind me, so I decided to introduce them.

"Sophia, this is my friend RJ, RJ this is Sophia Dra..." RJ jumped right in there before I even had chance to finish.

"It's nice to finally meet you. Kaz has said nothing about you to any of us. I think she was trying to keep you to herself." I frowned at her, but Sophia looked more than pleased on hearing this.

"It's nice to meet you too, but I must confess I have the upper hand as Keira has told me all about you. I do love your hair." RJ was just about ready to sell her soul to this girl just for the compliment alone. RJ was a sucker for flattery, but to have someone as superhumanly stunning as Sophia, this must have been classed as an honour.

"Thank you so much, the colour's called 'passion for pink'." Sophia nodded and continued to say,

"Yes, I was admiring it before. I have seen you in the club a few times." At this, I couldn't help the snort that escaped. This was a huge understatement as RJ practically lived at Afterlife. But I couldn't help notice in Sophia's responses, the cautious replies and how she was always careful on how she worded things, wanting to create an illusion she was just like the rest of us. The way she had said "In the club" instead of "My club". After all, it was a family business.

They continued to make small talk, and RJ beamed over everything she said. I was the third wheel of course, but I didn't mind. I just wasn't looking forward to the ride home knowing it would be nonstop Sophia this and Sophia that. But she was smart. Even after RJ's bombardment, she never really revealed anything about herself. She just kept the conversation casual and kept enquiring about RJ, deflecting each question back on itself.

Of course, RJ didn't notice.

On arriving home, I waved goodbye to RJ and smiled to myself as it looked like she was still talking about Sophia. No one was home yet, so I decided to cook Spaghetti Bolognese as it was quick, and Libby and Frank could just heat it up in the microwave. I was like a robot on autopilot, not really thinking about what I was doing. My mind was on tonight and on all the things Sophia had said.

Why hadn't I just said 'no' to working in the VIP? Or maybe subconsciously I wanted to work up there, just to be closer to him. I was most definitely a glutton for punishment that was for sure. I wasn't concentrating and burnt my hand on the stove. It woke me out of my zombie state, and I ran over to the sink to put some cold water on it, but it was too late it was already starting to blister. Great that's all I needed... more scars!

I heard keys in the door and realised the time was getting on. I dried off my hand and examined the big red blotch on the side of my palm near my little finger. Thankfully Frank walked in instead of Libby.

"Oh, hey Frank, how you doing?"

"Hey, yeah I'm good, better now I've come home to this...

mmm," he said, smelling the air and went straight over to the pot to lift the lid.

"All she needs to do is cook the pasta, okay, and try not to let her burn it this time." I patted him on the back as I walked past making my way upstairs.

"Are you kidding me, that woman could burn ice cream!" He laughed at his own joke sounding like Doctor Hibbert from The Simpsons. I was running up the stairs when I remembered I was starting earlier and would have to get a lift, so I went back downstairs into the kitchen, where I found Frank burning his mouth with a spoon in his hand.

"Ah-ha caught ya!" He dropped the spoon and held up his hands.

"Okay, you got me, I'm busted. What time you working tonight?" He was such a great guy, like a real brother. And that wasn't just because he would do anything for me. My sister was one lucky girl.

"They asked me to come in early, at seven if that's okay… oh and before you ask, no chauffeur driven car tonight." He laughed and joked,

"Why, who did you upset?" I smiled, then made my lips are sealed gesture across with my finger. It was time to go and get ready, so I jumped in the shower and let my worries continue under the warmth of the water that rained down on me.

I got to work in a fluster with only five minutes to spare. I wasn't sure what to do, so I went up to Jerry who was behind the bar with Mike. As soon as Mike saw me, he walked off to the other end without even so much as a head nod. What was his problem? Had it started already, was I forever going to be the outsider and shunned? Jerry came around from behind the bar and pulled me off to one side.

"What are you doing down here, you should be up there already! At least you remembered to wear black." He was not happy, but he kept his voice steady, although a little strained.

"Well, I didn't know if I should look in with you first or just go straight up there." He nodded as if this was normal, but he just kept looking around anxiously as though not wanting to be seen... this didn't help with my nerves.

"Okay, well you just go up the staircase that you went up last night, and they will be expecting you... go, go, you don't want to be late!" At this, he turned me around, almost pushing me out of sight. Then he walked off with his phone vibrating, and once again he looked as though he didn't want to answer it.

I shook off the feeling of dread, or at least tried to, as I took the same steps that I had done last night. I kept telling myself that it was just one night and if it was that bad, then I would leave. Yeah, I would just turn around and walk out. I could do that.

This little pep talk I was giving myself wasn't helping much, but it was the only thing making my legs move in the right direction. The club was quieter at this time, which made it easier. Not as many staring, gossipy faces as last night. The band members setting up watched me as I went by, near the door closest to the stage. One guy winked at me, but then his friend came and whispered something in his ear, and he quickly looked away. I wondered what it had been.

The same huge guys stood watch, but they didn't even look down at me this time, they just automatically opened the doors to let me in. I decided once inside to run up the stairs; otherwise, I might not go through with it and the last thing I wanted was to draw any attention to myself by being late.

This time there was no music and no comforting hum of people from down below. It felt more like I was entering a portal to a different dimension instead of just working the VIP in some swanky club. Maybe if there weren't as many weird-looking people that were drinking up here or at least some normal looking ones, then it wouldn't feel quite so daunting. It made me wonder even more about the type of businesses that the Dravens were into that would warrant such a strange array of people.

I walked through the doors at the top after taking more than a few deep breaths. Like before, everyone turned and stared but only for a split second, as if someone had flicked a switch that made them all turn back around at the same time.

I walked to the bar as I had done last night still not knowing what to expect. My heart rate went up yet again when I knew I would have to pass the top table. I bit my lip as I always did when being unable to control my nerves, and gripped the strap of my bag tighter over my shoulder. I put my head down and promised myself mentally; I wouldn't look.

I… Would… Not… Look.

This I repeated over and over in my head until I had passed, completing the ultimate goal of self-discipline.

I finally took a much-needed breath when I got to the other side and was safely at the bar. I held my eyes closed and raised my head slightly as I inhaled.

"Well, look who's back. Hey honey, you ready to start your shift?" My eyes opened to find the kindest face looking back at me. There was nothing I needed more than a friendly face right now as my confidence was at an all-time low.

"I'm ready. Put me to work." He motioned for me to come behind the bar, and I followed to where he pointed for me to get through. Behind the bar was just like any other bar, apart from it being immaculate. You could have done surgery behind there it was so clean. There was a place for everything, and most of the glasses were so fancy I was scared to touch anything.

There were masses of green bottles all lined up on their own designated shelves. No two bottles the same. All were different in shape, size, label, and even material, some being glass, others being made out of metal, and even wood. Along with the many different bottles, there were unusual glasses to match. Even goblets, tankards and sake cups lined the shelves below. Most of these were made out of different materials, ranging from stone to copper, silver and gold. Some were plain, and others looked as though they belonged in the Tower of London with the rest of the crown jewels.

Karmun saw me looking and said,

"Ah yes, we have a lot of different liquors that you won't have seen before, we import specialised drinks for each of our customer's needs." *Needs?* That was a strange way to put it, but he was foreign, so maybe he meant something else.

"You can put your stuff back here in this little room." He nodded down to a few steps from behind the bar into a small office style room.

"I'll give you a minute," he said, smiling.

I looked about the room taking in my surroundings for a moment, amazed for the first time to notice the lack of things, rather than the splendour I was used to seeing in this place. There was a desk with no paperwork or computer. There were shelves with no folders, just old-looking books. Also, there were no personal belongings from any of the other staff members, so I wondered what this room was even used for, and why was I the only one that seemed to be using it?

I put my bag down and took off my jacket, hanging it on the back of the only chair in here. There was thankfully however, a gilded mirror that looked far too much like an antique to be in this tiny back room. I studied my face, quickly realising that instead of my usual deathly white skin, my cheeks were flushed, giving me a warm glow. I placed the cold backs of my hands on them to cool them off and curled a stray strand of hair that had escaped from my twist. I took another nervous breath, knowing it wouldn't be my last one tonight. So, with my head held high, I walked back out to take my shift by the horns!

For the first night, Karmun thought it best if I just took it easy and collected empties as I did downstairs on my first shift.

"It will also give you chance to get a feel for the place, but you must understand, up here we do things differently." I was not surprised. Nothing about this place was normal, so why should the work be.

"I am the only one who gets the drinks ready, and the girls take them to their assigned tables, but they never change tables, you understand? That's our one main rule, okay?" It was the first time I had seen him serious, so I took the rule as set in stone.

"No problem," I said, assuring him I understood. But I wondered if I was only collecting empties then who would be serving my tables?

"You're going to be doing the tables nearest to the bar. There are ten tables in your section, and these are over here." He pointed to the ones surrounding the bar area. The tables went from one side of the bar to the other, ending up near the staircase I used when leaving last night. They were all along the same wall, and thankfully none of them went near the top table.

"We have six girls in total, including you, and they too all have their own sectors. See the small Asian girl with the pigtails? She does the same sector as you, but on the other side leading from the main staircase you see there, to the staircase at the back where you came in. Her name's Akako." He pointed to the staircase where I had first seen Dominic Draven and his bodyguards walk up, to the other end of the wall where I had just come from.

The girl I spotted was like a china doll, she wore what looked like a black school girl dress, but then I remembered there was a name for people who dressed like her... what was it called...? Gothic Lolita, yeah that was it. She looked adorable until she turned around showing scary yellow contacts that were haunting to look at. She saw me and bowed her head in respect.

"Then there's the middle, which is split into three sectors. The parts that are not raised both have six tables that sit Mr Draven's more important members."

"Members?" I asked wondering what type of club this was exactly?

"Clients," he corrected, and then pointed around the large raised area that only had the one table on it. This one, of course, I knew well.

"You can see the girl with long green hair, that's Zarqa. She covers the left side, and the other girl with the short black hair, that's Rue, and she covers the right," he continued, and I wondered how I was ever going to remember so many strange names in one night. He pointed towards each girl in turn, and I couldn't have picked a group of girls so different in all my life.

The one that worked on the left with the green hair was very beautiful with green eyes to match. She wore a black corset with green ribbon tied up each side. The black trousers she wore looked like leather and the heels she had on made me wonder how she made it through the night without limping.

The other girl looked more boyish, but the bust she had under her tight black T-shirt proved just the opposite. She looked like a punk skater with long shorts and army boots that reminded me of the 'Avril Lavigne' look, only she had short spiky black hair that was shaved on one side. I could now only see the back of her, so I didn't get a look at her face, but I did, however, notice the blonde bombshell who was dressed like a high-end prostitute buzzing around the top table.

Karmun noticed me looking and continued on with his introduction to the VIP area.

"Ah, that's Layla, and the other girl with black and red hair is Lauren but everyone calls her Loz, they both work the top table." I looked up at him sensing there was more he wanted to say.

"What? They have two girls for just the one table?" I said in disbelief, not understanding why on earth they would need two waitresses for what... no more than seven people!

"Yes, and you are never to approach this table, if you have anything to ask then come to me first, okay?" He said this in a firm yet steady tone. It was most definitely a warning, but it just made me even more curious as to who this man Dominic Draven really was. And unfortunately, in this case, the internet had proved useless. Apart from a few local sites mentioning their thanks for donations, the Dravens were off the social grid. There wasn't even a damn picture, something I had developed Tourette's syndrome over for a good hour cursing my screen.

"So, there you have it, it's as simple as that. Just stick to your tables, and you will be fine." He walked back to the bar and as I followed, I noticed that RJ was right, it was a lot bigger than it seemed from downstairs. Looking to the back of the room, there stood a pair of double doors that I hadn't noticed the night before.

They were huge and carved the same as the grand oak doors at the front entrance. At each side of them were magnificent stone pillars that framed the entrance and joined the ornate stone arch above. Unusually though, there wasn't anyone guarding these doors. There was, however, just something about them that looked threatening and imposing. Almost as if they took on a life of their own, something Demonic that sent shivers down my spine.

"What's in there?" Normally I wouldn't have even asked, but it was like staring at Pandora's Box. There was something inside me that needed to know more.

"You should stay clear of those doors." And that was all that he said on the matter. It was as if I was being tugged from either side, good versus bad. The good girl side of me wanted to take his advice and stay away, but the other side, the side I suspected the monsters fed from, was daring me to run towards the doors. I wanted to tear them open and run to whatever they were concealing. I could even hear the voices... *do it... do it*. I wrestled with the Demons inside me and walked away...

For now.

CHAPTER 19
BEAUTIFUL PAIN

I t didn't take me long to get into the job at hand, as a monkey could have done it just as well. The tables contained the same colourful characters as the rest of the place, but luckily for me, my tables seemed to seat the friendlier groups. The people that sat at all of my ten tables were nice to me and smiled as I took away their empties. Some even passed over the glasses that were hard to reach.

One table had people friendlier than the rest and even asked my name and introduced themselves as the family of Shinigami. Of course, I didn't know what this meant, but they seemed pleasant. They all shared the same striking eyes of the lightest blue colour, almost as if they were transparent, but they held a depth and sincerity to them, I couldn't help but feel at ease as they stared back at me.

The band started to play, but for the first time since working here, I heard a woman's voice over the microphone. It was a more mellow sound than what usually came from the speakers, but it still held a rocky edge to it. She sang about an infatuation with a dark-eyed stranger and how within 24 hours, the love would turn bitterly into death. The message being that he would inevitability become the death of her.

For reasons out of my body's control, I looked at the table

that I had been avoiding all night. What I found there was both alluring and terrifying.

As always, whenever I saw him not in my dreams, he was wearing a suit, this time black with a dark red shirt and black tie. For some reason, this added to his dominating features. His face looked even crueller and more unimpressed than usual. Maybe it was my added presence that did it. I couldn't seem to take my gaze from his eyes that were exhibited as cold and black like the darkest of winter nights. He sat in his chair with a masterful grace, his strong shoulders set back against the stone that mirrored his muscles. He looked deadly and indestructible.

He made me shudder.

Karmun kept a close eye on me the whole night, but this wasn't in an intimidating way, more like a friend who wanted to look out for me. He shouted me over as I had just finished clearing the last of the tables with empties on it.

"What's up?" I said, just as one of the other waitresses came over to the bar. It was the one with short hair, what was her name again... Rue, that was it. She turned to me and extended her hand, but I couldn't keep the shock from my face when I saw her eyes. They were the freakiest eyes I had ever seen. They were all white apart from the tiniest of black pupils left in the middle. There were scars, and what looked like burn marks around her eyes, creeping their way down the cheeks.

She was blind.

"Nice to meet you, I'm Rue, and you're Keira, right?" She said in a cocky voice as I took her hand and shook it, noticing a strange tattoo of an eye in a tribal style on the palm of her hand. I looked at the other hand to find another identical one in the same place. She looked directly into my eyes, which I found amazing considering she couldn't see them.

"Hi, nice to meet you too." She smiled and let go of my hand, turning towards the bar with no problems. She didn't even need a cane. She was quick and nimble and grabbed her tray of drinks from Karmun, turning one last time to my face and said,

"Welcome to the House of Crazy, I hope you stay." And that was it, she was gone. I knew blind people's senses were heightened, but she was truly gifted, to look at her you would never have guessed she couldn't see as well as the rest of us.

"So, how's it going?" Karmun asked me, as though it was my first day at a new school. I suppressed a little laugh and told him the truth.

"It's been fine."

"Okay well, why don't you take a break and get some air." He handed me a bottle of water from under the counter and nodded for me to take it.

"I'm really okay, I don't need a break. After all, I've not been here for more than an hour." His lips curved up into a knowing smile and said,

"Keira it's nearly ten." What? It felt like I hadn't long since started. This place was like a time warp. I grabbed the water and went to duck under the hatch behind the bar when he stopped me with a hand and said,

"Why not go get some air, the balcony will be quiet."

"Okay," I said, confused as he had a strange look in his eyes when he said this, just like when someone is told to say something out of character. Or maybe I was just being paranoid. Either way, I walked over to the staircase I had used last night and knew the doors to the balcony were next to them.

I was about to push them open, assuming they were just like any other doors, but oh no, not in this place. As soon as my hand came into contact with the cool glass, they disappeared into the wall out of sight. I walked through the opening into the dead of night and shivered as the air hit me like a cold shower after swimming in a heated pool. I closed my eyes from habit, something I always did when first walking out into a winter night. Although technically it was Autumn or 'Fall' as they called it here. But to me, whenever the weather got cold, and the rain or snow showed, it was winter's way of saying a premature hello.

I heard the doors closing behind me with a gentle hum, and the noise from the VIP was abruptly cut off. The balcony was huge, a room of its own. It was framed with marble pillars, and in between was a wall of stone balustrades. The top part was wide enough to sit on if you were brave enough, which I wasn't. There was no seating of any kind and the floor was spotless, even though there were massive ferns in Chinese pots either side of the doors, not to mention the surrounding woods. Yet not a stray leaf or needle from the ferns was to be seen.

Vines worked their way around the pillars, hugging them tightly, yet there was no evidence of where they came from, so I guessed they had made their way up the side of the house, mixed with the ivy.

The view in front of me was a blanket of deep surrounding blackness. There was no moon out, and if it hadn't been for the lamps on the walls, I wouldn't have been able to see my hand in front of my face. The lights cast an eerie glow that reflected off the marble floor making me feel uneasy. It was not an ideal place for someone with an overactive imagination, that was for sure.

I unscrewed the top of my bottle and took a couple of long swigs, not realising just how thirsty I was until I had felt the cool liquid slide down my throat. So, it took me by surprise when I heard my name being spoken from behind me.

"Keira, so here's where you've been hiding." I turned around to see Sophia for the first time tonight. I don't know why, but whenever I did get the guts to look over to the top table, all my eyes managed to find, was his face.

"Hi Sophia, how's your night?" She smiled and looked over her shoulder as though she heard something there. She smirked and turned back to answer me.

"It's productive, and as it just so happens it's about to get even more interesting, but enough about my night, how's your first shift going? Are you going to come back for more?" I thought for a moment and answered truthfully.

"It's been a piece of cake. I'm a bit surprised as you were right, nothing to worry about." I screwed the cap back on my water bottle and pulled down on my top, feeling like a shabby homeless person compared to the beauty before me. Her hair hung in perfect spiral curls and the purple dress she wore fitted like it was tailored to her goddess-like figure.

"Good, that's great! Well, why don't you join me for a drink after work to celebrate your first shift?" I looked down at my scruffy black flat shoes and knew the answer I would give her wouldn't be one she'd want to hear.

"I don't think that's a good idea, Sophia."

When I heard the response I was about to give not coming from my own lips, but from those of the man I was both terrified of and obsessed with, I kept my head down even more. My last breath caught in my throat and it actually felt as though my blood had stopped flowing through my veins. It was just like before when all I wanted was to be invisible, a fly on the wall, never to be seen until it was time for him to leave. I just wanted to look at him from a distance... that was enough, but stood here I was too vulnerable.

"And why not? She did well, and I think she deserves a drink!" I liked Sophia but right now, I just wished she would back down from being my new spokeswoman. I had to add something before I ended up being the reason for these two to battle it out.

"I...I appreciate the invitation, but your brother's right, I will have to pass, but thanks." I did it. I did the unthinkable. Okay, so I did it with my head down, but it was the first time I had spoken in front of him without needing to say the word 'Sorry'. Hell, I was just lucky it made sense and was in English, although I had stuttered a bit.

I looked only at Sophia, and she pulled a face as though I had just stolen her favourite doll, ripped its head off and then threw it to a Rottweiler to play with. So, because of this, I felt like I needed to add something more.

"How about another time, okay?" She smiled a little, and I could feel Draven's eyes on me, but I still couldn't look. I was just wishing this could be over so that I could get back to my job.

"Alright, but soon, and I won't take no for an answer." She seemed happy with this last little demand, but I found it more adorable than serious.

"Sophia, you're needed." He said this with such authority,

however, Sophia just shrugged her shoulders and nodded, but before leaving she hugged me and said,

"See you tomorrow." At this, I was sure I heard her brother's disapproval in the form of a low growl. I hugged her back but went bright red at the embrace. Normally I would have been fine but under the scrutinising eyes of her brother, the blood in my cheeks gave away my feelings only too clearly.

She left us alone, and I found myself playing nervously with the bottle in my hands. After a moment of silence, and him clearly not moving, I went to go around him when suddenly he grabbed my arm, stopping me.

I felt the heat as the first touch rushed through the thin material of my top and through the gloves underneath them. It penetrated my skin and pierced my heart as though he had been made from a pure sexual current. I was taken aback, to say the least, and didn't know how to respond, but the shock made my hand drop the bottle. Before I even had chance to bend down to retrieve it, he had it in his other hand passing it to me.

"Here you go," he said with a hint of softness in his voice as a prompt to take it. This was what made me look up into his eyes for the first time, and I regretted it instantly. His eyes were filled with so many emotions; it was hard to pinpoint just one. They were so intense I felt as though I could look into them for hours, getting lost in their beauty, they were truly mesmerizing. He looked back into mine, and without releasing my arm, he ran his hand down its length until he got to my fisted hand. He lifted it closer to his face as though about to examine it in detail.

"I…what are…?"

"Ssshh." He interrupted me with a gentle tone and started to uncurl my fingers with his much larger ones. Once my hand was flat, he turned it over by my wrist making me flinch. His eyes shot to mine in question as his grip tightened over the scars, he thankfully couldn't see. After a moment of searching for the answer in silence, he finally let it be and turned his attention back to my hand. Then he ran a single finger over the burn he found there, and I closed my eyes at the beautiful pain it caused.

"How did you hurt your hand?" His question made my eyes

snap open. I shook my head at him with a little motion, hoping this would be enough, but then he frowned.

"Keira, I asked you a question." This caused me to swallow hard before needing to clear my throat to voice my answer.

"I cook," I blurted out and then quickly realised how dumb that just sounded. So, I added to the dumb with a little more dumb, 'cause evidently, if your name was Keira, you could never have enough dumb!

"I mean I did it… earlier that was… eh, Spag Bol for my sister and Frank, he's my brother-in-law, you see I like him to have a good meal, and my sister isn't the best cook and…"

"I know who Frank is," he stated, and I just thanked the Gods his voice had shut me up.

"You do?" I couldn't stop myself from asking.

"I do," he answered simply, and I felt like slapping myself upside the head saying a loud 'Durr'! But of course, he knew who Frank was. Frank was the guy who provided security for downstairs.

"Of course, you do," I said quietly, although in my head I was screaming 'IDIOT!' to myself.

"Next time you will be more careful, yes?" The way he asked didn't sound anything like asking, but more like demanding. I could only nod in response, and when I did, he dropped my hand. This broke the connection as though cutting the wire that powered my heart for a short time. I lowered my eyes to hide my shame.

"Sophia tells me you expressed your feelings to her on being driven home." On this 'oh shit' moment I looked straight up at him.

"Well I…I… did say something, yeah but I'm… I mean, I did say I was really grateful, and I am… really grateful that is but…" He held up one hand for me to stop speaking and put me out of my misery.

"I understand. However, your safety is a concern as a member of my staff. Therefore, I will forgo the *embarrassing* chauffeured car…"

"Thank you, I really…" He cut me off abruptly as I made the cardinal sin of not letting him finish his sentence.

"But in return, I expect to be notified if Frank or your Sister is unable to provide you with transportation."

"Okay, that shouldn't be a…"

"I am not finished." My eyes widened as I bit my lip. I felt like a kid being told off.

"If this happens, then I *myself* will drive you home, is this clear?" In this moment I just hoped my mouth hadn't dropped open. Was he serious?! I could barely get my wits in order before he started speaking again.

"Karmun tells me you did well tonight." I nodded, not knowing what to say in response. I still couldn't look into his eyes, again feeling that if I did, I would never be able to escape them.

He moved a step closer to me, and I could feel the heat from his body. I closed my eyes not being able to prevent my shy habit, but I don't think he noticed my weakness. He leaned down slightly as he had done so many times before in my dreams.

He was more than a full head taller than me, but he closed the distance between our bodies to mere inches. I could smell his skin and wanted to inhale more deeply to take in every scent. But I didn't. No, instead I froze, locked into my position like a scared animal.

"Come back tomorrow then, if that is the case." And that was it. The delicious torture was over with those words still lingering in the air as he left me standing alone, nearly hyperventilating.

One thought was all that was needed…

My heart was in big trouble.

I was still thinking about my encounter with Draven when I was at home getting ready for bed. I had been in a zombie-like state for the last hour of my shift and the ride home with Frank.

I was still in shock that we had actually spoken to one another. Okay, it wasn't actually a really long conversation, but it was better than him just insulting me while I stood there not saying a word. But more than anything, I was in a numb state of shock that he demanded to know when I was without a ride so that he could drive me home! Himself... personally. He and I, in a car together... alone! How had this happened? One thing was for sure, my need for a car just reached desperate levels.

I could still feel goosebumps appear on my skin whenever I allowed myself to think about how close he had been, so what would a drive alone with him make me feel? I had thought that the real thing would have been more realistic than in my dreams, but as it turned out, my dreams had been spot on. The smell was the same, the heat and connection I felt whenever he touched me. It had all felt just as real as it did tonight. I couldn't understand how that could be, but whatever it was, I wasn't complaining.

Deciding to try and unwind, I picked up Jane Eyre and started to read where I had left off, but I kept imagining Draven as Mr Rochester. The similarities were starting to mount up. He too had been harsh calling Jane a witch the first time they met. But she soon warmed to him after a time, chipping away his rock exterior to find a soft centre that loved her, even though she was plain, penniless, and above all... *Broken.*

I would love to believe that my own story could hold such possibilities like that outcome, but in an age obsessed by beauty, money and greed, I doubted even for a second that Draven would ever think of me the way Rochester did about Jane. But it was harmless to fantasise... wasn't it?

After only three pages I put down the book, frustrated that everything had to come back to Draven. I turned off the light, and said a silent prayer for sleep to come without visions of the monsters that had now decided it was the right time to come back into my life. As if my life wasn't complicated enough!

I drifted in and out of sleep, but woke up when the tossing and turning was too frustrating to even try to sleep. So I got up and went into the bathroom thinking that my sleeping pills might help, even though they hadn't last night but who knew, tonight could be the night for change.

With two pills in my hand, I was about to swallow them when I heard something. I turned to face where the noise was coming from and stood deadly still, trying not to breathe. I waited, but there was nothing, so I put it down to my imagination.

I swallowed the pills and walked back into my room, were I heard the rain start to lash against my window panes, and put the noise down to that. I went over to the window seat and sat down, listening to the rain until the pills started to make me drowsy. I looked out at the angry night sky and jumped when lightning erupted, illuminating the clouds and silhouettes of the trees. This made me put my hand to my chest and I laughed nervously at my jumpiness.

I counted the seconds until the thunder, and knew it was close when I only got to six. Even though I knew it was coming, I still jumped again when it cracked the silent sky, filling it with a boom. I shook my head and laughed again at myself at how jittery I was. Then the lightning hit again, only this time it didn't just light up the sky.

As I looked down into the garden, for a split second, I could see a figure under my window looking up at me. I didn't take my eyes away from it but now without the lightning, it was too dark to make out who it was.

Straining my eyes, I waited for the next flash of light to reveal the mystery. The storm was getting closer as now I only got to three seconds until the thunder erupted. I could see the figure moving slowly, and it looked as though it was motioning me to come down to join him. I could just about make out that it was a man, being far too tall and bulky to be a woman. He moved his arm up and his hand was waving at me.

I waited and waited for some more light. If only the moon had been out, I could have seen him clearer. Whoever he was, he wore a long jacket to the ground, and a hat. The hat was like one you would have seen from those old corny detective shows, called a trilby. I could only see his mouth and chin as the hat concealed half his face, but my mind was processing where that hat looked familiar.

I was sure I remembered someone wearing one like that, but where? I didn't have to wait much longer to find out, as the sky lit up in three different places giving me more than enough light as the storm was now directly above the house. What my eyes saw there was scarier than any nightmare or any monster I had ever seen.

For there, under my window, beckoning me to join him...

Was my past.

CHAPTER 20

A TRIP DOWN HORROR LANE

I screamed and screamed until my lungs needed more air. I was gripping something as it felt like I was being smothered. I must be in a bag... That was it! He had found me... it was happening again... No, no, no! I had to get free. Someone must hear me... they had to hear me! I screamed again and again. I could taste the material over my face, and I could smell the sweat from my body as I twisted and turned.

I was scratching and clawing at it in hopes of escape. Not again, not again! The screams just kept coming. I was using all of the air left in my lungs and then the material lifted from my face as I heard a familiar voice saying my name.

"Kaz, Kazzy, it's okay, it's okay, it's just me... calm down, you're okay now, it was just a dream." My sister was smoothing her hand across my forehead, looking as pale as I must have been. She helped me sit up as my mind started to fight its way back to reality. My breathing slowed, and the tears started to flow from my sore eyes.

"I'm sor...sor...sorry," I mumbled through hiccupping sobs. She smiled and took my head into her arms, letting me cry freely into her shoulder.

"Is she alright?" Frank stood near the door with a baseball bat in hand looking like he was ready for action. She waved an arm behind her back at him in response, and he nodded once before leaving me in Libby's arms, like a small frightened child.

"Feeling better?" she said after ten minutes of hysterics.

"I'm sorry for that, it was just... I haven't had a dream like that for a while. I guess it really hit me." I took the tissue out of her hand and wiped my eyes and runny nose, feeling a little embarrassed.

"It's fine honey, but the way you were screaming I think Frank was ready to bust the door down, and it wasn't even locked. I think sometimes he thinks he's Jack Bauer from 24!" We both laughed, and I instantly felt better.

"Poor Frank, he looked worried," I said, feeling guilty.

"Well, at least you know you have a big brother in the house to protect you." That was more comforting than she'd ever realised.

"Was it about him?" she asked carefully, not wanting to upset me any further. I just nodded, feeling my eyes fill again. Her face looked both angry and sad at the same time.

"Try and get some rest, do you want to take some pills?"

"It's okay, I already... oh no wait, that must have been in my dream. In that case yeah, I better had." She got up and went into my bathroom but then came back out again with the bottle in her hand but no water. I was about to protest that I could never swallow pills without some form of liquid, but she handed me an empty prescription bottle.

"But how...? That's strange, there were loads in there yesterday." I couldn't understand how the bottle was empty. I had only taken some the night before and the bottle was over half full.

Libby glanced at me with a weird look, obviously not knowing what to believe, but clearly, she was worried, so I told her about the part when I had taken some pills in my dream.

"Maybe I was sleepwalking and tipped them away. I really don't remember." Her face softened and she got me some she had been given when she pulled her back out about six months ago.

"These will knock you out so take two now, and I will wake

you in the morning, but you know this means you're going to have to speak to another therapist to get any more pills, don't you?" I nodded, not liking where this was going. The last thing I needed now was to 'talk about my feelings' again. It was beginning to look like my old life was trying to catch up with my new one... *again.*

~

The next time I woke, it was morning and Libby was waking me up with a cup of tea.

"How are you feeling this morning?" I looked at her through blurry eyes and saw that she was all ready for work, which could only mean one thing... I was most definitely late! RJ would be here any minute. I jumped out of bed and raced towards the bathroom, but Libby stepped in my way.

"What's the rush?"

"I'm going to be late, how come you didn't wake me sooner?" I said with a croaky voice from last night's 'Sob-a-thon.'

"Because I thought you would want to sleep in, as it's a Saturday." Oh, I must have been more confused last night than I thought. I assumed when Sophia had said 'See you tomorrow', she had meant in class, but she had really meant at work.

"Oh yeah, so it is, but you're dressed for the office?" I stopped rushing to get ready and went to sit back down on the bed to drink my tea. Meanwhile, Libby was picking up some clothes and putting a pair of my shoes back in the wardrobe.

"I'm sorry, I know we were supposed to spend the day together, but this client is breathing down my neck to get this job done, and if I do a good enough job on this one, then I might have six other show homes, so it's a big deal." She smiled with enthusiasm but also looked guilty as well.

"It's fine, Libs. I have loads of studying to do and plus, I'm thinking while the storm's passed I will take advantage of the dry weather and go for a walk." I needed to go and clear my head after last night, and I couldn't think of a better cure.

"Okay, but tonight I will make up for it. We will order some pizzas, pop some corn and watch a girlie movie." I laughed at her take on an American accent. I loved the idea of spending some quality time with my sister, so I was disappointed to have to tell her that I couldn't because I was working, she looked wounded.

"I'm sorry, but hey, I'm off tomorrow, let's do something then, okay?" She nodded and added,

"Okay, but I still think it's all too much, all this work for college and the club... you're going to collapse." She was a little bit right. If I didn't get some decent sleep soon, I was going to drop.

"It's only until I have enough to get a car and then I will cut some of my shifts. Besides, I can't expect you and Frank to keep chauffeuring me around, back and forth." I held up my hand to stop her from continuing with her protests. I also mentally added on the part where now I had Dominic Draven to contend with and the threats of him driving me home.

"I know you don't mind doing it, but I do, it's not right that you have to keep picking me up at such late hours and plus, I don't want to push my luck with RJ." She admitted defeat and gave up.

"Okay, I get it. Plus, I know you must want your independence back." I smiled at her, knowing she only said all this because she worried and because she loved me.

"I will see you later... and Kaz..." She paused on her way out of the room as she held on to my door frame.

"Yeah?"

"Try and relax today, you know... take it easy, okay?" I replied with a 'Scouts honour' and saluted.

~

I spent some of the day catching up on college work and 'trying to relax' as Libby had instructed, but I found it hard to concentrate. My mind would wander over to darker thoughts that solely consisted of the dream. It was irrational to think this way, but I couldn't help feeling crushed under the weight of disappointment. It wasn't just that last night he had managed to worm his way back into my life, no, it was more the lack of someone coming to *rescue* me from it.

In my last nightmare, Draven had come to save me from the monsters, which made the nightmare less petrifying. But in the one last night, that was the one where I had needed him to save me the most and he hadn't shown. As a result, I couldn't keep my mind off my past, no matter how much I tried. It was so bad at one point that I was half considering the bottle of vodka that Libby had down in the liquor cabinet.

Though that was a bad place to go, and I knew it, but sometimes just the thought of going that low to numb the pain was all I needed to knock me back out of it again. I decided this was the right time to go for a walk and try and find the place that Libby and I had hiked to. It was a nice clear day at least, despite the cold, but once I started walking I would soon heat up.

I grabbed my jacket, which had a big hood, just in case it decided to pour it down. I put my mp3 player in my pocket, turned it on, placed the headphones in my ears and grabbed the keys. I knew the direction I was heading for, so I set out, losing myself in the music and the scenery around me. I half wondered if I would see that girl in the woods again, and realised I hadn't thought much about her since those first few days when I arrived. At least I hadn't seen her again, which made me wonder if she had followed me that day or if it had all been in my head?

I mentally shrugged my shoulders and followed the rough pathway that led deeper into the forest. I continued until I got to the part that forked, but for the life of me, I couldn't remember which way we had taken. For some reason, though, I had the biggest urge to go left, as though something was pulling me that way. There was that little voice inside that said it wouldn't be a good idea, but I didn't listen to it. No, instead, I listened to the rebellious voice that told me not to be so cautious.

After about twenty minutes along my chosen path, the forest floor started to get a bit more hard work. As if this had once been a regular walking spot but that had been a while back. It looked as if the earth hadn't been disturbed in quite some time. There were a lot of branches to duck under and pull back to allow me to pass, and at one point there was a fallen tree that made me change course due to its size. It looked freshly up-rooted and the air was filled with the scent of freshly dug earth. Maybe it had been from the storm last night.

Another twenty minutes or so of walking in this direction was all it took to make me regret my decision, fearing now that I would never remember my way back. I stopped and pulled my headphones from my ears to find that I could hear the sound of running water and realised there must be a stream nearby. As soon as I heard it, all I could think about was how thirsty I was. I followed the sound a little off the track I was on, and it wasn't long until I found it. The little scene was so pretty, I wished I had a camera with me.

The ground around it was softly covered in moss, and it curved its way around each little rock and stone like a blanket. The forest echoed the sound of the water rushing along and I bent down closer to take a drink. I rolled up one of my long fingerless gloves, freeing my hand to cup the crystal clear water.

I made a noise when my skin came in contact with the freezing liquid, as it was a shock but at least a refreshing one. I got up once I'd had enough and followed the stream upwards for a while before coming to an opening. The light pierced through the trees as they separated, creating a clearing like the one that I had seen in my first dream about Draven.

I stepped into the light, screwing up my eyes as they had grown accustomed to the shade the forest provided. I walked forward and soon realised that I was at an opening by the cliffs. There were trees that surrounded a log cabin, which was on the very edge of a sheer drop, and the National Park opened up in front of me, reaching for miles. It reminded me of the view outside my bedroom window with wave after wave of lush green forest.

I couldn't help but smile at the beauty and started wondering what the people who must have lived in the cabin were like. Not only must they have liked to live life on the edge 'literally' but they must have loved the forest and its beauty. It was one of the best views of scenery I had ever seen.

The log cabin looked long abandoned, with windows smashed and cracked wooden panels as though it had once been kicked in. The door was nearly hanging off its hinges and had also seen better days. I walked closer, feeling that I should be shouting to see if there was anyone else around. I don't know why, it was obviously a long time since it had been lived in, but I just felt that maybe I wasn't as alone as I should have been.

I put that thought to the back of my mind, and put my foot on the wooden steps leading up to the front door. The wood creaked under the weight of my foot, and I looked around, making sure I wasn't being watched. Seeing nothing but the wall of forest looking back at me, I walked onto the porch and looked through one of the windows by the door. One of the panels was missing so I crouched down and peered inside, telling myself that this was as far as I was going to take it.

It looked as abandoned on the inside as it did on the outside. There were a few bits of handmade furniture, but most of the stuff looked broken up and piled up near the doorways and windows. That's when I noticed the rest of the windows that faced out towards the cliff had been boarded up in what looked like a hurry.

The front door had the most furniture next to it, but it had been pushed backwards. Like something had burst through the front door spreading it along the floor in its path. I couldn't understand why anyone would do this, what were they trying to keep out?

I got a weird feeling in the pit of my stomach as I felt like it was time to leave. A gut feeling had me believing something really bad had happened here. I started walking backwards off the porch, not wanting to take my eyes off the door. Almost as if I did, someone might come bursting from behind it at any moment. This, of course, wasn't the brightest of moves as I caught my foot and fell backwards off the steps.

My body hit the floor sideways and I hit my head on one of the rocks that lined a path towards the front door. I closed my eyes as a shooting pain exploded around my skull. I tried to get up, but failed a few times as the ringing in my head made it hard to focus. I finally got up to my knees and felt for any damage.

My hand went to the cause of the pain and found a sticky liquid. Great! Now I was bleeding. I looked at my hand covered in deep crimson and tried to remain calm. I wasn't going to die from a little cut, and I had overcome my fear of blood years ago, with little choice on the matter.

I made it to my feet, wiping the blood off my hand on the ground as I rose. I could now feel it trickling its way down my cheek. I took off one of my gloves, wiped my face and held it to the rest of my cut, hoping it didn't need stitches. That's all I needed for my shift tonight, a big gash on my head and a blue bulge to match it. I just prayed it didn't look as bad as it felt. I started to walk back in the direction I had come from, and I was hoping that nobody was home when I got back. Libby would freak out as it was, but if I could at least wash the blood out of my hair, that would be a bonus.

Then I remembered the stream and that I could use that to clean myself up a bit just in case she was there. But where was it? Had I gone wrong somewhere because it was near the cabin, wasn't it? I turned in every direction, but I couldn't make out anything familiar. How far had I walked away from the path I came along? My head was starting to feel really fuzzy and my vision clouded with the pain. I quickly stuck out my arm, holding myself steady on a tree until I regained my balance.

It was then that I heard it. I couldn't understand where it came from, but I followed it anyway, knowing that it must lead to people. Someone was singing faintly in the distance, or was it music being played? I couldn't tell the difference as it didn't sound like anything I had ever heard before. It was a beautiful hum that changed into words I couldn't understand. Maybe I would come across some hikers that had a map… and obviously a stereo.

I twisted around branches and foliage, following the sound that echoed through the trees. Whenever I would go slightly off in the other direction, it would momentarily get louder in the direction I should be going.

I was in a daze and couldn't feel the throbbing in my head any more, all I could feel, taste and think was the noise that I followed. For all I knew it was leading me deeper into the forest and I would be lost forever, but for some reason, I wasn't worried. It was as if I was on some sort of mind control drug. I was completely hypnotised, and I was mellow and calm as I picked up the pace to find this astonishing sound.

I wasn't sure how long I walked, but it didn't feel like more than mere minutes. It was just getting louder but I still couldn't see anything that would make that noise. I was now on a path and my feet didn't have to work as hard to move along. I broke out into a run as it felt like I was getting closer and closer.

I could hear more words now, but still, it was a language that I had never heard. I was nearly losing my breath as my chest ached with the strain. I wasn't the fittest of people at the best of times and I hardly ever ran, but there was just something spellbinding about the sound that filled my ears and took over my brain. I was nearly there now, I could feel it. I could see an opening in the trees, as the light got brighter with every step.

Then the sound was gone.

The entrancing song had stopped as though the power had been cut, just as I walked out of the trees into the front of the house I knew well. I couldn't understand any of what had just happened. I looked around for signs of life, maybe a passing car or music that Libby had been playing, but that still wouldn't have explained it. I followed music that led me home. I was sure of it.

I went into the house and walked upstairs, dumping my jacket on the bed and kicking my shoes off. I don't know when, but I'd lost the glove I used to soak up the blood. I removed my remaining glove and pulled my ruined top off, ready to get in the shower. I knew nobody was in, so I walked to the bathroom and grabbed a fresh towel from the cupboard on the way. Once in the bathroom, I examined the damage in the mirror.

Thankfully, it wasn't as bad as I had dreaded. It looked worse because of the dried blood on my face and hair. The cut wasn't deep enough to need stitches, and I knew I could get away without needing to see a doctor. There was an angry bruise around it that I could hide with my hair, and with a skin-coloured plaster, I thought I could get away with it without anyone noticing.

Libby was back when I got out of the bathroom, and I didn't have time to hide the evidence of my fall.

"Oh my God, what happened to you?" She ran over to me and fussed around my head, tightening her fists and sucking air through her teeth, the way people did when they could imagine the pain.

"It's fine, Libs. Honestly, it's not as bad as it looks." This was a bit of a lie. Actually, it was a big ass lie because as soon as the music had stopped, the pounding pain began again.

"Tilt your head and let me see, you might need stitches." I tilted my head in her hands and said,

"It's okay, I looked in the mirror, and it's not that deep, I will be fine with just a plaster." She grabbed my hand and started to pull me down to the kitchen, where she kept the first aid box.

"Sit under the light." I did as instructed, and she pulled a box down the size you could have fit a Christmas turkey in! What did she keep in that thing? Spare body parts?!

"So, are you going to tell me how this happened?"

"It was no big deal. I just tripped and hit my head on a rock." She was cutting up little strips of tape into tiny lines and was passing them to me to hold.

"This might sting a bit." She sprayed some antiseptic on the open wound, and I cursed like a pirate.

"Nice… very ladylike," she teased.

"Sorry, next time it feels like my skin's melting off, I will calmly say 'Oh fiddlesticks, terribly sorry, my dear, but that did sting a wee bit.' She laughed at my posh accent, and carried on by pulling my skin together before sticking it in place with the little strips she'd cut, acting like makeshift stitches. She covered that with a bigger plaster and said,

"There, that's better."

"Thanks mum." I gave her a kiss on the cheek and left to go back upstairs.

"So, do you want me to call work for you?" I turned and looked at her in disbelief.

"Why on earth would I want you to do that?" I laughed at the thought.

"Because you hit your head and could have a concussion or something." I shook my head and smirked at the idea.

"I didn't break my neck, Libs, I only bumped my head. I think I'll be fine for work." She shrugged her shoulders and said,

"Okay, only making sure."

Once I was ready, I studied myself in the mirror and tried to position my hair so it covered the plaster completely, only every time I moved my head, my hair would move with it. I gave up and decided just to keep my head down and hopefully, no one would notice.

Just before I was ready for leaving, the phone rang with RJ on the other end. She wanted to ask me if I was working tonight and if I needed a lift home as Jack was the designated driver for this evening. I accepted the offer as I knew Frank couldn't pick me up tonight anyway as he was working late, and I didn't like the idea of Libby driving in the dark or worse still, getting a lift home with Draven.

"Tell Jack, thanks," I said as the conversation was coming to an end and I needed to leave so as not to be late for work.

"It's okay, you can tell him yourself later, as I'm sure he would much rather hear it from you anyway." She finished the sentence with a naughty giggle and hung up. I put on my jacket and took my bag from Libby as she held it out to me.

"You ready?" I thought about the question for a minute and wondered, was I ever ready to be in the same room as Draven?

The answer was always the same...

Never.

CHAPTER 21
A DRIVE NEVER TO BE FORGOTTEN

B y the time I had arrived at work, my headache went from a light throbbing to someone going at it with a jackhammer. I was regretting not taking Libby's advice. I tried to ignore it, but it was persistent, so I took a couple of the painkillers that I kept in my bag before I started work.

Once upstairs, I pulled the short bits of my hair forward to try and hide the huge bruise and lump that had now fully developed. It was amazing that in one short car ride it had changed so much. It was now different shades of blue and purple and also had crept its way down one cheek along with a little scratch. There was no getting around it, my face looked a mess, and no amount of hair across my forehead was going to conceal it.

I walked in front of the tables with my head down, letting my hair flop limply around my face. I didn't look up until I bumped into the bar.

"Hey sweetheart, how are... Wow, that's a real shiner. Now that looks painful. What did you do, lose a fight with a bus?" I smiled timidly at Karmun, not wanting to draw any attention to myself.

"I fell," was all I said before going around to the other side and into the little room in the back. Looking in the mirror, I lifted my hair again to re-evaluate the damage but, Eek... It didn't look pretty. The lump had grown and was making the plaster lift on the side that was near my hairline. I tried to pat it down, but it had lost its stickiness and wasn't co-operating. I rolled my eyes to the ceiling and inhaled a deep breath before walking out to start my shift.

This was great, only my second night at this job and I already looked like I'd been in the ring with Rocky Balboa! As I was just about to walk through the door into the bar, I heard my name, only it wasn't being called, it was being spoken. I couldn't see who it was without showing myself, so I waited. I didn't recognise the voice as the band had started, but I was sure it was male. I waited but didn't hear anything else, so I walked out. There was no one there apart from Karmun.

"Are you sure you're okay to work?" I wanted to tell him no, but knew that wouldn't look good, so instead, I lied.

"Yeah, I'm fine, it looks worse than it is." He didn't look convinced but gave me a tray of drinks anyway and pointed to the table. After about an hour of waiting tables, my head was starting to spin slightly, so I went into the back and took a couple more tablets as they didn't seem to be touching it. I knew this wasn't safe, but I just wanted the pounding to stop drumming against my skull. The music wasn't helping, being that it was a very heavy rock band called 'My Pretty Little Nightmares.' Well, they didn't disappoint being as they were, at this very moment, my nightmare. The drum and bass mirrored the pain I felt, and I sat down for a minute holding my head in my hands. I needed to get a grip.

I could do this! I was only doing a short four-hour shift tonight anyway, and I had three more hours to go before I could go home to bed. But then I was forgetting that Jack was taking me home tonight and Frank was working late. Well, I would just have to call Libby and ask her to come and get me, because I didn't know how I was going to last another three hours let alone the rest of the night downstairs socializing.

When I went back out, I noticed most of my tables had been cleared for me and Karmun's worried face was waiting for me.

"You need to go home, you don't look well." I was about to

agree when I noticed Draven's cold, hard eyes staring at me, making me change my mind. I didn't want to give him the satisfaction of being right. He didn't want me working up here in the first place, and after only one night, being sent home would prove him right. Nope, I don't think so. I would rather slog it out.

"I feel better now, I've just taken some pain killers, and they should start kicking in soon." He shook his head a bit, but I knew he was caving. He handed me the tray again and added,

"Okay, but if you feel dizzy or sick, then you are going home and no buts." I nodded and took the tray, trying to hold it as steady as I could.

The customers started to look at me strangely and I wondered how many times I had bumped into their tables. I was losing my perspective on my surroundings as my vision kept going blurry. It had only been another hour, but I was fading fast. Maybe Libby was right, maybe I had suffered concussion.

I got back to the bar and nearly fell but managed to hold myself up without dropping. I was feeling sick and needed some air badly. I grabbed my bag and told Karmun I was going to get some air on the balcony. He just nodded but I wasn't sure it was to me. I had never felt this dizzy before and kept shaking my head to make it go away, but it was having the opposite effect and making me want to vomit.

Once outside, I couldn't help what was coming and ran over to the huge plant pot that was closest to the door and threw up in it. Luckily, I hadn't eaten much throughout the day, so what came up was mainly liquid and bile. My throat burned and I took the bottle of water out of my bag and took a large gulp, only it felt like liquid fire as it went down.

The cold air on my skin was welcoming as the heat from my body was causing little beads of sweat to form around my temple. I wiped them away with the back of my sleeve and dug into my bag for some more tablets, knowing now it would be all right as I must have thrown up the last lot. I was just about to get two out of the bottle when the door opened suddenly, letting out a burst of warm air and music. So, I put the hand that was holding them behind my back and hid them from sight.

I was about to say I would be back in a minute, thinking it was just Karmun who had come out to check on me, but I was wrong. It wasn't Karmun, and no amount of wishing would make it so.

Draven walked through the glass doors and looked around finding me leaning up against the wall using it for support. I lowered my head quickly so he couldn't see my face and felt the heat rush to my cheeks, making my head spin even more. Why me?

Of all the times for him to need some air, I would have to be out here, after just vomiting in his plant pot moments before and looking like I had been hit by a car! I looked truly awful, and even though I knew it wasn't the best of times to be worried about what I looked like in front of Draven, it was just hard not to.

"Keira, what are you doing out here?" God, why did I have to love how my name sounded on his lips? I couldn't believe that my obsession didn't falter even when I was feeling as bad as this. My sickness for Draven obviously ran deep to the core.

"Sorry… I…I was just getting some air but… I'm umm… I'm done now." I turned to walk back in still keeping my tablets out of sight, when his large solid arm came out in front of me. I quickly stopped in my path and was rooted to the spot. His hand stretched out resting on the stone wall. His arm had become a barrier of solid muscle preventing me from leaving. I noticed he wasn't wearing his usual suit but a black T-shirt that clung tight to the curves of his defined chest and rippled stomach. A long black jacket that went to his knees added to a 'badass' exterior.

"What do you have in your hand?" His voice was hard and stern, making my lips quiver in response. Then his tall body leaned in towards mine slightly as it had done last night, and I got the same sensation of energy coming off his skin. My head started to spin even more, and I held the wall for added support. Now with my back fully flat against the stone, my heavy breathing became the issue.

"It's…It's nothing." I curled my fingers around the bottle tighter, but my palms were sweating, and they were starting to slip. I tried to put them in my pocket, when his other hand snaked around my back. I couldn't help the gasp at the feel of his touch as he gripped my wrist in a vice-like hold, pulling it back round to the front of me. My pulse went through the roof and I looked up at him for the first time, meeting his terrifying black eyes.

He took my hand in his and peeled my fingers from around the orange bottle, and looked down with disappointment in his eyes. I, on the other hand, was trying to string two words together, but couldn't due to the tingling heat that travelled its way around my body from his touch.

"I do not allow drugs in my club." I shuddered at the sound of his authoritative voice, which filled the night air. I wanted to defend myself. I didn't want him thinking I was some kind of junky! So somehow, amazingly my lips formed the words.

"It's not drugs, I mean… well yeah, it's drugs but just normal pain killers. See, I hit my head today and just have a bit of a headache." This in fact was a huge understatement. It actually felt as though my head was going to crack open allowing my brain to come oozing out in something that resembled a strawberry smoothie. I could also feel that I was fading fast, and my head looked down so that he couldn't see, also I was going slightly cross-eyed trying to stay focused and that was never a good look.

"Let me see," he ordered as he lifted his hand to my head. I thought I was going to die with shame. I was saying over and over in my head, *'Please don't, oh please don't'*. And for a split second he actually stopped as if he had heard my secret plea. But then his hand touched my chin, lifting it up so he could see my face better.

God knows what colour my cheeks went but they felt on fire, so it couldn't have been good. I couldn't look at his eyes, so they found a spot on his shoulder to stare at. But his hand didn't stop there, it moved up to where the lump was as he now pushed my hair back. I bit my lip so hard that my teeth almost pierced the skin. His fingers touched the cut very gently and when I thought that it couldn't get even worse, I realised that the plaster must have come off at some point.

He sighed as though upset with something, and said in a softer tone,

"This doesn't look good. You shouldn't be here, you probably have concussion." Oh great, now him too. Well, wait until Libby heard this one, something Draven and she agreed on. Only then I remembered I was yet to tell Libby I was working in the VIP, and knowing what her reaction might be I decided this was one story that was better left untold.

I didn't want to back down now I'd come this far, so I decided to be brave and tell him no.

"I'm going to be fine, I only have another hour or so and I will be okay until then." I moved to walk back inside, but because I'd been stood in the same spot for a while, I hadn't noticed that the only reason I was still upright was thanks to the wall. My feet gave way and I would have stumbled if it wasn't for Draven who had caught me by the waist. His strong arm was circled round my stomach and his other hand was gripping my side sending sparks of pleasure up my skin.

"I don't think that's going to happen," he said with a hint of smugness to it. Was he making fun of me?

My top had risen slightly, and his skin was now in full contact with mine. The heat off his fingertips left marks of intense stimulation on my back, and this was made worse when his grip tightened against me. I closed my eyes as the rest of my legs finally gave way and I was soon fully in his arms. He lifted me effortlessly, pulling my body closer to his.

I was so embarrassed, I started to object. Shaking my head slowly and saying,

"No, it's okay… I can walk, really," in a pathetically weak voice, as my head was now spinning.

"Easy there, I've got you now and I'm going to get you home." His face was full of concern as he stared into my eyes. It was the first time I had seen this softer side to him, and it gave him a different, yet sexy look. But then I knew I must have been dreaming, as surely he wouldn't take the time himself to care for me, an important man like Draven. I must have fallen asleep in that little room. That was it! I just prayed that Karmun found me and no one else.

It felt so real though, and would there be this much pain if it wasn't? I was vaguely aware that we were no longer alone. I could hear Draven giving orders to someone, and I was pretty sure it wasn't me as I was still nestled safely in his arms. Arms that felt solid, as though they had been fortified with steel, and I wondered if this was how Lois Lane felt when she was in the arms of Superman. By now, anyone else would have just put me down due to the strain.

I could just make out bits of what was being said and I heard the words *'Car'* and *'My Lord'*, but I must have imagined this last part unless there was something more to Draven than I knew.

When I heard the door shut, I knew we were alone again and waited for his next move. He leaned his head down and pulled me up closer to his face as he whispered,

"Close your eyes." I did what he asked, as if the warm scent of his breath hypnotised me. He turned my face inwards so it was against his solid shoulder and he moved his jacket so that it covered my head, shielding me from what was about to happen. I couldn't prevent the shudder that crept its way up from my spine at the feel of his large hand gripping the back of my neck.

"Now don't look or this will make you feel worse." I didn't understand what he meant, but I nodded under the material that smelled like warm leather. Then all of a sudden we were moving but I had no clue as to where. I mean, we were still outside, I was almost certain of it. I couldn't hear the music and the noise of people inside.

Also, there was still a chill in the air even though I could only just feel it, as I was next to Draven's soothing warm skin. In these arms I felt as though nothing in the world could ever harm me. I almost fell asleep with the calming effect of being moulded to his body in this protective cocoon. It was only the blazing pain in my head that kept this moment from being the most blissful experience of my life.

I couldn't explain how we were moving, as it didn't feel as though Draven's body had any movement at all. It felt as though maybe we could have been gliding but it was probably down to the fact that I didn't know what was real or what was fantasy anymore. Then whatever it was came to an end as I jolted slightly in his arms, as though he had just jumped and this was the landing.

He was walking now, and I couldn't contain the urge to look anymore, so I turned my head slowly so as not to draw his attention. However, he must have felt my movement under his jacket because he pulled me in tighter still. I could feel his heart beating against me and my own heart quickened because of it. This just felt so intimate that it was hard not to get carried away.

By the sound of his footsteps, it appeared as if he was walking on a stone floor and the chill was taken out of the air. I knew we must have been inside somewhere, as now it felt as though we were moving down a staircase. My body jolted slightly with each step and I couldn't help my hand grabbing on to the material of his T-shirt as though to steady myself. I was also sure that I felt him look down at me when I did this, but I couldn't see his face as my head was still buried into his shoulder.

When we unfortunately stopped, I held my breath waiting for him to put me down. His arms must be killing him by now as I was sure no man could carry a body for this long without any pain. But surprisingly he didn't put me down. No, instead I heard the creaking of a door's hinges and he carried on, letting it slam behind us. I jumped at the noise and he squeezed me tighter as though telling me through his actions that I was safe.

We carried on for a while longer and as if hearing my thoughts, he finally spoke

"Not much further now." His voice was strong and steady, and amazingly wasn't even strained slightly from the weight of me. I mean, I knew he looked fit, but I had no idea he was superhuman! The guy was a machine.

We went through another door into a room, and I knew this

was the end of our journey as his arms and grip loosened around my body, allowing me to turn my head and peek through.

We seemed to be in what looked like a car dealership. There were so many new cars I couldn't name them all as there must have been at least twenty. It looked more like a museum considering some of them were on their own display mounts. Some were covered in sheets and there was one that looked extremely old. But the strangest one of all looked like it was in its own glass room. I knew then that I was most likely dreaming, as I was sure I could see it shake as though trying to get out. What the hell was going on in my head?

We weren't alone, and Draven was walking up to a man who wore a flat hat and a long grey coat.

"Will it be the Enzo or the Phantom, My Lord?" I had no idea what he was saying but I think he was asking Draven which car he should take me home in, and then there was that *Lord* thing again. I just couldn't get my head around it. I was getting ready for his hands to let me go and even though the pain was now creeping its way across the back of my head, I was still encountering more pleasure in Draven's arms than I had ever known. Pleasure I wasn't ready to let go of yet.

"No, I will take her back in the Aston," he said in his usual commanding tone. The man nodded, adding,

"Very good, Sir," and went off to open the door to a very low silver sports car. It looked more like a panther than a car, with its sleek curves and angry grill. I was almost scared to be put into it.

"It looks as though I get to drive you home sooner than *you* thought," Draven said with a soft tone and a smirk I could see clearly.

"Oh… umm… it's okay, you don't have to… I know you're busy and… with stuff… I have my phone in my pocket, Libby can be called… she has a phone…" I said all this knowing my brain wasn't making much sense, and at the same time I wanted to smack myself for sounding so stupid… although my head hurt enough already.

"No." How he said that one word was as though it was final and made me bite my lip so I wouldn't argue against it.

With my body still curled in Draven's arms he walked up to the Aston and lowered me into the seat. He was so careful, as though I was made from fine china and he was scared of breaking me. As he put me down, his hands slid from under my legs and his face nearly touched mine, he was so close. I couldn't breathe and again closed my eyes, being scared that I might find his gaze fixated on me.

"Are you alright?" Once more his voice was soft and steady as he said the words so close to my own lips. I kept my eyes closed and could only nod in response as I still didn't believe this was happening to me.

"Good girl," I thought I heard him whisper, but then the door closed making me jump. Had he really said that? I opened my eyes and tried to focus them to the light.

Inside the car was like nothing I had seen before. The seat that I sat in was curved up around my body and it reminded me of a racing car. I think they called them bucket seats. In between the driver's side there was a curved middle console with controls I didn't recognise. For all I knew he could have been James Bond and this was where you fired the rockets and ejector seats.

The rest of the car was black leather and cream interior, with a chrome finish. The steering wheel looked more fitting for a master's hand like a sword to a warrior. It wanted to be driven, as if beckoning or daring you to touch it, to see if you could control its power. The silver wings that were embedded in the middle just added to the feel of the machine, as though created by the Gods themselves.

This car was definitely made for a man like Draven.

I didn't know much about cars, but I would bet my life on it that this car cost a small fortune. I jumped when the driver's side opened and Draven's long muscular legs stepped in. The car was facing a stone wall and it didn't look as if there was going to be enough room to pull forward to turn around but thinking about it, I couldn't see a garage door of any kind so I wasn't sure how we were going to get out. Draven must have noticed me looking around and read my thoughts.

"Put your seat belt on," he said while looking at me, and he soon had me biting my lip again. Then the lights went out plunging us into darkness. I couldn't help the uncertain noise that escaped, and his voice remained calm and said,

"Don't be afraid. Trust me." I don't know why but I did trust him. If there was one person I didn't trust, then that was myself.

I lifted my hand to my head and held it there trying to stop the aching. We were still in the dark and thankfully he couldn't see the discomfort in my eyes.

"Try to relax and the pain will ease." His deep voice cut through the silence as he killed any ideas I had that he couldn't see me in the dark. I looked over to him and for one tiny second, I could see a purplish tint where his eyes would be, and then it disappeared as the engine burst into life.

The beast came alive around us, sounding like a hundred thousand warriors charging into battle. Then the stone wall in front of us reappeared in the blaze of the headlights, only now seeming closer than it had before. He revved the engine as though taunting the beast and all of a sudden, I became disorientated by the thunderous roar and the immense force that pinned me back in my seat. Then in fear, my mind focused on the wall, I closed my eyes and gripped the seat ready for impact!

But it never came, instead we seemed to be getting faster and I never could imagine death to be so painless. I wondered if Draven had been my Angel to deliver me to Heaven or my Demon to drag me to Hell. But as I started to compose myself, I realised I was still breathing and in one piece.

"You can open your eyes now," Draven said with no emotion in his voice. I did as I was told and opened them to find we were on a road, but we were going so fast that I couldn't make out where, as everything was a blur outside my window.

I couldn't help but ask,

"Where did the wall go?" A quiet laugh came from his lips and a smile that I hadn't seen before. It was hard to tell in the dark with only the faint glow of the dash to show the expression on his face, but his eyes changed from their usual cold black to the hint of purple that I had seen before.

"That wall was the door and it opened just like any other,

which you would have seen if you hadn't had your eyes closed." The blood rushed to my face and I was glad that the light in the car wouldn't pick it up. I truly was going crazy and now Draven knew it too.

"Let me ask you, do you really believe I would have driven us both through a stone wall?" He laughed again at the thought and I was getting hotter. He was making fun of me and rightly so, but I had to defend myself in some way.

"Well, how was I supposed to know you had your very own bat cave? And considering it didn't look like a bloody door and I've had a knock to the head, maybe you could cut me some slack?" Oh my god! What did I just say? Where did that come from? And more importantly how was I ever going to take it back? I looked out of the window and once again was nearly pulling all the skin off my bottom lip. I was now wishing more than ever that this was a dream. What must he be thinking? The man had just carried me God knows how far and was driving me home in this awesome machine, and that's what I decided to say! What an idiot... IDIOT!

"Bat cave?" I shot him a look and thought I could just see the hint of his lips twitching as though trying to contain a smile. My only answer was a groan that couldn't be helped. He must have seen my head drop shamefully, so his next words were gentle and sincere.

"You're right. I'm sorry, you weren't to know. I hope I didn't scare you too much." I was also sure he sounded a little bit guilty as he asked me about being frightened. I was scared to open my mouth again in case something equally stupid came rushing out like verbal diarrhoea. I coughed, clearing my throat before saying,

"It's okay, I guess my mind just plays tricks on me sometimes." He turned his head towards me, taking his eyes off the road. I wasn't sure this was a good idea as it felt like we were going over a hundred miles an hour. He looked as if he wanted to ask something but stopped himself. I was burning to know what it was, so I turned and asked,

"What?" I didn't know where all this new-found confidence

was coming from. Then I started to worry about the bang to my head and wondered if that was the reason.

"You don't think like other people, do you?" His face was serious, and I realised that he wasn't making fun of me anymore. He actually thought I was crazy. This was like a flaming arrow to the heart. I was so sensitive about my mental health it was like my Achilles heel. When I didn't respond he looked at my face for the reason why. I must have looked like a spoilt child because I just folded my arms and looked out of the window. I mean, what did he want me to say, 'Yes, Mr Draven, I am a freak!'

"Trust me, Keira, that's not a bad thing." He said this, and his hand moved as though he wanted to touch me but instead, he let it drop to rest on the gear stick. I was about to answer him, but the car filled with the sound of ABBA and my heart almost stopped. The words "Gimme Gimme Gimme" sang over and over, and when I didn't move, he said,

"I'm pretty sure that's yours," and laughed again, only this time he couldn't wipe the smirk from his face.

I fumbled with the phone in my trouser pocket and said a weak,

"It's my sister's phone." But I doubted he believed me. I looked at the number and I knew it was RJ. Shit! I had forgotten them completely and answered the phone wishing this night would just end and my humiliation with it.

"Hey RJ, look I'm sorry… Oh… hey Jack, I thought it was, oh no I had to go home, I wasn't feeling too good." Draven all of a sudden went very rigid and his hands tensed on the wheel. I didn't understand why the sudden change, but I carried on with the conversation, wanting to get off the phone as quickly as possible.

"Yeah, I'm sorry I was going to call, no it's okay I'm nearly home." Jack didn't sound pleased and Draven didn't look happy.

"No, I'm fine, I just hit my head, No, no, in the woods not at work. Look, I will talk to you later, okay? Honestly, I'm fine it's just a scratch." Draven shot me a look as if to say *liar*.

"Okay yeah, well I'll talk to you tomorrow then, sorry what?

Who am I driving home with... uh..." Shit, shit, shit, I didn't know what to say? I didn't think that Draven would want anyone to know about this, so I said,

"Frank, yeah... okay then... see ya." I let out a sigh and put my head back against the seat. My head felt like it was splitting in two. I could feel a pair of eyes staring at me, but I didn't want to look. The atmosphere had changed since the phone call and I wished I hadn't answered it and had called from the house instead. I felt as though I should say something, although I couldn't think of anything but,

"Sorry about that, I forgot that I was getting a lift home with some friends." My voice went back to its usual embarrassed tone. I knew the confidence thing wouldn't last.

"Frank?" I had to think for a second, then it hit me, maybe he wanted to know why I had said it was Frank driving me home instead of him, but why would he care?

"I didn't... uh... didn't think you would want anyone knowing... you know." I nodded to the dash to indicate the car, and his sharp gaze locked on to mine.

"You think I would have an issue with anyone knowing I was driving you home?"

"I... well, what I mean is, you and your family... you know that I don't say things, I can be discreet, and I know you like your privacy and rightly so, I just figured..." I just figured I really needed to stop babbling! Thankfully though, he visibly relaxed and then even smiled.

"Keira, it's fine, and I know you don't talk about me or my family." Hearing him saying this gave me a warm feeling that was deep enough to penetrate my bones. After all, this didn't sound like the words of a man who hated me. I wanted to say something more, but we were pulling into the gravel drive and I knew I would soon be getting out, saying my goodbye. I told myself that I wouldn't linger, I would just say thanks and get out.

He stopped the car and cut the engine. Then it hit me, the very last thing that I wanted to do was...

Get out of his car.

CHAPTER 22
DRAVEN AND DOCTORS

raven got out of the car and walked around to my door. He did all this before I had time to react, so I grabbed for the handle but couldn't find one. He opened my door and looked as though he was about to carry me out.

"I'm fine to walk now, thanks." He backed away slightly but leant with one hand on the car over my head.

"Alright, prove it," he said being cocky, as if he knew I would fall. Of course, he was right. As soon as I tried to stand, I nearly fell back into the seat. He grabbed my hand and pulled me up, then in one swift movement had me safely back in his arms once again.

"I told you I was fine," I muttered in a pathetic attempt to save face. I felt his lips get close to my ear and he muttered right back,

"And I told you to prove it." Okay, so he had me there.

"I'm really okay though, just a bit wobbly, but I'm good now." His hold tightened in a way of answering me without speaking and if I was being honest, I had no real desire to leave his arms. It was now I realised for the first time he didn't have his jacket on anymore. He must have taken it off before getting in the car, but I was too shocked to notice much back then. We both should have been freezing in the cool night air, as I too was

255

without a jacket, but being snuggled up close next to him there was no way that would happen. He seemed to radiate heat and I sucked it in like it was warming my soul.

I could feel the definition of forearm muscles and large sexy hands that held my body in an iron hold. My heart did another one of its trademark flutters as I wished for this gesture to be for another reason, one of a more erotic nature. He walked up the steps and the door was opened by my poor sister, who I might add, was already in her pyjamas with bunnies and carrots patterned over them.

Ah, it looked as if it could have been worse after all. I could be in his arms right now wearing that. But the look on her face was one that I would never forget. Her jaw actually dropped open. I doubted that she had ever seen Draven before, so the sight of me in the arms of the most astonishingly handsome stranger was enough to make any woman's jaw drop. Hell, mine did and that was just in my dreams.

Draven smiled at her and I decided to speak, as Libby hadn't yet.

"I'm fine, it's just my head was… well you were right." She shook her head slightly and moved out of the way, letting Draven come in with me still in his arms. Then he spoke and I thought Libby was going to pass out.

"She fainted at work and has been a bit unstable on her feet, so I brought her home… to get some rest." He said this last part as a hint to get some sort of clue as to where he might put me down, but she still didn't say a word. However, we did get a semi-response as she pointed to the stairs.

"It's okay, just put me on the couch." I was already embarrassed enough as it was, but picturing him in my bedroom made me blush, along with wanting to attack him and tie him to my bed where he could never escape. The thought of him lying on my bed was enough to make my mind burst with pleasure and I didn't know if I could hide my secret fantasy about him without moaning and giving myself away. As it was, I was going to have no choice in the matter as he ignored what I had said and went for the stairs, carrying me up them as though I weighed nothing at all. My sister followed behind like some bunny loving robot.

He reached the first landing but kept going as if he knew where my room was. He leant down to my face and said softly,

"Is your sister Libby alright? She hasn't spoken a word."

"Yeah, and it's a first," I said under my breath so only he could hear. He tried to hide a smile. I was in shock... did he just find me funny?

When we got inside my room, he looked around for a moment before finding what he was looking for... *my bed.* I knew this was the end, so I inhaled deeply taking in his scent for the last time, wishing more than anything in the world that I could keep this intoxicating smell with me forever. This was the moment I was both dreading and dreaming about. There was just something about a man who carried you to bed, that made my body tingle. But this man, well there was no other who I could imagine ever topping this, even if I wasn't going to remain in his arms for much longer.

He placed me down tenderly and said,

"Here you go." And that was enough to make me close my eyes and bite my lip, yet again. But he hadn't moved. Did he want to say something more?

"You'd better watch that lip of yours or before long you won't have anything left of it..." He leant down closer and I received the next shock of the night, when he continued,

"...and that would be a shame indeed." One side of his mouth curved up into a mischievous grin and my heart was in need of fanning itself. Was he...? Did he...? *Flirt with me?*

"Would it?" I asked under my breath, so he wouldn't hear.

"Definitely," he said over his shoulder, as he had turned to face Libby, who had now joined us. How had he heard me? I was pretty sure I had only mouthed the words more than actually saying them. And had he really meant that?!

Poor Libby must have regained some life back when walking up the stairs, as she was now smiling at him.

"Thank you so much for bringing her home, but my God Kazzy, what are you trying to do, scare me to death?" Oh great, she was back. And she just had to call me Kazzy, like I was five all over again. Draven smiled at this and went to stand next to her.

"It was no trouble, but I would get her to a doctor tomorrow as she might need an X-ray," he said as though they were a parent and teacher talking about me as if I was a bloody child.

"No! I mean… no, that won't be necessary, like I said I will be fine, no doctors… I wo…" I nearly shouted this, but the pain cut me off and my eyes watered. Draven frowned and Libby noticed.

"She doesn't like doctors, ever since… well…"

"LIBBY!" I shouted, warning her not to add anything else to that sentence or my life would have ended there and then. Now Draven's full attention was on my face. I could almost see the cogs turning in his head. He looked as though he was burning to know why I had just reacted this way. Luckily, the conversation was interrupted by Frank running up the stairs shouting about the Aston Martin parked in the drive.

"Libs, have you seen that car? Man, whose is…" He was cut short once he entered my bedroom and saw the answer to his question standing there with his wife.

"Oh shi… I mean Mr Draven, Sir." At this Libby froze in horror, as she'd finally twigged who he was. But Draven turned to Frank and held his hand out to him and calmly said,

"Please, call me Dominic." Frank shook his hand as though he was meeting a celebrity. Libby also shook his hand but once more she couldn't speak. I couldn't help thinking that this was a blessing.

Frank looked over to me in the bed and said,

"Hey kiddo, what's up with you? You alright?" Great, now it was Kiddo, what was next, a bottle before bedtime and nursery rhymes?

"It's no big deal, I fell and now everyone's fussing." I couldn't look at Draven anymore. It was hard enough believing any of this was still happening. Nope, there was definitely no more worries about this being a dream! Frank stepped closer to see for himself what all the fuss was about, and then made a face like he tasted something sour in his mouth.

"Damn kid, that don't look good, where did you fall? In the ring with Bruce Lee?" Great, the one person I thought I could count on and now he had turned to the dark side. And just when I thought it couldn't get any worse, Libby found her voice again.

"No, she did it in the woods and then she went to work with concussion, collapsed, and Mr Draven here was good enough to bring her back... *himself.*" She added the last part as though it was some secret code she was trying to get across. One that said Draven *did* in fact drive me back here, and why the hell would he do that!?

"Well, I will leave you all and, Keira, I don't expect to see you working back in the VIP until you get the all-clear from a doctor... understood?" Draven said with his authoritative tone firmly back into place. Great, well this night really couldn't get any worse if it tried. Oh no, I was mistaken, because what came next was far worse than anything that had happened this night, because Draven's next words would haunt me for the rest of my life.

"Oh, and if I were you, I would give her a bucket just in case, she was a bit sick earlier." Oh dear god! He had known all along that I had vomited in his plant pot! Life just couldn't get any worse.

"Oh my, okay I will do that... and thank you very much for taking care of her but wait... did you say the VIP?" Libby unfortunately hadn't missed that bit and now I was going to pay for it.

"Yes, this was Keira's second night working the VIP area. Did she not mention it?" Draven's eyes looked questioningly at me, but I looked away from his gaze.

"No, it must have slipped her mind," Libby said, keeping her voice steady and smiling.

"Goodnight Keira, and get some rest." Draven said this as if he knew I didn't sleep well. I could only nod in return and his gaze flickered down to my bitten lip, before he turned to my sister. He said his goodbye and left my room with Frank walking him out. I could hear Frank saying,

"Umm, could I just ask what model the Aston is…?" Then his voice trailed off downstairs.

I wanted to die of shame! It was so bad that tears started to well up in my eyes and thankfully, Libby put it down to the pain. She came over and sat on my bed to feel my temperature.

"Oh Kaz, it will be alright, I'll get you some pain killers." And then I remembered, Draven had taken mine away and he still had them. But then I noticed Libby opening up a bottle of pills that was on my bedside table. It was the same bottle he had taken, but how? He must have put them there when he put me down and I had just missed it.

Libby went into the bathroom and came back with a glass of water in one hand and an empty bin in the other. I raised my eyebrows and she said,

"Just in case."

She handed me the water and I finished it in one, along with the two pills. Strange, they looked different somehow, but I looked at the bottle and it was the same one as before. So I shrugged it off, putting it down to my spinning head and immense headache. After all, this was one of the weirdest nights of my life, so why should it start suddenly making sense?

"Try and get some rest but wake me if you need anything or if you start feeling worse." She kissed me gently on the forehead and I told her I would be fine as she left the room, leaving me with the confusing images of tonight's events.

No, I would never sleep, that much I was sure about. I lay there and wondered how on earth I was ever going to face Draven again. What must he be thinking of me? The most ironic part was that if I had just left when Karmun asked me to, then I could have avoided all of this humiliation. Then my mind drifted to the nicer parts of tonight. The part where I was in his arms for so long and the way he held me close, as though needing to protect me in some way. Wasn't that worth all the humiliation in the world?

He now knew things about me. Like where I lived, who I

lived with and even where I slept. But wait, I was missing something here. When had I told him any of that? I hadn't told him any directions to my house but, yet he knew exactly where it was. I didn't tell him my sister's name yet on the stairs he mentioned it. And most of all, how did he know which room was mine? How would he have known that I slept on the top floor in the attic? This wasn't making any sense. There was something different about him.

He wasn't like everybody else, and by everybody else I meant... *human.*

I laughed off my ridiculous thoughts. What was I thinking? Not human? I needed help. Maybe this bang to my head had affected me more than I thought. I'd probably told him these things but didn't remember because I was in pain. Or the best explanation was he'd looked at my records. I mean, I don't remember filling out a form, but I did get the job thanks to Frank, so maybe he filled something in for me.

I still had all my clothes on, so I kicked off my shoes and wormed my way out of my trousers. I was about to take off my top when I stopped myself. I lifted it up to my nose and inhaled, allowing my senses to be overwhelmed with the delicious smell of his body. I pulled the top over my head, only leaving my underwear and a vest on, but I held the top in my hands and then positioned it close to my head so that I would fall asleep with nothing but that scent to consume my mind.

I woke up the next day to find that I had slept through the whole night having only one dream, and it had been perfect. I only had vague images and flashes of Draven being back in my room. But while he was there, I would feel the soothing touch of his hand at my temple brushing the hair from my bruise. I would feel his lips graze softly over the damage and then his kiss would linger as if it wanted to travel to other areas of my skin.

I felt his fisted hand bracing either side of my body, taking his weight on the bed and I would hear gentle words being murmured sweetly into my hair. In my dream, I didn't know what he was saying as it was in another language, but just by the way he spoke told me enough to know the deeper meaning. He felt protective.

After this I was even more surprised that I had managed to fall back asleep, but when I had it was down to Draven's words telling me to do so.

I looked at my bedside table and noticed a mug of cold tea, as it must have been sat there a while. I looked at the clock. Oh wow, it was nearly one in the afternoon. I hadn't slept this much since being in the hospital. It took me all of two minutes to realise that what had happened last night was in fact not a dream. And a mixture of pleasure and pain rang deep in my mind.

There was a little tap at my door and then it opened without waiting for a reply.

"Hey honey, how are you feeling today?" My sister's kind face poked through the doorway and when she realised I was now awake, she walked right in.

"I'm still a little sore but I will live to humiliate myself for another day I'm sure," I said in reply, and she smiled and looked a little confused.

"What is it?" I said, wondering what else could have gone wrong last night.

"Well, I think you will need to get dressed, as the doctor's here." What! No way, never going to happen... what was she thinking?

"Aww Libs, why did you go and call a doctor? I said I was fine and..." She cut me off, holding her hands up in defence.

"I didn't call a doctor."

"What! Then who did?" She smiled, clearly amused with the answer.

"He said that Mr Draven sent him." Oh no, was she serious? This wasn't some cruel trick, instead it was just a cruel reality. What the hell was Draven doing by ringing a doctor?

She left the room giving me some privacy to get changed, telling me she would give me ten minutes. But my mind wouldn't concentrate, as it was still fuzzy and lightheaded, and not just with the huge lump protruding from my forehead. I got up and wobbled like one of those inflatable clowns you hit for fun. My brain wasn't up to the simple task of walking to the bathroom. Once I finally got there I washed and brushed my teeth, but my throat still burned from last night's vomiting and the thought once more made me shake my head in shame.

Once I'd finished in the bathroom, I grabbed a pair of black sweatpants from my drawer, and put on a fresh pair of grey sleeved gloves and a maroon coloured top with a faded football logo of my dad's old university team. I brushed through my hair, quickly pulling it into a ponytail, and then went to sit back on my bed waiting for a doctor I didn't want.

"May I come in?" a voice at the door asked, and begrudgingly I agreed.

The man who walked in was at least in his fifties and had a familiarity about him that I couldn't put my finger on. His kind eyes were very dark blue and deep-set. He had a square jaw and a caring smile that lit up his face, making him look like a sweet guy. This made me relax slightly but I was still cautious. I hadn't had a lot of good experiences with doctors, and as a rule generally stayed away as much as I could help it.

"Keira, I presume. It's nice to meet you my dear, I'm Doctor Spencer." He held out his hand for me to shake, and smiled showing an impressive amount of very white teeth.

"Hi, it's nice to meet you too." Okay, so I lied, but what was I going to say, 'I'm dreading it so please get it over with'.

"Mr Draven tells me you took a nasty fall in the woods and was feeling some ill effects of it last night." This wasn't really a question, so when I didn't answer he came over to the bed to look for himself. He carried a black leather bag, one you might expect from a doctor, and placed it next to the bed as he sat opposite me.

"Do you mind?" He nodded to my head and I shrugged my shoulders in return. He then lifted my hair out of my eyes, very much the same way Draven had done, and the memory made me shiver.

"I'm sorry my hands must be cold. If you could tilt your head back for me, I will take a closer look." I did as instructed as he poked around the lump and cut that was in the middle of it. Then he took out a small torch, stethoscope, and then the thing I was dreading the most… something to measure my blood pressure.

"That looks nasty. You should really have gone to the hospital and got some stitches." He tutted and shook his head as though I was a disobedient child. So, I said the only thing in my defence, which so happened to be the truth.

"I know, but I kinda have a thing with hospitals," I said as his eyes fell on mine with a weird look of empathy.

"Bad experience I take it?" he replied as he shone the flashlight in my eyes to measure my responses.

"Something like that," I said before he wanted me to follow his finger. It was peculiar, his eyes looked at me in a heated way and I felt something strange around him, the same as I felt around Draven. It made me wonder if they were somehow related. I could imagine Draven looking like this when he got older. He was handsome for an older guy, like Harrison Ford or Robert Redford.

He asked me about my symptoms last night, and how I was feeling now.

"I feel a lot better today after a good night's sleep," I said, knowing he would be the one I would have to convince to let me go back to work. He raised an eyebrow and asked,

"Do you usually have trouble sleeping?" Ha, what an understatement!

"Yeah sometimes… well I mean lately." I wished he wouldn't pry. That was the worst thing about doctors, they had a way of picking up on everything. And they were usually right on the money.

"Do you take any medication for it?" Shit! I knew if I went down this route, I could easily predict where it would end.

"No." I don't know why, but he looked at me as if he knew it was a lie because he repeated my answer, which was usually a pretty clear indication when someone doesn't believe what you're saying.

"Yes, well let's take your blood pressure." Great, the bit I was dreading. This was the point they all thought I was a nut job!

"If you could just roll up your sleeves for me." He was getting the strap ready to put on my arm and I paused, not knowing what to do. He nodded to my sleeves when I didn't react, so I gave in and did as I was told and rolled them up over my elbow. He looked down at the gloves and frowned.

"Are you cold?"

"I suffer from bad circulation, cold feet as well. Do you mind if I keep them on?" He didn't seem convinced and said,

"It won't be for long." And he was about to roll them back when I whipped my arm from under his hands.

"Look, I'm sorry, Doc, but I have this thing with people touching my arms. Let's just put it down to an accident and leave it at that... okay?" He nodded and looked sad, getting my full meaning on the subject. After all, he was a doctor and I gathered he had seen this type of behaviour before.

"Alright, let's measure it on your neck, should we?" His jaw tightened when he looked at my arms and then softened when he touched my neck.

"I appreciate it and I assume that all this will remain confidential?" I nodded to my arms and he knew what I meant. I was at least happy to see we were on the same page.

"You mean Mr Draven?" He smiled, and I didn't understand the meaning behind it. I nodded, not wanting to say his name in front of him.

"Mr Draven is only concerned and wants to know when you will be fit to go back to work, anything else will go no further than this room," he said, making me relax my tensed arms and sigh in relief.

"Thank you," I said with strained emotion. I don't know why but I trusted this man and I couldn't for the life of me understand why. He handed me some pills to take that would help with the swelling and pain. He also cleaned up the cut, taking Libby's make-shift stitches off and re-applying medical ones. He then left the cut uncovered, letting the air get to it. I also noticed him studying me, and I could see his eyes lingering on my father's old sweater for a moment before my voice pulled back his attention.

"So, this means you will tell Mr Draven I'm fit for work?" I asked in the hope that his answer would be the one I wanted to hear.

"Yes, after three days of rest, and depending if you're fine in that time and have had no more dizzy spells, then yes I will." That was not what I wanted to hear.

"Aww come on, Doc. Look, I feel fine, great even, and I don't want to lose my job or anything." I was hoping guilt would work but with the smug look on his face he wasn't buying it.

"I very much doubt that would happen, and if I find out that you haven't taken my orders on board, then I will ring up Mr Draven and tell him you're not fit for a week." Oh great, a doctor with a PhD in manipulation as well as medical.

"Okay, okay, three days off work." I shook my head at the thought of not seeing Draven till then and the pain once again came back to my head.

"Not just work, college too." I pulled a face as if to say hell no, but he continued with 'Doctor's orders' and gave me a note to be handed into the academic office at college.

"I can't. Look you have never met my History teacher! You have to be dying to get away with not turning up for one of his classes." He laughed as though I was joking.

"I will speak to Mr Draven. I know his sister is in the same class, so I'm sure she could have a word with him for you." Oh God, that was the last thing I wanted. I had caused too many problems for Draven as it was.

"No...! I mean, no thanks, that won't be necessary, I think I have caused more than enough trouble for Mr Draven without involving him in any more of my problems." He looked hurt at this and again I was baffled by it.

"That's not how Mr Draven thinks. I have known him a long time and he has always taken care of his staff."

"Oh, I have no doubt, but he was very kind to me last night and considering it was only my second shift, I think he has done enough for me to last my lifetime. I wouldn't like to push my luck," I said with the memory of me in his arms hitting me again like a battering ram.

"Never enough." My head whipped round to his, on hearing the words that were barely spoken.

"Sorry, did you say something?" I asked, wondering if I had mistaken what he had said.

"I said, fair enough. Well, in that case, I will be off to report back to the man in question." He got up and held his hand out again to shake mine goodbye. I placed my hand in his and the heat coming from his skin shocked me.

"Goodbye Keira, it was a pleasure meeting you and until next time," he said, and then let go of my hand, leaving me feeling confused. Why would he say until next time? What a strange thing for a doctor to say, because let's face it, when was going to see the doctor ever a good thing?

As soon as he was out of sight, I fell back on the bed and covered my face with my hands, saying out loud,

"What must he think of me?"

"What must who think of you?" Libby's voice sprang from behind my door as though she had been waiting for the doctor to leave. I was not in the mood to talk to Libby about any of this, so I said,

"Sorry Libs, but my head is still killing me, so I'm just going to take some more pain killers and try and sleep it off... can we talk later?" She nodded and closed the door, leaving me alone to fight with my thoughts.

I grabbed the pills that the doctor had left and pulled the covers over my head as little tears started to fill my eyes.

Tears that screamed...

Heart-breaking trouble.

CHAPTER 23

OBSESSIONS

S unday was what I thought was going to be day one, but I learned later that day that the doctor had told Draven that I should only go back to work on Thursday night. Sophia had phoned to tell me this and asked if I wanted her to come around with any history notes from the lessons I would miss. She had also reassured me that Draven hadn't said much about last night, only that it wasn't an inconvenience and that he hoped I was feeling better. I almost fist-bumped the air but doubts soon took over any excitement. Maybe she had just said those things to make me feel better. Although, considering he had sent me a doctor in the first place, surely that was enough proof he cared on some level.

Unfortunately, my obsessing over the whole thing didn't end there. I wanted to speak to Libby about it but didn't know if I could. I finally dragged myself out of bed being lured downstairs by the most amazing smell of pizza. No offence to Libby but I just knew it was takeout. I realised that I was starving. I hadn't really eaten much on Saturday and what little I'd had, I'd thrown up. It was now nearly seven in the evening and I was so hungry my stomach ached as it growled angrily at me.

"See Libs, told ya, once she smelled the food, she'd come down... how you feeling, kid?" Frank was sat on the couch digging into one of the two pizza boxes grabbing a massive slice, and Libby was on his other side eating hers from a plate.

"I'm feeling better thanks, and guys, good call on the pizza, I could eat a horse." I sat down and dug in, taking one without anchovies. I couldn't get my head round anchovies on a pizza. In England you never got them as an option, and it turned out that I wasn't missing out. But Frank loved them. Actually, there wasn't much Frank didn't eat.

"So honey, I thought now would be the time to… umm… discuss last night." Libby said this in a quiet, timid voice as though not to upset me, and I knew she had a right to know, but it was still so fresh in my mind I really didn't want to go into it.

"I don't really know what to say," I said, which just so happened to be the truth.

"Well, you could start with why you didn't tell us that you were working up in the VIP." She was trying to keep her voice calm, but I could tell she wasn't happy about being kept in the dark.

"I'm sorry I didn't tell you, but I knew how you felt about me working there in the first place and I thought it would just make you worry even more." Frank nodded, as he actually knew what I was talking about, but Libby noticed and punched him on the arm.

"What?! It's true, you have given her a hard time over working there and you would have given her an even harder time if she'd have told you," Frank said sticking up for himself and me.

"Not necessarily," Libby said sulking.

"Come on, babe, sorry to say this Kaz, but ever since, you know the 'Thing', you have been a bit paranoid over your sister and I can understand why, I really can, but it's time to let her live her life without making things more difficult." Wow! This was the longest speech I had ever heard from Frank and it made me want to get up and kiss him! It was sweet the way he defended me and what he was saying was right. But my sister hadn't always been like this, it was just ever since she nearly lost me and now, she was simply terrified of it happening again.

Libby didn't say anything, she just pouted, and I half expected her to start sucking her thumb.

"Look, you know I appreciate everything you guys are doing for me and you were right, this really was the best move for me. And I know that you worry because you love me, I would worry too if…" I stopped, not being able to carry on. I would never ever be able to imagine if it had been Libby instead of me, so I physically couldn't continue that sentence. Libby looked around at me and saw my emotion, and her features softened.

"What I'm trying to say is that I understand, and I just want to start over. I actually enjoy working at the club and with the amount of security, I'm sure it's one of the safest places on the planet." She smiled, and I knew that her bad mood had passed and the gossip side of her was coming through.

"Sooo, can you explain how on earth you even got that job? Because I'm not being funny, but no one from this town has worked in the VIP." She sat looking at me as if I had achieved some sort of a miracle, when really it was just a case of my being nice to his sister.

"Well, I *am* being funny when I say I am not from this town." She laughed, getting my humour, and then I went on to tell her the story of when I met Sophia in history and how I had to take some bottles up to the VIP area and that's when she saw me. I told them how she had offered me the job, leaving out the part when Draven was rude to me. That wasn't enough for Libby's appetite for gossip, so she asked me about last night.

"What do you want to know?"

"Well for starters, how did it come about, that he would drive you home? I mean, that would be like Alan Sugar driving home his cleaning lady after a tough day!" She was so right, but if I couldn't understand why, then how was I going to explain it myself?

"I don't really know, I mean I was outside feeling sick, and then he was there."

"What do you mean 'he was there'… you mean he followed you?" Libby said, clearly loving this story.

"No, no, nothing like that, no I mean, why would he follow

me? No, he was probably just getting some air." She smiled like she had hit a nerve and then looked at Frank making sure he was still listening. That's when I knew the two of them had obviously been talking about this. She made a gesture with her hand to carry on, so I continued.

"So anyway, he found me and then I don't know, he just decided to bring me home himself." I tried to make it sound light-hearted and like it was no big deal, but she wasn't buying it.

"Oh come on, I need details!" Her hair bounced as she shook her head and I rolled my eyes.

"Like what? That was it… he just picked me up and carried me to his garage, we got in his car and he brought me home… end of story." I picked up another slice of pizza, but Frank responded to the magic work of "garage" and turned to get in on the act.

"Garage, you say? Okay, now we're talking, what type of garage? How many cars would you say? Did you recognise any?" Frank had now turned down the volume on the TV to listen to the rest of the story.

"Oh, I don't know… I guess I saw a couple of red ones that could have been Ferraris, but there were loads of them," I said trying to finish off my pizza, but Frank was determined to get more information out of me.

"Okay, so you saw Ferraris, what else? And when you say loads, do you mean more than ten?" Libby was rolling her eyes and I tried not to laugh at him. He was, after all, being serious.

"Umm… more like over twenty, they were everywhere, but I don't really remember which ones… maybe a yellow one… umm, with a logo of a bull. What are they called?" He smiled and shouted the answer as though we were playing a quiz game!

"You mean a Lamborghini?!"

"Yeah, that's it, but really, I don't remember any others apart from one in its own glass room, but I have never seen one like it before and it looked really old." Frank was close to salivating as he leaned over Libby to get closer to me, so he could hear me better that way.

"Man, I would love to have seen that room. I mean that

271

Aston Martin last night, what a machine! What was it like inside? Did he open her up?"

"Open her up… like her bonnet?" I asked teasing.

"It's called a hood, and I mean did he put his foot on the gas?" I bit my lip mischievously to prevent from laughing as I said,

"Well yeah, he got me home, didn't he?" Libby burst out laughing when Frank threw up his hands thinking I was being serious, so I put him out of his misery.

"Yes Frank, he went fast… thinking about it, I think we even went over a hundred." I laughed when his face beamed back at me, and I had never seen Frank so enthusiastic.

"Well, I don't like the sound of that," Libby said frowning, at which Frank and I both burst into raucous laughter.

"What?" Libby demanded.

"This coming from, Miss Speeding Ticket herself," Frank said, and my mouth dropped open.

"You have speeding tickets?" I asked in shock to which I was met by Libby's sheepish face.

"Only one."

"Two," Frank added before receiving a scowl from his wife.

"I gather Mum and Dad don't know," I said smirking as now the teasing tables had turned.

"No, and if you tell them I will hide the teabags."

"You wouldn't!" I shouted in mock horror.

"Aww, come on girls let's get back to the car, I'm glad I came home early. I asked him what model it was and when he said a One-77 I had never even heard of it, so I did some research on the internet, guess what I found?" He didn't give us time to guess, as he carried on like a steam train.

"Well, there's a reason it's called that! Because there was only 77 of them made! And you'll never guess how much, Libs." He nudged her arm, and she winked at me and then turned to him saying,

"Oooh honey, how much?" I couldn't help but laugh at her patronizing tone, one he didn't notice.

"1.7 million dollars, that's how much was sat on our drive

last night! I mean it's a 7.3 litre V12, which means it's got twice as many cylinders as our car!" He looked pleased with himself as Libby whistled at the price.

"Well, that's all double Dutch to me." He frowned, obviously wishing we were guys at this very moment. Still, I was a bit in awe of the price. I mean, why bring me home in something that cost so much… It just didn't make any sense.

"You were so lucky, that was like one in a million type thing!" He shook his head as it was obviously wasted on me, but the one in a million thing I did agree on, but just not for the same reason Frank was referring to.

"You mean one in 1.7 million, sweetheart." Libby patted him.

"Anyway, let's get back to the more important things, like how did he smell?" She then turned to me with a wink.

"What! Oh yeah, 'cause that's more important, his body hygiene?" With that, Frank turned up the TV and continued to watch football.

"The one thing I do want to know is why he drove you home… I mean, him personally?"

"I don't know, Libs, but he is known for taking good care of his staff." Frank laughed when I said this, and we both stared at him to elaborate on his outburst.

"Yeah, I bet he is, ha, ha." He chuckled some more, and Libby was shaking her head as though he was some rude, naughty little boy.

"Aww come on, isn't it obvious? He has a crush on her!"

"WHAT? I don't think so!" I shouted in disbelief

"Why do you say that?" Libby asked not wanting to hurt my feelings, but she was clearly with me on this one. Frank sighed as though we were both born yesterday.

"Oh no, he just makes sure she is the only one picked up and driven home in a freakin' chauffeured car. Then gets promoted after like what… one shift…?"

"But I…" I tried to cut this down, but Frank was clearly on a roll, and besides, it was clear Libby was all ears.

"Then she has a bump to the noggin, and he just picks her

up into his arms, after she puked in his plant pot I might add, and carries her off to his millionaire's car. Drives her back, whisked her up to her bedroom like some damn knight in shining armour, and then called a doctor to make sure she was alright. Oh no, couldn't possibly be sweet on her, no course not... must be Boss of the friggin' Year, that's the only explanation!" Frank laughed again as Libby and I sat in silence, gobsmacked.

Then Libby turned to me with a huge grin on her face, and said,

"Maybe he's got a point, Kazzy." Frank again seemed pleased with himself at his conclusion, but I was definitely not buying it. What the hell would a man like that want with someone like me?!

That night I thought that I would never sleep but thanks to the pills, I was out like a light. And again, I had no nightmares and only a few times did I dream. The dreams would be very brief, only lasting for a second when I would open my eyes and see that the bird was back and watching me from the window.

Every morning I would awaken disappointed that I hadn't dreamed of Draven, and the days seemed to drag on and on making me more anxious to see him again.

My three days off were all starting to merge into one. By the third, I was slowly going insane with boredom and Saturday night kept crawling its way back into my mind, making me both cringe and swoon every time.

Draven had become like a drug, and I was a junky needing another score. This time away felt like my rehab. I was most definitely ready to overdose on my obsession, because there was only one thing that I wanted, and it was the one thing that I would never get... *Dominic Draven.*

But going cold turkey wasn't exactly working for me either. Even his name brought goosebumps to my skin. After that night of being so close to him, I couldn't think of anything else. I replayed the scene over and over like a favourite movie. Only I couldn't decide whether it was a horror or a romance.

I also couldn't keep from thinking about what Frank had said and wondered if he did, in fact, have a point. But no matter how much you wanted something, I knew I would be a fool to get my hopes up for such a thing. People did nice things for others all the time and it was usually the people who read too much into these things that got themselves into trouble.

I spent Monday doing course work for every lesson, so at least I would be on top of things when I went back. Libby had rung the college informing them of my accident and they reassured her that they would pass on the message to my tutors. It was just a shame that they couldn't also reassure me about Reed not getting a guillotine ready for my return. I also had Jack call me to see if everything was alright. I told him about my fall and he insisted on coming over that night to see me, but I made my excuses, telling him I was still feeling groggy.

Tuesday was a clear day with the sun shining, enhancing the colours of the trees, making the autumn leaves look as if they had been made by the sun. I decided to grab a blanket and do something I hadn't done in years. I sat outside in the back garden and painted the view in watercolours, hoping to capture the beauty I saw each day. Painting to me was like riding a bike, a little strange after years of not doing it, but as soon as my hand held the brush, it was like being reunited with an old friend.

When I had finished, I couldn't help the tears that ran from my eyes. I used to love art, either creating an image from my mind or painting a view like this, capturing the essence of its purity. It was my escapism, one which I thought I'd lost.

That night the doorbell rang, and Libby showed the beautiful Sophia to my room. I was surprised to find her wearing jeans and a hooded sports top rather than her usual glamorous attire. But she still pulled it off, looking as though she was just modelling for a different fashion label. She also wore her hair up in a ponytail, making her look cute and even more doll-like.

"Oh, my brother wasn't kidding when he said it looked bad." The thought of Draven saying anything about me made me smile, one I couldn't hide. Even if it was about how bad I looked.

"How are you feeling now?" She walked over to my bed, where I was sat reading 'Sense and Sensibility'. I was always amazed watching her as whenever she moved, she always did so with such grace and elegance. It was more like dancing than walking. I was just glad that my room was still tidy. That had been one of my only saving graces on Saturday. At least he didn't think I was a slob.

"I feel fine, a lot better. You know I could start back to work earlier." She grinned at me, knowing it wasn't going to happen.

"Nope sorry, doctor's orders and Dom wouldn't allow it." I loved it when she called him that it made him sound just like an everyday, average guy. And clearly, he was never going to be just that.

"Here you go, the notes like I promised. Oh, and you don't have to worry about Reed, my brother took care of it." The words were like being doused by a bucket of ice.

"Oh no... why did he do that?" She frowned at me as she handed me the pages of notes and printouts.

"Why not? The doctor mentioned you were worried about it, and Dom asked me about Reed, so I explained that he could be somewhat difficult. He didn't like the sound of someone giving you hassle and wanted to make sure that didn't happen." She shrugged her shoulders as if it had been no trouble.

"I just don't want to cause any more problems for him, after all, he is my boss, and he has done more than enough already. He didn't need to do that as well." I played with the material on my gloves and looked down feeling embarrassed at being the cause of all this fuss.

"Look, you really don't need to worry, he knows you're my friend and well... I don't have many friends, so I guess he's going to be extra protective." Her eyes looked sad and didn't match the smile she put on.

"Well, I don't understand how a lovely girl like you couldn't have many friends, but I'm glad you're mine," I said in reply and her face beamed at the words.

"That means a lot to me. I have moved around so much, and everywhere I go, people just want to be my friend because of who I am, not what I am if that makes any sense?"

"Sure, I get it because of your name." She nodded, and I noticed a slight tinge of something brighter shining in her eyes. But I thought it must have been a trick of the light.

We continued chatting about other stuff for about an hour before she had to leave and again, she hugged me before she left. This time I hugged her back, feeling my body go warm when I touched her skin. She smelled like her brother, only the girly version replacing the woody, earthy smell for ones of flowers and honey. But again, the scent did strange things to my mind, making me want to hold on to it as long as I could.

Wednesday was very much the same as Monday, as in the weather had gone back to wet and stormy. I also had some more work to do for history, but thanks to Sophia, her notes held all the answers I needed, so it didn't take me very long. I would have to thank her for that on Thursday. Only one more day of solitude and I would be a free girl again. I couldn't wait to get out of the house. But more than anything I couldn't wait to get back to the club. I didn't know why, but I just felt so safe there as if nothing could ever penetrate those walls, not even my past.

Jack and RJ paid me a visit in the evening, and I told them about my new job. RJ's and Jack's reaction to this were very different.

"Oh my God, that is seriously the coolest news! Now tell me everything!" RJ said as Libby brought us some sodas into the Den where we all sat. On the other hand, Jack looked as though he was going to throw up as if he had something foul in his mouth and had to get rid of it.

"Why, when, how?" RJ continued, and I told them how it all started but she clearly showed her disappointment that I hadn't told her sooner.

"I thought I was going to turn the job down," I said in my defence.

"You should have," Jack said in a cool manner, but he was clearly upset.

"And why should she have, sounds like a dream job to me," RJ said backing me up.

"Because Keira is too nice to be a slave to that asshole King of Sacrifices," he continued as if I wasn't even there and I felt a sudden urge to stick up for Draven. Jack didn't even know him, so what was his big problem?

"What's that supposed to mean?" I said, getting defensive. But he turned to me and his features softened as he replied.

"I don't mean to be rude when I say this, but you don't know what we know... well what *I* know. There are strange things that happen up there, things that are... just...just wrong." This sent a shiver up my spine, and he noticed my reaction, feeling as though he had relayed a clear message to me. But all he had done was add questions to my mind, not answers.

"Well, why don't you fill me in if I'm obviously so clueless." I was getting frustrated now and was losing my patience.

"Look, I don't want to go into it but just trust me on this. If you stay up there, you're gonna get hurt." He said this as he placed his hand on my shoulder as though trying to will me to understand his secret meaning, but I was coming up empty.

They left shortly after that, leaving me more confused than ever before. I mean, this was getting ridiculous. I was going to have to find out from RJ what happened to make Jack hate them so much because from the way he was acting, it was like I had crossed over and joined a fluffy bunny killing cult!

I went to bed still frustrated about what he had said and how I couldn't make sense out of any of it. I was just hoping for the one thing that I really needed right now.

My drug, my obsession and...

My dreams of Draven.

CHAPTER 24
SENTENCE OVER

The next day I woke up after yet another dreamless night, but I was more positive when I realised that today I was finally allowed back to work. I got up earlier than necessary, so it was still dark and misty outside. I pulled on a big thick sweater and went over to sit at the window seat. The fog filled the air, covering the forest like another entity. It looked thick enough to hold in your hands.

I sat there thinking about seeing Draven again, and I wondered what would happen. Would he talk to me? Or would he just act the same as he had done before that shift? The way he had been that night was just so out of character, it would be hard to see him go back to treating me as if I didn't belong there.

The thought gave me an ache in my chest, and I circled my arms around myself as if trying to protect my body from what was yet to come. I was in a no-win situation, but I had come too far to turn back now. If only I could just walk away from it then maybe I would have a chance at a semi-normal life. But my heart had fallen, and fallen hard, for not just a man, but something more.

I was ready an hour before expecting to hear RJ's comical little car beeping its horn. I was dressed warm, wearing my denim jacket with a zipped hooded sweater underneath as layers were definitely needed today. It seemed as if I had waited ages for today, which was why I was eagerly sat by the landing window, looking out and waiting for my friend like a sniper.

And then as if by my will alone there she was.

"Bless you, RJ," I said looking up at the gods and blessing them for giving RJ her love for gossip, as that was no doubt the reason she was early. I ran down the stairs and flew out the door as her wheels were still turning.

From the moment I got in the car, there had been a constant stream of questions and I had to be very careful how I answered them. I didn't want to give too much away and there was no way I was telling her about what really happened that night. She was freaking out as it was, acting as though I was her new idol. She had even told me that her phone had not stopped ringing since the word got out that the new girl in town had landed the job.

As we walked to our classes, she told me about how she was being asked, or better begged, to be introduced to me. When I asked 'why', she had simply replied,

"Because the club is the hottest thing to hit this town for decades and people travel for miles around to go there. And every year people try everything to get a glimpse of the man himself, and every year they only get two chances. When he first arrives and when he leaves. This is the first year that they have stayed longer than a couple of weeks."

"How long do you think they'll stay for this time?" I asked as a new fear pierced through me. I hadn't realised that this wasn't a permanent thing and wondered how my obsession would carry on without the power source.

"How the hell should I know? You work there, remember? But his sister has started college, so who knows? Anyway, here's your chance to ask her."

I looked through the door to my next class and saw Sophia already at our usual seats, looking as perfect as ever. It always astounded me whenever I saw her, as her beauty was always breath-taking, and as always, I felt self-conscious. Thankfully, Reed had not turned up yet, so we still had time to chat.

As soon as I entered the classroom all eyes were on me like a swarm of bees to the hive. It was only Sophia that looked kindly at me and on a sigh, I walked up to my seat.

"Hello Keira, how are you feeling?" she said softly.

"I'm feeling a lot better, thanks, how about you?"

"Can't complain. The bruising has gone down a lot, that's good." Again, these were the right type of compliments, as the last thing I wanted was for Draven to see me that way again. My cheeks flushed at the thought.

"Yeah, it looks better now, and the rest I can hide with my hair at least." I pulled my hair to cover my cheek as evidence and she nodded. I noticed the boy behind her was staring at me and taking in every word I was saying. It looked as though he wasn't himself. I remembered the boy from last time and he was one of those types who kept his head down looking bored, with his hood pulled way over his head to hide the headphones in his ears. But now he was fully alert and had a strange tint to his eyes. Was he on drugs? What was his problem?

Sophia noticed me looking and turned to see my line of sight. When she saw the guy, she pulled a face I didn't understand but whatever it meant, it had taken effect, as the boy turned back to stare at the front. Only every now and again I would notice his eyes looking back at me. Did he know me from the club? Maybe it was due to the gossip about me that RJ had mentioned earlier.

Reed walked in, followed by a lackey student pushing a projector. I sighed in relief at the prospect of an afternoon free from Reed's droning voice.

"Today's class is about the understanding of observation. You are going to watch this documentary on World War 2 and write a paper on your interpretation of the events. I want constructive views on what you think about the issues surrounding the lead up to the breakout of the war."

Everyone in the class relaxed as they thought the same thing. An afternoon off from Dictator Reed! I, on the other hand, had thought of peace way too soon as Reed called my name.

"Miss Johnson, a moment if you please." The rest of the class turned and stared at me once more as though I was part of a freak show. The only one who didn't seem surprised was Sophia. This had been the class that I had been dreading, and for good reason.

I got up out of my seat and a hundred eyes followed. I even felt as if I should do a little dance down the steps for all their effort. The film had started and thankfully our conversation would be drowned out by the sounds of fighter pilots and gunships.

"I understand you had an accident?" he said looking unusually uncomfortable.

"Yes, and I'm sorry I had to miss any lectures but the doct…" He cut me off waving his hand saying,

"Yes, yes, I know. I heard all about it and I wanted to say that just because you have been fortunate enough to be in the good graces of the University's Dean and that he asked me to treat you differently…" This time it was me that was to interrupt.

"I'm sorry, but I don't know what you're talking about. I haven't even met the Dean."

"Don't play coy with me, Miss Johnson. I know that your employer is the University's benefactor, and that you are somewhat of a favourite of his, but that does not mean that you will receive instant A's without putting in the work!" I think my mouth actually fell open, as I was stunned!

"I don't know where you have your information from, Mr Reed, but I most certainly intend to work in this class, and any grades I get I want to have received them fairly and above all, legitimately. Mr Draven had nothing to do with my absence and why he thought it best to speak to the Dean on my behalf without my knowledge, is beyond me. So, if you will please excuse me, I am missing the reason for me being here… to learn!" I stormed off back to my seat shaking with anger. I couldn't believe that Reed had thought I was expecting special treatment and I was furious if Draven had implied as much.

What did he care and why go to the effort? My questions were soon going to be answered as I went back to sit next to the very person who could answer them.

"Are you all right? Did he upset you?"

"I'm fine! Well actually I'm not fine. I would like to know why your brother decided it would be a good idea to speak to the Dean about me."

She nodded and looked over her shoulder at the boy behind. What did it have to do with him?

"Sophia?" I said again through gritted teeth, trying to keep my voice down.

"It was my fault, I asked Dominic to speak to him because I knew that Reed would take it out on you if you missed his lectures. I guess he took it the wrong way."

"Yeah, that's a bit of an understatement, he thinks that I should be getting all A's without any work and a pass in each class! Reed was furious at the thought."

"Oh... okay well I'll have it straightened out, but I'm sure that my brother wouldn't have asked for anything like that. The Dean probably has it all wrong." I felt a pang of guilt as I had been ranting like a child at Sophia, who was only trying to help me out.

"I'm sorry and I appreciate you helping me, I really do, it's just I don't want to be treated any differently, just because I'm your friend. I feel bad enough that your brother has gone out of his way for me but he really doesn't need to. I bet he thought life was a lot simpler before I turned up on the scene." I lowered my head in indignity at the thought. I was like a pest, or some virus that was clinging on. No wonder he didn't want me around, look at all the bother I had caused him already.

"I sincerely doubt that." She laughed before carrying on. "Besides, I like having you around and really my brother doesn't mind, you just need to relax." She nudged my arm and I couldn't help but smile back at her.

"Okay, but no more special treatment. From now on I'm just an everyday friend who doesn't expect anything but regular friendship in return." She laughed and said,

"Regular it is, only in my life, I'm not sure I know what that is exactly."

"You'll be fine, we will take it one day at a time, and it just means I don't expect you to keep doing me favours. I'm going to be your friend regardless."

"Well, I like the sound of that," she said, and I noticed she wasn't the only one smiling, as the boy behind had also found something amusing in our not so secret conversation. Great, was this going to be added to the next lot of gossip?

∼

"So, back to work tonight. Will you be okay?" Sophia asked as we exited the classroom.

"Yeah, as long as nothing else goes wrong and I can refrain from making a fool out of myself for at least one night, then yeah sure thing, piece of cake." We both laughed, and the boy that was sat behind Sophia walked past me giving me a wink. I frowned, wondering what to make of it. I mean why wink at me when I was stood next to Sophia, surely that was like preferring a glass of Perry over a vintage champagne.

I said goodbye to Sophia and started to walk over to where I was meeting RJ. She told me earlier she would be busy chasing up a book from the Library, so I said that I would meet her at the car. I walked out the doors and I pulled up my hood and zipped up my sweater due to the cold.

It seemed that I had done this just in time as the heavens opened letting down big drops of heavy rain. I started to walk faster but didn't know why, as there was nowhere to provide shelter. I noticed the boy who had winked at me had now re-joined his friends and they all looked the same. Baggy jeans and hooded tops with rap star logos on the front. I tried to change my route but a large muddied green area was in my way so I had no option but to keep to the path. I walked past keeping my head low when I overheard the same boy talking about Reed's lesson.

"Yeah man, it was weird, I was like totally out of it! Dude what was I smokin' last night?" He looked different than he had done in class, and when I finally walked past his eyes spotted me but there was not a hint of reaction, as if he didn't even recognise me. Had I got it wrong? Maybe he winked at someone else.

The rain was getting heavier now, quickly becoming a downpour. The raindrops dripped off my hood onto my nose and I tried to shake them off when I heard footsteps behind me getting faster as though someone was running. I turned to see who it was but bumped into some screaming girls who were worried about their hair and holding books over their heads in a poor attempt to keep dry. I apologised but it fell on deaf ears and I continued along my path. Then I felt a hand grab my shoulder and I screamed in response.

"Whoa, hey Keira, it's only me." Jack stood opposite me wearing a baseball cap that hid most of his face and the hood of his jacket over that for extra protection.

"Oh, hey sorry, Jack, guess I'm a bit jumpy." He smiled down at me, but I could barely see his eyes. He lifted a hand to my face and brushed my hair off my forehead that was covering the evidence of my fall. I blushed at the feel of his touch and one side of his mouth curved into a smile as he noticed.

"That's looking better every day." He let his hand drop and I shook off the drips that had rolled down my cheek from my hair. He linked his arm around mine and said,

"Let's get out of this rain, you'll freeze in that jacket!" He was right, today was not the day to be wearing lightweight material, especially one that wasn't waterproof. He led me over to the trees near where RJ had parked and we huddled close under a large overhanging branch that acted like a protective green canopy.

"Look, about the other night, I'm sorry I acted like that I was being a bit of a dick."

"Only a bit?" I teased and lightly punched him playfully on the arm.

"Oh, it's like that is it?" he said, and his long arm reached up above my head and grabbed the branch above as he was about to shake it.

"Oh no, don't you dare!" I reached above trying to grab his

285

arm down before he could soak me, only it backfired. I lost my footing and fell into his arms, making him shake the tree anyway, soaking us both. We giggled like adolescents and his other arm wrapped around my waist steadying me. He leaned his head down and said in a deep smouldering voice,

"Do you know how cute you look all wet like that?" I stepped back and shoved him gently backwards in the stomach.

"Stop teasing me or I will get revenge," I threatened, not being able to keep the smile from my lips as I tried to act serious.

"And what might this revenge be... umm?" he said as he took a step closer.

"How about I set RJ on you?" His face changed and I continued,

"Ha, I've got you there because I know that she can beat your ass!" I joked, and he held up his hands to then place them on his heart in a dramatic way as though what I said had hurt. I giggled back as he replied,

"That's cold, I mean that hurts, Keira. How could you be so mean?" He tried to look like he was about to cry but couldn't keep a straight face and we both surrendered to laughter.

"What did I miss?" RJ's pink head came into sight as she moved an umbrella out of her way, seeing both Jack and I standing there laughing.

"Apparently, Keira here, is under the impression that you can kick my ass and she finds the thought heartlessly funny."

"Well, naturally I can take you, but that's common knowledge, bro." He then lunged for her, taking her off guard, making her drop the umbrella. He got her head in a headlock and started giving her a noogie.

"Say the words!" he said as he dug his knuckles deeper into her head.

"Never!" she said as she squirmed to try and get free.

"Say the words, Little Pink!"

"You're a homo!" she shouted.

"Now that's homophobic, RJ, and not nice, just say the words and I will let you free."

"Okay, okay ALL HAIL you, Master of the Rock, who can always kick my butt. You happy now Jack-ass?"

"It wasn't your best grovel, but I suppose it will do." He released her and she swung around, punching him in the stomach. It was like watching a Punch and Judy show at the beach. The rain had eased off a bit allowing us to get in the car without getting drenched even more. I waved goodbye to Jack as he winked at me, and it seemed to be my day for them.

Once I was home, I started on my assignment for Reed as now I was even more determined to make the point that I didn't require special treatment. No matter who my boss was!

I had made notes in class but considering I had already seen the documentary once before on the Discovery Channel, I already knew what I was going to write about. The notes had been mainly ideas and a few reminders on important dates, so I got to work and before I knew it, I was finished.

Shutting down my laptop I looked at my bedside clock to see I had enough time to get ready, starting with something to eat. I examined myself in the mirror and thankfully my hair had survived most of the rain, with the exception of a few curly bits around my face. My hair had a habit of going really wavy when wet and it would tend to dry this way if not brushed straight.

I let down my hair, giving it the once over with a hairdryer and repositioned it up once more, off of my face. I pushed the clip through, but little bits escaped and hung down, curling by my neck. I redid it again and again until I gave up, as it obviously wanted its own way.

I pulled the hair in front of my face hiding the now greenish-yellow bruise and a small cut that I was hoping wouldn't scar. My hair looked different, but it did kind of suit me with some tendrils hanging down giving me a softer look. I put on my normal uniform of black trousers and a long-sleeved plain black top to which I added black fingerless gloves, thus completing my outfit.

～

When I made it to the VIP, I decided to walk in-between the other tables trying to delay the inevitable. I now knew where I was going and could get to the bar without having to walk past the top table. Okay, so I knew I was completely chickening out here, but I just couldn't face him yet.

I noticed the other waitresses looking at me, and the only one who waved was Rue. I was still dumbfounded that she knew it was me, seeing that she was blind. Maybe it was my smell, but when I had smelled my skin before leaving, checking I didn't smell of B.O from not showering, it had smelled differently because of the rain so I added some of Libby's perfume.

Once past the scarier tables of people that took looking different to a whole new level, I walked up to the bar to meet Karmun. I wondered if he ever took a day off.

"Here she is, back to fight another shift, how's the coconut?" He pointed to his own head as if I needed an indication to where it was, but it was sweet just the same.

"Not one you can make a cocktail from…" I gave him a wink and he laughed.

"But seriously, I am fit and healthy and ready to be put to work."

It didn't take me long before I got back into the swing of things and everybody had asked if I was feeling better. Apart from the obvious, the ones that weren't part of my table plan and, of course, Draven.

I noticed him at his table surrounded by his usual entourage. There was his sister to his left and his brother to his right. I had never really noticed his brother before, only seeing him briefly when they first arrived, as I could never usually get past watching Draven. His brother was very handsome, but that was no shocker there. Their gene pool must have come from one Hell of a mix of handsome DNA.

His eyes were a combination of Sophia's and a bit of his brother's, but I could never imagine anyone in the world having the same eyes as Draven's. He was fair-haired, unlike his sister or his brother. His hair looked like gold and it was cut short in a halo of tight curls, giving him a purely angelic look.

Only his eyes suggested otherwise. They looked cold and heartless when the person next to him spoke. He looked bored and un-amused. I shuddered at the glare he gave them. His body was only slightly smaller than his brother's, being leaner, but he too looked powerful. He also looked younger with a softer skin covering his face, and his chin was not as square as Draven's. However, again his eyes revealed there was nothing soft about him. He was also in a suit, but he didn't wear a tie or waistcoat like his brother did. His look was more, smart/casual, whereas Draven's look clearly stated that he was the one in charge.

Sophia once again looked radiant in a black dress that was cut across the shoulders and went down into a pencil skirt around her perfectly shaped legs. The others around the table consisted of a mixture of people.

There was another beautiful young woman with flaming red hair that reminded me of Libby's, only she was very tall and athletic looking. She had a long swan-like neck and amazing brown eyes that looked like dark chocolate. Her skin looked as if it had seen a lot of sun as it glowed with a golden hue. She was wearing a red suit as if ready for a day at the office. I felt a pang of jealousy, as though a snake had bitten me and the venom was making its way around my body via the bloodstream. That was the life I would never have, so why did I even bother thinking about it?

I pulled my eyes away from her perfect features and looked at the others. There was a Japanese man who wore a long black and red robe over black trousers. The material looked embroidered with symbols that were encircled twice, creating a pattern. He held his hands together in his long sleeves and looked content, not smiling, but also not frowning like the others. I counted one more guy and one other woman but they were out of my view, so I couldn't make out any details.

The rest of my night went by without incident, or more importantly without any notice from Draven. My tables were cleared of empties and I was just serving the last one before it was time for me to leave. Like before, my night went by so quickly that I thought Karmun was joking when he had told me that I only had fifteen minutes left. I went up to the bar to get my last tray of drinks when the blonde waitress, the one called Layla, pushed into me saying,

"MOVE IT!" Her face scowled at me, and I could have sworn I had heard her hiss. She grabbed her tray and flicked her hair back as she strutted back to the top table.

"Whoa, what is her problem?"

"Don't you mean what isn't her problem? It would be a shorter list." I laughed at Karmun, who obviously thought the same way about her as I did.

I picked up my tray, but before I could leave with it, Karmun grabbed my hand and said the words that had my chest expanding in a silent gasp.

"Mr Draven wants to see you out on the balcony before you leave." Hearing this, only one thought screamed out in my head…

Oh shit!

CHAPTER 25
UNKNOWN TERRITORY

A s soon as Karmun had said the words, I found it hard not to bolt. Since Saturday, I had wanted nothing more than to see him again, but now I was very tempted to just make my escape. He made me so nervous, just the thought of going out there had my palms sweating.

As I went to deliver the drinks to my last table, I noticed Draven was still at his. Well, at least I could get out there first and get some fresh air. Maybe that would help steady my nerves. I handed out the drinks, and as I walked past the bar, I put down my tray. I pulled my fringe down covering my damaged skin and walked towards the balcony. The last time I had been out there, unbelievable things had happened, both shameful and blissfully wonderful.

I opened the doors, only to find myself not alone as Draven was already there waiting. He had his back to me and was looking out into the dead of night. I took a step closer trying to remain quiet, but the glass doors closed behind me making a whoosh that gave away my presence. He turned to face me and I couldn't find my voice. Had he always looked this tall or was it just because now I was even more nervous, and it made him look even more imposing?

He took a few steps towards me and I couldn't help my

actions as I took one step back. One of his eyebrows raised and he tilted his head slightly as if confused by my wariness.

"Sophia tells me you're feeling better," he said, as yet again he took another step closer, however this time I forced myself not to move. I couldn't say anything, but I managed to nod my head to indicate a yes. He looked as though he was trying very hard not to smile at my behaviour, which just made my annoying blush deepen. What was wrong with me? I would have to say something soon or I would just end up even more embarrassed. He carried on closing the distance between us, and with every step he took, my heart rate kicked up a notch.

"You're looking well, indeed a lot more colour than last time." His face looked controlled but there was a slight smirk edging its way to his lips. He was so close now that if I were to see his face I would have to look up, as it was, I didn't have the nerve.

His hand reached under my chin, pushing my face upwards to meet his eyes. They were as black as the night behind him, but they had a softer touch. He then looked away from my eyes and moved his fingers to my cheek. I must have stopped breathing because my chest felt tight, as though I was running out of air.

"Wh…What… are you…?"

"Ssshh, be still," he whispered gently as one of his fingers touched my lips briefly before going back to inspect my injury.

He was looking for my bruise and he pushed the hair hiding it out of his way. My hair fell in between his fingers and I couldn't help but close my eyes. The trace of his warm touch left a heated trail on my skin and I had the strongest urge to put my hand to his. He continued to brush the hair away from my face, so he could follow the red line with his thumb. He moved it over the cut from one end to the other and I bit my lip to hold in a moan. I could feel his eyes staring down at me, but I wouldn't meet his gaze.

Abruptly he dropped his hand and stepped back saying,

"I am satisfied." I didn't understand what he meant by this, but when did I ever understand anything in the world of Draven? I knew that I would have to speak, or I would never forgive myself. So, with this in mind, I inhaled as much air as my lungs could take and then spoke without trying to sound as nervous as I felt.

"I…I would like to thank you for what you did the other night, and I'm sorry that I have been the cause of so much trouble." There, it was out now and there was nothing I could do about it but wait for his reaction.

"Trouble? I don't know about trouble, but it was definitely eventful, wouldn't you say?" I was pretty sure he was teasing me, and I smiled back, still chewing my bottom lip.

He turned towards the door and my heart dropped when I realised that this was the end of our little meeting. However, my heart started hammering again in my chest as he stopped next to me.

"You're more than welcome, *Keira,*" he said, saying my name with such passion I thought I would need holding up again. I instinctively bit down so hard on my lip that my teeth nearly went through the skin. He hadn't left yet, and I wondered if he was waiting for me to say something. I only had seconds to find out. He leant down to my ear as if he had forgotten something and looking at my face had just reminded him, and he whispered,

"Oh, and Keira… such a shame you're biting your lip again." And with that he left me standing there alone trying to control my thoughts about not passing out. I felt a sudden chill as soon as he left and didn't know whether it was down to the cold night air or the fact that Draven wasn't there anymore. Every time I got close to him, the warmth I would feel was like being covered in an electric blanket from head to toe, resulting in the opposite when he left. It was like it was being torn away from me, leaving me feeling not only cold but also empty inside.

When I finally composed myself, I went back inside to get the bag, that I had left here last time, and my jacket ready to leave. I noticed the nasty blonde glaring at me from Draven's table. She only dropped her foul eyes when Draven noticed it too.

~

Once I was at home, I felt exhausted and my body ached. Not from working, but after four days of doing nothing my body had become used to relaxing. No, working at the club was one of the easiest jobs I had ever had, all things considered. I thought about work and why it always seemed to go so fast? I realised it must be down to the fact that I spent most of my time thinking about Draven and what I would do if he spoke to me.

Which was why I found I didn't have any more mental power left to think about what time it was. Being around him was a drug, and the longer I was there the more I wanted to stay. I'd only had a four-hour shift tonight but that was better than nothing, as I had learnt recently.

I was about to get into bed when the phone rang, and Jack was on the other end.

"Sorry to call so late but RJ's come down with something and isn't going in tomorrow," Jack said.

"Oh no, is she alright?"

"Yeah, she'll live. She's only got flu or something, but it hasn't shut her up yet so it's not that serious! So I was wondering, do you want me to pick you up tomorrow?"

"Umm, yeah… I mean that would be great, but only if you don't mind?" He laughed and said,

"Why would I mind? So, I will pick you up at the same time she does."

"Cool, thanks Jack. I will see you tomorrow then." He said goodnight and hung up the phone, sounding a bit too happy about RJ's condition. I went to say goodnight to Libby and Frank before going back to my room to catch an early night.

~

I was back at the club for some reason, but I didn't know why. Had I forgotten something? I sifted through my thoughts for the explanation but came up empty. I had already walked up the steps to the VIP and was standing outside the door, not knowing what to do next. It was as if I had been in dreamland getting here, and now someone had just clicked their fingers and awakened me.

I stood leaning up against the door and placed my forehead against the warm, wooden panel. My head felt as though I couldn't stop it from spinning. The muffled noises behind the wood were getting louder, and in turn making my head reel faster. I needed to get out, but I didn't want to go back downstairs, as it would be no better there.

As soon as the thought had entered my head, the door opposite unlocked and opened slightly. I couldn't help but be startled at the sound, as if waiting for something to burst through it at any moment. After staring at the opening for a while, I finally got the guts to go inside. I pushed it open cautiously, still half expecting something to jump out from behind it, but there was nothing there. I walked through, knowing I was making the wrong decision, but I couldn't help myself, it was as if I was being called... *or summoned.*

The night air hit me as, instead of walking into another room, I had entered a long open balcony. It was part of the house and it had a roof connecting it to the main building. I could make out a door at the other end, but I didn't want to go that far yet. I went over to the stone balustrade that rose up in arches connected to the roof, allowing you to lean over the top of the stone wall and see the open space.

There was a massive portion of the house cut out like a giant courtyard. I looked around to find the same balcony on all four sides, which seemed to go on for miles. This wasn't a house, it was a bloody castle! I looked down to see in the middle and strangely found a huge domed roof that reminded me of a mosque, sat at the bottom. It glimmered in the moonlight, making it look like polished copper. There was a sculpture at the very top of the dome, but I could only make out a pair of wings, so imagined it to be a bird.

I was astonished at what my eyes were seeing and couldn't get over this actually being here. It felt wrong. As though I should be somewhere in Europe, but then looking at the domed section more like the Middle East. None of it made any sense. I felt a sudden chill up my body as though I wasn't welcome here and this was something I shouldn't have seen.

I turned to walk back through the door I had just entered but it had no handle. My hands went up and down the wood searching for something, but there was nothing to be found. I pushed with all my body weight, but it didn't budge. I was stuck! I was trying not to panic, but I could tell it was coming, and soon. I now had no choice but to walk down the rest of the open hall and try the other door. I couldn't help but think about the trouble I was going to get into because of this.

What had I been thinking?

Unfortunately, the moon was going behind a cloud and I was about to be plunged into darkness. My breathing started to get heavier and I couldn't stop my hands from shaking. I walked forward only a few steps when, as if by magic, the lamp on the wall closest to me lit up in a rising ball of fire. I yelped out my shock, and then watched as the blaze calmed to smaller flames at the top. I clamped my hands over my own mouth to hold back from screaming out.

The lamps were made of wrought iron cages which came down into long, deadly sharp points at the bottom. The iron twisted up in strips curling round iron bars, which held burnt glass in between the gaps. The flames licked the air as if the oxygen was making them angry.

I continued forward, and when I reached the next lamp it did the same thing, as though working off a sensor. There were five in total and they all lit one after the other, illuminating my way down the hall until I reached the door. Thankfully this door had a handle and when my hand touched the cold metal, the door opened automatically.

I turned around before entering and saw all the lamps die one by one making a popping, cracking noise, followed by the sound of glass falling to the floor. It was as if they were exploding, so before the last one was extinguished and rained deadly shards on top of me, I quickly stepped through the door.

Once inside, I tried to calm my breathing the way the doctor had shown me to control panic attacks. I slid down the door and put my head in between my knees and concentrated on counting my breaths. I hadn't even seen where I was or what room I was in, but from the warm air, I gathered I wasn't outside any more. I finally looked up and once again I was in the dark. I was really frightened now and just wanted to get back to a safe place, one where I wasn't so exposed.

I stood up on shaky legs and heard a door open, but knew it wasn't the one behind me. I freaked out and tried to get back out onto the balcony, as at this point, I would take weird exploding lamps over not knowing what was hiding in the dark any day. However, my hands searched in vain as it was identical to the last door… no handle… which meant no escape!

"Who…who's there?" I said trying to control my shaky voice, but with the rest of my body trembling I didn't have much hope.

"You shouldn't be here," a surprised, deep voice growled from the shadows, and I jumped at the words.

"I…I'm lost" I stammered, hoping the voice belonged to someone who would help me.

"Oh no, you're not lost… you've been found." The voice was getting closer and made my skin give way to goosebumps. I was trying to move but something had me frozen to the spot.

Then the harsh voice ordered,

"Hala Olmak." ('Be still.' In Turkish) I couldn't even move my arms, hands, or any part of my body apart from my head. I tried to block out whatever it was manipulating my mind, and concentrated on pushing out the controlling force that was trying to take over me. I tried to think of a way to free myself, so I started by drawing in my mind an image of me moving. First my fingers wiggled and then one of my arms was set free, it didn't take long before my body was my own again and I quickly shifted to the side.

"How did you do that?!" the voice snapped with what seemed like barely controlled anger. I didn't answer, not wanting to give away my location as I was still edging sideways.

"Here, let me give you some light, we wouldn't want you

bumping into anything and hurting yourself again. I know you have a habit of falling down." His voice was smooth but finished with a rough edge. A candle lit somewhere close by and I could only see the space around me. An orange glow spread out, fading into the darkness, and my eyes squinted to adapt to the small circle of light. I moved a little bit more, thinking if I could find another door, I could then make a run for it. My foot knocked on something, but I steadied myself on the wall behind me.

"Careful, Keira." The voice knew my name? It was definitely a man's voice, as it was far too deep to be a woman's, yet I still didn't recognise its roughness. It moved around the room making it hard to pinpoint a location. I couldn't just wait here for him to get to me even though he obviously knew where I was, as the light was bouncing off my skin making me glow. Another flame lit up my way, but I could only make out the wall and floor. I kept side-stepping, feeling my way along when the voice spoke, reverberating around the room,

"I wouldn't keep moving that way if I were you." It sounded like a threat, but it didn't stop me. No, I could feel I was getting close to something as the air had changed.

"What do you want?" I said gaining some courage.

"Isn't it obvious...? Why, the very reason you came here... *back to me.*" I took four large steps away from the voice, but in the dark, I couldn't see as the candlelight didn't reach as far as I had travelled. I hit something waist height, and nearly tumbled over it when a hand reached out and grabbed me, stopping me from falling. Strong hands pulled me back, and in one swift movement had me twisted around and pressed solidly up against the wall.

He gently held the back of my head with one hand, so I wouldn't bang it against the stone my body was now pressed against. His body leant in close, and his hand slid down from my head to my neck making its way to the front. Now he held his thumb on my throat without applying too much pressure.

It seemed to be calming my breathing, as I was panicking on the inside, but on the outside my body remained calm. We were still in the dark and I couldn't see the face in front of me, but I felt as though I was outside again. I wondered if the thing I had nearly fallen over was another balcony. If that was the case, whoever was stood opposite me now had just saved my life. I relaxed my muscles and the voice responded.

"That's it, easy now." I responded to this in a negative way.

"I'm not someone you can control, so get your damn hands off me!" I shouted, but his other hand held my shoulder back as I tried to wrestle free from his hold. He gripped my shoulder like a vice, but he never once hurt me.

"I can see that," he said dryly.

"I asked you, what do you want with me?" I said, trying to sound more angry than scared.

"Don't be frightened, Keira, I would never hurt you." I don't know why but I trusted his words. Maybe it was down to the calming effect the movement his thumb was still making on my throat. His hand relaxed on my shoulder and moved down to my waist, but again when I tried to move away his hand flashed to my side, holding me still against the wall.

"Be still!" he said with clear frustration in his voice. Then, it seemed as though he was fighting down his anger as he inhaled a deep breath.

"You want to know what it is I want, but first you will answer one of my questions." His face bent down to mine, and felt so close I could smell his sweet intoxicating breath invade my senses.

"What...what do you want to know?" I shook my head as I couldn't think of anything I could offer him.

"Why did you come here?" he asked softly. I hesitated and tried to look away, but his hand slid up my top to get to my sides sending sexual sparks up my body. My chest rose heavily with the sensation and I let out a whispered moan, which made him show his teeth. I couldn't help but stare at a perfect white set, but with larger canines, ones that had me gulping.

Did he really have fangs?

When I didn't answer he tried harder to provoke one from

me, and with his other hand he released my neck and stroked my cheek.

"Come now, little one, tell me," he uttered softly trying to coax it from me. I tried to think of a different answer than the truth, but in the end, I just admitted the reason.

"I came here to find Dominic Draven," I said, and I was sure I could hear him smile at my answer.

"Is that right? Well, lucky for you… *you found him."* I tried one last attempt to move from under him, but he was too quick, and he grabbed my wrist pulling me back to him.

"Oh no, you don't." His voice held a hint of the truth, but I didn't want to believe it!

"You're lying! Draven wouldn't keep me here like this. He wouldn't even…" I trailed off, stopping myself before I said too much.

"He wouldn't what, Keira?" he demanded, and when I didn't answer him, I received a little shake.

"He…"

"Tell me!" he shouted, getting impatient.

"He wouldn't care!" I shouted as I tried to see into his eyes, but the black night behind only enhanced the dark shape in front of me.

"Oh really… you know me that well, do you? Well, have you ever thought there is a reason I care to keep you here like this?" His voice sounded different, an anger now mixed with hurt.

"No, why?!" I shouted still trying in vain to get free. When he had finally had enough of trying to prevent me from escaping, he pushed his body flush with mine, shocking me into remaining still. His frame felt solid with his muscles tensed against my smaller frame. His head bent down to my face and he said in earnest,

"I'm trying to keep you safe, as I said before, you shouldn't be here… not alone with me anyway." I heard the desperation in his words, and I swallowed hard.

"Then let me go and I will leave," I said on a whisper.

"I'm afraid it's too late for that, I will have to deal with this in a different way." This didn't sound good, so I tried one last plea.

"I'm sorry that I came but please don't..." His hands left my body and grabbed my wrists like lightning as I said this.

"Don't do what... hurt you?" He didn't sound happy.

"Don't get rid of me," I said as a tear started to form in the corner of one eye. He laughed without humour and replied seriously,

"Why would I ever want to get rid of you? What would make you say that to me?" His hands tightened around my wrists. It was as if he was dumbfounded by my admission.

"Because I'm... *I'm broken,*" I said as the tears got too heavy and fell down my cheeks. He released my wrists suddenly, as if knowing they were the source of my pain. He took a step back as if I had struck him, and I took my chance to move.

"Oh, Keira." I heard my name as sweet as a lover's caress against my cheek before I had chance to get in a step. I shook my head, but he stopped this by framing my face with big hands. He then used his thumbs to wipe the tears of pain from my skin.

"Well, if that is the case, then I guess I will just have to fix you..." he said with his forehead bent to my cheek, his voice hoarse as though it pained him to think of me this way. Then something changed. The very air around us seemed thick, too thick to breathe and I knew the reason why when I heard a rumbled moan. I looked up to see him looking down at my body, features still in shadow but there was no mistaking that sound.

The sound of hunger.

His hands left my face and travelled slowly down my neck. They only lingered for a moment before they journeyed further. The size of his hands covered the space of my chest as he palmed my breasts, lingering his thumbs longer on hardened nipples. This sent sparks of liquid desire straight down to the junction of my thighs. I couldn't help throwing my head back and releasing my own moans into the night. Then his hands continued onwards, spanning my lower stomach and holding himself back from dipping further. This was when he spoke.

"...but before I let you go, I owe you an answer to your question," he said stepping away from me, making me want to scream out in protest.

"You asked me what I wanted," he said, repeating my earlier question, but I could barely hear him as the moon had come from behind the cloud revealing the wonderful truth, the truth I had known all along.

It was Dominic Draven.

He was removing something from the long jacket he wore, and metal flashed in the moonlight. I froze as he brought the implement closer to my face. I was about to run, but as though reading my thoughts, he grabbed me once more around the waist picking me up with one arm tightly curled around my torso. He lifted me up to the level of his face until our lips were at the same height. He leaned forward until they nearly touched, and his mouth moved over mine as he whispered the answer,

"I only ever wanted you."

Then suddenly he stabbed me in the neck, jabbing me so hard that I cried out in pain before everything went blurred and my body went limp in his arms.

Arms that want to keep me.

CHAPTER 26

CAT FIGHT

T felt the pain in my neck and cried out, bolting upright, nearly falling out of bed. It took me a few minutes to understand what had happened. I was here back in my room but how did I get here? I rubbed my neck where there was a tiny pinprick of pain as though I had been bitten by something. I turned on my lamp and looked around the room, but there was no evidence that I had moved.

It must have been a dream, but surely it couldn't have been? It had felt way too real. The most real dream yet. I could still smell Draven on my skin and around my waist was warm from where he had held me so close. I got up and went into the bathroom. As I turned on the light my eyes stung at the brightness, so it took me a moment to focus on what I was looking for. I faced the mirror and arched my neck finding a little red lump with a tiny red dot in the middle of it. I rubbed it with my thumb trying to understand what I had just experienced.

The next day went by in a daze, as if I was a drone being controlled by another part of me, the part that had to conform. I answered when people spoke to me, with the right yes's and head nods but it was as if this was my dream and last night had been my reality. I played with the red dot on my neck all day, as if checking it was still there.

Jack had asked me a few times when driving me to college if

I was alright and I had answered him as though I was on autopilot. I walked into history like a ghost. I was still aware that I was being whispered about, but the difference today was I just didn't have the energy to care.

I sat down next to Sophia and she looked at me with a worried frown.

"Keira, are you alright, you're very pale and you look tired? Didn't you sleep well?" I couldn't help the reaction I gave as I let out an almighty laugh. I turned to look at her and she frowned as if I was losing it. Maybe she was right.

"I'm sorry, that was rude of me. The truth is I don't really know if I slept last night." Well, if she didn't think I was crazy before, she most certainly did now.

"What do you mean, you don't know?" she said but her face held a hint of something more, as if she was worried and not just for me. Then she seemed to notice the red mark on my neck, and I was sure I saw her shake her head. Maybe she thought I had turned to injecting drugs into my neck and this was the result. One doped up, nutty ass Keira!

"Never mind, I just had a bad dream or a good one, I can't really explain it, but I'm fine, don't worry." She looked sceptical, but she let it go as Reed entered the class.

At the end of the lecture, Sophia asked me if I needed a lift home as she had noticed RJ wasn't in today.

"Thanks, but it's okay, I have a lift. Jack picked me up this morning."

"Oh Jack... as in the 'not' boyfriend but wants to be, Jack?" She said this as she looked round to a passing student, and he stared back at her with a strange knowing look in his eye. I hadn't noticed the student before, but he was coming out of our class, so maybe it was someone she knew from there.

"Umm, yeah well, I mean he's just a friend."

"You really need a car, don't you? I bet you would love to have the freedom and not to have to rely on other people all the time," she said as we walked outside together.

"Yeah, I would, but I think I will need a few more pay packets before that happens. Besides, I'm just happy that I have a job, and a good one at that, so it won't be long." She smiled as though once again I had missed something important. She said something else that sounded like 'We'll see' and left, waving as she got in the huge black beast of a Range Rover. I couldn't help but wonder if Draven was also in there. I lowered my head as memories of last night flooded back to me, making my waist feel warm again from where his arm had wrapped securely around me.

I had regained some normality on the drive home and Jack seemed happier about it. He asked if I was working tonight and when I replied yes, it was obviously not the answer he'd been hoping for. I thanked him for the lift and waved goodbye as he pulled away.

∾

Whilst at work I remained quiet and, most of the time, unresponsive. I worked the hours that seemed more like minutes and Draven didn't approach me all night, and for once, I was happy about it. There was a new feeling I now held for him and I didn't want it to show through. I was now a bit afraid of him. I knew I was being stupid, but I couldn't help it. He had been so powerful and commanding in my dream last night, and I had felt powerless and weak against him.

I saw his eyes find mine as I walked past his table to go home, but I lowered my face in what must have looked like disappointment. Of course, I still felt as strongly for him, if not more so, but I didn't know if my heart could take much more, or my mental health for that matter. I didn't feel like myself anymore. Somewhere along the way I had lost control of my thoughts, and it was ever since I had first laid eyes on Dominic Draven.

I went outside to wait for Frank's car to come into view and I sat down out of sight of the doormen. The stone wall was cold, and I could feel the wetness soaking through the material of my trousers, but I didn't care. I needed to get my head straight. I needed to feel like I was in control of my own thoughts and more importantly, my own actions. This dream had been different. There was no one trying to steal it away from me, making it blurry and I didn't know if this was a good thing. I went through so many different accounts of last night and it all kept boiling down to one thing I had said.

I was broken...

I knew that I could never be 'fixed' as he had called it. There was no hope and I couldn't do anything about it, so it was about time that I just accepted it. Surely then, I could move on? Tears were slowly following others and before long my cheeks were wet with salty water. I wiped them off with the back of my hand, angry at myself for being so soft.

"Pull yourself together, Keira," I said out loud. Frank would be here soon, and I didn't want him seeing me upset. I was good at hiding my feelings. Hell, I was a pro. I was a terrible liar but through lots of practice I could have won an Oscar for acting as though I was fine.

When Frank turned up, I played my usual trick of asking him about a game I knew he had seen recently. This lasted me all the way home with just having to nod and say the occasional 'Umm' and 'Ah' when it was needed.

I don't know why, but that night I cried myself to sleep.

I felt better the next day after a dreamless night's sleep, however I was still worried. My dreams had been getting out of hand, and after how much better I felt after that one good night's sleep, I decided I had to do something about it. Even though I dreaded seeing them, I made the decision to make an appointment and speak to a doctor in order to get some more pills. If I was going to beat this obsession, the dreams had to stop!

I kept that frame of mind all day as I helped Libby with housework and we both cooked a pie together for tonight's meal. Well, I say 'we' in the loosest sense of the word, as it was more like I cooked and she talked, keeping me company.

Every now again I did slip up, and when Libby asked me

what had happened to my neck, I dropped the knife I held in my hand, nearly severing off a couple of toes. I told her what I had first thought it could have been.

"Bug bite," I said passing it off as nothing, which was far from the truth.

For the whole two hours leading up to my next shift, I tried to convince myself that I was a waitress and nothing more, and I needed to get this sickness out of my head before it got me into even more trouble. Because primarily, that was what Draven was for me...

Trouble.

Of course, as soon as I walked past his table for the first time on my shift, all my logic went out of my head as though someone had flicked my obsession switch. I scorned myself for not being strong enough to not want him. Damn him! Why couldn't I find the strength? After all the things I had done and been through... this I couldn't do!

I was fighting with my mind and my heart, trying to get them to co-operate, but they were rebelling, and as a result I wasn't paying attention to what I was doing. I kept making mistakes, taking orders to the wrong tables and bumping into the other waitresses. In the end, I told Karmun that I needed five minutes to sort my head out and he threw a bottle of water for me to catch.

Once outside, I nearly downed the whole bottle, as I couldn't get rid of the thirst nagging at my throat like I'd swallowed barbed wire. I needed some sort of pain to bring me back down to the earth I didn't feel part of. I let the anger course through my veins and build up and up until I broke. I punched one of the trees by the door making it shake under the pressure. I had hit it with everything I had, and sharp twigs scratched at my hand and knuckles.

It didn't bleed but it left a mark and I had accomplished my goal, as now I was fully alert to the pain. I knew it wasn't the best idea, but it had worked. I now went back to my job without making a pig's ear of it, as my mother would say.

I buzzed around, as I was now back in the zone. I cleared all my tables and replenished them all with drinks again as though I had downed a few espressos. The throbbing in my hand only made me concentrate more and I pulled my glove over my hand to hide my blazing red skin. Okay, so it was going to leave a bruise, but I didn't care.

My shift was soon over, and I was saying goodbye to Karmun, when my night changed for the worse. It was like being on a roller-coaster with a constant stream of ups and downs. Okay, so mostly downs at the moment, but considering my foul mood, this didn't surprise me.

I had turned too quickly and knocked straight into the blonde... *Layla*. She dropped her tray, which thankfully was empty, she looked down at it and then back up at me with fury in her eyes.

I held my hands up saying,

"I'm really sorry." Though that would never be good enough for her, and I started to walk away, giving her space.

"Where do you think you're going, vermin?" she hissed at me. I wondered what it was about me that she hated so much. I turned around and said,

"What did you say?" with my outrage brewing and showing its ugly head.

"You heard me, you parasite!" Her lips curved into a sadistic grin.

"Leave it, Layla!" Karmun was now getting in on the act, trying to convert tension into peace.

"Stay out of this, Kokabiel!" I didn't understand what she called him, but it had been effective. He left to stand at the other end of the bar, leaving me alone with this nutty girl, who was gladly putting my crazy to shame. She looked down at the tray that was still on the floor. She nodded to it and snapped,

"Pick it up!" Her words slithered through blood-red lips and I half expected a snake's tongue to come out of her filthy mouth.

"No!" I said folding my arms, determined that this would be one night that I wouldn't back down.

"Pick it up, now!" Her eyes burned, turning red and bloodshot.

"I said NO!" I shouted back, and was about to walk away from this rude girl's tantrum, but she grabbed my arm and dug in long fingernails, twisting them deeper into my skin. I squinted my eyes as the pain was making them water, but I still couldn't bring myself to pick it up.

"Do it, I know this hurts," she sneered at me, curling her lip in pleasure, which was sickening to see. I tried to free my arm, but she twisted more, and I could feel her nails digging into my skin piercing the flesh. I couldn't help the moan of pain, but I still managed to say,

"I have felt more pain than your little cat scratch! Now. Let. Go!" I warned, even though I knew what was coming and waited for the pain to increase, as I could already feel little drops of blood on my arm soaking into my glove. I made a fist with my other hand and got ready to swing it at her.

She smiled at my reply and the vile bitch looked happy about it. I tensed my face, not wanting to give her the satisfaction of seeing me hurt, when she suddenly dropped her hand to her side. Her face abruptly turned to stone.

"Is there a problem, Layla?" Draven's strong authoritative voice boomed behind me, and it was quite clear he was not happy.

"Nn…o…no, My Lord," she said as she lowered her head in respect. I rubbed my arm as you could see the imprints on my gloves where her nails had gone through the material. Damn it, another pair of gloves ruined.

"Keira, would you like to add anything to this?" I turned to face him, and looked at him with an over-emotional face as the anger I felt for them both hadn't yet subsided.

"No, she dropped her tray and that's about the end of it," I said, not wanting to make an issue of it. Layla looked at me shocked as to why I hadn't given her up to Draven. I just figured that there wasn't much point as he didn't look a bit convinced. He soon turned back to her.

"Back to work, Lahash, Eu vou tratar con vostede máis tarde!" ('I will deal with you later!' in Gaelic) He spoke the words so fluently, but I didn't have a clue to what he had said or even what language he had used.

She understood though, for what he must have said made her cringe and look frightened. I almost felt sorry for her, remembering never to get on the bad side of him. She was about to leave as she backed up, lowering her face like he was some kind of sultan. And what was with the 'My Lord' bit?

She was about to turn, when he pointed to the floor at the tray saying,

"Pick it up!" And this time she did so without hesitation. I didn't blame her because compared to Draven, her anger looked like a kitten next to a sabre tooth tiger.

Once we were alone, he pulled me to one side, grabbing the arm that she had dug her nails into, so I couldn't help moaning at the feel of pressure. It was also the hand that I hit the tree with, so it didn't look good for me. He loosened his grip once he heard the groan that slipped out. He didn't ask me what was wrong, he just lifted my arm and examined it. I pulled it away from him and said,

"It's fine," and held my hand behind my back.

Draven looked furious and I felt scared being there to witness it. I swallowed hard, trying to mask my fear with bravery. He turned his head towards the direction Layla had left and gritted his teeth saying,

"Kelba!" ('Bitch!' in Maltese) But again, I didn't understand. I wanted to leave but his tall frame blocked my way. I had never seen him so angry, and I could have sworn that I saw his eyes flicker to purple but returned quickly to jet-black.

"I'd better be going," I said as I tried to pass him, but he didn't move, and my hands started to shake behind my back.

"Wait," he said in a softer tone, as though my words had pulled him out of his rage.

"Let me see your arm," he asked, and when I didn't move, he looked down at me, meeting my eyes, but I wasn't going to falter. I'd had just about enough of being ordered around tonight and I was done with it!

"I told you it's fine and if I don't go now, I will be late for

Frank," I said finishing it with a deep breath, only it didn't sound as steady as I had hoped.

"He can wait," he said, pushing it further, and the smart thing to do would be to give in, but I just couldn't, so I stayed firm and replied,

"But I can't, so if you'll excuse me, *Sir.*" And with that, I turned my back on him and went to leave down the main staircase. Only my plan didn't work very well as when I got there, I was stopped by two of Draven's huge guards. They stood in my way, but with my blood boiling from all the humiliation my bravery didn't fade.

"Excuse me," I said through gritted teeth, and they looked over me to their Master. I turned, looking in the same direction to find Draven's eyes burning into me. His gaze stayed on mine for longer than ever before. I was just about to give in and go back to him when he broke away first, nodding to the men that stood like a wall blocking my path.

They parted and let me through, but I had a feeling I was going to pay for this at a later date. I nearly ran down the steps and out of the building that felt as though it was consuming my soul. I was sure I could still feel his eyes staring at me until I was out of the main doors.

I couldn't believe what I just did. What was I trying to prove? I had just disobeyed a man like Draven. I really was crazy.

It was raining, and I ran for the car parked with the engine cut. Frank had been waiting. This time I couldn't fake anything to Frank, so instead, I turned to him and said,

"I think I just made a big mistake."

"I doubt that, but what happened?" he said, giving me far too much credit than I deserved. He started the car and pulled out onto the main road.

"I just really pissed off my boss."

"You mean Mr Draven?" He was serious, but he didn't look as worried as I did.

"The man himself," I said as I held my head up with a fist to my cheek and my elbow on the side window.

"Aww come on, it can't be that bad, he likes you remember?" he said nudging me on my other arm.

"Well if he did, I doubt he does anymore after the show I just put on."

"Christ, you didn't take a swing at him, did you?" he said as he'd just noticed my red fist. I laughed at the thought and his worried face straightened.

"No, but haha. I got in an altercation with another waitress, who is a raging bitch I might add…"

"And you hit her?!" Frank said, getting excited at the idea of me sticking up for myself.

"I wish as I came close, trust me, but then Draven saw it all and intervened."

"Don't tell me he took her side?" Frank asked no longer smirking.

"No, he sent her on her way but when he had asked to see my arm, after what the bitch did with her nails…" I said, pausing to show him the holes in my glove before continuing,

"…I then told him no and walked off." He grinned and then his eyes fell to my gloved arms and sadness replaced his smile.

"Well, I'm sure he admired you standing up for yourself, I can't imagine that happens a lot around someone like him."

"No, never more like, but he didn't look happy about it."

"I'm sure he will get over it and hell, if you tell a man no, then it damn well means no!" Frank was great, a real big brother. He knew what I had been through and felt the pain just like the rest of my family had, so I knew that he meant what he said. He leaned into me and said,

"Well, I have something to cheer you up."

"What's that?"

"Libby's in bed, so you're safe." We both laughed and I was glad that I had confided in Frank, as it felt good and comforting offloading some mental weight.

❧

I sat on my bed and pulled out the clip that held my hair up, and ran my fingers through it, feeling the ache of having it up all day. It fell down my back in one big tube from spending the day twisted. I played with it, separating it into smaller pieces until it hung in waves down to my waist.

I examined my hand, and a bluish bruise was starting to form at the knuckles. What was I thinking? I had just got rid of one, only to replace it by another. I pulled down my gloves and ran my fingers over four little half-moon shaped bloody cuts. Well, at least they would fit right in with the others.

I barely ever looked at my arms, as when I did, I would usually get upset at the memory of how they came to be. I touched the lighter scars at the top first and then moved down to the deeper ones near the wrist. These were larger, thicker and had never really made it back to skin colour. They were deep red as if a reminder of the blood that once poured out of them. I did the same on the other arm and placed the two side by side. What a mess. I counted eight slits on one and six on the other. I looked as though I had been mauled by a lion.

This was the reason I refused to obey Draven. I never wanted anyone to see my scars, and I most definitely never wanted to explain how they got there. Well let's face it, as soon as anyone saw them, they would make up their own conclusion anyway, so what was the point? They were a reminder for me every day, for the rest of my life, of what happened. I didn't want that for other people. After all, I had come here to get away from all of that.

Needless to say, I didn't get much sleep that night.

~

The next day I spent looking after Libby, as she had come down with the same bug that RJ had, and the way my week had gone, I was just hoping I wouldn't get it next.

"How are you feeling, Libs?" I asked as I sat on the couch opposite her. She looked terrible with her skin all pale, making her red hair look as though it was on fire.

313

"I'm okay, I guess, I just can't seem to keep anything down though."

"Yeah, RJ had the same thing, but she rang earlier and said she was feeling better, so it must only last for a few days. Do you want any soup or anything?" As soon as I mentioned food, her face went a greenish colour and she bolted for the bathroom waving her hand at me.

"I'll take that as a 'no' then," I said when she was out of sight. I was just about to go into the kitchen when there was a knock at the door. Maybe Frank was back, but it would be way too early yet. He had gone over to 'The guys' house. The guys being a bunch of mates he went to high school with and they now all watched football together whenever they could. He hadn't wanted to leave at first, but Libby and I both convinced him that she would be fine and as I was staying in anyway, there was no point him missing it.

I opened the door to a man wearing a black suit and a black chauffeur's hat. But there wasn't a car in sight. Maybe he had parked around the side, but why would he do that? He held a long black envelope under his arm and asked,

"Miss Johnson?" He was a bit creepy looking, so I stepped back from beyond the door frame in case I needed to slam the door shut. I know this was an odd response, but I couldn't help but be wary.

"Letter for you." And with that he held out an envelope for me to take, and then he promptly left.

"Who was that at the door?" Libby had re-emerged from the downstairs loo and was cocooning herself back into the bedding on the couch.

"Just a letter for me. Do you think you could hold down a cup of tea?" She nodded like a child and continued to watch some cheesy daytime drama.

I walked into the kitchen and placed the letter on the table while I filled the kettle. Once I had clicked it on, I went to sit down and stare at it as though it would bite me if I touched it again. I turned over the black rectangle and saw that it had been sealed by red wax. I looked closer and noticed the seal was the family crest of the Dravens. It was the same as on the doors and the back of Draven's chair at the club.

Maybe this was about my behaviour last night. Oh shit... maybe I was getting sacked!

I couldn't bear it any longer, so I tore open the seal and pulled out the contents. The sound of the kettle boiling hid the small scream that I made, and I dropped the paper back on the table.

I just couldn't believe it, what the hell was going on?

There must have been a mistake!

Was this real?

CHAPTER 27
GIFT OR DEMAND

I stuffed the letter under my armpit as I carried the two mugs into the living room. I passed Libby hers and I sat back down still in shock.

"Good news?" she asked over her mug.

"I… don't… know," I said slowly, as I was still trying to make sense of it.

"What's wrong?"

I handed Libby the envelope and said,

"This is what's wrong." It didn't take her long for her eyes to widen in shock at the wad of cash she held in her hands.

"WOW, where the hell did you get that from?" I nodded to the letter that was still inside. She pulled it free from the cash and scanned the letter, finding the words that stood out.

"That's your wages? $4000 in a month!" She shouted the words and I stared at the pile of green notes in her hand.

"But that's… that's crazy… you are a waitress, right?"

"Of course, I am! What do you think I do there?" I said getting frustrated!

"I don't know, lure them all sacrifices… Kidding, kidding," she said, but I didn't laugh. How could I… I mean, what was this?

"Well, at least you can get a new car now."

"I'm not going to spend it, there's been a mistake and it's

316

going back!" I hissed, slamming my hand down on the arm of the chair and then picking up my tea, gulping it down and burning my throat.

"Really? You're not going to spend it?" she said in disbelief.

"No, I'm not... in fact... I'm... I'm going to sort this out right now," I said getting up to go back in the kitchen, ignoring Libby as she asked what it was that I was going to do. I picked up the phone, grabbed the number that was on the fridge and called the club. It rang four times before someone picked up.

"Hello, Club Afterlife, Jerry speaking."

"Hi Jerry, it's Keira."

"Oh, hi Keira, what's up?" he asked in a wary voice. He must have thought I was calling in sick and maybe he was dreading the thought of telling them upstairs.

"Don't worry, I'm not calling in sick, I just want to know, could you put me through to upstairs?"

"Umm, I don't know... can I ask what this is about?" Oh yeah, he was wary all right.

"Well, it's a bit personal and I don't think they would want me disclosing any information to anyone about it so..." That did it! Before I knew it, the phone was ringing again and this time a familiar, happy voice answered.

"How can I help you, Keira?" Karmun asked.

"How did you know it was me?"

"Lucky guess. I'm assuming you got your wages?" Ah, so he knew I would call. I started to relax, as they must have realised their mistake.

"Oh, right so you know it was wrong then. It's okay, I will bring it back later and we can sort it out then, but wow I was shocked..." He cut me off when he said,

"Wrong...? Keira, there's been no mistake."

"What!? But I... don't understand, I..." I mumbled my words, when he said,

"There's someone here who wants to speak to you, hang on." Oh no, this was bad... this was a very bad idea.

"Hi Keira." I let out a sigh of relief when I heard Sophia's voice on the other end. I was just thankful it wasn't her brother's.

"Hey Sophia, I was just telling Karmun that I think there has been a mistake." I was about to explain but like Karmun she already knew.

"No, there's been no mistake, we have just added a bit onto your wages, like an advance, so you can get a car." What!? Was she joking? They were giving me money to buy a car? I couldn't speak. I couldn't think of anything to say. Not even when all I heard on the other end was…

"Keira, are you still there?"

∾

Sophia had told me how she and her brother felt it was important that I had my own transport, as my shifts might be getting later, and they felt it was unfair to ask me to do this if I had to rely on other people. In the end, I had no other option than to agree to keep the money, but I stated that I would pay it back monthly. This was something she didn't fully agree to, but I decided it was best to approach it in person.

It didn't help that Libby's smugness lasted the rest of the day as she had been right in thinking I would spend it. When Frank came in it was the first thing out of her mouth.

"Guess who's buying Kazzy a car?"

"He's not buying me a car! They have loaned me an advance on my wages, and I am paying it back!" I said this last half directed back at Libby, with the temptation to stick my tongue out at her.

"Cool, how much are we talking about here?"

"4000 bucks!" Libby said in a corny American accent. Frank's face lit up and replied,

"Nice, but babe, leave the American to the pros, yeah? So, when do you want to go and spend your hard-earned dough?" he said mocking me, but it was hard to stay in a bad mood with Frank and his huge teddy bear cute smile.

"Does this mean you'll go with me?"

"Of course. I'm not letting you get ripped off, coming back

318

here with a piece of crap like that rusty tin can your friend's got!" He put his jacket back on and I asked,

"What, you want to go now?" He raised his eyebrows and lifted up his hand as if to say, 'Well duh!'

~

We were in his car and I had put the money in my bag stuffing it down into the bottom, paranoid that it would fall out or that I would lose it.

"You've got your new licence, right?" Frank had already gone over everything that I needed before I left the house.

"Yeah, got it, but are you sure this guy is gonna be open? It is a Sunday."

"Trust me, this guy never shuts. You'd better let me do all the talking because this guy... well, let's just say he's a bit of a ball buster." I didn't have any problems with that. I wasn't exactly brimming over with car expertise.

"No problem," I said as we pulled up to a set of traffic lights.

"Sooo... I guess this means you couldn't have pissed him off that much," Frank said, giving me a wink, and I shook my head in denial.

"I don't know what you mean," I said rolling my eyes and looking out of the window casually.

"Yeah, sure you don't... well, okay if you want to play it off as nothing then I'm game, but you have to know that this isn't the normal behaviour for a boss... *right?*" Well yeah, of course I knew that, but was there anything normal about Draven? I mean, I couldn't imagine he was spending his Sunday 'watching the game and drinking a Bud'! If I thought about it, I couldn't imagine him doing anything average.

Thankfully, he dropped the conversation as we pulled up to an intersection then took a left into 'Bobby's Used Car Lot' as the sign read. Frank parked the car near a guy washing a big pickup truck. He looked about sixteen and there was no meat on him whatsoever. In fact, he resembled a beanpole.

There was a gritty office, and a man emerged from behind a

door that had seen better days. The man was short and stocky, with the shiniest bald head I had ever seen.

Frank leaned into me and whispered,

"Man, look at that head. Bowling, anyone?" I nudged him in his ribs and tried not to burst out laughing.

"Now remember, let me do the talking."

"I don't think that's going to be hard," I said swallowing the laugh that was still there.

"Hi there, Bobby Brown at your service, what can I do you for?" he said giving me a wink that made me smile, but not for the same reasons he was thinking. I couldn't help it. He was like some comical but slightly slimy uncle from a sitcom. He wore a tweed jacket with a pair of light blue jeans that were too long for him, so they were rolled up at the ankles. He topped off the look with a crooked smile and yellow teeth.

"We're looking for a reliable car for my sister here," Frank said, and I loved the way he never added the 'in-law' bit.

"Sister, eh… lucky for me then." I nearly choked trying again not to laugh.

"Well, let's go and take a look should we, pretty lady?" he said, and motioned for us to follow him. Frank frowned at his attentions towards me, but I just found it hilarious. For some reason he had kind eyes that made me want to smile back at him. However, Frank pulled back my arm and whispered in my ear,

"There's something wrong… he's never this nice!" I shrugged and followed him around to the cars.

"So what's the budget?"

"$3000," Frank said before I could speak, and I shot him a look.

"$3000 you say… umm, well if that's what you've got, then that's what you got, let's see what I can do," he said as though he didn't believe the amount.

I let him walk ahead then I whispered to Frank,

"Why did you only say $3000?"

"Trust me, this is how the game is played, watch and learn kiddo." He walked on holding his head high as he caught up with Bobby.

"Hey, what about that one, the red Chevy?" Frank said pointing to a sporty coupé.

"What, the Camaro? Dodgy transmission that one," Bobby said scratching his smooth head. He started to walk over to the bigger vehicles when Frank stopped him as he had spotted another one.

"Now, here we are, Kaz, this one's perfect! It's a Toyota Starlet, right?" he asked Bobby, who didn't seem that interested as he just nodded.

"Go on, Kaz, give it a try," Frank said opening the door to a little white hatchback.

"I wouldn't do that if I were you." Bobby leaned into Frank and said,

"Someone died in there you see and... well... we never could get rid of the smell." I pulled a disgusted face and let go of the car door, rubbing my palm down my jean's leg.

"Nice," I said sarcastically, and I saw Bobby looking at me, grinning. Frank pulled me back away from the car as if I would get infected standing so close.

"Okay, what about this VW Golf?"

"Nah, you don't want that one, look over here, I have something perfect for the lady," Bobby said walking back in the direction of the big boys, where a line of pick-ups and 4x4's sat.

"Here we go, the Ford Bronco, now this is your girl, and it's midnight blue to match the pretty girl's eyes," he said giving me another wink, and I giggled, not knowing why. From anyone else I would have found this creepy, but there was something strangely familiar about him. Maybe he reminded me of a regular from the pub I worked in back home. They were always flirting with me, but it was only banter... plus I got great tips at Christmas!

"Hey, look pal, if you think that by putting us off all the other cars is going to make us pay $6500 then you can think again! Come on, Kazzy, let's check out the Mustang over there." Frank started to walk off, but I just walked around the huge blue 4x4, slowly falling in love. Bobby watched me wide-eyed, smiling as though it was a slam-dunk. He opened the door for me adding,

"There we are, *my* lovely." Then winked at me, but there was just something in the way he said 'my', like he really meant it.

"Uh… thanks," I said getting in the driver's seat and holding the wheel.

Frank walked back to the Bronco and stood next to me looking as though I had lost my mind.

"Look, I will do you a deal. I'll let her go for $4000." Frank and I both looked at him in amazement, and Frank shouted an animated,

"What?!" While looking back at me. I just shrugged my shoulders and got out, walking around it trying to find the damage.

"Are you kidding, what's wrong with it?" Frank asked picking the words out of my head and frowning as if Bobby was trying to sell us something dodgy.

"Nothing at all, she runs great and the lady needs something strong that will protect that pretty little bone structure. She's a 1995, 5.8 v8 engine and she's a beaut. Start her up if ya don't believe me." He handed Frank the keys as though he'd known all along this was the car he would sell me, or more astonishingly be the one I would want. I didn't say anything as Frank took the keys and started her up, while I stroked the hood like I was in front of a horse.

Frank got out and said,

"I told you we only have $3000." What? I couldn't believe he was still haggling with the guy! He must have thought that there was something wrong with it for that price.

"Ah yes, so you did. Well, I will tell you what, how 'bout I let ya have her for $3000 plus a kiss," he said motioning to his cheek, and my mouth dropped open. Frank looked at him as though he had lost his mind.

"What is wrong with you!? Come on, Keira, this guy's crazy." And he started to walk away, but I smiled and said,

"So, let me get this straight, not only will you drop the price from $6500 but you will knock another $1000 off just for a kiss on the cheek?"

"A kiss by the prettiest girl I have ever seen. So yeah, I'm old and bald... humour me," he said, and I couldn't help but laugh first at his compliment and then his joke. I mean what an old charmer! But I had to admire his spirit. So, I went up to him and kissed him gently on the cheek, seeing something in his eyes that brought back a memory I couldn't explain.

Frank saw this and held up his hands like Bobby wasn't the only one who had lost their mind.

"Ah sweetheart, now that was worth every cent," Bobby said grinning like a Cheshire cat. Frank came up behind him and said,

"Alright Casanova, let's sort out the damn paperwork."

I got in the car after Frank showed me the basics, and I started to follow him home. It felt strange driving again, more so because not only did it feel like a tank, but I kept wanting to change gear as I had never driven an automatic before. Also, I had to keep repeating to myself the most important rule about driving an automatic and that was to only use one foot. So, I kept my left foot tucked firmly away under the seat so that I wouldn't be tempted to use it for the clutch that wasn't there.

I smiled all the way home and if I'd known the town much better, I would have gone for a longer drive. There was so much room in this thing, I think I could have moved in and still had room for a sink! Frank, on the other hand, was still expecting it to blow up or something. Well, I loved it!

When we got back, Libby had disappeared along with her car and Frank got worried, so he rang her mobile, which she didn't answer.

"Maybe she went to the pharmacy," I said, trying to be helpful and not panic. He, on the other hand, was imagining things that included the words 'Hospital' and 'Emergency.'

He tried her again on her phone, over and over, and as before she didn't answer. Okay, so now I was getting a bit worried. Why hadn't she left a note or just called us back? This wasn't like her, unless her stomach pain had turned more serious and she did in fact go to the hospital. I walked into the kitchen and was just about to tell Frank to call the ER, but he was already on the phone, and it wasn't to Libby.

"No, okay, well thanks anyway, if you hear anything you got my number," he finished, and put back the handset on the wall.

"She's not at the hospital."

"Alright then, maybe something at work came up?" I said, and he grabbed the phone again, punching in the numbers impatiently. But before the phone could register, the front door opened.

"Olivia, where have you been?!" Frank said in a relieved but angry tone. Libby looked innocently at our frowning faces and put a plastic bag behind her, Frank didn't notice but I did.

"What? I just popped out for some Pepto Bismol. Jeez, paranoid much," she said as she walked past us and went straight to the bathroom, leaving Frank and I with the same expression.

"Well, I called your cell like a million times, babe, and guess what? You didn't answer!" Frank was upset, that much was clear.

"I was driving!" she shouted from inside the bathroom.

"Since when has that ever stopped you?" Frank snapped back.

"Well, aren't you the one who's always telling me to be more careful? And what's with the third degree?" she asked through the door. I had gone into the kitchen to put the kettle on and also to give them some privacy.

"Well I was worried, I mean you're ill, so I just thought that something could've happened... I mean Christ, Libs, I called the hospital."

"Oh honey, I'm fine, look I'm sorry if I made you worry." And with that I knew it was over as I could hear the sound of kissing, so I got up and closed the door, which made them giggle like teenagers.

I couldn't help but think that Libby was hiding something, as the rest of the night she was acting... well, kind of weird. For starters, she stuffed her face full of the beef stroganoff I made and then she tucked into a tub of Ben and Jerry's Phish food.

"Well, it looks like someone is feeling better," Frank had said as he too dug his spoon into the tub, pulling out a lump of brown gooey chocolate. Frank had filled her in about our trip to Bobby's and she laughed until she cried, especially when Frank added,

"Yeah, should have seen his shiny head, it looked more like a solar panel for a sex machine! Horny old bastard!" Then we were all in hysterics.

"Well, it looks like Keira is catching everyone's eye," Libby said, nudging Frank as they shared a not so private joke. I just rolled my eyes and took my plate back into the kitchen, saying,

"Kids," as I passed them.

The truth was, I was still a bit freaked from what I had seen in Bobby's eyes. I just couldn't put my finger on it, but there had been something deep and lurking about the way he looked at me. I tried to shake it off as I did with most things these days, but it still remained at the back of my mind. To be honest, ever since I had met Draven, I had felt something in my life had changed. Almost like my mind was being controlled by another entity. It had confused my senses, making me feel like I was being watched by other people. It was making me see things that I couldn't explain, and who knows, it could even be controlling my dreams.

I know thinking this was crazy but considering the facts, what else was there?

That it was just all down to me and my imagination? Maybe the fact that I had seen monsters in people since I was seven years old had something to do with it.

Either way I looked at it, the same conclusion always came up...

There was something wrong.

CHAPTER 28

WEEKS GONE BY

T hings at the club changed after that Saturday I had walked away from Draven. Weeks had gone by and yet not a word from him. It seemed that he didn't take kindly to being disobeyed and my punishment was being ignored. He didn't even look my way when I went by, and the pain of this got worse, not better.

The one time I thought I was close to receiving a reaction was when he walked past me at the end of my shift one night. Only instead of a friendly word, I got a hostile glare, which made my fists clench and my heart pound in my chest. I was very close to screaming at him but thankfully, I was still scared of him and the bravery from that night hadn't lasted.

Apart from my nights of being ignored at the club, my days had found a good routine. I would spend my time juggling college and working, with the occasional night off, spending it with RJ and the rest of the gang. My problem was that the more time I spent with Jack, the clearer he was making his intentions. I tried to talk to RJ, but it fell on deaf ears as she would have liked nothing more than for me and Jack to become an item.

I had soon got used to my new car and loved the new-found freedom that went with it. I took it in turns with RJ driving to college, and it didn't take long before my glove compartment was filled with RJ's favourite CD's. Of course, she preferred it when I took my car, as unlike hers, it didn't sound like a lawnmower on crack!

She showed me all around the town and I took her out to eat at a Mexican restaurant to say thanks. It felt good to do this again, making me feel less like a teenager and more of the adult I was. We all went to the movies one night, and they all laughed at me when I had called it the flicks. However, Jack's flirting never went unnoticed as he made every effort to be near me.

I felt as though I belonged. A feeling I hadn't felt for a very long time. But at the back of my mind were my own demons inching their way to the surface, never letting me forget the sense of security that I felt when I was near Draven. It would only stop when I was at the club, making me feel as though I had come home. A piece of me was empty, and that hole would only be filled when I was there. It was like the building itself was one giant entity which fed from my emotions. I felt as if it wanted me there, it needed me there, and it used Draven as the key to keep me there.

Then one day everything changed, and I was once again thrown into a world I didn't understand. It had started just like any other day, the only difference being that Jack had asked me on a date, and this time I couldn't find any more excuses to make, so I agreed. I was caught in the middle of a war with my mind and heart. Both wanted different things. My brain convinced me that after two weeks of silence and being ignored, Draven didn't want anything to do with me and no amount of wishing it would make it so. My heart, of course, didn't want to give up, so it hadn't been an easy decision. I just kept telling myself, it's only a date, what's the worst that could happen?

We had arranged for Friday night, as I had the night off due to the day shift I was going to do on Saturday. I had never worked the club in the day before, so I wasn't really sure what to expect. I wondered if Draven would still be at his table, as surely they couldn't just sit there every day and night, could they?

I had two separate friendships with Sophia. There was the

usual everyday one in class, and the other very different one at the club. She had tried to explain it once, but I told her that she didn't need to explain anything and that I fully understood why this was. She had a position to uphold and couldn't spend the time talking to me when I was working. After all, she was one of my bosses.

It wasn't as if she just wouldn't acknowledge me. She would always wave, and occasionally she'd come up and say 'hello', but you could tell it was frowned upon by her brother. In class though we acted like normal friends, laughing and joking about Reed. She would do her usual trick of asking a million and one questions about me but never really revealing anything about herself. She remained a mystery just like her brother. She never once mentioned him and I never asked.

She did, however, ask about Jack the day that he asked me out.

"I noticed you were talking to Jack before class, any development there?" she said as she twisted a black barrel curl around her finger.

"Yeah kind of, he asked me out this Friday night and I finally said yes." She didn't look shocked as if she had been waiting for it, knowing all along what he felt for me.

"Umm that's nice, you're not working then?" There was something off about her tone, but I couldn't put a finger on it.

"No, I have the night off, but I'm in on Saturday," I said, trying to figure out her expression.

She quickly dropped the conversation as Reed entered the room. My relationship with Reed had smoothed out after the misunderstanding was rectified and the evidence that my work was always handed in early, and above all, always received a good grade. This wasn't only down to the fact that I wanted to prove a point, in truth it was more down to whenever I spent any time alone with myself, my thoughts would be consumed by Draven. The only way to stop this was to set my mind on a different course and as a result, I was ahead in all my classes.

It was Thursday and I was working at the club tonight. I got in from college to find Libby already home and cleaning again. Lately, Libby had been acting weird, ever since her stomach bug. She would clean constantly and eat everything in sight.

I didn't understand her behaviour, as she had never been one of those cleaning freaks or one for over-eating. Granted, before I came to live with them there was mainly junk food and a microwaveable meal on every shelf of the freezer, but they were also fitness fanatics. But Libby had stopped doing yoga and gave up her Pilates class at her health club.

I was on my way upstairs after saying 'hello' to the bottom part of her, as her head was stuck in the oven cleaning it like a woman possessed, when it hit me! I ran back down the stairs flinging my body around the corner so fast that I almost slipped and shouted,

"You're pregnant!" Her head emerged from the foamy oven and she smiled.

"I knew it! Why didn't you tell me?!" I shouted not being able to contain my excitement. She got up and pulled off her rubber gloves, throwing them into the sink. I couldn't help running up to her and giving her a big hug.

"Whoa, too tight, too tight!" she said as I squeezed my arms around her.

"Oops sorry, but come on tell me, does Frank know?"

"No and I don't want you to say anything, not yet," she said, holding me back by my shoulders, so she could look me in the eyes.

"I won't but why? Is he not ready?" I asked not believing the question. I knew that he was ready to be a dad. Anyone could see that when he was around other people's children, he adored kids.

"It's not that, look there's a reason I haven't said anything about this, and you have to promise not to say a word!" she said, holding out her hand for the special secret handshake that we had made up as kids. I placed my hand on hers and did the moves she knew so well, ending in a disgusting spit in each palm rubbing them together. Of course, back when we were kids, we would just wipe our hands on our trouser leg but now we both got up and washed our hands at the sink, laughing.

"So come on, spill it."

She took a deep breath and said,

"Frank's got low sperm count." I couldn't help it but I laughed. I knew it was wrong and Libby didn't look happy about my reaction, but I laughed more about the way she said it than the actual meaning behind it.

"I'm sorry, I didn't mean to do that. It's just the way you said it. I half expected you to tell me that Frank's a spy or something." She rolled her eyes and continued.

"Well, I have my first scan next week and I wanted to wait until after then, just to be sure… I don't want to get his hopes up."

I nodded and held her hand, saying,

"But when did you find this out and why didn't you tell me?"

"I don't know why I didn't… I wanted to. It's just that I thought I would be jinxing it if it told anyone." She squeezed my hand back before getting up to make tea.

"I found out when you and Frank went out to buy your car, when you left it got me thinking about why I was sick and then I remembered I hadn't had my period for a while, so I had to get a test."

"And that's why you were all weird about it when you got home?"

"Well yeah, I mean I even heard my phone go off in the car and was about to answer it when I thought… no, I have to be extra careful now, as I might be living for two. It even slowed down my driving."

"So, you went to get a test and it was positive?" I said passing her the milk out the fridge.

"No, I bought four tests, and they were *all* positive." I couldn't help my eyes welling up at the thought.

"Aww Libs, that's great news. God, Mum is going to freak out." She shot me a look, and I quickly said,

"Don't worry, my lips are sealed as long as you promise me I can be here when you ring her."

We sat and chatted about baby stuff until Frank walked in and I realised that I would be late for work if I didn't get a move on. I ran upstairs, grabbed my stuff and ran out to my car. I turned up five minutes late but because I was still wearing the stuff I'd had on for college, it made me even later as I had to change in the back room before I could start.

"I'm sorry I'm late, Karmun!" I said as I whizzed past him taking my first tray to my tables. When I came back for my next one, he stopped me.

"Umm, sorry honey, but Mr Draven wants to see you." My heart dropped. This had been the last thing I was expecting. I couldn't help but ask,

"What about?"

"I don't know, but he wants you to go over to his table right now." He said it as if he hated being the one to tell me this. Once again, I felt like running. I had never been over to his table before and it was somewhere I never wanted to go. Not only did I have Draven to face but now I had to face a whole table of unfriendly faces! Sophia was the only one I wasn't scared of but against six others, I didn't think it was going to make much of a difference. So, I placed down my tray and took a deep breath, feeling as if I was about to be thrown to the lions.

It was like walking towards the electric chair, I couldn't stop from shaking, and I could feel my pulse pumping under my scars at what I was about to do. I could see them all as I got closer and their faces became clearer. But my eyes focused on the man who had requested my presence at his table.

I decided that I wasn't going to speak. I would just nod. This was because I didn't think I could have formed the words even if I tried. I walked up the steps to the same level of his table and was stopped by the biggest guy I had ever seen. It was one of Draven's bodyguards, but this guy looked like he ate other bodyguards for breakfast.

It was the same guy who I had seen briefly twice now, once when they first arrived and the second was when Draven had come to my aid in the carpark. His face was scarred and full of potholes, his eyes were small and dark but rimmed with red. His hands looked as though they could have crushed the head of a cow and he reminded me of a Viking warrior. He stood in my way with his arms folded, which looked like hard work considering how big they were.

"Ragnar, let her through!" Draven's voice ordered. I shuddered as I walked past him.

Once I was next to the table, I froze. It was like being in front of a king and his court. His sister looked up and smiled which gave me a bit of courage, but not enough to get me to move or speak. I looked at the other two, whom I had never seen fully, but I didn't hold my eyes to them long as everyone was staring at me as though I was their next meal. It was like being in a confined space with every type of deadly creature and they were all thinking the same thing…

Snack time!

"Why were you late?" Draven said without looking at me and the others raised their eyebrows at the sound of his words. I still couldn't find my voice and Sophia was about to say something to her brother, but he held up his hand to stop her. She gave up and turned back around to face the front.

"So, let's have it," he said with no emotion, and my heart sank at his coldness. The anger I felt from this replaced a bit of my fear, so I gritted out,

"It's personal." Which wasn't a lie, but my angry voice made it sound like one. I bit down on my lip and tasted the blood as it cracked inside.

"Right, well in that case, you *will* work tomorrow night to make up for it." Sophia looked up at me, eyes full of sorrow, but my face must have got the message across that I wasn't happy because she quickly looked away. The way he had emphasised the word 'Will' was a clear indication there was no getting out of it.

"Fine! I could do with the extra shift, so that's just great, it's just dandy," I said with my anger take over in the form of sarcasm and the man next to Sophia shot me a disapproving look. He was very serious and the huge scar that went down one cheek wasn't the only thing that added to his frightening look.

All of one side of his face was covered in a strange series of tattoos which snaked around the scar and ran the full length of his face. The black ink passed through the damaged skin, but the ink disappeared when it reached the injured tissue. It made it look as if there were pieces missing from the design.

Apart from this, he had a very serious but handsome face, with long, platinum blonde hair that fell down under the black hood he wore over his head. He was ice white and scary. He was also the first albino man I had ever seen. So, when I received this look, I couldn't help but find my feet with my eyes before braving another glance. Draven shot him a glare and his eyes looked elsewhere. Then Draven spoke again.

"That will be all." And then he picked up a shot glass shaped like a claw that had been defying gravity by staying up on a single point. He shot it back and placed it back on a tray that Layla was holding out to him. Again, the claw stood up, floating as she took it away. Ragnar, the giant, motioned for me to leave and I did gladly, without looking back!

The rest of the night I worked in a red mist of anger. I couldn't believe that ten minutes of being late warranted that! Jack was right, what a stupid rich pompous ass! Who the hell did he think he was? I just didn't get him. One minute he was acting like the most amazing guy, and the next he was some scary, badass godfather type, getting pissed off because I was all of ten minutes late! It was ridiculous.

I finished my shift and changed back into my normal clothes, as if to make some point when I walked past his table to go home. Okay, so I didn't know what type of point I was trying to make but his eyes followed me all the same. When I got downstairs, I was met by Jack and the rest of the gang. RJ had wanted to catch this band playing that was called 'The Dizzy Bandits' who were a mix of punk and rock.

"Hey, what's wrong with you, you look tense?" Jack said as he joined me at the bar. I looked back at the VIP area and glared in the direction I knew he could see me from up there.

"Yeah, tense is a good word but pissed off is a better," I said as I ordered a coke from Mike and then changed my mind saying,

"Ah hell, give me a shot of tequila."

"Whoa, aren't you driving?"

"Yeah, but one won't hurt and trust me, I need it!" I said downing it in one without the lemon or salt.

"Wow, you're hardcore baby!" he said giving my chin an affectionate little squeeze. Then, I don't know why, but I did something so out of character that I shocked myself, as I went on my tiptoes and kissed Jack on the cheek, not being able to help the look towards Draven as I did this.

"Well, the band might be crap, but it was definitely worth coming tonight. But I have to ask, what was that for?" he said with the biggest smile on his face.

"For being sweet and cheering me up," I said as I ordered a more sensible coke.

"So, come on, what happened... leader of the vamp pack been throwing his weight around?" he said as we walked back to the others.

"Something like that, yeah! But hey, I'm really sorry I'm going to have to cancel our date."

"What? Well that sucks! But it's nice to see you all worked up about it. What can I say? I bring out the fighting spirit in every girl." He laughed, leaving me feeling guilty. I excused myself and went to the ladies to compose my thoughts. Of course, it didn't help that I felt like I was being watched everywhere I went.

I looked in the mirror back at my reflection and didn't like what I saw there. I shouldn't have used Jack to get to Draven. I mean, why would it even affect him anyway? He had made it perfectly clear on his feelings for me and if not by treating me like a leper for the past couple of weeks, then most certainly tonight's humiliating torture.

It had felt like 40 lashes to my heart and I hated that I still felt the same for him. I was like a magnet for the worst type of men, they would dig their claws in and I couldn't escape their clutches. Only with Draven, he would suck me in again and again and then spit me back out whenever it suited him.

I splashed some cold water on my face and rubbed the back of my neck with my hands. What a fool I was. Here was Jack, who thought that I was angry because I couldn't go on a date with him, when secretly, I had been relieved. There was nowhere I would rather be than at the club. The reason I was so angry was the way Draven had spoken to me. His coldness, his disrespect and disregard for anyone else's feelings just because he was angry was excruciating and completely unacceptable!

I stayed later than I had expected to, but I knew that if I had gone early, I would have just spent the time in my room stewing over 'Lord Draven'. So, only when the band finished and RJ had flirted with every member including the sound technician, we said our goodbyes and I walked to my car.

It was one of the only ones left in the shadowy car park and it made my truck look sinister. I fumbled with the keys in my bag trying to get into the safety of my 'tank'. I found them but only to drop them on the wet ground, which I could barely see. I bent down, feeling around for them as they had gone a bit under the truck. I felt the cold metal and grasped my fingers around them. I straightened back up and tried the lock but when I looked through my window, I noticed I wasn't alone.

Staring straight back at me, was the bird perched on the top of the next car. Its eyes were glowing purple and it spread its wings as though ready for flight. It made a high-pitched screech and put its head down making its razor-sharp beak shine in the moonlight. I screamed at the noise, dropping my keys again.

Damn it! I bent down again quickly and whipped them from the gravel floor as they had fallen by my foot. I came up like a shot and rammed the keys in the lock. I looked to check the bird hadn't moved closer but it had gone. I didn't wait around for it to reappear, so I jumped in my car, locking the doors and turning the ignition. I drove out of there like a bat out of hell!

When I got home all the lights were off and I knew Frank and Libby would be in bed. I sat in my car for a while, still feeling too freaked to move. The bird was the one thing I knew wasn't in my head because Jack had seen it too. I sat there tapping my hand on the wheel trying to pluck up the courage to walk the short distance to the front door. I mean, it was only a bird, what was I so frightened about?

Okay, so it was the scariest, biggest most Demonic looking bird on the planet, and it looked like it could rip out my jugular with one swipe but hey, apart from that! I counted to three and bolted out of the car, not even bothering to lock it. I ran to the door with my key already in hand and shoved it in the keyhole. I pushed open the door and slammed it shut, forgetting about Frank and Libby in bed. I listened but there wasn't a sound, so I gathered they hadn't heard.

I just wanted this night to end, as it had been one thing after another. I walked over to the liquor cabinet and poured myself a drink of whisky and then I went into the kitchen to get some ice from the dispenser. I just needed a drink to calm my nerves and seeing as I hadn't yet made an appointment to see a therapist it was the next best thing to sleeping pills.

I took my drink upstairs and the first thing I did was close the blind above my window seat. Knowing that the bird was out there somewhere and seemed to have a tendency to keep finding me, I thought it best to hide. I knew I would never sleep right away so I took myself and my glass over to my desk and pulled out the drawing pad that I kept my secret Demons in. I tore out a page and began to sketch.

∾

I woke the next morning to find Draven's face staring back at me. I didn't remember at first that I had sketched a picture of him, so I was shocked to see the perfect features that I had burned to a memory slot in my brain. It was his deep-set eyes, his strong jawline, even down to his stubble and his shoulder-length hair styled back off his face. I had captured every bit of him as though I had copied a photograph.

Just looking at it gave me goosebumps and I quickly put it away in my desk drawer, hiding his cold glare. I had drawn him the way he looked last night, and the memory made me close my eyes and push it back into the far corners of my mind, next to the other bad stuff I stored there.

I got to college early, as RJ wasn't in today due to a hangover she called 'study day'. I went to the library to kill time and to get out a few books on American History, as it was the one subject I was going to be in the dark about. Of course, when it was time for British history then I would be back in the game but for now, seeing as pretty much everyone in the class except me was taught it in school, I was going to need to learn it all from scratch. By the time I found the right section, I only had time to grab one book and run to my first class.

While I was in history, Sophia had apologised for her brother's 'bad mood' and asked me if everything was all right at home? I explained that everything was fine, not wanting to disclose any details. I thanked her for her concern and lied about being okay with what happened last night.

"Sometimes, I don't understand Dom's reasoning, but let's just say he likes things the way he likes them, if that makes any sense?" she explained, and I nodded but I really wanted to say, 'Well actually, it makes no sense whatsoever but hey... I guess cryptic clues must run in the family.' Instead I just stuck to,

"Don't worry about it." She dropped the subject, not mentioning her brother again.

Before she went, she told me that I could start at eight instead of seven if I wanted but I didn't want to add more fuel to the fire, so told her seven was fine. I didn't want to give him the satisfaction of another showdown.

When I got back, Libby reminded me that she and Frank were going to Frank's parents for dinner and were staying the night, so not to worry when I returned to an empty house. It was going to be the first time I stayed there alone, and the idea didn't have me jumping around in excitement shouting 'Party'... if anything Freddy Kruger came to mind.

I had a feeling that this would be one of those nights, and the dread washed over me like sticky black tar. With these thoughts, I had a shower and it helped, but even Libby's honey milk shower gel didn't make me feel clean. I dried the top part of my hair putting up the rest that remained damp. I put on a black vest over my black underwear that I only wore when I needed to do some more washing.

I pulled out a pair of black long-sleeved gloves and slipped them over my scars, placing my thumb through the hole. I put on my black shirt that did up with a few hooks at the front and tied at the back as it wrapped around my waist. It showed my curves as the material clung to my skin. I added a Gothic black and purple tie that RJ had given me as I was sick of being the only one that didn't make an effort on weekends. I even decided to add a tiny amount of mascara that I had borrowed from Libby. She looked as shocked as Frank when I asked her for it.

"What's brought this on?" she said as she handed me three different types, getting overexcited to see me making an effort again.

"Nothing, it's just most of the waitresses dress smarter at the weekend, so I didn't want to stand out."

"Well you look great, really smart with the whole tie thing," she said, waiting for me to pick a stick to use.

"I only needed one."

"Yeah, but what do you want to go for, length, fullness or curl?"

"What?"

"Here, go with this one, you already have the length and fullness, you lucky cow!" she said handing me the one with a blue lid that had the words curl and waterproof written down one side. Well, I guess that was good considering the amount of strange shit that had happened to me while working the VIP, tears seemed to be an everyday occurrence... well, at least I wouldn't look like a panda if anything else went wrong tonight.

"Thanks, and you're sure I don't look... well, I don't want to stand out and look like a plonker." She shook her head saying,

"Kazzy, if anything you will stand out for being beautiful, you look great... and look at that skin... flawless," she said, laughing when I cringed at the compliment.

I applied the mascara, making my lashes even blacker and

curl upwards slightly. I examined myself, pulled my shorter bits of hair down over my face, putting them to one side, and looked at myself in the mirror.

I felt different…

I felt exposed.

CHAPTER 29

DANGEROUSLY EXPOSED

I got to the club with plenty of time to spare, knowing I would never make the mistake of being late again. I walked through the main doors after my usual head nods to Cameron and Jo, but I couldn't shake the feeling that something was going to go very wrong this evening.

I crossed the massive hall, snaking in and out of the early arrivals for the band that was going to be playing. It was one of the better-known bands, but no matter how many times RJ had told me, I just couldn't remember the name of them. I noticed my friends sat ready at their usual table and they waved when they saw me. Jack looked shocked at the sight of me and I suddenly felt self-conscious. I should have just stuck with my regular look.

I ran up the stairs before I chickened out and pushed open the door. For some reason it seemed busier tonight than any other night I had worked. I was about to walk around the back out of view when Akako the Japanese waitress stopped me.

"Sorry no go, no go, walk round," she said and then dipped her head, leaving me feeling less than happy about it. I had already taken my jacket off and had it over the strap of my bag, so I would look strange putting it back on when I was already here. Some of the scarier clientele were starting to stare at me, so that made me move my feet in the direction of Draven's table.

I purposely remembered how mad he had made me last night, which made me hold my head high instead of letting it hang down pathetically. So, when I walked past, I finally looked as though I had some balls. However, I couldn't help looking at Draven for a split second, but it was enough to catch the different look he was giving me. I had never seen this look and I had to say, *I liked it.*

It was a mixture of surprise and shock with the smile adding a different edge to his eyes. The look he gave me made me feel... well, kind of sexy. But as soon as I passed, so did the feeling.

"Umm, hi Keira, you're looking... good," Karmun said clearing his throat. I felt my face get hot and I wished I had changed before leaving the house dressed like this.

"Thanks," I said as I walked past going to put my bag in the little room. I dumped it on the chair and threw my jacket, not caring where it landed. I just wanted to check the mirror, worried that there was something else on my face apart from mascara. But there was nothing but my pale skin with the hint of red cheeks and very dark blue eyes that were now framed with thick lashes. I could see that there was something different about me and it wasn't just down to the lashes, but I couldn't figure out what. Giving up, I went out there and started my shift.

Sophia was waiting for me when I walked out and she too did a double-take at me, which made me blush even more.

"Keira, you're..." I interrupted her saying,

"Yeah, I know I'm early," I said in a loud voice and unbelievably Draven shot me a look as though he'd heard.

"That's not what I was going to say but yes, you are, and it hasn't gone unnoticed, along with *other things,"* she said looking me up and down. By this time, I was the colour of a cherry.

"I would like to invite you to join us for a drink at our table after work," she said as Layla walked past looking as though she was swallowing her own tongue.

"Umm thanks, but I don't know if that's a good idea," I said, as now I probably looked as shocked as Layla had, only it was making it hard for me to swallow!

"It was at my brother's request, he feels as though he was a little hard on you last night and would like to make up for it, if you'll let him of course," she said smiling, as though she'd had something to do with this.

"Well, that's very kind but I don't think…"

"Come now, surely you wouldn't deny him this?" she said in a very persistent tone.

"I guess not," I replied, only realising that I had agreed to it when she clapped her hands together as she spoke.

"Excellent! Till later then," she said with glee, leaving before I had time to recall the 'yes' I had sort of said. Great, now I was going to spend the rest of the night worrying about spending social time with the Dravens!

There I was again, more confused than ever. One minute he hates me the next he wants me to join them? What the hell was going on?! This wasn't right and if I went over there at the end of my shift, then I would most definitely be playing with fire.

I spent the rest of my time serving drinks and picking up empties feeling as though I wasn't the only one who knew about this strange twist of events. It seemed they were all waiting for this to play out. Of course, the end of my shift was coming along quicker than I had hoped for, and with only ten minutes to go I was starting to panic big time. So much so in fact, that when a fight broke out, it took me more time to register what was going on.

One guy in a black military jacket was flinging another guy across the table, smashing glass all over the floor which spread as far as my feet. It wasn't in my section but the one next along, so this put me in the firing line. I stepped back to move out of the way. Although, little did I know I was moving in the way of someone else…

Someone who hated me.

Layla had been stood against the bar with a tray of slim vile looking glasses that reminded me of test tubes. She was looking straight at me with even more hate in her cruel eyes and I instinctively took a step back from her. But in turn she took a step closer to me with a murderous look that twisted her features and made her eyes blood red. This terrified me as I knew the awful truth.

I was seeing her in Demon form!

I didn't have time to react and all the other eyes were on the fight that was still going on. I was trapped in front of this crazy, evil bitch and one thing was clear without having to hear her speak… she wanted me dead and gone.

Before I had time to turn, she closed the gap pushing her hand into my side, sending a searing pain through my body that spread like a plague eating my flesh. She leant her face down next to my ear and whispered,

"Good luck with that one, Elegido!" She spat out the final word, and this was one language I knew well, she had called me 'Chosen One' in Spanish.

She walked away smiling, leaving me standing there in the worst agony I had ever felt. I staggered about and looked down to find that she had stabbed me with one of the thin glasses she had held on her tray. Only this one was metal and looked more like a round hollow knife. I couldn't scream, even though I tried, but my voice was lost in the crowd that was still trying to stop the fight.

I put my hand to my side, but the metal was in the way. I looked back at my hand and my skin had been replaced by the colour of the blood that now poured freely from my body. It was warm and thick, reminding me of the last time I had seen this much blood on my hands. I could feel acid in my mouth and my knees gave way as I tried to move away from the bar.

I fell, putting my hands out to save myself, but one slipped with the blood on it and flew into the glass that covered the floor. It dug into my palm as though my skin had been made from tissue paper. I tried to pull out the razor shards with my other hand, but I couldn't focus on where my other hand was. Things were going blurry as I heard someone shouting my name.

"Keira…! Keira, look at me!" A strong voice was shouting in a controlled yet desperate voice.

"I… my side, I can't…" I said trying to make sense, but the words wouldn't come out right.

A hand went to my side, and I heard what sounded like a growl when he obviously found the problem.

"Keira, can you hear me? You're going to be fine, just don't close your eyes. Okay... Keira, look at me!" I opened my eyes at the voice and saw Draven leaning over me. He had a mixture of fury and pain in his eyes as he barked out commands in a different language I couldn't understand.

"Find her, I want her alive!" he said to the figure standing behind him, who looked like one of the men from his table. I kept feeling this stabbing pain as I moved, so my hands went to the cause as I tried to pull it out, but hands found mine before I could get there.

"Oh no, don't touch that, little one. You have to leave it, or you will bleed out. I promise it will be gone soon." His voice was smooth, and it had a calming effect on my mind. But the pain was overtaking it and I wanted him to talk to me more. I could feel myself being lifted as an arm slid under my legs and another arm went under the upper part of my body.

"Keira, stay awake and talk to me," he said blowing more scent my way and I breathed deeply letting it take the pain away for a brief time.

"I don't want to go..." I said hoping it made sense. His hands gripped me closer to his hard chest.

"You don't want to go where?" he said trying to get me to keep talking.

"Hospital." I mouthed the word and the glass in my hand pinched as I moved it, forgetting there were shards still embedded in my skin.

"Don't worry I'm not taking you to hospital."

"Why?" I said wondering if that wouldn't be the smart thing to do.

"Because there isn't any time and because I can help you now," he said, and I was sure I could feel him running.

"Doctor?" I said meaning to add the 'Are you' at the front of that question but he understood.

"Something like that... oh no, come on, Keira, open your eyes for me." He gave me a quick shake to get me to respond. I opened my eyes, but it was getting harder as I felt as though I was falling.

"Nearly there, come on, keep with me now!" he said and it felt as though we were flying, he must have been running that fast. My eyes couldn't focus. It was like driving at death speeds and watching it all go past in a blurry vision. Amazingly, I managed to find some humour in the situation,

"You said that last time." He let out a tense laugh and said,

"So I did."

We were slowing down now and I heard a pair of big doors opening.

"Have you got everything ready?" he snapped out, and I didn't like the sound of the word 'everything'.

"What everything?" I said, wondering if he was asking me but then another voice spoke, and I knew the answer.

"Yes, Master," a woman's voice said in a quiet timid way.

I opened my eyes and saw that we were in a large room, but my mind switched back to the pain consuming my every function and I screamed as I was put down on what seemed to be a couch.

"Ssshh you're okay, I know it hurts but it won't for much longer," he said standing up and taking off his suit jacket.

"You promise?" I said, and the back of his hand caressed down my cheek as he replied,

"Yes, Keira, I promise." He then demanded, "Leave us!" to the girl who was still in the room. He pulled up a chair right next to me and pulled a small table closer to him that held lots of things I couldn't yet make out.

"Now, I'm going to pull you up slightly, but it will hurt... you ready?" He got closer to me and held both hands under my arms to pull me up.

"No but do it anyway," I said waiting for the pain to come. And boy did it come.

"AHHH AHH! Ouch, okay...okay, now that hurt!" I said trying to not cry but my cheeks were wet, so I think it was a little late for that wish.

"I know. I know it did, but you won't have to do that again."

He moved to the table, and now I could see a green bottle that I knew well. He then picked what looked like a sugar cube out of a glass jar with some silver tongs and placed it onto a strange slotted spoon, which had a design of wings cut out of it. This was then placed over a glass with a fancy silver bottom that curled up like a thorn vine overtaking clear glass.

He took out a tiny glass bottle and popped off the lid, then dripped some strange red liquid onto the sugar. Then, picking up the green bottle, he poured it over the sugar until the liquid ran over it into the glass below. He filled the glass then dripped some more red liquid onto the sugar before making me jump slightly as he set it alight. I didn't even see how he did this, as there was no lighter or a match in his hand.

After the sugar bubbled and caramelized, he dropped it in the glass making the mixture turn from green to red. He stirred it before passing it to me, but he must have added yet something else to it as it was now black. Or did he just blow into it and it changed colour? My mind couldn't control what was real and what wasn't.

"I need you to drink this, but careful, it's hot," he said as he pressed it to my lips.

"What is it?" I asked, pausing before drinking the contents of the glass.

"It's absinthe and it will help with the pain... drink," his voice took on a more authoritative tone, making me obey. The liquid burned my throat but not because of the temperature. It felt like acid tickling its way down inside me. But within seconds of it hitting my stomach the pain started to change into a numb ache more than the stabbing, ripping feeling I was used to.

"Better?" he said as if feeling it too.

I nodded, and automatically my hand went down to grab the implement that was still embedded in my side. He stopped me again just like the last time.

"Oh no you don't, let's not get too hasty. I need to stop the bleeding first, you're still losing a lot of blood." His hand let go of my wrist and moved to where the metal was sticking out of my skin.

"How come I can't feel the pain anymore?" I said, and his eyes flicked to me, looking up from my side.

"Because I didn't like seeing you in pain, however, you will feel the side effects soon enough."

"Side effects?" I looked at him with wide eyes and a worried frown.

"Hold very still... okay?" he said gently, ignoring my question. He placed his hand down on my stomach, stopping me from moving suddenly, while his other hand was positioned around the metal ready to extract it.

"Will this hurt?"

"Do you really want to know that?" he said as he yanked it hard away from my body, not giving me chance to answer. My question was answered as my body arched upwards from the agony and I screamed once more. His hand pushed down on my stomach and won the fight with my body's reaction. I was flat to the couch and panting from pain.

"Good girl... Ssshh... It's alright now, that's the worst bit over with," he said as he smoothed my hair back from my wet forehead and then slid his hand down to wipe the tears from my cheeks. It took me a moment to come back from that one. I remained silent trying to catch the breath that his quick action had stolen from me. He turned back to the table and grabbed a piece of thick, white gauze, holding it down on the now open wound.

He had examined the weapon for a moment with a dangerous glint in his eyes before crushing it into thin shards. It shattered in his hand and he threw the evidence away in an angry gesture. I looked on in amazement but still didn't speak. The white material had turned red but thankfully the pain hadn't returned.

"I need you to stand." His face was soft and full of tenderness. His hand went under my body again and he lifted me with ease. I was soon upright and in a pair of arms so strong I felt safely caged in iron girders. I stood facing him and my blood was on fire from being so close. His hands were coming up around my neck and I didn't understand why.

"What...what are you doing?" I said flinching backwards.

However, he just took a step into me, moving closer, and I could hear my breath hitch as though trying to play catch up with my erratic heart. His hands started on removing my tie from around my neck.

"I have to get to the wound. Do you have anything on under your shirt?" he asked, and I thought I would pass out, and not from extreme blood loss. He wanted to undress me?

"Umm… yes… why?" I said timidly.

"Because I need to take this off," he said as he put his hands around my back, closing the space between us completely. My head only came up to the top of his chest, and he bent his head down slightly, looking over my shoulder. His hands found the knot of material where my wrap shirt was tied behind my back. I couldn't look into his eyes, even though they were obviously scanning mine. His arms encircled my body and I had never felt so protected. His body being this close did strange things to my senses, making me want to touch his skin in the places his clothes concealed. The sexual tension emanating from us both was clogging the air, making me tremble with need.

When he had untied my shirt, he lingered there for a moment before removing the rest of it, peeling it away from my skin and exposing my bare shoulders. His touch was soft and gentle as though any sudden movement would scare me. He threw it to one side as if it should never have been there in the first place. Then he moved back, picking up a long red velvet scarf, and came towards me with it held out as if he was about to put it around my head.

"What are you going to do with that?" I asked, stepping back.

"Don't you trust me?" he said, cocking his head to one side as though trying to read my thoughts. When I didn't reply, he stepped towards me and placed the velvet around my eyes, knotting it at the back of my head.

"The drink I gave you will start the after-effects soon and I don't want it to frighten you," he said smoothing out the material over my eyes with gentle thumbs, making sure that I couldn't see.

"Frighten me?"

"It will make you see things that aren't there... it acts as a hallucinogenic."

My eyes were no longer a sense I could use, and my heart started hammering out a beat at the raw power he had over me. I heard him moving, and then I jumped when his hands touched my waist.

"We both agree that your top is ruined, right?" he said as his hands stopped moving.

"I guess," I said, not getting the question. Then his hands grabbed a handful of the black cotton and ripped it open just under my bra, so my stomach was exposed. Again, I jumped at the noise and also the air that hit my skin. His hands were back over my stomach and it felt like his head was level with my navel. Maybe he had sat down but because I couldn't see, I didn't know anything other than his touch.

Then something strange took place. He placed his palm to my wound and held it very still. I was about to move as I didn't understand what was happening, but his other hand caught me, holding me in place by my side. He then gently applied enough pressure to secure me from moving backwards. I was quickly being pulled closer to his body before he spoke.

"Now be still." His hand released its tension on my side, but I was still unable to move.

Then it happened.

A wave of fire entered my body and coursed through my bloodstream, making me convulse. It felt like someone had injected me with a mixture of morphine and a burning aphrodisiac. The remainder of pain was being washed away, but leaving behind the sands of desire. My body lit up like every sexual switch was being flicked at once and nothing could stop the moan coming from deep within. I felt the evidence of such scorching need dampen my thighs and sizzle along my nerves as though Draven's fingertips were right there at the core. I gasped for breath just as my knees gave out.

"Draven!" The plea broke out before I could grasp it back to the safety of unknown yearnings.

"I've got you... I've got you now, Keira," Draven hummed softly in my ear just after he caught my body from caving in on itself. I shook and then the storm of fiery passion calmed, turning into a deep feeling of euphoria. One only found after the sweetest sexual release.

Now, every fibre and molecule felt strong, as if another energy had entered my body making me feel reborn. A metallic taste filled my mouth as if I had been struck by lightning, and my eyes filled with tears but not from pain. It was as if my body couldn't contain the sensations without producing evidence on how magical it had been. My muscles tensed as I felt them grow powerful. I felt strong, as though I had been genetically altered.

His hand felt my body respond to whatever he had done to me because he whispered,

"Easy there." He held me still for a moment before making sure I was steady.

"Now, let's take care of that hand." He took hold of the palm that still had glass embedded in my skin. I had forgotten about it, as the pain had long gone. Although, now my hand shook in his as another fear hit me.

"Are you still in pain?" My other hand went to my wrist stopping him from removing my glove.

"No, but I don't... I mean... oh God, please don't!" I said spluttering out the words, wishing I could see his face. I lowered my head and I could feel the material go damp from tears that started to form as my old fears became too much to handle.

"I won't remove your glove, Keira, just the thumb... okay?" His voice sounded sympathetic, and I continued to hang my head in shame.

He knew.

He pulled the hole over my thumb and peeled it back, folding it over the wrist. I bit my lip as my nervous tension gave me away. I had to control the urge not to yank my hand from his. It didn't take long as I could barely feel the glass being picked out. If anything, it felt as though he just moved his hand over mine and the glass all came out at once. Like metal filings to a magnet, leaving me with a tingling on my skin.

"Are you alright?" I startled when I felt his breath brush my cheek, not registering where his large presence was standing once again. I nodded, biting my lip, thanks to what his close proximity was doing to my mental state.

"Good, now raise your arms for me." Okay, so if I was biting my lip before, now I was close to tearing the damn thing off!

"Wh…what?"

"I know you heard me, Keira," he said whilst fingers lightly peeled a strand of hair from my forehead.

"But… why?" my stunned voice stammered again, to which he merely responded with a short command,

"Now Keira." So with the voice of my boss turning hard, my arms shot upwards with little thought.

"Good girl, now place them firmly behind my neck while I lift you." I couldn't help the little sigh I released as a result of both the endearment and order I received.

He must have bent his head down for me to reach him, as my fingers grazed the cords of his tensed neck. I swallowed the hard lump in my throat, one I named 'this is crazy' and wrapped my arms tighter for a better hold. Once this happened, he lifted his head, momentarily taking my body with him as I clung on. I yelped at the sudden shift, but then his arms swept out and took my legs from beneath me.

"What happened?" I asked on a whisper, referring more to everything that had happened in the last hour.

"That was me saving your life," he simply stated.

"And now?" I asked as he started to walk with me tucked away safely to his chest.

"And now, I am going to clean you up."

"Clean me… you're going to…"

"Yes Keira, do you like being covered in blood?" he asked in a new voice that I was fast learning was Draven being amused.

"No, of course not," I said quickly, and I heard a quick short rumble of laughter.

"No, I thought not," he replied with a smile in his voice. I decided to remain quiet at this point so as not to embarrass myself any further.

I felt him walk just a few steps before I heard a door being opened. Then sadly, I felt myself being lowered from his arms, arms that I felt far too comfortable in. He positioned me so that my back was pulled in tightly to his front and I felt the hard rim of a sink at my belly.

Without saying a word his arms came around me to turn on the water and they remained that way, trapping me to his frame.

"Tell me, Keira, what is your full name?" His question caught me off guard and this wasn't helped when his hands circled my wrists. He pulled my hands from gripping the edge of the sink and plunged them into soothing heated water. Meanwhile, my mind went into full panic mode… did he know? God, I hoped not!

"My full name?" I asked trying to gauge his reaction.

"Yes Keira, your full name," he repeated directly in my ear, making it hard not to shudder, especially when his hands were scrubbing gently in between my fingers.

"Well you… um, you know my name," I tried to say more, but it was getting harder to think when he started rubbing our hands together now washing them as one.

"That might be true, but I'd like to hear you say it all the same," he insisted again, not moving his lips from my ear. I wondered where his mind was at with this question and I just prayed it wasn't anywhere near the truth.

"Keira… John… it's Keira Johnson," I said more forcefully the second time, after clearing my throat and his hands tightened their hold on top of mine for a moment.

"I see. Very well Keira Johnson, let's get you clean." He repeated my name like the lie it felt, and I was just happy that I was facing away from him and my eyes couldn't see what my lie did to him. I tried to keep my breathing even as his hands continued to wash away the night's horror from them. I just knew that if it hadn't been for the bloody water I imagined running off my skin, this would have been one of the most erotic moments of my life.

"I need to get to your injury now." His voice sounded thick, with some emotion I prayed to God to be shameless erotic

352

hunger. He lifted my hands from the water and gave them a little drip shake, which should have woken me from this mindless addiction. That was until his hands started to rip what was left of my vest top, exposing me to just my bra. His fast action wasn't enough to miss the feel of him brushing against my breasts, and I inhaled sharply.

"Easy now, I won't hurt you. I just needed it out of the way. Be brave for me a little longer, okay?" His fingertips danced little circles across my ribs in a soothing manner, and I nodded as my voice had left me. Well, that's not exactly true, it didn't leave me, more like it was put on lockdown. One so I didn't end up sighing his name on a carnal whisper.

"That's it, just relax into me and let me take care of you now." Oh my God! That one thought slammed into me thanks to his delicious words skimming across my skin, mirroring the very fingers belonging to my dream man.

"Yes." This one word slipped past my barrier and came out as I turned my head against the neck I found there. I felt a moment when his body grew tense at hearing this escaped word but then I relaxed back into him, causing him to do the same. I felt as though this was *our* moment. No dreams, no nightmares, no balconies and no social status between us. It felt like I had made a crack in the hard shell in which my Draven was locked deep inside. And I wanted just a moment, a second in time to stop the world spinning and hold on to this feeling.

And oh my God, didn't it just feel so freaking good!

Draven seemed to understand the moment of need as we both remained still, just breathing in sync, bringing us closer together with every fill of our lungs. I could swear I felt him whisper something into my neck, but its understanding was lost on me. Then things started to move along and if I felt good before, then now I really felt the fire!

His hands stretched across my skin so that he held as much of me as possible.

"Arms up, sweetheart." His words barely penetrated my euphoric state, and because of this he had to physically take control. He held my gloved arms, and lifted them up and back to hold on to him behind me. This new move caused my body to bow outwards, thrusting an already heaving chest further on display.

"By the Gods," I thought I heard him mutter, or it could have just been in the hope that he was feeling anything close to the Heaven I was rising to. His palms ran along my upstretched arms and then continued down the length of my body, brushing along my sides in a torturous way.

I decided right then that his hands were pure magic, that I was starting to seriously need over every inch of me. I could barely think, even as he started to use what must have been a cloth to wash me. All my mind would sing was the chorus of us being skin to skin. Anything else was mute at this beautiful point as I was now dependent on his touch to keep my body singing. Obsessions of the mind now being supercharged by obsessions of the body.

I don't know how long it lasted but I knew without question it was over far too soon. Hell, I could have died in his arms of old age and it still wouldn't have been long enough!

"You're all clean," he said, and was it my imagination that his voice now sounded strained and hoarse? I reluctantly lowered my arms, and not feeling the ache told me it definitely hadn't lasted long enough.

"Uh… thanks," I said shyly thanks to the aftermath of a hot as Holy Hell moment with my fantasy guy.

"You're welcome, Keira. Now turn around while I bandage you up." He had manoeuvred me further into the room, using his hands to guide me at my waist. He remained a constant strength around me and even now when he was once again sitting in front of me. Then he started wrapping strips of bandage around my waist and his hands worked with skill as if he had done this many times. I mean, who was this guy, a doctor in another life?

Once this was done, I let out a short squeal when I felt my body being lifted again and then swiftly carried back out of the bathroom. I tried to get my reactions to his touch to calm down now that our moment was over, but this was proving difficult when he kept sweeping me up and holding me impossibly close.

He moved me over to the side telling me to sit down, once letting go of my legs and allowing my body to slide slowly down the hard length of him. I did as I was told but I had the biggest urge to reach up and find his lips with my fingers, swiftly followed by my mouth. I wondered what he tasted like, how his tongue would feel duelling against my own in one of the most glorious battles between two people lost to lust.

But this was where that thought process took another turn, as now instead of pure sexual hunger powering my body, another essence filled my veins, making me feel strong. As in 'bitten by a radioactive spider' strong!

"What did you do? I feel… different."

"I gave you a drug to help heal you, so you will feel a little more… *energetic,*" he said with a smile in his voice.

"A little? I feel like I could take on the heavyweight champion!" I said still feeling the buzz of the drug.

"Well, you did beat the crap out of my tree, so I wouldn't put it past you," he said laughing. I had never heard him fully laugh and I wished I could have taken off my blindfold to see it.

"How did you…? Oh, forget it. There's nothing you don't know about, is there?" I said, letting my defences down and being completely honest.

"There are… *some things,*" he said with both concern and regret lacing his words.

"Do you need to call your sister to explain why you won't be home?" His voice felt closer to my face, as he trailed his fingertips down my cheek stopping at the tip of my chin. And once there he used his thumb to silently extract my bottom lip from my teeth. Teeth that found my bottom lip because of the question he had asked.

"No, there's no one home tonight, they won't be back until tomorrow… but why, what… do you mean I won't be home?"

"You need to rest before I let you go anywhere tonight," he said, before I could hear him doing something else but was at a loss to know what. I had to admit to myself how much I relished hearing him say this, and gave into the little chills of happiness assaulting me as a result.

"I feel fine now," I said so he didn't see me as weak.

"You say that a lot, don't you? Keira, you were just stabbed and nearly bled to death, I think the least you can do is sleep for a few hours." His voice held a hint of humour mixed with disbelief.

"But I ..." He cut me off saying,

"I'm just going to give you a shot and it will help..."

"No, don't!" I said putting my hand out to stop him. My hand had found his shoulder, and I could feel his soft skin over solid muscle twitch with the contact. Where was his shirt? I moved my hand slowly up toward his neck and could feel some material from what must have been a vest. This was the first time my skin had found this much of him, and I bit my lip at the feel of his strong frame under my fingertips. I couldn't help my actions as I traced them right up to his jawline.

His body had gone rigid under the feel of my touch but then after what seemed like minutes of us both being still, his hand grabbed mine pulling me closer to him. I could feel his face so close now, and like so many times before, I stopped breathing. I was now destroying my bottom lip again, with good reason, and I swallowed hard.

"Why are you so nervous, Keira?" His soft voice invaded my concentration and I couldn't answer at first. I just loved the sound of my name from his lips and right then wished he had said another name, one that was long forgotten and left behind. I finally shook my head slowly and lied,

"I'm... not nervous." But my broken voice proved otherwise.

"Then tell me, Keira, why are you biting your lip again?" he said in a smouldering voice that contradicted the sharp pain that shot in my arm. I knew then it had all been a ploy to inject me all along when I wasn't paying enough attention.

"Ouch, that wasn't fair!" I said pulling back and rubbing my arm.

"Would you have let me do it any other way?" He sounded amused and I didn't answer. The effects of the drugs were already making my head feel heavy and I tried to fight it by pulling the scarf from my eyes.

What I saw in front of me must have been from the drugs in my system as there was no other way to explain it.

Draven was glowing, and the vast space behind him was taken up with an impossible image…

Wings.

CHAPTER 30
THE FRIGHTENING TRUTH

I woke up surprised to find I wasn't in my own bed, and it took me a minute to remember what had happened. My head ached as I sat up in what was the biggest bed I had ever seen. I was covered in black satin covers and I seemed very high up, as though the bed was on a platform. I looked around and there were thick brocade curtains all around with a tiny amount of light coming through the cracks. It didn't take a PhD to realise that I was sat in an enormous four-poster bed and the curtains were drawn.

I sat there, afraid to move as the drugs had now worn off and I was fully awake. But then I felt down to my side which was still bandaged and there was no pain. I decided that I was going to get up, as I was stupid being scared. What was I afraid of? Draven had clearly saved my life.

I moved back the curtains, expecting someone to be behind them. I was faced with semi-darkness, lit only by a few candles and the moonlight that poured through glass doors opposite the bed. My eyes had already adapted to the light and I noticed that the bed was indeed on a higher section of the floor. It reminded me of the way Draven's table was in the club.

It had three steps around the platform, and I swung my legs over the side ready to get down. I stopped, checking I was alone before moving. The room was in shadows, showing furniture but not allowing the details to be seen. There was a candle lit on a small table that was closest to the bed. The candle illuminated a small space around it but stopped me from seeing further into the room. I stepped down off the bed and held on to the frame to steady myself. My legs felt like runny eggs and my muscles ached as though I had recently run a marathon.

I turned to look back at the bed where I had just been sleeping and was amazed to see it looked even bigger. It was a huge, wooden four-poster and the posts looked more like tree trunks, being massive carved spindles holding a wooden roof that looked as if it had been carved by Da Vinci himself!

From there, hung luxurious fabric that matched the gothic bedding. I pulled them back revealing more of the bed, which could in its own right, have been an American state.

I turned to the table and noticed a glass filled with the same liquid that Draven had made me drink, and there were two pills next to it. I picked up the paper that was next to them both and read the words that looked as though they had been written in calligraphy,

Keira, take these when you awaken.

And that was all it said. I decided that wouldn't be a good idea, so I left them there and walked further into the room. The room was long and from what I could see, which wasn't much, it was split into two sections. The first part was like a living room/office and the other was clearly a bedroom. From what I remember about it, it had been very grand, with old antique furniture. But my memory of what had happened was unsurprisingly vague. I had only really remembered the way I felt being so close to Draven. Or maybe that was all my mind chose to hang onto, and rightly so.

I took the clip out of my hair, letting it fall down in a mass of waves. It was still slightly damp and smelled of forest fruits, thanks to Libby's expensive shampoo. I rubbed my head where it ached from being slept on. I looked down, expecting to see blood-stained trousers but all I was wearing was my black underwear set. This certainly brought colour to my cheeks, not only knowing he had seen me like this but to know he had been the one to undress me.

Thankfully, I still had my gloves on, but I was still too exposed.

I examined the bandaged area expecting to find blood, but there wasn't any. Come to think of it, what had Draven actually done to it? I only remembered him placing his hand across it, but there had been no sealing of the wound, no anaesthetic, and certainly no stitches. So how had he stopped the bleeding?

And then I remembered something... What Draven had looked like when I had removed my blindfold. Draven had told me that I would see things, but I had never expected anything like that. It was strange to have seen Draven as anything but his usual perfection, so I had to keep telling myself it had to have been the drugs.

It was deadly still and silent in the room with only the flicker of the candlelight. Someone had removed my shoes before putting me in bed and only my socks remained. My heart started to skip a beat at the thought that it might have been Draven to once again carry me to a bed...

This time his bed.

I looked around and noticed something black and folded at the bottom of the bed. I discovered my black trousers, that had obviously been washed, and a woman's black T-shirt that I had never seen before. My first thought was that it was Sophia's, but either way, I was just glad the next time I faced Draven, I wouldn't be dressed in only my underwear.

My feet were soundless as I moved over the stone floor, making my way to the glass doors. There was no handle, and when my hand went out to push them, as soon as my fingertips touched the glass, the doors disappeared into the stone wall. I jumped at the sound and waited to gather my senses. But as I hesitated, they slowly crept their way back, concealing the entrance once again. Now I knew what to expect, I touched the glass again and walked through onto another huge balcony.

The balcony was very similar to the one outside the VIP,

only on a grander scale. It held the same marble pillars, but the difference was it didn't have marble balustrades in between. Instead, it had wrought iron railings in a black and gold design. Metal vines intertwined through the bars, with huge black roses and deadly, black claw-shaped thorns.

There were also two large trees up both sides of the doors in massive Japanese pots that reached my hips. My eyes took in the rest of the space and I noticed a staircase to one side. It looked as though it went up to the roof as it spiralled around a stone turret. This place was definitely more like a castle or a monastery than a house, or a nightclub for that matter!

I walked a few steps closer to the edge, and the full moon lit up the surrounding view of the forest. But as I stepped even closer, I noticed that we were higher up than I had first thought and the closer I got, the more I realised that we were hanging over a cliff face. The valley opened up like a crater below, as though the land had been struck by God himself. As soon as I realised the immense drop below, I stepped back, as I wasn't the best when it came to heights. Okay, correction, they terrified the living shit out of me!

I heard a noise behind me and automatically hid behind one of the trees. The noise came from the room and I was about to step out, but I stopped when I heard a voice I didn't recognise. I could barely see as I peeked around through the foliage, but I could hear a man's voice and it wasn't Draven's.

"Where is the girl?" the man's voice said.

"She was here a moment ago, I can still feel her, and the doors won't open for her. She couldn't have gone far," Sophia's voice answered the man, but it was different to how she normally sounded. Her voice was strained, as though angry or upset. I couldn't help but peek my head round to take a look but as soon as I did, I wished more than anything that I hadn't. What I saw was petrifying on a whole new level!

Sophia's face had changed into a monstrous sight, her skin was cracked as though made from hard desert sand under the hot blazing sun. It was grey and lifeless as though she was a living corpse. Her eyes were all milky white, like they had been burnt and she was now blind, but there was a black substance oozing from cracks in her eyelids. Her mouth looked like a pair of knives had slit it on either side, making it wider and more of the black liquid was holding it together.

I couldn't believe what I was seeing. My body was shaking and I held my hands over my mouth, locking my scream securely inside my body. My eyes filled with tears, as the fear overtook my mind. I pulled my head back out of sight, hiding from this horror. How could something so beautiful have turned into something that nightmares were bred from? I tried to stay quiet as I could still hear them in the room.

"My brother must be informed… go!" she snapped, and I heard the two separate doors close. I waited for any sound to be heard but the room was now empty. I peeked around again to confirm this, and my breath calmed slightly when it was clear. I was still clutching onto the tree like it was a lifeline.

This could not be happening. It just couldn't! Not Sophia, I just couldn't grasp onto reality. Maybe it was still the drugs in my system, as Draven had said it would have strange side effects. But deep down I knew the truth. After all, I had seen this type of thing most of my life, and what I had seen in Sophia was purely Demonic!

My Demons had come home.

I was just trying to compose myself when another fear threw me. I was missing in their eyes and they were trying to find me. The last thing Sophia had commanded, in true Draven style, was 'my brother must be informed', which meant something more terrifying than the sight I had just seen.

Draven would soon find me, and what if the last thing I had seen in him hadn't been down to the drugs?! Oh God, this couldn't be happening! I was still behind the tree with my mind racing on ideas on how to escape. Surely, I wasn't a prisoner? This whole thing had just been one huge mistake. Once again, a dreamlike experience with Draven had turned drastically into my own personal terror. I was about to go back into the room when something very dangerous caught my eye, now making this nightmare a very real one indeed.

The bird was back and flying past, gliding in the moonlit air as though it owned the night. And it too had changed, just like Sophia had. The bird's feathers had turned to solid black rock and the ends of them looked like rows of daggers. Its body was producing a flaming red energy that was moving like lava throughout its veins, leaving a slipstream of power in the sky.

I ducked as it flew over my head missing me by inches and I couldn't stop the little scream that erupted. I watched as it swooped down, landing on a smaller lower balcony and it made its usual ear-shattering screech into the night. I couldn't take my eyes off the bird as if it was drawing me in, which meant I saw what it wanted me to see. The cry was intended to alert its master, who had now walked into view.

Draven came out onto the balcony and approached the bird as though it was a pet of his. I hid yet again, and I watched as Draven extended his hand out to the bird and stroked his fingers down its hard body. But the bird no longer held my stunned gaze, as it wasn't the only one that had changed.

Draven looked as though possessed by something crawling around his body under the skin, making him glow a powerful deep purple colour. It was as if his veins were pumping it around every organ and therefore taking over. But even this wasn't the most striking difference. No, the real change was what followed behind him, following his every move as though very much a part of his body.

Draven indeed had wings.

I looked on, slowly getting closer as I tried to see more of what I couldn't explain. I could taste the same acid in my mouth as I always did when witnessing the impossible things that I saw, but this was like no other. It was terrifying as much as it was excruciatingly painful to witness.

The tears rolled down my cheeks, as I didn't want to believe my eyes… my cruel, cruel eyes. Why was this happening to me? What had I done to deserve repeatedly getting my dreams shattered in the most horrific ways? This wasn't reality! This was me… it had to be all me… I had to be the one making this happen… it had to be my own madness showing me all this…

Draven and his pet were no longer alone, as someone I couldn't see clearly approached. I knew then that my time in hiding was soon to be up as they must have told him about my disappearance. The person left as Draven's hand went up in what looked like fury. The bird was about to give me up as Draven's eyes followed the direction the bird's head moved to. They were now both looking directly at me and my first impulse kicked in, as my mind shouted one command…

Run!

I turned, and my legs found the staircase that led to the roof. I hadn't realised that the Heavens had opened, and it was now pouring down with rain making the stone floor slippery, and I struggled to keep upright. My body was wet through and my cold skin was fighting the urge to shiver. I didn't know what was happening behind me, but my shaking body wasn't about to stop to look.

The steps seemed to go on forever as they went around the wet stone wall that wasn't adding much support. My hands slipped from it again and again, but I kept going. My hair hung wet and limp around my waist clinging onto my skin as though it was also afraid. I finally made it to the top as it opened out in front of me. The large flat roof was surrounded by an impenetrable stone wall that looked as though it had trapped me in.

The moon was providing the only light, but the clouds that had filled the skies had dampened its power and my eyes tried to focus on any means of escape. After what seemed like a crushing eternity, they eventually found a door. My soaking feet slapped their way across the wet floor, and I ran until the pain in my chest grew tighter. Then I heard it, the sound of giant wings moving in the air above me.

I flung my body round to face the man who was controlling them. Draven was in the air, flying down with such speed that my eyes barely registered the sight. He landed hard, knelt on one knee, dark wings spread wide with his hands fisted to the ground beneath him.

The floor shook under me at the power and his head snapped

up to meet my frightened face. I saw the roof had cracked and crumbled under the pressure of his landing and it rippled out like veins. My head moved, looking towards the door then back at him, trying to judge the space between us. I thought that I could make it, but he must have thought differently, as he shook his head from side to side, telling me a clear no!

I looked one more time into those blazing eyes that seeped through the curtain of wet black hair covering part of his face. I swallowed hard, mentally counted to three, and turned to run for it but when I did, my body found his instead, blocking my way. I didn't know how he'd got to me so damn fast, but I knew my need to get away was now.

His face was so close, his purple eyes burned into me and the light coming from his skin reflected the water off my own. His dripping hair was as black as the stormy night above and it was now all pushed back behind his ears, making his face look even more serious. He looked at me as though he wanted to rattle me to death, and my reaction of terror showed in response.

I didn't wait for him to move, instead, I ducked under and around, surprising myself at my quick reactions. I gave every ounce of energy I had left, directing it to my legs and making them run towards the door, faster than I had ever moved before. The door came closer and I knew I was going to make it. I had to make it because this was it... I had nothing left in me!

I grabbed the door handle and prayed that it would open and when it did, I let out a premature breath of relief. Draven's hand then came out from behind me, slamming the wood back against its frame, making it shake under his extreme strength.

"Oh no you don't!" he said in controlled anger. I stared at the wood, unable to turn my eyes to him, but his voice again filled the night with a daunting order.

"Turn around and look at me!"

I turned with my head down, both hiding my tears and horrified face. However, this wasn't good enough for him,

"Keira, look at me. Now." His voice was softer, but it was still clear that this was not a request.

My head arched up to his face and my back pushed itself

against the door as my fear was too much and I needed the space between us. I wasn't safe and this was my instinct following through.

"Wha...what are... yyy...you?" I stammered, wishing I could replace my fear with anger. His hand came out towards me, and I screamed,

"DON'T TOUCH ME!" as I ran to one side trying to get past him.

There was a loud whoosh in the air as one of his wings came rushing forward from his body so fast, blocking my path with a wall of black feathers. I turned to escape the other side and he did the same thing, cocooning me in this small space with my back against the door. My heart felt as though it would burst through my rib cage and I panted to try and regain some control.

"Calm down and please... *do not try that again,*" he said, frustrated at my defiance. My face was wet, not only from the rain but mainly from the tears that were now flowing freely.

"What do you want with me?" I bravely asked.

"What I wanted was for you to have stayed asleep until the effects had worn off," he said remaining calm. This, however, had the opposite effect on me.

"EFFECTS! This isn't from any drugs, this... what I am seeing... is real!" I shouted as my hands motioned towards his body, which was fully exposed as he wore nothing but trousers. His defined chest and stomach showed the muscles of a bodybuilder, only made more by nature. Whatever Draven was, he was clearly different, and his body screamed out those differences in abundance. The veins housed the energy that flowed, showing purple under his skin. I realised that I had been wrong, he wasn't possessed... this was him. It had been all along!

"What are you?" I demanded, still holding on to my bravery as though it was the only thing keeping me alive.

"It's complicated and you are not ready."

"Complicated! Is that a joke? You're telling me it's complicated, and here you stand with bloody wings on your back and purple blood running through your veins! And all I get from you is 'It's complicated'!" I was shaking, I was so angry, and his purple eyes fed from my anger. His wings still held me captive, cutting off all the light from the moon making Draven the only light source in this dark situation.

"What do you want from me?!" he shouted back, scaring me, but it didn't show as I shouted back in return.

"The *truth* would be nice!"

"As I said, you're not ready," he said shaking his head, making the light move quicker under his skin fuelled by his emotion.

"Well, you have to give me something, because I'm *not* going to put this down to me being crazy... no! No way... not this time, Draven!" I spat out the words like venom.

"I'm afraid you have left me no choice in this, Keira." He said my name, and for the first time it made the reality seem all that more real. It was me that was here, it wasn't the dream part of me. This was real. This wasn't an illness sucking me under. A madness consuming my mind and warping a truth into horrors of the underworld.

This. Was. Real.

"Why... what are you going to do to me?" I asked as my voice clearly spelt the words panic.

"I would never hurt you, I have told you this, but you have to understand... *this*... this you have seen, it is not a good thing for either of us, and I have to resolve it before it gets any more out of hand and if I don't, trust me... *you* will get hurt!" His warning was as clear as the water that continued to fall from the sky. So, this was it, this was to be my end? Question was, was it to be by the hand of the man I was clearly falling in love with, or the Demon that faced me now? I couldn't help my response as I started to cry my despair.

He leaned in closer to me, placing a hand either side of my head on the door. His face came so close, I could feel the warmth from the energy that coursed through him. My body couldn't help but still yearn for him the way it had always done. I wanted him and no matter how scared I was, the yearning was still there... I needed him.

"Hush now, don't cry, little one." His mouth came to the level of mine so that the words were said over my quivering lips. Then he moved slightly to capture a falling tear in a kiss on my skin, tasting my fear for himself. His body was leant in, consuming the rest of the space between us, and closing his eyes, he inhaled deeply as though trying to take in my scent. He let out a groan and his eyes looked into mine with such intensity, I couldn't breathe.

"Keira, you just don't understand what it is you do to me. ¡Por Dios y el Diablo como mi testigo, ella será mía!" ('By God and the Devil as my witness, she will be mine!' In Spanish) he said with such passion, and my mind tried to translate the words, but it wouldn't work, it would only allow my senses to react to how he made me feel.

He looked me up and down as though he wanted to devour me with his touch, and my body trembled at the thought of his hands finding my wet skin. So, instead of trying to run, I did something very stupid. My hands moved up slowly, first to his wide strong shoulders, then they moved down his large biceps, feeling the raw power move under my hand.

I bit my lip ready for him to pull away from my touch but instead his eyes closed, and he looked as though he had to concentrate very hard not to react.

"Only you, Keira." He spoke in what sounded like pain, and his closed eyes tightened with the force of such pain.

"I… Draven." His eyes flashed open at hearing his name coming from my lips, and the intensity I saw there was soul-consuming. Then a hand cupped my jaw and he lowered his forehead to mine. I didn't know what he was or what he was going to do to me, but at that moment I saw it for what it truly was.

Heartbreakingly beautiful.

Then I broke the spell when my hand dropped at the noise behind us, waking me from this trance I was locked in. It seemed as though the bird had found us, and his face turned towards the sound, as if seeing it through his own wings.

"I'm sorry, Keira, but it is time," he said as if answering an unsaid question. I didn't like the sound of that, knowing that this would end. I wasn't ready to let go yet, so I stepped into him eliminating the last shred of space between us. I put my arms around him, pulling our bodies together and pressing myself up against him. He reacted in the way I hoped and held me tight, wrapping his strong arms around me. He took my breath away, and his wings wrapped around the both of us fully so all I could see was Draven's face. He looked down into my eyes and said,

"Goodbye, my sweet Keira, until it is our time." And then, before I could protest, his lips found mine, kissing me tenderly as his mouth opened, letting the air that had passed through him now enter me.

It whirled around my mind, making me feel dizzy. I tried so hard to focus on bringing myself back to this perfect moment, but I was falling into an abyss of darkness. It sucked me in until I couldn't feel my body anymore, until I couldn't feel Draven's body anymore and until the only thing I could feel was death…

Again.

CHAPTER 31

GOODBYE DRAVEN

Slowly my eyes opened as I regained consciousness. A blurry white light brought me round and I blinked a few times in order to gain focus. Certain things started to become clearer, and the first was the sight of a window seat with cushions askew.

Sitting bolt upright when too many things became familiar, I was confused at how I was now back in my own room. I jumped up and ran to the mirror on wobbly legs to examine myself. My clothes were all still intact, there was no ripped vest, no bloody trousers and even weirder, I had no bandages. I looked for a scar or a mark, anything to indicate what had happened last night, but there was nothing. I lifted my hand turning it over and over, but it too was just as clear as it had been the day before.

"No! It…it can't be!" I shook my head in disbelief. This was not happening! There was no way that what had happened last night was a dream. Not this time! However, there were still things that backed my theory. Okay, they were small, but they mattered. My black shirt and tie were missing. My hair was still damp and loose from running around in the rain. And most importantly, I could still smell Draven imprinted on my skin.

No, this was not a dream!

I begrudgingly had a shower, washing away the last traces of last night from my body, and after drying myself, I got dressed. I noticed it was 10:30am and I was due to start my next shift at twelve. It was when I had finished in the shower that I realised I was ravenous. I could have eaten a bloody horse and its rider! I went downstairs into the kitchen, and was about to shout out to Libby or Frank when I remembered that they weren't back yet. It made me wonder who had brought me home... or how for that matter. I ran to the window and my mouth dropped open as I saw my car sat there as if I had parked it myself.

Once I had raided the kitchen cupboards for anything I could get my hands on, I only had just enough time to get ready for work, and this was one day that I would be determined to speak to Draven about the truth!

It was as though my body and mind had hit a limit to how many different emotions I could feel all at once. The more I replayed the night's events over and over in my head, there was no doubt in my mind that it had happened. He must have brought me back here and tried to cover up last night, hoping I would just put it all down to a bloody dream. Well, this time he wasn't getting away with it. I would demand the truth.

Hell, I wouldn't leave until I got an explanation, and not just for last night. No, now after what I had witnessed, it only convinced me more that none of them had been dreams. Something was going on here and I had a right to know. Draven had been coming into my room at night, of this I now had no doubts left. All that was left were the reasons why.

As soon as I stormed into the club, I got a weird sense that it didn't want me there anymore. As though the pull it once had over me had been put into reverse, making me feel unsure and unwelcome. It was strange to see the club this way, like a deserted old Wild West town that had lost its sheriff. There was no security at the stairs like there usually was and it was deadly silent.

I took a deep breath and made for the main staircase, trying to retain my annoyed state. I would not let him intimidate me, not this time! Once upstairs, I noticed that most of it was now empty with only one waitress, Rue, and with about five tables occupied. Draven's table wasn't one of them. I walked over to the bar where Karmun, as always, was working. He noticed me, and for a split second I thought I saw a nervous glint in his eyes. But it was quickly replaced with an even friendlier smile than I normally received.

"Hey Keira, I think you're needed mainly downstairs today," he said as he was wiping down the bar with a wet cloth.

"Karmun, did you see what happened last night?" I said, coming straight out with it. He looked uncomfortable again and I knew the answer, but he remained calm in his reply.

"Umm… I'm sorry, Keira, I'm not allowed to talk about it," he said, trying to palm me off with the no gossip rule, but I wasn't having any of it.

"And why not? Considering it had something to do with me, I think I'm entitled to the facts!" I said, getting irate quicker than I thought I would. He held up his hands, about to say something else, when I gave up saying,

"Okay then, fine, I want to speak to Draven about it!" I couldn't believe where all this bravery was coming from, but I just hoped it lasted until I was in front of the man himself.

"Are you sure that's a good idea?"

"It's a damn good idea considering I think it's the only way that I will get the answers that I am looking for," I snapped holding my head high.

"As you wish… I will tell him. Why don't you wait on the balcony for him to arrive?" he said, probably shocked at anyone demanding such a thing. I nodded in return and stamped angrily out on to the balcony. Being back here brought back a flood of memories from last night. What was it with this place and balconies anyway? Everything seemed to happen on them.

The cool air nipped at my skin as I pulled my long black jacket closer to my neck, zipping it up the whole way. It was the one with a big hood and also had a big neck which acted like a scarf. The thought of a scarf also brought me back to last night, before things had turned darker and more surreal. I let my mind drift in and out of last night's events, so when Draven finally did arrive, I wasn't as prepared as I had been.

"Keira, you wanted to see me?" He said the words in a hard tone, and my pulse went up a couple of notches, as usual. He stood back from me, unlike all the other times we had been brought together. Now though, it was clearly going to be different as his face said as much.

He was wearing black trousers with a black suit jacket, only underneath he wore a more casual faded grey T-shirt that once again showed his washboard stomach, one that I had seen so intimately last night. However, this more casual look didn't reflect his mood.

"Yes... I wanted to talk to you about last night," I said trying to remain strong, only he didn't even look bothered that I wanted to speak to him. It must have been an act surely?

"Ah yes, well, it was an unfortunate accident and I'm glad to see you're feeling better after your fall," he replied, changing back to his usual 'boss' routine.

"What fall?" I asked shaking my head, feeling the warmth invade my cheeks.

"You must not remember. Well, that's understandable, you went out like a light. I do apologise for what happened and I assure you, I do not tolerate fighting in my club. But well, this is what is expected when drugs are involved. Trust me when I say the matter has been dealt with." *Trust him?* How could I ever trust this man who now stood in front of me? I didn't even know him! He was cold, and my heart froze from its bitter aftershock. This wasn't Draven... This wasn't my Draven! The anger came back, building up inside of me like a firecracker ready to burst.

"That's...That's bullshit! Don't lie to me!" I shouted feeling myself shake with emotion.

"Excuse me?" His voice sounded shocked and also very pissed, but I no longer cared! So, I carried on,

"That didn't happen... Goddamn it, I didn't fall!" I yelled the words, and his cold heart reflected in his expression, looking at me as though I was no one… I was back to being *a no one.* Well, I don't think so, I wasn't having it!

"And what is it that you believe to have happened exactly?" He crossed his arms, making his scepticism all the clearer. So, I did it. I did what I had come here to do, and I wasn't about to back down now. I didn't care how much my mind screamed no, I wasn't going to lose this fight.

"Fine, play it like that! We both know what happened last night, but considering you're playing it down as though it was nothing but a 'bump to the head' then you go ahead and do that! But I will never, and I repeat *never* believe that, and no matter how much you try to trick me… I'm here telling you now, it won't work!" I said, and the tears welled up but didn't betray me as they stayed firmly in place. I had to tense my fists when I said this so as not to shake with hurt.

He stood glaring, his black eyes holding no shred of the passion that I had seen flow so freely last night.

Then the doors opened and the beautiful redhead who sat at his table glided in. She stopped next to him, and there was something different about her that I hadn't seen before. But no matter what I braced myself for, what I saw next would crush my heart and every hope I had ever foolishly allowed myself to feel.

She curled her body into him, and his arms embraced her, returning the affection. She then looked at me as though I had been made of invisible matter.

"Oh, you must be Keira, the waitress who got knocked down due to the fight, how's your head feeling today?" she said in a voice that sang with the same beauty that radiated off her. I had to use every last breath in my body to answer without showing the tears that just wanted to run freely out of my fragile body.

"I'm fine, thank you," I said, and Draven for some reason, probably in disgust, turned his face away.

"That's good. Well, I'm sorry Dominic, I will leave you to finish and trouble you with wedding plans later." As she spoke those cruel words, I was sure you could actually hear the sound of my heart being ripped apart. I wanted to look away. Hell, I wanted to run and never look back, but I was trapped like a bird in a glass room. I was being blinded by the light and couldn't find my way out of my own personal cage of nightmares.

She lifted herself to the height of his face and kissed him. This was enough to unleash the tears from my eyes, leaving behind a salty road for others to follow. I looked away and wiped them off my skin in vain.

I didn't notice when she left, but to be honest my mind was a blur, consumed with the pain of self-pity. I just want to drown in it.

"I'm sorry, that was rude. I didn't introduce you to my fiancée. That was Celina," he said still holding on to his unemotional countenance, and I had lost all of mine. I couldn't speak, fearing what I would say in reply. Then, when I thought the pain couldn't get any worse than knowing he was getting married to one of the most perfect creatures this world had ever seen... he spoke.

"I understand there has been a misjudged account of affections that do not exist. Perhaps this was partly my doing as well, as a young overactive imagination can sometimes twist the truth. In light of your clear feelings, I would think it best for you if you no longer work up here in the VIP." He finished this sentence, thus sealing my fate into a pit of misery. He could see the tears, and yet his arrogance was still stronger than ever. We were miles apart, and the difference was that he didn't care and all the time I was fighting my way to get back.

"Right... you're right, clearly... what a stupid mistake to have made!" I said this out loud not realising, as nothing made sense, but nothing ever does when you're lost.

"I think you're a hard worker and..."

"Stop, just stop!"

"Keira, I..." He said my name and even though this time it was softer, I had already lost it. So, I interrupted him with my final decision.

"I quit." I heard him sigh and utter something I didn't catch under his breath.

"There is no need for you to quit."

"Oh, I think there are more than enough reasons for me to quit... don't you?" I shot back, making him frown.

"No, I don't. Not considering I know how much it will upset my sister."

"*Sophia.*" I uttered her name under my breath, forgetting how she would feel about all this. It didn't matter to me how I had seen her last night, all I could think about was the friend I had made and didn't want to lose.

"She thinks very highly of your friendship and has been good to you, are you really willing to repay her kindness by quitting because of unreciprocated feelings?" This felt like an arrow to the heart, and he saw me wince when he delivered the final blow.

"*Don't...!* Just don't." After everything that had happened between us, I couldn't stand here and continue to listen to his lies.

"*Fine.* I will continue downstairs for Sophia's sake, but only until I have paid off this car..."

"Keira, that's not necessary," Draven said, but I held up my hand and then spat with venom,

"Oh, but it is as I want *nothing* from you!" This time, he winced, but I carried on.

"Don't worry I will never be stupid enough to set foot up here again or be foolish to show any of my *young overactive imagination* towards you ever again. I can promise you that!" I said as my last attempt at saving my face. When I said this, there was the first tiniest bit of emotion I saw in his soulless eyes, but I looked away from it, knowing that if I saw anything that would give me hope, I would fight for him...and clearly it was a one-sided battle. One I could never win.

I walked past him to the door, and something made me stop. I turned to face his back, as his eyes did not follow, and swallowed back the sob, saving it for when I was out of this Hell!

"Oh, and congratulations... *My Lord!*" I managed to say before my voice completely broke down.

"Keira, wait, I just…" I heard behind me, but I didn't wait around to hear the rest. Just being in the same space with him was torturous enough. So, these were the last words I heard before I ran from the balcony, down the stairs, out of the building and across the car park, as fast as my legs could carry me.

Once I got to my truck, I couldn't even wait until I was in the safety of its metal frame. My body sank against it and I cried till every part of me hurt. I don't even remember getting into my car or stupidly starting the engine. But my body's need to feel safe again was greater than the risks. I could barely even see the road ahead but somehow, as if another body had taken hold of me, it made me drive. I didn't even feel like I was moving, as my body was numb. I should have been shaking uncontrollably but my limbs just kept going until I reached my home.

Once in the drive, my possessed hand cut the engine and then that was it, I was back to me again and it hurt all over. My body convulsed and I sobbed so much that I couldn't breathe. I gasped for the air in hiccups to fill my lungs, but it was proving hard as the tears wouldn't let up, and trying to do both was difficult.

I don't know how long I sat there, but the pain continued to overwhelm every part of me, and I only realised it must have been hours as it was now dark. Luckily, Libby and Frank had still not come back, and I finally gathered my senses long enough to make it into the house. I noticed there were two messages on the machine and I reluctantly pressed play.

"Hey Kazzy, hope you're having fun with the house all to yourself as me and Frank are staying another night. Be back tomorrow around noon, love you!" Libby's happy voice filled the air and tears rolled out of my tired, sore eyes as the word 'fun' had been painful to hear. The other message made it ten times worse, as it was Jerry confirming my new shifts and how Draven had spoken to him telling him that I wasn't needed today, and wouldn't be for a few days, so I was to start back on Wednesday. This had me falling to my knees in a crumpled pile on the floor, and I cried so hard that I must have passed out.

I definitely exhausted myself as the next time I woke, dawn was breaking outside. So, I dragged my heartbroken body to my bedroom and I fell into bed, covering my head, never wanting to see the light of day. I wanted to stay in my safe little cocoon where no one could ever hurt me again.

How could I have let this happen? How could I have allowed myself to believe such things? Draven had never wanted me. He had never cared, and all those nights that it had seemed as if he did were all a terrible lie my mind had created. I had seen things that weren't there. I was swept away by a man who had never really existed, and the result of my mistake was the broken shell of who I was.

My mind had deceived me.

I sat up, not being able to sleep, even though I was utterly drained. I wished that I could have just got in my car and kept driving until I came to an end. That end being when the hurting inside finally stopped. Coming here had been a big mistake. I was stupid to believe I could ever have belonged here! I didn't belong anywhere. I just left an aftermath of destruction in my path... I was poison!

In the end, I rang RJ telling her I wasn't feeling good and that if I felt better then I might make it in later for History. She had asked what was wrong and with the sound of my broken voice I got away with telling her it was the flu. Of course, after looking at myself in the mirror, my voice wasn't the only evidence of it. I had no colour to my skin, only the red blotches that remained around my eyes making it look as if I had lost the fight. Which was right in more ways than one.

My eyes were the scariest thing as they had no whites left, having been replaced by bloodshot lines. My nose hurt around the edges from being rubbed so frequently that not much skin was left there. My lips were cracked through the constant biting, making them bleed. This was so that some of my pain was directed to the outside of my body, therefore relieving some from the inside.

In the end I couldn't face college, as seeing Sophia again was going to be too much to bear. The wound that Draven had inflicted was still too fresh and exposed. I finally got out of bed and dressed, only without looking at the clock I had no idea how long I had just sat there thinking about what a fool I was.

Once I was dressed, things started to get clearer, and I needed to make a change to get past this. After all, I had come back from worse than this, hadn't I? It didn't feel like it. I might have the scars from my past that showed on the outside, but Draven had also left his scars, and they ran deep inside to my core.

So, what was worse...? I knew the answer to that question.

I pulled on my father's old college football sweater and grabbed two things before leaving. One was my car keys, and the other was the picture I had drawn of Draven.

I got in my car, driving faster than I should have been. I let the sound of the engine drown out most of my self-pitying thoughts. Jack had told me about a place and I drove in the direction that, thankfully, was far from Afterlife. That name... was that what it meant? That Draven would steal my heart and my soul, and this was to be my Afterlife?

Thinking about the pain didn't bring tears anymore, as if there was nothing left in me. He had taken everything, and all I could do was try and resurrect myself to how I was before I had ever seen him. I had to be re-born and there was only one way I knew how to do this, and it was going to be hard. A lot harder than last time...

I found the dirt road after the warning signs for cliff faces, and I knew where this would lead me to. I thought of Jack for a moment, wondering how this would have all gone if I had seen him first and he had been the one in my dreams.

The road came to an end in a big semi-circle where the cars usually parked. I turned off the engine and got out. The cold hit me, and the wind whipped around my face as I realised how high up I was. The cold was a good thing.

It kept things clearer and I had my goal firmly set in my mind. As scared as I was of the drop below me, I walked to the edge. After all, what did I have to fear anymore when they had all come true in my life? One after another I had been used and thrown away when I was no longer needed... but this time I would change it all. I would never go back to that... *never!* And this was my proof, no matter how small an action it seemed.

The trees swayed around the forest and I knew this was a perfect place to finish this obsession once and for all.

I pulled the picture of Draven out of my back pocket and sat down crossing my legs, getting close enough to the edge to be able to get rid of the problem. I took one long hard look at the pencilled sketch, knowing that I had already seen the last of its original. So now my re-birth would begin by getting rid of every last bit of him, including any of my thoughts about him.

I had the mental capability to cast my Demons from my mind by drawing them, locking them into the page, thus banishing them from entering my mind again. But I had always kept the pictures and I never really understood why I did this. So, it got me thinking, maybe the only way to get him out of my mind completely was to remove him from my memory.

With this in mind, I kissed my hand, placing it gently on his face. Then, before I could back out, I began tearing into it with so much fiery passion, that before long it was in tiny pieces in my hands. Then I waited for the reason I had come here.

I closed my eyes and held myself still, trying to judge the air around me, feeling it coming closer. As I couldn't help but think, that if this helped once before, then maybe I would have a chance. Even if it just got a little better, then that could be enough to get me through this, making the most horrific pain I had ever felt turn into a mind-numbing existence. So, I sat waiting patiently for the exact moment when it felt right to let go of him forever.

It came over me, blowing my hair up around my head and I lifted my hands, opening my palms, feeling the pain being taken away with the pieces I had left of Draven. They blew upwards, carried into the sky where they belonged... *where he belonged.*

I watched as they blew into the green abyss of the forest and my eyes strained as I waited until every last piece was out of sight.

Now, I could move on and finally…

Say goodbye.

CHAPTER 32
GRASPING REALITY

After that day, I did get slightly better as I pulled myself together and carried on. The pain never fully went away. Instead, it was replaced with a dull ache, as my mind was usually numb. But I went on with my life as you have to. Sophia never returned to History. I didn't even know whether she dropped out or was ill, but it seemed too much of a coincidence that she disappeared from college life.

No one was allowed to talk about it and the only one who had been nice to me from the beginning was Jerry. But even this, I think, was staged. I completed my shifts like a machine being controlled by the need more than the want part of me. But the more and more I worked, the less painful it got being there. Then even the others started talking to me again and Mike and I were once again friends. We even flirted with each other on occasion. I finally started to relax.

Nothing happened again, there were no more nice dreams that included him. However, my dreams didn't just stop. No, instead they had taken on a darker turn. I decided that after the fourth time of waking up in the house screaming, I would finally give in and see a counsellor.

I had made my appointment with a Doctor Goff and I was now sat in a waiting room with peach walls and crappy pictures of summer flowers in pots and a little girl playing happily with

382

her dog. If this was supposed to have a calming effect, then it most certainly didn't work. After my nightmares, I had seemed to have taken a gloomier approach to life and I tried desperately to control it. I found nothing fun or good in anything anymore, and it was starting to scare me.

The only peace I would find was whenever I went back to the cliff face. I would sit there for hours looking out to the view, thinking about where it all went wrong. I knew this wasn't the best way to think and that everything happened for a reason but when your heart is torn, and your body broken, it is very easy to hate that logic.

The woman behind the desk looked over her thick-rimmed glasses and spoke out my name in a squeaky voice.

"You may go in now."

I walked into a room that had been furnished to try and give a homely feel. As though trying not to intimidate you or make you feel even more uncomfortable about the reasons that had obviously brought you here in the first place. The room had a big couch and a smaller armchair next to it. There was shelving around the room with different 'Self Help' books and a few family photos.

Doctor Goff was a middle-aged man with a full beard that had a mixture of ginger and grey bits in it. He wore small glasses and looked like every other shrink I had ever seen. It was as if when they started to develop into adults, people would turn to them saying 'You know you kind of look like a therapist or a doctor,' and they would reply 'Okay, then that's what I will do'.

He motioned for me to sit, as he himself was sat behind his desk, which held a laptop and piles of paperwork. He didn't look very organised for a professional person.

"Miss Johnson, I am pleased to meet you, sorry for your long wait but I have found it difficult finding any of your medical history. Where did you say you were from?" he said as he stroked his bushy beard.

"This is the deal, Doc. I don't want anyone to know my background as I left it behind me where I want it to stay. I don't want to bring all my old problems into this because that's not why I am here," I said, getting all that I had rehearsed out of the way before I forgot. Shrinks had a crafty way of getting information out of you and I knew if I didn't set the ground rules straight away, then I could slip up.

"Then why are you here?" he asked in a non-aggressive tone.

"I'm here because I can't sleep and when I do sleep, I wake up screaming for help from my nightmares," I said not taking a breath.

"Help from whom?"

"Sorry?" I said, wondering why he asked me that.

"You said you cry for help, I was just wondering who from?" Again, this question I didn't really understand, and I wasn't about to tell him who exactly I was crying out for. So, I lied and said,

"My sister, or anyone really." He raised an eyebrow as if he didn't believe me but carried on without questioning it.

"Why don't you start by telling me about the dream?"

"Okay well… I'm at a club and I'm about to start my shift, as I work there you see…" I was stalling, and I didn't know why but his eyes had turned very dark and intense making me not want to speak any further.

"Go on… what happens at this club?" he urged.

"Well, I go into the back room where I always put my bag and jacket. There's this gilded mirror and I always give myself a once over before starting my shift," I said, stopping, but his face got more intense and his hand lifted, motioning for me to continue. So, I took a deep breath and explained the rest.

"I'm looking at my face in the mirror and I see someone else instead staring back."

"Who?" he asked, and I repeated the same question back at him.

"Who?

"Yes, who is staring back at you?" he asked, and I didn't want to say.

"Just some guy, but anyway…" He stopped me again.

"Just some guy? Someone you know or someone you work with *or for?*" he asked, and I froze as he hit the nail on the head with the last one.

"My boss... so anyway... I turn around quickly to find the room is empty and the door is still closed. So, I turn back to face the mirror and it's me again. Only something is different and very wrong as I don't look the same. I have my hair down which I never do, and I'm wearing different clothes."

"Do you recognise your other self from a different time?" he said, looking over his glasses as if to judge my reaction to the question. I wondered if he knew I was lying when I replied,

"No."

"Alright, then please continue," he said as he wrote down some more notes in a red leather-bound book.

"So, the girl... well I mean me... she is staring back at me with hate in her eyes and I'm always so scared to look at her. I move my face away but then I hear a tapping on the glass, so I look back to find a broken piece of the mirror in her hand." I almost shuddered thinking back to how haunting the image always was to find.

"I see, and it's from the mirror you're looking into?" he asked, and I nodded.

"It's a long piece that's thicker where she holds it and it goes down into a deadly point that she is using to get my attention. I freeze to the spot and scream 'What do you want?' She then mouths the word 'DIE' to me, and her arm comes out of the mirror and slashes at my arms over and over, cutting my wrists so that when I look down I am covered in blood again and screaming. That's when I wake up." And there it was. Of course, I knew what the dream was about and didn't need any doctor telling me his theory of interpretation. All I needed were the pills.

"Ah," he said looking at my arms, finding nothing but my sweater's sleeves.

"Any suicide attempts before?" he asked bluntly, and I coughed, as I couldn't believe what he had just asked. Weren't doctors supposed to be delicate about this type of thing?

"No!" I shouted as I was now clearly upset.

"I'm sorry, did that bother you?"

"No, but it took me by surprise."

"Sorry, but I have to be sure, and considering I don't have any records on your medical background, I'm in the dark here. So, you said about seeing the blood on your arms *again,* what do you think that was referring to?" Ah, so that's why he had asked. I had slipped up when telling my story, damn it.

"I don't know, I must have just made a mistake that's all."

"Of course. So, you said you can't sleep. Has anything traumatic or emotional happened recently?" His eyes looked deep into me as if trying to hook out the lies that he knew were coming from me.

"No, I have a lot on at college and I work nights, so maybe I'm just wired from it all, but I need to get some sleep," I said rubbing my tired eyes, hoping this was enough to convince him.

"Okay, so you said you work nights, is this at the club in your dreams?"

"Yes, but that really doesn't have anything to do with it," I said, getting defensive and he knew it, so he decided to keep pushing for it.

"You also mentioned your boss in the dream. Do you have feelings for him?" Oh, come on! Now he wanted to know about my non-existent sex life.

"He's my boss," I said, trying to state the obvious.

"Yes, but things can still happen between an employer and an employee."

"Yes, I know, but nothing happened." I was so close to caving that I could feel the tears coming back for the first time in weeks.

"Umm... I'm not so sure. You say that nothing has happened but whenever I mention the idea, you look upset... I'm here to listen, Keira, so please give me that chance." And that was it, the way he said my name reminded me of Draven so much that I could have sworn I was talking to the man himself. A tear rolled down my cheek and I said the words I didn't want to admit.

"Fine, you want the truth then here it is... I fell for my boss and I stupidly mistook that he had some feelings for me too, but I was cruelly exposed to reality and as a result, I am trying my hardest to get over it," I said, and I wiped the tears from my face with the tissue he had handed to me.

"Right well… in that case I will prescribe you with some Benzodiazepines which will help you relax, but this is for a short time only. I don't want you becoming dependant on these, and I want you to come and see me once a week for four more sessions, then we will take it from there," he said, looking strangely sad from my little outburst.

I got up, happy that my time was over. He handed me the prescription and shook my hand giving me a weird feeling when I came into contact with his skin. It was like a familiar memory that I couldn't quite remember.

After meeting with the doctor, I knew that I wouldn't be returning for a second visit. He was very good at analysing my dreams and I knew it wouldn't be long before he got me telling him my sad and gruelling past. Most doctors had a way of digging for the truth, as they believed that to face our problems head-on was the only way to deal with them. I had already faced 'my problem' head-on before, and I was not about to do it ever again.

Libby had told Frank the good news about her being pregnant after a scan confirmed what she already knew. Frank had gone crazy with happiness, telling everybody he knew and even some he didn't. As soon as the phone went, even salespeople would hear all about it. So, unless they were selling baby cribs and strollers, as they call them here, then most of the time they would be the ones to end the call. I had been there when Libby had told our mother, and she had cried so much she'd had to put my dad on the phone.

These were the reasons that I hadn't told Libby or Frank about what had happened at the club, or about me seeing any doctor. They just carried on believing that I was still working in the VIP area and they had not seen any change in me. And I wanted to keep it that way. This wasn't too difficult as sometimes people become so absorbed in their own happiness, that they fail to see the truth behind a lie. It wasn't that I thought they wouldn't understand but I had felt so guilty from the last time I was broken, that I never wanted anyone to look at me like that again.

I lied to those who I couldn't hide it from, like RJ and Jack, because they were going to see me working downstairs in the club. I told them that they didn't need me anymore, as the girl who I replaced was now back. This of course wasn't a complete lie as they didn't need me anymore... well painfully more like *he* didn't need me anymore.

Jack had been great, a true friend, whereas RJ didn't let it drop for a while, as every time I saw her she would bring it up. Jack thankfully intervened one night when we were at the club and my shift had finished.

"RJ, give it a rest. Can't you see she's sick of talking about it?" he said fighting my corner.

"Well, I just don't get it!"

"No surprise there!" Jack said being sarcastic. RJ hooked out an ice cube from her glass and threw it in his direction, only it missed him and hit some poor girl that was innocently walking past. The girl turned to see who had been the culprit and RJ pointed to Jack keeping a straight face.

As soon as the girl saw Jack's handsome, Brad Pitt look, she smiled as if throwing an ice cube at her was a good thing. I couldn't help but laugh. I mean, okay it was cute when you were about ten. A boy that fancied you would then throw stuff to get your attention, but in your twenties, it was a bit pathetic.

"Hey bro, I think you're in there, why don't you ask her to the Halloween Gig?" she said not even lowering her voice. The Halloween Gig was held here at the club, when lots of bands were going to compete. It was a huge night that happened each year and the Goth scene loved it.

"Yeah thanks, but I will pass, Butt Munch!" he said playfully. They were just so different you forgot that they were even related. I left early that night, but Jack walked me to my car. I was so relaxed around him that it didn't seem out of character when he would flirt.

Consequently, when he put his arm around me as we walked out of the club, I didn't give it much thought to why people were staring. I guess we looked like a couple but because I had made it clear on my 'no dating' rule, Jack hadn't asked me out again. I just gathered he had got the message. So, when he stopped me from getting in my car, I was confused.

"Keira, I've been meaning to ask you something, but well, I guess that you were going through a tough time regarding why you left the VIP... not that I want to pry," he said, and I realised he knew the reason I had given had been a lie. Was Jack the only one that really knew me?

"It's none of my business and I get why you wouldn't want to talk about it... trust me, I know how it feels... more than you think." He said this with sadness in his eyes and I knew that his feelings ran deeper than I realised. He was talking about what happened at the club.

"Jack, you know if you ever want to talk then I'm here, okay? I too don't want to pry either but if you ever need anyone, then I'm a better listener than a talker." We both laughed lightly trying to change the glum mood.

"I know. You're a good friend but I..." He wanted to continue but he couldn't find the words which I now understood he wanted to say. So, I did something so out of character, that I shocked myself when the question came out.

"Jack, will you go to the Halloween Gig with me?" His face dropped in amazement, as if this was the last thing he had been expecting.

"You want to go with me?" he said, checking he had heard it right.

"Yeah, but hey, I understand if you are going with someone else," I said, now worrying that I had it all wrong.

"Hell no, I was going to ask you all along, but I've been waiting for the right time," he said with the biggest smile across his face.

"But hey, won't you be working?"

"No, I have been given the night off so I'm free as a bird." And this was true, for some strange reason, creepy Gary had told me that I wasn't needed, even though it was going to be one of the busiest nights of the year! I didn't understand it, but I wasn't going to argue, although I did double check it with his brother, Jerry, just in case.

"So, you will be my bird for the night?" he teased, going back to his usual flirty ways. I smirked at him.

"Yeah, Jack, I will be your free bird for the night," I teased back, granting myself a gorgeous smile from one handsome Jack.

I left the car park after arranging times for Saturday night's date with mixed feelings. Was that the best idea, going on a date with Jack? I mean, of course I liked him, who in their right mind wouldn't? But I couldn't help the fear that I was betraying my own feelings. I clearly was not over Draven, but thinking about it, would I ever be?

Of course, that didn't mean I had to live my life as a nun! I had to move on, especially as I was now sleeping again and wasn't living my life as a zombie.

By the time I got home I decided that what I had done was for the best. I needed to live my life, not shy away from it. I would now embrace every opportunity, and tomorrow night would be my first show of this; one thing was for sure, I was going to dress for the occasion! I was going to knock Jack's socks off… well at least try.

When I got in, I was glad when I saw Libby was still awake, because there was something important I needed her help with, and this was one request that I knew she would most definitely enjoy.

"Hey Libs, I've got a huge favour to ask." She raised her head round from leaning it against Frank as they were watching some action movie. I think she had even fallen asleep.

"Yeah, what's up?"

"Well, don't go all weird or anything but I kind of have a date tomorrow night and well, I need help with a costume." As soon as I said the magic word "date" she was now wide awake, and even Frank was looking at me and leaving Van Damme to his kickboxing.

"Oh, yeah definitely, of course I will but I have to ask… who with?" she said as she was out of her seat coming to face me.

"It's Jack."

"But I thought you'd been turning him down ever since you got here?"

"Well yeah, but I sort of asked him." She and Frank shot each other a look as if they thought I had been taken over by pod people.

"Okay... umm... so one other thing, what are you going as?" she said, trying to keep the grin to a minimum.

"It's kind of just the usual Gothic theme," I said as she followed me into the kitchen. But as soon as I had said the words, she had clapped her hands, scaring me into looking back at her.

"Is that a good thing?" I asked, and I could almost see the cogs turning in her head.

"Oh yeah, I have just the outfit, but I think I will need to change a few things," she said, but I wasn't even sure if she was talking to me or herself.

"Why, what are you thinking?" I asked, hoping I wouldn't regret it this time tomorrow night.

"Well... I have this old costume from when Frank and I went to this fancy-dress party last year, it was a medieval theme, and I have this black and purple dress with a corset top." Forget about tomorrow night, I was regretting it now!

"Oh no, no corsets!"

"Oh, come on, you will look great, plus if you dress the way you always do that's not the point of Halloween."

"And what is, exactly?" I asked with my arms folded.

"It's the one night that you can get away with being someone else. It wouldn't be you dressing up... it will be the Halloween you."

"That makes absolutely no sense, you know that... right?" She shook her head at me.

"Look, what do you think other people will be wearing? You hate standing out, right? And I can guarantee that if you don't dress up as a sexy Goth then you will be the only one who doesn't... hence *Kazzy standing out.*" What she said in a crazy way made sense. So, I gave in and agreed. She had free rein to do whatever she wanted. Which I found out also included makeup and hair. I knew I was making a categorical mistake, but she was just so happy with the idea of playing 'dress up' that I couldn't crush her enthusiasm. So, with that I kissed her goodnight and went to bed.

∾

The next day all hands were on deck as far as Libby was concerned. She started with bringing me tea in the morning, waking me up a lot earlier than I would have liked. She marched me into the bathroom and ordered me to shower. When I started to complain that I was hungry she passed me the soap and said,

"Here eat this," and closed the door, leaving me to shower. Once I was inside the cubicle, I heard a tapping at the door and had to turn off the water to hear who it was.

"What?" I said shouting through the glass and bathroom door.

"Use the stuff I put in there for you," Libby shouted back through the wooden door, as I shivered now the hot water had stopped warming my skin.

"Okay!" I shouted back and continued to shower with the new products that smelled like passion fruit and felt like cream covering my body. It had little seeds in it that exfoliated my skin, making it feel soft when I got out and dried myself.

Libby dried my hair while I sat there and ate breakfast, and Frank came in grabbing a can from the fridge.

"Having fun ladies?" I tried to turn to say something sarcastic, but Libby pulled my head back around with my hair and I complained.

"Oww…! God, Libs, don't go into the beauty business, will you?"

"And why not?" she asked, hands on hips, brush still in hand.

"Because I don't want you to get sued!"

"Shut up!" she said in a playful manner that made me smile.

Once she'd finished drying my hair, she put it in huge curlers until I looked as if I could pick up a radio station.

"What are these for...? I'm not wearing my hair down."

"I know, but when I put it up, I want the ends curly, anyway don't you trust me?"

My answer in my head wasn't the one I gave.

"Of course, I do but..."

"No 'buts', leave a master to work please," she said, waving the comb round as if it was her magic wand.

After my hair was done I was allowed to leave the torture chamber, which was better known as the kitchen, and do what I wanted while she worked on my Gothic attire. She had already taken my measurements, which weren't far out from her own, and lucky for me she had the same shoe size so I could borrow some of hers.

To be honest, I didn't have the most productive day, as it was hard to do anything with what felt like a transmitter on my head. The day went by surprisingly quickly and after having my nails done and my eyebrows shaped, I was ready for my makeup. I felt like a big kid's doll as Libby was clearly loving every minute of it. She spent what seemed like ages doing my makeup, and my face started to ache from holding it so still.

"What time is Jacky boy picking you up?" she asked as she was applying powder to my pale cheeks.

"We said about eightish... why?" I said in a worried tone.

"No reason, just wanted to know how much time I had."

"Libs, it's only six."

"Yeah, but I still have to do your hair and then we have to get you into your dress." I still hadn't seen the dress as she wanted it to be a surprise, but I knew her true motive behind it was so it would be too late for me to back out of wearing it. She also wouldn't let me look in the mirror once my makeup and hair were done. She hadn't left out a thing, from curling my eyelashes to matching the hair clip with the colour of the dress.

When everything was done, I only just had enough time to get into my dress as Jack was now sat downstairs with Frank, and from the sounds of it, they were both watching a game.

Libby had timed it to a tee, as when I finally had been strapped into my dress, I only had enough time for a quick look in the mirror.

I was speechless. I was completely blown away, and Libby looked at me with tears in her eyes and her hands covering her mouth waiting for me to speak. I could barely believe it was still me.

I looked... well... sexy!

I was wearing a tight fitted corset that looked as though it had been moulded to my skin as the black and purple velvet material snaked around my frame, making it curve in all the right places. It was tied with a thick purple ribbon that went all the way down my back touching the cheeks of my behind and to the top part on the skirt. The skirt carried on the design, twisting to the front of my leg where a big slit ran up exposing my thigh.

The rest of the skirt rippled down in layers, some bits nearly reaching the floor and others in a net material that gave the skirt body. It moved gracefully around with me when I turned in the mirror. One leg was completely on show while the other was hidden under the multiple layers of black.

But this wasn't the part I was most worried about. No, because the stiff boned corset was creating an eyeful of bust that I usually concealed. I had also been conned into wearing knee-high black leather boots with a tall heel, but it wasn't as hard to walk in them as I would have thought.

I had already put the gloves on before Libby helped me into my dress. They were purple velvet to match and they went up all the way past the elbow, which I was more than happy about.

After dragging my eyes away from my dress, I looked at my face, seeing someone different staring back at me. I was still pale, but my skin looked like it was made from porcelain with a hint of a blush at my cheeks. At this point, I didn't know whether that was from the makeup, or my reaction to seeing myself like this.

My eyes were dark and smoky with a long black line across the eyelid that followed down and flicked out at the end. They were black underneath also, giving them a dark and mysterious look. They were framed with long curly lashes that tickled the tops of my eyelids.

I licked my lips, but the dark red colour remained, making them look full and like a cupid's bow. I turned my head, looking at my hair and seeing the shine of a soft gold as lighter streaks were caught in the light making them look like silk. It was swept back into a high twist, which overflowed with curls hanging down to my neck. The shorter bits hung down curling around the shape of my face.

"I don't know what to say..." I said very quietly, but she just held the biggest grin.

"You don't need to say anything... and well, you don't have time anyway." She was right, as now it was time for the hard part, now I had to face people. But even though I promised myself I wouldn't do it, the one thought slipped in and stuck around the edges of my mind...

Would Draven see me?

CHAPTER 33
TO BE NOTICED

Libby checked me one last time, fluffing my skirt out and then remembering something, she came at my neck with a red lip liner.

"What's that for?" I asked as she was coming closer to my neck.

"Well, if anyone asks what you are, you can say 'a victim' see!" she said, turning me to face the mirror again, pointing out the two red dots on my neck she had just put there. Great! Well, that just gave me images of a certain dark someone pinning me down and biting me on the neck.

I grabbed my long black jacket and zipped it up before going downstairs.

"What are you doing?" Libby asked protesting.

"I don't want Frank to see me like this... don't worry I will be taking it off in the club," I said nudging her as she looked hurt, so I added,

"Thanks Libs, it's amazing." And I soon had her smiling again. I transferred my purse out of my bag into my deep jacket pocket and Libby added some red lip-gloss in there as well.

"Just in case," she said, making kissing noises like she was five. I couldn't refrain from rolling my eyes.

I walked downstairs with more than butterflies in my stomach. It felt more like giant beetles. Jack and Frank were sat in the lounge getting animated about the game. But they both turned when Libby cleared her throat. Jack's mouth actually dropped, and Frank looked as though I was someone else. No one said anything. They just kept staring at me, which didn't go down too well with Libby.

"Well, what do you think?" she said speaking for me. Jack was the first to find words.

"Oh, wow, you look... I mean you look, great, amazing... just wow," he said, and I blushed. Frank on the other hand nudged him as they were both now standing, and whispered,

"Smooth... real smooth." And I smirked.

"Thanks, but shouldn't we get going?" I replied, making my way to the door still blushing.

"Yeah Kazzy, you look fantastic, good job, Libs... hey, you kids have fun tonight!" Frank shouted to us on our way out of the door.

I was so full of mixed emotions, but embarrassment was definitely the big winner. I only noticed what Jack was wearing, in the car. He was dressed in a long black leather jacket with ripped jeans, and ripped T-shirt with fake blood on it. He had white makeup over his face and his eyes had thick black around them making him look Goth sexy.

"Nice costume, but you're going to have to give me a clue," I said motioning my hand up and down.

"Ha, well naturally I'm a rocker zombie victim... Durr," he said making fun at me.

"Ahhh... yeah, now I get it. That must have taken you umm... all of five minutes to come up with," I said teasing him back.

"Well, we can't all be as naturally beautiful as you, some have to work hard at greatness... plus this was the only thing I could put together in an hour." I blushed at the first part but laughed at the second.

"Been working today then, I gather?"

"Yeah, but I had enough time to buy some fake blood in my break," he said, showing me his ripped T-shirt that exposed bits of his toned skin underneath. It wasn't surprising that Jack had a muscular six-pack under all those clothes. It was, however, a shock seeing it. I wondered if he noticed my gulp.

It didn't take long before we were queuing to get in, as tonight was definitely going to be packed inside. There were lots of Goths but also some actual costumes, the usual devils, witches, black cats and loads of zombies.

"Oh, look Jack, it looks like only a few hundred people copied your idea," I teased again. We got inside, and I knew it was time to remove my jacket, but I was just so nervous I was still clutching onto my collar. It did, however, bring me comfort to see that Libby had been right. Everyone was dressed up and I doubted anyone would notice me. I also couldn't help where my eyes seemed to be drawn, as I looked up to the VIP area. There, I saw a tall black figure standing at the edge of the top floor balcony. I couldn't make out any features but there was just something in me that knew it was him. This was enough to give me the guts to remove the black fabric that was hiding away my body.

As soon as I did, I regretted it, as now everyone was staring at me, including Jack. Even weirder, the lights above seem to flicker as though searching for some more power. What was that all about?

"Oh my God, Keira, you look… I mean you really… wow." Again, it didn't make much sense, but it was incredibly sweet all the same.

"Thanks Jack, come on let's get a drink," I said, linking my arm in his as we made our way through the crowd towards the bar. Once there, I was about to get out my money when Jack stopped me saying,

"Hey gorgeous, first round's on me." And with that he flagged down Mike, who didn't even recognise me.

"Keira… is that… no way, you look great," he said, and Jack rolled his eyes at Mike's attempt at a compliment. Personally, I found it nice but I was starting once again to get burning cheeks from all the attention. I was going to have to get a few drinks down me for some liquid courage.

"What can I get you?"

"I will have a coke, and the lady will have a shot of tequila and a Corona," he said without having to ask me. He really did know me well. I downed my shot and swigged back my beer, tasting the lime around the neck. It was as if I could feel myself relax with every taste.

"You're not half Mexican, are you?" Jack asked joking about my preference of drinks. I just poked him in the ribs in a playful way before giving in to giggles.

"So, come on then, what are you supposed to be? Hell, not that I'm complaining." I smiled and tilted my head to one side, showing him my red dots.

"Well isn't it obvious? I'm a Gothic Vampire Victim... durr!" I mocked, and he laughed shaking his head as we walked off, but I was sure I could have heard him say the word 'Damn' under his breath.

We found the rest of the gang, and RJ came running up to us dressed as an evil fairy. She wore a ripped tutu with a pink net top that didn't leave much to the imagination. She also had a pair of ripped wings that matched the furry boots, also bright pink.

"Kazzy... Is that you? You look fantastic... who would have thought you were such a sexy bitch?" she said as she hugged me smiling.

"Come on, let's dance," she said, grabbing me away from Jack, who looked less than happy about it. We walked into the middle of the dance floor, finding Lanie and her older sister Katie. They were both dressed like Alice in Wonderland, only one was good and one was evil. They looked great and both said the same about me. It was the first time in a long while that I had felt this self-confident, and it felt good.

We all danced, taking breaks here and there, doing shots at the bar followed by more beer. Luckily, I was far from a lightweight when it came to alcohol. Spending years working behind a bar you learned to take it, and in England the drinking age is eighteen not twenty-one. But I knew my limits and never pushed it, not enjoying the feeling that I couldn't control myself, or more importantly, my visions.

The battle of the bands was fun, after each small set a band

STEPHANIE HUDSON

did, the audience would vote by screaming the loudest for their favourite. It finished with the winner doing another set and the band that won was called the Stone Crows. They played one of their most popular songs, *'blood in the midnight alley'*. The place erupted as not one soul was left sitting down. I found myself jumping up and down with the rest of them, getting lost in the heavy music.

After a night of drinking, the effects of it were starting to make me feel braver and when Jack moved his body closer to mine, I didn't shy away from him. So, when they played their last song which was a ballad called *'Ever after and over the beyond'* he put his arms around my waist for a slow dance. My heart started to beat quicker and when I found him staring down at me, I knew what was about to happen.

"Keira, I really like you, you're not like anyone I have ever met before," he said as his face got closer to mine, and I still hadn't decided what to do. I wanted to, but it felt wrong. Draven popped into my head for the first time, quickly followed by the memory of him kissing his fiancée... so with that image clouding my decision... I let it happen. I let Jack place his lips upon mine and I kissed him back. His hands found my face and mine curled around his back, pulling him closer, which he responded to by kissing me harder.

Then something happened. All the lights went out as if every one of them had blown a fuse. There was a loud smashing sound coming from up above, like tables being upturned, and I shuddered in Jack's arms. He pulled away from me and said,

"What the Hell was that?!" But I replied by pulling him back to me for another kiss. To be honest, I didn't know what it was, but considering it had something to with the VIP, I found myself just not caring!

The lights all came back on after a few flickers and the band then started back up. I parted from Jack and saw his happy face smiling back at me. But I couldn't help the guilt that I felt, the guilt I just couldn't understand. This made me excuse myself and I went to the ladies before Jack could realise my regret.

As soon as I got in there, I tried to sort myself out. I had to pull myself together. I would be stupid to mess this up. Jack was a really great guy who liked me and was the easiest person to be around. I had never felt that relaxed around anyone before, so surely that counted for something, didn't it? I stared at myself in the mirror for what seemed like ages. It was only when another girl came in that I woke up out of my trance.

"Hey, nice dress!" she said, and I smiled back not really taking anything in.

"But there is one thing... and I hope you don't think I'm being rude... but if I had hair like yours, I would never wear it up, it's too nice to hide." I thanked the girl before she left, leaving me once again alone with my thoughts. I studied myself in the mirror but the alcohol was doing strange things to me. I was trying to focus on whether or not I was doing the right thing by kissing Jack but in the end, I said to hell with it!

I applied some more lip gloss, pulled my gloves up and did something I never do... I let my hair down. It was now a mass of golden bouncy curls that fell down my back to my waist. I took one last look in the mirror and walked out, back to Jack.

People's eyes followed me as I worked my way through the crowd. I even heard one girl whisper 'Man, look at that hair' and I couldn't help but smile at the compliment. So, what was the big deal, I was allowed to feel good for one night... so why did I feel this nagging pain in the back of my mind, like I was doing something wrong?

When I finally made it back to the group there was someone missing.

"Where's Jack?" I asked RJ, who was flirting with some guy dressed as a zombie bunny.

"Umm... I don't know... wasn't he with you?"

"Yeah, but I came back from the loo and he was gone," I said looking everywhere. RJ whispered something to the bunny and came with me to look. We both started at the bar and I asked Mike if he had seen the guy that I had come in with.

"Yeah, I saw him, but I think there must have been a problem 'cause he was being escorted out by security."

"What!" I shouted, but Mike just held up his hands saying,

"Hey, don't shoot the messenger!"

"Sorry Mike," I said before leaving.

"Maybe he got into a fight or something?" RJ said looking worried.

"I don't know, but I'm going to find out." I had a strange feeling this might have something to do with that kiss!

"How?" she said following me to the front entrance. I didn't answer her but just kept moving in and out of the people who stood in my way. I didn't stop until I came to the two men who could tell me what I wanted to know.

"Cameron, Jo, How's things…? Oh, and why did you have my date thrown out?" I said hands on hips. They both looked at each other then looked back at me with guilty eyes.

"Look we only did as we were told, okay."

"No, it's not okay. I want to know why?!" I demanded, not backing down as I felt the rage roll over my skin in a heated flush.

"Because we were told he was trying to sell drugs, and we did our job," Jo said trying to sound firm. Meanwhile RJ was looking at me in awe as it must have looked like watching a Chihuahua go up against a Bull Mastiff!

"What! That's ridiculous, I was with him all night!"

"How dare you! My brother doesn't even take drugs, let alone sell them!" RJ screamed at the idea.

They both tried to calm us down and said,

"Look, we do as we are told, if you don't agree then take it up with the management!" Cameron was, of course, referring to Draven, so he didn't expect me to say,

"Oh, don't you worry, I bloody well will!" And with that, I turned around and stormed right back inside the club, with RJ on my tail.

"Err… Wait, Kaz… Kazzy, just hold on a sec… think about this, you can't just go up there and start demanding why. I'm upset as well, but come on, be serious!" she pleaded, but there was no way I was going to let him get away with this! I went to the doors that I knew would be my safest bet of getting through and turned back to RJ.

"Oh, I have never been more serious in my life! He can't be allowed to get away with this. I don't give a crap who he is! But you had better stay here because this is not going to be pretty," I said letting the rage fully take over.

"Hell, you don't have to ask me twice! Anyway, I'm going to try his cell and see where he is," she said, leaving to go back to where we had left our bags and jackets with Lanie and Drew. I, on the other hand, marched straight up to the two massive guys by the bottom door and said,

"Draven wants to see me," with such confidence that they both looked at each other then back at me, so I continued,

"You can go and ask him if you like, but I can tell you now, he doesn't like to be kept waiting."

This was enough to achieve my goal as they parted to let me through the doors. Once inside, I took a moment to think about what I was going to do. Was I really going to walk straight up to his table and demand a reason from him as to why he would give an order for Jack to be taken away?

"Shit! Yes, I was!" I said out loud. It just didn't make any sense and there was absolutely no way I believed any of the accusations against Jack were true. No, this had to stop, and it would stop tonight!

The liquid courage helped me get through the doors and walk straight over to his table. I barely noticed anything else as I could feel my blood boil, I was so angry. I was shaking at the thought. I reached the front of the table standing directly in his view and stood there fuming.

Oh, and didn't he know about it. Draven's face was controlled well, but I could see the underlying surprise in his dark terrifying eyes. There was also something more there, but it was a look I had never seen before. However, this just added fuel to the fire that was scorching inside my belly. I was burning hot at the very sight of him. I walked straight up to the table but was stopped by the giant Ragnar. Even then my courage didn't fade. No, if anything it had the opposite effect. I folded my arms across my chest and looked up at the brute.

STEPHANIE HUDSON

"Excuse me!" I said through my teeth when what I really wanted to say was 'Get the hell out of my way, you big oaf!'

He didn't move but he did turn his head towards Draven, waiting for a command, like a dog to his master! I, on the other hand still hadn't taken my hateful eyes from Draven's. I was standing there getting ready for the escort downstairs, thinking how much this would make me snap. I knew how Draven would not like a scene. But what he did next surprised me.

"Let her through." At this, his dog backed down letting me pass. I ran a frustrated hand through my hair as I walked by and I could swear I heard him growl at me. Draven and the rest of the table came into full view and my heart missed a beat at the sight. I tried to control the pounding in my chest, but I knew that I couldn't falter now I had come this far.

Draven was wearing all black, which enhanced his terrifying beauty. The rest of the table were also dressed very grand, as though they were celebrating something of their own. My eyes scanned the table and I realised there was another man present who I had never seen before.

He had long straight hair that looked almost like ice as it was whiter than white. His face was long with a thin, straight nose to match, that reminded me of a crow's beak. He looked older than Draven, or anyone else on the table, for that matter. This gave him a very wise and knowledgeable looking face. I scanned his frame and saw he was wearing an unusual suit that looked like half a robe with a long hood at the back and a cape that came around to one side.

He looked as if he could have been royalty or someone very important. He even had his own bodyguards, who looked equally as terrifying as Draven's men. They stood behind his chair on their guard as I approached. He must have sensed their unease as he held up one long white hand at them without turning his head. There was something strange about him as I found myself drawn to him but couldn't understand why.

I got to the edge of the table and all eyes stared at me like the intruder I was. Sophia's eyes were the only kind ones I found, but I couldn't let this influence my objective.

"You have something to say?" Draven's voice was the first to slice through the silence. Okay, so now I was here I was going to have to find the words. So, with that in mind I took a deep breath, and came out with it in the strongest voice I had in me.

"Yes, I would very much like to know why you had my date removed under false accusations." The pale man to the side of me eyed me curiously and held on to his amused grin.

"Well, I think even I can answer that, my dear," the man said in a very hoarse voice, sounding more than happy about this new turn of events. I turned to face him, and Draven looked beyond furious.

"With a beauty like yours, you are more fitting for a king than a mere servant boy, wouldn't you agree, Dominic?" he said, and I was surprised to find him calling him by his first name, as if making it clear that these two were equals in power.

"Keira is just a waitress who works for me downstairs," Draven said in the coldest manner, twisting the arrow he had once again shot into my heart. I couldn't believe the audacity of this man! This was slowly pushing me over the edge with fury.

"Really, just a waitress… umm, alright, if you say so. My dear, I am very pleased to meet you, a rare creature you are indeed," he said, standing to take my hand in his, lifting it to his lips. I let him do so freely as the look in Draven's eyes filled with hate at the sight, so I happily complied as if this was my little bit of revenge.

"Malphas!" Draven hissed what I assumed was his name. Malphas, however, didn't seem anything but happy about Draven's reaction. His eyes met mine over the hand that he still held in an icy grip.

"No, I didn't think so," he said smirking, as he finally let go of my hand.

"Keira, I think it's time for you to be getting home," Draven said, glaring at me as though I was made from dirt.

"Well, that would be a great idea but unfortunately someone unjustly kicked out my date, therefore leaving me stranded and without a ride home… so you see my predicament!" I snapped, folding my arms again showing him my bravery, which was now mixed with fiery passion.

"Well, I think I have seen enough to satisfy my curiosity. My Lord, I will now take my leave, but my dear please allow me to escort you home, for it would be my great pleasure." Malphas' very deep, gravelly voice offered.

"Thank you that would be very kind," I said looking at Draven, who now looked as if he wanted to shake me to death.

"That won't be necessary. Zagan, take Miss Johnson home, *now!*" he ordered to one of the men who sat at his table. He was the one who always wore the hooded jacket and had the scar and tattoos upon his face. He stood at this command but stopped when Malphas' men got closer to me. I didn't really understand what was going on, but Draven's voice ended it quickly before things got out of hand.

"Malphas, you *DO NOT* want to push me on this!" He said his name with a clear warning behind it, and in return Malphas' hand went up again as it had done before.

"But of course." He came closer to me once again saying,

"It was a pleasure to meet you, my dear Keira." He stepped forward, close to my ear and whispered so no one else could hear,

"I will be at the front of the building waiting to drive you home… meet me." He then kissed my cheek as if that was what he was planning to do, for everyone watching.

But I jumped back at the sound of Draven's fist going down on the stone table with such mighty power it not only shook but also cracked under his hammer-like hand. His voice roared out making everyone look on in fear, including me.

"ENOUGH! Keira, go and wait for me on the balcony! *Now girl!*" he demanded on a bellow when I hadn't moved quickly enough for him. His black eyes flickered with the same purple I had seen before, as he stared at Malphas as though he would soon rip his throat out. This was one order that I would not disobey, and I left but not before I could just hear Malphas saying,

"Fear not, My Lord, I would not hurt the girl, not after what I have seen with my own eyes… After all, she is…" But his voice trailed off and I didn't hear the rest as I was heading towards the balcony. However, on the way there my mind flipped, hearing his cold voice calling me *'Just a waitress'* and snarling *'Now Girl'* like saying my name would taste foul on his tongue.

This decided it for me, and now away from Draven's evil glare, I was clear to think for myself. Hell, Draven was my boss and that was it. He had no rights over me whatsoever, so why did I have to go and do what he said when I would just end up getting another ear-bashing on the balcony? No, not this time! I was my own person and I would do as I pleased, and if he didn't like it, then he would just have to sack me or better still, I would quit!

So, with that in mind, I waited until I was out of sight and sneaked down past the guard, and shot down the stairs like an Olympic runner. Once I was on the ground floor I ran up to where my jacket was and said a quick bye to the rest of my friends, not waiting for a reply. I bolted for the front doors, scared of looking back. My heart raced with panic, knowing I had gone against him and knowing that I would seriously have to pay for it.

Once outside, the cold air hit me, making me remember my jacket, which I then put on. It didn't take long for my senses to realise that what I was about to do was an extremely stupid thing and a very dangerous one at that. But before I could back out, a black limo came around to the front and the door opened. I took a deep breath, knowing I was making a categorical mistake, and entered the car. Malphas looked at me with curiosity as I tried to calm down inside. The car pulled onto the main road towards the direction I lived, although I hadn't yet said a word.

"I certainly admire your spirit, there aren't many who would defy a man like Dominic Draven, but maybe that adds to the appeal for him," he said as he stroked the smooth white skin on his chin. The limo was very dark inside with only a few small blue LED lights that made his skin bright white.

"I can guarantee that I hold no appeal for Mr Draven

whatsoever," I said looking out of the window, seeing nothing but the black night.

"I highly doubt that," he said as he flicked a switch, making a little bar appear. He poured himself a drink and offered me one, which I turned down, before asking,

"What makes you say that?"

"You really don't look at yourself in the same way as others of your kind do, do you?" he asked and I didn't understand what he meant by 'my kind'.

"All I know is the way Draven treats me, and like he said, I'm just a waitress," I said trying not to look hurt at the memory, but he just smiled as though what I had said had been funny.

"Have I missed something?" I asked looking him in the eye.

"Draven clearly has a hold on you, and you in turn a hold on him… that much I can be sure on." He swirled the golden liquid around in his brandy glass before taking a sip.

"You're wrong, I have no hold on him and you saw for yourself, I'm just an inconvenience."

"On some level you're right but not in the way you think. I saw with my own eyes indeed, a man who is trying to protect something he holds very valuable to him, and that, my dear… is you," he said as he tipped his glass towards me, pointing me out.

"Well, I think his soon to be wife would find a problem with that, I'm sure!" I said but his face changed at this news and he laughed at the thought.

"Umm… interesting. Well, I will give him this, he most certainly knows how to put the needs of others before his own… Ha…What a saint!" he said, this time throwing his head back to laugh heartily, and I really was at a loss to know why.

"Well, they were certainly quicker than I thought, and I guess that just confirms my conclusion," he said as he pressed another switch above him making the black screen between us and the driver come down.

"You'd better pull over before this gets… *out of hand*. I have made my point, and they theirs," he ordered the driver, and he did as he was told, pulling up by the side of the road.

"What's going on? Why are we stopping?" I asked in a panicked voice.

"Don't fret, my dear, but pray tell me, if you truly believe that Draven has no feelings of want for you, then why would he send a car to follow us and be flagging us down to get you away from me?"

I looked round in horror, as his statement was confirmed by the headlights behinds us…

Draven was here.

CHAPTER 34

JACK'S PAST

I looked around in surprise to find a figure walking to my side of the car ready to open the door. I looked back at Malphas to find him releasing the lock on my door, and I jumped at the sound. Why had I been locked in, in the first place?

"Well, I bid you farewell and will look forward to our next meeting, when the moon is right of course." And with that my door was open, ready for me to exit the Limo. I didn't fully understand what he meant by the moon, but at this point I was just glad to be getting out of the car and away from this chilling experience. Only when I got out of the car, I heard him say in one of the most disturbing voices I have ever heard, one that made my skin crawl over cold flesh.

"See you soon... Keira." The door then slammed shut, and the man stood before me caused my mouth to drop open in astonishment. The Limo drove away, and I suddenly wished I were still inside it. I couldn't help but state the obvious.

"Vincent Draven."

"Keira, please get in the car," he said, holding his arm out to the huge black Rolls Royce behind me. It looked like a deadly panther in the dead of night, and the man who held the door open was just as forbidding.

"What are you doing here?" I asked, annoyed at my current

situation and also hoping his brother wasn't in there waiting for me.

"The car, if you please," was his repeated response, so I gave up, feeling that this whole thing was ridiculous as I got in the car. I slid over the cream leather interior to the other side as Vincent got in after me. I sat there like a spoilt child with my arms folded tightly across my chest.

His brother was also incredibly handsome, with tight curls of blonde hair and the most amazing smouldering eyes that you could get lost in. His face was softer, but still, I wouldn't want to get on the wrong side of him, which was apparently down the road I was heading.

"So, like I said, what are you doing here?"

"I am here on my brother's orders and he is not happy with your conduct," he said without looking at me, but my fury doubled.

"I don't care! He can't do this. I was perfectly fine where I was!" I said, thinking I was close to stamping my feet but glad I didn't, as it would have looked more funny than serious.

"I doubt that. I do not understand why you continue to make things so difficult?" His calm voice just angered me more.

"Me, make things difficult! I think I could have made it home without all the theatrics."

"You do not know the man who was taking you home, like we do. You do not know what he is capable of or who he works for... You were not safe." He said this, and a chill went up my spine, making me feel stupid. Why had I got into a car with a complete stranger who could have been a psycho? I lowered my head knowing what he said was right... I'd been foolish.

"And I'm safe here with you?" I challenged.

"Yes, we don't mean you any harm, Keira. My brother is trying to protect you. Why can you not see that?"

"Why would he even care?" I said to the window, absently running a velvet finger down the steamed covered glass.

"Well, that you will have to take up with him as he wants to see you tomorrow," he said, and the thought of how that was going to go made me shudder. We pulled into my gravel road and the house came into view. Jack's car was parked there, and he was sat on the porch steps waiting for me. Vincent noticed and simply stated,

"That boy should not be here. If I were you and didn't want to anger my brother further than you already have, then I would get rid of him." He looked serious when he said this, but I couldn't resist the urge to say what I did, as my back was up at the idea of any more demands.

"Well, you're not me! And I have obviously pissed Draven off, so what the hell does it matter? He's made it perfectly clear I mean nothing to him, so why should I obey him!?" I said before getting out of the car. I slammed the door shut but the window rolled down and Vincent said,

"Don't forget, Keira, tomorrow... oh, and I really wouldn't keep him waiting," he said, not once raising his voice to anything other than a controlled calm tone, which in itself was annoyingly frustrating!

"Fine!" I shouted as I stomped off towards Jack, who was now watching this little scene play out. I stamped up the steps in frustration before shouting,

"ARRGGHH!" And he looked at me as though I had lost it, which I was very close to doing.

"Hey, are you okay? Who was that?" He got up and came up to me, putting his arms around me, making me calm slightly at his concern. The car had now turned around and was pulling away, but I could still see Vincent watching through the open window.

"Yeah, I am now they've gone. Look I'm so, so sorry about what happened. Are you okay?" I said, pulling away from him to see his face.

"Yeah, I'm fine, they just got the wrong guy, I guess, but I was more worried about you, about how you would get home. Then RJ said she saw you getting into a limo, so I drove straight here."

I told him what had happened, and he looked on in horror. I left out a few parts not wanting to cause any more problems than I already had mounting up. He told me how he had been driving around looking for me until RJ rang to tell him her version of it, which made him smile.

"I have never had anyone fight my corner before, but, babe, now that is impressive... RJ said you were unstoppable." He laughed and put his arm around my shoulders as we sat down on the top step of the front porch. Then something struck me. Why the hell did Draven have him thrown out in the first place? If it wasn't because of me, then it must have something to do with Jack's past. So, I decided now was the time to ask.

"Jack, I hate to ask but I really want to know... what happened to make you hate them so much?" His arm fell from my body and he turned to look at my face. His features were first hard at the memory but then they softened when he looked into my eyes.

"It was over two years ago now, the summer before I was to start my first year of college." He paused, playing with his hands and his elbows rested on his knees. He looked out to the surrounding forest, as if his story was locked away there and he was searching for it.

"I met a girl. She was so Goddamn beautiful and incredibly smart, which I like in a girl. I like a girl you can have a conversation with, a laugh with... not one of these 'airhead' types... a girl with depth," he said looking round to find my face, as if trying to judge my reaction to his words. I smiled, so he continued.

"She came into Airtime, the store I work at in the mall." I nodded as I had heard him talk about the shop before.

"Well, we hit it off straight away, and amazingly I found the guts to ask her out. Even more amazingly though, she said yes!"

"I can understand why," I said nudging him and he grinned back, but his eyes remained sad.

"Cutting a long story short, we became tight, went out and were inseparable all summer. She lived with her aunt and was starting college the same time as me, so it all felt perfect. We had such a strong bond that my body would literally ache when I wasn't around her." Of course, this I understood perfectly, as it was how I felt all the time I wasn't near Draven.

Even though, now, it felt like I wanted to slap some sense into him.

"So, what happened to her?" I asked softly.

"We went to the club for the first time together, as then I was the legal age to drink, it was the same night that the Dravens always made their first appearance. Of course, back then, I was just like the rest of them. You know, getting mixed up with all the gossip, wanting to see them just like everyone else." He rubbed the back of his head with his hand, and I felt bad that I was making him talk about it as he was clearly finding it hard.

"We all waited like idiots for them to arrive, but she was the only one who was looking awkward, kind of agitated and I couldn't understand why... the way you acted that night brought back so many memories I was so sure the same thing would happen to you, that I couldn't witness it again... so I left, do you remember?"

"Yes, I remember." The truth was, how could I ever forget? My life hadn't been the same since that night... Not that it had been much before it.

"You remind me so much of her, it's scary sometimes... I'm sorry, I shouldn't say that," he said backtracking, but it didn't offend me, so I reassured him.

"It's fine, really, I don't mind." He looked at me, smiling at my reaction.

"Well, apart from the hair of course, but your sister Libby has similar... she was a redhead, but some days I would be amazed looking at it, as it looked as though it was on fire," he said, and I could almost see her in my head.

"Please go on," I urged.

"Well, Dominic Draven did the same thing, as though he was Master of the Universe looking down on all that is beneath him! He walked past that same table and he looked at her the same way he looked at you but, unlike you, she didn't look away." I shuddered at my own memory of that night. I could just imagine how he made her feel, how I felt... of course it would have been the same.

"So, the night went on and she was acting very strange after she saw him, so before I could ask her what was wrong, she turned to me and kissed me with more passion than we had kissed before. Then she told me goodbye, she had to go. She pointed to where the ladies restroom was, and I said okay, letting go of her hand thinking it would be only minutes until it was right there, back where it always was." He looked down at his hands as if he longed for them to be refilled with those same hands once more. He looked as though he would have killed for it.

"But of course, she never came back. I looked everywhere I could go, but there was one place I wasn't allowed and when I tried to get up there, I was escorted out of the same doors just like tonight."

"That's terrible... what happened to her?" I asked but no matter what idea I had in my head, the next words out of Jack's mouth were never what I could have imagined!

"Draven took her!"

"WHAT?" I said, realising it came out as a shout. "What do you mean he took her?"

"Exactly that... he took her from me. I waited all night for her to come back out, but she never did. When I spoke to some friends I was with, they said that they had seen her being escorted upstairs by two of his men. After that night, I never saw her face again..." The awful truth came out, and now his sadness was quickly replaced by pure hatred for the guy in question.

"What do you think happened to her?"

"I have my suspicions but at heart I know the truth..." He swallowed hard before saying the unthinkable.

"I think that's she's...she's *dead!*" I gasped and my jaw dropped in shock just thinking about it.

"Not just that she is dead though, but that Draven... well I think that he killed her!"

"What? No way!" I shouted, and Jack turned to face me seeing as I had reacted this way.

"I'm sorry to say these things, Keira, but think about it, she was never seen again! EVER! Her aunt moved house the next day. The next day, for fuck sake! I rang the police, but they said because she was of age that they couldn't do anything. But think about who owns the police! The Dravens of course," he said, standing up now in front of me marking all the points on his fingers as he carried on.

"I broke into her aunt's house after she left but there was nothing there, there wasn't even any evidence that anyone had ever lived there!" I could just picture all these things in my head, as I had days when I just couldn't understand why things didn't add up.

"That is weird, I agree, but come on, Jack, think about what you're saying... murder?" I said, trying to reason with him.

"Look, believe what you want, but she loved me and she would never have just left without saying something, without trying to get to me... she just wouldn't have," he said as the sadness fully devoured his heart.

"I'm so, so sorry, Jack, that is just terrible. I don't know how you can... I mean, doesn't it?" I struggled with my words, but he knew what I meant.

"You mean how do I stand being there?" I nodded, and he came back to sit next to me again, placing his hand gently on my knee.

"Because I always wonder that if I keep going back there, that maybe one day I would be proven wrong and that I might see her again," he said, and my heart melted for him. I placed my hand on top of his and he took it, wrapping his fingers in between mine.

"That's why when it happened again tonight, I panicked... I thought it was happening all over again and I couldn't bear losing you too." His other hand stroked the back of mine, making little circles around it with his thumb.

"So, was that *him* in the car or one of his lackeys?" he asked bitterly.

"Actually, it was his brother." I saw his face and said, "Yeah, I know, I was just as surprised. I'm sorry our date was ruined but hey, up till then I was having a great time." At this, his face lightened, looking hopeful.

"Me too, maybe next time we could just go to the movies or something."

"I think that would be safe enough," I said laughing, and he smiled making his face paint crack and peel. I playfully grabbed a piece, pulling it off and flicking it back at him.

He laughed back but came at my sides, tickling me, which unfortunately made me snort! My hands flew to my mouth, but it was too late, Jack pointed at me and laughed mockingly.

"Now that seriously is the cutest thing I have ever heard!" he said, pulling my hands away from my face keeping them locked in his.

"That's because you didn't do it!" I said as my cheeks were now glowing red.

"Hey, I didn't notice before, but you bite your lip," he declared, and my heart sank at the memory of Draven. He always commented on me biting my lip, so it didn't feel right when Jack said it. It was as if it belonged to Draven and him alone. This pulled me together a bit and made me remember my warning from Vincent. Maybe this was the reason all along. Maybe this was what he didn't want me to find out. Jack's past...

I stood up and Jack looked hurt.

"Did I say something wrong, because you know I love the snort thing, right?" I couldn't help but smile down at him. He was just so damn charming and loveable that I wanted to give him the biggest hug. But this wasn't enough, and I knew it... I couldn't kid myself. I just didn't feel the same way as I did when I was with Draven. No matter how much I tried.

"No... no you didn't, it's just, well, to be honest I'm so tired I could drop," I said, which was half true. He relaxed at the thought that it wasn't him and I felt my guilt double.

"Well, you'd better get to bed, beauty queen, but how about a kiss for Prince Charming?" he said bowing and taking off an imaginary hat.

"Well I don't know, you will have to point one out for me," I said teasing him again. He put his hands up to his heart and pretended that I had just shot him. Then he fell to the ground making me jump and run over to him. I shook him, but he didn't move.

"Jack! Stop fooling around... Jack!" But then he just raised his hand and pointed to his mouth, keeping his eyes closed. I couldn't help but laugh.

"Oh, for God's sake," I said, bending over him and kissing him lightly on the lips, he responded by sitting up while he had his hands on my face pulling me to him. Once we had finished, I looked at him seriously and said,

"So, does this make me the Prince and you Sleeping Beauty?" We both laughed and he kissed me quickly on the cheek before pulling me to my feet.

"If you like, but I'm warning you... I don't do dishes!" he said as he tickled my side again.

Once I had said goodnight and had received one more kiss, I watched Jack get in his car and drive away. I was about to turn to go inside when something caught my eye. In the trees ahead, I wasn't surprised when I found a pair of glowing purple eyes staring back at me. The bird was back, and it looked as though it was ready to move, so before it could, I ran inside slamming the door behind me, shutting it out.

The next day I was up early, as I couldn't sleep after everything that had happened the previous night. It had been such a roller-coaster of events that it took me a while to process it all. First, there was the date part of the night with Jack, which I had to admit was making it difficult not falling for him.

But then I was dragged back into the weird life of the Dravens, and was once again thrown into his world. Then the next thing I knew, I was being escorted home by first a mad man, according to Vincent, then by Vincent himself. He then left me with the bombshell that his brother demanded to see me today, and if that wasn't enough, to then warn me against seeing 'the boy'. So, all in all, a typical Keira night with little sleep to follow it.

Of course, when Libby asked me how my night had gone, I had saved her from the wild night's adventure and lied, saying it went great and was loads of fun. I got in the shower to try and relax my muscles as I was tense from the thought of what I had coming to me today. My meeting with Draven was not going to be pretty and I didn't trust myself not to speak my mind, which knowing Draven's temper wasn't the best of ideas.

I looked at myself in the mirror as I was now back to my usual plain self. Well, apart from the panda eyes I had going on. I had scrubbed my face last night about three times but no matter how much soap I used, I still had black eyes this morning.

When I got out of the shower, I was feeling refreshed, and more importantly, relaxed, but it didn't last long as Libby came into my room telling me about the phone call. Apparently, I was now required to go to this Draven showdown early, so I only had an hour to get ready, which was just great! Of course, I couldn't look disappointed in front of Libby or she would know something was up.

"I didn't think you worked Sundays," Libby said before returning downstairs.

"Yeah, but there's loads of clearing up to do after last night, it was packed." She nodded taking this as my answer, and as soon as she was out of sight, I sat down on my bed letting out a huge sigh.

I knew I wasn't really working today as the only reason I was needed was for Draven to give me an ear-bashing, which evidently couldn't wait till Monday's shift.

So, with this in mind, I pulled on some jeans, a grey T-shirt, some grey gloves and a zip-up maroon coloured hoodie. Once I dried my hair and put it up in its usual style, I grabbed my bag making my way out of the door.

Ready for my nightmare date with Draven.

CHAPTER 35

SHOWDOWN

When I got there, I sat in my car for a while trying to decide whether or not to go through with it. I could just walk in there now and say to Jerry 'I quit' and then I would never have to see Draven again, but that thought hurt me more than I wanted to admit.

Then there was the other part of me that wanted to stick up for myself. I mean, who was Draven to tell me what I was and wasn't allowed to do on my night off? He said last night... his very words being, 'She's just a waitress' so why the hell go to all this trouble for one? This was the reason I wanted to go in there.

I wanted answers, once and for all.

So, I took a deep breath, got out of my car and made my way inside Afterlife. It was quiet, and I had deja vu from the last time I'd had to see Draven as I remembered how that had ended. Well, at this point I had nothing to lose. I mean, what could he possibly have to say to me that would hurt more than he already had done.

I walked up the stairs, and as soon as I entered the room, eyes stared at me as though I was a dead man walking. I tried to ignore it, but it was hard when some even rose from their seats to get a better look.

Actually, this did help, as it made my blood pump around my veins faster as my anger was mounting again like last night. I tried to hold on to it but as soon as I saw Sophia's sad face, it melted away. She was stood near the bar waiting for me and as soon as I approached, she looked away as if ashamed.

"Sophia, are you okay?" I asked but she just nodded and replied,

"This way, Keira."

I was stunned that she was being so cold towards me. Was that it from now on? Was I to be hated by every Draven? We walked up to the huge double doors and my heart quickened. I thought semi-neutral ground was going to be the balcony again, but it looked as if I was mistaken, as I entered through what looked like fortress doors. The immense carved wood creaked angrily as they went back, and I followed Sophia in silence. The wide, luxurious hallway looked as though it would go on forever and I was getting ready for a long walk, when Sophia stopped at the first door not far from the entrance.

I stood opposite her sad face, and asked again,

"What is it?"

"Why did you do it?" she asked frowning at me, before adding more, "Why put yourself in danger like that?" Her face looked like a small child, and I felt guilty but didn't know why.

But before I could answer, there was a booming voice that was unmistakably Draven's, from behind the panelled door. She led me through as we both walked in.

The room was a huge office, surrounded by an open plan balcony that was like a veranda. Two sides of the walls that faced outside were large stone arches that went up to the ceiling. They were open, and the cold air filled the room. That wasn't the only thing giving off a chill as Draven's icy stare was enough to make me want to run home.

"Leave us!" Draven commanded his sister, who gave me one sympathetic look before closing the door behind me, sealing my fate. Draven sat at a big oak desk that was the size of a bed. He sat in a hefty wooden chair to match and I stood frozen at the sight. He turned to look at me but still, neither of us had spoken, so I decided I was going to be the first to speak. I wanted to get this over with sooner rather than later.

"You wanted to see me?" I asked, already knowing the horrible answer to that question.

"I wanted to hear you explain yourself!" he snapped, staring at me as though I had committed treason. I didn't know what to say but I couldn't keep the frown from my face. So as if wanting to make it worse, he yelled again,

"Well, let's hear it!"

"Hear what?" I said, and now his anger grew.

"Do not toy with me, Keira. I am on the edge, so I suggest the best course of action is not to push me too far! I want to know why you disobeyed me?" he asked, clearly trying to keep calm, which didn't look as if it would last much longer.

"I'm sorry, but no one informed me that I had to take orders while I wasn't even at work!" I said, not keeping the sarcasm from my words and deliberately ignoring his warnings.

"What a shame that is, because maybe then you would stay out of trouble for longer than a day!" His body was almost shaking, as his temper flared up at me. He looked terrifyingly strong under the dark T-shirt he wore, which got tighter at the arms as he flexed his muscles under the material. I was almost expecting it to rip open under the strain. He also wore faded jeans, and this was the most casual I had ever seen him. But still, it made it harder, as all I wanted to do was get close enough to touch him. I tried so hard to hate him, I needed to, right now, or I would lose yet another battle. I swallowed hard, trying to bury my carnal feelings for him but with him looking the way he did, was I ever going to accomplish this?

"Well, maybe if you hadn't had my date thrown out, then this could have been avoided. Did you ever think about that?" I shouted back, holding my fists into tight balls to control my shakes.

"That *boy* had no business being in my club!" he said, emphasising the word boy.

"What utter bullshit! What was the real reason you had him kicked out?" My voice rose with the injustice of it all.

"I do not want this conversation to be about that boy you call a date!" He let out an angry half-laugh when he said the word boy, and it was starting to grate on my very last nerve.

"Stop calling him that! And the whole reason I came up to confront you about it, was because of what you did!" I said, holding my hands up at him. I mean, what did he want from me?

"That *person* is of no concern of mine!" he barked out on a snarl.

"And I am?!" I shouted back, but he lowered his face, not wanting to answer that one. He remained quiet for a while, and all that was heard was the sound of me panting for air. But then his voice cut through it, making me shiver in fear.

"Tell me why, Keira?" It was an icy tone, full of reprimand and disapproval.

"Why, what?"

"Why you got into that car with Malphas?" he said through clenched teeth, and his hands gripped the side of the wooden desk, which looked as if it wasn't up to the task.

"Because I wanted to!" But this was most definitely not the right answer as he erupted out of the chair, kicking it back behind him with so much force it hit the stone pillar and crumbled into splinters.

My body pushed back against the door in horror as I couldn't hide my fright. He stood facing me, and the fear was now so clear in my eyes that it seemed to bring him down to a calmer level. My palms were flat on the wood behind and I wanted to turn and run. It was only his face softening that made me stay. I don't know how, but I knew he would never hurt me, still, that wasn't enough to make my shaky hands stop vibrating against the panels.

"I didn't mean to frighten you, Keira. Forgive me, but I would just like an honest answer... please," he said with genuine need in his eyes.

"I got in the car because I wanted to piss you off, as revenge!" I said being truthful.

"And that is the reason you put yourself in harm's way, to get to me? This isn't a game, Keira." He raised his head up and held the bridge of his nose with his thumb and forefinger. He looked in pain, but the guilt got too much so I shouted out,

"Then maybe you should stop playing it like one! What the hell do you care anyway what happens to me? You made your feelings perfectly clear and just as you said yourself, *I am just a waitress!*" I hissed this last part in the only way I could repeat such words, words that shot me down to the ground last night. My voice was getting louder as the hurt in my eyes filled with liquid emotion. The pain returned back in his eyes also.

"I said that to Malphas so that he wouldn't take notice of you, but I didn't really have much of a chance of that, now did I...? You certainly made sure of that!" he snapped back, and his black eyes invaded my senses.

"And what do you mean by that?"

"Well, let's look back. Not only did you have the courage to come up to my table in the first place, but then you added to that, the nerve to push it by challenging me in front of him... and well, I don't even need to mention how you looked." He finished this and I was gobsmacked.

How dare he!

"So, what is this? The result of a bruised ego? And you have no right to comment on how I looked... I mean, this is coming from a man surrounded by tarts and I get persecuted for dressing up the once, on Halloween," I huffed, shaking my head in disbelief.

"That's not how I meant it," he sighed and started again, using more delicate words.

"I meant, that for a girl who normally dresses not to be noticed, you picked a hell of a night to look..."

"What?" I snapped.

"Irresistible," he said without a note of mockery behind his words, and this shocked me into silence. Did he really think that? He had stepped closer to me and I could feel the heated power from his body once more, bringing back all my dreams and at the same time, overpowering my sensible mind.

"I don't understand you, Draven, one minute you're treating me like I don't exist, and then the next minute you're going out

424

of your way to protect me," I said in a quiet voice, which seemed to make his frown turn from harsh to non-existent.

"I wish there was an easier way but…"

"But what?" I pushed for more. I needed to know what was going on here. I needed to know what this was between us more desperately than breathing.

"But there isn't, and I'm afraid that if you're not prepared to stay out of harm's way, then you will just have to listen to me and learn to obey." And with that, my calm went crashing out the window.

"Obey…? Obey…? Really, Draven… *Obey?"* I asked completely stunned. He just crossed his arms over his chest and simply replied,

"Yes Keira, obey!"

"Unbelievable… And please explain to me, Mr Draven, Sir… why the hell should I when you give me no answers, no explanations, not one single clue as to why this type of thing keeps happening to me?!" I shouted, still stuck on that one word, *obey.* I was close to spitting venom at this point. I turned my head from him, as I couldn't look any longer. He would never tell me the truth, that much was clear.

"You're not ready for the truth, Keira, and I'm not the only one keeping secrets, now am I?" he said looking down at my arms, and a flush of blood ran to my cheeks at the mention of them. I put my arms around my back and spat out the words with everything that was in me, amongst this world of hurt he had created.

"You don't know anything about me!"

"Likewise… presumption is, after all, the mother from where all mistakes are born," he said adding more cryptic messages my way.

"Well, until I get the truth, why should I listen to you? Oh no, I don't think so… I will live with my own choices, thank you very much," I said, making my full feelings known and crystal clear.

"That's not an option anymore," he said moving away as if this was the end, but to hell it was!

"Draven, I think you're forgetting that you're not my father, my brother, most certainly not a lover, and well, not even a friend. So, I think it's best if you get a clearer definition of the word BOSS!" I shouted as I was about to leave, but before I had chance to open the door, he was behind me holding it closed with his hand in front of me. This again brought back memories of that night on the roof, adding to my anger.

"You don't intimidate me," I said holding my voice steady, which only worked because I wasn't looking at him. He leaned closer to the back of my ear and blew his scent around me like a cloud of doubt surrounding my words.

"I think we both know I'm more than any of those things," he whispered, and my body agreed with every word. However, my mind was screaming at me. I shook it off, looking back over my shoulder, and replied firmly,

"I don't think your wife-to-be would be very happy to hear that." Then I shrieked as he hit the door with his fist, before pushing away. I felt the wood shudder next to me.

"Celina has nothing to do with this."

"What, just like Jack's girlfriend had nothing to do with it!" I said, regretting it as soon as it was out. He turned around to look at me with the anger back, slowly killing me with his scowl.

"Oh, what has your charming little knight been saying this time?" This hurt, but not for reasons he would think. No, for it wasn't that long ago I considered *him* to be my knight. My dark protector from hordes of past Demons, but now... now he was just adding to that horde.

"He told me how you stole his girlfriend from him," I braved on, and he let out a callous laugh.

"And you believed him of course! So, what, he is scared it will happen again I suppose... by me taking you away from him? Parásitos!" he shouted getting more irate.

"Don't call him that!" I said, knowing it to be the Spanish word, vermin. He turned around in surprise, so I stated,

"I speak Spanish," with satisfaction, but he just rolled his eyes.

"Anyway, he's my friend and I am going to come here with

him again, whether you like it or not." But this was like lighting dynamite as he nearly exploded with rage.

"YOU WILL NOT!" he roared with blinding fury, but I didn't back down.

"You're saying that I can't bring him in the club?"

"I'm saying that the boy is never to set foot in my club again, and that is final!" he said folding his arms across his wide chest, once again straining the material that covered them. I gulped at the sight of muscle upon muscle. He was a pure mass of dominant alpha male, and I couldn't believe my little self was even here stood arguing against him. Half of me wanted to shy away and just whisper my submission to him, but the fighter in me screamed out with rebellious spite.

"Right, well in that case, you won't have to worry about it anymore."

"Good, finally you see sense," he said prematurely as though he had won a round.

"You misunderstand me, Mr Draven, it won't be a problem anymore... because I quit!" I said firmly, and before I could judge his reaction, I grabbed for the door and left him in the room alone once more.

I heard an almighty crash from the other side, but I just kept going, walking past Sophia without saying a word. I also walked past Karmun at the bar and the rest of the bodies that were all sat around at their usual tables. Eyes all around locked on me as always, and this is when I snapped.

"Yeah, that's right, have a good look, everyone!" I shouted, holding my arms out and spinning on one foot for everyone to see. Then I kicked a chair out of my way before storming out of this Hell.

I don't think I stopped once to take anything in until I made it to my car, when I was once again crying. This time though, it was from anger rather than pain. And it soon changed into me swearing like a sailor all the way home.

"Asshole! What a complete egotistical asshole!"

I was so confused I could hardly breathe. I gripped the steering wheel as though I was going to lose control if I didn't. It made me want to go running into Jack's arms just at Draven's commands alone. It was as though every time he demanded me to stay away from him it had the opposite effect, making me want to rebel.

It was as if even though he didn't want me, he also didn't want anyone else to have me either. But I was still at a loss to understand why. I was too wired to go back home, and I didn't want Libby to see me upset. So, I drove to my favourite spot and sat there, letting my mind drift to easier times.

I wanted the truth but all I got were more puzzles that I couldn't decipher. After my past warped my life into starring in my very own horror movie, all I would do is ask myself why me? And now this time all I seemed to be asking myself was, why *not* me?

I wanted him so badly like the ache Jack described was much more like agony, and now I had given up all my chances of seeing him again by quitting. I thought back to when I had mentioned Jack's girlfriend and he hadn't denied it, so maybe it was true? Maybe the only reason he wanted to control me was because I had been with Jack. Could there be more to the two of them, more than either of them had told me?

Whatever it was, there was no way I would believe murder! I knew the Dravens didn't live life like other people and whatever they were in to, I still couldn't see it being anything that serious! But on the other hand, what did I really know about them?

Very little.

Sophia had always been more than careful about disclosing any information about their past. I didn't know where they came from or how they made their money. I mean, I didn't even know how old any of them were. Nobody did, and in a town that they half owned, I found that astonishing.

Once I had sat there for a few hours, stewing over questions I had no answers to, I decided to get in my car and call Jack. It only rang twice and he picked up, sounding happy.

"Hey, Keira, what's up, you missing me already?" He laughed heartily on the other end, and my mood quickly lifted.

"I was just wondering if you're free tonight?" I said, suddenly worried he'd say no.

"Yeah, I have a date with a pretty blonde, but I don't know where to take her. Maybe you could advise me?" he said, and I couldn't keep the grin from my face.

"Oh, well I reckon the movies might be a safe bet."

"Mmm, I don't know anyone there that will buy all the copious amount of drugs I'm selling but I do have a truck full of guns so maybe I will get lucky... you could help me sell them if you like?" he said, and I was laughing so hard another snort nearly reared its ugly head.

"Ah-ha, nearly had another one from you there... I could feel it!" he carried on, making me chuckle... well giggling was better than the Miss Piggy impression.

"I will pick you up. What time are you free?" I asked, hoping it wouldn't be long.

"Now is good, and if you're lucky and give me good compliments, I will even treat you to a not so great meal at the diner!"

"Well, I have always liked your hair."

"Sold to the girl in Umm... what're you wearing?"

"Red."

"Sold to the girl in red, mmm red," he said like Homer Simpson.

"Okay, see you in a bit, *Homer.*" And after he laughed back, he said bye. I hung up and started the engine. It didn't take me long to get to RJ's house, I had already been there a few times, but mostly we hung out somewhere else. Once I pulled up, I didn't have to wait long as Jack was sat on the steps waiting for me. He was back to his usual ripped jeans and rock T-shirt, and today's choice was the 'Ramones'. His hair was slightly damp, it looked as if he had just got out of the shower and when the car door opened it, smelled like it.

"Hey cuteness, how was your day?" he said putting on his seatbelt.

"It's been better, so you will have to try extra hard to cheer me up," I said pulling away and heading towards the town.

429

"I will buy you a crummy dessert for after your even crummier meal."

"Mmm, I'm really looking forward to this place," I said as he directed me left at the lights.

"At least the sodas are cold, for me that's a big plus."

Once we parked up and went inside, Jack grabbed us a booth while I went to the toilets. I was just on my way out when a waiter walked past me, glaring at me with a strange tint in his eyes. I wondered if he was in any of my classes, but I couldn't remember him. One thing was for sure, he didn't look happy about seeing me here.

I slid in opposite Jack and I already had a coke waiting for me.

"Sorry about ordering already but they're never that quick, so I did panic buying." I snorted my coke out as I laughed, and my cheeks nearly made the drips boil I was so embarrassed!

"Well, that was gross."

"Thanks, next time you wanna make me laugh, make sure I don't have anything in my mouth!" I said wiping my face with a napkin.

"Duly noted," he said giving me a salute. "So, are you going to tell me why you had a bad day, or will I have to interrogate you Jack Bauer/Thomas style... you see what I did there?"

"Yeah, that was really clever, but answer me one thing, what is it with men and Jack Bauer?"

"It's a guy thing, he's like a father figure to us all, and come on, who wouldn't want to be a CTU agent?" he said, passing me the grubby menu.

"The waitress told me the specials and I could tell you them, but if you want to hear them with attitude then I'd better call her back over."

"I think I will pass, thanks."

"Suit yourself. So, bad day?" He waved one tanned hand in the air to prompt me.

"Oh yeah... I quit," I said looking over my menu.

"Really?! How come, was it after last night?" he asked, and I didn't know whether to tell him.

"Let's just say last night was the straw that broke the camel's back."

"Aww and you have a lovely back as well... but look, all joking aside, I don't want to cause any problems for you, although I must admit I am glad." Well at least one of us was, I thought as he said this.

"Yeah, anyway let's eat something, so what would you recommend?" I asked, and Jack replied,

"The place across the street." And we both laughed as the waitress gave us dirty looks.

∾

After Jack paid our bill, we walked out to the car, where there was another guy walking towards us giving me the same rude look the waiter had. They didn't have anything in common, but the look they both gave me was identical. Even Jack noticed, as he said,

"Jeez, what was his problem?" I shook my head and didn't say anything until Jack's voice pulled me out of it.

"Earth to major Kaz, hello!"

"Sorry, what did you say?"

"Just that you need keys to enter the vehicle," he said, shaking imaginary keys at me.

"Oh yeah, that might help," I said laughing, this time without humour. We got in my car and I followed Jack's directions to the cinema. We were both joking about the food we'd just eaten and the terrible service, when I asked,

"Why do you even go there?"

"Oh, me and Celina used to go there all the time," he said as if it had been yesterday but I, on the other hand, nearly slammed on the brakes. My mind automatically flew to Draven's red-headed fiancée!

"Did you just say... what I think you just said?"

"Yeah, Celina... why?"

431

CHAPTER 36

VISIT FROM A DRAVEN

As soon as Jack had said the name, I couldn't focus, my mind was everywhere and nowhere. Surely it couldn't be? But the more I thought about it, the more it made sense. I mean, how many red-headed beauties called Celina were at Afterlife…? It must be her!

I wasn't concentrating and bumped the curb, so I thought it best to pull over.

"Keira, you don't look well… maybe taking you to that diner was a mistake, you're not immune like the rest of us," he said looking concerned.

"I think I had better drop you off and go home, I don't feel so good," I said, and it wasn't a lie.

"Yeah, no problem but, babe, you really don't look good… you have gone a bit green." And I could only imagine the truth of it. I turned around and drove towards his house after convincing him that I was fine to drive but he still watched me like a hawk.

I pulled up and before he left, he told me that he would text me later to check on me, which I thought was sweet. He lifted my hand to his lips and kissed it before leaving the car. As soon as he left, I felt better, and not because I was suddenly bored with his company.

I was just so scared of saying something or letting it slip as to the whereabouts of his long-lost love… or more like, now suddenly *un-lost Draven's love*. Well, at least it was confirmed that Draven didn't do anything dreadful to her like commit murder. No, he was going to bloody marry her!

I made it home but was glad the roads were clear as my reactions weren't up to the challenge of catering for other motorists. The lights were on and I wondered if I could just get away with going upstairs without going into a conversation as to why. Well, I would soon find out.

I knocked on the door as I had left my house keys on the hook inside. I waited and could hear laughing behind the door, but one of the voices was female and it certainly didn't belong to Libby.

"Hello Keira," Sophia said as she answered the door looking at ease in my doorway.

"Umm… Hi," I said, not wanting to be rude and come right out and ask her what she was doing here.

"Sophia's been waiting for you, since you weren't at work?" Libby said, confirming I was now busted.

"Umm yeah, I went out with… mates," I said, stopping before I said Jack's name, only I didn't know why I wasn't just being honest. It wasn't as if it mattered any more.

"I'm guessing she means Jack," Libby said to Sophia, and I was suddenly aware that Sophia had been waiting for me, so what had Libby said to her, or vice versa? I was immediately on my guard seeing her here, since it wasn't long ago she was giving me the cold shoulder. I walked into the kitchen to grab a bottle of water, and said to Sophia,

"Do you want to come upstairs?" I then walked on without waiting for an answer, knowing she would follow. Libby went back to join Frank, who had fallen asleep in the lounge watching one of Libby's period dramas, as she preferred watching them rather than reading them.

Sophia and I were silent all the way up until we entered my room. I went to sit on my bed, and Sophia sat at the window seat opposite me.

"You have a great view from here, Keira," she said in a sad tone, but my mood remained the same… *sceptical.*

"I hate to be blunt, but why are you here, Sophia?" I said looking at her, but she was still staring out of my window as if searching for something. I gave her time, but I was biting my lip when she finally came out of her trance.

"My brother didn't mean for things to go that way," she said coming to join me on the bed.

"And what way was that? Demanding things of me that were not his business to try and control, or the fact that I quit over it?" I said in an emotional voice, as I always did when it came to Draven.

"My brother deserves to be happy, it's just a shame it was never going to be that easy," she said, and I didn't understand a word of it.

"Look, I'm really tired of all these cryptic messages that seem to come out of all three of you. Your brother has made his feelings very clear, crystal in fact, as to how he views me… and anyway, I'm sure his new wife will make him very happy," I said after rubbing my forehead in frustration, even if I was trying to press for any information. But knowing Sophia's reluctance to talk about anything personal, I doubted I would be satisfied.

"I understand why you are vexed and…"

"Vexed? Sophia, I am pissed!" I interrupted, but she chose to ignore that and carried on.

"Yes, and I can only apologise for it, but do you really believe that my brother only thinks of you as nothing but a waitress?" she said, shocking me at how blunt she was now being.

"To be honest, I have absolutely no idea how your brother looks at me, and I'm not even sure if he looks at me at all." I couldn't hide the sadness in my voice and Sophia picked up on it.

"But you know how you feel for him… *yes?"* Her head tilted to one side as though urging me to speak the truth to her, but I wasn't about to fold so easily.

"Why do you even ask? What does it matter how I feel, when my feelings are not returned in the same way?"

"If there are feelings there then they still matter, regardless of my brother's actions, you will learn this soon enough," she said in nothing short of a promise, only I was at a loss to understand the hidden meaning.

"Why have you really come here, Sophia?" I asked, tired of playing this game.

"I want you to come back to work at the VIP... *where you belong,*" she said, and it felt strange when she said this last bit, as though she was trying to influence me to feel the same way.

"I don't think I can do that," I said, but it felt as if I was going against nature by rejecting the idea. Ever since I had left the VIP, all I wanted was to get back there. I wasn't whole unless I was near him and if working there was the only way, then that was what I wanted. But there was another part of me, the part that was responding now.

The part that was trying to save my sanity.

"Why not? Dom wants it too," she said, and my look said it all.

"I'm not lying to you, Keira."

"There's just been so much that has happened. I don't know if I can do it. I don't know whether I could even face him again." At this she found her key to cracking me as she was getting up and buttoning up the thick crisp white jacket she wore.

"Well, sleep on it and meet with him tomorrow night to discuss it. This is at *his* request... and don't worry, he won't lose his temper again," she said as she walked to my door.

"I will think about it, but I'm not making any promises. Will you be back at college tomorrow?" I asked, and she paused as if trying to find the right words, and then smiled saying,

"Ah, I knew there was something else... there was a fire... oh no, don't worry, no one was hurt, but our part of the college is closed for the next few days due to the investigation."

"Oh my God, that's terrible... was it done deliberately?" I asked, as she obviously had all the facts.

"Deliberately...? Oh, most definitely. See you tomorrow, Keira." And with that she left, smiling a scary wicked smile. That was weird, almost as though she not only knew it had been done with purpose, but also that she knew who and what that purpose was.

Once she was gone, I picked up the phone and called RJ to see if she had heard anything.

"Oh yeah, but it's only just started so how did you hear the news so quickly?" she asked, and it was just another confirmation, something strange was going on and Sophia was involved.

"Sophia told me," I confessed in a quiet voice.

"Oh well, I guess she would know with her brother being so involved in the place. Shit, I bet this means more money to cough up from them," she said, but I could hear Jack in the background trying to get to the phone.

"Sorry Kaz, but Romeo wants to talk to you, hope you're feeling better." And then Jack's voice came on the phone before giving me a chance to say goodbye to RJ.

"Hey, how are you? You thrown up that gourmet meal yet?" he asked, and I heard RJ saying, 'Nice Romeo,' in the background, which had me smiling.

"Not yet, but here's hoping," I said before continuing with my enquiry.

"So, did you hear about my building?"

"Yeah, it's a right mess, so it looks like a few days off for you, 'cause aren't most of your classes in there?"

"Yeah, all of them for the next few days, but doesn't it seem strange... I mean, why would anyone do that?" I asked, and he laughed saying,

"You do have Reed, don't you?" I laughed again, letting it go.

"Well, at least no one got hurt, that's the main thing," I said trying to be positive, but I couldn't help this nagging feeling I had in the pit of my stomach. Something that screamed the Dravens weren't what people believed them to be.

Soon after the phone call, I went to my room with a mind swimming in an ocean of thoughts. Actually, it was more like drowning in them! In one day, I had quit, then been asked to go back, and also found out that Draven's fiancée could be Celina, the girl who went missing from Jack, two years ago. My life had turned into a Gothic drama and I couldn't decide whether to pull the plug or to keep watching.

I went into my bathroom, looking for what I wanted or in this case, *needed.*

I popped back two sleeping pills and downed the rest of the water before doing my usual night-time routine. Once I was ready for bed, I could feel the pills taking effect. So, by the time I got into bed, I fell asleep thinking about what tomorrow's meeting would bring, hopefully the opposite of today's…

That would be nice.

~

By the time I woke up the house was empty, as Libby and Frank had already gone to work. I strolled downstairs, still in some old sweat pants and a long T-shirt that I usually wore for bed. I walked into the kitchen, and there was a message waiting for me on the fridge in Libby's handwriting.

Call me when you get up, Libs xxxx

I popped the kettle on first and grabbed a breakfast bar down from the cupboard along with a cup for my tea. In England, people drink tea like the Americans drink coffee, so my brain didn't work without my tea in the morning. I made it and finished my bar, before picking up the phone and dialling Libby's work's number.

"Olivia speaking," she said in a professional tone.

"Hey Libs, what's up?" I asked.

"Umm, I've got something to tell you, I was supposed to last night, but I completely forgot," she said in a guilty tone, and I didn't like where this was going.

"Okay, what's wrong?"

"Well, Frank and I have been invited to spend the week at Frank's parents' Lakehouse with the rest of the family, but I didn't think I could get the time off," she said, and I could hear her taking a gulp of something before carrying on.

"Right, sooo…?" I said, already foreseeing what was coming next.

"Well, I got a call last night saying it would be fine as one of my clients has put back the finishing date by three weeks, so we're now clear to go… but I wanted to ask you if you would mind?"

"No, not at all, of course I don't mind. I mean, you go every year, don't you?" I said, trying to sound more positive than I felt about staying in this house by myself for a week.

"Are you sure? You could have anyone over to stay, I'm sure RJ or *Jack* especially wouldn't mind," she said giggling.

"It's fine, Libs, I think I am old enough to cope in the house alone for a week!"

"Umm… That's not all," she said like a child about to ask their mum for candy.

"What do you need?"

"I was wondering, could you do me a huge, mammoth favour, and put some of my laundry in the washer and nip to the store and get a list of supplies for me?"

After I had written a list as long as my arm of what Libs wanted at the supermarket, I picked some dirty clothes out of her hamper and put on a load before getting ready to go out.

I got changed in record time, as I wanted to get back to finish off Libby's mountain of washing. It didn't take long to get to the store and as it was a weekday, it was nearly empty. I was making my way up and down the aisles, grabbing loads of junk food that was on Libby's list when I spotted someone I knew. He was heading straight for me and I pushed my trolley past until he looked me in the face, but there was no reaction. So, I said,

"Hello Doctor Spencer, how are you?"

"Eh… fine young lady," he said frowning, with no recognition on his face whatsoever.

"You don't remember me, do you?" I asked.

"I'm sorry, but I do see a lot of patients," he said in an unfriendly tone.

"I bumped my head and Mr Draven asked you to see me?" I said, but his face remained a blank.

"I afraid you must be mistaken, my dear. I don't even know a Mr Draven," he said as he was about to move away, but I stopped him as I placed my hand on his trolley.

"I'm sorry, but... but that's impossible... you have to remember, you came to my house and you said that you have known Mr Draven for years!" I said getting panicked, but he just moved his trolley in a rude manner, and said,

"Well see, that's where you're wrong, it couldn't have been me because I don't do house calls! Now, if you will excuse me!" And with that, my hand dropped from the metal and I moved to the side, letting him pass. I stood there as though I was having some sort of meltdown. It was definitely him, I was sure of it. I mean, he didn't look as healthy as the last time I saw him, as his face now looked older. Even his eyes were a paler grey with a face full of lines, showing the stress he had mounted up over the years. But there was no doubt it had been him. I had said his name and he hadn't denied that.

I got the rest of the stuff in a daze. Maybe he suffered with short-term memory loss, but I doubted very much that a doctor's profession would be the way to go if he did. Even when I had paid for my stuff and was loading it into my car, I was still thinking about it.

The man who I had seen had been kind and gentle, but this man had been rude and definitely not a people person. And how could someone have aged so much in such a short space of time? I just couldn't get my head around it and I knew it wasn't just me going crazy, as Libby had also met him that day.

Once again, it had become one of those things that I tried to forget or put to the back of my mind, but it kept crawling its way forward, scratching away at my brain.

I was back in the kitchen munching on a tuna sandwich I had made myself when the phone went again. I picked it up trying to swallow a mouthful of bread.

"Hello," I said, but there was nothing on the other end but heavy breathing, so I said it again.

"Helloooo." But then I heard a guy who sounded like he was in the background, saying in an agitated tone,

"Hey, you have to pay to use that!" And with that, the phone went dead, leaving me shaking my head. Must have been a wrong number.

After I finished my lunch, I did the rest of Libby's laundry, and I decided to run a bath and try to relax, before I did what I knew I had to do tonight. I poured in Libby's fancy bottles of bubble bath under the running water, and it filled the room with the scent of a Tropical Delight. I lit a few candles and pressed play on the CD player that she had fitted in the bathroom wall. It had the sounds of the forest, with birds and waterfalls transforming the bathroom into a relaxing haven.

It was a huge room with a massive free-standing bath that you could fit more than one body in. I let my robe slip to the floor, and I placed one leg in, letting my skin adapt to the temperature, feeling the slight itch as it was too hot. I then braved it and dunked the rest of my body under the scented water, feeling it soothe my muscles into relaxation. I tried not to think about tonight, and concentrated on the background sound of the forest, but no matter how I tried I couldn't help it.

I kept seeing Draven's harsh face, the way he had looked at me yesterday and it made me shiver, even though my skin was hot. Being in the bath was reminding me that Draven was like water, I didn't know when it would be ice cold or scalding hot but either way, I needed it... I needed it to survive.

Once I had finished relaxing, I did all the usual girlie things, shaved my legs and any other areas that needed attention. I scrubbed my skin with a rough sponge and the soap that smelled like strawberries until I glowed. As soon as I was done in the bath, I rinsed off in the shower and washed my hair, as I could never wash it in the bath with it being so long. By the time I got out, Libby and Frank were back and frantically packing.

She popped her head round my bedroom door after about an hour of running around like a headless chicken.

"Hey honey, we're off in a minute, thanks for sorting out my washing and going to the store for me, you're a doll!"

"No problem. I just used all your fancy products in the bath to make up for it!" I said and she laughed.

"Oh well, I will get you to scrub the decking outside for that one, Cinders. Seriously though, you know you can help yourself. Are you sure you don't mind us going?" she said, looking at her watch as though they were going to be late, so I got up and hugged her saying,

"I told you, I will be fine... now go and have fun, and don't worry about Cinderella, but if I'm not in later when you ring then just leave me a message, I've gone looking for my glass slipper." She laughed at my joke.

"Okay, well I will ring you, and if you have any problems then it would only take us two hours to get back home. I love you, Kazzy," she said, hugging me back before leaving, and I shouted down to Frank to have fun before I heard the door shut.

I closed the bedroom door and put some tunes on my laptop, the first song on my playlist being a band called 'Shinedown,'. I thought it was quite apt when the first song was called, 'The Sound of Madness' which seemed to express my situation perfectly, especially considering I was listening to it while I got ready for yet another meeting with Draven.

I put on an extra vest, that had lace at the top and thick lacy straps, under my black T-shirt, with matching fingerless gloves that met the sleeves of my top. I wore tighter-fitting jeans that were one of my nicer pairs, well one of the only pairs that weren't ripped around the edges. I dried most of my hair but thanks to using Libby's new shampoo, it went extra wavy. I put it up, but some bits kept escaping so I decided to leave them, as it added to the look.

By the time I was finished '30 Seconds to Mars' had made it on my playlist with 'Stranger in a Strange Land' playing, which once again reminded me of the Dravens.

I checked myself in the mirror and when I was slightly satisfied, I grabbed my jacket, my zip-up sweater, and keys with shaky hands and left the house. The rain battered down on my car's windows mirroring my mood, the closer my car got to Afterlife.

Sophia had said that this meeting would go better than last time, with Draven's temper firmly in check, but I could never predict anything in that place. It was as though it had its own parallel universe and any other rules of the world just didn't apply. I mean, Sophia had asked me to come back to work at the VIP, and that was what Draven wanted too, but could I do that? Could I just go back to normal, after everything that had happened?

There was definitely something between Draven and myself. Some unnatural bond that kept on throwing us together, one *he* kept denying. So, I decided this would be my last try. I needed answers and I didn't care how I got them, whether it was in a calm conversation or a stormy argument.

Of course, I preferred the first one but no matter how I got them, I wasn't leaving until I was satisfied. This time, this was going to be the end.

I just hoped that this time I could finally...

Let him go.

CHAPTER 37
CAPTURED

Well, here I was, back again, ready for the same thing I had done yesterday. I was just hoping this time, I would get better results. Only tonight there was going to be an important difference, as now I wasn't an employee of his and he certainly wasn't my Boss.

I walked inside past Cameron and Jo, as they eyed me curiously. I wondered if everyone knew that I had quit. Even so, I seriously doubted they knew the cause. Hell, I wasn't even sure why, but I knew one thing, and that was I just couldn't pretend any more. Seeing Draven every day was like feeding my addiction, one I knew was bad for me, and little by little I just kept on wanting more. I was finding it harder each time I saw him to pretend that I didn't crave him as badly as I did, and it was exhausting.

The VIP came into view and my heart skipped a couple of beats as I walked to the bottom of the staircase. The two security guys didn't even bat an eyelid at my approach, they just moved aside without a word and I made my way up, biting my lip.

I reached the top and the room fell into a hushed silence, and I automatically put my head down in shame. Well, if they didn't know the reason I quit downstairs they most certainly knew up here, that much was obvious!

I walked over to the bar and noticed that none of the Dravens

443

were sat at their table, but most of the regulars were sat at theirs. It was odd without them there, like a vital organ missing.

The heart.

I had already decided that I wasn't going to make the same mistake twice, so when one of Draven's men, the one I now knew was called Zagan, came up to me and asked me to follow him, I told him a firm,

"No."

"Excuse me?" he said in a calm manner that was as equally hypnotic as Draven's. I could see him eyeing me cautiously under his long black hood and this added to the intimidation.

"I said, no. I will meet him out here or not at all," I answered, remaining strong and trying to concentrate on my own voice and not his.

"Very well, I will go and inform him of your terms. Please wait here," he said smiling, as if this amused him greatly. He left through the huge doors that I had vowed I wouldn't walk through again. The memory of being trapped in there with Draven was both terrifying and exhilarating. Yesterday, seeing Draven just proved that I couldn't be trusted. Every time I saw him, it was getting harder to control the urges I had. All I wanted was to go skin to skin, to touch, to taste and to be close to him in ways that were obviously forbidden to me.

Meanwhile, the band had started up, and downstairs was getting busier with college students piling in to hear the live band. Karmun came over to me with a friendly smile as if he'd missed me.

"Well hello there, Miss Johnson, can't get enough of us I see," he said before downing a shot himself.

"Hey Karmun, missed me?" I said being cheeky.

"Of course, my dear, but how about a drink?" he offered, but after what happened the last time, I had downed liquid courage, I decided to pass.

"Suit yourself," he said, before leaving me to get the phone that was now ringing. I watched him pick it up knowing that this rarely happened. The whole time I had worked up here I had never heard the phone ring once. So, it didn't surprise me when I saw the confusion on his face. However, what did surprise me was Karmun's reaction, as he was now bringing the phone over to me.

"It's for you," he said passing me the cordless handset. I put the phone to my ear expecting to hear a familiar voice but instead, all I got was a voice I only ever heard in my nightmares...

It seemed my past had finally caught up with me!

"Hello Ca... Umm... no I guess it's Keira now." A deep voice spoke straight from my memories, but I was unwilling to accept the unspeakable truth.

"Who is this?"

"Oh, my dear Keira, *you... know... who... this... is!*" the voice said in a mocking tone, dragging out the words and extending my pain. My heart crumbled at the sound, causing tears to form in my eyes and overfill, falling down my cheeks in seconds.

"NO, NO, NO! IT CAN'T BE!" I screamed, and everyone in the room shot me a look.

"I'm back, Keira, and guess what? I will be seeing you... very, very soon," he said, and I screamed louder than my lungs could take. I threw the phone down, smashing it to pieces. But I didn't care as everything seemed to happen in slow motion. For blurred seconds, I watched people's stares turn into a mixture of confusion and what looked like pure joy. Then, my head came up at the sound of a door opening and suddenly there was Draven.

Our eyes locked enough for a blink to release a terrified tear to roll down my cheek. There, his penetrating gaze honed into that single drop that felt like a razor blade cutting deep due to its reason for being born. I saw his lips move but his black depths never left me. Then one foot moved in my direction, and this shook me from the captivating spell Draven had caged me in.

I had to run.

So, I ran.

I turned as fast as I could and ran for the staircase, not stopping for anything or anyone. I just had to run. I had to get away from this place... *run*... He knew where I was... *run* faster, Keira... he was here... *Run!*

I kept this life-saving mantra going, and would do so until I was free. I had to stay free, I just had to keep going and stay free this time. I couldn't let him get me... I wouldn't survive it. Not again.

So, I pushed into the security guys, breaking through before they had time to react. I ran down the steps letting gravity help me, using my body's weight to do the same at the other end. I launched myself through the middle of the two men that stood in my way. I crashed through them, landing on the floor with an almighty thud. I didn't even react to the pain that shot through my limbs on impact with the solid stone floor.

The guards tried to grab me, but I crawled out of reach before getting to my feet once more and running through the crowd. My head whipped around trying to weigh up my options of getting out of here. But with Cameron and Jo taking orders from Draven, I didn't like my chances with that exit. So, I ran towards the bar knowing there was one exit that wasn't guarded. I found who I was looking for and ran towards Mike who was serving somebody.

"Hey Keira... what's wrong... you..." I cut him off, trying to control my panting and said,

"Please Mike... he, he, help me... I have to get out of here... *Please!*" I stammered but he just pulled me out of sight and in through the back.

"Okay, okay calm down, I will help you..." he said making his way through the back to where I found a familiar door.

"Go through here and keep going right around the building, you will then see your car... *go!*" he said, opening the big metal door I had used once before.

"Thank you," I said, giving him a quick kiss on the cheek before bolting through the door and down the metal steps. The door slammed shut behind me and the security light illuminated, showing me the way. I grabbed my phone out of my pocket and rang the number that I had burned to memory.

"Merseyside Police," a woman answered in monotone.

"Inspector Matthew's desk," I said in a clear panicky voice, only the woman didn't seem to respond to it.

"I'm afraid he's not at his desk at the moment," she replied, and my heart sank deeper at the news.

"Fine, but could you get him to call me? It's very important! Tell him it's Keira Johnson, he will know what it's about!" And with that, I hung up and put the phone in my back pocket just as she was asking for my number. He already knew it, so I didn't want to waste any more time on the phone when the first thing I needed to do was get away from here!

My car came into view, but it was even darker now and the few lamps that were dotted around didn't offer much light. Still running, my mind was trying to think where I had gone wrong... how did he find me?

I had to fix this. I had to get as far away from this place as I could. And then the thought hit me... if he knew where I worked then it was more than likely he also knew where I lived. Then it came to me, of course he knew where I lived because he had been the one to call the house today... he had been the heavy breather. Oh shit!

Once I reached the handle to my truck it didn't budge, I realised it was locked and I fumbled for the keys out of my pocket. I was finding it hard to focus, so when I finally found them, I dropped them on the floor as I was trying to get the key in the lock. I bent down to pick them up, seeing the gravel minus silver keys...

They were gone.

"Looking for these?" a voice said, and I jumped, nearly having a heart attack at the same time. I stood up seeing Vincent Draven, who was casually leant against the hood of my truck, holding my keys.

"Umm... yeah, thanks..." I said, trying to sound calmer than I felt as my heart hadn't yet recovered. I held out my hand to retrieve my keys, but he didn't pass them to me. Instead, he enclosed all his fingers around them, concealing the metal bunch. My pulse started to speed up as the panic was building.

"I think I'd better hang on to these for the moment," he said in his usual smouldering voice that was like his brother's, and it had the same effect as it invaded my senses. I took in a deep breath and pushed the calming sound from my mind, becoming in control once more. I still hadn't said anything, so he spoke again, but this time I started breathing through my mouth so as not to let the scent in.

"Where are you going, Keira?" he asked, and I took in two more deep breaths before answering him.

"Something has come up… a family emergency and I have to go." I tried to make my voice as steady as possible, but it was proving hard with the way my blood raced around my body in a blind panic. I continued, adding,

"If you could please give your brother my apologies and tell him that I will meet him some other time."

"Why don't you tell him yourself?" he said nodding in the direction I had just come from. There I saw a tall, dark figure striding towards me and closing the gap between us quickly. He wore a long black jacket that was close to the floor, and he looked more terrifying than I had ever seen him look before. He had two men walking behind him further back, and one of them I knew to be Zagan. My body felt like it was being rattled as I couldn't help but shake. I decided to make a run for it as I knew if I didn't, I wouldn't get another opportunity. So, before he could get any closer, I dashed to the side Vincent wasn't blocking.

But in the time it took for my body to turn, I was facing Zagan, who stood there blocking my way. His face scared me as the long thick scars on his face looked deep and angry. I couldn't be sure, but it looked as though his tattoos were moving around it.

I didn't know how this was possible or how he got to me so fast, as he must have moved at an impossible speed. But he wasn't the only one with this amazing talent, as when I looked back towards Draven, he was now stood opposite me. Close enough for me to feel the heat coming from his imposing body. My body pressed back against my door and I could feel the cold metal seep through my clothes, freezing my skin. My head looked up slowly, taking all of him in through my fear.

"I wouldn't do that again if I were you," he warned, making me quiver at the sound of his controlling command.

"I have to go!" I said trying to sound strong, but he wasn't buying it.

"And where would that be?" he asked looking down at me, but I couldn't meet his eyes, knowing that if I did, I might tell him everything.

"As I told your brother, I have a family emergency."

"Really? I don't think so, Keira." He looked to his brother and held out his hand to him and without saying a word, his brother handed him my car keys.

"Please! You don't understand I have to go..." I decided to plead with him. I finally looked up at him with tears rolling down my cheeks. His features didn't change, but he didn't look as angry anymore, no, if anything, he looked eerily in total control.

"Who was on the phone, Keira?" he asked me the question I didn't want to answer.

"You can't keep me here against my will!" I shouted, finding some bravery that was buried deep.

"I think you will find that I can..." he said, leaning into me and finished with,

"...*Quite easily.*" This was said with so much confidence that I could do nothing but believe him. My phone started to vibrate in my back pocket and I jumped when I felt it. This was my chance and I knew which card I would play.

"That's the police ringing me and if I don't answer it then he will send the cops to look for me, he knows I'm here," I said warning him without moving. But he leant in closer still and I flinched when he started putting his hand on the metal frame of my truck above my head. I mistakenly took a deep breath through my nose, letting my body fill with his warm scent. I closed my eyes and more tears fell in the path of those before them. He got close to my ear and said,

"Well, we'd better not keep Inspector Matthews waiting then." And then he wrapped his strong arm around underneath my jacket and my top. I sucked in a quick breath when he placed his palm on my skin, pushing his hand down the curvature of my spine until reaching down into my pocket, retrieving my phone. By this time, I couldn't breathe at all with the feel of his touch, amazed to find even in this situation, I was still ready to explode from the feel of his skin on mine.

I then let the shock from this new information sink in. How did he know who Inspector Matthews was, had he overheard me ringing him? He pulled back from my body and stood as he was before. He flipped open my phone and answered with ease.

"Inspector Matthews." As soon as he answered, I let out the loudest scream for help I could, but my voice didn't follow through with my mind's instruction. Instead, Draven's hand reached up lightning-fast, so close to my face. He held out his palm to my throat without touching me and then he squeezed his hand into a tight fist as if taking my voice from me, locking it away in his iron grasp.

I couldn't speak!

My mouth would move, but in vain. Not one sound came from my lips and I held my hands around my throat, as all I could feel was a tingling in my larynx. I tried to run, but as soon as the thought entered my mind, Vincent's hand went to my shoulder, holding me still and restraining me back against my car door.

Draven just shook his head telling me a firm 'no', while he continued on the phone.

"Yes Inspector, she is fine… a little worked up as you can understand, but she will be better when she has had some rest." His hand was still held into a fist and I had stopped struggling, giving up under Vincent's superior strength.

"She will remain here at the club, it is safer that way," he said, and I shook my head at him in defiance. *Safer*, what a joke! I wasn't safe with this insane, controlling man and his brother. I had been so wrong about him. He had been the enemy all along and I had been too blind with love to see it!

"I will get her to ring you when she has calmed down, as I am sure she has many questions… No, that too has also been taken care of." I was now wondering what else he had 'taken care' of. I couldn't help the tears that flowed freely, and I wiped them away with my sleeve, feeling like a helpless frightened child.

"I thank you for your prompt delivery of the case file and please, give my regards to your Chief Superintendent for me," he said before hanging up and placing my phone in his jacket, along with my keys.

He finally unlocked his fist, and this released my voice back to me. I coughed at the feeling it made, making my eyes water more. I tried to move away when his fingers started to caress my neck, but his grasp tightened until I stopped struggling. He did this until my breathing resumed some semblance of calm before letting go.

I couldn't believe what was happening, *it couldn't be real.* How was he doing these things...? What was he? I wanted to scream out, but I was afraid he would take control again, so I remained quiet and he must have read my thoughts, because he lifted his hand to my face and swept my wet cheek with his thumb.

"Good girl," he whispered gently, then turned to Vincent, who removed his hand that had been keeping me restrained.

"Now, are you going to come with us quietly?" Draven asked keeping his tone soft, but I had other ideas, as soon as I got another opportunity, I was making a break for it!

"Umm, I didn't think so... *pity,"* he said, as once again he must have read my thoughts before I had time to realise my mistake.

"I think we should finish this as the locals are getting restless," Vincent said to his brother, nodding in the direction of Cameron and Jo who were still admitting people into the club. They were looking over to us and I wanted to scream out, but once again I didn't as Draven would undoubtedly react to it.

Draven turned to Zagan, whom I had forgotten, but was still stood close enough to have seen this all play out.

"Zagan, you know what to do... take care of it," he commanded, and I didn't like the sound of it, so I shouted,

"Please don't hurt them...! I'll...I'll come quietly," I said, not knowing if that was true, but I didn't want anything bad to happen to them because of me. Draven turned back to me with his eyebrows knitted together, frowning. But my pleas fell on deaf ears and Draven turned to Vincent as if he had asked a silent question.

"Well, be my guest, but I doubt you will get the outcome you're looking for," Draven said to his brother. Vincent responded by placing his hand on the side of my head. I tried to duck out of the way, but it was now Draven's turn to restrain me so that Vincent could continue.

He stepped into me until his body was flush with mine against the truck. His hands shackled my wrists and held them firmly to my sides. I also didn't miss the way he lifted the bottom of my top up slightly, so that he could make contact with my skin. I shivered at the flash of electricity that coursed through me. Then his thumbs started to make small circles, offering a comforting touch.

His brother gripped the bottom of my chin and turned my face to his. He looked deep into my eyes and I jerked at the sound of his voice which had entered my mind, although no sound came from his lips.

I wanted to get away but was held in a vice-like grip by not one, but two Dravens. So, I did what I always do when trying to cast out bad things. I pushed with everything I had. I pushed his voice to the back of my brain not focusing on his words. I let them mingle into one long mumble, like the sound of voices through a thick door or wall. They were trying to get louder, and his eyes looked more intense, so in turn I closed my eyes tight, pushing further and further until eventually it stopped and there was silence.

I let out a long, exhausted sigh, and found I was once again trying to control my breathing. When I opened my eyes, Vincent was frowning at me, like Draven usually did.

"Frustrating isn't it?" he said to his blonde brother, who couldn't take his eyes away from mine.

"Extremely," he responded with irritation dripping all over the word.

Draven let me go when his brother did, and I slumped back against the door. I was exhausted and completely drained. Whatever Vincent was, he was damn powerful that was for sure. I didn't know what exactly they were trying to do but I had an awful feeling I was about to find out.

"No matter, we have other means... Takeshi," Draven said holding out his hand to the Japanese man who appeared from behind him. I had seen this man before, sat at Draven's table, wearing the same as he wore now. He pulled out a black square of fabric from one of his long sleeves, before breaking a vial on to it, spilling the liquid and soaking the material. He then passed it to his master, and I had a feeling this wasn't going to be a good thing for me, so I took my one last chance.

I was hoping, with it being a last-minute decision that it could work. I ran to the side as it was now free with Zagan gone, dealing with other things. I could feel some distance grow between Draven and myself but in my haste, I slipped, losing my footing. I waited to feel the ground below my knees, but I was still upright as Draven had grabbed me from behind.

"Oh no you don't, my little one." His arms held me tight as I started to fight against his body. One of his arms circled my waist, which was holding my torso still as I tried to twist. So, I decided to let out a scream for help instead, but this plan was also obstructed by him clamping his hand over my lips. He had the fabric covering half my face so that my nose and mouth would have no choice but to inhale the strange scent.

I held strong, not breathing and using all of my strength to hold on. I tried to break free, clawing at his hand that was clamped over my face, but it was obviously an impossible task and he knew it. My eyes streamed with tears and I couldn't believe that my nightmares were coming true... I couldn't believe this was happening again!

"Don't struggle, Keira... just breathe now," he whispered in my ear. But this had the opposite effect as I tried to twist away more from my muscled cage.

"Stop fighting it." His voice was soft, gentle and also soothing. My body began to react to it, giving up the fight I had

no chance of winning. He could feel it too as he didn't crush me so tightly. My lungs had finally run out of air and if I didn't inhale, I was going to pass out anyway, so I took in sharp little breaths that were shallow and out of control.

"That's it... good girl... calm yourself and take deeper breaths," he said softly, and his arms were soon taking my weight instead of fighting against it. I felt his hand leave my mouth and start to smooth back my hair, caressing me against him and pulling me tighter into the cradle of his body.

"My little Keira, sleep now. You are safe." I heard his voice in my head and then I was floating. A rosy mist flowed over me and his voice was the last thing I remembered before falling asleep in his arms once again,

"You're mine now."

CHAPTER 38

HELD AGAINST MY WILL

"Did you get a trace on the call?"

"No, he just wasn't on long enough. Don't worry, Dom, we will find him. She is safe now... Do you think she will fight against it?"

"Undoubtedly."

That last voice that spoke, I knew belonged to Dominic Draven, and the other was his brother, Vincent. I hadn't opened my eyes, but I could now hear the voices clearly. I didn't want to alert anyone that I was fully awake, so I kept very still and waited.

"What will you do about the girl if she does not co-operate?" Vincent asked his brother, and I held my breath waiting for the answer.

"She will obey... she is stubborn, yes, but she can be controlled in this," Draven said, and I had to control the urge not to get up and punch him! *How dare he!* I didn't understand why they were doing this, but I wasn't about to stick around to find out. The first chance I got, I was so out of here! That's if I could find my way out of this fortress before they caught up to me.

I had to get out of here... I just had to!

Then I heard the door open and my chance presented itself.

"My Lord, there is something you should see," another voice spoke, this time one I didn't recognise. Then I could hear footsteps coming closer to me until they stopped next to where I lay. I could feel, by the usual heat and drugging scent, that it was Draven standing over me. I continued to breathe evenly, as I would have done if I had been asleep. He leaned down, and I felt his hand come to my face. Two of his fingers touched my cheek moving down my skin, and I didn't move, hoping he would believe my act. He seemed satisfied as he moved his hand away and walked across the room.

"Very well, show me."

I heard the sound of several people go out of the room and the door closed. This was my signal to move, so I opened my eyes slowly until it was confirmed I was finally alone. I knew they would be back soon, so I didn't have long. I was in a room I hadn't seen before, which was long and full of grand chairs and luxurious sofas positioned everywhere. There was a massive fireplace in the middle of the room that you could have fit an elephant inside. Two statues of winged angels stood abreast the fireplace and reached half the way up the wall, taller than your average man. It was all made from carved pale marble, which seemed to be the theme of the room.

In fact, there was marble everywhere. Candlesticks, the moulding on the ceiling, chairs, tables, even figures of winged Demons sat on their own stands. I didn't take long looking about the room, just long enough to find what I was looking for. I saw there was another door on the other side of the room, so I ran for it and opened it slightly without going through it. I then ran over to one of the tall windows that were framed with thick red and gold embroidered curtains hanging to floor. I stepped behind one side, letting the material shield me from sight. I then waited for them to come back, knowing this was my best chance to escape.

I didn't have to wait long as I heard footsteps and a door opening. I counted three different voices, and it didn't take Draven long to notice that I was missing. I bit my lip as I heard his anger erupt.

"She couldn't have gone far I can still feel her near... FIND HER!" He thundered the order, which echoed in the room like the Devil calling. I heard one person leave after saying a quiet,

"Yes, My Lord."

"When you find her, bring her to me at once... I will be in my quarters." Draven's order must have been directed at his brother, and I shuddered at the thought of being recaptured.

"Of course, Dom, have no fear for we will find her," Vincent said in reply before leaving. I waited to hear one more door close and then I would make my move. As soon as it did, I peeked around the fabric, seeing that the room was empty once again. I dashed out, looking for another door. There were three in total, one in the middle and one either end, so I chose the one I didn't think anyone had used.

I ran to the door at the far end, hoping it wasn't locked. Thankfully it wasn't, so I opened it cautiously before walking through. Once inside the other room I looked around to find a small storeroom of sorts, filled with trunks and boxes. There were piles of newspapers stacked high and some furniture that was covered with large white sheets. It was darker in this room with only the light coming from the small crack under the door. It was enough for me to see and feel my way around.

Well, one thing was for sure, I couldn't hide in here forever. They would soon find me. I traced the walls until I found yet another door. Bingo! I stepped quietly around the piles of files on the floor and finally got to it. I turned the handle, but it was locked... *Damn!*

I waited a minute, thinking what I was going to do next, when I heard a strange noise as if someone had just unlocked it. I froze, waiting to be discovered, but nothing happened. The door didn't move nor did the handle, so I tried it again and this time it worked.

I opened the door cautiously and again peeked through, checking it was all clear. I entered a hallway that was at the top of a staircase. Looking over the balustrades, I found that I was higher up than I first imagined as the stairs went on, continuing down until I couldn't see the bottom. I was starting to panic now as I wasn't sure I would ever find my way out of this stone maze. And what was to say that the next door I opened didn't lead right to Draven himself.

My mind started to whirl around making me feel dizzy, so I backed away from the immense drop I was still staring at. I fell back to the wall, holding myself up using the different stone boulders jutting out which made good hand rests. What was I going to do? How was I ever going to get out of here? And when I finally did, what then? Was I to run from one horror straight into my own personal Hell?

I must carry on moving. I couldn't just wait here for them to find me. At least if I kept going then I had a chance, didn't I?

I walked along the hallway that was badly lit by only a few candles held in holders on the wall. I kept going until I stopped at the sound of voices. I held my body still and tried to quieten my laboured breathing. Once the sound moved and went silent again, I carried on until I came to another door at the end. I was just about to open it when I felt a hand grab my shoulder and a scream erupted out from my lips.

"Ssshh, it's only me!" Sophia stood opposite me holding an antique oil lamp that hung on a brass stick.

"Sophia?" I said as if to check.

"Yes, now come with me," she said, grabbing my arm softly, pulling me back down the hallway.

"Where are we going?" I said, not trusting her.

"I'm getting you out of here, but you must be quiet... follow me," she said letting go of my arm, and I followed her until she stopped at a large tapestry that hung from gold hooks on the wall. I stood looking at her, confused as to why she was now staring at it. She turned to me and passed me the lamp.

"Hold this," she said as her hands flowed over the woven material without touching it. Her hands went around in patterns and I was about to ask her what she was doing, when I heard the sound of stone grinding against stone. I couldn't see anything but when she lifted the tapestry back, she revealed a passageway in the wall. She took the lamp back and motioned with her hand for me to follow.

"How did you do that?!" I asked astounded, as she led me up the narrow tunnel.

"Do what?" Her voice sounded steady, as if what she had just done had been an everyday normal occurrence. The walls were wet, and the floor was slippery as my footing nearly gave way a few times. But every time this happened, Sophia saved me by grabbing my arm, steadying me.

"Careful!" was all she would say before letting go. I was suddenly aware of how strong Sophia was for such a small delicate frame.

"How much further?" I asked, as my legs were growing tired from working so hard to stay upright.

"Here we are, just through this door," she replied in monotone. The door opened without her laying a finger on it. I jumped at the noise and my eyes squinted to adapt to the brightly lit hallway we were now stood in. She carried on, but now I could see her fully, I was beginning to get wary as she was acting strangely. I had a job to keep up with her as it was obvious she was in a rush.

She was nearly at another door when I had finally caught up to her, stopping her with my hand on her shoulder. She turned to look at me and her face was frightening until it softened at my reaction of seeing her looking so angry.

"Sophia, what's wrong?" I asked warily.

"Nothing, I just want to get you out of here, that's all," she said looking around, but I didn't trust her words, so I asked,

"Why are you helping me anyway?" My suspicious voice was getting louder.

"Because I do not always agree with my brother's decisions..." she said opening the door for me to walk through, and stupidly I went inside.

Once inside the room, Sophia stood next to me, but I couldn't take my eyes away from the man that now stood opposite us.

"...But that doesn't mean I would ever disobey him, Keira," Sophia whispered to me, before going up to kiss her brother's cheek and returning to the door.

"Thank you, Sophia, you have done well," Draven said, before his sister left out of the same door we had just come in. As soon as the door shut, I turned quickly to try and run back through it, but the door made a locking sound, sealing me in with Draven. I banged my fist hard on the wooden door, expressing my full feelings about being trapped.

"That won't help," he said in his smooth, deep voice that I had quickly grown to hate, as he was no longer the Draven I knew. He was now my captor and I his prisoner, and all I wanted was to escape!

"Then what will?!" I shouted back at him, as I turned around.

"Co-operation might be a good idea," he said sarcastically, but I just bit my lip, and this time it was in anger.

"What you really mean is *submission*. To obey blindly your every command, is that it?" A shrug was all I received as an answer.

"I might consider that, if everything wasn't on your terms!" I snapped back.

"Well, if you were left to your own devices, then I doubt you would last long, especially with what you've got in mind," he said keeping a cool manner. I on the other hand was not.

"And what the hell is that supposed to mean?!"

"I think you know what it means… you're obviously not safe to deal with this alone," he answered rubbing the back of his neck, as if this was all very frustrating to him.

"What, and I am safe here, *with you…?* Oh, I don't think so!" I said, feeling my skin get hotter as my anger was multiplying with every word out of his perfect mouth. He let out a short laugh at my words, and said,

"And have I hurt you?"

"Not yet, no, but you are keeping me here against my will!"

"Well, if you weren't always so difficult, then things might have gone differently, but I am only keeping you here for your own safety," he said, slowly losing his calm exterior. I decided to play it a different way, as I knew if I pushed it, we would just end up in another shouting match, and his temper wouldn't help me right now.

"Look, I have to go. You don't understand how important it is… Please let me leave," I said, pleading once again with a man who had a will of iron.

"I understand more than you think… *Catherine.*" He said the name I hadn't heard for the longest time, so that it felt foreign to me even though it was my own. My mouth actually dropped as I couldn't believe it had come to this.

He walked over to his desk, and I finally had chance to take in my surroundings, realising I was in the same room I had seen before. It was the room I was brought into when Layla had stabbed me. The night that Draven tried to make me believe was all a dream. But this only confirmed it… it had all happened! I could see the bed at the far end of the room on a higher platform, which was the same one I had woken up in that night. I looked to the side of me and noticed the couch that I had laid upon, bleeding.

I wanted to cry out at my realisation. I knew deep down it had happened, and I wanted to lash out at him for making me feel crazy. But there were more important matters to deal with. Like for starters, when did he find out my real name and what else did he know…?

Meanwhile, Draven had retrieved a folder from on top of his desk and was bringing it closer to me. I already knew what it contained, so I looked away in shameful disgust.

"I don't want to talk about that," I said feeling the emotion building up.

"What you mean is you don't want to talk about your past!" he said as he threw the folder back down on the desk making the contents spill out, scattering my life on pages across the polished wood. I kept swallowing, as I could taste the acid that my stomach produced. The anger started to replace my shame. What right did he have to do this to me?

"My past is none of your business! How dare you judge me! So, you think because you found out my real name that this proves something…? You don't know anything!" I shouted as my hands shook.

"Don't be foolish, Catherine, I'm not judging you, damn it! I'm trying to protect you, if you would only let me," he said trying to calm me down, but it was too late for reason, we were well past that now.

"Protect me from what?!"

"From that!" he shouted pointing to the file spread out like a collage of my life.

"Well thanks, but I don't need your help. I coped on my own last time and I can do it again!" I said, but he looked down at my sleeves and came back with the ultimate hurt.

"Is that what you call coping?"

I looked down at my arms that were covered with numerous layers as I still had my jacket and zipped hooded sweater on. I was so angry I could feel the tears developing and I wanted to scream out at him, but instead, I calmed my breathing and said in a controlled way,

"You think you know everything, just because you have read some stupid file filled with evidence pictures and test results, but you don't know anything about how I coped. You just take one look at me and you come up with the same conclusion as everybody else does! After all, it was you that said presumption is the mother from which all mistakes are born!" By the end of this little speech, I couldn't stop the beads of water that escaped my eyes.

"Then tell me," he said, his voice filled with compassion at seeing me cry.

"What?" I said nearly sobbing.

"Well, you say I don't understand, you say that I don't know the whole story, and this is true, I don't." He flipped open the file and continued, "I have read this file over and over and there is not one statement from you, so why don't you tell me what happened?"

"NO!" I shouted quickly, shaking my head as if it would erase this new nightmare. There was no way I ever wanted to relive what happened, but he walked closer to me, stopping only a foot away. He tilted his head to see my face, but I kept my head down.

"All I want to do is go... I...I just need to get out of here," I said without meeting his eyes, as I could feel them burning into mine.

"Alright then, we will strike a deal. If you tell me what really happened, I will let you leave," he said, and my heart rate shot up a couple of notches.

"You wouldn't?" I asked keeping on my guard.

"I give you my word that if by the time you have finished, and you still want to leave, then I will allow it but…"

"But?"

"I have to be satisfied with the truth," he said, placing his hand under my chin and then bringing my face up to see his. My skin tingled under his fingertips and I mentally scorned myself for still feeling like this around him. I bit my bottom lip again, and he smiled at the sight before letting go and stepping back away from me.

My body instantly started to cool down with the distance he put between us, and I almost wanted to go running back to him so that I could feel warm again. What was I thinking? NO! He was the enemy. I had to get that through to myself, he wasn't safe… he was dangerous!

Although, he hadn't hurt me, and he did keep saying how he was protecting me. God, this was so confusing, like being pulled one way by logic and the other by need and hope. And Lord knows how much I was in need of a protector right about now!

He moved further back, putting a distance between us I didn't like, and motioned for me take a seat. I did as I was told, as with the story I was about to tell I didn't know if my legs were up to the task of holding me up.

"What do you already know?" I asked, not wanting to tell him any more than I had to, but he must have realised what I was thinking because he just gave me a warning,

"Keira… please be reasonable," he said, quickly going back to calling me the name I was used to. I instantly felt better hearing it. I nodded, and he let out a sigh before he answered me.

"I know your name is really Catherine Keiran Williams and that you're twenty-three years old. You were born on the 7th day of the 7th month in 1987 in Liverpool. When you were seven years old, you had something very unusual happen to you and you started seeing things you couldn't explain. You soon learned to control it and lived a semi-normal life until you went to University, moving to Southampton at the age of twenty-one. There, you were to become a victim of a kidnapping." Once he was finished, I couldn't find my voice.

That was my life in a nutshell. The very one I had been running from for over two years. And this was the night that I had finally hit a brick wall, preventing me from running any more. I wanted to scream out in pain at what he knew.

He was the one person in the world that I wanted to keep this from and now my fake world was crumbling around me, leaving me standing in the rubble of my horrifying past.

So, I took a deep breath and started to do the one thing that I didn't want to do…

I stopped running.

CHAPTER 39

SCARS OF MY PAST

"My family all called me Keira or Kazzy, as my dad was convinced I was going to be born a boy. So, my middle name is Keiran, which is what they would have called me if I had been. This was after my grandfather. It was only when I went to Uni that I dropped it, taking on a more adult sounding Catherine, you know, like a new start," I said calmly, wishing I could have stopped at that, but I knew my chances of getting out of here lay with the story I had to tell. But his next words surprised me,

"I like the name Keira and its meaning."

"Its meaning?" I had to ask as even I didn't know what my name meant. He gave me a half-smile which looked far too good on him.

"Another time perhaps."

"Right," I said with disbelief. When did this guy ever tell me anything, I thought dryly?

"So, I was studying History and Spanish, as I do now, but I also studied Art. For the first few months we had a guy teaching us who was due to retire. He was waiting for his replacement to arrive and unfortunately, he did. His name was Hugo Morgan." At the sound of me saying his name, it seemed I wasn't the only one affected, as Draven's body went rigid at the thought. His now intense stare wasn't helping, so I lowered my face to continue.

"He was renowned for his love of surrealism, which at the time I also had a passion for." I shuddered remembering the day and hating that I had no clue at the time what it meant. Draven's eyes never left me, and I found this a strange mix of both comforting and unnerving.

"At first, he seemed charming, and it was clear his love for art had made him a very popular tutor among all of his students, including me." I laughed without humour as I continued,

"I remember my friends being jealous as he seemed to single me out as his favourite pupil. Time went on and it started getting more serious. I would see him following me everywhere, every time I turned around, there he was. At first, I put it down to being paranoid but then it soon became clear that he was stalking me. So, as a result, I found myself skipping classes to get away from him but soon he confronted me." I closed my eyes briefly as my mind drifted back to that day.

"He fed me this story, telling me how he was sorry if he had been a bit weird, it was just down to the fact that I reminded him of someone dear to him and that he didn't want it affecting my work. I decided to forget about it, feeling sorry for him and I went back to class, stupidly thinking it was now sorted. *Little did I know it was far from over,"* I added quietly.

"Even my flatmate, Charlotte, wasn't convinced and didn't trust him. She thought that I should have gone to the police or spoken to someone at the university. But I didn't want to cause problems, so again I stupidly ignored her advice. Of course, I was about to realise my mistake and pay dearly for it." I paused wiping away a stray tear at the thought, but this made Draven look at me full of concern, so he stood up and said,

"I think that's enough for now, we should continue this later, after you have had some rest." But I didn't want to rest. I needed to get out of here as quickly as possible. The more time I was here, the less chance I had of giving Morgan the slip.

"I'm fine. I would prefer to carry on... *Really,"* I said

nodding, so he sat back down to listen to the rest of my dark drama, looking as if it caused him pain.

"You said you knew about my visions. I don't know how you do and even if I asked, I doubt you would give me any answers anyway. But I guess I'm used to the fact you seem to know impossible things about me without ever explaining why," I said to him, but he didn't react the way I thought he would. He just smiled and then shocked me with his reply,

"You will have your answers too, if you are ready for them."

"Really?" I asked not hiding my surprise, but I quickly gathered this was just another tactic to keep me here, and I was soon proven right.

"Yes... if you wish, but after you have finished, and I am satisfied with all I need to know," he said in a way that made me believe him.

"Well, one night it all changed. You see, I used to have visions of what I can only describe as creatures. I see everyday, normal people and then they would change into things I couldn't explain. So, I figured if I had to live with it, then I would at least try and find a way to control it and well... I found a way," I said, and Draven held a fascinating grin and was looking at me, not like I was crazy, as he should have been, but in awe and amazement. As if I had mastered the secret to immortality or something.

"How?" he asked shaking his head in bewilderment. Which got me wondering what he knew about it? Could he be the same as me?

"I would sketch what I saw, kind of locking it away, I guess, so it couldn't come back. After a while the visions only came to me in dreams and pretty soon, I learnt how to control these too. The visions calmed through years of concentration and persistence. But this particular night I had a nightmare that I had no control over. This happened sometimes and unfortunately still does..." He nodded his understanding, and I continued,

"That night I saw Mr Morgan, not as a Demon, but being terrorised by one. It was everywhere he went, following him like a plague that was slowly killing him. It's hard to explain but I got the impression that it was sucking the life from him." Draven reacted to this new bit of information and finally it looked as if I had told him something he didn't know. He rose up from his seat suddenly, looking agitated.

"I have to leave you momentarily, but I won't be long," he said moving towards the door, but he stopped. Then he turned and took a few steps that placed him in front of me to then run a hand along the side of my neck. He held me there and when I looked down escaping the intense moment, he simply used his thumb to apply pressure under my chin. I had no choice but to look back up at him.

"Please stay here and wait for me, Keira." And with that said, he quickly left me alone to calm the pounding of my heart. I wondered why this bit of my past affected him so much.

I got up and decided to explore the room. It was like something you would find in a king's bedchamber. There were tapestries that were of different war scenes hung about the room over stone walls. There were battles with Japanese warriors mounted on horses fighting what looked like winged soldiers, flying from the Heavens.

The sitting room section of Draven's quarters consisted of comfortable furniture that screamed this was a man's room. It was both masculine in its heavy wood and iron fixtures, but also luxuriously expensive with its rich colours and plush materials. It was one of the most beautiful rooms I had ever been in, but it was also years beyond its master's age. This I found surprising.

I went over to the couch that I had been placed on and noticed a dark red stain that looked as though it could have been from my blood. I leant down to touch it, when I jumped at the sound of the door opening. I expected it to be Draven coming back, thinking how quick he had been, but it wasn't him.

A small girl walked in, with short black hair with blue streaks in it. She had a young, kind face and wore a long, black skirt, with a blue corset on top of a shirt she wore underneath. She held a tray of drinks and fruit, which she placed on the table next to where I had been sitting.

"My name is Candra. My master said you might be thirsty or

hungry. If there is anything else I can bring you, then please just ask, there's an intercom on the side of the door I came through," she said so sweetly.

"Thank you, Candra," I said, feeling awkward at a servant bringing me drinks, as after all, it wasn't long ago I was doing the same job. She smiled and then left out of the same door, which I heard lock immediately. So, Draven *didn't* trust me. Of course not, why should he? I mean really, just how many times had I run from the guy.

I suddenly realised how dry my throat was and I nearly ran to the tray to get a drink. I poured some water from the silver jug along with some ice cubes that fell in my glass, and downed it in one before refilling it. I also grabbed a few grapes from the bunch and went back to exploring the room.

I walked over to the large mahogany desk situated against one wall, that was now scattered with bits of my life. I moved the papers around until I came to two pictures that sent dread up and down my spine. It felt as though I was being electrocuted by a loose wire I wasn't holding. I picked up the first photo, which was of me in the hospital, taken by a nurse for the police. I looked like death warmed up.

I was an utter mess, covered in cuts and bruises marbling over my broken body. I had a sheet that covered my chest, but my shoulders were exposed, showing ugly red marks and angry welts that went across my neck. Bruises ran around my arms like bra straps, only these were from restraints of a different kind. My face however, only had marks from where I was still traumatised, as my eyes were red and sore from the tears that had flowed for days.

But this wasn't the worst sight. No, what made me feel sick to my stomach was seeing both my arms in bandages wrapped from wrist to elbow. Every slice in my skin was showing through by the blood weeping from their many stitches.

I pushed it onto the floor in disgust, knowing that Draven had seen me this way made my heart break a little. The other picture had the opposite effect. It was Morgan's mug shot. Well, of course, Morgan wasn't his real name, but during my experience it was all I had known him as, so this is how he remained.

In this photo he looked like he did when he had taken me... pure to the bone evil. When I was in class I had once thought he looked friendly, and even kind of handsome, but now that memory made me feel sick at my foolish first impression.

He was young for a tutor, being only in his late twenties. He had bronze-coloured hair cut back and short, and he usually wore a trilby hat when first coming into lectures. He had a longish face, with a pointed chin and a long straight nose to match.

However, his eyes were the most outstanding feature, as no matter what feelings were behind the smile, his sage green coloured eyes never lied. They were always cold, as if frozen in a time of pain, one he wouldn't let go of.

I hadn't seen this face for two years, yet I could still remember the horror which it caused as if it had been only hours ago. I felt as though I couldn't breathe, as reality hit me once more.

This monster was back, and it was clear...

He was coming for me.

"Are you alright?" Draven's voice broke the spell Morgan's face held over me. I turned, still holding the picture in my hand. My wet cheeks were proof enough for what I grasped in my hand. He walked over to me slowly, and he looked concerned at the knuckles turning white from crushing the picture in my fist. He approached cautiously, like you would a frightened doe caught in a trap. I bit my lip, looked up and saw him raising my tense hand to take in his own. One hand held my wrist gently, while the other started peeling back my fingers, using just enough strength to get the job done.

"Let go, Keira," he uttered tenderly, and I knew he wasn't just referring to the crumpled face in my hand. I gave him a small nod and let him take the object of my distress away from me. He let it drop to the floor, and I couldn't stop myself from placing my foot on top of it and kicking it back behind me where I wanted it to stay... forever.

"Keira, I…" His voice brought me back to what needed to be done, so I interrupted him before his words could affect me further.

"I'm fine, Draven. Let's just get this over with," I said as I walked past him, resuming my seat and wiping the angry tears away with the back of my gloved hand.

"I'm not sure you are ready, why don't you…" he said, but again I just cut him off,

"Look, I just want to get this over and done with, so I can get the hell out of here and unless you're going to let me go now, I think we should proceed."

"As you wish," he said sitting, trying to keep his face neutral.

"Yeah, I didn't think so," I said under my breath, but from his expression it looked as if he caught it and its full meaning although he didn't comment, so I continued with my story.

"So, where was I?" I asked out loud. For the first time since meeting Draven, he looked uncomfortable. He raked his hand through his thick dark hair, and I watched with wide eyes. It was unbelievable. Here I was, telling the haunting truth behind my life of lies, and I was fantasising about being the one to run my hands through his hair. Was it as soft as it looked?

"You were locking out Demons," he stated calmly.

"Ah yes, well… now I had a sketch of his monster that was haunting him daily in black ink, firmly locked away in my notebook. Only, what I didn't plan on was the next day there was a fire drill, and we all left our bags and jackets in the class. Of course, at that time I was in Art. So, when I got back my notebook was gone, along with Morgan. I didn't give it much thought until I was walking to my dorm later that day and he approached me." I shook my head remembering what happened and all the mistakes I made.

"What did he do?" Draven asked on a growl that sounded close to the edge.

"He was trying to get me to go with him, talking about running away together. This was the final straw, so when I finally got away from him and safely back to my room, I told

Charlotte about my plans to talk to the authorities." I looked down as I knew this was the bit that was going to get ugly and I hated looking weak!

I was playing with the edge of my gloves and tried not to visualize the actual night I was taken.

"How did it happen, Keira?" And there it was. With that one question asked in that gentle yet demanding tone, I could barely deny him anything. But saying my name like that... Hell, I would have given him the world with my soul attached and wrapped in a bow if I could!

"I had been dating this guy called Tom Robertson, who I had been seeing for a few weeks. He was a nice guy, funny, smart, the type you could introduce to your parents. So, when I got a text from him asking me to meet him, I replied that I would as I needed a nice distraction to take my mind off Morgan." If only I could have gone back, I wouldn't have waited another hour before going to the police, I thought bitterly.

"See, I still felt bad that I would have to report Morgan for his behaviour. I knew what it was like to see things, and I remembered how utterly alone I felt when I couldn't control it. I just wished there was another way, but what I didn't realise was that Morgan had his own idea of dealing with it... Or more like, *dealing with me.*" I stopped to clear my throat, and Draven looked as though he was about to move towards me but stopped himself.

"Drink," he said with smooth control that sounded as liquid as the water that went down my throat. It cooled my insides that felt as though they were burning from the memories. I placed one hand at the back of my neck and closed my eyes, knowing this was going to get even more difficult. I noticed Draven's eyes scanning me with obvious concern, and I reassured him before he could ask,

"I'm okay." He didn't believe me, you could tell with the one raised eyebrow he was sending my way, but he must have accepted it as he nodded for me to continue.

"He had used Tom's phone, tricking me into believing I was

472

meeting my new boyfriend, when really he had directed me to exactly the right place where he could easily take me... He stole me away and I didn't have a chance! The next thing I knew he had his arms around me, injecting me with something, taking me against my will. So, you can see where I would have a problem with being taken like that!" I added this to prove a point, hoping he would get the message, and from the look on his face... he did.

"I didn't realise the extra pain that would have caused you," he said looking guilty, but I coldly asked,

"Would it have made a difference?"

"No. It would not," he said unashamed.

"I didn't think so," I replied back sardonically.

"I do what I have to do but my reasons are far from your nightmares, Keira," he said in such a way I knew it to be true, so I couldn't stay mad at him. Draven and Morgan were miles apart... Good and Evil... or so I foolishly thought.

"Fair enough," I gave him before continuing,

"So, when I woke up, I was in my prison. A concrete Hell that was the basement of his house where I was to remain for forty-three days, caught between wanting to die and fighting for every hour of them." I couldn't help but look down at my concealed scars and caress them absentmindedly, as though at that moment they needed a loving touch.

"See, he believed I was possessed by the same Demon that haunted him, and no matter what I said or how I pleaded, nothing got through. He was obsessed with the idea that I could be fixed!" I wiped the tears again, and Draven looked as though he felt every one that fell.

"He called it trying to save me, but what I really needed to be saved from was the madness that consumed him. At first, he would try little rituals that were mainly harmless, including the burning of incense, sprinkling of Holy Water, reading different scriptures, that type of thing. But because his Demon never left him, it also meant that in his eyes it never left me either. So, things got worse, after weeks went by, he started doing more research and finding more radical and dangerous methods." I closed my eyes briefly, shuddering as if seeing myself back there.

"I would normally just wait for each day to come and go before someone would surely find me. On the weekdays he would go to work, and I would be left to wonder on ways to escape but there was no way out. He had thought of everything! I would sleep on an air bed that he inflated more each week. My food was brought to me on a child's plate and I was only allowed to use a plastic spoon. He always said this was so the Demon couldn't force me to hurt myself, and this way he could keep me forever." At this Draven couldn't help but react. He got up and walked over to a table that held a large glass decanter. He poured the red liquid into a wine glass and downed it in one, then poured himself another. He looked over to me before up turning another glass and filling that also.

"Here, drink this, it will help," he said passing me the glass. I looked down at the red liquid as I swirled it around before wanting to drink it. Draven spotted my hesitation and informed me,

"It's red wine."

So, I took a sip and let the flavours evolve in my mouth, tasting the berries used, mixed with an acidic after-tone. He watched my every move as though he was waiting for me to break down and fall into pieces. My skin was burning, and it felt as though I was going to melt under all my layers, but I didn't want to take them off, as I wanted to remain firm and show I was ready to leave as soon as possible.

"So, as I said, weeks went by and still no rescue, and I was soon to realise why. He had thought of everything. He told the University that I had left due to personal reasons, and he had forged my handwriting. He had also written letters to my parents telling them one excuse after another why I hadn't called. But my parents must have been getting worried because one night, he drugged me and forced me to read what he had written into a recorder."

"What did he force you to say?" Draven asked through gritted teeth.

"He made me tell them how I wanted to be left alone. How I was safe but I had run away with Tom to get married, and how I wouldn't call again, as this was all I wanted. He made me do it over and over until it sounded right." I shuddered remembering it all.

"That must have been hard," he said with empathy as I sipped my wine.

"It was, that's why I would have to do it over and over. Sometimes I would just shout for help, but I soon learnt that this wasn't a good idea." I shivered at the memories.

"What did he do?" he asked, making the armrests groan under the pressure of his grip.

"Well, let's just say after a few good hits to the face, I learnt that there was no getting around it, so I did as I was told."

"Я буду ему подавить!!" ('I will crush him!!' In Russian) He erupted from his chair and roared in another language that sounded like Russian, making me jump. He prowled back and forth with one hand clasped firmly behind his neck, looking like he was close to destroying something with his fist. After a minute of this he finally stopped to look at me.

"Forgive me, it's just this… well, it is not easy for me to hear." He was trying to calm his temper, this much was clear, and once again, I couldn't force my eyes away from his muscular frame as it tensed uncontrollably. He looked close to exploding into a full rage. He saw my worried face, and his features smoothed as he regained his control.

"Please continue." So I did, but I frowned as I knew it was going to get much worse.

"Are you sure you can handle this, or do *you* need time?" I asked, turning the tables back on him and giving him a small smile to relieve some of the tension. I think we were both in need of it. He took a deep breath and released it with a heavy sigh, letting go of the pressure his anger was building.

"I am fine now, thank you," he said bowing his head as though I had helped in bringing his temper under control. He then motioned for me to continue.

"I thought that that was it. I thought that he had fooled

everyone! The people at Uni thought I was home, and my family at home thought I had run away to be with Tom. I knew it was only left up to me and if I had any chance to escape, I would have to find a way. Then things got even worse."

"How?"

"He started once again with the rituals. He had now got it into his head that maybe I wasn't possessed like he thought but instead maybe I was a witch! Of course, I knew my history about the witch-hunts and how they always ended. But this was where he had a problem. Most witches were burned at the stake, drowned or tortured so brutality they wouldn't survive, and he wanted me alive, that much was clear. But one night he came up with an alternative... And that night was one I would never forget."

I realised I had finished my wine, but it was soon refilled by Draven, as he knew that to continue I would need it. And he was right, it did help as I could feel my body relaxing with every drop I swallowed. It must have been a strong wine to be taking effect so quickly after just one glass. He still loomed over me, making me take a large swig of my wine for different reasons. I could feel his gaze penetrating me from above, but I refused to look.

"Keira." He said my name like a warm caress over my body and I wanted to sink myself into the comfort I found there. I tried to look at my feet, but his hand shot out, preventing me from lowering my head anymore. He took a firm hold of my chin and raised my face to look up to his towering frame.

"You don't have to do this, Keira," he said so softly it was barely more than a whisper, and I closed my eyes, letting the captured tears fall. His grip left my chin and took the tears away with his touch.

"You wanted this, Draven... so you're going to get it. *All of it.* I accepted the deal to spill my gruelling past to you, so no matter how hard it is to tell, by God I am not backing out now," I said fiercely. Something in me had snapped, and I found that if I didn't finish now, then Draven would never fully understand why. He would never truly see the blind justice to my actions, and I didn't want them to remain in the shadows any longer.

"Very well, little one." I felt his touch leave me and I waited until I could hear him resume his place in the room, then I opened my eyes and carried on.

"This particular night I woke to find myself strapped to a chair at the wrists, feet and neck. The restraints also went under my arms and around the shoulders, preventing me from moving. I was still feeling woozy as he must have drugged my food, because I don't remember anything after eating. I was scared and upset. I don't think I stopped screaming throughout the whole thing. I just remember the searing pain of heat on my skin and the smell of my own flesh burning. I think I eventually passed out through the pain." I automatically felt for the small burn marks on my back and scratched at it through my layers. I couldn't look at Draven, but stopped when I knew he was watching me.

"When I woke, my wound was wrapped up and I could smell disinfectant. He was stroking back my hair telling me how sorry he was. I mean I just wanted to kill him, and here he was acting as though he was trying to help! Of course, his delusions convinced him he *did* help. Telling me how he thought it must have worked, as he couldn't see them anymore. I tried to pull away from him, but I was too weak, and he must have given me some more drugs as I kept needing to throw up. He told me how he had read that witches possess something called the 'Devil's Mark' from where they had been touched by one of his minions and when applying a red-hot poker to it, they would leave a screaming body."

"Vade retro Satana!" Draven said in disgust, shaking his head and looking away from me, as though trying to deal with his repulsed feelings.

"What does that mean?" I asked, wanting to go over to him and touch his face as he had done so often to mine. To soothe the line he had in between his brows when frowning.

"It means, 'Go back Satan.' It is a medieval Catholic formula for an exorcism, but in my case, I meant it as something else as

477

it also means the threat not to tempt me!" I didn't quite understand what he meant by that last bit, but I didn't push it as he looked furious. So, I continued with the last part of my miserable story.

"Then he started talking about us being together forever and that he was soon going to take me away from that place, somewhere we could be married and start a fresh new life. I wanted to scream at him and lash out, but I knew I had to use this as an opportunity and play it smart. So, I went along with it as if it was something I wanted too, thinking I would soon get a chance to make a break for it. But again, I was wrong." I took a moment to sip on my wine before continuing.

"I found out that not only was he going to drug me again, but he also started talking about taking care of my family, as they were becoming a problem. This made me panic more than I had in the entire time I had been locked down there. I knew what he was capable of, and knew that my family could be in danger. So, this gave me the strength for I what I would have to do next," I said, looking down at my covered scars wishing they could stay that way forever.

"What I didn't realise was, this was when I would find my opportunity as he started bringing down boxes to store, while he was getting ready to sell the house. Of course, any time anyone would come to look around I would be tied up and gagged so I couldn't cause a problem." I shook my head thinking back to how many people had walked above me and could have been my saviours.

"It was in these boxes that I finally found what I had been looking for, my chance to end it all. I waited for him to leave for work and started to open each one. Most of the boxes were filled with old newspaper clippings and childhood toys. But in one of the boxes was what looked like personal items of a young girl. I saw a picture of her and found she looked very similar to me, with long blonde hair and the same eyes. She was also sat next to a young Morgan and they had their arms around each other in an embrace."

"What did you find?"

"At the very bottom, I found a large wooden box with a key still inside the lock. I opened it to find it was a music box with one of those little ballerinas twirling round to the sound of Nutcracker's Sugarplum Fairy. But my eyes weren't fixated on the doll, they were fixated on the large square mirror behind it." I lowered my eyes as though ashamed of where his thoughts would go hearing me say this and when he next spoke, I knew I was right.

"So, you used it to try and kill yourself," he said in a sad voice, finishing the end of my story for me. Hearing this, my anger shot up along with my body as I was now standing in resentment.

He looked shocked at my reaction, but he was soon to know why…

"I never tried to kill myself!"

CHAPTER 40
MY END... OUR BEGINNING

"Why am I not surprised that you wouldn't think differently? No! I didn't bloody try to kill myself!" I held out my arms, and said,
"I did THIS to save myself and my family!"

"Calm yourself... I didn't mean to upset you, please explain," he said standing from his chair also. I inhaled deeply and every time my lungs refilled, I calmed down more. Enough to continue...

"Look, Draven, you have to understand that if I was the cause for those who I loved to come to any harm, I would never be able to live with myself. I would stop at nothing to prevent Morgan from hurting them"

"I understand that more than you know," he said, motioning me to sit back down as though I had clearly made my point, so I carried on after throwing myself back into the seat behind me.

"I knew how long it took for him to get from his car and down to me. I counted it every time he returned back to the house. I knew it would only be a moment before I would hear his footsteps above, and the first thing he always did was to come down to the basement to see me. I knew exactly how many minutes I had, so I sat and waited until I heard the car." I trembled at this, the hardest memory of all. The pain I created. Oh God the pain!

"It was hard to do at first as I was shaking with fear, but then the adrenaline kicked in and my hands plunged the mirror shard into my skin. You see, my plan was to try and make it look worse than it was. Lots of shallow cuts to create the illusion that it was more serious, but you see it wasn't working, there just wasn't enough blood. So, I started to get clumsy by this point and cut myself too deep a few times at the wrist. Of course, it was too late, I couldn't stop the bleeding, but at least my plan had worked because as soon as he saw me, he panicked. I used the last of my strength to play him at his own game. I told him how I didn't want to lose him, how it was the Demon that made me do it. That it was jealous of my love for him and it wanted me to suffer and die." I looked up to see Draven's eyebrows were raised and he was giving me a look I couldn't decipher, so I carried on.

"Of course, he believed me, and for the first time in over six weeks, I saw daylight as he put me in the car. But I must have passed out because the next thing I knew I was being placed outside the emergency room doors, 'don't say a word and I will be back to get you' he told me. And of course, it didn't take long before I was found by the hospital staff."

"And you informed them of what happened?" I laughed without humour before answering,

"Oh yeah, I informed them alright. Once inside, I screamed bloody murder as loud as I could for the police to be called as I had been kidnapped! Well, it didn't take long before they finally took me seriously and my parents confirmed it, as they had been looking for me for over a month. They arrested Morgan when he came back trying to get me, as the receptionist told him I was in a different room, which was full of cops waiting to take him down."

"That was an incredibly brave thing you did, Keira, but there is one thing I still don't understand... Why didn't you give a statement?" At this question I turned away.

"I have my reasons, which are personal, but it helped that I didn't need to as when they went to Morgan's house, they found enough evidence to tell my gruelling story for me.

481

Unfortunately, this also led them to more dead bodies." He didn't look surprised at this and I gathered considering he had read the police report, there wasn't much after this he didn't know.

"I found out later that he had killed my roommate Charlotte, making it look like suicide. They found Tom's body dumped in the woods near the University. He'd had his throat cut so deep it nearly severed the head, so naturally the police were already investigating his murder." I winced at the memory of breaking down when the police told me all of this. This was the hardest news to take in as I could do nothing but blame myself and had done ever since.

"He should have been caught sooner!" Draven snarled in loathing. I decided to finish this once and for all, getting rid of this past burden in full, and then I could fully concentrate on how the hell I could get away with not living through it all over again!

"Yeah well, they didn't really have much to go on, and for a time even I was a suspect in Tom's death as I had disappeared. They also found the body of the real Hugo Morgan, as he had taken on his life and fooled everyone. They had told me his real name was Douglas Brone and his background was a sketchy one. They knew he had a sister who was also called Catherine and that he thought of her as more than a sister, if you know what I mean. They don't know how she died but just that she was the one in the picture that I had found."

"So this was why you didn't need to give a statement, they had more than enough evidence against him."

"You can say that again, but if that didn't seal his sentencing, then the room they found most certainly did," I said sarcastically, swallowing down the feelings of revulsion in the form of bile at the back of my throat.

"What room?" he asked on a growl, as though he couldn't take much more.

"They also found a room in his attic that was dedicated to his obsession with me. They found hundreds of pictures of me, ones he'd taken and ones he'd drawn and painted. There was also my hair, some of my clothes and some other sicker things that he had removed from my trash. But the worst thing they found was my body double."

"Body double?" Draven asked as he leaned forward, resting his forearms on his knees.

"The frozen body of a murdered girl who looked just like me was found in a locked chest freezer…" I felt sick saying this next part as the horrors even continued after my freedom.

"One that was stored in the very basement I had been kept in."

"By the Gods," Draven muttered, shaking his head in disgust.

"She had also gone missing close to the same time as I had, and they believed at the time that they could have a serial killer on their hands. But then they realised why her. See, the police believed he was planning to fake my death and for this, he needed someone that fit my body type. He thought that he could just take me and that we could disappear, but my family were making that difficult. They got the police searching for me and people at the university were being questioned. Morgan was also questioned and quickly became a suspect. It wasn't going to be long before they found me but of course I didn't know any of this. Naturally, as soon as he was caught it was clear to everyone that he was insane and instead of going to a secure prison, he pleaded insanity and was sent to a high-security mental institute."

"Fools… he deserved to hang!" Draven shouted in anger as I had now clearly come to the end of my near-destruction two years ago. He lowered his head, clearly thinking things through.

"Hanged? I don't think that's been done in a long time, Draven," I said not knowing what else to say but his head shot back up to look at me.

"In England, the last hanging was in 1964," he stated, shocking me as to why he would even know that. I decided to let it drop and move on to more important things.

"So now you understand why I have to go?" I stood and moved towards the door, knowing this would be the last time I would see him. I swallowed the lump in my throat at the thought and tried to ignore the desperate feeling that was chipping away at me. I didn't want to let him go. But in this, I had no choice, so made the last step and tried the door, which was still locked.

"No, I do not! No, if anything, that story just confirmed my justification for keeping you here," he said standing himself, folding his arms across his chest making his stance more powerful, but I wouldn't back down to his intimidation.

"What?! That's not fair… you…you gave me your word!" I threw at him, but he didn't bat an eyelid.

"I gave you my word that if I was satisfied with the truth, then I would let you leave."

"Yes, but I told you the truth!" I shouted back.

"That you did, Keira, so bravely, and you will never know what it means to know you have entrusted it to me…"

"But I…" He held up his hand to stop me and swiftly carried on,

"However, your story just confirms how afraid you are of being caught again, and I won't be satisfied until that threat no longer exists, as you will *never* go through that again… *EVER!"* he replied, retaining his cool countenance after shouting the last word.

"You have no right. I want to leave! I have to!"

"And why exactly is that? Do you want to keep running forever, Keira? Because if you think this will keep you safe then you're more wrong than you realise!" His black eyes stared at my face, searching for some reasoning there.

"I'm not trying to save myself, damn it! I am running away to save the people I care about. If I leave then he will follow me, and I might just have a chance to not only save myself but more importantly those I love… don't you see, I have no choice!" I was crying fully now at the thought of losing them, this was all my fault. I was a freak of nature and should never have been born! I just caused pain to everyone around me, like a disease with no cure.

I could see his expression soften through my watery vision.

And then there was another look. One I couldn't quite place, but I got the distinct impression that he didn't like seeing me cry.

"And this is the only reason you want to go? So you can prevent the people you care about from getting hurt?" he asked coming closer to me, but I stepped back with every step he took forward. I didn't want him to cloud my mind's decisions and I knew that as soon as he got close to me that I would be lost under the power he had over me.

"Don't come any closer!" I warned with a jittery voice.

"Answer me," he said, ignoring my request as he still kept taking steps towards me.

"Yes, of course it's the only reason! You really think I want to go on the run? Knowing that I will eventually get hunted down and my nightmare will start all over again!" I looked behind me, but I wasn't heading to the door as I thought, he was backing me up against a wall. I couldn't even see one door left in the room where previously there had been two. What was happening to me...? What was he doing to me? He was getting closer and my heart responded with panic. How was he doing any of this?

"Please don't!" I said again, which seemed to work as he stopped before getting too close.

"If that is the truth, then you have nothing to fear and therefore no need to leave." He looked hurt at the sight of my fear towards him but if only he knew the reasons for it, and that I feared my own reactions to his touch.

"But didn't you hear me, I have no choice!" I shouted out at my last attempt at getting him to see reason.

"I have taken care of it. As soon as I was informed of his escape, I took measures to see that not only you but also your family were safe," he said, taking off the suit jacket that he wore over a faded, dark grey T-shirt, making my legs weak at the sight of his solid torso.

"Taken care of it how?" I asked feeling some shred of hope.

"I have my people watching Libby and Frank, making sure they stay safe. I also have people watching your parents in England, just in case, and I have even taken measures to keep your friends here safe... So you see, you have no reasons to leave." When he had finished, I couldn't believe it... *was he right?* Were they all safe? Was *I* even safe from that monster who wanted to destroy my life? He must have seen the shock on my face, as he said,

"I can guarantee your safety here, but not if you run from me, *Keira."* His voice was soft and beseeching. The way he said my name was like the night I had dreamt of him when he had placed a warm blanket around my shoulders, pulling me close and keeping me safe.

"But I don't understand... why? Why would you do all this for me?" I asked, hoping he would give me an answer that would finally make sense.

"Is it not obvious?" he said, looking at me like I had never seen him before. He looked at me as though he needed me like he would his next breath. As if he wanted to consume me.

I looked down at my hands, as his stare was putting a different kind of fear through me, one of blinding passion and my own overwhelming need. Christ, I wanted him so badly that even now, at the mouth of my own Hell, all I wished for was that first real kiss between us.

Then something snapped. A clear line that was once there like an impenetrable wall had just been stepped over and left long behind, all with one word,

"Enough!" he demanded abruptly, and before I could speak, he made his move. He had clearly waited long enough, and cut the distance between us in seconds. His body came up to mine, framing my face with both of his hands, lifting it up so that my lips could meet his before he devoured me whole, kissing me with more passion than my body could take.

I quivered under his touch, unable to help the storm of emotions that took over. I had waited what felt like an eternity for this moment and if I had dreamt of it every night for all of time, it still wouldn't have come close to the Heaven he took me to. I couldn't stop my hands from lifting to anchor his face to mine by holding his neck. I never wanted this feeling to end and I think if I had died right now, then I would have died knowing the true meaning of lost in lust, faith in fate, happiness in hope, and finally, locked in love.

Upon realising this, I couldn't hold in a cry of bliss, one captured in his mouth. As a result, this was where my legs were about to buckle as every muscle went soft. He reacted to this by grabbing my waist, wrapping one solid arm around it and picking me up to the level of his face. Then a greater passion exploded between us when I placed my elbows on his shoulders and used my forearms at the back of his head to secure his lips to mine.

"By the Gods, woman!" He pulled back to growl at me and I murmured a sound of protest from being apart for even a second. His eyes sparked purple before he pushed me further into the wall and took our kiss from explosive to soul-consuming. His lips moulded to mine, taking everything he wanted from just one kiss. He parted my lips, invading my mouth with every sensory fibre he possessed.

At this very moment in time, he owned me, dominated me, and I gave myself to him like the most willing of sacrifices. His free hand moved to the back of my neck while his other hand gripped my side tighter in his hold. It was a purely possessive gesture as his tongue thrust deeper in an act of insight to come. And just when I thought it couldn't get any more intense, he deepened the kiss, tasting me until my insides were on fire and he could practically lick the flames!

He lit my veins with utter carnal desire, and I never wanted to cool down from it. Tilting my head even further to the side, our noses touching, he explored every last inch of me. I couldn't help the moans that just proved how I felt about him and what he was doing to me. I felt him smile over me before he pulled his lips from mine. I didn't like it. I wanted him back to me. I had to control the urge not to find them again myself. But he had other plans, seeing that my legs weren't up to holding my bodyweight when he was so close.

He carried me over to his desk, still holding all my weight with just one arm, and used his other arm to clear the top of all that lay upon it. He swiped it all onto the floor, and my past was now scattered around my feet where I wanted it to remain forever. He placed me down so that I remained the same height as his perfect face. His eyes were still alight with the clear ache of his sexual craving.

His hand snaked up to the back of my head, and his palm stretched out around the back of my neck with his fingers entwined in my hair. There, he could control the position of my head, tilting it to the side so that he could bring his mouth to my exposed neck. He kissed me there, and the feel of my cold skin where his lips left imprints sent tingles down my spine. I closed my eyes as the room started to spin.

My body was close to sizzling, which he must have felt as his hands found the collar of my jacket, pulling it back over my shoulders and letting the cool air bathe my overheated body. That's when I noticed the doors that led to the balcony were now open, letting in the night breeze.

He pulled off my jacket and threw it to one side, as though it should never have been allowed to conceal me away from him to begin with. Then he looked back at me and my heart skipped a few beats at the sight of the lust in his dark eyes. One corner of his mouth quirked up, exposing a confident smile as his hands gripped the back of my knees. He held them firmly, moving them to the side and separating them. Then he gave them a quick tug, making me slide closer towards his body, eliminating the space between us. I couldn't stop the gasp when I felt the hard evidence pressing back into the place I wanted his body to join mine. I wasn't just ready for him... ready for him to take his rightful place inside me, but I had been ready for what felt like my whole life.

And it was beautiful.

But my gasp ended as he crushed his lips to mine once more and I could taste the scent that I had craved. I had never experienced any feeling like it. I had never been kissed like this before as it felt like we were designed for each other. My hands finally found the courage to touch the hard curve of his shoulders as I gripped on for dear life. They were received with a stronger need for my body. His hands curved around my

AFTERLIFE

back, trying to get to my skin through the layers that obstructed them.

He pulled back slightly as his kiss became soft until his lips left mine altogether. Now he was looking at me and I felt self-conscious as his serious face studied me. He was looking at my hair and, then he frowned.

I was just about to ask him what was wrong when he moved his hand to the back of my head. Then unbelievably, my clip opened and jumped into his hand without him even touching it. His eyes widened when releasing my hair down like a golden waterfall. He put down the metal clip and then let his hands feel the mass of hair through his long fingers. He looked in awe.

"Clavis aurea," ('Golden Key,' in Latin) he said in a rough voice, that still held the hunger he had for me. I didn't know what it meant but I responded by putting my head down, causing my hair to fall forward and hiding an embarrassed face.

"A beauty like yours should never be hidden," he said as he lifted my face up to his eye level with a single finger at my chin. His hands then lifted to my face where he pushed all my hair back from blushed cheeks.

"I told you once never to hide from me, Keira," he told me with such intensity that I had to blink. He told me that in a dream once, a dream I now had confirmed had been real.

His hands brought me back from those thoughts when they went down to my sweater. Once there, he pulled down my zip slowly, making that single noise echo and scream out what was about to happen. I could hardly believe this wasn't a dream, and for the first time, I allowed myself to rejoice in the fact they had never been dreams. He was really here with me, and his hand proved this when he found bare skin at my waist.

An intense feeling shot up my body, making me a puppet in the hands of a master. He pulled me back to him and his smile lingered over my mouth, toying with my logic of right and wrong. This was most definitely wrong... so wrong that it made sense in my life!

A life that brought me to this moment in time when I had never felt such blissful agony. Blissful with his hands on my body getting ready to strip me of every piece of clothing I wore, but pure agony knowing I would have to stop him. This man, the man of my dreams, wasn't even mine to touch. He belonged to another and my heart hated the fact!

I knew I had to stop it, and I knew that I would never accomplish this if I let him kiss me again. So, before he could add any more pain to my decision, I placed my hands on his chest and pushed him back, but it was like pushing a stone wall with pillows.

"Draven... We...we can't do this!" I found my voice, but he wasn't convinced as when he slid his hands down to the base of my spine, close to my underwear, I let out a moan, which provoked his mouth to turn into a satisfied grin.

"Really...?" he said, tilting his head to see my eyes which I tried to hide. However, I remained strong and pushed him back again, which he finally took seriously, and his hands let go of my body. I had to use every ounce of self-control I had to jump off the desk and walk away from him. I was trying to calm my breathing and with that, the other parts of my body that were affected by his skin touching me.

I mean, was I crazy? This was all I had been dreaming about ever since I had first let my heart beat in the sight of him, and now I was walking away. If I didn't go to Heaven over this, then the Pearly Gates were going to have problems!

"This is wrong... we can't do this...we shouldn't have..." I said trying to find words that felt right, but no matter how strong my morality was, it felt as though I was going against God himself by walking away from Draven.

"I disagree and so does your body. Stop fighting it, Keira," he said with intense eagerness to have me back in his arms. But I couldn't, it was morally wrong, why couldn't he see that?

"Draven, you're going to be married... I can't. I just won't be the other woman in this picture!" I said feeling the pinch of hurt this caused me. She could have this. This was hers, and I was so jealous I could almost taste the green air around me! But Draven didn't seem to feel anything but amusement by my reasons.

"And this is the reason I don't have you in my arms where you belong?"

"Isn't that enough of a reason?" I asked frowning at his reply.

"I guess in your eyes what I am doing is a sin?" he asked, smiling at the thought.

"What would you call it?" I snapped getting annoyed.

"An inconvenience… One I will soon rectify." He walked over to an intercom that was mounted into the wall, pressing a red switch.

"Send Celina in here immediately," he said, and my heart sank at his request. What was he doing? This wasn't what I meant!

"Draven, what are you…?" I started to ask after a moment to get my head around what he was about to do, but then the door opened, and his perfect fiancée entered the room looking, as always…

Radiant.

CHAPTER 41

IMPOSSIBLE TRUTH

Celina didn't look surprised to find me in her fiancé's bedchamber, nor did she look upset. What was going on here? If that had been me, I would have lost it! She walked up to Draven but not in the same manner as she had done last time. No, this time there was no embrace, no kiss and I silently thanked God for it, knowing I wouldn't have been able to cope at that sight again… not now. Not after that kiss.

"Celina, you remember Keira?" he said, nodding to me.

"Yes, but of course. Hello again, Keira," she said politely. I was still standing there in shock, frozen in front of these two who were playing with me.

"Hello…" I managed but it didn't sound like me.

"Celina, please tell Keira if we are engaged," Draven asked her outright, and I shot him a look as if to say, 'what the hell?'

"No, we are not, My Lord," she said as certain that the sun will rise again.

"Have we ever been?"

"No."

"And one last thing, have we ever been romantically involved?" Draven's eyes were on me at this last question, but I was numb from the answers she was giving. What type of trick was this?

"No, My Lord, never… will that be all?" she said with her

perfect complexion remaining a calm colour, whereas mine felt as though it was glowing crimson!

"Yes, that will be all... Thank you, Celina. You may leave us now," he said dismissing her, and once again we were left alone, but my acceptance to this news was not going down well.

"What the...?" I said, barely refraining from dropping the F-bomb then looking away from him.

"I apologise for the deception. Unfortunately, it was necessary."

"Unfortunately, it was necessary!? Oh really... 'cause I'm just dying to hear this one, Draven!" I shouted, feeling my passion for him change into distaste for all the lies I had been allowed to believe.

"How could you do that to me?!"

"I had little choice at the time... only now it seems to have been in vain," he said keeping calm in the face of my resentment.

"And why is that exactly? Because tonight you decided that you want me and then tomorrow, I will be cast aside, so you can be engaged again?" I asked painfully as my true feelings came flooding out through the dam of denial. He, at least, had the decency to look guilty but it was still clear he remained strong in believing his reasons.

"Everything I have done with regards to you, has been for your best interests, whether you choose to believe me or not, I speak the truth. Sadly, I could not take your feelings into account."

"And why not?!" I enquired irritably.

"Because it was your feelings that I depended on for my plan to work," he confirmed, making me remember how much my heart filled with pain the day he was referring to.

"I needed to hurt you so you would stay away from me. I needed you to hate me, Keira... it was the only way I could keep you safe." He was almost pleading with me, but I wasn't about to cave in yet.

"Safe from what?"

"From me! By the Gods, girl, do you not see!?" he cried out, exasperated as if he really believed it, but I wasn't buying it. It didn't make sense.

"That night you got stabbed was because of me, because of what I am and what I have to be... I wanted to spare you from the weight I have to bear." And for the first time I saw Draven as a torn man. The power he held was reduced to nothing more than the single thread of a spider. Still, I couldn't help but think that I was the one twisting on the end, unable to ever get away.

"I don't understand... what are you even saying? Who...who are you?" I asked, but his face was full of sorrow for where this night was now heading.

I mean, did I even care what he was? I knew I was too far gone past that same line he had stepped over when he kissed me. So, did I really want to turn and go back to that safe point? I knew the answer, even as I asked myself that very question. There was no going back. Never, and this I'd known long ago. I loved him, and in the end, that's all that mattered.

So, before he could answer, I made a lifetime's decision right there and then. Because right at this very second, I knew life would never be the same from this moment onwards. And that's when I finally got it!

I knew the answer after all this time.

Where love takes you, and the choices you made on which road to travel down... that wasn't the point. And it wasn't about the destination either, it was down to who you wanted on that journey with you, and who you *needed* standing next to you when you finally arrived. So, with this new-found knowledge, I walked straight up to him and let love take me...

To Draven.

"Actually, I don't care," I said before I reached up on tiptoes, took his face in both hands and crushed my lips to his, finding my home...

I had arrived.

At first, he was in shock and remained still until my hands went from his face, then round to his hair, pulling him roughly down to me. This woke him from his trance, and once again he took all control, reverting back to the powerful Draven I had only known him to be… *and I liked it*. He was, after all, my master, and I was his willing slave. And oh God, I wouldn't have had it any other way. Thankfully, I was about to understand the full meaning of why this was a damn good thing!

After twisting his fists in my sweater in a sign of sexual frustration, he quickly peeled away the material that was keeping me concealed, leaving me in my little black T-shirt and gloves. He put his head down, inhaling the smell of my hair and he groaned as my arms locked around his waist. There, I was finally brave enough to lift his T-shirt up at the bottom, feeling the soft skin on his back. His body responded to my touch just as mine did to his. I felt my power over him, and I revelled in the fact.

For the first time, I had some control instead of it all belonging to him. However, it didn't last long as he tried to remove one of my gloves. I pulled my arm back from his hands and held it firmly behind my back.

"Keira, I told you, do not hide from me… *Ever.*" His smouldering voice ordered me to obey him, but I just couldn't do it. I never showed anyone my scars, and Draven was most definitely the last person I wanted seeing them.

"Don't fear me, Keira," he said leaning his forehead to mine, enveloping me in that drugging aroma. Then he reached around me and grabbed one of my arms, pulling it gently back round. I tensed in his hold, something I could tell he didn't like.

"Please trust me," he asked as he started to remove the tight material, rolling it down until the first scar came into view. I couldn't help my reaction. I tried to pull back, but he wouldn't let me. I pleaded with him with watery eyes, but he knew as well as I did, that he needed to do this. His control wouldn't allow him to have anything between us. He wanted to know everything about me, and I knew, for a man like Draven, that I had to give him this. So, as my scars came into view one by one, my breath held. I swallowed hard and my body tensed as his eyes noted every line.

Once my arm was fully exposed to him, he did the same to the other until they were both on show. I tried to pull them away again, but he held them firmly in front of me. He studied them closely and I could feel them getting hot, as this was the first time anyone had ever touched them.

His fingers traced each line as if trying to take away the memory of the pain that created them. He didn't say a single word about them, and I was glad when I saw there wasn't pity in his eyes but silent wonder. It was as if now by knowing the full story on how they came to be, it made more sense to him. Almost as if he was now looking at the evidence of *giving* life, instead of the evidence of *taking* death.

I liked this look.

A lot.

I can't say how long he stood there, just holding my arms and caressing the scars I'd created with a broken piece of mirror, but I didn't care. The moment was beautiful and felt like freedom for my soul. Then the beauty he gave me intensified when he raised them up and kissed each scar so softly, as though now taking away the memory of the self-inflicted pain, one by one.

After this, he slowly lifted my arms and put them around his neck before lifting me over towards his enormous bed. He kept his eyes locked on mine and I wanted to close my own against the intensity of it all. Then I inhaled sharply as all the lights died at once, only to be replaced by a warm glow as every candle in the room came to life. How did he do that?

"That's better," he said as he set me down on the top step to the bed, which put us at the same height once more.

"How did you do that?" I whispered looking at him in awe. Everything he did was magical, but I had no answers to any of it. He didn't say a word, as this would prevent him from kissing me, which he soon proved he would rather be doing. I kissed him back as if my life depended on it. My lips were hungry to taste him again.

This was my drug and I never wanted to stop. My elixir to life was drinking in this man and I wanted every last drop, the question was... would I ever be sated?

I soon forgot about my exposed arms as it felt natural to be like this and as he said, I didn't need to hide anything from him... not anymore. I wanted him to have me, to take me and keep me here with him forever in his castle. I knew that at any moment he could reject me. I knew that with every breath I took in his arms, it could be the last, and I would be left more broken than ever before... but I just didn't care. It would be worth it.

The tears, the heartache, the soul-crushing pain... all of it!

Then, when I thought it couldn't get any better, it multiplied. His hands ran up my sides under my top, pulling it up, and I held my breath as he pulled it off over my head. I could feel my hair raining down against the skin on my back. He looked down at my body hungrily before tossing my T-shirt away. I was just wearing my bra, which luckily was one of my fancy black ones.

"So beautiful, ma déesse parfait." ('my perfect Goddess.' In French). I blushed at the part I understood and was left only to imagine what the French meant. When Draven spoke in a different language he did so with such ease and flawlessness it had me gasping in wonder. It also did magnificent things to my insides, making me shiver in anticipation.

His fingers traced the lace around the top of my bra, and I couldn't breathe. My nipples pebbled under their confinement as if trying to get to his touch, and lucky for me, they didn't have to wait long. My eyes closed as I felt a single bent finger run down the middle curve, and my breath stuttered when his knuckle flicked over the hard, sensitive point.

"Look at me," he demanded, his voice thick and heated. My head went back, and I opened my eyes to look into his. There, I found purple fire, and when he suddenly took both my breasts into his hands, my reaction fed the flames. My mouth opened for the moan to be heard, and in return he growled low before he tore open my bra, ripping it down the middle.

Discarding it from my shoulders, he freed what looked like a feast to behold in his gaze, and I shuddered as he finally touched my bare nipples. This ignited that invisible fuse that ran straight to the hidden bundle of nerves I couldn't wait for him to find.

"I need to take you, Keira. I need to take you... *Now!*" he said after quickly grabbing the back of my neck and hauling my body into his. His rumbling voice almost shook with the proof of his words. I felt his lips at my neck, and sucked in a quick breath when he sucked at my skin before holding it with his teeth. I could feel my heart pump quicker, sending even more blood to my face. It was exquisite torture.

Then abruptly, he picked me up, forcing me to look at him. God his eyes! There was purple light encircling the darkness, consuming every emotion until it was all one and the same.

Pure... Raw... Passion!

He placed me down on his bed of silk as though I was the most precious of gifts and the cool material made me shiver. He didn't once take his eyes from my body and I found my uncertainties come flooding back to me as I lay half-naked, knowing what I wanted to happen. He must have realised my thoughts as he grinned sinfully, pulling his own T-shirt from his perfect body. I couldn't make my lungs work at the sight.

Jesus Christ!

His body looked impossibly strong, as though it could crush me to death if he wanted to. Of course, one look was all it took to know this wasn't what he had in mind, although his muscles were going to come in handy for what was about to happen next. I wanted to trace each and every line his perfect body displayed. I was almost desperate to lean up and touch him, to taste him.

So, I did.

I started at the top, running my fingertips along a set of wide shoulders, down to the centre of square pectorals and over the hard ridges of his clear cut abs. His muscles twitched and the hard planes of his stomach clenched as though he was holding back a ravenous thirst in tasting my skin. The candles' warm glow cast his skin in the most delicious and exotic shade, giving him the appearance of some unruly warrior. He certainly had the build for wielding a sword or an axe. Christ, he looked like he could lead an army into battle, carrying a whole arsenal on his back!

He moved to the end of the bed, determined to remove the rest of my clothes, leaving me on show and hiding nothing from him, granting him something no other had seen in a very long time. He pulled off my jeans slowly, peeling them away like skin from a fruit. Then, holding on to my legs, he tugged softly, sliding my body under his and holding all his weight above where I lay. My breath caught before he leaned down and kissed me once more.

Our bodies mingled together creating our own heat source, skin on skin and my nerves were soon replaced by utter bliss. I found myself lost in the hurricane that Draven created. The waves of sensation crashed into me with every delicious touch and I wanted to drown in him. My body reacted to every move he made, causing me to groan, moan and writhe beneath him with wanting more. His hands slid down my arms finding my wrists, which he then held securely above my head, locking me where he wanted me. It was as if he knew I could barely contain my reactions towards him. I felt like I was going to explode and disperse in his arms.

His kisses started to trace down from my mouth onto other body parts and I closed my eyes trying to control myself. All I wanted to do was scream out with pleasure. He was gentle, yet created a brutal assault on my senses as he kissed, bit, sucked and nipped at my skin as far down as he could reach. It was clear he had a favourite when he took as much of my breast into his mouth to bite causing a beautiful pain that turned to a pleasure I had never known. He worked me to a near frenzy while expertly playing with my nerves like fine-tuning an instrument.

I didn't know how much more of this I could take and when my body started to bow, pressing myself further to his control, he smiled against the side of my breast he had been working on. He nipped at me one last time, making it harder to breathe, then he worked his way down, until eventually he had to unshackle my wrists from his grip. I knew where he wanted to go but my inner self-conscious wouldn't let me get that far, making me pull him back to my lips instead.

Surprisingly, he did as I demanded but he groaned at not being able to carry on his exploration of my body. My face burned with embarrassment which he found amusing.

"Why would a Goddess be embarrassed with her own perfection?" he said, making my shame double.

"I haven't… Umm… done this in a long time," I said quietly, feeling as if it was my first time all over again.

"I'm glad to hear it. Don't worry, little one, I will be gentle with you," he said giving me a wink. I laughed, easing some of the tension from my shoulders. I tried to not start over-analysing it or I would have just worked myself up into a state of self-consciousness. He was obviously more experienced in this department than I was but from the impressive size of him pressing against me, I wouldn't have said I was doing too badly myself. I blushed at the thought of how something that size was even going to fit. I wasn't a virgin by any means but let's just say it had certainly been a while.

Then he shocked my mind to silence as the sound he made can only be described as pure primal. He had me trapped in a cage of muscle, looming above me as he growled down at me. I couldn't speak.

"That colour on your skin makes me want to bite you. Every look, every bite of your lip, every blush… Every. Single. One…" He shook his head and closed his eyes at a memory I couldn't see.

"What is it?" I asked timidly, barely a whisper. His eyes flashed open, and for a brief moment they were completely overwhelmed by blazing purple.

"Makes me want to do exactly what I am going to do to you right now!" And with that he crushed his lips to mine in the most dominating way a man can take a woman. Of course, I crumbled into his masterful hold like the prisoner I felt. Like the prisoner I was. One who couldn't escape this. Not now. Not ever. There was no more running from him… not now I was caught. I was his captive for as long as he wanted me.

Then something happened that plunged me into a world that was both utterly stunning and terrifying at the same time. He held me as though he was commanding my body, bending me to his will before I felt his need pressing harder against me. I took a deep breath and closed my eyes waiting for the fullness to push me over.

"Look at me." It was another demand, and one I found I couldn't possibly disobey.

"That's my good girl," he praised before he entered me in one swift movement. I cried out at the intensity and he swallowed my reaction in a kiss. Then there were no more words as we found ourselves connecting. Like puzzle pieces finally fitting together, only creating a clear picture of the truth.

Two truths making one beautiful certainty.

So much so, that I found my mind nearly bursting with the consuming fire of raw, untamed need. I had never experienced anything like it, not even close to it. If I thought that his kisses were intense then this was something not of this world. It felt enchanted as my body arched upwards, thrusting back against him inside me. His hard length hit every nerve in just the right place, and his precise movement dragged out the bliss for as long as my mind would take it.

I was lost in a world of ice and fire. So, so hot. My body was melting as if I would soon self-combust and then his skin would change, making me cool. It was like the two extremes of temperature were fighting inside under his skin, causing it to have the same effect on me.

As soon as he had entered my body, something had happened. A different force had taken over my soul making it react to things I didn't know I could feel. It multiplied every touch, making my own personal pleasure keep going and going until my body couldn't take any more and I wanted to explode over and over.

But I don't know how he kept preventing it, making it intensify with every new wave. He was controlling my release, keeping it back for when he was ready, but my God I didn't care. I was just being transported to a different world... one I never wanted to leave!

After what seemed like hours of ecstasy, my body cried out as I couldn't take any more.

"Draven... Draven, please... oh please." That's when I realised I was begging this God above me to take me away. To take me to the

same promised land he would find. The promise that had been on the horizon the entire time he had been inside me. I'd been begging over and over for what he continued to deny me. But I couldn't hold on any longer, it needed to erupt, waiting to feel the aftermath, and as if by reading my mind he looked down at me and whispered,

"Alright, little one, are you ready to be mine?" And all I could do was nod, silently praying his words to be forever true.

"Say the words." I nodded again not finding the mental ability to form words, but he wasn't satisfied.

"I need to hear you say the words, Keira. Say them now!" He sounded strained, as though he couldn't physically continue without my compliance. So, I dug deep and mustered the only words that mattered,

"I am yours, Draven, take me... please, Oh God take me!" And that was all that was needed for him to do just that. I braced myself but there wasn't much point to this as what happened next was totally out of my control. His body moved in such a way that the feeling made me need to bolt upright. He must have known that this was going to happen as Draven's hands held me down by the wrists, so I could continue riding out the full force of my orgasm. It was the most amazing experience of my life.

Therefore, I couldn't help the scream that erupted, followed by a moan as I turned my head into the pillow, crushing it against my face to catch any more screams. I tried to contain it all, but it was just too much. It was as if something was bursting from within me and had grown to such a fever pitch that it would have killed me if not released in the most brutal of ways.

I was like a woman possessed as my body bowed up and down, all the while screaming with every aftershock and wave that wouldn't stop hitting my body. I bit down on the material, and my hands gripped the pillows wanting to rip them to pieces. It lasted for the longest time, until finally the euphoria enveloped my senses, making my body collapse from the fight as my muscles gave up against duelling with his control.

I still had my face buried in the pillow trying to catch my breath, as I was exhausted both physically and mentally. That was without a shadow of doubt so much greater than I could have ever imagined it would be, and being it was with Draven, then I'd imagined it a lot!

I felt his hand smooth back my hair, exposing one side of my face. He pulled from me and I whimpered at the loss. I think I heard a small laugh, but I couldn't be sure of anything at this moment. Hell, my whole family could have walked in the room right about now and I don't think I could have found the strength to bat an eyelid. Grandma included!

He was lying down next to me on his side and he pulled the covers over me, cooling my hot skin, causing me to suck in a breath. He put his arms around me, lifting my head on to his shoulder, resting it against his chest. I could feel his heartbeat, and the rhythm was making me drift away, until his voice was the last thing I heard,

"So long... so many lifetimes waiting, and now I have you, Keira. Now I have you. Now you're finally mine... *sleep, my girl... sleep now, I have you.*" I wanted to ask him what he meant but his words were intoxicating my senses, until I had no control other than to do as he asked. And my exhausted body didn't find a single problem with this request, as falling asleep wrapped in his arms just added to the immense bliss...

From the man I loved.

CHAPTER 42

NOT A DREAM THIS TIME

When I awoke, the light streamed through my room, brighter than ever before. I only had one window, but the light filled the room making my eyes squint as they tried to adjust to the sun. My bed also felt strange and my body ached as if I had spent the night running. Suddenly, the events of last night shot through my mind, and I nearly jumped a mile at the body that moved next to me.

Last night, sex with Draven had been the most perfect moment of my life, that much I was certain. And thankfully this time, I knew that it most definitely hadn't been a dream, as I didn't usually wake up to find him lying next to me.

I froze, not wanting to wake him but I wondered what I should do now. I could see my top and a torn bra but nothing else, so getting out of bed was out of the question. I leaned gently around the bed to try and locate anything else I had been wearing last night before Draven had expertly removed it. I noticed a T-shirt he'd been wearing that was within reach as it was at the bottom of the bed, near one of the huge posts.

I managed to stretch out, with my eyes squinting and holding my breath from effort so as not to move the bed enough to wake him. I slid the top over my head, thinking that my hair probably looked like it was a home for woodland animals. I couldn't help my next action as I lifted the material to my face, and I inhaled his scent as the memories came flooding back of last night's 'sexcapades'. The smell had me almost groaning out loud.

"It looks better on you," Draven said, and I shot round to find him fully awake and leaning on his side, propped up by his elbow causing a bicep to bulge. He was smiling, and I went bright red at obviously being caught. I didn't know what to say, so I started biting on my lip nervously.

"Quiet this morning, Keira. Any reason for that?" he said being cocky, and a cheeky grin that I had never seen before broke out on his lips. Then he grabbed the T-shirt I was wearing, gripping the fabric into a bunch with his fist. He pulled me back to his arms and soon the scent of the T-shirt was nothing compared to the real thing.

"Morning," was all I could whisper as I was still embarrassed and well… in complete shock! I don't know what I expected the morning after, but for some reason, Draven's devastatingly handsome smile wasn't it. Maybe, because subconsciously, I had convinced myself that I would only be lucky enough to have him for one night. Well, if that smile was anything to go by then on this occasion, I was thrilled to be wrong!

"Finally, you found your voice, I was worried there for a moment," he teased, and I turned my head to see he was clearly amused.

"You seem happy," I said, making it more of a statement than a question, and doing so in a shy voice.

"And why wouldn't I be, with you here, in my bed… in my arms, where you finally belong?" he said, smoothing my wild hair back from my face, making me remember how crazy it must look. I quickly put my hand to my hair pulling it back behind my neck, trying to contain it like a beast. He laughed pulling my hands away.

"Don't, I like it. Wild and free, as it should always be," he said tipping his head lower to catch my eyes. However, new worries set in as I remembered my exposed scarred skin that he held in his hands. I looked down, and in the light of day they looked so much worse. I tried to pull them away yet again as I had done last night. But like last night, he held onto them, pulling them closer to him.

"Ssshh now, don't fret, little one," he assured when I started to squirm in his hold. He lifted them to his lips, and he kissed the red and white marks, making each one feel the cool breath from his delicious mouth. I closed my eyes as the same sensations from last night came tiptoeing back, which was magnificent but also not the best idea right now in the daylight. Too exposed. Too vulnerable.

When he was finished with the inside of my arms, I felt his hand glide along my cheek, making me openly look at him. I was about to say something when Draven spoke first, only it wasn't to me.

"You may enter!" And with this, I heard the door open and my reflexes took over, making me hide like a kid under the covers. Draven let out roaring laughter at my reaction, making the bed vibrate. In fact, he was still laughing when the person approached the bed.

"Brother, you remember Keira?" he said trying to control his amusement. I, on the other hand, was filled with so much shame all I could do was put my hand over the covers and give a little wave.

"Keira, pleasure to umm… well, sort of see you again," Vincent said coughing back a laugh like his brother.

"Dom, there has been a development, something you will want to see."

"I will be there momentarily," Draven said, then seconds later I heard the door close. Moments after, the covers were whipped back from my face and Draven was already out of bed and dressed in fresh clothes. I was amazed at how quick he had been and where he'd got his new clothes from.

"I would appreciate it if you didn't hide your face, as it's something I take great pleasure in admiring, and when there's a sheet in the way, well… you can see my problem with that." He leant down and kissed my forehead, and said,

"I have to go, but I won't be long." His voice was a spine-tingling smoulder.

"It's okay, I can just get ready and leave," I said sitting up, but he looked furious at the idea.

"NO! No, I don't want you to leave, of course not… why would you think that?" he asked, looking hurt.

"I guess… I just expected that last night was just well… last night," I said hoping, no, more like praying I was wrong. Draven appeared startled and jerked back a bit.

"What, you thought that all I wanted was one night?" he said in amazement before turning, amused at the idea.

"Well, to be honest I didn't know what to expect and around you, no offence, but that's something I'm used to," I said feeling confused and also very truthful.

"I see… well, in that case, let me make myself clear for you right now. I have not waited all this time to only have you once. I asked you last night if you were ready to be mine and that is what I meant. You said yes. You are now mine. So what I want…" He cleared his throat, and the corner of his lips turned up as he rephrased his statement.

"Excuse me… what I would *like,* is for you to stay in my bed until I return. Now, can you do this for me, Keira?" he finished, and I just hoped my jaw hadn't dropped to my chest like it felt it had. Was what he said true? Did he now consider me his? Oh God! Oh God! I didn't know what to do with this new information, therefore I could only nod as my answer.

"That's my girl. Besides, you need more rest and time for your body to adapt," he added with a caress of my cheek before going to leave me, using the same door his brother had. I wanted to ask him what he meant by my body needing time to 'adapt' but the only question I asked was,

"Umm before you go… do you have a bathroom?" I said blushing.

"But of course, there is a door behind the tapestry in the corner, please make yourself at home here, Keira." And then with that he left. I loved how he said my name and how it created little bumps on my skin every time.

As soon as I heard the door shut and decided I most definitely was alone, I got up out of the enormous bed. My legs felt like they had been hollowed out and my bones replaced with jam! My muscles ached, so it took some time to steady myself, wishing I had become a gym bunny before meeting Draven.

I walked around the bed, and gathered my clothes so that I could change out of his T-shirt that I still wore. I wobbled over to the other side of the room where he said I would find another concealed door. It was behind a tapestry as he said, but this one wasn't of a battle scene like most of them were.

It had an enchanting Angel holding an urn, but strangely she looked as if she was turning into a statue as the bottom half was a light grey as though it were stone. However, her face looked serene and calm as she waited for her fate. I moved it to one side and opened the door she hid.

The bathroom was huge and, like Draven's bedroom, was also extremely grand. There were different sections to the room. At the very end was a giant stone arch that led up some steps to the biggest bath I had ever seen. It looked as though it could have been a room on its own to accommodate at least ten people! It was flooded with light as there was a floor to ceiling window behind, which also shaped into an arch.

Nearer to where I stood, was a white marble block that looked as if it could have weighed a tonne. It was carved into a bowl with black taps. I shuddered when I thought back to that night and how Draven had brought me in here to get me clean. Before last night, it had been the most erotic experience of my life, one that was cruelly taken from me by the man himself, when trying to make me believe it never happened. Well, now it was mine again I thought on a smile I couldn't hold back.

Behind the sink was a lush gilded mirror that was the same design that was on the balcony railing. It was the vine with black roses, and it was stunning. Until I looked into it and saw my hair! Oh God, I looked as if I had been dragged through a hedge backwards after a mad hairdresser decided to freak out, giving me a backcomb! It was then that I spotted that opposite the sink was a walk-in shower, which was also the size of another room.

It comprised of a five-foot stone wall and shower head bigger than a Frisbee, which again was black. There was a wooden cabinet to one side that I opened to find it full with crisp white towels. Why not? After last night I most definitely needed a shower. Although, the thought of washing away Draven's scent from my skin wasn't that appealing. However, the thought of him coming back and seeing my bad case of sex hair again was definitely worse.

So, I slipped off his T-shirt and walked behind the wall. As soon as I did, the water automatically came on and I squealed in surprise. It must have been on a sensor as there were no controls on the wall. The water felt amazing and was the perfect temperature. It rained down as if I had my very own personal rain cloud above me. I couldn't keep the satisfied grin from my face.

I looked around for anything I could use, and found a hidden shelf in the stone wall containing glass bottles filled with different products. I didn't know what each of them was, so I opened them taking a whiff. I think I got it right. First washing my body with one that smelled of jasmine and lotus flower, then I washed my wild hair letting it lather up before I rinsed it until it squeaked clean.

Once I had finished with scrubbing and conditioning, I grabbed the two towels that I had put over the wall, using one for my hair and the other for my body. I dried myself with what felt like a billion cotton thread towel that was designed with 'soft as a baby's bum' in mind, and then wrapped up my hair.

I looked around for my clothes but realised I must have left them on the couch before I came in here. I wrapped my towel tighter and poked my head around the door. I was more than a little surprised to find a familiar suitcase waiting for me. It was the one that I'd used when I first moved here.

I opened it up to find most of my clothes, and more importantly, my hairbrush, along with a new toothbrush and tube of paste. These I was very thankful for, as the last thing I wanted was to see Draven again with morning breath. Although, I did briefly wonder why I had a bag packed at all… what was Draven planning?

I grabbed the items I needed along with a new outfit and

clean underwear, thankful now that I had a bra that wasn't useless. When I was finished getting changed, Draven still hadn't returned, but there was a tray of food and a steaming pot of English tea, to my utter delight! I was close to doing a little victory dance but was too scared Draven would catch me, so refrained.

I was starving and sat down to eat to quieten my grumbling stomach. Once I had my fill of toast and tea, I decided to do something with my hair before Draven came back. I had dried it as much I could with a towel but now I needed to put it up. After searching through my bag for anything to put it up with, I remembered that Draven had removed my hair clip last night and put it down on the desk. I found it and twisted it round and round securing it with the metal clasp.

I decided to pick up all the papers from the floor and put them back in the folder which had my full name printed on the front of it. My fingers ran over the printed name for it was the first time I had seen it in years. I closed my eyes to shut out the memories, before I started to cram the papers back inside.

I cringed at the haunting pictures of monumental amounts of evidence from his house. There were photocopies of letters that he had written pretending to be me, and worst of all, a picture of what had been my cell. I shuddered at the memory and stuffed it angrily back into the folder along with the rest of the crap!

I looked down to check I had got everything but there was one piece that was out of place on the floor by my feet. It didn't look as if it should be there as it was a piece that had been torn from a note pad. I bent down to pick it up and turned it over slowly to reveal the picture. It was a sketched drawing of utter perfection in every sense of the word. And I knew it well but couldn't understand how it was here now.

Not only had it been created but also destroyed by my hand.

Impossibly, it was my vision of…

Draven.

denim-covered legs, it took everything not to say, oh to Hell with it!

I shook my head to get my mind back on track.

"Everything! How you do the things you do? How you know things about me? The truth about why you feel the need to protect me and why you felt you had to lie to me to do this?" I blurted out in a ramble.

"That's a long list for one conversation," he commented dryly.

"I'm sure you will manage," I said, not helping the sarcasm that came with it, making him raise one eyebrow at me.

"I understand that you're upset, but you have to realise that everything I did was for this very reason. I was trying to save you from the truth, which I'm not sure you will understand… *yet.*"

"Well, there's only one way to find out now isn't there?" To this he tilted his head in agreement.

"Alright, as you wish. But first I need to ask you an important question… Catherine Keiran Williams, do you believe in God?" he asked so outright that it threw me.

"Umm… I don't know, maybe, but I guess after all the bad things that have happened to me, I find it hard to believe in something so good, when God allows so much evil in the world." This was me being honest, but he looked shocked.

"Really…? This surprises me from you. You humans are all the same. You choose to believe in God when life is good, putting it down to *His* work but as soon as things are out of your control you quickly stamp out your beliefs or blame *Him.*" He said all this, but my mind was still lingering on the word 'humans', saying it as if he wasn't one.

"Then let me ask you this, do you believe in free will?"

"Yes, of course," I said, wondering where he was going with this.

"Then, if that was to be taken away, you wouldn't be you, right? You would be someone else's idea of you… do you understand?" he asked as I must have looked confused.

"Yeah, I get it, so what you're saying is that we would all be like puppets."

"Yes, something like that. You must understand that God gave life, but that it is your gift to do with it how you choose to live it. He does not dictate how you do this, nor does he negate your decisions. You must realise that he is neutral when it comes to your free will, you are a product of your own choices and this sometimes, no matter how terrible, well... they just happen for a reason," he said looking at my arms and I knew what he was referring to.

"So, you're saying God is real?"

"Well, that depends on the individual. If you want to live your life in denial, then no he wouldn't be, but to a man of faith, then yes he very much exists."

"Wait a minute, how can you answer that by saying yes and no?" I asked, frowning.

"Everyone sees things through different eyes, Keira, and it is as simple as yes and no. It always has been. Religion means something different to everyone. For some it's an excuse for war and greed, or to fuel the minds of men with hate and create a passionate reason to kill for others to then gain. Some use it as a comfort in life's struggles or a push to do good or to be a better person. But no matter the race, gender, age or stature in life, it all amounts to the same. Every single one of you throughout time has viewed God differently, but they have all had something in common... they all had free will in that belief, Keira. That is the difference." His dark eyes tried to judge my reactions, but he didn't look satisfied.

"What are you thinking?"

"So, you're saying that God is real, but only if we choose to believe that he is and if we don't, then whatever he does won't affect us anyway?" I said wondering if now I was making sense.

"Of sorts, yes, but anyway now for another question... do you believe in the Devil?"

"No, no of course not!" I said, feeling that it was obviously my answer. But he laughed at me, shaking his head as if I was wrong again.

"And why not?"

"Because I know it's wrong." Okay, now I felt like a naïve child saying it out loud causing him to laugh again.

"Really and why is it wrong to believe in a balance?" he said crossing his arms once more, as it seemed like a habit when he didn't agree with me.

"Balance?"

"Then answer me this… how can you know the good without the understanding of evil? How can you know happiness without experiencing misery, pleasure without pain? These things are essential parts of life that need to be faced and endured."

"I guess so," I said, knowing he was right. How could someone believe in the good and not the evil? Again, I was being naïve.

"So, before I go on, do you, Catherine, believe in God and the Devil?"

"Deep down, yes, I think I do. I think maybe I always have," I said, feeling a weight lifting as I admitted it, as if it just confirmed my every belief in one short conversation.

"Right, well now comes the big one… Do you then believe in Angels and Demons that walk amongst you?" he asked, and I had a feeling he was about to confirm my fears.

"I find it hard to believe," I said the words, but did I really?

"This surprises me considering all that you have seen. I don't think you are being true to yourself, Keira." And he was right, I wasn't. After all, I believed all those years ago in what I saw, and I knew as each year went by, the less I saw them, then the less I believed in them, as though maybe it was me who had created them subconsciously. Well, at least this was confirming once and for all I wasn't crazy! Now that is what I call a silver lining.

"You have your gift for a reason, don't turn your back on it now, not when it can help you the most." I knew the meaning behind his words. He needed me to believe, because without it I would never accept what he was. So here it was, the big question,

"Are you an Angel?" I asked, finally getting out what I had

wanted to ask from the very beginning. Something deep down told me this is what he was, but I foolishly chose to ignore it.

"No."

"No?" I repeated, making sure I had heard him right. Okay, so now this shocked me! And then it crashed into me like being hit by a freight train. If he wasn't one... Was he the other?! No, he couldn't be... could he?

"I am something different, but what you saw of me that night, the night you were stabbed, well that was my true form. That is who I am, Keira," he said, moving closer to me with a fear in his eyes that I had never seen before. It looked exactly like the same fear I had held so many times when thinking of Draven... *the fear of loss.*

"Heaven and Hell are not at war as the stories would have you believe. The war is here on Earth, as it has been since the beginning of time. Fallen Angels and Risen Demons are mainly the result of deviance. Angels go against God and they are banished to Earth to do good. To be granted favour at the hands of their work, but sometimes they have other ideas. You see sometimes they want to stay." He moved around the balcony, letting his story unfold and I could do nothing but look on, listening to every word that flowed so freely from him.

"It is the same principle with the 'Risen'. Demons that defy the Devil will be cast out, only being allowed back when they please him. Rogue Angels and Demons have always been a problem, as they often wreak havoc on your world and they disturb the balance, not only for your kind but for the world you cannot see. However, there are many that do not, as there are many different forms of us and not all strive to cause destruction. Some of us are here to help control it."

"You said 'us' but if you're not an Angel then... no... it can't be!" I couldn't finish it. It felt to wrong to say.

"What, you don't think I could possibly be a Demon?" he said bitterly, hurt at my reaction but I couldn't help it, he just couldn't be. All these years of hating what I saw, he couldn't be part of that!

"I don't know anything anymore," I said weakly, and I could

feel the tears waiting to arrive. How could someone show me all that compassion when they were born from a place of pure hate? I wanted to turn away from him, but I couldn't. I was locked by my fate and only Draven held the key.

"Well, I see I'd better explain before you go back on your promise," he said with resentment.

"I told you I wouldn't run"

"No, my dear, and you wouldn't get very far even if you did," he started, making me bite my lip at the thought of him chasing me. The vision it painted was both exciting and terrifying.

"I was sent here to control the balance as I am the only one of my kind. You see, my mother is an Archangel, which is a high-ranking Angel. She fell in love with my father who is of the First Hierarchy in Hell. This was utterly forbidden and completely unheard of. They kept their love secret for a long time until it became clear that my mother was pregnant," he said, watching me as my face dropped in shock. WHAT?! What was he saying? I couldn't help the question I had to ask,

"Angels and Demons can reproduce?"

"Yes, although rarely. But not in the same way as humans. They are created as souls and then the fate of these souls is decided upon in a divine court. Some are allowed to stay, some have to fall to a human host, only this time it was different."

"Human host?" I said, trying to control my urge to ask a million and one questions at once.

"I will get to that soon, but first I will explain why I am here and not in Heaven or Hell. There was not to be only one ruling on this decision as it was not only on one plane. It was a matter to be dealt with from both sides. Heaven and Hell both came to the same conclusion. Our souls, especially mine, were too precious to waste. My mother had triplets, one pure Angel, one pure Demon, both incredibly powerful and very strong thanks to their heritage. With our parents being of the highest rank it was in our bloodline, so to speak," he said, as though he was talking about his mum and dad being accountants or something!

"Okay, so Sophia is the Angel and Vincent the Demon... but

what does that make you?" I asked, but he smiled as if I had made such a mistake by that remark.

"It is funny how you would think that, I suppose to humans, Sophia would look more Angelic than the powerful Demon she is." He laughed at my reaction. I was shaking my head, not wanting to believe her as a Demon... all this time, but then looking back to that night... well now that did make sense.

"She is not bad, Keira. I know it is hard to understand as you only can go on what history has taught you, but not all Demons are bad just as not all Angels are good."

"Okay... so like I said, what are you?" I was almost too scared to ask. *Almost.*

"I am a product of two souls fused together. A combination of the most powerful forces of both Heaven and Hell merged. I am part Angel and part Demon," he finished, then waited for I don't know what... my screaming, running, maybe my attempt at jumping from this balcony. I know he was trying to assess my mental state but when I didn't do any of these things, I think he found his answer. And so, he carried on,

"As I said, this was a shock to all as this had never happened before, and hasn't ever since. I am the result of a forbidden love that was so strong it divided every existence in both our worlds. I have the power of the two and this made me an asset, so I was chosen to keep the balance here, making sure both sides played an equal game." Okay, so this was an 'oh shit' moment but not necessarily in a bad way. So, he was half Demon, but he was also half Angel, which would account for his wicked mood changes, I thought, suppressing a chuckle.

"So how do you do that?" I asked referring to this job of his. He smirked and ran his hand through his hair, giving me another 'oh shit' moment, but this time one of a different kind. One that made me wish we were both naked.

"Being more powerful than the rest helps. Mainly my word is enough on the matter, but there are some who like to be more... well, shall we say... difficult," he said, but not in an arrogant way, which considering what he just told me, he would have been entitled to.

He moved closer to me, being cautious in case I was frightened by him, but when I didn't move away, he had another of his answers. He closed the distance in a heartbeat and held the tops of my arms to look deep into my eyes, searching for my true feelings on all that I had just heard. And there he found them as I looked tenderly back.

I wanted to kiss him, to let him know that no matter what impossible truth I had just heard, I still needed him more than the air I breathed or the blood that flowed through my veins. Because without him it would all have been for nothing. I finally knew the reason for my visions and those reasons no longer scared me.

His fingers traced the crease of my mouth before his lips followed, and his kiss was gentle this time but I was no less affected by it.

"Come inside… you are cold and it will rain soon," he said once he had finished kissing me. He placed his hand on my back and guided me into the room. Once inside he motioned me to sit, and there was a new tray of food and drinks on the table next to where he wanted me to sit.

"Eat, you must be hungry," he said, once again being worried about me.

"Do you eat?" I asked as I grabbed a peach from the bowl of fruit. He looked as if he was trying very hard not to laugh at my question.

"What? It's a good question," I said getting defensive. So, he got up and grabbed an apple from the bowl and bit into it grinning like a bad boy, so I couldn't help but smile.

"Yes, it is, and to your question, yes, I do eat. I don't have to as often as you, but my body still has most of the same functions as yours." After last night I highly doubted that, but I remained mute from saying so.

"Really, so were you born with that body?" I asked, biting into the nicest peach I had ever tasted and I had to catch the juice that dripped down my chin… next time I would have to choose the grapes, less messy and embarrassing.

"Yes, in a way. This body was given to me from a willing

sacrifice and I have had it ever since." I coughed a bit of peach that shot down too quickly. Did…did he just say sacrifice?

"This was a great honour, Keira. He became an Archangel for his faith in God. You see, the bodies that we possess act like a vessel, but we still have to take care of them. Like a plant to nourish, but our power keeps regenerating the body's cells making it last longer. But they are not infinite, they don't last forever, eventually they grow old and that's when we move on." Okay, now this was weird!

"How long have you had your body?" I asked thinking that one day he may look like someone different. I didn't like the idea. He was perfect the way he was and I never wanted him to change, so when he said,

"Since the beginning." I was confused but happy.

"But you just said…"

"Yes, I know, but I am different. For some reason, my body has only aged about five years since I was first reborn. But Sophia and Vincent have changed a few times, well quite a lot throughout the centuries." At this I tried not to choke again!

"Centuries? How…how old are you?" I asked gulping hard.

"I don't think we should bombard you with too much information all in one go. After all, I don't wish to give you any more reasons for me to have to chase you, although that idea is somewhat appealing," he said winking at me, then smirked when he saw me gulp. He came over to me and poured me a glass of iced water before kissing the top of head, as my face must have told him I needed it.

"I told you, I won't run."

"I know, that's what scaring me, so far you have taken this all eerily well." I guess he was right, and I wondered why that was. Perhaps if I had met him yesterday and found all this out, then maybe I would be screaming. But looking back, first on all those years that I'd seen the unimaginable and then the gradual build-up of all things I have seen whilst being here… well, the first thing that comes to mind, is that it all kinda made sense now.

"Okay, well what if I changed the questions?" I asked, looking at him over my glass and he looked intrigued.

"Ah, let me guess, would these questions have anything to do with you?" He grinned knowing the answer.

"Umm maybe… okay yes, but you can't blame me!"

"I never would," he teased and pushed his hair back with both his hands, and I couldn't speak for watching him. Man, he was so hot I couldn't think when he did things like that.

"What was I saying?" I confessed, and he laughed at my incoherence.

"You wanted to know, why you?" I nodded without replying. I wanted to know but I was also scared of the answer in case it was something I didn't want to hear.

"When did I first meet you… really?" I asked, as I wanted to be sure it was when I thought it was.

"When it was near to our visit here this year, my sister was acting strange, as if she was waiting for something or someone… So when she left early, I went to find her. I followed her to an open part of the forest where I found her creating her own version of the Garden of Eden. I usually indulge her, letting her get away with these things as we can manipulate what humans see, so it wasn't a worry if this was ever found. But then when I turned up, she ran off and I didn't understand why, until I saw you."

"You saw me there, that wasn't a dream?" I asked, feeling that I had known it all along. But this made me wonder again if they had never been dreams?

"No, it was real. The first time I saw you, I was mesmerized. You had me locked in from that very first second and I couldn't get away. I watched you from afar first of all. You were so timid, like Alice fallen down the rabbit hole. I couldn't believe you could see what my sister had done, even though I tried to control it. I couldn't help coming closer to you as you didn't seem real to me at first. And then you literally fell at my feet like you had dropped from Heaven." I blushed, not even trying to hide my smile.

"I couldn't help but touch you. I had to use every last bit of self-control I had, not to sweep you up in my arms and take you away with me, keeping you mine forever. You don't know how hard it was. *How hard it has been,"* he said, and out of everything he had ever said to me, this shocked me the most. Did he really feel like this? I mean he couldn't... could he?

"I wish you would have taken me away with you," I whispered shyly, looking up at him from where I sat. Seeing him standing there with intense emotion clearly showing and with what he was telling me... I knew all he said was true.

"I doubt that would have been a wise move... for you at least. So the only thing I could do was to make you think it had all been a dream. I tried to walk away and leave you alone, but I couldn't. I needed time to make it safe for you. Of course, it didn't exactly help when it turned out that you were working at my club right under my nose, but even this was never enough. I had to keep seeing you, but each time it was getting harder to make you believe it wasn't real." It was like listening to the confessions of a desperate man or should that be desperate stalker Demon?

"I would come to you when you were asleep just to watch you, but you always seemed to wake. It was as if you knew I was there. And of course, then there was the night I saw you having a nightmare... I couldn't just watch you go through pain, you were so frightened. That was when it was the hardest to try and make you believe. I have never known such a stubborn mind in all my years!" He laughed at my frowning face being called stubborn, but he carried on.

"All I could do was watch from a distance, but it drove me crazy. It consumed me, like every day had turned into my own personal torture in a world that usually I help control, but over this I had none." He looked as though this was a painful memory, and to a man or 'Being' of his importance, it probably had been. I was amazed to find his feelings had mirrored my own.

"I had no idea you felt like this, the same way I felt. I can barely believe this is happening. But if this is all true, then why did you treat me so badly when you saw me in your club? Why did you object to me working in the VIP?" I hated talking about these times as it seemed so long ago now, and things had changed so much since then, but I needed to know the truth.

"Because I was trying to keep you a secret, Keira. Like I said, I needed time to do this. I wanted to keep you at a safe distance from a room full of Angels and Demons. I was scared they might have been able to feed from your emotions, and this I could not have. But mainly, I wanted to keep you safely away from me!" At this he looked guilty.

"Wait... what do you mean, feed from my emotions?" Okay now this I didn't like the sound of. He took a deep breath before starting to explain.

"Demons and Angels survive on the emotions of humans. It's where they get their energy, their power. The stronger the emotion the more powerful they become, that's why I allow humans into this place, making it a Gothic nightclub. The emotions of alternative people are a strong mix of both positive and negative, satisfying everyone's needs." I heard the words, but I couldn't help feel bad for all us unsuspecting humans.

He said the word *feed* and something painful clicked. Was this the real reason behind him choosing me? God, it was too excruciating to even think about, but unfortunately too important to ignore. Then I thought back to all the times he could have fed from me and it made me feel sick.

My pain from sharing my story must have made for a good feast surely! I suddenly felt betrayed. I had trusted him, and this was the reason all along, the reason I was here now... the reason he'd picked me. Was anything real about how I felt or was it just manipulated to suit his needs!?

I stood up, needing to get some air as my head spun from the facts. Why else would a man like Draven want me? I had been so foolish. So Goddamn foolish! Of course, it wasn't me he wanted, it was just the pain of my past!

I moved towards the glass doors and Draven had been right about the rain, it was now lashing it down against the balcony.

"What's wrong, Keira, you look unwell?" Draven moved towards me, but I put my hand up to stop him. I could feel the same pain in my heart again, as the realisation finally hit me. I walked up to the doors and put my hand on the glass, waiting for it to move but it didn't budge. I knew Draven must have been keeping them closed, ensuring I remain here to continue to feed from my pain no doubt.

"I need air, Draven… let me out," I said in a dead voice that didn't belong to me.

"Keira, tell me what's wrong, look it's raining out… please just talk to me," he said placing his hand on mine, but I just shook it off.

"Let me out, NOW!" I screamed at him, knowing I was just adding to his enjoyment. The doors opened and I walked out into the lashing rain. I just didn't care. I needed to feel something… anything but the feeling that I was food for him!

And that was all it was, just a way for him to become more powerful. Had he been playing me from the start, trying to provoke these emotions from me to increase his high? Tears rolled down my cheeks mixing with the rain that fell on my face. I could feel Draven behind me, but I couldn't move. I was locked in this place with nowhere to go. I wanted to go back to before I knew any of this, back to a safe place, back to his safe embrace, one where it wasn't purely for his gain!

"Please talk to me… what did I say?" he said with panic in his voice and I let out a sinister laugh, one that didn't sound right coming from me.

"So, all this time that was the reason. I was just one big high for you to suck the life from! Oh look, here comes a girl that's broken, let's see how much I can mess with her and feed from her emotions! I bet an attempted suicide was a big turn on!" I couldn't help my reaction. I pounded my fist down on his stone chest, and I hit him, and kept hitting him until my fists were red. And he let me until I had gotten it all out.

"HOW COULD YOU?! How could you?!" I screamed at his hard face until it was his turn to take over. He grabbed my arms and shook me until I regained control.

"KEIRA, listen to me… LISTEN! I can't feed from you. It's impossible! No one can… it's not been allowed… you're the

Chosen One!" He shouted back at me, and before I realised it, his arms had caged me in an unbreakable hold. I was then being taken back into his room by force, where he was to make me understand...

The only way he knew how.

CHAPTER 44

SOMETHING DIFFERENT

" **G** ET OFF ME!" I screamed, but it was no good, he had my body in his iron hold, his arms locking around me with an incredible force. I was like a frightened bird, squirming to get free. His face looked both calm and controlled, but I knew that was soon to change. My hair hung wet around my face and my clothes clung to my skin. I had only been out there a moment, but it was long enough for me to get soaked.

He finally put me down, up against one of the huge bedposts at the end of the bed. I was stood on the second step and when I tried to move, he grabbed my hands and pinned them above my head. His face was level with mine and he leant his body into me, making my pulse quicken with both anger and the hunger I still felt for his touch.

He was wet too, and water dripped down from his black hair onto his face. His hair came forward making his features look all that more chilling, his black eyes twitched with hints of purple as the Demon inside was screaming through.

I was furious, but at the same time something else burned inside me and I couldn't stop it... Damn it but I wanted him!

"Let me go!" I screamed again, and his hands only increased their pressure on me.

"NO!" he shouted back, and I knew I was his to do with as

he pleased. There was a light tap at the door and this didn't go down well with Draven as he wanted me to himself.

"Leave us! We are *not* to be disturbed!" his voice thundered, and it truly scared me as it was not a command to be reckoned with. His hard eyes sliced back at me slowly. With the sight of purple piercing through his icy stare, his head lowered, and his lip curled slightly, there was only one way to describe him, for he was truly predatory. I bit my lip at the sight of what seemed as if he wanted to consume me. This look of fright must have brought him to a calmer place.

"Why do you refuse to trust me? After everything I have done, you still think I want to hurt you?" He moved one hand away, but when I tried to take my chance and move, he just transferred both my wrists into one large hand.

"Because it is nothing but lies, everything you have said is just one big lie to get what you want!" I couldn't contain my anger. I had to get it out. It had to be freed. He laughed once without humour.

"If I wanted you purely to feed off, as you so wrongly think, why would I have waited so long? I would have taken you there and then!" His free hand was gripping onto the wooden post near my side. His breathing became as heavy as mine, as he wrestled with his anger.

"Maybe you just enjoy playing the game!" I said to be cruel. Why was I pushing him and most of all, why was I enjoying it? What I said hit home, literally, as he hit the post with annoyance, and the bed shook behind me as he shouted,

"Tanrı ve Devils el sizin tarafınızdan aptal kız vardır!" (Turkish)

"Speak English!" I shouted back, hating it when he did that in rage!

"I said by God and the Devil's hands, you are a foolish girl!"

"You're right I am a fool… for trusting that you could ever just have wanted me for me." Again, this hit him hard, but he reacted differently this time. He shook his head at me, and his free hand went to my waist that was now exposed from having my hands still held above my head. As soon as his skin came in contact with mine, it sent fiery pulses up my side, making me feel weak.

"You think that I would have gone to all this trouble just for a good meal? There are sadder cases than yours, Keira, but none that would ever have touched me in the same way. The only reason you are here is because I want you... no, not just want, but *need you* and I know you feel the same." His hand moved further up with his words.

"No, I don't!" I shouted, but the words were a lie, and he knew it too. His sinful grin under his dripping hair and his black, deep-set eyes that were searing into mine said as much.

He leant his head closer to my face, holding it there. His hand circled round down to my thigh and it moved inwards slightly making my body thrust against his with want. His lips were so close, I could almost taste him.

"I know you do, and I will prove it," his lips whispered over mine, but he still wouldn't kiss me, and I was going crazy inside knowing that if he didn't put his lips to mine soon, I would scream out. I wanted him like never before and if he didn't take me, I would be proving him right. Then he made this a million times worse. He lifted my leg up so he could step closer to my body and in that position, I could feel his length rub against my sweet spot.

This was more than I could bear, and I caved in to the power he had over me. I crushed my lips to his and they parted, letting me in. Once there, the taste of him was an unbelievable high that spiked with every touch. It must have had the same effect for him as he dropped his hold on me, taking my body in his arms as the kiss intensified. He crushed our bodies together so that I could barely breathe, but every breath I took was blissful torture.

I was losing my battle against why I was so angry. But I wanted to remain in control. I wanted to be heard and know the real reason for me being here. He had called me the Chosen One outside, what did it all mean? The questions that floated around my mind brought me back down from my high, and I found I could concentrate once again. As soon as he broke away from the kiss, and said,

"See, Keira, your actions are proof enough, don't you think?" And with that he broke the spell. My anger doubled, and I couldn't help what came next as if some of his rage had flowed into my very pores making me strong.

"How dare you!" I shouted, and then slapped him across the face. I was so angry that he was right. I hadn't been strong enough to say no. Well, now that was about to change! He could only look shocked for a moment and then he gave me another grin as if he enjoyed my reaction. I walked away from him, passing the bed when he grabbed hold of my arm and yanked me roughly back to him.

"And where do you think you're going?!" he said as I was back in his arms again, where I was going to stay no matter what! He kissed me furiously like he had never kissed me before, and my body went like putty under this new aggressive passion. That was it! My logic vanished along with my will. I was his for the taking and my hands fisted in his wet hair, pulling it forcefully to keep him where I wanted him.

His hands travelled the length of my spine before curving over my cheeks. Once there he gripped me forcefully, lifting me up to his groin, wrapping my legs around his waist and locking them at his back. I don't know how, but my hair was loose again, flowing down in wet waves, and his fingers ran gently through the strands until getting to the base of my neck. There he grabbed a handful, twisted and pulled my head back suddenly, so my neck was taut. Then his face descended, and his lips took the offering provided. He ran his tongue up the length of my neck and made his way over to the side, where he held me immobile with his teeth. My heart pounded at what he would do next and he seemed to be fighting with himself.

All I heard was a Demonic growl rumbling against my jaw before he released me. Then there was no more being gentle, as he threw me on the bed proving this. My breath left me at the unexpected, making me even more excited at this new side of Draven I had never seen before. He flipped me over, so I was lying on my front as his hands explored my back. I heard him remove what must have been his clothes as the next time he touched me I was sure he was naked.

My clothes were irritating him too as he couldn't get to my skin freely with them in the way. That's when I heard a ripping sound as he wasn't patient enough to remove them the conventional way, as he had done with his own. He had torn them apart as if they had been made of paper, proving his strength. I jumped at the sounds of my clothes coming away at the seams and I grabbed for the sheets, just for something to hold on to whilst I was being manhandled in the most blissful of ways.

My back was now naked, and his fingers took on a softer role as they traced from the top of my neck, down to the base of my spine. My body arched up like a stroked cat, increasing the energy that he created inside me and when I did this, his hands grabbed me from underneath, twisting me back upright to face him. He removed the remaining strips of material that were covering me and threw them away like rags. His eyes grew wide and hungry for my exposed breasts, as if he needed to taste them, which is exactly what he did.

He leaned down and bit my sides softly but enough for the pain to be turned into pleasure. He worked his way up over my nipples, sucking and torturing each one until I nearly came apart beneath him. He looked up at me with a heavy purple gaze before continuing on round to my neck making me groan under each bite. I placed my hands on his back and couldn't help but rake my nails down, digging into his skin, and he too groaned in response.

My jeans were all that remained, and these would be a problem for what he wanted to do next. He gripped me roughly by the denim on the waistline and pulled me up to his groin, suspending me and creating a space underneath my body. This was so that with his other hand he could pull the jeans, ripping them away from my thighs and making the material separate all the way down the sides.

Now I was as naked as him.

I couldn't tear my eyes away from him as he reminded me of

some Demonic wild beast, and I was the only victim he wanted to feast upon. And I let him. I let him have me, giving myself gladly to his needs as they were also my own. He was kneeling and looking down at me, helpless under his domination. He tightened his hands around my arms and pulled me up to him, wrapping my legs once more around his waist. He sat back off his knees and lifted me up slightly so that he could enter me.

I screamed out as soon as he did but he fought my body's reaction, restraining me back to him, pulling me down at the shoulders to take his full length. Once again, his size shocked me and made it hard to take as I let out more screams of intensity. The pleasure evolved inside me, getting stronger with every move he made. I could feel his muscles clench at his own pleasure, and I in turn let out moans of uncontrollable rapture.

I don't know how long we were locked together in this unbreakable bond and, like last night, my mind was consumed with the ecstasy that I felt. I could only feel, but I couldn't think. My brain wouldn't let me.

Draven's hands were everywhere. Controlling my every move. He would hold me in the tightest embrace like he never wanted to let me go, and then the next minute he would hold me at arm's length just to look at me in admiration. All the while pounding into me with such power, making me feel like he possessed every inch of my body. I didn't know how my body survived the onslaught as my mind was finding it hard keeping sane.

I felt him move his impressive grip down from my breasts to my hips in an almost bruising hold before I felt myself being moved. I had my eyes closed the whole time but when I finally did open them, I was again lying on my front. He was still firmly seated deep inside me and his hands held me tightly in an embrace. Once again, I couldn't control what I needed to happen after what felt like an eternity of maddening ecstasy. His hand found the front of my neck, holding the length and used it to turn my head upwards. I could feel his strong jaw against my face, and he placed his lips at my ear.

"Tell me what you want, Keira?" he said in a forceful tone. I closed my eyes and bit down on my lip, not wanting to speak. So he reacted by multiplying the feeling inside me and my body tensed under his weight, as he thrust harder inside me, hitting my G spot again and again.

"Is this what you want?" he whispered, and I could feel the mischievous grin behind his words. When I still didn't answer he did the same thing, only making it last longer, then cutting it off abruptly at the last second making me scream. He was toying with me to get me to obey him.

"Keira, I can keep doing this until you speak to me," he warned, and I knew my body couldn't take it anymore, so I gave in to his unusual demand.

"Yes." The answer escaped my lips barely making a sound.

"Say it again," he said gripping my neck tighter.

"Yes," I replied, this time louder but still, it wasn't enough.

"Say it again!" he shouted masterfully, and this time his other hand found a nipple to twist and I nearly went off like a rocket, so I screamed,

"YES!" Finally satisfying him.

"Good girl," he said finding the response he wanted, and he showed me his gratitude by making my body erupt, crying out, along with his own roar of release. Once again, he fought against me, holding me down until I calmed. This took time, as it didn't stop until he knew my body couldn't take any more and I was pleading with him out loud. I went to bury my head again, but he wouldn't let me.

"No you don't, I want to see the pleasure in your eyes," he said, firmly holding my face up. I went to bite down again on my lip, but he stopped me by placing his thumb in the way of my mouth as I probably would have bit through it. And then it was all over as I again let out one last scream to finalize it, opening my eyes to look at him. My muscles collapsed into arms that still held me.

He lowered me down gently, letting my head roll into the covers as I hid my shame. He waited patiently for my body to regain control and my breathing to calm. All I wanted to do was sleep, and the feel of him stroking the back of my hair was making it worse. I followed the rhythm, back and forth, and he kissed the top of my head, saying,

"Forgive me, I was too rough with you." I was about to disagree when he interrupted my chance.

"Sleep, Keira," he whispered gently after easing out of my used body. But this I wanted to fight against, so I opened my eyes again, only this time without looking at him. My skin was sticky from sweat and my cheeks burned from my screaming. He covered me with the silk covers, cooling me down as he had done last night. I was still on my side, my face remaining out of his sight. His hand stroked down my shoulder and my arm. His skin was now icy cold making my skin react.

"You need rest... *my love.*" I knew he was right as I was exhausted, but my stubborn nature came through. Also, did he just call me... *my love?* My inner-self was screaming out with glee but my exterior remained calm. A term of endearment that was all. I kept repeating this over and over.

"I don't want to sleep," I said timidly, and he let out a small laugh.

"Your body is not used to all it has endured. You need time to adjust," he said, back to a soft velvet voice. I turned to face him as I couldn't hide from him any longer. He was smiling, all traces of the beast gone.

"I'm fine, you weren't too rough but that was... well... *different,"* I said putting it diplomatically.

"I think they call it make up sex, Keira." He smirked at me.

"Does this mean we get to argue every day?" I said only half-joking, and I stretched out like a lioness after a long sleep. He laughed again filling the room with the sound I was quickly becoming addicted to.

"If you would prefer, your wish is of course my command."

"And you, how would you prefer it?" I asked intrigued but also self-conscious.

"Keira, I would take you any way I can, but I would never want to hurt you... I know what my limits are," he said, and I took his words seriously having tasted his strength only on a minute scale.

"I do, however, apologise for your clothes. Maybe getting me roused up like that would be better for when you are already naked." I laughed looking down at my once normal clothes now torn to shreds.

"It was worth it... I am sorry for hitting you," I said sheepishly, looking down and feeling guilty that I had been so worked up. He lifted my chin to see his wide grin.

"Keira, you are the only one ever to be allowed to do so and if you choose, you could chain me up and beat me. I can imagine, coming from you, I would enjoy it immensely." His grin changed into a mischievous smile and I hit him lightly on the arm, teasing him.

"Oh, and you think I have a temper, you were downright terrifying!" he teased back. I frowned but it wasn't quite so effective when a yawn followed it.

"Come on now, you are tired, try and get some sleep."

"I'm not tired." He raised one eyebrow at my lie and I fought back another yawn so as not to give him any more proof.

"But there is one thing... I'm kind of hungry," I said, and just then my stomach proved it by rumbling.

"Of course, I am sorry, I forget that you need more food, especially after... well, such a physical work out."

"Is that what you call it?" I teased again, but he replied by kissing me gently. When he pulled his face away, he looked more serious, and I was instantly worried.

"Keira, you can't do that to me again. You have to start trusting me, no matter what your own insecurities tell you. You must listen to me and know that from now on, what I say is the truth," he said, and I felt ashamed of my behaviour, no matter how amazing the outcome had been. I think this had been enough to prove to me that I was here because he wanted me to be, because he really did care about me. After all, like he had said, there were sadder cases out there and if he was purely doing this to feed off me, then why me? Why not some even more messed up soul? I didn't say anything, but I nodded in agreement.

He was getting up to leave when I stopped him.

"Where are you going?" I said, sounding hurt that he was leaving me, and shamefully feeling a little needy.

"To get you some food before you collapse, you need to get your blood sugar level up so that you won't feel so weak," he said, and once again by the time it took me to turn away and back again, he was fully clothed in a fresh long-sleeved T-shirt and jeans.

"How do you do that?" I asked shaking my head at him.

"Keira, there are lots of things I can do, being very fast is only one of them." And to prove this he was back next to me holding out the bowl of fruit for me to choose. I hadn't even seen his body move. He was that fast. I picked a lush green apple out of the bowl and took a bite. He watched me, his deep eyes followed every move I made, causing me to feel nervous.

"What?" I asked

"I love watching you eat... it makes me want you all over again," he said eyeing the juice that overflowed from my lips. This prompted him to move my hand that held the apple away from my mouth and kiss the side, tasting the juice for himself. I shuddered, feeling the sensations all the way down to my toes.

"Mmm, it tastes better off your skin," he said making me blush.

"Umm... I kinda need to do something," I said after I had silently finished my apple. But knowing what I was going to have to ask him, added to the embarrassment I already felt. He nodded for me to carry on with my question.

"I need some clothes. I have to do the whole girl thing." And I pointed to the bathroom.

"Ah, well be my guest, it's not like I haven't studied every inch of you already. There is nothing you need to hide." He was smiling, knowing this was most definitely something I wouldn't do. Before I answered, he got up and was back again with a long, dark red silk kimono over his arm. He passed it to me saying,

"I will give you a moment alone." Like a perfect gentleman. I slipped it on as soon as I was alone and went over to get a fresh set of clothes, wondering if they would last until the night... part

STEPHANIE HUDSON

of me hoped not! Once I had used the bathroom and made myself respectable again, I walked back into the room, disappointed to find it still empty. I picked up some more fruit and poured myself some water.

Then I jumped at the sound of the massive grandfather clock that was stood in the corner. The wooden sides held another carved warrior scene and it too, looked Japanese, matching the tapestries and other bits of furniture. It struck four times, telling me that it was almost evening and I still hadn't spoken to Libby. She must be freaking out. I started to search through my bag but then remembered that Draven still had my phone.

"Goddamn it!" I said out loud

"That's a sin you know." Draven's voice made me jump, and my hand went to my chest feeling it thump erratically under my palm.

"This is never going to work if you keep creeping up on me and nearly scaring me to death!" I said, realising how funny that sounded seeing as I was talking to a half Angel/Demon! He looked amused and came over to me, holding out my phone in his hand. I went to take it, but he put it behind his back.

"And what do I get in return?" he teased looking playfully down at me. It was so surreal seeing Draven this way, when the only way I had been used to him was such the opposite.

"And here was me thinking that you were the type to just take whatever you wanted... oh well," I said turning away, knowing that I might win this round. But he was fast and by the time I turned, he was back in front of me again, grinning like the cat that got the cream. He held out the phone again, which I took from him but in turn he took me. He pulled me to him, spinning me around so he was now behind me. His head arched downwards, and he moved my hair back off my neck making my own head spin.

"I do take what I want, Keira... will that be a problem?" he asked whispering in my ear and then he moved his lips down my neck tilting it to the side with his hands. My hands however were shaking at the feeling and I dropped the phone. In a heartbeat

Draven's hand shot out, leaving my neck, and grabbed my phone mid-air before it could crash to the floor.

I turned to face him and took the phone. He was trying to contain his smug smile, but he wasn't doing a very convincing job.

"You know being too cocky isn't good for the soul," I warned, playing with him as I walked away, putting a safe distance between us. I was never going to be able to ring Libby with Draven even standing this close to me, let alone kissing me.

"Maybe not, but I know a lot of other things that are definitely on the list," he replied winking at me, which made me melt.

I flipped open my phone and pressed the quick dial to Libby's number.

"Kazzy, where the hell have you been?! I have nearly gone out of my mind... I left you about a hundred messages and..."

"Libs, calm down, I'm fine, I just haven't had chance to..."

"Oh what, spend two minutes calling your panicked sister!" She was not happy, and I felt guilty that I had left it this long. I tried to reason with her without having to answer the most obvious questions that were no doubt yet to come.

"I'm sorry, but Libs, you're on holiday. I didn't want you to think I was scared on my own or anything!" I said hoping this would work. Draven was sat staring at me finding the whole thing very entertaining. I frowned at him and he bit back a smile.

"So, you have been at home?"

"Umm well, yes and no..." I said trying to worm my way out of it.

"Well, which is it, Kaz?"

"Jeez, Libs, what's with the interrogation? I said I'm fine, why are you so upset?" I asked as I could hear her getting a bit emotional.

"I was worried, and I think that all things considered I have a very good reason too!" She was, of course, right, and my guilt came through.

"I know, you're right I... I should have called sooner, I'm sorry."

"So, where have you been?" And this was the question I was dreading, so I tried to bypass it.

"So, how's the family, is Frank enjoying himself?"

"Kazzy, why won't you tell me where you have been... where are you now?" she asked not believing a word I said.

"I'm at home," I said way too quickly. Man, why did I have to be such a shit liar! I could see Draven finding my lying funny and I shot him a look.

"Well, that's funny, 'cause I just called there about five minutes ago and guess what, Kaz... no answer!" My God she was unstoppable!

"Well, I just walked in." I threw back at her, but Draven shook his head warning me against where this was going. Because he knew that I was walking into a trap and I was about to get caught out.

"Oh really, so you're there now?"

"Umm... yeah," I said, knowing I was already busted.

"Okay, so how many messages have I left on the answering machine?" DAMN IT! This question was too much for Draven to contain the roaring laughter that erupted from him. I only now guessed that one of his other gifts was great hearing!

"Who was that?" Libby asked as she to, had the gift.

"It was nobody, just the TV, one of those annoying sitcoms... it's nothing," I said emphasising on the annoying part, which Draven didn't miss. He just mouthed the words, *'is that so'* at me with a raised eyebrow. I tried not to laugh.

"Was it, Jack?" she asked, and Draven replaced the good humour with a low growl, at the sound of his name. Before I knew it, he had my phone in his hand and to his ear. My dread doubled and pure panic set in.

"Hello Libby, its Dominic Draven here," he said with such ease and confidence that I was in shock. Why would he admit to where I was?

"No, she's fine, she's obviously not at home, but I think she was a little embarrassed to tell you herself," he said, and I couldn't hide my horror, what was he doing? I could just hear Libby ask,

"Tell me what?"

"Keira and I are involved," he said, and I stood looking up at him like he had lost it. But just when I thought it couldn't get any more shocking, it did! When Libby asked,

"Involved how?"

Draven replied with the last thing I could have ever imagined out of his lips…

"I'm in love with her."

CHAPTER 45
LOVIN' BEING INVOLVED

I couldn't speak. It was as if Draven had once again stolen my voice, only this time it wasn't done intentionally. So, when he had finished on the phone to my sister, he passed it back to me, saying,

"She wants to talk to you." He looked down at me, but I still couldn't comprehend what had just happened. Did he just say he loved me? Why? How? When?! My mind was overloaded, as if my mental dam had just been blown apart, flooding my mind with too many questions to process.

"Keira," Draven said louder, bringing me around, but I was still in a semi-daze when I put the phone to my ear.

"Kaz…Kazzy, are you still there?" I nodded but knowing she couldn't see me, I found the words I needed.

"Umm, yeah, what's up?" I said trying to sound casual which was so uncool, it would have made The Fonz from Happy Days slap his forehead.

"What's up…? Are you freakin' kidding me? Kaz, your Boss, Mr Zillionaire and the most powerful man in the town. Hell, not just the town, but well, you get the picture… Kaz, he just said he was in love with you!" I swallowed hard as she confirmed that I wasn't hearing things. This was impossible, wasn't it? How could he be in love me? When I didn't answer she carried on, and I could feel Draven's eyes on my face, but I couldn't look at him. I just couldn't!

"Keira, what the hell is going on? He said you're there with him and have been since Monday... well seeing as it is Tuesday, that could only mean one thing!" Oh GOD! She couldn't be allowed to know, to think... oh God!

"What? So, I... um... stayed the night," I said clearing my throat, feeling it start to close. God, were my cheeks melting from the bone like they felt they were?

"OH, COME ON! Look okay, just answer me two things and I will leave you alone, as you are obviously in the safest place imaginable." I shook my head, but I kept forgetting she couldn't see me.

"Look Libs, I don't have time for this!" I said trying to put her off with irritation.

"Okay, well, you want to play that game, if you don't, I will call Mum!" Oh shit! She did not just go there!

"Oh no, don't you dare pull the mum card on me... You wouldn't!" I said testing her, knowing that bloody hell she would if she didn't get her way... she always did this! I heard Draven laugh, and I finally found the strength to turn to him and I held up my hand and shot him a look as if to say, 'this is all your fault!' He didn't look as though he took my threat seriously. No wonder, 'cause apparently he loved me! Oh my God!

"Libs, we're not kids any more, you can't just pull that crap on me!" I said trying to make her see sense, but it was like reasoning with Joseph Stalin!

"Well, you have your choices... pick one," she said as if this was set in stone.

"Or I could just hang up," I said playing that card but seeing as I was playing against a master, I wasn't surprised when she said.

"Yeah, but you can't hang up on Mum... So try me!"

"FINE!" I shouted turning away from Draven as he was making this harder, acting like a child himself, as if this was the funniest thing he had seen in years.

"Alright good but remember that I will know if you're

lying… First question… did you do it?" she asked getting excited, and this just made me want to chuck my phone over the balcony and see how long it would take to smash to the bottom!

"Do what?" I said feeling my face tense.

"Play scrabble! What do you think I mean… sex?" As soon as she said this, I wanted the earth to swallow me whole. The last thing I wanted was to be having this conversation with my sister when I had just heard Draven say that he loved me!

"Fine! Yes… next question!"

"Oh my God… no way! Way to go, Kazzy! How was it? Was it as incredible as it looks like it would be?" She sounded like she would soon hyperventilate, and I cruelly wished she would, so I could get off the phone! Draven burst out laughing at this and I scowled at him.

"Was that him laughing?" she asked, and I turned from him to get my own back with my next words,

"Yeah, he's watching America's next top model." I tried not to laugh when I heard the Demon in him release a low growl. Yep, payback was a bitch I thought smugly.

"He is not!" she said on the other end.

"So, is that your next question?" I asked sarcastically.

"No, I will drill you on the dishy details later when I'm home but what I really want to know is, just answer yes or no, as I know he's there, but tell me… do you love him?" Of course, as soon as she said it Draven was up out of his seat coming over to me, waiting for my answer as well. Libby was not to know that he could not only hear my side of the conversation but hers as well.

I looked up into deep pools of emotion, seeing the eyes of a desperate man. I knew my heart, but he didn't, so for all he knew I might not have loved him, but come on… that wasn't going to be likely now, was it?

"Yes, I love him," I said, feeling every word as though my heart had finally spoken the truth to the one it mattered the most. Draven swiftly took the phone off me as I could just hear excited screams from Libby on the other end. He raised it to his ear, and said,

"Bye Libby, she will call you later." And then he snapped my phone shut. He turned to me with his eyes ablaze, took me into his arms and kissed me so passionately that I could feel the tears welling up. He then placed his hands on either side of my head, his fingers embedded in my hair and his thumbs on my cheeks. And we fit together so beautifully it was hard to breathe. It was the sweetest kiss I had ever known.

I was still in shock when he finally put me down. I didn't know what to say, from the first time I saw him, the obsession began. I couldn't think of anything but the man who stood opposite me now, but I would never have believed in my wildest fantasies that he could be thinking about me too. However, for him to be in love with me! Now that was a gift.

"What are you thinking about?" His soft voice brought me back.

"I umm… well, I'm in shock," I admitted.

"Why?" His voice sounded confused.

"Because I don't understand why… why would you ever love me?" I blurted out before I could stop myself.

"And why not? Why is that so hard to believe?" He looked hurt and a little bit angry.

"Because it's just me, and I have been in love with you this whole time but I'm just some plain looking, messed up girl with no right to have you!" I said looking at the floor, ashamed at all I blurted out by admitting how I felt. But it was the truth. How would I ever feel good enough for a man like Draven, who was swimming in a sea of beauties, and I was just the outcast looking in? His hand rose to my face, and with a fingertip under my chin he lifted my face to his.

"Keira, why do you simply refuse to understand what you mean to me? I have waited for you for far too many lifetimes to mention. You were made for me, and for years I have searched in vain only to find bitter disappointment. Until the day I finally found you… and trust me when I say, I would fight Heaven and Hell to keep you!" His hand now gripped my neck to lift all of my face to see the truth in his eyes and at the sight, as hard as this was, I could do nothing but believe him.

"But if that was the case then why have you been determined to keep pushing me away?" I asked in my shy voice.

"Because you have become the only weakness in all of my years. I have many enemies, Keira, and up until now they had nothing to use against me... I had nothing to lose... *until you.*" He motioned for me to sit and I knew now I was about to hear the rest of the story. The reasons behind every lie he told, as now there was nothing left to stand in my way, now all cards were on the table.

"Are you ready to continue our earlier conversation?" he asked, sitting next to me, with my hands in his.

"Yes, but can I still ask questions?" I asked, and he let out an easy laugh making me smile back at him.

"I wouldn't expect anything else from you." He touched my nose playfully with one finger.

"So where did I get to before... we?"

"Before I wigged out?" I said, knowing now he was trying to be diplomatic.

"Let's just call it a misunderstanding that ended with an interesting twist." Now it was my turn to laugh. Well, that was one way to put it! I, on the other hand, would have said 'the most amazing sex of my life!'

"You were telling me why you weren't happy about me working the VIP," I said, grabbing a handful of grapes, and getting more comfortable by bringing my feet up and putting my arms around my knees. He watched me curiously, making me once again feel self-conscious.

"As I explained before, for some reason my kind cannot..."

"*Feed...*? It's fine, I won't go all weird again, but can you explain it more?"

"Feeding is not harmful to humans, except when some do it to excess and this is forbidden as it's one of the rules. But with every rule, there are those who break them. Positive and negative energy can cause different effects on us, so we usually stick to what we prefer. For example, a Demon is more inclined feed from depressed people or humans that might feel lost in life. With Angels, it is the opposite, they prefer the more positive emotions. But as I said, the pendulum swings both ways. It is not as clear cut that Angels are always good and Demons are always bad."

"What do you prefer?" I asked, and he frowned at my question.

"I am different. I do not need to feed like the rest, *but...* occasionally, I still do. It would feel unnatural if I didn't. Like, say if you didn't need water to live," he said filling my glass and passing it to me. "I hold this out to you and the very idea of it makes you thirsty, so you will still drink it even though you don't need to." And he was right, as soon as he passed me the glass, I was thirsty and couldn't help but take a sip. He shot me a knowing grin.

"I am both Demon and Angel, so I am inclined both ways, therefore I feed from both energies. Like I said, there are some that do this to excess, which is forbidden because they then manipulate human emotions purely for their own gain, like feeding an addiction. They will keep a human down and depressed just to feed on, and thus taking away their free will."

"Okay, that makes sense so far... then what about me?"

"When you came to work in the club, I forbade anyone feeding from you. I would not allow anyone to even try, as I shamefully looked on you as if you were mine and mine only. But my curiosity got too much for me one night, and I soon realised that not even *I* could feed from you. But not only could I not feed, most of my powers wouldn't work, as if you were locking everyone out, including me." I couldn't help but smile at the thought.

"That must have been frustrating for you," I said without being able to keep the self-satisfied look from my face.

"Oh, believe me, it was! I had never been unable to see into someone's past or thoughts before. I wanted to know everything about you, but you kept it all locked away, keeping it just for yourself. It was very selfish of you, Keira," he teased bringing my hand to his lips so that he could kiss each of my knuckles.

"I would say sorry, but I would be lying," I teased back, making him playfully start biting my hand. I couldn't help but be turned on by the sight. I mentally whipped down my libido, saying 'down girl!' and then asked,

"So what did you do?"

"I had to do things the conventional way, which was difficult for me. You have to understand, I am very used to getting what I want, and when you walked into my life, it consumed me that I couldn't get you the way I wanted. I started by seeing you at night, but you would then wake, and it would get harder each time to try and make you believe what I wanted you to. As they say, I was trying to have my cake and eat it, but as I told you before, you were very stubborn," he said as he pushed a stray bit of hair back behind my ear.

"Why am I different? You mentioned something about the 'Chosen One'... what does that mean?" But as soon as I mentioned this, he stood up abruptly and turned very serious.

"I should not have said that to you, it is not the time and there is more you need to know. Besides, that is something I am forbidden to discuss."

"Forbidden?" I shook my head, not understanding how a conversation could be forbidden. I mean this was like waving a red rag to a bull!

"Please, Keira, forget I said that, let just this one thing slide, please... it is not something you need to trouble yourself with, not yet anyway." This made me want to ask more but I knew it would not be wise, so I stayed silent.

"I do not know why you are different. But I would never have you any other way, no matter how frustrating it has been. Of course, Sophia made it her duty to try and force the issue." At this he rolled his eyes, making me smile.

"Sophia? But why would she...?"

"Because I am not the only one who has been waiting for you to come to us. She loves you and she knew that this would finally be the year. That's why she started college, to get close to you."

"But I don't understand, why would she go to all that effort?" All these confessions were making my mind whirl. Was this all true, and if not, then what would he ever gain from lying? No, I had to believe him.

"Because she loves me dearly and wants me to be happy. So evidently, she decided to hurry things up. She was the one who had Jerry make you bring up those bottles. I knew nothing about her plans, and then when I saw you walk past me…" he shook his head as if reliving the memory, "…well, let's just say, I very nearly stole you away there and then. It was like waving drugs in front of an addict." I shuddered. As soon as he said this, it was as though my own feelings were being projected back to me.

"So, that's why you seemed so annoyed?"

"At the time, I was furious! She went against me by involving you in our world, but pretty soon I was also thankful for it. I would spend my day watching you through the eyes of others and waiting for you until I could finally do it through my own."

"Wait a minute, eyes of others, what do you mean?" I was now panicking, wondering what else he had seen. I mean, it was like having some supernatural stalker confess his sins. I was still processing all of the dreams I had of him being in my room as being real, but now I had so much more to contend with.

"Another one of my gifts is that I can view things through the eyes of others. Almost like a semi possession. They still have their functions, but I own their mind for a short time. And then they awaken as if it has all been a daydream. Of course, I have had my fun with it also." He laughed at a memory I couldn't see, so I couldn't help asking,

"Fun?" before folding my arms as if what I was about to hear were the tales of a naughty boy.

"Well, you might be angry, but you have to know it was my only way to keep a watchful eye on you." Now he looked guilty, like he had just been busted by… well, by his girlfriend! Now that sounded strange in a wonderful way.

"Draven?"

"I will tell you, but please try to keep an open mind, Keira."

"Why, so you can make me do the 'can can' in my

underwear?" I asked teasing, and I saw his lips twitch trying to deny me the smile.

"As nice as that image is, I think you're safe... for now." I blushed and had to clear my throat, before saying,

"Umm, please continue." This time he didn't deny me the smile.

"At first, I just used to see through the eyes of your fellow students, but Sophia would often frown upon it, as of course, she would know when I did this." I couldn't help but laugh at all those times when I had seen someone looking at me funny, it had been Draven all along. Then I froze in horror as I realised the others he had used. My hands flew to my mouth, but he couldn't keep the badass grin from his lips as he knew I must have realised who else he had seen me through.

"The doctor?" I said under my hands.

"Which one?" he said, waiting for me to freak out.

"WHAT? Both of them? You...you... oh God, no wonder he looked at me like I was crazy!" I said, shaking my head at him.

"I'm going to take a wild stab in the dark and say you met one of them, when it wasn't me." I just nodded, and he let out a roar of laughter at which I jabbed him in the ribs. However, it didn't do me much good as it probably felt like I was tickling him with a fine paintbrush!

"I'm sorry, I shouldn't laugh but come on... it is kind of funny," he said pinching my cheek playfully, making me cave in with a smile.

"Okay, but that's it... right?" I checked, but I knew from his face that it wasn't.

"Come on, who else?" I demanded, trying to be firm.

"Okay, but you will find this one funny and like I said, it was worth every penny!" He couldn't keep the smirk off his face, when the penny dropped.

"No way! Bobby the car guy. I knew it!" I shouted turning fully towards him and pointing at him.

"I knew there was something weird about that guy. First to drop the price and then knock off one thousand for a kiss on the cheek!" I said, not being able to contain the laugh after it, one he joined in.

"I would have gone for a kiss on the lips, but I think Frank would have knocked poor Bobby out and I didn't want him to wake up with a black eye. But I must say, I was slightly shocked when I gave you four thousand dollars and Frank said you only had three... he knows how to play the game," he said seeing the funny side, but I felt guilty for poor Bobby, as he must have woken up wondering why he practically gave a car away.

"Poor Bobby," I said voicing my thoughts, and Draven's hand stroked my face as if finding my concern for Bobby sweet and endearing.

"Oh, he didn't do too badly, waking to find himself ten thousand richer."

"What?" Was he joking?

"Well, I couldn't let him wake and find he had very nearly given the car away, and I was determined that you were going to have the Ford Bronco, even if it was for only three thousand." He said this like it was obvious.

"Oh great, even more money I owe you!" I said putting my head in my hands, but it shot up again when I heard him let out an almighty laugh, which made me jump.

"I don't think so, Keira. But we can do a deal and you can pay it off in other ways." He winked, giving me another mischievous grin as he leaned down and kissed me before I could object. I realised why this was so funny to him as compared to his wealth, whatever it may be, ten thousand dollars was most likely pocket change to him.

"So that's why Bobby seemed to be so horny, it was you all along! Well, that explains it." I laughed back at him as he kissed me again, smirking, just proving my point.

"Well, could you blame me for trying to sneak a kiss from the prettiest girl around, plus I don't think he will mind the memory."

"What, he will remember?!" I asked feeling embarrassed again.

"It's like I said, they just fall into a trance and then wake being semi-aware of what has happened." I looked at him frowning, so he added,

"It doesn't hurt." But I just continued to look at him sceptically.

"Did it hurt you?" he asked.

"What?! You have not done it to me? Have you...? Oh no, When? Why? I thought you couldn't do things like that to me." Okay, now I was really panicking.

"For some reason, I can only access your mind when you are emotional. I found when you let your guard down, when you are upset or frightened, this can be done. I first did it when you locked yourself outside the club when that dumpster nearly broke your fingers. I have never had to watch someone so closely before. You are so accident-prone." He said this like it was an endearing quality, and I got the distinct impression that he liked taking care of me.

"You made the lid go back, and my fingers... you made them open the door!"

"And did it hurt?"

"No, it just felt tingly, like when you usually touch me," I said, and one eyebrow rose.

"Tingles?" I went red when he repeated the word, as obviously I had said too much.

"Umm, never mind... carry on," I said as he laughed from seeing my embarrassment. But then he let go of his amusement and I soon found out why.

"And the other time... well, it was downright painful to witness."

"Draven?"

"The time I achieved my goal. When I lied to you about Celina and I..."

"I remember," I whispered, silently pleading him not to continue.

"When I saw how much it affected you, I was destroyed. I was also in shock that you felt so hurt. That you could actually feel that way for me. I never knew until that day. So, when I saw you by your car, too upset to move, I took over your body and

got you home. I knew otherwise you would never have made it."
This actually looked agonizing for him to explain.

"Thank you, and what I said to you…"

"Your words cut through me like Excalibur. The last thing
you said, calling me, *My Lord.* I will never forget that feeling if I
live for ten thousand lifetimes. But it was all my own doing. You
see, after that night on the roof, after you saw the real me, I
knew you wouldn't let it go, that you couldn't be convinced or
controlled. So, I decided the only way was to hurt you, to make
you hate me, make it so you would want to stay away from me."

"But I didn't, I still couldn't let you go!" I cried out.

"Well, when I saw you at the cliff face, I thought otherwise."
It looked like he winced at the memory.

"You were there?"

"Yes, I didn't leave your side after I got you home. You were
so upset that I could access that part of your mind so you
wouldn't see me." I frowned at him, but his face looked too hurt
for me to continue to be mad for long.

"I know what you must think. It was a great intrusion to your
privacy, and trust me when I say I was punished for it, but I
could not be torn away from your side… not with so much
pain." My face shot up to look at him, and I shuddered at the
thought of him being punished from seeing me like that.

"What do you mean… *punished?"*

"My punishment was great indeed, as I witnessed the hurt I
put you through. I wanted to make it right and take it all back,
but I was torn between your safety and your happiness. In the
end, I made my choice, which was the lesser of two evils. But I
wanted to be there for you even if you couldn't see me, even if I
couldn't touch you and comfort you. However, I thought it had
all been in vain when you went to the cliff face." I raised my
eyes at him, and the back of his hand stroked down my face and
rested on my neck before he carried on.

"When I couldn't control your body, I thought I was going to
have to reveal myself and stop you as I thought you were going
to jump."

"You thought I was going to kill myself?!" I shouted at him.

"Consider why I would think that, Keira... As far as I knew, you had tried to once before. It was obvious you were hiding something, and it wasn't that hard to guess," he said, looking at my concealed arms, and I pulled down my long-sleeved top past my hands.

"As I said, I thought I was going to have to stop you, but as always I can never predict anything when it comes to you. You don't act like normal humans do, but I guess that is down to your own gifts. It makes you unique. Your mind doesn't work the same." I frowned, but he smiled, saying,

"Don't look at me like that... this is not a bad thing, my love." And with that one endearment spoken, my face softened.

"You have to be different, Keira, or think how difficult this would have been. If you weren't used to seeing the things you do, then one look at the real me, you would have run far away and never come back!" I knew what he meant. I reacted to it at first but still, I came back to him... even after what I saw. The very next day in fact.

"Okay, so you have me there, but how did you get the picture I tore up?"

"Ah, my portrait. Well, I was intrigued to know what it was you were ripping up. So when you left, I summoned back the pieces and made them whole again. That's when I first realised how you controlled your gift... you were trying to get rid of me." He was now looking out of the glass doors when he said this, as though still searching for those small pieces dancing in the wind.

"I was trying to make it easier. To let you go as you wanted me to... at your hand remember?" I said, reminding him and therefore taking away my unjustified guilt.

"I know, but trust me, it didn't make it any easier, not when I still had to see you every day in the club, and it would get harder... thanks to that boy, *Jack!*" He hissed out his name on a snarl.

"Wait a minute, it was you?!" I said, thinking back to the dive of a bar we all went to that day.

"To which are you referring, Keira?" This time I could poke fun at him.

"You were the angry drunk at the bar who didn't like Jack sitting so close to me!" Draven let go of the growl, he had obviously been holding in, at me mentioning it.

"The *boy* needed cooling off," Draven snarled letting jealousy seep through.

"Well you certainly took care of that, didn't you?" I said, folding my arms before adding,

"So, I guess Halloween wasn't such a big hit then?" At this, his reactions to how he felt became more obvious. He turned to face me, and the Demon part of him came through at the thought. His eyes flashed deep purple fire which had me wincing back.

"No... it wasn't." He growled the words, and for a suicidal moment, I wanted to get closer to him and smooth out his frown with my fingers. Which, at a guess, would have been the same as pulling a thorn from a lion's paw. He was clearly angry about the memory of me with Jack, but come on, he had gone and done the very same thing with Celina. Right in front of me, no less!

"Now who's being unreasonable? I was a single girl and Jack is a very good friend but nothing more... you have to know that by now! And anyway, you acted like you hated me, remember!"

"Do you let all your friends kiss you like that?" he snapped back, making me jump, and ignoring my comment about him acting badly towards me. I frowned, but if I were honest, his actions made me slightly happy about the idea of him being jealous. I mean, it was ridiculous really, the idea of Draven, who I have been literally obsessed with since I came to this town, being jealous over me and Jack!

"Oh, and you can rightly talk. I seem to remember you starting the whole thing by telling me you were engaged to one of the most beautiful women that I have ever seen, of course not until after you kissed her in front of me! Let's not forget that!" I said now getting up, feeling like this conversation was a little one-sided! Draven turned to me once again, raising his eyebrows, until finally admitting I was right. He had acted first, and knew that he pushed me into Jack's arms as a result.

"You are, of course, right, but also very wrong on one thing in particular."

"And what's that?" I said folding my arms over my heaving chest.

"There is no one, not one Being, that compares to your beauty, and no man alive that could resist such a pure heart." He was over to me in half a second, his hands finding my face before his lips followed, all this before I could even speak a word. Maybe this was because he knew I would have disagreed. I was never very good at receiving compliments, as a rule you have to believe in them, to accept them. And I had just about enough self-confidence to get by in the world but to be with a man like Draven…

Well, I was still amazed.

Once he had finished kissing me, I was my usual incoherent self and I opened my eyes to see him smiling again.

"I am so sorry I hurt you, Keira," he said, making my heart melt. He was so sincere I couldn't think of anything but forgiveness.

"And I too am sorry if I brought you any pain by kissing Jack," I said, but even at the very name of him he flinched.

"That night of course changed everything."

"How do you mean?"

"Well, no doubt it is the reason you are here now. I instructed Jerry to give you the night off because it was the one night I wanted you as far away from here as possible."

"But why?" I asked, remembering wondering why I had been allowed to have the night off in the first place.

"Because you have never been in more danger in your entire life." He looked then as he had done that night. Face set in stone. Stern and powerful.

"I would never have imagined that by removing that boy you would turn into a fiery temptress. When I saw him kiss you, my reaction, well… you no doubt noticed?" I nodded, remembering the lights that blew and the loud crashing sound from above.

"Well, I couldn't tolerate that! And trust me when I say throwing him from my club was the kindest course of action, considering what I wanted to do! I mean how dare he... *you were mine!"* he shouted as his temper flared, and for a second, I thought I saw his skin change colour, or was it the Demon part of him trying to get out?

I took a step back in reaction to it, but he didn't allow that, for he gripped the top of my arms to hold me to him. I frowned and made a disapproving noise at his outburst. But deep down it also sent sparks of pleasure to my heart, secretly liking the idea of belonging to him.

"Forgive me, it's just..." He made a low rumbling noise, which I knew was down to his Demon side.

"You must understand... It... well it is hard to control emotions I have not felt before." He looked up to the ceiling for what I can only assume was to find control over his fiery temper.

"So, when I had him thrown out, you did the complete opposite of what I thought you would do. I mean, I knew you would be upset, but the last thing I imagined was you coming up to face me! I knew how much you'd had to drink, but it was not enough to think you capable of such bravery! You had always been so shy and skittish around me." He shook his head at the memory.

"Well, that will teach you to underestimate people."

"Not people, Keira, just you. I have never known a human to be so reckless before. As a general rule, humans are attracted to us yes, because of the hold we have on them, but they are also afraid of us, and for good reasons. Up until then I believed you to be the same, and although I hated the fact, it was, at the time, a necessity. I was clearly mistaken." He grinned at the thought. I must have looked like an angry cub going up against the Alpha!

"You made me angry," I said in my defence.

"Oh, there was no doubt in that, my little one! Any other time and I would have found it endearing but that night was very bad timing."

"Because of Malphas?" I said, saying his name cautiously, but I knew it was the reason before I saw Draven's reaction.

Again, it was like watching a granite statue wanting to crush the very name from existence.

"Yes," he said through gritted teeth.

"I knew it was too late as soon as he saw you, as humans are never allowed upstairs, it was my rule, and for me to break it, it would have to be for my gain only. He knew this, and if I would have had you ordered back down, he would have just found you and forced you to speak." I shuddered at the thought. What had I been thinking?

"So the only thing I could think of, was to pretend that you were nothing to me, which turned out to be impossible, as he knew how to push me. And with that, so did you."

"Well, could you blame me? I mean, how confused do you think I was? First you treat me like I was just some stupid little girl getting in your way, then you want to take care of me from a little bump to the head? That was going from one extreme to the next. So then, after all of that, you pushed me over the edge and well... let's just say I was pissed off! I mean talk about mixed signals here!" I said not taking a breath.

"So, that's why you didn't obey me?" His eyes opened wider as he looked down at me, finding out my reasons for such a stupid mistake.

"Well, it doesn't help when you use words like 'obey', I can tell ya!" I said, making my full northern accent come out as it usually did when I got animated. He didn't miss it either.

"That's adorable, you know."

"Draven!" I shouted at him, as I wasn't trying to be adorable! I was trying to get my point across.

"Alright little one, I'm not saying I don't understand your reasons, but what I am saying is that you don't realise what a catastrophic mistake you made."

"Why, because he's a bad guy?" I said talking like I was watching cartoons.

"No, because he works for the most dangerous Demon in my world. *Lucius*... my only equal in power and my mortal enemy. As a result, I will have to spend all of my time trying to keep you safe."

"Safe? What has it got to do with me? I'm just a human," I argued, while thinking a big ass 'oh shit' on hearing this!

"Yes, but you're *my* human and as a result, you have now become the most wanted human on the planet!" I must have looked stunned because Draven had his arms around me as though I might fall. And boy did I now have reasons to fall...

I was Wanted.

CHAPTER 46

BAD DECISIONS

"Okay, so can't we go back… I mean… make it out like I died or something?" I said in a panic. I mean I was already being hunted by one crazy human, but I could imagine a powerful Demon was going to be another thing entirely! Draven still had his hands around me whilst I went into full meltdown.

"Keira, it will be alright. You don't need to worry yourself about anything anymore. I will take care of you and I will deal with this. You have far too much on your mind as it is… here sit." He led me to the seat, but my mind was now racing with the thoughts of being in the middle of a war I couldn't see. Was this the price I had to pay to be with him?

Okay, so this calmed me slightly, as I knew I would have gone to Hell and back to be with Draven… and it was starting to look like I might just be taking that trip! I must have been nearly hyperventilating because he had put my head in between my legs, and I was soon breathing more calmly.

"Feeling better?" he said rubbing my back, calming me in minutes.

"Yeah, sorry, I am still trying to adjust… you know?"

"But of course, Keira, I can't imagine what hearing all that I have told you has been like, but you are taking it all in amazingly well. However, I think that is enough for one day."

"No, no really, I will be fine… oh, but wait, what time is it?" I still asked, even though I was looking around at the clock.

"Why would you need to know that?" He raised one eyebrow at my question.

"Because I have to get ready for work," I said, standing up and walking over to my bag. But his hand grabbed my wrist, making me tense as I still wasn't used to being touched there.

"I'm sorry, but did you get another job in the one day you quit?" He gave me a wicked grin and stood over me, making me feel small like a Hobbit.

"No, but are you really telling me that I can't have my old job back? After all, that was the reason I came here to meet with you in the first place. Okay, well we didn't even start that meeting, I will admit, but it still ended in my favour," I said, wondering how it would have really gone if I hadn't had that phone call.

"Well, you weren't thinking that when I was holding you against your will, as you put it." He was trying to distract me, and I was trying to squirm away to my bag, but he wasn't having any of it. He held my wrists like manacles and was keeping me still.

"Alright, so what would have happened if I hadn't had that phone call from my psycho stalker?" He squeezed my wrist tighter at the thought of the mad man who also wanted me.

"Simple, I wouldn't have needed to go outside to get you."

"What do you mean?" I shook my head at him in confusion.

"Keira, as soon as you turned up here, you sealed your fate. My intentions were never to let you leave. But as usual, you were stubborn and refused to co-operate, wanting to meet me on the balcony. Either way, it would have made little difference to me. I would have just taken you there," he said so matter of fact.

"Taken me… *you don't mean?*" As soon as I asked, I knew he hadn't meant it the way I thought he had, as now he was making me shake with the laughter that erupted from him. I took great offence to this and tried to pull away from him, but he wouldn't have it. So in return he pulled me up, still holding my wrists and raising them above my head, bringing my face closer to his.

"And where are you trying to get to, exactly?" he said looking down at me, not even trying to conceal the humour.

"I'm glad you find it so funny!"

"Keira, I find the idea a little amusing, yes, but consider why... what would you have done if, as soon as I saw you, I had ripped your clothes from that soft skin of yours and made love to you, especially after how our last meeting went... what would you have thought?" Okay, so he had a bit of a point, and I got past my bruised ego.

"Enjoyed it," I remarked on a smirk, as it was too hard being angry with him, especially when I got to see that heart-stopping smile. He finally released his hold but not to let me escape, only so he could bring me closer for an embrace. He wrapped his arms around me like steel bands and I had never felt so safe.

"Really, well maybe we will try that one another time, but for now, why do you want to go back to working for me?"

"I don't want to be treated differently because we are... umm... well, because I'm being favoured by the boss." Did that make sense?

"Favoured... is that what you call this?" He looked amused at my choice of words.

"Well, what do you want me to call it... are we... *dating?"* I said feeling the humour in the idea. I couldn't imagine Draven taking me to a restaurant and buying me chocolates.

"Well, considering taking your body last night wasn't a date and the second time I *really* took your body was after a heated argument, I think we can skip right past the dating thing and let's just say we're in love and together." With him putting it like that I had to agree. It was so much stronger than anything I had ever experienced, so I was like a fish out of water. However, I still wanted to jump up and down and start shouting about love to the world. Yes, I was *that* insanely happy.

"Well anyway, I am still going to work in twenty minutes, regardless!" I said being firm, but he looked back at me as if to say 'Oh, I don't think so!'

"That's going to be difficult when you're tied to my bed," he teased, and I fell for the bait.

"You wouldn't!" I said feeling a little excited by the idea.

"Well no, I wouldn't tonight... but I have to say the idea is appealing. However, the answer is still no." He let me go, and I pulled back so that I could see his face.

"No? Really... so let me get this straight, I am asking you for something and you are refusing me this?" Ha, I knew once I saw his face that I had him with this one.

"Keira, don't do that, you know I want to give you everything I can, but not that. I'm trying to keep you safe, so don't make it difficult!" he said turning his back on me, but I knew I was on the verge of winning.

"You have to be kidding, this place is a fortress and how can anything happen with you watching over me? Plus, I will be right downstairs and..."

"Downstairs, I thought we were talking about you having your old job back, why would you be downstairs?"

"Because that is my old job, remember? You kind of sacked me from the VIP," I said, laughing that we were even having this discussion.

"I did not sack you! I advised you to work downstairs, but nothing more... anyway, we are not having this conversation any longer." And this was Draven's way of dealing with things. He says how it is going to be and expects that is how it is going to be. Well, he was in for a shock dating a human then!

"You're right, because I need to get ready." I walked over to grab my bag and took it into the bathroom, leaving him in the room, probably stunned that I wasn't *obeying*. But really, when had I ever done as I was told by Draven? I couldn't help but smile as I closed the door behind me.

"And what do you think you're smiling at?" I turned, and he was leaning against the shower wall with his arms crossed. I nearly jumped out of my skin!

"Damn it! Stop doing that!" At this he just looked amused and raised one eyebrow at me.

"Fine, I will just get changed in front of you!" I said, pulling out my black trousers and a black top with a fresh pair of gloves to match. I waited for him to be a gentleman again, but he remained there and just extended out his arm.

"Be my guest..." he said being cocky again. So, I took a deep breath and pulled my top above my head, leaving on just a white bra. I was still looking at him and when his eyes widened, I felt as though I was the powerful one... had I just found his weakness? I was sure I also saw him swallow hard, and it was making it difficult to keep the smirk off my lips.

So, I went a step further. Instead of putting on another top straight away, I stayed topless while I removed the next item. I turned around for this bit and before removing my jeans I let my hair fall down my back. I then unzipped my jeans and pulled them down slowly, almost in a teasing way. I had on a pair of little white French knickers, which I'd chosen on purpose knowing they were one of my sexier pairs. I could hear him groan at the sight of me flicking my hair back after pulling my foot out of the last leg. This was enough to break him.

"Come here!" he commanded, but I just looked over my shoulder at him, trying to be seductive for the first time in my life.

"Are you going to change your mind?" I asked, trying not to show how intimidated I was at the sight of the Demon coming through, as his eyes were intense and hungry.

"I will do anything you want, if only you come to me *now!*" I jumped a little at the sound of the growl that came with the last word. But it worked, as I turned around and my hair fell forward, covering the top part of my very exposed body. Looking at him now was making the blood rush to my face, and this seemed to excite him even more. I walked slowly towards him and he watched my body move, like a bird of prey.

His hand touched my face first, then travelled down as he brushed my hair back with his fingertips, giving him a clear view of one side of my near-naked body. I couldn't help my heavy breathing as my chest moved up and down under the hand that was now making its way across the front of my neck and down to my breasts.

I closed my eyes after his black eyes flashed purple and scared me slightly. The feeling was so erotic, I wanted to fold my body into his and let him take me. Then he leaned down to my neck and kissed me so softly it could have been the wings of a butterfly. He moved his lips up to behind my ear, and then whispered,

"I will let you get ready for work now but remember that later I will get what I want in return... and Keira, *later*... we will be playing by *my rules.*" Then by the time I opened my eyes he was gone. The thought of what was to come made my body fill with liquid fire.

I got dressed and redid my hair ready for my first shift back, but I still couldn't stop thinking about what was in store for me once my time was over. I bit down on my lip just thinking about it.

When I went back into the room Draven wasn't there, but instead it was the servant called Candra, wearing what she wore last time only it was in black and red.

"Hello again, My Lord would like me to escort you back to the VIP area, so you can start your shift." I nodded but I really wanted to ask her why people were calling Draven 'My Lord'. Only I chickened out of that one.

"Umm okay, thanks." I followed her out of the same door that I had entered what seemed like a lifetime ago. We were in the same hallway I had been in with Sophia, but I only started to recognise it when I got closer to the huge doors at the end. I had seen this before, but now I was coming at it from the other direction. I noticed the door on the left as the one I had gone through on Sunday when I had confronted Draven. It looked as if it could be his office.

As soon as we approached, the double doors opened and filled my lungs with the familiar, comforting smell of Afterlife. I walked past all the obvious stares, as it was apparent that everyone knew about Draven and me. Hell, they probably knew before I did!

It was strange, knowing that they were all Angels and Demons, but it was like deep down I had known. After that dream I had, showing me their true forms, I'd had my suspicions, but cast them deep, banishing them to the back of my mind.

I found Sophia eagerly waiting for me by the bar, and I was sure I even saw her jump with joy at the sight of me. I walked over to her, knowing I couldn't hold anything against her for deceiving me. After all, she was his sister and that was her first priority… plus, in the end, it had all been for the best.

"Keira… you're not angry with me, are you?" she asked cautiously.

"No, I understand why," I said, and she practically threw herself at me. I braced a step back as her body hit mine and I hugged her back, feeling the same heat that I got from her brother.

"Good, well now that's all cleared up, why don't you finally join us?" she said holding onto my now gloved arm. Again, I was trying to get used to it but it was taking its time, so I couldn't help but flinch.

"Oh, sorry," she said looking down, feeling me tense. No doubt she already knew the story along with her other brother. This thought didn't exactly fill me with joy, so I tried to ignore the fact.

"Umm, maybe after work, I have to get downstairs and…" I said, but her face was telling me not a chance!

"Sorry honey, but Dom's well against the idea. However, you can work up here, you know… where he can keep an eye on you." She finished this off with a wink. Then a thought came to me.

"Jack's downstairs, isn't he?" At this she gave me a wicked grin.

"Yeah, pretty much." I rolled my eyes and gave her a little head shake. Sophia laughed, and then leant into me to whisper,

"But I will give you a heads up, so you're not too hard on him, He is not yet used to not getting his own way and is still trying to adjust to *your* ways… just count yourself lucky you're not locked away in a tower somewhere as he first wanted." At this, I choked on a swallow.

"You're kiddin' me... *right?!*" I asked on a loud whisper.

"Knowing my brother, do you doubt me?" she replied smiling, and I swallowed hard again, luckily not choking this time. I decided to shake off this conversation as Sophia just pulling my leg, or in this case more like messing with my head!

So, with me working up here, I hadn't won as I thought! Well, he was going to pay tonight, if he thought he was going to get all his own way now then he could think again! There was just one slight problem with this theory, when it came to Dominic Draven, I had zero self-control.

"I will see you later, Keira. It will be nice having another girl at the table... you can sit next to me," she added sweetly, making it even harder to picture her as a Demon.

"Okay, see you later," I said, secretly dreading it before going over to the bar where Karmun's happy face was waiting for me. A tower... *really?*

"Ah, she's back. How you doing, honey?" He was filling up a tray for me, but his eyes drifted over my head looking towards the top table, he nodded once.

"He's staring over here, isn't he?" I said, making Karmun's face drop.

"Ah... I wouldn't know," he said, looking away from me sheepishly.

"Yeah, right, sure you don't," I said with my hands on my hips, knowing that Draven's eyes were watching my every move. I, however, refused to look at him.

"Hey Keira, you've got some funky energy going on, you must be happy," Rue said as she came up behind me, taking her new tray from the bar.

"Thanks Rue, I am happy, how about you?" I asked, knowing that this was probably one of her gifts.

"Can't complain but washing your hands when you see through them isn't great, ha, ha!" She said doing jazz hands and laughing to herself as she walked back to her section. So, the tattoos of eyes on her hands weren't there just for effect, she saw through them?

How strange...

Karmun was smiling, as my face must have been a picture, which got me thinking, was he Angel or Demon? I would have to remember all these questions for Draven later. There were still so many things that I needed to ask.

I started to work, and everyone was friendly as usual, but my concentration wasn't fully on my job. I couldn't stop thinking about the last thing Draven had said to me, and it was making me quiver at the thought. Also, now thanks to Sophia, I had the image of Draven locking me in a tower and having his wicked way with me with no escape. This was definitely making the top five fantasy list!

As for what tonight would hold, I was both excited and scared, because even though I knew he would never harm me, there was still that element in him that terrified me, and shamefully… *I liked it.*

I still hadn't looked at him, but it was becoming harder. It was as though he kept trying to enter my mind and make me look but I kept denying him access, which was probably making him crazy with frustration. The night was flying past as quickly as it usually did in this place and I realised I only had an hour to go, but for Draven, it seemed that he had finally hit his limit.

I was standing at the bar waiting for my next tray of drinks, when hands came around and leant on either side of me, blocking me into the solid body behind. I had my back to him, and a whimpered whisper left my lips in surprise. He leaned into me, not caring about all the eyes that watched us. Karmun came over to me with my tray but one flick of Draven's hand sent him on his way.

"Time's up, little one," he said, blowing his scent down my face giving off its usual drugging effect. I inhaled and tried to keep my voice steady.

"Not yet," I whispered, going back to my usual shy self and pushing a stray bit of hair behind my ears.

"Remember what I said, Keira." His tone was even tenser than it had been in the bathroom. Only now, I was the one who was swallowing hard. One of his hands came at my side and he moved my top up to get to my skin. I had to brace myself on the bar in front of me. I couldn't believe he was doing this here! Didn't he care who saw us?

"Draven, not here!" I said, coughing first to get back my speech.

"My game and my rules, Keira," he said in his rough, smouldering voice, which again made me quiver. His touch went up even higher until it reached the bottom of my bra. This made me react by grabbing his strong hand and pushing it down.

"Does that mean you're mine yet?" he said, with the trademark bad-boy grin I could feel against my neck.

"Draven please... be reasonable," I said using his words against him.

"With you teasing me, I don't think that's going to be a possibility."

"I'm not teasing you." My skin went hot at the thought of who could be watching. How could he do this to me...? Was this my punishment for wanting to work?

"No Keira, this isn't your punishment... that comes later my love," he said, and I turned around to face him. Again, he took my breath away, as what he was now wearing made him look like a dark Gothic Armani model! He was wearing a black suit but he had a deep red shirt and tie to match. His hair was controlled back and well-groomed, but this made him even more irresistible.

"How did you do that?" I couldn't understand how, when he had said...

"You must be letting me in, heightened emotions work well enough for a distraction. And so it would seem that you have been thinking about our little bargain we made for most of the night now." This made the liquid fire come racing back to my already pounding heart. Once again, I saw the purple glint in his deadly black eyes, and I knew the Demon in him wanted me.

"Yes, he does... so, Keira..." He leant in closer, and whispered over my cheek, *"I wouldn't keep him waiting."* Damn it! He could still hear me, okay, focus... I needed to calm down before I regained control, but his smile told me he could still hear me. So, I mentally pushed harder and harder until bang! I knew it had worked as he frowned in frustration. I suddenly felt better knowing I was back in… well, sort of control.

"Anyway, we can't go yet as I sort of promised Sophia that I would join her for a drink."

"She will get over it," he said, now touching my neck, but I moved out from under his hand and put some distance between his body and mine, knowing that his touch was the hardest argument to resist.

"But it's rude!" I said, and he softened into the Angel part of Draven, giving me a smile as if what I had said meant more to him than I realised.

"Of course, I was forgetting your pure heart… well come on then, let me introduce you to my council."

"Umm… Council?" I said nervously, thinking maybe this wasn't such a good idea any more. But he had already put my arm through his and was leading me towards his table.

A table full of very powerful Angels and Demons…

Shit.

CHAPTER 47
DRAVEN'S COUNCIL

raven walked me up to the top table, and it felt as though I was being led into a pit with a load of deadly vipers. Why hadn't I just given in to Draven when he wanted me to go back with him? They must have been expecting me as there was now a spare chair waiting next to Draven's, ready for my body to fill it. It was one of those situations where you really wished you'd downed a bottle of wine, or vodka in my case, as one bottle of wine probably wouldn't have worked.

Ragnar for once, was not in my way as I stepped up to the level of the table. I still couldn't believe I was actually here doing this. It was like meeting the family for the first time, only in a weird horror film kind of way.

I stood a little back from Draven, trying desperately to hide behind him, but he wasn't having that. He pulled my arm around so that we were side by side and I was now in everyone's clear view. Then they all stood up at our presence and I wanted to die with shame!

Draven held out his arm and motioned for me to take the seat in between him and Sophia. I had never felt so out of place before in my life, and I wanted to just get up and run away from how bad I felt. Why had I agreed to this? I was surrounded by

569

handsome scary guys and the most stunningly beautiful girls. It was a bittersweet pill to swallow.

Sophia was, as always, breathtakingly beautiful in her red, bell-shaped dress with perfect lips to match. And then on the other side was Celina with her amazing red hair that twisted down to one side, making a cascade of curls that lay on her shoulder. She wore a black corseted dress that went up to one side, mirroring her hairstyle. The black satin material made her hair look more wild and alive, like she had a head full of fire snakes.

I looked like the thorn amongst the roses and I couldn't understand why, on an Earth full of such beauties as these, he would want someone as pale and plain as me? I couldn't swallow the self-conscious image I held of myself, even when someone as Godlike as Draven sat here next to me. I wanted to turn to him and just scream out why…? WHY ME?!

I knew the reason I had flown off the handle when Draven had described the feeding habits of Angel and Demons, because it would have made perfect sense in a world that was completely void of all normality. Finally, a reason I could comprehend, something I could grasp on to. One that made me understand what it was he was getting out of it.

"Lauren!" Draven had called over another beauty just to seal the lid on my pit of jealousy. He leaned into me, putting his hand on mine, bringing me out of my mental breakdown.

"Keira, what would you like to drink?" I turned to face him, knowing exactly what I needed.

"Tequila with salt and lime please," I said, and his face exhibited shock.

"Really?" he whispered, and I just nodded, but the rest of the table looked amused.

"Bring a bottle we will all have a drink," he ordered, and then he turned to me and kissed me on the top of my head making me stare at him in amazement, *why would he do that in front of everyone?*

"So Keira, now you know about us, are you very angry at me for burning down our school?" Sophia asked me very sweetly.

"What?!" I shouted in shock, and every eye stared at me, as this was the most noise I had made. I instantly regretted it but come on! She couldn't drop a bombshell like that on me and expect me not to react like a… well, *like a human!*

"Sorry to shout, but what? You did that…? Why?" I asked, and I could hear her giggling along with a few others.

"Sophia, I hadn't got around to that yet," Draven grumbled at her, and I shot him a look. Of course, he had known.

"It wasn't just my idea, Keira, and besides, we have paid so much into that place over the years it was about time we got some fun out of it," she said, sounding as if she had done this type of thing a few times before.

"You just love the pretty flames, don't you Zagan?" She nudged him in a teasing way, but he just shot her a look from under his hood and then playfully pinched her nose. I couldn't help but laugh at the sight.

"So, are you going to tell me why?" I asked, but she was like a child and she reached across me and poked her brother's arm.

"Nope, but he will now he's not boring anymore."

"Sophia, try to behave," he said trying to be stern but failing miserably. He then leaned into me again, and said, *"I will explain later."* And he gave me a smouldering look. What was it with this man and what he could do to me with just one look? Of course, this feeling amplified when he raised his hand to my neck to grip it gently. It sent a bolt of sexual sensations right down my spine and straight to my girly bits, making me tighten my thighs. It was such a mark of possession by the most powerful man in the room, there was only one reason for it…

It was clearly a warning.

Then Loz came with our drinks. She set down the shot glasses all bunched together near me, and then the bottle, which was topped with a pouring spout. So, when I stood up to pour the shots, everyone looked at me in shock. Draven's hand was on mine and I looked around, then couldn't help saying,

"What? Everyone wants one, don't they?" Draven laughed at me light-heartedly and the rest did the same. I lined the glasses all up in a row as I used to do on busy nights at the pub back home. I ran the Tequila over the top of them making sure that just a drop hit the rims of the glasses. I then sprinkled the salt back and forth over where the liquid had hit making the salt stick.

Then I held the bottle more firmly in one hand and filled each one to the same amount near to the top. I moved it back and forth until each one was ready for consumption. I then placed a piece of lime on each glass, resting across the top, and I was finished. When I finally looked up, everyone stared at me as though *I* was the supernatural being!

Draven was also surprised but his eyes held something more for me... *lust.* Everyone passed them around, and then we all held them up before knocking them back. I then casually sucked on the lime and Draven leaned into me, moving the stray hairs that had rested on my neck to whisper in my ear,

"What you just did... well, I would like to request a private show later but be warned, Keira, I have other ideas for that lime," he said, and I think I nearly swallowed it whole at the thought. I couldn't believe he was flirting with me... here, now!

I turned back round to find my glass refilled, and I shot it back again with ease.

"Yuck, I don't know how you do that, it's foul!" Sophia complained, calling Lauren back over for another drink.

"Well, Dom, the girl can drink, that much is clear," Vincent said smiling, clearly amused, and Draven punched him on the arm in agreement. I was a little amazed watching Draven and Vincent have such a normal brotherly moment. But I also couldn't believe how at ease I was now starting to feel. Then a corona was put down in front of me thanks to Sophia, as she nodded towards it.

"Thanks," I said to Loz, and she smiled at me.

Zagan was about to grab my shot glass and refill it when Draven's hand took it before he could.

"She's had enough," he said firmly, but I wasn't happy about this. He didn't know my limit and it was a hell of a lot more than two shots! I turned to him and frowned, which was enough for him to change his mind. He threw it to him, and I didn't even see

Zagan's hand catch it, he was so fast, but I had it back in front of me, refilled, by the time I looked back down.

Once again, I shot it back, but now I was being cocky myself as I dropped the glass, doing a trick I had learnt years ago from one of the regulars back home. I dropped it behind my hand, making it disappear, and transferred it to my other hand so quick, the glass was upturned on the table in seconds. Of course, to a table full of Angels and Demons this probably seemed really lame. But I didn't care.

"Where did you learn to do that?" Draven asked me in wonder, but instead of giving a shy response I just winked back at him.

"I'm guessing this isn't the first club she has worked in," a new voice spoke acidly. There was one seat that had been empty up until now. I had seen her before but never up close, and oh how I wished it would have stayed at a distance.

She was the most stunning creature I had ever seen, but the most striking difference to her and the rest was that she was also blonde, making my shabby hair look more like straw than her lush locks of spun gold.

"Keira, this is Aurora," Draven said in an icy tone as she sat down. Now *she* looked like a bloody Goddess!

"Hi," was all I could say, as I quickly went back to my sombre self. I gulped back my corona as I went quiet again.

"So, Keira, it's my party tomorrow night and you will join us here, won't you?" I found it hard to hear what Sophia had said when I couldn't take my eyes off Aurora's perfection. Her low-cut dress concealed just the right amount, but also showed enough that said 'look, here's what you could have!' It was an emerald green colour, one that I could never have got away with. It hugged her every curve like it had been designed with her body in mind. Hell, for all I knew it had been!

"Yes, we will be here, Sophia," Draven spoke for me as he must have known what I was thinking, after all, this was very emotional, and couldn't he read me when my guard was down? Well, that was most definitely the case now. Aurora had, in fact, ripped my guard to shreds. I felt his arm on mine, but I couldn't look at him. I just wanted to curl up into a ball and stop feeling so damn jealous. It was ridiculous.

"Good, but Keira, you will have to borrow one of my dresses," she said, clapping her hands together at the thought.

"Dress... uh... I don't really do dresses," I said, keeping my voice down. But I could have sworn I heard Aurora laugh at this.

"Sure you do, I remember Halloween, and I'm sure my brother definitely remembers it." She winked at me and I blushed at the memory.

"What's the occasion?" I asked, being polite, and I also wanted the excuse not to look at Draven.

"It's mine and Vincent's birthday!" she said smiling at her brothers who both rolled their eyes at the thought.

"Really...? Oh," I said confused, wondering how that worked. Weren't they triplets?

"It's not our birthday, it's more like our bodies' birthday," Vincent corrected her. I looked at him but couldn't stop my eyes following around the table opposite me, where they found Aurora staring so intensely at Draven, it made my blood boil. Then Draven stood abruptly and lifted me by the arm, raising me too.

"Keira and I are retiring for the night," he said sternly and started to move me away, when Sophia giggled, and said,

"Yeah, I bet you are!" Draven tapped her on the head as he moved past her. But it was long enough for me to see the burning desire in Aurora's eyes at one Dominic Draven.

He walked me calmly to the back of the VIP, which was the entrance to their fortress-like home. He had hold of my arm, and wouldn't loosen his grip until we were through the doors and they were firmly closed behind us. I had a bad feeling about this, as he didn't look too happy. I followed him in silence to his bedchamber but stopped before the doors. I wasn't going to go in there with him like this.

"What's wrong?" I asked him, and he finally turned around to look down at me.

"Inside," was all he said, barking out his order. I didn't

accept this, so I didn't move, even when he opened the door and gave me a 'do as your told' glare.

"Keira!" He shouted my name, making me jump, so I gave in seeing as he wasn't going to budge. I walked through the doors and went over to the desk to lean on it, as I didn't want to sit before I knew what this was about.

"What did I do this time?" I said folding my arms, but he turned to me with arrogance in his manner, which in his suit, he reminded me of Mr Darcy.

"You were brilliant out there, but it was just a pity you tarnished it by not believing in yourself." He looked over to me before helping himself to a bottle of something that had been placed where the bowl of fruit had been. He poured out one green glass for himself and then poured me a glass of water. He downed his in one, and then poured himself another before turning back to me. He held out the water for me to take but I was feeling rebellious.

"I don't know what you're talking about," I said, taking the shot of green liquid out of his hand instead of the water. I knocked it straight back, keeping my eyes to his. He raised one eyebrow at me, waiting for my reaction to the horrific burn I could feel like acid travelling down my throat. I tried so hard not to react and give him the satisfaction of seeing my regret for doing something so stupid. This stuff was foul and tasted like its only purpose in life was to strip paint or clean toilets!

My eyes started to water and my need to cough was getting too much. He held out the glass of water that I really wanted to take but my stubbornness wouldn't allow it, so I just shook my head, knowing I couldn't speak at the moment without sounding like a croaky old man. A small smirk appeared on his lips before he turned his back to me and refilled his drink. I took this moment to scream silently, mouthing the word *'Fuck'* before I saw him swig back his own shot, after muttering,

"Stubborn girl." I looked for a slight reaction to the liquid fire going down his throat, but the cocky ass showed none.

"I'm not stubborn!" I said stubbornly, knowing it was true.

"Really... and I suppose you're going to tell me next that you are not over-sensitive either!" he snapped back at me.

"What do you want from me, Draven?!" I said knowing he was right. I was over-sensitive, but I couldn't help it, his perfection made my insecurities double.

"DAMN IT! Keira, I want YOU!" he shouted at me as he still hadn't calmed down. He threw his glass to the floor, and I jumped at both the sound of breaking glass and his arms that were now round my waist lifting me up to his face. He kissed me, merging his lips to mine, proving this was all he wanted to do and had wanted all night. I had once again been such a fool, no wonder he had been angry at me.

His hands spanned up my back and were about to start undressing me, when they stopped abruptly and put me down.

"What's wrong?" I asked, panting after such a kiss. He moved away from me, which was a first for him. He didn't answer me, he just removed his jacket, throwing it to one side. He sat down on a luxurious sofa, one that was covered by a thick, black velvet material, making his dark red shirt look all that more striking. He casually undid his top button and loosened his tie with one hand, while his other arm rested along the back of the chair. My heart, on the other hand, felt like it was going to give up on me. Holy shit, it was one of the sexiest things I had ever seen!

I hadn't moved from the desk that I was using to keep me steady, probably looking more confident than the bag of nerves I was! His eyes held the same look he had for me in the bathroom, and I gulped. He wanted another drink, so he held out his hand to the deadly looking shards that were scattered along the floor. Then as if by using magic, they all shot back in his hand, reforming the shape of the original glass. When it was completely fused together, he poured himself another drink, and I wondered if it ever affected him like alcohol did with humans.

"Come here!" he ordered, and when I didn't move towards him quick enough, he moved the desk behind me, pushing me closer to where he sat. I let out a little scream, so I moved from it, and as soon as I did, it shot back into place. I looked back at him and he extended one finger, motioning for me to come closer.

I stepped forward a few steps but stopped when he held up his hand for me to do so. With his hand still there, I heard the clip in my hair unclasp and it flew to his hand as if returning to its master. He placed it down on the table next to him and then looked back at me wide-eyed, as my hair was now the way he wanted it. He nodded for me to continue. I did, but very slowly, being both scared and excited at the same time. However, it swung more one way than the other when he gave me another command.

"Take off your clothes," he said, and my heart stopped for a short time.

"Ss...sorry?" I stuttered, not knowing if I had heard him right.

"Strip, Keira," he said in a more demanding tone which just kept getting deeper.

"Why?" I asked, being a coward again.

"Because, it's my game and my rules, remember?" Oh god! This was what he had in mind, at least in the bathroom I had found that the low lighting helped! As soon as the thought entered my mind, the room was plunged into darkness and then the soft glow of candlelight ignited the room.

"Is this better?" Well, yes it was, but it still didn't control my shaking hands that didn't want to move from behind my back.

"Come, come, Keira, you can't be shy... not after the show you put on in there." He nodded towards the bathroom and gave me a sexy, sinful grin. I was suddenly wishing I'd had more Tequila! Draven cleared his throat, showing me that he was waiting, and I knew there was only one way to go, so I slipped off my shoes to indicate I was ready. Well, as ready as I would ever be.

I gripped the bottom of my black top, crossing over my arms getting ready to pull it over my head but then I stopped, thinking I could regain back some control. Well, if he wanted a damn show then he would bloody well get one! So, I lifted it, showing my stomach, and very slowly pulled it up and over my head as I twisted my body slightly. Once again, my hair rained down in waves, half covering my bra and my back.

I did his usual trick of throwing it to the floor. My eyes burned back into his, only I doubted mine matched the Demon coming through. I knew what came next, and as my black trousers were tighter than my jeans, I knew I could play this to my advantage. I wasn't going to turn around like I had done in the bathroom. I wanted to tease him, but he had other ideas about who was in charge.

He held up one finger and made small circles with it, taking back control. I obviously didn't do this quick enough for him because he added his smouldering voice to the action.

"Turn around," he ordered sharply, and I shuddered at his dominating manner which seemed to vibrate around the room. The power in this man was startling. So, I complied and turned around so he could see my back as I had done earlier, only this time, I pulled all my hair around so he had clear view of my skin and what was to come.

I undid my trousers and gripped them from behind, pulling them down slowly, flattening my palms over my own cheeks, making him release a low growl. I turned back around once I had removed all my clothes, just leaving me in my underwear.

"A bene placito," ('one who has been pleased well,' in Latin) he said with his voice thick with desire. Again, I didn't know what it meant but I hoped it was something good, so I bravely asked,

"Are you pleased... *Master?"*

"Come here now, Keira," he said, nodding to his lap and I obeyed gladly, walking over to him and placing one knee either side of his waist, then sitting down feeling his pleasure for myself.

"It is you that is the master, and I but your willing slave... and yes, I am indeed, very pleased," he said, before devouring me with a mind-blowing kiss. His hands ran up my spine, making me arch backwards as his lips found my neck. When I opened my eyes, he was naked and so was I, as now my underwear was nowhere to be seen. I still didn't understand how he did that!

He lifted me up and positioned me over his erection before driving me down, taking the length of him deep inside. He did this with such force, my body nearly crumbled with the first thrust of him inside me. I couldn't help but throw my head back and let out a lustful moan. His hand grabbed a fistful of my hair and used it to control my head, making it move to where he wanted it to go. He pulled it to the side so he could bite my neck like a starving beast. I could feel the exquisite pressure build inside me but then he held himself still as if fighting something.

"Draven... ohhh please," I moaned, pushing him over the edge where I wanted him to fall. His fangs lengthened against me and then suddenly plunged into my flesh. I cried out in pain that quickly morphed into immense pleasure. He then sucked hard, taking not only my body, but now my very essence. With each pull his lips created, I could feel it draw out my orgasm to a fever pitch. Thankfully, this time he let me have it, and I screamed when he hit that delicious spot inside me, causing my body to explode in such a beautiful way. I rippled around his length, clutching tighter to him, making sure he continued to find pleasure being inside my core.

"Gods, Keira! Fucking delicious!" he said, swearing for the first time in front of me, but Holy Hell that just made me want to come again! He licked where he had bitten as I could feel a trickle of blood come down my neck, but it didn't hurt. His tongue had sealed the puncture marks he made, healing my skin instantly.

It had felt so amazing that I wanted him to do it over and over, but he released my hair and lifted me up, and I wrapped my legs around his waist making him groan again. Before I knew it, I was sat on his desk with him still locked firmly inside me, where he took control over all of my body as well as his.

He gripped me tightly, fingers embedded at my hips, pulling me closer into him. The build-up started to form as quickly as if he had said 'now', but this time I knew he wouldn't give it to me until he was ready. He was powering into me, and all I could do was hold on and enjoy the wild ride.

He gripped me by the shoulders, and I let out the moans of rapture with every deep thrust he made inside me. It felt as though I would die from it all, and Draven was most definitely my executioner as he pounded into my body, pushing me through all my limits. I thought I would have called out 'no more' but it seemed my mind had other ideas, when it would only shout out,

"More!" I had to grip onto him until my muscles ached from fear of falling into an abyss. He was my anchor in the raging storm that was my building orgasm. I lost all sense of time as my exhausted body quivered under his hands that touched me everywhere. My head fell back as I let out little screams of pure overwhelming stimulation. This was the most intense my body had ever felt, and it couldn't cope for much longer, so I sat up to be closer to his body. I buried my head in his neck to tell him what I needed.

"Please... I can't take any more... give me what I want," I said in a whisper, and his hands gripped around my body tighter, getting ready to keep me restrained for what came next.

"Your wish is my command," he said, before making me erupt in what was the most mind-blowing experience I had known. I now knew that up until now he had been tame with me. This was much more than I could take. I cried out, screaming over and over again, and in a feeble attempt to control it, I pressed my face into his hard chest, trying to contain my body's reactions. It wanted to do things he wouldn't allow. It wanted to convulse at the throbbing pleasure, but his arms locked me in a prison of muscle.

So when I bit down hard, I found it was his flesh I wouldn't let go of. This must-have caused a reaction within him as in the midst of my wonderful delirium, I heard Draven roar out his release. I felt him pulsate inside me, causing mini shock waves along my channel. My fingers found the skin on his back and dug in deep, scratching him under the strain. My body felt broken, like it had shattered under the pressure of too much ecstasy.

"Ssshh... just breathe, calm my Keira," he whispered in my ear as the frenzy was slowing down and euphoria was taking over, covering me in a cloud of confusion. I was trying to convert my panting into slower, deeper breaths but my body vibrated under his hands as I trembled.

"Are you alright?" he asked in concern. I couldn't help but let out a short laugh. Was I alright...? I had just had the most incredible experience and it seemed that it just kept getting better every time. And he was asking me if I was alright! Where were his mind-reading powers now?

I swallowed hard and smiled at him.

"I am more than alright. I felt like I was flying and now I'm floating in a mist of euphoria... so yes, I am fine," I said laughing again. He kissed my now salty lips before picking me up into his arms and placing me on the bed. He moved away from me but before I could complain, he was back again with a large goblet of water.

"Drink, your body is dehydrated," he said smiling at me, looking as satisfied as I felt. Then he produced a cloth and moved to go in between my legs.

"What are you...?"

"I am taking care of you, as I did the first time when you slept," he said, like this was a normal thing for a man to do. I inwardly cringed knowing he had cleaned me up after I had passed out the first time, but on the other hand it was a sweet gesture. That still didn't stop me from slamming my legs shut.

"Keira!" He said my name in warning and then took matters into his own hands, hands that started to pry my legs open. I shut my eyes and tried to let go of the shame as he gently wiped me clean and discarded the cloth.

"My sweet, shy, Keira, thank you for allowing me to tend to you," he whispered in my ear, making me bite my lip. I nodded, trying not to acknowledge what he had just done and move on before my cheeks exploded like lava bombs.

There was, however, one question that was burning inside me to get out.

"What we did… was it… the same for you?" I asked, wondering if my cheeks were now glowing. He grinned, showing his perfect white teeth.

"I can imagine it's much better," he said, but I frowned thinking there was no way that could be true.

"I doubt that very much," I said thinking, how could it be? What did I do for him… because I am pretty sure he did most of the work!

"Keira, why do you think I bit you? I am sorry about that, by the way," he said looking guiltily at my neck, where his thumb gently stroked.

"Don't be, I liked it! Well, more than liked, actually." He looked back up at me, raising his eyebrows in surprise.

"It makes me understand why my kind breaks the rules," he said, and I shook my head in confusion.

"What do you mean?"

"It is utterly forbidden for Angels and Demons to be with humans like that," he said as if I would have known this.

"Then, why are you with me? Why did you just…?" I stammered. But he just let one side of his lips turn upwards, giving him a smug grin.

"Because it is different with you and like I said before, you were sent to me… *born for me.* I can't go into why as of yet, but you will understand in time. All you need to know is that it is allowed… well, more like expected." And he added a low rough laugh to this last part.

"Wait a minute, so let me get this straight… I was your first… *human?"* I asked, getting giddy at the idea.

"Yes, of course," he said, as if this was common knowledge.

"So, you were like a… *human virgin?"* I asked, not helping the giggle that came out at the thought. He rolled his eyes at me and then shook his head frowning.

"If that's what you want to call it… yes, but you were the same, may I remind you."

"I wasn't a virgin," I said before I had chance to think about it.

"Why, have you slept with many Angel/Demon half breeds lately?" he asked sarcastically.

"Oh well, if you put it like that, then no, just you... but humans..."

"YES, yes I don't want to know about that!" he said, cutting me off with all the humour gone. I think I could take a wild stab in the dark and say that Draven was a wee bit possessive.

"Sorry, but I guess I'm not the only one, I mean, you must have had your fill of... well you know," I said not liking this conversation any more.

"Yes, and would you like to hear about them?" he snapped, again with the sarcasm.

"NO!" I shouted, and he shot me a look as if to say, 'well then!'

"Okay, I get your point... but just to clarify, humans... well, no comparison," I said, giving him my own version of a cheeky grin that made his fierce gaze melt.

"Well, for your information... being with my kind can in no way compare even in the slightest, with what your body does to me... your soul is like nothing I have ever felt before... even the taste of your blood..." He groaned and his hands tensed on my shoulder.

"Forgive me, I shouldn't say that. But one thing's for sure, it looks like I was wrong about knowing my limits... I will have to control myself next time," he said as his thumb circled where he had bitten me again.

"Please don't, I enjoyed it. But I still don't understand why being with humans is better?"

"Not humans, Keira, just you. It is hard to explain as there are so many things you still don't know. But the most important thing is for you to understand, is my feelings for you. That was not pleasant for me to hear you think those things in there." He nodded over his shoulder to the door, and his voice had gone back to being stern with me.

"I'm sorry, but I never asked you to listen in and I can't help feeling jealous," I said frowning and getting defensive.

"Keira, why on earth would you be jealous?" Was he joking?

"You were at the same table, right…? I mean, you did see all the gorgeous women sat around you?"

"There was only one gorgeous creature that I couldn't take my eyes off and she is now lying in my bed naked, where she belongs!" he said as he playfully flicked my nose, at which I continued to frown.

"Come now, Keira, you have nothing to be insecure about," he said before getting up, and the sight of his naked behind made my stomach flutter. The candle flames flickered making his skin look warm and inviting, so much, in fact, that I had to bite my lip to contain the urge to go running after him. I rolled over and buried my head in the cool silk sheets, thinking what had I done in my life to deserve such perfection to want me the way he said he did? It was only then that I realised how exhausted I felt, but I just didn't want the day to end.

"You need rest," Draven said, pulling the covers from my face.

"I'm not tired." But the huge yawn that followed told him I was lying, and he laughed saying,

"Really, could have fooled me."

"Why are you dressed?" I asked, as he was now in his full suit once more.

"Because I have some business to attend to, but don't worry, I won't be leaving you alone for too long." He bent down and lifted my face up to his warm lips, filling me with his intoxicating scent that made me feel even more worn out. It felt as though he was trying to invade my senses, forcing my mind to let go and give in to the sleep I desperately needed.

So as a result, I was asleep as soon as his lips left mine, with the last words I heard him whisper over my skin…

"Mine now."

CHAPTER 48

NOT ALONE

I woke up in an empty bed, and the only light was from the moon outside casting an eerie bluish glow to the room. It reminded me of the night I had been stabbed, and I had to think for a moment if it hadn't all been a dream. But considering I was still naked from my last encounter with Draven, I knew it had all happened... thankfully. I was miffed to find I was still alone, though maybe his business was taking longer than he originally thought.

I decided to get up and use the bathroom, knowing I would never get back to sleep now, not until I was in Draven's warm, solid arms. I shuddered at the cold floor beneath my feet as I grabbed the kimono that was draped across the bottom of the bed. I wondered if Draven had been in to check on me and left it there, knowing I might want to get up. It made sense as he seemed to know every move I made or would make.

I slipped the cold material over my skin, wishing I had my warm pyjamas, even though I wouldn't want Draven seeing me in old sweatpants and a holey vest top. Once inside the bathroom, I fumbled around for a light switch at the wall but there was none. It was far too dark in here to see, so I left the door open letting in what little light there was. It felt strange in here, like the air was thicker, making it harder to breath, and my heart started to beat faster from fear. I didn't like the feeling that came over me. It was the feeling that I wasn't alone…

I decided that I wasn't that desperate to use the bathroom after all, so I turned around to leave but the door slammed shut, sealing me in. I went to grab for the handle but when I pulled my hand away it was now wet. I rubbed the dripping substance between my fingertips and it felt thick and gooey. It looked black from what little light that was coming in from the window behind the huge bath. I looked back at the door and it was now completely covered in the weird black tar that fell down in clumps, slapping on the tiled floor.

What was going on?

"Draven!" I called out, but then my heart stopped as I heard a low laugh behind me. It was a laugh I had heard before, only this one didn't belong to anyone I loved.

No… This belonged to someone that I *feared*.

I whipped my head round to face him, but the bathroom still held the one occupant, and that was me.

"Wh…who's there?" I asked the darkness, with my voice trembling so much it sounded as if I was being shaken. I stepped further into the room as the black tar was coming along the floor nearer to my feet. As I walked past the gilded mirror behind the sink, I noticed two glowing dots that were getting brighter in its reflection. They stood about Draven's height and were getting closer as I in turn, edged closer to the sink. I took a deep breath and turned quickly to face it head-on. I soon realised that the two glowing dots belonged to a body and were in fact eyes staring back at me. I could just see the shadow of a man at first, but when the moon came from behind the clouds, I realised it wasn't the shadow of a man… it was the shadow of a Demon!

The sight was so frightening I gagged, my mouth tasting the acid of sick my stomach produced. It was horrifying, with skin that cracked and bubbled, bleeding the same black tar. Its lips had been sewn up crudely with some thick wire that looked as if it had been snipped open with bolt cutters. The glow from its eyes turned fiery red at the sight of my fear. Its face was long and misshapen as though it had been squeezed in a vice making its eyes bleed, only this time it was blood and it trickled down to its mouth.

"So, you must be Catherine, the rose that I have heard so much about from my young friend over there. I believe you two are acquainted," he said, spitting out the blood that flowed freely to the floor below him. I turned to where one long, deadly, black rotting nail attached to a deadlier looking hand pointed towards the window. There, Morgan was leaning against one of the marble pillars, casually holding a large blade in his hand that he used to wave at me. I let out a blood-curdling scream and I saw the flash of a jaw full of teeth as he smiled.

"I told him he wouldn't need to bring that thing, but he knew your passion for sharp objects and insisted." I turned back round to face him and now Morgan wasn't the only one smiling. His mouth was hideous just like the rest of him. Each row only held six teeth, but they were more like fangs, all separated, coming down from his bleeding gums. His cloak curled around his body as if it too was alive, until I realised it wasn't a cloak at all, those were his wings!

"GET AWAY FROM ME!" I screamed at him when he took another step closer, making my back lean against the sink that I was very nearly sat in.

"Come, come, my dear... your Dark Prince can't save you now. I have taken care of that!" he said, making the blood from his mouth hit me in the side of my face. I wiped it away using my sleeve, but as soon as it touched the fabric it turned into little black and red spiders that went running up and down my arm. I tried to shake them off, but they took cover, scurrying under my sleeve and biting into my flesh to hold on. I couldn't contain the screams, as they seemed to multiply, making my skin burn and itch.

I decided to make a run for it, but the black ooze was everywhere on the floor, making my feet stick as it worked its way up my toes, gripping on like black cement. I tried one last time, only to find myself screaming at the ink-black arms that had now burst through the mirror behind me. They grabbed me by the shoulders roughly, trying to restrain me for their master who was still coming closer. He extended one flaky hand out to me and his mouth opened, as if readying himself to sink row after row of bleeding fangs into my skin.

"NO, NO, NO, GET AWAY!" I screamed and screamed, feeling my face wet from sweat and tears. Then the arms from the mirror started to shake me, becoming more forceful.

"KEIRA!" My name was being shouted by the voice I had desperately wanted to hear.

"KEIRA, WAKE UP!" Draven's arms were those from the mirror and the sight of the bathroom had now been replaced by the view of the glass doors held at the end of Draven's bed. I was sat up and his arms circled around my shoulders, rocking me slightly to make sure I was definitely awake.

"Keira, it was just a bad dream... Ssshh, try to breathe," he said this last part as I was sobbing like a frightened child into his chest. He stroked his hand down my hair, letting me soak his skin with my salty tears that I couldn't control.

"It's all right now my love, you're safe... I've got you," he said in a soft and soothing tone. He positioned my body so that he was cradling me in his arms and he let me weep until I regained my voice.

"I...I woke up but...but you weren't here," I said, but I didn't sound right, my speech was strained and scratchy as my throat burned from screaming.

"It was all just a dream, Keira. I came back from leaving you after only ten minutes, but you were sound asleep. You didn't even stir when I slid in next to you," he said gently.

"So you didn't leave... you didn't... leave me?" I said through broken sobs that caught in a hiccup.

"Ssshh, I am here now, and I won't let you go, you're safe, my little one." The use of my pet name worked its magic and I relaxed more into his hold.

"That must have been a bad one. I tried to get through, but I was being blocked by something very powerful. Do you think you're alright to tell me about it?" he said looking down at me, trying to see my face that still found comfort in his chest. I finally calmed enough to look at him and he wiped my wet cheeks with his thumbs.

"I have to get up… I have to draw it before he comes back!" I said looking around for something to change into.

"So, once you have drawn what you see, you lock it out?"

"Yeah, but don't ask me how it works because I have never understood it." I grabbed all my hair around into a twist and knotted it at the back, knowing it wouldn't stay like that for long.

"Umm…" I was about to ask for something to wear when he pointed to the kimono at the end of the bed, but just the sight of it brought back the nightmare. He noticed my shuddered hesitation and must have realised.

"Perhaps something more comforting?" he said before pointing to my pyjamas from home; my sweatpants and holey vest.

"How did you know?" I asked in amazement, but he just reached for them and slipped the vest over my head and passed me the pants. I swung my legs out and pulled them on thinking how I must look in them. Then the lights illuminated getting brighter, and my shame doubled as I thought I had at least the dark to hide in.

"Why did you do that?" I asked pulling down my vest like it would in some way help.

"Well, can you draw in the dark?" he asked, and it was the first time I had seen him pulling on a pair of jeans. It was strange seeing him do something so normal and regular. But I was glad when he didn't add anything else to it, as I loved to look at his naked torso even if now wasn't the time for my erotic fantasies to enter my head. But damn, he looked good.

"Okay, good point… do you have anything I could use to umm, you know…?" I waved my hand in the air like I was painting. He nodded towards the desk and there were supplies of different kinds spread out for me to take my pick. Draven walked over to the chair and pulled it out for me to sit. I smiled at his gentleman-like manners and I took my seat, which he then pushed in for me. I couldn't help but pick up the long feather quill and hold it up to him.

"Anything after the 1800's?" I teased, and he rolled his eyes at me, but he couldn't keep his smile hidden for long.

"What? So I will admit, I am a bit old fashioned, but you try and use something since the 6th century and then switch to a basic pen," he said as he took the quill from me and spun it round in his hand quickly, morphing the feather into wood and then handing a pencil back in return.

I ignored the 6th-century comment before my mind started to do cartwheels thinking about his age. I decided he must be joking of course and started to sketch the monster from my dreams. I then told Draven the story. It seemed to affect him, as I could see he was trying very hard to control his temper. It was most definitely the most terrifying nightmare I had experienced so far, but when Draven saw the finished picture it seemed it hadn't been a dream after all.

"Sammael!" He ground out the name under great strain from keeping his voice from growling. I noticed his jawline twitch under the grinding of his teeth and his hands were fisted by his sides. He looked as though he wanted to burst into flames, and that night on the roof came slamming back to the forefront of my ever fragile mind.

"Sammael?" I asked standing up to face him.

"He is an Angel of Death! His name means 'Venom of God'." He said all this through gritted teeth and had to crick his neck to one side before continuing, giving him the look of a gladiator getting ready for the deadly arena.

"He joined forces some centuries ago with a Demon named Belphegor," he said as he walked over to the intercom at the door.

"Have my brother sent here immediately!" he ordered to a timid voice on the other end. I didn't fully understand what was going on, but I was too scared to ask, as Draven looked almost savage at this new information. I had a head full of questions, but the only one I needed the answer to was if this Demon was coming for me.

Vincent was striding through the door within only minutes of his brother's request. He was dressed casually as though he had just been woken up, which was likely as the clock in the corner told me it was four in the morning.

He wore black trousers and an open shirt that revealed a washboard stomach like his brother's. He wasn't as large as Draven, more of a slim, athletic build, but still powerful with rippling muscles that tensed when Draven spoke the name of my terrorising Demon.

"I believe he is going to try and get to me through Keira and he's using this Morgan to do his will."

"You think he will try and seek revenge for our part in Belphegor's plan?" Vincent asked, not looking as worried as his brother.

"Oh, of that I have no doubt! He was the one, after all, to help the human escape." Draven was pacing back and forth, but his brother put one hand on his shoulder to stop him.

"Dom, calm yourself, he cannot get to her. She is safe as long as she remains here." He walked over to the desk where he found me leaning against it listening to this conversation, one I didn't fully understand.

"Keira, you do not need to be frightened we will keep you safe, but is there anything else you remember?" he asked in a calmer voice than his brother and like this, it was easy to see the Angel in him.

"Like what?"

"Did he do anything to you?" As soon as he said this Draven let out a heart-stopping growl that put more fear into me than the dream had.

"Dom, please... you will scare her!" he said looking over his shoulder at him with a scowl.

"Keira, you need to tell us, did he hurt you in the dream or touch you in any way?" His eyes were soft and trusting, but I didn't know where these questions were leading to?

"Well..." I said looking over at Draven whose eyes were burning full of hate and Hellfire!

"Go on, Keira, and don't worry about him... he will behave," he said smiling at me, filling me with ease. Draven looked ready to explode with a venomous rage, but Vincent purposely moved to block him out of sight.

"He spat blood from his mouth at me and when I tried to rub it off, it released loads of little spiders that started biting me," I said in a low voice, as this part I had left out to save Draven any more pain than was necessary. I heard a sharp intake of breath behind Vincent.

"Where did they bite you?" I was already holding my exposed scars behind my back, as I was used to Draven seeing them but not his brother.

"On my arm," I said shamefully.

"Let me do it!" Draven shouted at Vincent, but he turned to face him, placing his hands on his chest and stopping him from coming any closer to me. I couldn't help but flinch back at the sound. Draven's voice had taken on a rougher, deeper edge as though it was coming from another part of him. It made me wonder... was this his Demon voice? It could definitely be classed as Demonic.

"Dom... Dominic! Listen to me... you will not see straight and will only frighten the poor girl! She has been through enough to experience your temper as well! GO! Go and calm down, brother, I won't be long with her." At this, Draven's eyes softened slightly when they met mine. The purple haze lifted slightly as he leaned down to kiss my forehead, before walking over to the glass doors and exiting on to the balcony.

"Forgive him, but he is finding this difficult. He doesn't like things to be out of his control. He is not used to the feeling." Vincent actually shrugged at this, which made him look so human it was hard to see him in any other light.

"What happened, I mean why is he coming for me?" I asked, trying to find any answer that I could comprehend.

"We played a part in his undoing long ago and well... it looks like the years have not been of the forgiving kind. You must understand when something of this world tips the balance one way more than the other we have no choice but to intervene. And let's just say that Sammael tipped the scales in a big way."

"So now he's using me to get to Draven?" He looked amused

at me still calling his brother by his last name, but he remained quiet on the subject and just nodded his head.

"What do you need me to do?"

"I would like you to trust me... do you think you can do that?" He held out an outstretched palm and I knew exactly what he wanted me to put there. I closed my eyes and tried to remember how to breathe. How could I do this?

"I won't hurt you and I understand your reluctance, but it is the only way for me to see the dream for myself." So, I bit down on my lip and found the deep breath I needed, knowing there was no other way around it. I placed the arm that had been bitten in my dream in his hand, scars facing upwards. His eyes looked down at the lines of my past and with his other hand he held it over them but stopped, meeting my eyes with his.

"I must warn you that I might see more than is needed. Your scars are deep, as are your memories from how they came to be. So it might take me back further than I need to see and for this, I am truly sorry." And before I could back away from the thought of him seeing more than he should, his hand clamped down on my skin making the connection.

"Beautiful soul," Vincent whispered in awe before the sensations began. It felt like my arm was being held under an icy river making it go numb. His grip refused to let go as I tried to pull away, but he wasn't going to do that until he had seen all he needed to see. I watched his eyes flicker as though he was in a trance and his mouth moved speaking unspoken words so fast, I couldn't make out what they meant. It was only a faint whisper, but I was sure I saw my first name escape his lips.

Then the visions started to hit me like a flicker book of uncensored pain. I saw years of fear from my childhood in nanoseconds. Me hiding under the bed armed with nothing more than a Care Bear flashlight saying, 'It's not real' over and over. I saw myself hiding in the supply cupboard in high school shaking back and forth. I saw myself hiding under the staircase in a dark basement biting trembling lips, praying not to be heard crying to the calling of my name.

Always hiding... years and years and a lifetime of hiding!

STEPHANIE HUDSON

Then the last vision. The tragedy in this Gothic play. Only there was a difference… this time *I had nowhere to hide.*

The Angel in front of me saw all that was needed, and his eyes closed. The feeling started to flow back through my veins with the rushing of blood warming my skin back to its usual temperature. He still held my arm but not in the same way. He was now stroking my scars, full of emotion in his crystal eyes.

"You are very brave, Keira, and have an incredible will to do good by others, you truly have been made with the purest of hearts and you were born to walk amongst us… someday you will agree and believe this also," he said, before he leant down and raised my arms to his lips, kissing my wrists like his brother had done. His eyes looked up into mine, making my own water with the emotion that mirrored his.

His brother was witness to this, but he remained silent until Vincent let go of my arms. Taking a step back, he nodded to me in what looked like great respect and I was stunned into numb silence. Only a single tear escaping displayed my true emotions on what had just passed. It didn't go unnoticed, just unspoken.

"Dom, it seems that our past is also going to pay us a visit along with Keira's. You are right, he is using the human's connection to her to find her whereabouts, but she is strong and has blocked him out. He has already tried to conquer her mind again but has been denied access." At this, Vincent affectionately smoothed the back of one finger down my cheek, as if I had done well. Draven walked closer, looking as if he might explode with even more rage than what already consumed him. So, I decided to be braver than ever before…

I moved away from the desk, accepting that all my body wanted was to feel safe in the arms of my Dark Prince. So, with a beating heart and a silent prayer that I wouldn't get rejected, I marched right up to him and put my arms around his neck pulling his face closer to mine. I could feel his muscles soften their indestructible stance and he weakened to my control.

"Please don't be mad," I said trying to use my own take on his very effective smouldering voice. His arms wrapped around my waist picking me up, so he could kiss me more freely.

594

"I am sorry if I frightened you," he said with eyes burning with passion once more.

"She certainly has an effect on you, brother. I haven't seen you come down from one of your trademark rages since the same blood ran through both our veins," Vincent said full of humour, and it took me a while to decipher what he meant. He had never seen anyone affect his brother like this in all the time they had been brothers.

"I will make the arrangements... she needs you, brother. She has been through enough to hide alone any longer," he said sadly before leaving us to continue where we left off. I bit my lip to hold back the tears that threatened with that parting statement.

Draven lifted me up into his arms and carried me back to the bed, making the room dark once more with only the light of the night sky.

"My brother was gentle with you?" he asked keeping his voice to a low whisper.

"Yes, but I think he was taken back with what else he saw," I said shamefully.

"My brother and I have seen much brutality over the years, but self-sacrifice is a rarity that our kind doesn't come into contact with often. It is one of the most powerful and intense acts a soul can possess. Your soul is pure and therefore, when my brother became a part of that for a short while, it no doubt affected him greatly." He seemed to say this with such pride, but I couldn't help feeling embarrassed with the way they had both looked at me.

They made it sound as if I was some kind of saint, when I knew full well, I wasn't. Especially not after all the unclean fantasies I'd had about Draven since I first laid eyes on him. And well since then, acting them out was more explicit than I had ever imagined possible.

"Keira, will you do something for me?" he asked, pulling me closer towards his smooth skin, and I knew I could never refuse him.

"Anything," I whispered, resting my head on his chest and nestled under his shoulder.

"Will you allow me access inside your mind?" This made me look up at him in surprise.

"Why?"

"Please trust me and let your mind give in to what I ask it to do." I nodded, knowing that he was learning quickly how my mind worked and this was the proof. He kissed me, filling my mind with his control, and there was only one thing he was telling me to do...

"Sleep peacefully."

CHAPTER 49
AVA

I woke to Draven's touch as his fingers ran up and down my arm leaving a sensual trail along my skin. I opened my eyes to find him propped up on his elbow, staring down at me. I was wondering how long he had been looking at me and I just prayed to God that I hadn't been snoring or worse, drooling!

"Good morning, my little one... how do you feel?" he asked kissing my shoulder softly.

"Surprisingly good but I can imagine that's because I am waking up next to you," I said honestly, smiling back at him. Meanwhile, he seemed to be studying every inch of my body, making me nervous again. It was just such a roller-coaster of emotions being around him. One minute I would feel completely at ease and then the next I would change back into the shy waitress I was.

"Have you been awake long?" I asked, hoping he hadn't.

"A while," he said casually, as he continued to sear my skin with delicious heat under his constant touch. He was exploring down my back and lifting my vest to get a better view, but this made me giggle as his fingertips tickled my side.

"Ticklish, are we?" he asked with a mischievous grin.

"No, no, I'm really not..." I said, trying to control my laughter as he continued to move along that same spot again trying to provoke a response out of me.

"Keira, we are getting a little defensive, aren't we?" he said teasing me again, and his hand slid down and grabbed a handful of my vest, pulling me closer to him. I loved it when he was so demanding, as it felt as if I had some shred of control over him and I was quickly understanding ways to use it to my advantage.

"You know you have some adorable little freckles on your back, one in fact that resembles the star constellation of Corona Borealis."

"No there's not," I said feeling that he was making fun of me, but when I looked at his face, he was being serious. I had never heard of this star constellation, but his face held something deeper as if seeing the last piece of the puzzle fit for the first time.

"Well, I have been staring at you for hours now, so I think I would know," he said as a matter of fact. I couldn't help but cringe at the thought.

"No, you haven't!" Surely not... *well I hoped not.*

"Haven't I? I find you fascinating, and it has been so long that I have had to admire your body from a distance, now that you are here, well, I am taking full advantage of the time to study you." At this, I hid my head under the covers.

"Oh, please don't say that!" I said full of pure embarrassment! But he just laughed at my response.

"And what is wrong with what I just said, exactly?" he asked pulling the covers from me, but I still couldn't look at him. Why was he doing this to me?

"It's embarrassing," I mumbled hiding my face in my hands, as now I didn't have the covers any more.

"Alright, so you don't take compliments well... I find this astonishing, all things considered," he said, making me look at him. What did he mean by that?

"All things considered?" I asked, and he smiled as though he had accomplished something.

"Well, you don't have confidence to believe it when I tell you how incredible I find your body, yet you have enough confidence to give me a private striptease, *twice* may I add."

598

"Once! The second time didn't count... your rules remember," I said not being able to keep the grin from my face.

"What are you saying...? That you were *forced?*" he said, leaning forward and whispering the last word like it was forbidden, teasing me and doing a very good job of it.

"More like intimidated," I whispered, as there was a knock at the door, and I didn't want this conversation to be overheard. Once again, he let out a roaring laugh, before saying,

"Come in." Candra walked in, holding a tray full of muffins, sweet pastries, bagels, and baguettes. In fact, she looked as if she had just robbed a bakery! But most importantly, she had a pot of tea on her tray and my heart melted at the sight. Once she nodded at us both a good morning, she left us alone with the mountain of food.

"How many are joining us for breakfast?" I asked, getting up and picking the biggest chocolate muffin which I started to pick to bits. I also poured myself a steaming hot cup of tea and couldn't help but smile at the idea.

"Well, I realised that I haven't been feeding you properly, and today you are going to eat more than just a few pieces of fruit."

"You know you worry about me too much," I said munching away in chocolate heaven, which he couldn't help smiling at. I'd always had a sweet tooth, no matter what time of day, so the gooey chocolate and moist sweet baked goods in my hand was too yummy to wait.

"Actually, when it comes to you, I don't think I worry enough," he said, getting up and positioning himself opposite me to get a better view of me eating.

I started playing with my hands after I had finished with my sugary delight, and was thinking about how to ask all the questions that I still had floating around my mind.

"You want to ask me something?" Draven said, amused. I just looked up at him in surprise.

"What made you say that?" He nodded down to my hands and I dropped them.

"You always seem to play nervously with your hands or bite your lip when something is on your mind," he said as if this was common knowledge, and I couldn't believe how much he must have watched me in this short time to know all these little traits I had.

"Well… I was kind of wondering about some other things I still don't know," I asked sheepishly knowing there was one question that, since last night, had been burned to my brain and it was one thing that I was scared to ask.

"And they are?"

"You're not going to like it," I warned, and he now looked intrigued. So, I carried on before I got the Draven trademark frown.

"Well, I was curious about Celina, what happened with her and Jack?" I asked, thinking I would start off lightly with the interrogation.

"Why would I not tell you that?"

"Because that's just the start," I warned and then there it was, the frowning at me I was becoming so used to but this time it didn't last long, being replaced with a half-smile.

"Celina is a Demon, one that fell in love with that boy." Now I frowned at him.

"Jack, is that better?" he amended begrudgingly. I just smiled in return before he continued,

"Well, as you know, it's forbidden."

"She's a Demon… really? Poor Jack!" I said, but considering my past with Jack, Draven didn't look happy with my sympathy.

"Well, it seems he got over it!" he said cruelly.

"Don't say that! Jack told me how devastated he was. I mean one day he had the girl of his dreams and the next thing she sees you, and then poof… gone. He thinks you killed her, you know," I said, looking at him over the rim of my cup, but Draven couldn't control the raucous laughter that erupted from him. I had never heard him laugh so much and although I was trying to be angry at his reaction, I couldn't help but love the sound.

"DRAVEN!" I shouted.

"I'm sorry, but you have to see the humour in it, you see, I was the one who saved her," he said calming down from his outburst.

"Saved her?"

"She broke one of our laws. She was going to be punished, when she appealed to my better nature and well, since then she has been an asset, proving her worth on my council."

"Oh, I bet," I murmured being jealous again.

"She makes a good assistant, Keira, that's all I meant. It is better for her to be here than cast down to deal with *his* wrath!" he said pointing to the floor, and I shuddered at the thought.

"So you and her… never…?" I said still hiding half my face behind my fancy cup and saucer.

"You know, I do find this jealous thing strange… on one hand it is utterly ridiculous and on the other it is also adorable… still completely irrational, but adorable all the same."

"I'm glad you're so entertained by the whole thing, but I am not the only one who gets jealous, remember? Anyway, you didn't answer my question." I was now going red from that last comment.

"No, I thought I'd already made that clear."

"Well, she could have been lying, she is after all a Demon."

"Yes, and so am I," he said, getting defensive.

"My point, exactly. *You lied,*" I said, feeling that maybe I had finally won a round as he gave up with that one.

"Well the answer is still no… next." Thankfully, he was still in good humour, but I knew my next question would change that.

"And Aurora?" As soon as I said the name, I knew the answer and my heart sank… as in lying at the bottom of the ocean with the rest of the shipwrecks!

"Keira, this is getting out of hand!" he said getting up and throwing his hands up in frustration.

"That's not an answer," I whispered.

"Well, that's the only one you're going to get on the matter!" he said in such a way that I knew he would never back down. I had my answer already anyway, I was just minus the details. However, I couldn't help the feeling that with one of Draven's ex's still around, this was going to be an issue. I mean, how could I ever compete with such beauty? And a beauty that made it blatantly obvious she still wanted him back. Oh yeah, this was so coming back to bite me on the ass!

"Fine! But why didn't Jack get the chance to say goodbye to Celina?"

"Why, do you think it would have made it easier?" he said without leaving the sarcasm out of his tone.

"Yes of course. At least then he could have moved on," I said feeling bad for Jack, first Celina, then me, all at the hands of the same man... well sort of man.

"Does that mean you will break the boy's heart by telling him the truth?" he said, thinking he had got me with this, but I already knew that when the first opportunity presented itself, I would explain it to Jack.

"Yes, to a certain extent I will tell him, so then he can find closure and move on without thinking that one day she might come back or worse, think of you as her murderer!"

"You make it very hard to be mad at you when you think of others before yourself," he said coming over to me and kneeling at my feet. I was about to say something derogatory, but he started kissing me gently on my jawline once again, making me forget what we had been talking about.

"Okay, one other thing, what happened to Layla?" As soon as I asked, I wished I hadn't as his grip on my chin tightened, his face turned hard, and his eyes switched to flaming purple.

"That is not your concern. She was dealt with and this is all I will say on the matter." I decided not to push it any further, but I did look up at him with wide eyes making his features soften.

"Those amazing stormy eyes of yours could control the heart of any man." At this I blushed.

"There is, however, one female that I have wanted to introduce you to and she would very much like to meet you... *properly this time,*" he said pulling me up off the seat, which I reluctantly vacated. I didn't know if I could cope with any more beauty queen Demon/Angels, but I refrained from saying this.

He held my hand in his and I pulled back thinking there was no way I was meeting anyone in my sweat pants and scruffy vest!

602

"Can I at least change first and why are you pulling me towards the balcony?" But again, he found this highly amusing.

"I doubt she will care what you are wearing. Plus, I find you oh so cute like this," he said, poking me playfully in the stomach, which again tickled.

"Oh yeah right, pull the other one!" I said with my Northern English accent coming out thicker than intended, making him raise an eyebrow.

"Don't!" I warned, knowing he was going to pick up on it but instead of commenting out loud, he just mouthed the word 'cute' at me and laughed when I frowned.

"Okay, so you said that I need to meet her properly, so I have met her before?" But he just winked at me as he pulled me through the glass door to the clearest day I had seen yet. The view was breath-taking in this light with the sky so clear and the sun cast the scenery into a lush green utopia. But I noticed we were out here alone, so I automatically went towards the steps I knew led to the roof.

"Not up there. Just wait, she won't be long in coming," he said, and then let out the strangest noise...

But wait, it was one I had heard before, back when I first moved here. Back when I received a welcoming of different kind.

He stood behind me with his arms draped over my shoulders and looking easily over my head, due to the massive height difference. Then I saw what he was waiting for, as a black figure in the vast blue sky came into view and in this light, it looked more majestic than terrifying, as it usually did.

The bird was getting closer, and I glanced up at Draven who looked delighted at the sight of its graceful body swooping down, catching the wind as though it owned all of the sky until finally, it angled its body ready for landing on the railings. This close up it looked double its size, with its wingspan close to two meters wide. I couldn't help but take a step back into Draven at the sight as the railing shook with its body weight landing.

"Rara Avis, Quieta non movere... Ssshh," ('Rare bird, don't move, settled things.' in Latin) he said as it shook and

603

STEPHANIE HUDSON

repositioned its huge feathers, as if trying to get comfortable. I was now hiding behind Draven at this point, as it was extremely intimidating. It looked as though it could rip my face off with one swipe! Wolverine had nothing on this one, with its claws that were black razor curls of destruction.

"Keira, come here... there is nothing to fear," he said as he pulled me back round, placing his large hands on either side of my shoulders so I couldn't move. My heart was doing overtime, trying to keep me calm at the sight of this mighty beast.

"She will not hurt you, she is merely curious." At this, the bird tipped its head at me as if trying to figure me out.

"She?" I asked in surprise, as it clicked this was who he wanted me to meet... his terrifying pet. Oh God, why couldn't he just have had a cat, like a normal person! No, no, he had to have a dangerous creature that could do serious damage. What else did he have, a bear in his summer house?!

"Yes, this Avis or Ava for short," he said moving towards her and stroking her affectionately. She looked as though she loved it, moving her head up and under his hand. I couldn't help but laugh in shock.

"She's magnificent!" I said, not being able to close my mouth, and she looked as though she understood me as she squawked in response to Draven.

"She wants to know why you have been so scared of her," he said, as he now moved his hand to stroke her chest and at this, she ruffled her feathers, stretching out her wings making me jump back.

"Really, she wants to know that?"

"Ava is my eyes to the sky, when I couldn't see you for myself, I would possess her, and it would allow me to look over you while you slept," he said so matter of fact.

"You could see me? So every time I..." I said thinking back to all those times I had seen her.

"Not every time no, when I couldn't myself, I would have Ava watch over you, but you used to startle her when you reacted badly... she was a bit offended actually," he said looking

604

down at me, and so did Ava as if I was being judged by them both.

"Uh… sorry," I said feeling a bit guilty, but considering this bird could most definitely take me, I think I had been justified in being frightened.

"Do you want to stroke her?" Draven asked, and I instantly withdrew my hands around my back.

"Umm that's okay, I don't think she would appreciate that… plus she likes it when you do it… so I'll just watch," I said being a coward. He just laughed at me.

"You're not scared are you, Keira?" he said pulling the reverse psychology crap on me. I nodded quickly making him keep his knowing smile.

"Come, give me your hand," he said, and when I didn't, he gave me a stern look. Of course, when I *still* didn't move, it wasn't enough for Draven to just give up. No, now it was time to use force. He put both his arms around my back and bent his lips close to my ear making his hair fall forward. His hands found my wrists and gripped them tightly.

"Come now, you will upset her… she just wants to be friends." So, knowing guilt would most definitely work, I gave in and let my hands be led to the waiting bird.

"She will behave, won't you, Ava?" This was a command and she ducked her head forward for me to stroke her more easily. When my hand was about to reach up to her, I stopped, hesitating.

"She won't hurt you, Keira." And his hand overlapped mine and moved it to her soft, black satin feathers. I ran my hands over her back letting my fingers run through to her body, and she squawked again in what I guessed was pleasure. Well, all things considered, her beak hadn't yet removed my hand and flown off with it. I moved down under her neck by her chest where I had seen Draven go, and she made me jump as she flashed out her impressive wingspan at my touch.

"Ava, don't show off!" he scolded, and she turned her head at him, tilting it as if to say, 'why not?' I couldn't help but laugh at her expression.

"Yeah, why not... eh Ava?" I said in her defence, which seemed to seal the bond between us because I was now her new best friend. She walked along the railing, closer to my body and gently rubbed up against me, making her feathers tickle my neck. I giggled, stroking her back affectionately.

"Umm interesting... she doesn't usually like other women, but you seem to be the first," he said, and I shot him a crazy look.

"And you tell me this now?!" I asked through gritted teeth not wanting to startle her with shouting.

"Let's just say I had an idea she would love you as her master does," he said, making me want to melt into him. There it was again, him saying he loved me and I don't think I would ever tire from hearing it.

He took a step closer to Ava and whispered something to her that I couldn't hear. Then he did the unthinkable. He held out a bare arm as he still only had a pair of jeans on, and said,

"Aqui!" Which I knew meant 'here' in Spanish. Then she jumped on his arm digging her claws into his skin, which didn't even tear, and more amazingly, he didn't even flinch. He grabbed her beak in his fingers and shook it playfully making it an adorable sight to behold.

"Are you ready for it, baby?" he asked her, as he was now looking up into her beautiful face and her eyes widened with what seemed like excitement. She squawked an answer.

"Well, you wanted to show off, so you'd better make this good, old girl!" he teased before he produced something black and spiky in his hand. He then teased her again pretending to move his hand as if to throw it, catching her out. It reminded me of what I used to do to my grandparents' dog, Sandy, trying to make her go for a stick before it had left my hand.

The second time, however, he did throw it, making it rocket through the air and it went so far, I couldn't follow it for long. He then put his arm down and lifted it quickly to send Ava off into the sky after it in a graceful dismount. She flew off until out of sight, going so fast it was like trying to watch a bullet hit its target, too fast for human eyes.

"What was that you just threw her?" I asked as we walked back inside.

"You don't want to know," he said smiling to himself, as if I was missing something he didn't want to tell me.

"Yeah, sure I do," I said hoping that I did.

"It was a bird's foot." He laughed at my face, which was now screwed up as if I had just smelled something bad... like Frank's feet!

"She eats other birds, it's how she consumes her souls and well, for some reason she favours the feet, saving them for last."

"Yuck! That's really, really gross, how do you even know that?"

"Well, I did tell you that you wouldn't want to know. You see, Ava lets me into her mind, and we share it when I am there but sometimes... well... unfortunately for me, *she gets hungry,*" he said pulling his own yuck face.

"Okay, I think I just hit my limit on the weirdo scale!" He laughed at my humour, which sent little sparks of pleasure down to my stomach. I loved the idea that I could make him laugh.

"So, where did she come from?"

"Ava has been with me since the beginning, a gift from my father to keep an eye on us all. She is a Demon of course, her host being a cross between a raven and a golden eagle to you. She also has her own powers. But since she was sent, she favoured me from the start and this is why she doesn't like... well, you know?"

"You mean other woman you have been with?" I said rolling my eyes at him at his reluctance to finish that statement.

"Well yes, but I knew her connection with you would be different. She pleased me and trust me, she is never normally that well behaved and has given me the run around a few times in the past. When she was young especially, she went through a stage of terrorising small villages, scaring them and aiming for the younger ones... for some reason, she hated children." He shook his head at what looked like a memory and I looked on wide-eyed trying to imagine how terrifying that must have been, as not so long ago I was also in the same mind.

"But with age she has become quieter and grumpier, spending most of her time alone as she prefers."

"Aww, well I think she was sweet," I said putting my arms around his neck, which seemed to be a weak spot of his as he melted into me, doing what I wanted him to, which was of course, kiss me.

"I hate to put a downer on this good mood of yours, but you will not think so kindly of me in a few moments." He smirked at the thought of me turning into an angry kitten no doubt.

"And why is that?"

"Because any minute my sister is going to walk through those doors and take you away from me." He didn't look happy at the prospect.

"Why?" I said, hating the idea of even spending a minute from his side.

"She has it in her head that she is going to get you ready for the party tonight." Oh no!

"No, no, you have to talk to her, reason with her," I said pleading with him, but he just held up his hands in defence.

"I would love to, but she is very persuasive."

"But you're her brother and surely, she will do what you say… I mean reason with her… please, she has to be stopped!" I was close to begging at this point, which he was still smirking at.

"Keira, it is not that bad and besides, you think I am hardcore when I get angry… you have never witnessed Sophia's temper!" he said, and I couldn't be sure whether he was teasing me or not, so I put my hands on my hips to show him I wasn't going to accept this. But then, as usual, my display went out of the window when he put his hands on my sides and pulled me into him, kissing me on the forehead.

"Demon remember, and a determined one at that." He noticed my frown and continued, "It is simply best to let her have her way, after all she is excited as she has never had a sister to…"

"Use as a human doll?" I finished his sentence with sarcasm.

"I was going to say *to love.*" And as soon as he said it, I felt the guilt that he was counting on.

Then he moved away from me and walked towards the door, opening it before Sophia even had chance to knock. She strolled in, looking as if she had tried very hard to look casual but of course failing miserably. She looked just like she'd finished her photoshoot for Paris fashion week.

She wore skinny style jeans that looked as if she had either been sewn into or they had been painted on. She had added a long, dress style top that was white and fell off on one shoulder. Her hair was casually pulled up into a high ponytail, making her curls look contained yet fighting to get free. One thing was for sure, she looked bloody happy!

"Dress up time!" she said, clapping and smiling like the evil Cheshire cat from Alice in Wonderland. She turned around knowing that I would have to follow, and I couldn't help but drag my feet at the thought. I mean, she wasn't even giving me time to change. Oh, this was going to be a bad idea. I walked past Draven with my head down, but he stopped me, kissing me on the top of my head, saying,

"Play nice, my Keira." Of course, knowing that I was about to go and play with a Demon didn't make me think there was going to be anything nice about this game…

Not when Alice was getting pushed down that damn rabbit hole.

CHAPTER 50
DOWN SOPHIA'S RABBIT HOLE

I followed Sophia for what seemed like forever up and down staircases, along passageways and through God knows how many doors! Finally, the last door was opened for us by Zagan, of all people. He nodded at me, but I didn't miss the wink he sent Sophia's way, which she tried very hard not to react to. However, she was still smiling when we entered her bedchamber. Well, I say bedchamber, it was more like a whole floor of a department store and we were in the soft furnishing department!

She had different beds scattered everywhere, making it look more like a cabana club than a bedroom. She had different tent-style rooms to the sides which towered up into elaborate metal points giving it a Moroccan vibe. There were couches of all shapes and sizes and luxurious material framing the walls and furniture. I noticed there was even a bar in one corner, and this made me realise that this was a separate club of its own, *a private one.*

"Sophia, what is this place?" I asked, as I caught up with her as she was moving towards a more private part at the other end of the room. This was partitioned off by a wall of fabrics overlapping each other that hung down from a grand arched high ceiling. One look at it all and I wouldn't have known where to begin to try to get through it. But Sophia just held up her hand

and they moved apart, flowing up and down and side to side, allowing us a passage through the gap they created.

"This is my bedroom... amongst other things." She giggled before continuing, "I have asked Dominic if you would like to join us, but he is dead set against the idea, so you will have to miss out... he never did like to share." She shook her head at the thought, and then added,

"This way," motioning me through the last door, which finally must have been where Sophia slept. Now *this* looked more like a 'Sophia bedroom'.

It was a Gothic dark fairy princess room, with a huge wrought iron bed that was covered in the same fabric that flowed around the arched posts. It looked both deadly and cute at the same time. The room also had a punk vibe as the walls were papered with the most unusual design. It was black velvet with the biggest bright pink roses that looked lethal with pointed sharp petals, some tinted at the ends in crimson.

I knew one thing, and that was that RJ would have freaked out seeing a room like this! The furniture was a fairy tale design, but it was black lacquered, and it screamed out that this belonged to a girly Demon!

"Okay, first you need to take a bath," she said, opening a set of double doors into a massive bathroom that had a different feel to it. It was like walking from evil to pure good. This room was like a tropical paradise, with plants and flowers up the walls giving off an incredible scent of the rain forest. She must have seen my face drop.

"Like it?"

"It's amazing, I just... it's just... like the Garden of Eden!" I said as it finally came to me. At this she clapped her hands like an excited child.

"That's the look I went for but wait until you try my bath!" she said pulling me further into her private heaven. Around one corner was an actual waterfall that flowed down the wall behind her bath. The bath was sunk into the floor so you had to step down into it, and I realised that the waterfall wasn't just there for effect, it was the shower!

The whole bath was like an infinity pool that just overflowed into an abyss I couldn't see. She let out a laugh at my face, and I was starting to feel thankful that she wanted to share this with me. So at least if this makeover went horribly wrong, I still got to use the most awesome bath in existence.

"I will leave you to it. There is a bag there with all the usual stuff you use… you know?" she said, making me laugh as she pretended to shave her armpits. She was just the most unpredictable girl I had ever known.

She left me alone in paradise and I nearly ripped off my clothes to get in there quicker. I lowered my naked body in the water, which was the perfect temperature, and let the liquid caress my skin, making it soft and smell amazing. All I wished now was that I had Draven in here with me, and that thought alone was enough to make me start fantasising about all the naughty things we could be doing.

After a long soak, I decided that I should start on the reasons I was in here in the first place, so with that in mind, I reached over for the bag that Sophia had pointed out. It was filled with all the things I needed, but it amazed me to find it was the same make of razor I used and the same gel. I even found a new toothbrush for me to use later. It felt strange doing all the usual things you do in a bath, because in this one it felt as if it was only meant for two things, one was relaxing, and the other was purely erotic. One that I was getting desperate for. Draven was most definitely like a sexual drug, the more I had, the more I wanted… no, not wanted, but more like *needed!*

My hand wandered down on its own accord and it felt wrong and oh so naughty, which only added to the thrill. I couldn't stop thinking of Draven and all the delicious things that he could be doing to me right now. I mentally begged for him to come to me, and I opened up my mind to the possibility that he could hear my silent pleas.

My touch became more precise and my need for him became more intense. I found myself calling out for him in my head, screaming his name, so when I heard his voice, my eyes shot open.

"Electus... my Electus." I looked around the paradise I was immersed in, expecting to see his commanding figure stood watching over me, but I was alone. I sank back down under the water, more than a little disappointed not to see him. Had he really spoke to me or had my mind been playing cruel, teasing tricks on me?

"For my touch only... " Just as I was closing my eyes again, I heard his voice penetrate the room. Once more my eyes snapped opened, only this time they only found the darkness. I was thankful for the soft blue glow beneath the water, as I only now realised there must have been lights situated under the water of the bath.

"Hello?" I whispered, unsure of who would hear me, but my only reply was the sound of running water. The waterfall behind me drowned out the sound of my thundering heart, so when I heard his voice again, I wished there was a way to turn it off, so I could be sure.

"You called my name, Keira." I blushed, knowing it was possible my carnal desires had brought him here.

"Draven...? Is that you? *Are you in here?"* I muttered the last part as if I was speaking of a sin. My answer came to me, as the sight of two glowing eyes pierced through the dark. The purple fire told me it was Draven and I gasped at the reality. I watched his shadowy figure approach and I sank back in trepidation. I felt my body humming in anticipation for what was to come but I was also nervous at how exposed I felt. All these feelings combined, only managed to heighten my oversensitive mind until I was close to bursting, I was so turned on.

Draven's shadow loomed over me, looking impossibly tall due to me being sat below the level of his feet. He moved to the edge, and I could barely make out his naked form stepping down into the small pool that was Sophia's bath. I watched, completely mesmerised, as his body submerged itself deeper under the water, now becoming something I could see thanks to the cool glow of light that acted like a blue moon under the water.

"Dra...Draven?" I uttered his name as I broke the silence feeding the sexual tension in the room that was almost thick

enough to taste in the air. I gasped out in fright as his body was at me before my heart could register him moving, so it beat wildly in my chest. My wide, startled eyes stared up at him in disbelief as he shifted his body behind my own, cradling me from behind.

"I heard you scream for me, Keira," he whispered with his lips at my ear, and I let my head fall back against his shoulder as both his hands found my breasts. A moan that couldn't be contained escaped my lips as he pinched the nipples hard enough for pain to shoot straight to my clit. I could feel the strength of his erection behind me and I couldn't help my wanton body from reacting to it. I rubbed my behind against his glorious length, rolling my hips in an attempt to find a rhythm that would drive him wild.

"Now, I want to hear you scream for me as I bury myself deep within your body... can you do that for me, sweetheart?" he asked seductively, but he received his request when he suddenly impaled me on his erection, and I did indeed scream out his name.

"Draven!" He held my shuddering body locked to him as though he feared I would sever our connection. The beautiful sensations started to light up my body as he moved me the way he wanted me. Each drag of his length inside me rubbed and caressed the wonderful knot of nerves in a maddening way that had me screaming his name over and over. One hand held firmly over my breast and the other dipped under the water to rub my clit and it was only seconds before I was crying out my release.

Then I went wild against him, needing once more to chase the orgasm, finding the pattern I loved the most. I pushed my body against him, riding his erection from behind and working my body into a frenzy of need. I was lost and powerless to stop it, and the growl of pleasure behind me told me that he too never wanted it to stop.

But then the power exchange between us flipped, and what little I possessed was obliterated. He pushed me forward, holding the back of my neck in his strong grasp as he bent me over the edge of the bath. My top half was pushed flat against the tiled floor and the cold stone made my nipples harden as I was powered into from behind. He gathered up my hair in his hand and held on, pulling it for that sensuous tug of pain that morphed into pleasure. I arched backwards as he took me to a new height of pleasure, my breasts raised up from the floor as my head was forced back and they danced in the air with each thrust.

He locked an arm around my waist and as he drove into me, he pulled me back against him for a deeper connection. The water splashed up around our bodies like the waves of sea exploding around the rocks at the shore. It mirrored the force of pleasure I felt ripping through my body as I came for the last time and I felt our union finalise, as he too erupted inside my body as we found our release together. My insides clenched around him in a desperate attempt to have him never leave the comfort of my body and he continued to hold me close to him, wrapping his big arms around me as our hearts found a steady rhythm once more. The aftershocks made my body quake in his arms and I felt his smile against the skin on my neck.

"You scream for me and I will come... always." These were the last words uttered before light flooded the room once more, and I felt my body sinking under the water as I was no longer held there. My hands gripped the sides to hold me up, but I knew he was gone. I smiled as I felt the evidence of him being here slide down my leg and I reached down to gather it, pulling it from the water. I don't know what came over me, but I placed the thick substance to my lips and tasted him. I found myself moaning out loud once more at the sinful act I was relishing as his unique taste burst over my tongue.

"Oh God, I am in trouble," I said out loud smiling.

～

Once I had showered under the warm waterfall, I squeezed my hair, wringing out the last drops from washing it with the most marvellous smelling products. I got out as my wrinkled fingers told me that I had spent too much time in there already. I looked around for a towel as I dripped on the floor but couldn't find one.

"Looking for this?" Sophia's voice startled me, and my hands flew to my more private parts, as she held out a lush thick white robe.

"Sophia, I'm…"

"Yes, yes, you don't need to worry, you don't have anything I haven't seen before… well except them," she said nodding to my arms. But for the first time I wasn't blushing at the thought of my exposed arms, no it was at what I had just been doing with her brother in the bath. Did she know?

"Sorry, I didn't mean to be so blunt… I usually just say what I think without… well thinking about it," she said as I hid my nakedness away under the soft towel.

"It's fine. I guess it just takes some getting used to," I said quietly hiding my past.

"Well, we have work to do, or more like I have work to do, so come with me and we will get this show off the roof!"

"Isn't it show on the road?" I asked, laughing nervously at what she had planned.

"Not when you have wings, my dear!" She giggled, as my face dropped. She took my hand with ease and pulled me to what looked like a Moulin Rouge boudoir. There was a grand looking chair waiting for me in front of the biggest gilded mirror I had ever seen, which filled the whole of one wall. I swallowed hard knowing there was no way I was getting out of this, and Sophia knew it too giving me a sassy grin and wink.

"What are you going to do?" I asked, sitting down slowly and looking at the entire contents of a beauty counter on the table in front of me.

"Don't you trust me?" she said, pulling my hair from under my robe and holding out a pair of scissors. This did slightly unnerve me at the sight of someone I knew to be a Demon coming at me with a sharp implement in her grasp.

"Not with those in your hand!" I said, panicking at what my mother would say if I cut it all off.

"I'm only going to trim a bit off the bottom, don't worry,

Keira... try and relax. I'm only going to enhance the beauty that is already there," she said brushing my long waves, and for a Demon she was a hell of a lot gentler than Libby had been.

"Plus, Dom would have my head if I were to change you too much. No, I have had my orders," she said rolling her eyes at the memory.

"Sophia, can I ask you something?" I once again played nervously with the sleeves of my robe.

"About?"

"About Draven," I said looking down, feeling the heat in my cheeks.

"Keira, I think it is about time you called him by his first name, don't you?" she said amused at the idea.

"But I have always called him Draven... in my head anyway." At this she didn't comment but just nodded her head and smiled.

"Well, I wanted to know about Aurora?"

"I think that is a question best left for him, don't you?" she said stopping the comb for a moment, which told me she knew where I was going with this.

"But I have asked him!" I confirmed, regretting it as soon as it was from my lips.

"And?"

"He wouldn't tell me anything," I said deflated.

"Then what makes you think I would?" she asked taking pride in her grooming me, which made me feel a bit like a pet horse of hers.

"Because I have bribery in my favour."

"Oh really, and what bargaining power are you playing with?" she asked intrigued.

"Well, if you were just to answer a few of my very innocent questions then I will let you do whatever you want to me with no moaning about it... complete and utter free rein!" I said swivelling my chair around to face her.

"Or, I could just put you in a trance and do that anyway," he said bringing out her cocky side that reminded me of Draven.

"Sophia please... I won't tell him, and besides, wouldn't *you* want to know?" With this I had her, knowing that she would most definitely do everything in her power to find out, after all, she and her family had found out everything about me.

"Okay, well I can understand it when you put it like that... but, Keira, he is extremely powerful, and he will already know we are having this conversation." This shocked me, and I couldn't help but turn nervously towards the door as if readying myself for him to come bursting in the room.

"So, you won't tell me?" I said like a sullen child.

"I didn't say that but let me ask you, do you love my brother?"

"Yes, of course I do," I said full of certainty, and she smiled again.

"And he loves you, so what does it matter about his past?"

"Well, my past mattered to him," I said being firm and proving my argument with a damn good point.

"Your logic is hard to argue against and you are right, he did in fact go to great lengths to find out everything about you." Her hands were now running through my dry hair, even though I hadn't heard a hairdryer being used.

"So I gather he knows about every tiny last bit of my past and therefore, my past relationships. Why then should I not get the same privileges?" I said cringing at the very idea of him know everything.

"It does seem to be very one-sided doesn't it?" she stated, and I felt as if I had someone on my side for the first time and my triumph showed through, presenting itself as a wide cunning smile.

"Okay, I give in! Sorry Dom..." she said looking up at the ceiling before continuing,

"What is it you want to know?"

"Were him and Aurora ever, you know... together?" I asked knowing this was a no-brainer!

"Well if it helps, then yes they were involved intimately," she said shaking her head, but I didn't know if it was at me or the memory.

"For how long?"

"Oh, not very long and it was some time ago."

"Okay, so explain 'not long'," I asked hoping for weeks more than months.

"Oh, I don't know, ten or twenty years, give or take a decade," she said this so matter of fact. I on the other hand nearly swallowed my own tongue!

"WHAT?" I shouted at her, not being able to contain it.

"Keira, please try to understand that we view time very differently… that is really not that long." Oh no, not long at all, I thought bitterly.

"I don't think I can breathe. No wonder she hates me," I said, putting my head back giving me a full view of the spectacular moulded ceiling that right now I wasn't that interested in.

"Keira, she doesn't hate you, she is just extremely jealous of you," she said, liking this fact more than I knew.

"Why on earth would a Goddess like that be jealous of *me?*" I said feeling all my hope fade.

"Simple, because he ended things with her, and now he is with you, only the big difference is that he loves you dearly and he never loved her."

"He dumped her?" Now my ears pricked up at this new bit of information, and my fading hope was quietly creeping its head back around the corner.

"Dominic has never been happy, and he has never been in love before, so his distractions were just what they were… *distractions.* But he has been waiting for *you* since the beginning, and this was something Aurora could never accept."

"I bet it must make it even harder for her, looking at someone like me," I said, biting down on my lip considering what her thoughts must be.

"Keira, you underestimate yourself greatly! No doubt you saw the way she looks at my brother. She has done this always, but when you joined our table last night his eyes never left your face. I know Dom well enough to honestly say this is the happiest I have ever seen him, and he deserves to be happy… he deserves you, and you him." At this, she motioned towards my arms reminding me of my past and all I had endured. Was she

619

right? When it came to Draven, did she really think that I deserved him?

"Thank you, Sophia, I feel better now I know. I think he tries to protect me too much, when all I need is the truth."

"I think he keeps expecting you to run from him," she added, before carrying on with the next stage of my beauty regime.

"Why would I ever do that?" I asked amazed. Surely he didn't actually think this?

"Keira, you are a human, granted not like other humans, but still, he is what he is… no doubt you were taken back when you saw his other form?" she said, reminding me of the immense power that I saw coursing around his indestructible body.

"I learnt long ago how to deal with things I couldn't understand but I controlled the fear and well, that night I was more nervous than frightened. Not because of the way he looked, but because of the obsession I have on him. To find myself in that position with him, well, let's just say my heart pounded for other reasons," I said being completely honest, and she seemed not only shocked but happy with my response.

"You really were born for him, Keira. And I'm glad to have you for a sister. Now, let's get on with making him weak at the sight of you!"

"Umm, Sophia, can I just ask one more thing?" I asked being all shy again, and she nodded

"What is that big room for back there?" I asked referring to the private club we had walked through.

"Oh, that's my fun room but Dom is adamant that you won't be joining us." And I was soon to learn why not.

"He is very possessive over you, not wanting to share you with anyone… I guess we won't be seeing him there again either." And with this it suddenly dawned on me, making me let out a gasp in shock but Sophia just laughed at me and my innocence. The penny dropped and landed on a very 'dirty' floor…

It was for orgies!

∼

After what was most of the day, as it was now dark outside, I was finally ready. It felt as if I had spent the day at a posh health spa, all the time being waited on hand and foot. Sophia and I had giggled with girl talk over champagne and pizza, of all things! This was because she knew it was my favourite, and there wasn't an anchovy in sight. I'd had every part of my body worked on until everything was smooth and smelled luscious.

I still hadn't seen the finished product and well, my heart was proving how nervous about this I was as it was starting to sound like a pneumatic drill in my chest. Sophia was walking me through to the other room, the one with all the mirrors.

She had thought of everything, including very luxurious underwear that I was now wearing underneath my purple satin dress. Of course, this had been the only thing I had been allowed to choose. She held my gloved hand in hers and pulled me towards her full-length mirror. She told me to close my eyes as she guided me left a bit then right again until she clapped her hands with satisfaction, saying,

"There, now open your eyes, you beauty!"

I opened them and stared into the mirror as if searching for myself in the reflection looking back. It was as if I was looking at an impostor who was playing a beautiful version of myself. I mean, when Libby had made me over, I had been shocked but now, well now I was stunned into silence. I looked amazing!

Sophia had my hair half up in a mass of loose curls that came down in a golden cascade. My makeup was minimal but as she had said, it just enhanced what I already had. My lashes looked longer thanks to curling them up and they were doing that tickling thing on my lids again. My eyelids were now a soft purple with darker shadowing by the fold and this made them look more seductive, which I knew Draven would enjoy. My skin glowed, feeling softer than ever before and the colour of my dress emphasised it.

My dress was gorgeous, a deep purple with a satin corset top that tied at the back concealing the underwear beneath. It crossed over at the front with two thick straps that went over my shoulders and again crossed over around my back. These were a dark indigo colour that matched the underneath fabric part of the skirt.

It came down to a short skirt that flowed around my legs, showing one more than the other. It flared out longer at the back, spreading out the colours as I moved and twirled around. My legs looked longer than they ever had before, probably down to the fact that this was the most of them I had shown.

The shoes were made from the same two materials as the dress with ribbons that tied up and around my ankles making a pretty bow at the back. I looked like an exotic bird trying to attract a mate!

"I can't believe it…it's…" I stammered as Sophia stood back to admire her handy work.

"You look beautiful, Keira, but it wasn't hard to accomplish that," she said affectionately. I turned around to her and hugged her tightly.

"Thanks Sis!" I said winking and making the biggest smile come to her face as she hugged me back.

"Well, time to see what your Dark Prince thinks… maybe he will buy me another car, I haven't got a yellow one!" she said making me laugh at her optimism.

"Umm, I think he has to like it first before you start thinking about paint jobs," I reminded her as we walked back through the room that made me blush at the thought of what went on in there.

"I don't think we need to worry about that!" She laughed as Zagan's eyes saw me and looked again to check it was in fact me. At this my cheeks went from blush to full rouge which got me thinking, what were they going to be like when Draven saw me? How was I ever going to do this?

It didn't take us long before I realised that we weren't going back to his bedchamber, we were going directly to the club, and my heart rate flew through the roof.

"Why are we going straight to the club?"

"Because those were my rules, I knew that if he first saw you like this in private, then the both of you would never make an appearance. Dom can be quite selfish and well, when it comes to you, he becomes obsessed." That word took me back as it was exactly how I felt about him, but I wondered if she had added this last part for my benefit only.

We were soon at the double doors and I was just about to turn to Sophia and ask if she needed to get ready. I prayed she wasn't just walking me to here and then expecting me to go it alone, as I knew I would never have the balls to do that. But when I turned back around, she was fully dressed in her own beautiful gown, looking like a bird of paradise in midnight blue. It reminded me what a Roman Goddess would look like as the dress flowed down to her feet, moving gracefully with her body. Its halter neck plunged down showing her curves like mine did. It was only now, that I noticed Zagan looking at Sophia with nothing short of burning desire.

"Why didn't you just do that with me?" I asked, stunned at her ability.

"Because where would the fun have been in that... plus we had a good girlie bonding session." I couldn't help the huge grin that was plastered across my face at her response.

The doors opened as we approached, and Sophia's curls bounced excitedly as she walked with her arm through mine. As soon as we were in sight, every eye followed us as if there was an unseen connection they were trying to keep hold of. I hoped this was more at the sight of Sophia than me.

We strolled over to the table, where I could see the back of Draven's dark suit. I silently prayed he wouldn't turn my way, as in these heels I was scared I would fall on my face if I had his smouldering look to contend with. Vincent, however, was going to give me away as he hit his brother with the back of his hand on his shoulder. Vincent looked as shocked as Zagan had, but this was nothing compared to the shock I saw as Draven slid his dark eyes in my direction. I looked up at them staring and Sophia giggled noticing it too.

I could taste the gloss on my lips as I bit down on them, full of nerves. I walked up the steps and Draven's eyes followed every move I made, from the bottom starting with my legs, and moving upwards to the bit of my exposed thigh. He continued his journey up to my boned corset clinging tightly to my skin and making my curves more developed as I moved. Until finally he got to my face, and I swallowed hard at the desperate hunger I found in his eyes. The Demon in him looked as if it wanted to ravish me there and then, not caring if we were in a room full of intrigued eyes. I looked away like a frightened servant girl in the eyes of her Masterful Lord.

Draven was the first one to stand, with the rest following his lead. Aurora was already there looking breath-taking as usual and her eyes couldn't tear away from Draven, but it didn't bother me as much as it should. This, of course, was down to the look he was giving me, and I wanted to kiss Sophia for making this happen.

We were about to take our seats, but Draven had other ideas. He took my satin covered arm in his strong hand and walked past the table pulling me behind. I could just catch Sophia giggling at this while Aurora looked away with eyes full of disgust.

Draven was breathing heavy, and he wasn't the only one by the time we got to the balcony. As soon as we were out of sight, he whipped me around and pushed me up against the wall, making sure to be careful with my breakable body. His hands slid up my sides making me quiver under his touch.

"I take it you're pleased?" I said, but it came out as more of a nervous whisper through a mix of fear and the mind consuming ecstasy that was Draven, which always affected me down below.

"You put the stars to shame and make every Goddess shy away at the sight of your beauty," he said in a deep voice as his body closed the space between us, letting me feel for myself just how pleased he was. His lips were at my neck and I felt his teeth hold my skin as though he was trying not to bite me. I arched my neck more wanting him to, waiting for the rush of pain to mix with the pleasure that I felt last time. But his teeth released their hold and his lips took over, which I could feel smiling at my neck.

"You really are a temptress and the Gods will envy me

tonight as you are all mine and mine alone!" he said, both demanding and smiling at the thought. His mouth moved over to first suck my bottom lip into his before enveloping me in a deep controlling kiss.

I could feel him tasting me and his hand went to the inside of my thigh, moving upwards causing me to let out a moan, making my want for him as clear as where his hands wanted to be...

Everywhere.

CHAPTER 51

UNDER A SPELL

J ust before his fingers hit their mark I spoke, as I knew if he had made it there then I would have begged him to enter me.

"We can't do this… not now," I said trying to control my breathing to a slow pant. He, however, let out a low growl which startled me.

"And why not?" he said with the look of desperate man.

"Because I told Sophia that we wouldn't disappear and we would stay for her birthday, remember, you also promised?" I said, trying to get through to the Angel inside. The one hand he held to my shoulder travelled up to my neck and lingered there feeling every breath I took, fingers drumming at my pulse point.

"She will understand, Keira," he said, trying one last time as he brought his other hand into play. They now found their way down to my top, touching my cleavage and for a moment I thought he was going to tear my dress in two when he then started to grip the material roughly.

"Draven… *please,*" was all I needed to say to get him to come back to reason. His hands then went to my face and pulled me closer for another sweeter kiss. He was starting to sway away from his desires and listen to my words.

"You took me in Sophia's bath not so long ago," I reminded him, blushing at the memory.

"*I want more of you*," he whispered intensely.

"We will have all night," I said feeling the flutter of tingles at the thought. It made me very nearly give in, but then Sophia popped into my head and the day we had spent together. So in this, I didn't want to disappoint her.

"I will obey for now but after our time is done, I will bring you back out here and will have my way with you... *understood?*" he said, showing me the full meaning of desire as he once again kissed me making my legs turn weak and close to useless.

When we were back inside, he didn't even flinch at the stares we both received. No, instead he held me by his side proudly, guiding me back up to his table. Once again, they all stood out of respect, and Sophia shot me a look and mouthed a silent 'thank you' at me. Draven waited until I sat before sitting himself and again, I couldn't help but notice the look Aurora gave him.

"So you approve, brother?" Sophia asked looking past me to Draven, I however looked at Sophia as if to say, 'Please not now', but she took no notice of my silent plea.

"She is perfection as always, but you have added the frame to the masterpiece, well done Sophia," he said as he held his hand to the back of my neck. I, on the other hand, must have turned a very undignified colour of red. Sophia coughed as if he was missing something out.

"Very well, you can pick your new car tomorrow," he said, and he and his brother both rolled their eyes at their spoilt sister.

"Yes, well with that out of the way let's get the champagne here and start the party," she said nudging me. Almost immediately the champagne appeared, being pink for the girls and black for the men.

"I didn't know they did black champagne?" I said to Sophia, but she just replied,

"We do," and grinned.

"Did you enjoy yourself today?" Draven asked, looking down at me while he pushed a loose curl from my face.

"Yeah, we had fun and a good chat," I said, and Sophia

frowned at me, but I couldn't keep the smile off my lips. I mean come on, he already knew!

"Yes, so I heard" Bingo! Of course, he did.

"You should have just told me," I whispered as I took a sip of my pink bubbles.

"You're right, as usual I underestimated your persistence and to break Sophia, well now that is impressive." At this, Sophia just stuck out her tongue at her brother as if this was her tenth birthday!

"Next time I will be more honest with you, as now I know you can take things so well," he said, and at this, Aurora looked at him wide-eyed, but his eyes still only held me in their gaze.

"So, what about some more shots?" Sophia said clicking her fingers, turning around to Loz.

"Lauren dear, do get us something delicious," she said, and I wondered if she knew what to get her from that description.

"Cognac," Draven said making it clearer, knowing exactly what his sister found delicious. I was just shocked that they wanted to shot the stuff, but my surprise didn't end there. When it arrived, it came in the most amazing bottle covered in what looked like diamonds. Then she placed all the shot glasses down that matched the bottle. Draven nodded to her and she poured them all, this time doing it before I could get up.

She then went around with the tray passing them all out, and Aurora drank hers first giving Draven a wicked grin, which made me want to strangle the smile from her lips! Draven took two off the tray and handed me mine, checking first.

"Would you like to try it?" he asked, and I nodded taking the sparkling shot glass from his warm hands that I wanted all over me.

"What, no tequila tricks to entertain us this time?" Aurora said in an amused tone that didn't go with the glare she gave me. Well, if she wanted to play that game, then fine… bring it on, bitch!

"Not tonight, no, but if you know where I could get some cherries then I could show you another trick in under thirty seconds," I said, finally adding some of my own kind of humour to the table and I finished off my shot in one.

"Cool, what can you do?" Sophia asked, and Draven shot her a look as if not wanting her to ask me... umm maybe he thought I was bluffing.

"I can tie a cherry stem into a knot with my tongue," I said, watching Sophia's eyes light up.

"Oh really?" Aurora pushed, and Draven didn't look happy about her interfering.

"Yes really, I would show you if I had one," I said, not wanting to back down as I usually did in situations like this.

"Well Dominic, are you going to indulge us and let her show us her gift or are we but to assume?" Aurora said speaking to him, and I wanted to growl at the sound of his name from her lips. So I decided to play my advantage, turning to him, and for the first time calling him by his first name myself.

"Yes Dominic, let me show them," I said placing my hand over his heart, which made his glare turn to me in joyful surprise. He didn't miss me calling him this and his eyes grew soft before he gave me one of the nicest smiles as a reward.

"Are you sure you can do this?" he said leaning into me, whispering in my ear so the others couldn't hear, but it made me smile at his reluctance... he didn't believe I could do it.

"Me Miran!" I said, meaning, 'Watch me!' in Spanish. He continued to look at me in awe, and it seemed that this was my night for surprising not only myself but Draven too.

"Yes Dom, I want to see," Sophia said getting excited at the human performing tricks for her amusement. So Draven produced a gorgeous lush red cherry that thankfully had a long stem, as it was always easier and quicker the longer they were. I looked over to Aurora and she held out one elegant hand to indicate she was waiting. The rest of the table were also watching me, adding to the pressure, but considering I had been doing this trick since I was young, I knew it wasn't going to be a problem... well, that was if I didn't choke on the damn thing!

I plucked it from the fruit and held it up to prove it was straight, but for this one I couldn't look at Draven or I knew I would never be able to do it right. I placed it in my mouth and wiggled it around, holding one end secure inside. Then I folded the rest with my tongue making a loop, and when I had it positioned right, I pushed the end through. I pulled it out of my mouth gripping one end with my teeth so that it tightened the knot I had made. I did this in under twenty seconds.

I held it up for everyone to see, and dropped it back into my empty glass and slid it over to Aurora's place for her to have a closer look, feeling fantastic at my 'entertainment', as she had called it. I finally looked at the rest and I smiled at their shock, but Sophia nudged me saying,

"That was brilliant! You have some skills there, honey," she said winking at her brother, who I could finally look at. He had the biggest, badass grin on his lips, and he repositioned my head so that he could kiss me fully... in front of everyone! And it wasn't a simple meeting of the lips, oh no, it was head slanted, noses touching, tongues battling and lip sucking kiss! Once he had finished, he turned to Sophia, and said,

"Oh yes, skills indeed." And the whole table erupted into laughter... *all except one.*

He moved my hair off my shoulder and came to my ear to tell me his private thoughts on my act.

"To say that I am impressed would be a great understatement. I am sorry I doubted you, but I think the only way to make it up to you would be for me to show you my own talents... *with my tongue,"* he whispered winking at me, and I popped the cherry in my mouth trying to flirt back. Only it ruined it when his hand slid up my leg and I swallowed the stone in the middle.

Thankfully, he didn't notice as his hand rested there. I shuddered as his fingers flexed in and out on my skin as he drank the rest of his champagne. Of course, now all I had in my head was the image Draven had planted there and what it would be like having that masterful part of him on a more intimate area of my body.

I bit my lip at the thought.

This was by far the most relaxed I had felt, and after a while even the looks that Aurora was trying desperately to receive back from Draven didn't bother me. Sophia was right, he never took his eyes off me and I swam in a sea of bliss knowing this. I got to talk to his Council more and was included in all conversations as if I belonged. It was as though I was a part of them now, like one of the family.

As the night went on, I could tell Draven was getting restless as his flirting only increased and he just didn't care who saw us. It seemed like the most natural thing in the world and was if embarrassment didn't even exist in Draven's world. I just blushed at his attentions, which seemed to make him want me more. I tried not to tease but it seemed everything I did made him ask if time was up yet.

"Dom, try and behave as the poor girl can't have a conversation! You will have her all to yourself soon enough… try and show some self-control," Sophia said, loud enough that I wanted to bang my head into the marble table and bury it there! But he just laughed at his sister and leaned over around my back to get to her, pulling one of her curls down making it spring back up.

"Ouch! Dom, don't be a bully!" she said playfully, and it seemed as if I was sat at the naughty table at a wedding.

"Sophia, don't be a baby and stop moaning… you don't see Keira complaining," Vincent said back in a cool, collected tone, and I couldn't help but smile at the banter. Meanwhile Aurora looked at me as though she wanted to rip off my head and use it as an ashtray as she was smoking one long black cigarette.

Then something happened, shattering the night's ease. Takeshi broke his glass in his hands making everyone stunned into silence. I was the only one who didn't know what this meant. I looked over at him and his eyes were now glazed over in what looked like muddy water. They flickered, changing from black to clear like a stormy night. Then they cleared, resuming their normal state, and he rose from his seat and calmly walked behind Draven.

"My Lord, there has been a development you need to see at once," he said in the low steady voice he always used. Draven looked seriously at him, as if searching for what it was and when he found it, he first looked at Vincent who got up and stood next to Takeshi. Then he looked to Sophia to relay some silent message.

"Don't worry, Dom, she will be safe," she said smiling at me. Draven held my hand and pulled me up, walking me away out of earshot.

"What is it?" I asked, concerned at his stern features.

"It is nothing for you to worry about, my love. But I am afraid I will have to leave you here for a little while... stay by Sophia's side, can you do that for me?" he asked, and I knew this was a semi-command, one I didn't mind as I knew it was for my own good.

"Don't worry, I won't go anywhere."

"Good girl... I won't be long." Then he tipped my chin up with his thumb and finger and kissed me gently, leaving me by the bar to wonder what was going on?

I decided to get something else to drink as the champagne was going to my head and I wanted to have a clear mind for the treat I had been promised later tonight.

"Karmun, can I have a glass of water please?" I asked before he left to get some more bottles.

"Yeah, sure honey," he said in his usual sweet tone, which made me miss working with him as we had formed a good friendship over the time I worked up here. However, now I had the feeling he looked at me a little differently... being Draven's girlfriend. That word sounded weird as I couldn't quite get my head around what we were exactly. Like Draven said, I think we skipped the whole dating thing. Then my heart nearly stopped at the sound of the phone that was ringing, as my last memory came flooding back, making me gasp for air.

"Keira, it's for you again... someone called Frank." As soon as I processed the words, I could finally breathe normally enough to take the receiver from Karmun.

"Hey Frank, what's up?" I said wondering what emergency could warrant Frank ringing me.

"Keira, it's Olivia..." His voice sounded strange, panicked, and that was something I'd never heard from Frank before. Also, he never called her that, so my heart rate dropped in fear.

"What happened, what about Libs?"

"She's in the hospital, some guy tried to grab her and pull her into a car, I got there just in time to stop him, but he drove off... but..."

"Oh my god! Is she... the baby?" I asked feeling the tears start to form.

"The doctors can't tell, but she needs you," he said sounding upset, which was weird as he was normally so strong.

"I'm at the club and I don't know if Draven will let me come now, see there's..."

"Keira, there is no time! I have a friend coming there to pick you up, you remember my friend Andy, well he's a cop and he will bring you straight here... you will be safe with him," he said pleading with me, and I knew my sister would be asking, even begging for me to be with her. I had to get there, I just had to!

"Okay, I will try and get away, where does he want to meet me?"

"He will be waiting in the club near the back doors, he should see you," he said, and then the phone started to make a crackling sound like bad reception.

"Hurry Keir..." Then the phone went dead and I knew what I had to do. I had to disobey Draven's one rule...

I had to leave Afterlife!

My mind started to create hundreds of scenarios of how this could ever play out. I was torn between telling Draven everything and praying that it would swing my way and he would let me do what I needed to do, which was to run to my sister's side. But deep down I knew the truth... he would never let me leave. So that's when my time shifted into plan mode.

I needed to get away from the one place I felt safe and do what was right. Libby needed me and there was nothing on the planet that would keep me from my sister. Not even a Demon/Angel half-breed boyfriend that had an army of Supernaturals at his beck and call. But how do I give them the slip?

Then it occurred to me... couldn't I do both? Okay, so this was it, finally a plan was formulating and one that just might work. Before I went back to my seat, I had asked for what I needed from Karmun and stuffed it down my top out of sight. I had to play it cool or Sophia would see straight through me. I had to concentrate harder than I had ever before to keep her out of my head. This wasn't going to be easy. Hell, after all, I was trying to deceive a Demon!

"You okay, who was that on the phone?" she asked trying to play it cool herself.

"Oh, it was just Frank, my brother-in-law... Libby couldn't get me on my phone, so she rang the club," I said rolling my eyes and shaking my head trying to make out it was nothing.

"Was anything wrong...?" she asked, eyes full of concern for me, which made it all the harder to lie, but for Libby I would have to put on the best show of my life.

"Oh, it's just my gran back home, she slipped on the ice and broke her foot and I need to ring her to see how she is... my mum is worried," I said watching her face buy my story.

"Aww, that's a shame, well I hope she is okay... do you want to call from the phone at the..." I cut her off a bit quicker than I should but still kept my voice steady.

"Oh no it's fine, I will just wait until tomorrow, she's in the hospital at the moment and my parents will be driving down there... but thank you." I smiled at her, adding reassurance to my unsuspecting lie.

"Not a problem." She smiled back but now I had to ask something I wasn't sure she would fall for.

"Sophia, would it be okay if I use the restroom?"

"Yes, of course, you don't need to ask." And she motioned for me to go back to Draven's room, which I had a feeling she would, so I played my next card praying for an Ace.

"I know this is going to sound a bit wimpy but could I just pop downstairs to use that one... after last night... you know my dream... well I have really felt uncomfortable in there."

"I understand that it would affect you. I think it should be fine but don't be too long, okay?" she said not seeing the problem, and thankfully Draven had been called away or I would never have been allowed to get away with it!

"I won't be long," I said as I excused myself from the table. Zagan didn't like the thought of me leaving but surely he wouldn't go against Sophia's say on the matter? When he didn't say anything I instantly felt better as I headed for the back staircase. I ran down as fast as my legs could take me and I was soon through the doors at the bottom. There was a toilet close by, so I quickly ran to them and locked the doors behind me. I pulled out the paper and pen that I had stuffed down my top and quickly wrote the note I'd planned.

Draven,
I am sorry that I have left but Frank rang and told me that Libby has been attacked and needs me, as she's in hospital. I think it must have been Morgan, but he escaped before Frank could get to him. Don't worry, as I will be safe. Frank has sent a friend of his to pick me up. He's a cop! I have to do this. My sister needs me!
I love you and will be in your arms soon
P.S. Please don't be angry with me.
xx Keira xx

Once I had finished my letter, I knew there was only one person that I could trust with it and who would buy me enough time to get out. I had spotted Jack with the others at their usual table as Draven had, through my request, allowed Jack access into the club and well… now I needed him.

I ran over to him as quickly as I could in heels and luckily, he spotted me instantly. Under different circumstances I would have chuckled at the way his eyes nearly popped out at the sight.

"KEIRA! Where have you been? I have been calling but…"

"Jack, there's no time, I need your help, and this is going to sound crazy but please, I need you!" I pleaded speaking a million miles an hour, but I needed to do this quick or there was no way I was going to get out of these doors!

"Why? What's wrong? Why are you dressed like...?" He was trying to get more information out of me but there wasn't any time, so I had to cut him off again, pulling him away from the others who were now trying to talk to me.

"Look it's my sister, she's had an accident and well, I need to get out of here, but I need you to give this letter to Draven after I've left... Please, Jack, please do this for me and don't look at it," I said with such intensity that he seemed to understand.

"But they won't let me up there."

"They will if you tell them what it is about... please, Jack, you're the only one I can count on." I could just see the police uniform by the back door, and I recognised Andy, Frank's friend. So, I took my chance and stuffed the letter into his hands, leaving him still asking me questions as I ran to the back of the club.

"Andy?" I asked knowing that it was, as I had seen him in the house a few times.

"Keira, come with me, Frank told me what happened," He said, grabbing my arm and pulling me to the back door that he had entered through. Draven's men weren't guarding this door. They were the men Frank trained, so when they saw Andy, they opened the door without hesitation. As soon as we were outside, I wanted to pull my arm out from under his tight grasp but he wouldn't let up.

"You know, I think I'm safe to walk on my own," I said trying to sound calmer than I felt.

"Let's just get you in the car, my partner is waiting for us," he said in an eerily calm voice. The car wasn't far, and now Andy was making me run towards it as if we were being chased by something I couldn't see. He opened the door for me, and I slid in the back, falling slightly as he pushed a little too hard for my liking.

"Wow, you guys are efficient. Frank and you guys must go way back uh?" I said trying to make small talk but neither replied. I tried to look through the grating between me and the driver to see if I recognised him but in the dark, it made it difficult. He sped off onto the main road making the loose gravel spray out behind us, and I wondered why they were high-tailing it out of here as if they were in hot pursuit of a stolen vehicle?

Five minutes had gone by and still not a word from the two in front and my palms were starting to sweat through my gloves. I was starting to regret not demanding that Draven take me to the hospital himself, at least I would have felt safer. I quietly reached for the door handle just to check that I hadn't been locked in but considering this was a police car my chances weren't good.

"Umm, how long is it till we get to the hospital?" I asked, as I didn't recognise the road we were on, and it looked as if we were heading away from town instead of towards it. But still I received no answer and my sweaty palms were now itching into full panic. So, after another five minutes I asked again.

"Look guys. I know you live around here but I'm pretty sure we're heading out of town," I said, but when they still didn't answer I banged my fist hard on the metal, making the caged space rattle.

"That won't help, Catherine," a calm voice spoke, and my panic tripled making my headache with pain.

"How do you know my name?" I asked as the tears welled up instantly. This time however the driver spoke, and I leaned in placing my fingers in the square holes of the car's cage, trying to see the face better.

"Be good, Catherine, and don't make this difficult... *not like last time.*" As soon as his lips formed the words, a car approached from the opposite direction and his high beam headlights confirmed my worst nightmare, lighting up the face of my own personal monster...

Illuminating the face of Hugo Morgan.

637

CHAPTER 52
TEARS & BLOOD

"LET ME OUT!" I screamed, as I banged my fist on the windows and the cage, until they were red-raw.

"Calm down," Morgan said in an unemotional voice. But I couldn't stop. My body wouldn't let me. My heart was pumping pure adrenaline around my veins, making me morph into the most violent person I had ever been.

"YOU CAN'T DO THIS!" I banged on the glass of the side window, and I thought it might give at one point, so I tried a new technique and used my foot. I could see it would nearly go if I just kept at it, but this made them pull over, so I knew I didn't have long.

I was shaking with a lethal combination of both fear and anger. It made me want to scratch their eyes out at the thought of being in the hands of that mad man again. I had been so Goddamn foolish! Draven knew the dangers. He had warned me about this, and I was just too pig-headed, thinking I was in the right... and now I was going to pay dearly for it.

They stopped the car and I screamed and screamed as they both opened their doors. They were coming around to my side and I didn't know which way to attack, because they were both going to take care of me. I turned to Morgan's side as he opened the door first and lunged inside for me, but I kicked out hitting him with the point of my heel.

"Aaarrrh…! Damn it, Catherine! Don't struggle or this won't be pleasant!" he warned, and even the grating sound of his voice made me want to do even more damage. So, with that in mind I kicked out again. Only this time he counteracted my move by grabbing my leg and pulling me towards him. My skirt slid up and he looked down at me with hungry eyes, which made him loosen his grip.

I used this as my opportunity to lift up my knee, hitting him hard, right on the mark, making him howl in pain. I tried to struggle up past him but in his rage, he punched me across the face, knocking me down with a hefty blow. I was too stunned and dazed, which gave him back the advantage. I could taste the blood in my mouth, but the pain didn't fully register from all of the adrenaline in my system.

"We don't have time for this!" Andy said, now speaking in a different voice than before. It didn't sound like Andy, but more like the voice I had heard in my dreams. At this my heart nearly stopped, giving way to a whole new fear.

"Some help here!" Morgan snapped back at him as I squirmed around like a fish on a hook. He then opened the other door and reached in grabbing my wrists, pulling my arms above my head and holding them there in an unbreakable grasp. Then Morgan put a knee either side of me, straddling me and sitting down on my crotch. I wanted to be sick at the feeling, as his eyes explored my body with obvious lust. He held up a syringe that flashed silver in the small, car light. He was extracting liquid from a small medical bottle and I knew what was coming, so I tried one last effort as my body was failing from fear. I pulled my arms and bucked my body trying to worm my way out of his hold, but Morgan had finished now not needing his hands. He pushed me down and my arms got pulled out farther. making me scream in pain as it felt like they would soon be ripped from their sockets!

"Be good!" he warned, flashing me an evil grin. One hand was on my stomach and it worked its way up my body, pressing down making the bones in my corset dig in. He was enjoying every minute of this, not being able to keep that sick smile off his face. He held his hand on my neck and turned my head to one side, ready to stick the needle in.

"Draven will kill you for this!" I said, making his grin turn sour before he jabbed the needle in deep, making me scream.

"Draven will come for me... *he will... he...*" I said through the cloud that consumed me.

"Oh, we're counting on it, my dear," Andy said, only when I looked, it wasn't Andy anymore.

It was Sammael.

I woke in a mist that clouded my vision. I felt wrong, as though my body wasn't positioned right, and it took me a while to come to and fully realise why. My hands were tied and pulled above my head, but I was upright, unlike the way I had been in the car. The memories came back to me making my senses clearer. I was stuck and I wriggled about trying to move, but it was no use. My hands were tied round something making my body hang down like a piece of butcher's meat. I looked up, and there was a huge hook which hung down from a chain that was wrapped around a wooden beam. My feet just barely touched the floor making it impossible to get free.

"You're not going anywhere, Catherine... *not this time.*" Morgan's voice came from the corner of the room and I jumped at the sound, but it was drowned out by the sound of my chains rattling as I was going crazy trying to get free. I twisted and turned, trying to pull myself up but just not having the strength, so before exhaustion set in, I had to give up. Morgan came at me out of the shadows and his hand was held over my mouth, as I must have been screaming with all my struggling.

"SSSHHH... Calm down or I will have to sedate you again... Now, are you going to be good?" he asked, and I could taste his skin from where he held his hand over my lips, which made me want to gag. I nodded, to indicate a yes, as I just wanted him to stop touching me!

"Okay, no more screaming and I won't have to hurt you

again," he said in that creepy voice I'd had so many nightmares about. But when he moved his hand from my mouth it didn't leave me entirely as it moved down my neck, resting there as he looked into my eyes smiling.

"Oh, how I have missed you, Catherine. I have thought about nothing but this moment. They wouldn't even let me have a picture of you, so I had to draw you from memory," he said as his hand slid further down past my chest and down to my side. His other hand went to the opposite way and he pulled my body into his as it swung easily on the chain, making it impossible for me to move away. His face was inches from mine, and I held my breath and closed my eyes wishing Draven would find me soon.

"Do you remember what it was like when we were together? We were so happy, and we will be again soon, I promise you this time I will take good care... *such good care of you.*" His hands gripped my side until my eyes watered at the pinch. Then his lips hovered just over mine and I could no longer keep quiet.

"I wouldn't do that if I were you," I whispered before his touch infected me.

"And why is that, my girl?" he said smiling as he lingered over my lips so that I could smell the sour liquor on his breath.

"Because I am *NOT* your girl, and the one I do belong to is not going to be happy with you touching me!" I said trying to sound as serious as that threat was.

"Oh, and what will he do... take my soul?" He nearly spat out his words and I could almost taste the cheap whiskey.

"No doubt he will simply kill you," I said calmly as I knew this was true, knowing Draven, if he saw this he wouldn't bat an eyelid at ripping him limb from limb. But Morgan was back in control as he pulled a large blade from his back and held it up to my neck. I let out a moan at the sight.

"Ssshh, don't move or we might have another accident like last time, and well... this one we won't be coming back from. How did that feel anyway? I was always curious... it must have been excruciating?" he said, pulling away the sharp metal from my skin and pointing to my arms with it.

"It was worth it!" I said, feeling my blood boil under my skin and wishing I were a Demon for the first time in my life!

"Tut, tut, don't say that, Catherine, that's not nice and you will pay for it," he said as his free hand touched my leg and moved up my thigh making my skin crawl!

"GET OFF ME!" I screamed as I thrashed around, but the blade came back up to my neck, stopping me instantly.

"Behave!" he shouted back at me as his hand was trying to find what it wanted, and the tears started to fall down my cheeks, some landing on the cold blade beneath my chin.

"Don't... please!" I pleaded, and his face softened slightly but not enough to crush his fantasy, and I cried out as he found his mark in between my legs.

"MORGAN! Leave her!" A stern voice growled at him and he reluctantly removed his hand, but he winked at me before walking back to his corner, sniffing his hand. I could feel the bile in my mouth from the sick effect he had on me.

Sammael was back to looking like Andy but he was no longer wearing the uniform, and neither was Morgan. I looked around as there were a few camping lamps casting shadows about the room, making my fear double as I didn't know what was real or what was in my head anymore.

"She is strong, incredibly so for a human," Sammael said in a low, terrifying voice that made me sob softly. He was making the shadows move around me like sea serpents and I could feel them biting my skin, but it wasn't real! I was screaming with pain, but I was trying to concentrate, knowing this was my only chance against him.

COME ON, KEIRA, THINK! I shouted to myself in my head. I needed to be strong... hold it together... hold it now! I found where he was and pushed as I had done when Draven tried to enter my mind. The shadows evaporated into dust and the pain slowly disappeared. I could finally breathe, and my body flopped down feeling exhausted with the effort it took.

Sammael clapped his hands, as this was all very entertaining to him.

"Very good, my dear... I am impressed, a rare thing indeed.

No wonder Draven has claimed you for himself. You are a nice quirky addition to his following," he said, making it sound as if I was property. I still couldn't speak as I was panting after the breath had been wiped from me.

"I told you she was different," Morgan said as if being proud of me.

"Yes, you did well. Now, give her some water before she faints. I need her awake for this next part," he said, and my panicked breathing nearly started again at what the next part would be. Morgan came towards me and put a glass to my lips, but he couldn't resist where his other hand went, so when he pulled back the glass from my lips, I spat it all back out at him!

"BITCH!" he screamed, as his hand came crashing down on my face again, and I felt my lip burst open and the blood drip down my chin. I hung my head down from the blow but could hear the laughter from Sammael.

"She is feisty. Well, she would have to be to wet Draven's appetite," Sammael said, sounding more than amused at my outburst.

"NO! There is no way she has been with him like that!" Morgan shouted, and now I started to laugh but I wasn't sure why, maybe I had finally lost it!

"SHUT UP!" he barked at me.

"Make her see!" he demanded of Sammael, but he was unmoved by Morgan's denial.

"She already has the sight and she has seen him, Morgan, but she doesn't care what he is! Don't be naive... of course she has fucked him, he would not be able to contain his urge around such a temptation. He would have made her his at the first opportunity."

"I don't believe it!" Morgan was outraged at this which only made me laugh more. This was, after all, the only revenge that I had.

"Ask her," Sammael said, gesturing to me. Morgan came at me, breathing heavily under the strain of the truth. His face twisted with hate, and I found great pleasure in telling him something that would cripple him!

643

"What he says is true, he made me his and you know what… I loved every fucking minute of it…! Now I belong to him, dickhead!" I said smiling, as I enjoyed each word that came from my bloodied lips. But again, he hit me, making the burning pain heat my skin on one cheek. It was still worth it though, which made me wonder if I was getting used to the pain. He was about to do it again but stopped as he had a different idea. He walked over to Sammael and handed him the large knife.

"DO IT! We had a deal!" he said, but Sammael held up his hand, passing on the knife offered.

"We do, and I will fulfil my end of the bargain, but I will not be needing that." He grinned, and even though Andy usually had a kind face, this time it turned hard and terrifying. He had changed him into a killer, a murderous bastard and my body went into panic at the sight. I was giving up hope and I knew Draven mustn't be able to find me, for I had run out of time!

With each step he made, my heart rate increased, making the pounding in my chest hurt and my rib cage rattle with fear. The tears came without control and I shook, making the chains clang against the wooden beam. Morgan came up behind him getting a better view, as his sick mind enjoyed watching me squirm.

Sammael's eyes devoured my body admiring it for himself… no doubt taking his fair share of human girls over the years. His hand touched my waist and clamped it into a deadly hold. He forcefully pulled me close, and I could feel the wood give a little under the added pressure. This shot a pain through my side making me whimper, which he enjoyed even more.

"Just to warn you my dear… *this will hurt,*" he said, licking his lips and I could smell the black tar that I had seen in my dream on his breath. He found my arm and ripped my glove off, exposing my now red scars from the heat that coursed through my blood. Beads of sweat ran down my forehead, and they trickled to my lips to join tears and blood.

"Why don't we use your arm, as that seems to be your preference?" he said, flashing me his evil grin. He held up one hand and showed me the deadly claws growing out of his nails, and they reminded me of Ava's, black and razor-sharp. I screamed, knowing this was my time and the last word on my lips would be his name. He didn't do it quickly, but oh, so agonisingly slow. He tore four long slashes into my skin, and I howled in pain as this was like nothing I had ever felt before.

"DRAVEN!" I screamed out, and it echoed into the night leaving me breathless from emptying my lungs. The pain made my body convulse and I nearly passed out. I swung around making the wood splinter and rain little bits to the floor as the chain rubbed away at it. I could feel the blood gushing out of my arm making its way down through my dress, down my side, and finally dripping from my feet. My mind couldn't concentrate on what I wanted it to do. My head fell backwards, and my eyes rolled upwards, as all I wanted to do was blackout. I could hear words being said, but couldn't process anything but the immense pain and blood that was leaving my body.

He then pulled me back and placed his hand over the gushing wound, making the fires of Hell fill my veins. The feeling was similar to when Draven had done the same thing to the wound Layla had caused, only when he had done it I had felt no pain, only pleasure. Now, when Sammael touched me, my blood felt as though it was mixing with lava, burning evil, and I couldn't hear anything above the screams. Over and over, they erupted filling the forest with the noise of agony. It took me a moment to realise they were coming from me as finally the pain started to subside.

"He won't be long now, as no doubt he heard that and knows she is here," Sammael said, sounding pleased as if they wanted Draven to come. I hung down exhausted but couldn't feel my blood dripping to the floor anymore and when I looked up, I noticed my arm was glowing an angry red from the effect his touch had left. When I turned to face them both, I found myself screaming again at the true sight of Sammael.

His face was even more hideous than my dream had shown me. The black tar was alive around his face, moving in and out of his dead, grey looking skin as though keeping him together. The blood oozed from his disgusting lips and dripped like mine had onto the floor around him. His crude metal stitches that had once held his lips caged were now cut and bent outwards, sticking through the holes in his cracked skin.

I wanted to vomit at the sight, and knew I would if he came near me again. His wings wrapped around his body like cloth that had claws attached to the ends. They weren't made up from feathers like Draven's, they were like webbed fingers, black and also dripping with tar. This was what Morgan wanted me to see. He wanted me to see Demon forms thinking that when I saw Draven, I would run from him. He was foolish again, continuing his deluded state even after Sammael had told him.

"I will leave as he will be here shortly, I need to summon the others... but you remember your part of the bargain don't you, Morgan?" he said placing one long flaky hand on his shoulder, as Morgan couldn't take his eyes off me.

"Morgan!"

"Yes, I remember... *Afterlife,*" he said answering Sammael, and I couldn't swallow at the sound of the club being mentioned. What was he going to do? Then it hit me, maybe the reason they wanted Draven here was to get back to the club without his guard. Were they really going to try and bring down Afterlife? Oh no... it was a trap!

"NO, you can't!" I shouted, and Sammael started to laugh, spitting more blood to the floor and it sizzled, acting like acid as it hit the ground.

"You don't need to worry about it, my dear, you have played your part beautifully and maybe we will meet again in some other life but for now... well, I will leave you in Morgan's capable hands," he said, snapping his teeth shut which overhung his nailed lips. The wires were in the way and the sound of bone against metal was a gruesome noise.

"Why are you doing this?" I asked trying to pull my body up, but my wrists were bleeding from the skin that had been rubbed away by the rope.

"Revenge, of course. See, your precious Draven did this to me," he said, pointing to his wired mouth.

"He and his brother thought they had the right to meddle in my affairs like they are the LAW! After my partner Belphegor didn't need me any longer, he sought the help of your Dark Prince to silence me forever," he said with a bitter spark.

"But as you can see, I found a way and now, well thanks to you, I will finally get my revenge... he is not the only one with powers, and now I have an advantage. See I have nothing to lose, not anymore as they took that from me, but Draven... now he finally does and soon, oh so soon, he will feel the effects of what I endured at his hand. He took from me, and now it is time to take from him. And take I will!" He nodded to me with another evil snap of his fangs.

He left out of the door, and it was then I realised where I was. I was in the log cabin in the woods where I had fallen. It looked different as the furniture that had been piled up against the doors and windows was now all stacked in one corner. The moon was still bright in the sky from the clear day we'd had, and having no clouds to hide behind it flooded the cabin with light.

Now we were alone again, Morgan wasted no time coming back over to taunt me like the leech he was! His hand went to my scarred arm and he ran a dirty hand over each one taking pleasure in it.

"Now we will be alone forever, Catherine. I will take care of that," he said as if this was something I would want to hear, so I decided to try reasoning, if you could with a nut job like Morgan. I said his real name for the second time in my life and it felt like acid was burning my mouth at the infection it caused.

"Douglas, please, I am not your sister, *my* name is Keira not Catherine... you don't want me, it's Catherine you're looking for," I said, and his face first looked shocked then twisted into a red mist of anger.

"My name is Morgan, and you are not allowed to talk about my sister... she LOVED ME!" he screamed, and this could be my one chance to stall for time.

"What happened to her?" I asked him as he had now turned away from me, so at least with this I had accomplished something.

"NO, NO, NO!" he screamed, and then started slapping his

head over and over. I could only hope he would hit harder and knock himself out in the process!

"You don't get to speak her name... EVER! She didn't leave me!" he shouted, and I could see the tears starting to form. He bent down and gripped his head in both hands, pulling his hair to the point of obvious pain. It was at this moment that he had never looked more insane. He needed help, that was clear.

"Speak to me, Douglas, tell me what happened to her," I said in a soothing voice trying to calm him down.

"I loved her! And she loved me! It would all have been fine if *he* had never come in between us."

"Who came?" I asked, as I tried to squirm loose when he wasn't looking.

"That boy... *THAT RICHARD!* I hated him! I hated him, but she said for me to give him a chance. I couldn't look at him... the way he looked at my Catherine... SHE WAS MINE! Goddamn it!" he said as if seeing the memory there for himself, he shook and so did I, as I guessed what was coming next...

A twisted soul's confession.

"I found them together the way we used to be. She loved him now, not me. When I forbade her to see him again, she lashed out... *at me?* She couldn't understand, he didn't love her... not like I did! I was trying to keep her safe... I just wanted her to be safe!" His arms flew up dramatically as his story continued.

"I found her sneaking out to see him, so I followed them and tried to get them to stop. His car wasn't as good as mine... and neither were his brakes," he said in an eerie voice that held a hint of satisfaction. I shuddered at the sound, knowing this human was pure hatred and the evil sickness had consumed his mind long ago.

"I ran them straight into a tree and then parked up to watch, waiting for the flames. But I had to get closer. I had to look as I hoped his face... that perfect fucking face..." he snarled the words almost like they would choke him.

"I wanted it mangled, bone without flesh so that my sister could see the truth! But when I saw them, they were both still fine, still alive and breathing! My sister didn't call my name...

she called his… *HIS!* After everything I had done for her, after everything I gave her! He had poisoned her mind against me! They needed to be punished and it was my right to punish them. So I took out my father's lighter he had given me, and as the fuel pumped out all around them, I sent them to where they belonged!" he said finishing his past, and I cried for that poor girl's desperate attempt at real love, only to be murdered for it by the jealousy of her own brother. I wretched up bile and had to spit it to one side. It was sick, twisted, evil and unimaginably cruel!

"So you see, Catherine, you will not leave me again… not for another Richard. This time I will keep you safe and I will keep you always… keeping you forever!" he said now coming back closer to me, to place his hands on my skin as if staking his claim.

"Please, Douglas, you don't want to do this," I pleaded as his hands slid around my back and down the material of my ripped skirt. He was gathering it up in his hands and I couldn't bear the thought of what he wanted to do to me.

"Now it's my turn to have you, I was going to wait till we were married in the eyes of God but seeing as you have already mated with that *thing…* that *abomination!* Then I will take you here and now, ready for him to see when he arrives. Won't that be nice for him?" His hands pulled my skirt all up around me and I twisted again trying to get loose, but the pain in my wrists was making it hurt so badly I couldn't try for long.

"Calm down, my love, you will learn to love me back… in time… *lots and lots of time.*" He kissed my neck, working his way up to my face. His hands held my backside and he pulled my lips to his, crushing himself against me. I opened my mouth and bit down as hard as I could on his bottom lip, tasting his blood in my mouth. He screamed and backed away placing his hand to his bloody lips in surprise. I spat his blood out on the floor, not wanting anything from him to touch my body ever again. I didn't care what happened next as he may have taken my body by force, but my soul belonged to just one man, and one thing was for sure… I wasn't going to make it easy!

"That wasn't nice, do you know what happens to bad girls?" he shouted, slapping me again making my head whip to the side like a rag doll. Only now I wasn't as scared as I had been back then. I wasn't the same pathetic girl quaking in some basement cell. So the laughter came thick from my bloody lips making me look... *Demonic!*

"Stop laughing! What's wrong with you?" he screamed at me, and he slapped me again trying to knock some sense into me, which was exactly what I wanted to do to him only using a baseball bat!

Then I heard the most beautiful sound that made my sinister laughter turn to a full blood-curdling scream.

"AVA!" I shouted, and Morgan's head whipped round to the door seeing it flap on its hinges in the wind. I heard Ava cry out at the sound of my voice and I knew now it wouldn't be long.

"Are you ready, Morgan?" I asked in an ice-cold voice that I didn't recognise.

"Ready for what?" he snapped, coming back up to me with his knife in hand as if he had the advantage again. I just looked up with a detestable grin of my own, and said,

"For my revenge!"

CHAPTER 53

DRAVEN'S BAIT

I screamed at him before he grabbed me by the throat, closing my windpipe making it nearly impossible to breathe, but his grip was slipping from his sweaty palms and shaking hands. He wasn't the only one losing grip as I was quickly getting lost in the darkness that was trying to pull me under. I just needed to hold on... just hold on for a little while longer. Draven was coming. I could feel it, as every cell in my body started to ignite, and the connection was burning brighter the closer he got.

Then the walls started to shake, and the wood made splintering noises as if under strain from a storm. Morgan looked all around the room, as like me, he didn't know what was happening. Then we both heard a huge crashing noise as if a boulder had fallen from the sky, giving off an aftershock on the floor and causing a rippling tremor as the wood split.

That's when it all happened at once. The whole front of the cabin suddenly ripped from its foundations, moving at such high speed it made the logs crumble into the forest as if they were twigs. The roof was about to cave in on us, but my scream was premature as one half-peeled back as if it was just a tin can. It flew backwards over the cliff's edge behind, and you could just hear its destruction as it smashed to the ravine below.

The cabin was a mere shell with a few beams remaining and

only three walls. I shook with every movement it made as I was still attached to the beam by the chain. My wrists were beyond a bloody mess as my bonds had cut through the flesh, but at least my screams had been muted thanks to the mighty quake that had erupted on the forest floor.

When everything stopped shaking, I finally looked up to see Draven's other form…

And. It. Was. Godly!

He stood where he had landed from the sky, with his huge, dark wings expanded out on full view. The top part of his body was exposed displaying dominant energy powering his veins, veins that were glowing fiercely. His hands positioned outwards to control the rubble that was in his way, causing it to shoot through the air behind him, giving him a clear path. It was only now that I fully understood the intensity of the power he held. It was truly terrifying…

If I thought that I had seen Draven angry before, then that had only been the tip of the volcano that was about to erupt into full Demon fury. He moved forward, making the rubble part like the Red Sea, launching it out into the forest as if it had been made from foam. This was not the half Angel/Demon I had seen before… Oh no… there was no Angel in sight as his eyes found Morgan holding my neck in one hand and a large blade in the other, which he had positioned at my side.

As he got closer, his naked torso looked as though it would explode with the fire under his skin. You could see a raging red river flow around his body as it was destroying the Angel within him. It looked as if the Demon part was completely taking over and was most definitely winning the fight!

His muscles rippled as he tensed them at the sight of me. I must have looked as I felt… *which was broken*. My dress had been torn, exposing all my legs, and the straps were no longer. The blood down my arm remained as it had dripped all the way to my shoeless feet and as my face had been hit at least four times, I couldn't have been pretty to look at.

"YOU CAN'T HAVE HER!" Morgan screamed at him as the blade got closer to me, but Draven moved faster than either of our eyes could catch and was soon at Morgan. He just extended his arm out and flung him aside as if he had been a cardboard cut-out.

"Watch me!" he said in a controlled anger as Morgan's body flew through the air, crashing into the other side of the cabin. I jumped at the thud it made, making my body sway around on the chain. Draven's eyes found mine, but it was as if he was looking straight into the pits of Hell and what I was seeing was the reflection. The purple had all gone, being replaced by an inferno of utter rage, it would have had the whole Underworld quaking in fear.

His red irises scanned over me, and I could just see the hint of pain that touched them as he noticed every new mark on my shattered body. He came closer to me and I couldn't help the tears that still overflowed, only now they were tears of relief. Not just that I had survived but more than that, I could now see Draven's face once again.

"You came for me… you…*you found me…*" I sobbed, feeling the tears fall down my sore red skin. His hand went to my face and I was surprised when it felt icy cold. It was the only part of him that was now flowing back to his purple energy. He was controlling it to soothe my burning cheek.

"Of course, I came for you… I will always come for you, Keira," he said as he leaned his forehead to mine and he whispered,

"I love you."

I was just about to say the same back when I saw a flash in the corner of my eye of Morgan's blade.

"DRAVEN BEHIND YOU!" I screamed, and he turned into the blade that Morgan held out in his hand making it disappear into Draven's gut and now only the handle was showing.

"NO!" I screamed out as I saw Morgan back up to wait for Draven's fall.

Only it never came. Instead, Draven looked down at it sticking out of his flesh, making his hair fall forward in front of his face. I couldn't speak at the sight… I wanted to run to him and pull it out, driving it deep into Morgan's heart! But I never got the chance.

Draven flashed a destructive grin that was pure undiluted revenge, one that only wanted to hunt evil as he looked up to find Morgan's terrified face.

"My turn!" he said in a Demonic growl I had never heard before, and he pulled the blade from his body in one fierce swipe. He then grabbed Morgan by the throat and pinned him to the wall, lifting him with one hand. He started to choke him, being a near foot from the floor, and Morgan's legs fought frantically for the wood beneath him. Draven's eyes grew wider, enjoying the sight of his pain. He even licked his lips, and I watched his fangs grow as if he would soon attack like a hungry animal going in for the kill! I couldn't stand it any longer as the good in me couldn't let this carry on.

"Draven, please... he's sick... he isn't right... he needs help," I said as I watched the life drain from his body, and Draven shot me a fierce look as I had just interrupted his Demon frenzy. He dropped him, making him fall to his knees where he coughed and wheezed, trying to regain his breathing, clutching his throat with his hands. Draven looked down at him like he was disgusted with the parasite at his feet.

"You're right, my Keira, he is sick, and I know just where they can help him," he said sternly, back to his formidable Demonic voice. This made me shake to my very core. He was beyond petrifying. He was the place from where nightmares were born...

He was their King!

Then, like lightning, he had him back up straight and plunged the knife deep into his heart without even a shred of humanity.

"ENJOY HELL, VERMIN!" he said through the deadly smile on his lips... Oh yes, he was most definitely enjoying this. Morgan was suspended onto the wall behind as the large knife went straight through into the wood. He spluttered out blood, and I couldn't believe my ears when I heard laughter come from his blood-soaked lips. He turned to me and looked me straight in the eye.

"I will be seeing you soon, *Catherine.*" And those were his last words before the life left his body completely. Draven got angry at this and ripped the knife from his chest, and as his lifeless body crumpled to the floor, he kicked it, as if it had been a dead animal!

"CORPUS VILE!" Draven shouted at his victim ('Worthless body!' in Latin) He then came over to me, but I was still shaking from what I had just witnessed, so when his hands touched me, I jumped and let out a shriek.

"Ssshh, it's okay, Keira, I won't hurt you... I'm sorry you had to see that," he said so softly it was hard to believe the Demon I had just seen. His hands gripped around my waist, and for the first time tonight it felt good, as now I was finally in the right hands. He lifted me up gently as if I was going to crack and fly away like dust. He lifted me over the hook and set me down, clearing any debris before my feet touched the floor. His hand stroked my hot face and he shook his head at the state I was in.

"Keira, please tell me you are alright... tell me... are you in much pain?" he asked through closed eyes and gritted teeth. He looked as though he would soon lose the last thread of what sanity he had left. Then his eyes suddenly flashed open and he scanned my face then the blood on my arm.

"I'm okay, but my wrists," I said as I held them out for him to see. He looked at the bonds tearing into my skin, and then he pulled them off gently as he growled at the bloody marks they had made. He tossed the crimson-stained rope to one side as I winced at the throbbing.

"I'm sorry... I was so stupid... I thought... I believed..." I started to sob but he placed his hands on my cheeks, once again making them cool. He wiped my tears and my smudged eyes with his thumbs, and then pulled me into him to hold me safely in an embrace.

"Ssshh... You're safe now, I have got you... I won't lose you... not again, *not ever!*" With these last two words, his Demon came through, and I was happy to hear it wasn't only his

Angel side that wanted to protect me. His voice was full of granite-hard emotion and I could feel his muscles flex under my arms I had wrapped around his waist. Then they went harder still as he heard his enemy calling him out.

"OH, DRAVEN! Time to come out and play!" Sammael's voice echoed around the trees and bounced off the canyon wall. Draven let out a growl that sounded deadly to the core. He still had me in his arms like my dark protector.

"Keira, stay here," he ordered, but I held onto him and for the first time touched his wings, which were surprisingly much softer than they looked.

"Draven, don't, it's a trap! There is more than just him out there... I heard him talking about others and he also said something about Afterlife," I said, shaking my head and gripping onto him so tightly, as if I never wanted to let go.

"Keira, listen to me, I have dealt with his kind before, do not fear for me but you must stay hidden. Ava is outside. When I leave here, I want you to run over to her, she will keep you safe... do not move, Keira... you understand?" he said, fully aware that I was no longer to be trusted with my own decisions and rightly so, just look where they had gotten me.

"No, you can't go... please don't leave me!" I begged, wrapping my arms around his neck and trying in vain to hold on. He looked down at me and wiped the tears from my frightened face.

"Keira, do you trust me?" His eyes flicked back to their calmer purple and I think this was for my benefit.

"Yes... but..." He kissed me softly before I could finish, filling my mind with ease. I didn't even notice when he had lifted my arms above his head, freeing himself from my hopeless hold. He turned me around showing me where Ava would be waiting.

"Run to her, Keira, run and don't look back. This is something you will not want to see!" he said with the flames reigniting in his eyes as he was now leaving me to face his enemy.

He walked out of the ruined cabin and went around the side to where Sammael's voice came from. As soon as he was out of sight, I made a run for it to where I could see Ava's shadow waiting for me. I tried to run as quickly as I could, but I had to dodge around the rubble on the forest floor, so it took me longer than expected.

She was positioned opposite the cabin at the end of the clearing and when I finally reached her, she wanted me to follow her into the thickness of the forest, but I couldn't move. I could hear Draven's and Sammael's voices clearly, which made me stop in my tracks.

I couldn't leave him!

I hid out of sight as Draven had told me to, but I couldn't help but watch, going against what he had asked of me. They both stood at the side of the cabin and Sammael had his back to the cliff's edge. I found myself hoping he would just step too far and fall putting an ultimate end to this nightmare.

"It has been far too long, My Lord" Sammael said as if this was only going to be a peaceful meeting between colleagues.

"Not long enough it seems, you're back for another lesson seeing as my last one didn't get through," Draven said in an amused tone, it was almost as if he was going to enjoy this. He was stood opposite Sammael, and I had a clear view of them both from the tree I was glued against. Ava was nudging me with her beak again, but there was no way that I was moving from this spot, not until I knew Draven had safely beaten him back to Hell!

"What, this time no guard, no Council, and of course, no Vincent to back you up?" Sammael's bloody teeth snapped together at his pleasure.

"You are distinctly mistaken if you believe I would need anyone else to aid me in damning your soul, sending it back to the Underworld," Draven said with an arrogant smile on his lips.

"Ah well, in that case, let me introduce you to some of my friends... they're just dying to meet you!" Sammael let out a roar into the night, and I could see the mist of black tar flow from out of his mouth as if releasing an infection into the atmosphere. Then the ground started to vibrate as though something was trying to crawl its way through. I backed up closer to the tree and gripped tightly to the bark. I could hear noises from the cliff face as if there were hundreds of creatures scratching their way to the top, making their claws hit the rock like nails on a chalkboard.

The sound made me put my hands over my ears, as they now erupted into a high-pitched shrieking. Ava responded, making her own ear-piercing sound. I wanted to stroke her, comfort her, but one look at her in her Demon form and I chickened out. For one thing, all her feathers had been replaced by cooled volcanic rock, black and splitting at the wings. Red embers glowed beneath, like a raw energy breaking free. Her beak and claws had grown to even deadlier proportions and the moonlight glinted off the razor edges. No, I don't think stroking was a good idea!

Then I saw the creatures as they emerged from over the side, like a swarm of broken people. They were tortured bodies with eyes that had been torn out, leaving gaping, bleeding holes, and the rest of their faces were all locked jaws of huge teeth. Their skin wrinkled and split at the folds, making it look red-raw. They crawled closer to Draven, advancing on the forest floor, their limbs moving independently from the sockets that held them. Their heads rotated all the way around like Demon owls and they made the most disturbing noise, like giant crickets or as though their bones were cracking under each movement.

"Is this the best you could do, Sammael... Gorgon Leeches?" Draven said looking unimpressed and he repositioned himself accordingly, ready for the swarm crawling his way. I held my breath as these gruesome creatures scratched their way closer to the man I loved, and I couldn't understand why he hadn't brought anyone else to help him. Well, it seemed I was about to get my answer, as the first wave got within range.

Draven's body erupted into crimson flames and he used them against the parasites around his feet, setting them alight. They squirmed around, and their high-pitched squealing got deeper and sounded more like howls of pain. Then the flames erupted from his hands coming out in streams, hitting the ones further away and torching their bodies like kindling.

When every creature was alight, he pounded his fiery fist to the ground, making it crack and open up as once again the earth shook from the force. This seemed to release lava-like hands from the ground, as if the tortured souls of Hell had come to collect and to drag the flaming creatures back down to where they belonged.

The hands grasped at the scorched limbs, tearing them from their bodies, and the forest was filled by the cries of agony, ripping flesh and snapping of bone. I felt sick at the sight of hands full of bloody meat and body parts being ripped apart by Hell's residents.

The last wave of leeches were coming over the cliff, and seeing this massacre they took a different approach, spreading out from all angles. These were slightly different looking as their bodies were harder, like frozen blistered stone with blue light coming from their eyes and chapped limbs. It was like the first wave had been the fire and now it was time for the ice!

Draven's body changed at the sight, transforming the red fire that licked at his skin into an inner blue flame that I knew burned the hottest. He then let out an almighty cry into the night, making his body quiver and his flaming sapphire wings open up to their full span. At first, I thought Sammael must have done something to him and I nearly ran over, but then his cry turned into a roar and his head was back looking up in the sky. The clear night changed drastically, as it was now darkened with thunderous clouds making me jump at each crack of lightning that lit up the forest. My mouth dropped open at the sight of him controlling the sky. I was in stunned awe, and now truly believed that this one man could control Heaven itself!

And I was about to witness the proof.

I couldn't help but cry out when Draven was abruptly struck by lightning, making the flames around his body turn into veins of electricity that travelled along his flesh where it belonged. He then used this as he had done the fire. He shot it outwards in thick glowing arcs, picking off each creature in sight. For one unfortunate creature, the power coming from Draven turned into an electric lasso that cut its body in half, turning to dust as the two sides hit the ground.

I watched as now one had crawled onto the side of the log cabin wall, and I didn't think he was going to see it as he was facing the other way. It got closer and leapt out at him with its razor teeth that looked like deadly icicles. As it leapt off the wall it landed on him, sinking its teeth deep into his flesh. This, however, had no effect, as soon as its body made contact, it spasmed, turning into a black charred corpse.

This was then blown back with his impressive wingspan pushing the air outwards. In one massive gush it was taken away by the wind as it evaporated into ash. Draven continued moving his wings until the rest of the black lifeless bodies followed it, being caught in the whirlwind he created. They looked like soot floating away into the stormy night's sky. The clouds then started to evaporate, taking the remains with them, and now all that was left were the two to battle it out.

"Well, Sammael, I have to say that was a little disappointing, I would have thought years of solitude would have taught you more than mere parlour tricks," Draven said, brushing the remaining ash from his bare arms in a casual manner before reclaiming his normal purple energy. His wings then went back into their folded, interlocked position at his back.

"Come, come, now, Draven… that was just foreplay," Sammael replied, as it was now his time to get ready. His clawed wings opened up from around him and shockingly revealed a muscular body under his withered skin. He didn't look as weak as he first appeared to be, and now it looked as though the same power was coursing through his body. Only his was a clear light that was fighting against the Hellish red veins that were trying to take over. I put this down to him once being a servant of God who had turned evil for his own powerful gain.

His body started to shake as if trying to control the energy that was building up from inside his rumbling chest cavity. You could see his veins filled with the two liquids that were trying to mix as they moved to his outstretched hand. It was producing a long staff, growing as his power was adding to its size. It was at least three inches thick and was covered in interlocking symbols that blazed with the same energy. It looked alive, and for all I knew it was part of him.

At this, Draven erupted with a deeper purple and held both hands out at his sides. I then watched in utter shock as his own power burst free in the form of weapons of his own. Out of the two of them, Draven was hands down more equipped, as he now held two massive swords that also looked as if they were part of his body. They came from inside his forearms and grew until they were near the floor. He reminded me of a samurai warrior about to go up against a warlock. My heart was going crazy at the sight, as a human who has spent more years than not seeing the unbelievable... well this was just something else! I didn't want to believe it was real, but couldn't turn my eyes away from the supernatural reality!

Ava had given up trying to get me to follow her, as there was no way I was going to miss this. My eyes were glued to the two glowing figures as they moved around each other, as if calculating where to start. Then, I knew it would be soon as Sammael spoke in what sounded like Latin, and Draven's response sounded deadly.

"Ego te provoco!" ('I provoke you!'... Used as a challenge, 'I dare you' in Latin) Draven growled out, which forced Sammael to make the first move, swinging his huge staff towards Draven's head. But Draven was quicker than my eyes could take in and before I knew it, he was behind Sammael, taking his own shots.

Draven was graceful and moved like a well-choreographed fighter. Sammael was heavy-handed and flung his staff around above his head, making it come crashing down aiming for his opponent. Of course, by the time it came down it would only make contact with the ground forming a small crater from its impact. Then they seemed to change tactics, as now they were fighting at a closer range, making their weapons clash as they connected with each other. Sparks of energy flew out into the dark making it appear as a deadly light show.

At one point I thought Draven had been hit, as half his body fell backwards bending at the knees. But I saw the glowing staff swing round a fraction from Draven's bent body and I realised he was just avoiding it. He quickly pushed his torso back upright, swinging his swords round in both directions and missing Sammael's throat by mere inches. Sammael stumbled backwards but regained his footing, which Draven allowed and waited for. I couldn't believe he did this, as I would have used this as my chance to take him by surprise.

"You have learned some more skills since Belphegor's infusion of powers," Draven said seeming impressed, and now I understood why he waited for him to regain his stance… it was out of respect for his worthy opponent.

"That DOG got more out of it than I! My reasons were pure and yet you took his side!" Sammael spat out at him, and I didn't understand why, but he said it with more pain than hate in his voice.

"You broke the rules, he didn't," Draven said simply as he circled him once again.

"And you? What are you doing that is so different from what I did?"

"She is the Electus! You do not get to speak about my Chosen One!" ('Chosen!' in Latin) he shouted, and it was the first time during this fight that he lost his cool.

"Ah, favoured by the Gods, how very convenient for you!" Sammael snarled in an icy cold voice that made me shudder to my feet.

"I do not have to justify myself to you! You had your orders and you chose to deny them for your own gain, Sammael," he said regaining his control, but this made Sammael's energy turn blood red as his rage doubled.

"I LOVED HER!" he roared, before charging at Draven with his staff held high ready to strike. He ran at him and jumped, giving it the extra height for more of an impact. However, Draven simply crossed his swords above him, counteracting the move and making the sky bright with the lightning produced as the two weapons collided. I couldn't help the little shrieks that came from me as I watched on in horror.

Sammael was getting more frustrated with each attempt at landing a fatal blow on Draven, but he was unstoppable with his flawless technique. Each movement was a dodge followed up by an attack of his own and a lot more got through, making Sammael weaker with each strike of Draven's sword. This made Sammael cry out into the night as he had done in the beginning and again, I felt the ground vibrate.

More of the same creatures soon appeared, and now Draven not only had Sammael to contend with, but now a forest floor covered in what they called Gorgon Leeches. Draven's movements got even faster and I could hardly make out the blur of his glowing shape, twisting and slicing through body after body. Sammael looked as though he had something planned, as he held out one hand and directed some of the others to try and get past Draven… past Draven and straight to *me!*

"Electus!" Sammael shouted at them, and they whipped their rotating heads in my direction and then came scuttling towards me, making their horrible snapping noises as their monstrous teeth ground together. But Draven saw this and reacted before they could get through. He set his blades alight and cut into the ground, making a fiery barricade between them and me. This eliminated most, but one made it through just in time and was now closing in on where I stood shaking in fear!

Ava let out a warning cry to Draven, which made him send out a command of his own.

"AVA ANAR!" ('GO!' in Catalan) Draven shouted, Ava didn't need to be told twice and she took flight in her Demon form. The lava that flowed through her wings made her move at an incredible rate and she swooped down and picked off the Leech that was coming closer to me.

I could just see the bleeding eyes disappearing above me as she carried it off into the night sky. Ava then threw it up and played with it before ripping its limbs off to devour. I put my head down and gagged as I thought I was going to be sick at the sight of its blood being spilt, spraying out in a red mist of death.

Meanwhile, the fight had become even more intense as I watched Sammael smash down his staff, missing Draven, but striking a rock, which then glowed with the same energy from his weapon. It now appeared that it had just erupted from Hell as it bubbled with molten fire.

Draven had caught the staff, landing on it and balancing there before using his feet to grip it. He then twisted his body violently, thus flinging Sammael flying through the air and smashing into the side of the cabin wall. The wood splintered as if a bulldozer had just taken it down.

Sammael in turn picked up the hot boulder and threw it with his powers at Draven, who was quick enough to fly out of its path and land backwards behind the destruction it caused. Draven picked himself off the ground where he landed and straightened up his body before walking over to Sammael.

Draven looked possessed by the Devil himself as he cricked his neck either side as if getting ready for the next round. Sammael, on the other hand, looked as though he was chanting something I couldn't hear, but I could have sworn I saw him touch Morgan's dead body as it could now be seen amongst the rubble. It must have been his first realisation that Morgan could no longer help him in his revenge.

Then before my eyes could focus, Sammael was transported to the other side, next to the forest edge. Once there, he swung his weapon around letting it crash into a massive tree trunk causing it to split and sending at least twenty feet of solid wood to slam down into where Draven stood! It barely missed but it made him lose his footing long enough to be caught off guard. The tree was quickly sent hurtling into Draven's stomach and knocked his body off the cliff, followed by the trunk.

"NO! DRAVEN!" I screamed out as I ran from where I was hiding and launched myself at the edge. I didn't make it far before something caught me around the waist, pulling me back and stopping me from getting to him.

"NO…! LET ME GO!" I screamed at whoever was preventing me from moving, but the hands gripped me tighter until my ribs hurt.

"GET OFF, YOU'RE HURTING ME!" I shouted out through tearful eyes.

"I will do a lot more than hurt you if you don't come with me quietly!" That voice... No, no, no... it just couldn't be! Not again!

"It... It can't be... NO!" I screamed as I felt the cold blade of the knife held against my neck once more.

"That's right, Catherine, I told you I would be seeing you again soon." Morgan's voice sliced through my soul, making me want to finally give up the fight I no longer had the strength for.

I slumped against the cool blade when his next actions penetrated.

"And as you know..." His hand reached up and brutally grabbed a handful of my breast before his foul mouth whispered in my ear...

"I never break my promises."

CHAPTER 54

DRAVEN FINDS DEATH AT HIS HANDS

I screamed out as he bit down on my ear after he reminded me of his promise. Morgan's hand left my breast and clamped over my mouth making it impossible for me to cry out to Ava, who I could no longer see in the sky. Then, with one look to the canyon's edge, my heart burst back to life along with the fight inside me.

I saw Draven's body fly up from the cliff face and come crashing down at Sammael with his swords held out. He came down slicing into Sammael's body, crossing over his blades first through his head then catching his upper body, cutting through his arms and back through his torso. When Draven landed on one knee, his swords held behind him, he looked up to see Sammael's body fall in pieces to the ground.

This just left his black soul, which was trying to form again into a body, but it kept falling in heaps to the ground as it desperately needed a new host. The tar was all that was left, and he was trying to control it. Meanwhile, Draven stood back from him and pounded both his swords into the ground, sending a branched crack to open the Earth's crust. Once again this released a horde of tortured souls to take what was left of Sammael.

While this was happening, I got my chance to make my own move. Morgan was moving backwards towards the other side of the cabin, but he lost his footing on the rubble making the knife lower from my neck slightly. This was enough for me to stamp down hard on his foot, causing his hand to release my mouth.

"DRAVEN, HELP!" I screamed until my lungs gave out. Draven turned in anger at the sight of Morgan dragging me away from him. He pulled his arms back, his chest expanded and with his head thrown back to the sky he let out an almighty Hell-raising roar. I couldn't help but rejoice in Morgan's shaky hands, as he was most likely terrified at the sight of Draven's flaming body coming towards him. But then something happened, making Draven's body go crashing into where I had been hiding, causing the forest to shake under the exploding impact!

I screamed under Morgan's hand that clawed to my lips trying to keep me quiet. Sammael had used whatever power he had left and hurled himself onto Draven's body and was now attacking it. The black tar clung onto his skin as if trying to get inside and consume his soul. I could feel the blade cutting my neck slightly as I tried to fight to get away and go over to help him, not really knowing what I would do when I got there. But Morgan was doing everything in his power to try and control me, making my feet bleed where he was dragging me along and tearing the skin on my bare soles.

Meanwhile, Draven was fighting Sammael, trying desperately to get to me also. Draven's hand reached out to me, and I focused on the tips of his fingers trying in vain to touch my own. I pulled against Morgan as I too stretched out my arm in a despairing way, but we couldn't reach each other. It was as if time was standing still as our eyes met and tears fell from mine as I saw him mouth the words,

"I'm coming for you."

His body then fought even harder, rolling around as he tried to regain back control over the black ooze that was still trying to take over. Then Draven seized his opportunity by pounding his fist to the ground making the Earth split right beside him, once again releasing the tortured hands. They wasted no time in reaching up to Sammael's body which Draven had suspended over the gap. The hands found the black soul they had come for and peeled it off Draven like meat from the bone. It was like watching the hands of hungry beasts as their claws dug deep into Draven's body, tearing back out handfuls of Sammael's damaged, evil soul.

"Non Omnis Moriar!" Sammael's black form shouted out into the night! ('I shall not die. Not all of me will Die,' a phrase expressing the belief that a part of the speaker will survive beyond death in Latin)

"NO, BUT YOUR SOUL WILL LIVE ROTTING IN TARTARUS!" Draven thundered back as there wasn't much left of Sammael's infected soul left to be taken. Then Sammael let out a spine chilling laugh as if there was something Draven was missing.

"My soul may be taken but as for your Chosen One, well we will soon see if the Gods favour her mangled body at the bottom of the ravine!" Sammael spat out, and I could just make out this last threat as I was still in range to hear. Morgan had stopped pulling me as he had reached his destination… *the cliff's edge.*

"Afterlife, Draven! The boy has served me well… shame Is Reputo Is Has Pennae!" ('The boy thinks he has wings!' In Latin) Sammael said still laced with laughter in his voice, as the rest of his soul was sucked, ripped and dragged back down into the Underworld.

"I will live… on… you will… see!" His last words spluttered up in the last black gurgle before Sammael was no more.

"NO!" Draven screamed out as the Earth closed over Sammael's black soul. Draven reacted by flipping his body into the air and flying over, opposite to where Morgan had me held captive. He landed, making the ground shake, but it wasn't enough to cause Morgan to lose his footing as he planned. The knife started to dig further in, and I cried out in pain, preventing Draven from risking coming closer.

"Stay there or I will KILL HER!" Morgan screamed after proving his point, and Draven held up his hands as if to try and reason with him.

"Okay... Okay but just watch the fucking edge!" Draven warned, and it was the first time I had seen real fear in his eyes.

"You can't have her! She belongs to me and this way we will be together forever!" Morgan cried as his voice shook under the strain.

"You don't want to hurt her, not if you love her!" Draven stated, but it was no use against Morgan's infected mind, he was too far gone to ever find his way back to the land of reason.

"YOU DON'T GET TO TELL ME WHAT TO DO, RICHARD!" Morgan screamed with his clouded mind consumed by hate. Oh God! He wasn't looking at Draven... he was looking at Richard, and it wasn't me he was holding in his arms...nit was his sister, Catherine.

"I'm not going to kill her! I am going to take her away, so you can't have her, Sammael gave me a gift and I am going to use it!" he said as he dragged me closer to the edge. I could feel the wind blowing up the side of the canyon. I turned to look down at my rocky grave and felt the fresh tears rise.

"Morgan, listen to me, Sammael lied to you, his plan was for you to kill yourself and take the one thing I love with you! You don't have any powers!" he spoke urgently as he stepped closer, but this made things worse, putting Morgan into a boiling rage.

"YOU LIE! He said I was doing God's work. He said if I let you kill me, that God would bring me back and you would get punished for taking her away from me! Well, here I am. And you don't have the powers to enter my mind and stop me!" he ranted on at him, causing my chest to become tight as I knew this was to be my fate.

"You're right, I can't enter your mind which means you have a choice, Douglas, and that choice will decide your fate on the other side, for you will die if you try and *take her from me!*" His Demon came through at the end, as if it could no longer be contained and kept back from the exchange.

"Is that so, Demon?!" Morgan had one hand held securely around the handle of his blade that he held so close to my throat, that my blood trickled down it. His other hand wanted to taunt

Draven, who watched as Morgan's fingers invaded the skin on my body as he fumbled to get down below.

"PIG!" I spat out as I twisted away from him, making the blade pierce my neck deeper. Draven's Demon growl deepened and looked close to breaking free.

"Was she this feisty for you, when you fucked her?" he asked laughing, making Draven's body vibrate with rage.

"Well, it looks like I will find out for myself... say goodbye to your Demon lover, my little whore!"

"Dominic, no...! I'm sorry...! I love you!" I shouted out as I knew my fate had finally come when Morgan gripped me tightly around the waist and he made us both lean backwards, plunging us over into the deep abyss of the night.

"KEIRA! NOOO!" Draven's voice echoed, bouncing off the cliff face, making it the last sound I would ever hear as I fell to my death.

I knew this was my time. It would soon all be over, and the one thing I knew for certain was that I wasn't yet ready to face my own...

Afterlife alone.

CHAPTER 55
TIME FOR THE ANGELS

I could feel Morgan's hands release their hold, as now my body was falling independently towards death below. I wasn't as scared as I thought I would have been. No, instead I was covered in a warm blanket of security as my fate came closer to take me. I kept my eyes closed as I wanted the last thing my eyes to see was Draven and I held onto it tightly in my mind as I felt the pressure of the air push my tears back to my hairline.

It was strange to know death was but seconds away. Not anything like the first time. And if I was being brutally honest with myself, I had known all along that when I slit my wrists that it wasn't the end but now, well that was different.

So bitterly different.

Now, it felt like a cruel twist in a life lived with a sight into an unknown world of darkness, only to finally find my light in Draven, to then have that light extinguished. Yes, it was cruel indeed, but I also couldn't help thinking that I wouldn't have changed one thing of that life lived, if my prize at the end was those few short days with Draven in my life. That had been my balance, with Morgan and Demons on one side of the scale, and with Draven and Angels on the other.

Draven was my reason. He was the only thought I held onto, my last link to the world. He was my anchor to the other side. My beacon

671

to follow, and I don't know how, but I just knew that he would make sure I would arrive to wherever it was the Gods deemed as my fate.

But, although I was dying at peace, there was no mistaking the piece of my heart I left behind on that cliff face.

Dominic Draven.

The man I was obsessed with. The man who had changed me. Not just fixed me but made me so much more. The Man, the Angel, the Demon and the Lord.

Dominic Draven. The man I loved.

Always.

~

Then it happened and I... *I died.*

I felt the impact my body made with the ground and was thankful I was at least spared from the pain. I started floating up to what must be Heaven and wondered if this was because of who Draven thought I was... *the Chosen One.*

I couldn't help the sob that was torn from me at the thought of the man I loved, knowing I would never see him again. No, now it didn't feel Heavenly, it flipped on its axis feeling more like Hell! I was gasping for the air I no longer needed and the warmth I could feel got closer around my skin. I still didn't want to open my eyes, but I was sure I could feel something touching me, gripping onto my body taking it upwards.

Is that what happened? Had the Angels come to take my soul away from Draven's heart? I knew I shouldn't, but I couldn't help myself cry out goodbye to my only love.

"I don't want to leave Draven. I want to say goodbye... please let me say goodbye to him." I couldn't help the plea that escaped. I wanted to remain strong. Strong enough to let go.

"Keira, he's gone, he's dead!" A Heavenly voice spoke, and I burst into tears pushing my face into the body that held me.

"Draven..." I said his name like a prayer to the Gods and muscle-bound arms pulled my body tighter into his own, making my skin tingle and flood with warmth.

I was in Draven's arms once more and knew this must be my gift, they were letting me say goodbye.

"I know I mustn't have long, but you have to know... I love you... and...and I will always love you... God knows I don't want to say goodbye, Draven, I'm scared. I don't want to leave you!" I was spluttering the words out amongst sobs that I couldn't control. I didn't want this to be the last voice of mine he heard but I couldn't help it... I needed him so badly!

"KEIRA! Keira, listen to me, you're not going anywhere! I have you safe and I would never let you fall!" His voice was stern but held a soft edge as he was trying to make me understand.

"I'm not... *not dead?"* I asked, letting myself hope as I had never hoped before.

"NO! Of course not! Keira, I caught you... wings remember?" he said, and this made me cry out with a relief that I couldn't believe I was allowed to feel. I stupidly opened my eyes, and screamed out at the sight of being hundreds of feet up in the air with the black forest below. Draven cradled me in his arms, but he shook me a little trying to get me to look back at him.

"Keira, don't look, close your eyes until I tell you, or you really will be sick and that won't be pleasant for either one of us," he said with a bit of humour in his voice. I did as I was told, not having any want to see how high up I was, as my fear of heights made me feel nauseous. I could now feel the motion of his wings moving up and down and then gliding, catching the current of the wind. Because of the height, the wind hit our bodies with a greater force but the heat that coursed through him kept us both warm.

I had both my arms around his neck, and interlocked my fingers to hold on tighter. I nestled my head into his shoulder and the side of his neck, breathing in his intoxicating scent.

"I thought I was going to lose you," he said in the saddest voice I had ever heard from his sweet lips.

"I thought I had lost you too and wasn't going to get a chance to say goodbye," I said, and my reply was muffled as my head was buried safely into his neck.

"Is that what you meant when you said you didn't want to leave?" he asked, and I was shocked, what else could he have thought I meant.

"Yes of course but what else…?"

"I thought you meant Morgan," Draven said, pleased he had it wrong.

"So, Morgan's definitely dead then?" I asked holding my breath at the name that just left my lips for the last time!

"Oh yeah, and trust me when I say he is most definitely gone," he said gritting his teeth at the mention of him. I shuddered at the thought of his mangled broken bloody corpse on the rocks below.

"So, that means I'm free… I am finally free!" I said lifting my head up seeing his huge wings gracefully moving in the night air, catching the moonlight on his silky dark feathers. I also caught a glimpse of what must have been Ava flying close behind us and I smiled at the sight.

"Yes, you are, he is never coming to get you again, Keira. I can promise you that," he said kissing my head as my hair flew around his neck, touching his bare back.

"Now, let's get you home." His voice sounded tired from worry and now finally saying this brought us closure, making the nightmare end. But I just snuggled closer, and said in a satisfied voice,

"I am already home, Draven, I'm with you." He tensed his hold over me, and hummed tenderly in my ear,

"Home," causing a single tear to form. We descended down through the sky. He held me tighter and my stomach felt as if it was moving up into my throat. The same feeling you get in an aeroplane coming into land. But unlike a conventional flight, I didn't realise when we were safely back on the ground as his feet came in contact with the balcony outside his bedchamber.

"Keira, my love, you can open your eyes now," he said, chuckling softly as he tried to pry my fingers from his neck. He placed my feet on the ground, and I couldn't help but cry out in pain as the pressure to the cut skin beneath hurt at the slightest touch.

"Oh, Keira," he said lifting me again, holding me by the waist.

"It's okay, I will be fine to walk," I said through my teeth, as my feet were still stinging.

"Oh no, Keira, you won't as there is no need to be brave now, my little fighter," he said carrying me through the glass doors inside to a well-lit room. I couldn't help but cringe, as I must have looked as awful as I felt. He walked up to the bed and placed me gently down as if I was going to break into a million pieces. I had my feet hung over the sides like a child on a seat that was too big for me. Then the door burst open with Vincent striding in followed by Sophia.

Oh great, just what I wanted, an audience to add to my shame. Here I was, looking like a broken doll in a dress ripped to shreds, when Draven looked his usual Godlike self, completely unscathed and not a mark on him.

It shocked me seeing Vincent in his angelic form, glowing white with a huge pair of pure white wings, which came forwards at the bottom and curled upwards around the front of him. This was truly breath-taking, as it was the first time I had seen him like this. However, when Sophia followed him in, it was also breath-taking, but for another reason.

She too was in her other form, which shamefully unnerved me the most, as I had only seen her once as a Demon and that was from a distance. Now however, she was coming closer to me, and I had to use every ounce of self-control I had not to pull away. Her desert hard skin looked painful and her lips were split higher up her cheeks as if they had been cut either side. I swallowed hard as the soulless eyes took me in, they must change depending on her mood, because this time they were onyx black and void of any white. It was almost as if they had been injected with the ink that had started to spread out like poison under the skin.

Now, seeing her like this, I noticed something else I hadn't that night and that was she too had a pair of wings. Only the reason I hadn't seen them that night became clear, as they weren't your typical version of what her brothers had. No, Sophia's wings were like shadowy grey smoke that followed her back, always keeping their shape. The dark vapour came up over her head into sharp points and like Vincent's, also curled up slightly in front of her. They were fascinating to watch and reminded me of trapped smoke in a glass cage.

I didn't want her to know I felt this trepidation around her, so I concentrated hard on the Sophia I knew and loved like a sister, and that's when it happened! The strength inside me reached its full limit and I pushed harder than ever before with the love I had for Sophia, making her turn back to her human self. I didn't know how I did it but when I looked at each one it had affected my sight on all three of them. Now when Sophia came at me, I could finally breathe freely at the gorgeous Sophia I knew.

"Oh, by the Gods, Keira, are you alright?" Sophia ran up to me and hugged me tightly making my now bruised body ache, and I couldn't help the air that I sucked through my teeth.

"Oh sorry, sorry!" she said letting me go, and Draven shot her a look of disapproval. But she walked straight up to him and hit him with an almighty punch to the face, cracking his head back and to the side, while Vincent stood with his arms folded. I was in complete shock at the sight of a little doll attacking a bear and getting away with it. And man did she have one hell of a right hook!

"That's for your arrogant pig-headed mind, thinking you didn't need any help! Just look at her!" She pointed at me and shouted at him while Vincent finally took a step towards her to calm her temper.

"Sophia, it wasn't his fault... I was the one who was fooled, please don't blame him," I pleaded, and I tried to get up but as soon as my feet touched the steps around the bed Vincent's arms were around me grabbing me upright, so that I wouldn't fall. His face was hard lines that spoke of his controlled temper, but it wasn't at me, this was directed over his shoulder at his brother, as he must have thought the same way his sister did.

"Are you in a lot of pain, Keira?" he asked, placing me back down on the bed as softly as his brother had.

"No, I'm fine but please don't blame him," I said with pleading eyes as I looked into his Angelic crystal eyes.

"Keira, they are both right to be angry. I shouldn't have underestimated Sammael. You got hurt because of my arrogance and for this, I cannot be forgiven," Draven said as he turned away from us all at his own shame. My guilt was too much to bear and it made me shout at everyone!

"Look this is stupid! It's over now and what's done is done! But listen to me when I say this was my own damn fault, and if I had told you all the truth about who had called, then this could have been avoided! Now if you don't forget all this and drop it right now, I will leave and I won't come back until you all start blaming the right person... ME!" I shouted as my own temper was getting out of control. They were staring at me now in disbelief, and so this forced me to make my point as I rose off the bed and winced at the pain that shot through my feet. But Draven was now the one who flashed to my side picking me back up and putting me down on the bed.

"Keira, stop! You will hurt yourself even more!" he said holding me still.

"And I will, but only if you all stop pointing the blame at the one person who saved my life," I said, looking from Vincent to Sophia and finally back at Draven.

"You're right. It is not necessary to keep torturing the girl with events that have already taken place, but, Dominic, you must stop acting as though she only means something to you and you alone. You brought her into *all* our lives, so then you must learn to accept joint responsibility for her safety. No doubt this won't be the end of the difficulties having her involved in our world means. Let us help you both." Vincent came over to place his loyal hand on his brother's shoulder, and it was emotional to see the love they not only had for him but for me also.

"Yeah, Dom, why do you get to have all the fun? The one time I could have kicked ass in years, and you deny us both the opportunity, pulling that leader and head of the family bullshit!"

Sophia ranted, and I couldn't help but cough down a chuckle at the thought of her fighting. But then, after the punch I witnessed her land on her huge brother, I could very well see her coming in handy.

"Right, now that's all cleared up, could someone please get me some bloody tequila 'cause I was lying about the whole not being in pain thing!" I said, and Draven wasn't the only one who frowned.

"Right, I think we need to be alone for this next part." He especially looked at Sophia as he said this, and I knew he was going to heal me the way he did last time. Only he didn't know that I had the sight since Sammael had touched me.

All this time he must have thought I had just seen him and Andy fighting, without witnessing all the Leeches that were attacking. I couldn't help but laugh out loud as he was trying to save me from seeing what Sophia looked like as a Demon! After everything I had just seen I found this close to hilarious.

"Keira, what's wrong?" Draven asked as though he was not only concerned for my physical health but now my mental health as well.

"Draven, I have had the sight ever since Sammael touched me and made me see! I saw everything that happened back there." As soon as I said this, Draven's face dropped like it was the worst thing that could have ever happened. He actually looked pale for the first time, and added to this was mortification when I held out my arm to show him what had been done. The red marks still remained from where Sammael had cut me open to force the power of sight into me.

I looked towards Sophia who gasped and turned to hide away. This instantly made me feel ashamed that I had thought badly of her Demon form. After all it was who she was, and I should have just accepted it to begin with.

"Sophia, please don't turn away," I pleaded, wanting to go over to her but Draven still had his arms around me keeping me on the bed. She still held her head down and my guilt was overwhelming.

"Keira, can you still see us?" Draven asked his face full of concern.

"No, I have learnt to control it. I just pushed it out like I usually do, and you all changed back. So you see, Sophia, you don't need to hide from me, and anyway I saw you long ago as a Demon," I said shocking them all. She turned back to look at me and I could almost see the tears in her dark eyes.

"When?" she asked shaking her head as if she didn't believe me.

"I saw you that night after Layla stabbed me, I was outside on the balcony when you turned up looking for me." This new information made her laugh with disbelief.

"But, Keira, all this time you have still acted the same towards me, what you saw in me must have frightened you?"

"I won't lie it did at first, but I knew you were still you, no matter what you looked like on the outside, my feelings would still remain the same... you're my friend and like a sister," I said with tears welling up.

She marched right over to me and hugged me, but this time being more careful of my body that was slowly turning different shades of blue and purple.

"Thank you," she whispered in my ear, and she turned to her brother and said sweetly,

"Take care of her, Dom," before departing with Vincent through the door they came in, leaving me alone with Draven. His hand caught a stray tear that fell down my cheek and I turned to face him.

"Why didn't you tell me?" he asked softly as he was examining the shallow cut on my neck from Morgan's blade.

"I guess because I didn't think it was that big of a deal, and after nearly a lifetime of seeing your kind... well, now I guess I just understand it better. It doesn't affect me anymore, not like it used to." This was the truth, after years of not understanding and asking endlessly why me? Well, now I knew why, and all those years of terrified tears and hiding myself from being seen, now I knew there was a reason for it. And that reason didn't include me having to hide any longer. Because now I had a Demon at my back and that Demon I would never hide from. For now, I also had the light of an Angel to guide me through the shadows of my past who would never give me the chance to hide.

So, with a Demon at my back and an Angel leading the way, I could not be happier that these two great forces created one undeniable strength that stood at my side.

The man I loved…

Draven.

CHAPTER 56

HOME & WANTED

"Anyway, so what's the diagnosis, Doc?" I said trying to add a bit of humour to the situation, but he just frowned at me.

"You're a mess, my Keira," he said with frustration and I winced at this.

"Is it that bad?" I said giving him my best wide-eyed puppy look which amazingly seemed to work as his eyes relaxed and the crease on his forehead smoothed.

"Still beautiful, but a mess all the same, however I will soon fix that. Hold very still, okay?" he said as his hand went to my neck, as I gathered he needed an open wound for this supernatural voodoo to work.

I couldn't help but close my eyes as I felt the heat rush through my body using my veins as transportation. I arched my spine and my head fell backwards at the intense feelings produced. Draven lowered me back on the bed, so my head could find support. I could feel every muscle in my body relax as the energy inside me started to regenerate new cells and sparking them into healing the rest of me. My feet stretched out as it made its way down to them, and I could almost feel the cuts closing up giving me a tingling feeling just like pins and needles.

It made me feel drunk with euphoria as my mind swam in an ocean of warm energy making my skin change from warm to cold, over and over, again and again like waves touching the shore. It was Draven's touch that brought me back to reality. His hand slid up my side creating a different blissful feeling, one I wanted more than air. I let out a moan and the sound of his laughter made me open my eyes to find him smiling down at me.

"Feeling better, I presume?" he said with a cocky grin.

"Yeah, I'll say! Thanks for that but did you have to turn me on when I look like this?" I said laughing and covering my face with my hands to conceal my blush.

"I wasn't aware it had that effect and there is nothing wrong with the way you look." Was he joking? I looked down at what he could see. I let out a startled gasp at the sight. It was just as if the night had never happened! I was wearing the dress as though I had just put it on moments ago. I sat up too quickly, making my head spin.

"Careful," he warned but I was just amazed to find not only my dress intact but also my hair was the same as it had been. I could even feel the makeup that Sophia had put on me. It was as if I had never left the club. I laughed as my skin was now glowing a healthy shade rather than the bruised blue it had been.

"Oh, you're good," I teased turning to face him smiling. He just shrugged his shoulders as if it had been no trouble, but I could see the hidden smile behind that confident expression.

"I will be expecting a reward, not everything I do for you is for free," he teased back as he placed his hands on my face, pulling my lips to his. As soon as I tasted his mouth, I inhaled his scent making it hard to breathe. I could feel the energy that was still inside me, bursting with desire to have him take me. But almost as soon as I thought it, his hands released me and I let out a moan of a different kind, one he laughed at.

"I don't think we should push your body any more tonight, it has been through enough, and with you looking the way you do, I don't think I could control myself," he said, swallowing hard as his eyes scanned my body with hungry intent. I frowned at him and my disappointment was as clear as day.

"Don't look at me like that, Keira, you need rest not a full-body workout." He got up, swiped a hand roughly through his hair and left me on the bed as if to help control himself. A control I was trying to destroy like it was my enemy, and boy, did I know just how to do it!

"Fine, if you won't give me what I want!" I pouted before doing the unthinkable.

"Keira, what are you…" he started, but my next actions cut him off. I lay back down and started to lift my skirt slowly, feeling the warm skin on the inside of my legs. I moved my fingertips up them slowly and I licked my lips as I closed my eyes. I soon got closer up to where my pleasure burned, and my head went back on the pillow the second I made contact. I arched my body with the mounting pleasure.

I heard a low growl before I felt my wrists being restrained above my head and Draven was now on top of me. He held me down pressing them hard into the pillows above. I couldn't keep the satisfied grin from my face.

"Nobody pleasures this body but me… do you understand?" He ground himself against me making me bite my lip in response.

"Answer me, Keira!" he commanded in that controlled velvet voice that had my head spinning with incoherent thoughts. He pushed his hard length against me, grinding the head to rub in a delicious way that made me moan and writhe underneath him.

"Keira!" he warned, this time in a deeper growl. I knew I had him just where I wanted him but still, I pushed. I pulled my body up as far as it would go being restrained and whispered in his ear,

"Don't you have a promise to keep?" I finished by licking my lips, caressing his ear with my tongue.

"And you say you're not a temptress," he whispered back in mine before biting my neck, still keeping me restrained. Moments ago this would have hurt like hell but after Draven's energy was transferred inside me, my body felt stronger than ever before, and well, I wanted to show off my new power. Although the power of seduction I had in mind had quickly turned tables on me.

"It's not my fault your will is weak," I said, before biting him back playfully on the neck making him let out his own moan, which was more satisfying to hear than I could ever explain.

"You're right, my will, because of you, is nothing more than the ruins you leave crumbling around this bed. You hold all the power when it comes to my heart, Keira," he said seductively before proving I didn't exactly hold all the power after all. Not when he grabbed my fresh new dress with two hands over my heaving chest before ripping it off my body leaving me in just the deep purple underwear I had picked for this occasion.

This was no doubt done to prove the point that I was definitely not as in control as I acted. His eyes scanned every material covered curve, and for once he was the one to bite his lip first, granting me with just a hint of fang. Then I jumped when on a rumble his Demon form broke out, clearly ready to play. He looked up at me with purple fire in his eyes.

"Scared?" he said through an evil, wicked grin as he pulled me up by my arms till I was level with his face.

"Terrified," I mocked back before crushing my lips to his in excitement. I heard the sound of my underwear being torn away, feeling the sharp tug of impatience as the last barrier between us was eliminated. My legs wrapped around his waist and I held my body there using my new strength with ease. His hands held my backside and lifted me the right height before lowering me down as another kind of energy filled me.

I let out a burst of moans not wanting to contain my bliss from him making his teeth find my shoulder. He held my skin in his mouth, trying to fight the urge to bite down. So, when I turned my neck to the side submissively, I made the decision for him, as he sank his teeth deep into my skin, making the pain quickly turn into the most incredible sensations of rapture. Each pull of my life's essence being consumed by Draven was pulling me deeper into my pending orgasm until I was so close, I screamed out my objections when he stopped.

"Draven... I... I... need..." I begged shamelessly but his hoarse voice cut me off.

"I've got what you need," he said against the part on my

neck he had been drinking from and I felt his wet lips on my skin where my blood still flowed. His tongue then licked me clean, sealing the bite which sent beautiful shivers down my neck and back, making me shudder in his hold.

Then he showed me exactly what I needed as he powered into me over and over, leaving me with no other option than to hold on tight and let him ravish every last bit of me. This got even more intense when he pushed our bodies up against the wall behind the bed, pinning me against the wooden frame. Again, I thought this would have hurt me if his power inside me wasn't making me stronger and able to accept his Demon form making love to me now.

His wings help him push into me, and with every deep thrust his feathers shivered in a stimulated sequence. He held his entire body flush with mine, moving away only to pound himself back into me, punishing me with pure bliss and making me scream with the building pressure. It felt like his steel arms were the only thing keeping me from exploding and floating away.

"Say you're mine, Keira!" he growled in my neck. I couldn't believe he wanted me to speak now. I tried but I couldn't think about anything other than what his body was doing to mine.

"Say it! Speak the words *NOW!*" He was losing control and my body trembled under his hold as his Demon voice vibrated the last word on my skin.

"Y...yes... I'm *yours!*" I screamed out as my orgasm rocketed to the surface and shot out of me thundering my insides.

"MINE!" he roared, throwing his head back like the wild Demonic beast he was as he too found his release. His one hand on the bed splintered the wood as his fingers crushed the frame with his own pleasure, while thankfully the other hand on my body wasn't so brutal.

Time had been lost as our bodies were locked in fire and ice of sexual energy and when he finally laid me down to allow my body to convulse with exploding ecstasy, I knew it had finished.

"Did I hurt you?" His worried voice brought me back to his arms and his hands that were exploring my shoulder for any marks he'd left. I grabbed his hand and placed it over my beating heart.

"Not unless this gives out on me!" I said laughing as it felt it would beat right through bone, flesh and skin. He brushed back my hair that had fallen in front of my face and kissed my wet forehead.

"I would never let that happen," he said softly as if the very thought of it hurt him to think about.

We lay in each other's arms enjoying the sweet aftermath of unbelievably carnal sex, just listening for the point when our hearts and lungs worked at a calmer rate. Draven had left my body's heat and after making me drink some fluids and 'taking care' of me again, I decided now was a good time to get his side of the story from him.

"Draven, I have to ask, how did you find me?" I said as it was something that I had been wondering ever since I saw him outside the cabin.

"Whilst you were fooling Sophia into believing that phone call had been nothing, I was with Takeshi when I first realised what was going to happen." He sat up to face me, ready to tell me what happened on his side whilst I was being taken by Morgan and Sammael.

"You see, Takeshi is one of the Guardians. He is a powerful Angel who has a unique foresight of our kind. I had him watching out for signs of Sammael's activities, but he was being blocked by his power. Of course, this was until Sammael showed him what he wanted me to see." He spoke as he played with a curly strand of my hair that hung down my bare shoulder.

"What did he see?" I asked as if I was listening to a fairy tale more than the horror story it had been.

"He saw Sammael and me fighting in the forest, but he couldn't make out a precise location although he knew it was going to be tonight. Well as soon as I saw what he envisioned, it suddenly hit me that I couldn't feel you anymore, as if you were no longer in Afterlife. It was soon confirmed, as by the time I got back to the table you were nowhere in sight. I went a bit insane at Sophia," he said looking guilty at his memories, so I didn't ask although I wanted to.

"She told me how you'd had a phone call from Frank, and she explained the story you told her. I have to say I am slightly impressed at your acting skills, knowing what a bad liar you usually are, for you to fool a Demon like Sophia, well that is a power in its own right," he said, making my cheeks red from the intense stare his dark eyes gave me.

"Don't misunderstand me, I am still extremely angry at you for disobeying me like that! What were you thinking?" he asked lifting my chin up as I hung my head in shame.

"I'm sorry, but I knew you would never have let me go and I thought my sister needed me! She means the world to me, Draven, and when I was found in the hospital after being held by Morgan, she was there for me... she took a flight that night to get to me, so she could be there when I woke up," I said getting tearful from the memory.

"I understand, but why didn't you wait for me?"

"Would you have let me go?" I said, already knowing the answer to this question.

"No, of course not but I would have checked it was authentic and then driven you there myself, if it was the truth." To this I had no argument, at the time all my common sense went out of the window, being replaced by blind love for my sister.

"You have to promise me right now, you will never do that to me again! I have never been so worried in all my life and trust me when I say that is a long time." His fingers held on to me as though never wanting to part with me ever again.

"I promise I will be more careful next time."

"Next time? Why, do you plan on getting kidnapped again anytime soon?" he said sarcastically tilting his head to one side.

"Well, no, but this is me we're talking about... magnet for trouble remember?" I said playfully flicking him on the nose, but he just shook his head at me.

"That won't happen again, Keira," he said this as a warning to all that may try, as I remembered when he first told me about the dangers I would face for being the one he loves.

"So what happened next?" I asked, trying to bring him back down from his heavy breathing at the thought of me being taken again.

"Well, when I rang Frank and he told me everything was fine and how he hadn't called, that's when I knew Sammael had used Frank's voice to lure you into his trap. So to say I found my inner fury would be a huge understatement, I was blind with rage! I had the club searched for any clues but there was no trace! I had Ava searching the skies to find you but there was nothing." His eyes flickered purple as he remembered the feeling, then they grew softer at the next part of the story.

"Then that boy Jack came forward. He was trying to get up here to see me. One of my men caught him sneaking in. He was shouting about you, and I had him brought to me at once. That's when he explained and handed me your note, which honourably he hadn't read. This is what saved your life," he said as my mind went to Jack and how hard that must have been for him to do, and from the look of things Draven knew this too.

"This was all Takeshi needed to fit that last piece to his vision. He saw Sammael using the policeman's body as a host and then he was able to see the cabin. The rest you know…" he said about to finish this last sentence over my lips. Then the terrible thought came to my mind and I shouted,

"What about the policeman, Andy, I mean the real one?!" Draven frowned as if he really didn't want to tell me but when I nudged him, he lowered his eyes before speaking the sad truth.

"Keira, I am sorry to tell you this, but he is dead. Sammael killed him before entering his body days ago. There was nothing we could have done to change this." I could feel the tears well up at the thought of anyone but Morgan losing their life during these terrifying events, but it made it all the worse because he was a good friend of Frank's. He was going to be crushed!

I closed my eyes, and Draven caught the tear that ran from one and then kissed me softly as though I could break at any moment. Then my mind raced back to another fear, as it seemed to be my night for causing problems.

"But wait, what about Celina?" I said pulling away from

him, which he didn't like at all as his eyebrows knitted together and his strong jawline flexed. So, before he answered, he pulled my head closer to finish the kiss. This made me want to chuckle, after all Draven was very much used to getting his own way. He then continued after his lips left mine.

"Yes, well the boy... I mean Jack, well he of course saw Celina."

"Oh no, poor Jack!" I said feeling even more guilty at the trouble I had caused everyone. How could I have been so stupid, I should have given it to Mike or Jerry, anyone but Jack!

"Do not worry yourself, Keira, I have taken care of it."

"And what does that mean?" I said, getting a bad feeling about what had been done to Jack.

"Give me some credit, Keira, I am not going to harm the boy who helped me save the most important thing in my life! No, I took your advice and allowed the boy to find closure. I allowed Celina time with him to explain her reasons. So alright, not the full truth behind them, but close enough for him to move on." At this I threw my arms around his neck and kissed him all over.

"Thank you," I said, seeing the softer side to Draven's humanity come out. He held the back of my head with his strong hand as he rested my head in its little nook next to his bare shoulder. I couldn't help but be happy that at least one good thing had come out of tonight's events, but I wasn't about to disclose my feelings on this to Draven, who would no doubt, disagree with me on the matter.

"Can I ask something else?" This was a question I had wanted to know since I had told Draven the truth about my past.

"Of course," he said as if he would give me anything I asked for.

"How did you find out about my past and why?" I leant away from him, wanting to judge his expression for the answers he gave.

"What brought this on?" he said, but I frowned and shook my head.

"Let's just say that after tonight I want to find my own

closure but first, I would like some answers so that I can move on." He nodded taking this as what it was... *something I needed.*

"Alright, what would you like to know first?"

"Why? I mean, why go to all the trouble?" I asked looking down at my arms and found the marks that Sammael had made were now gone.

"Keira, after the very first time I saw you in the forest, I did everything in my power to find out all about you. I needed to know, but of course with the help of the authorities, you had changed your name, so you made this difficult... even for me. I couldn't understand at first why I couldn't find anything, then I realised you were hiding something when you never came to work without gloves. You even slept with them on and I knew the reasons you gave were false."

"What do you mean?" I asked looking confused, but he smiled as though this was amusing.

"You would always say you were cold or had bad circulation to those around you, but Keira, I could feel for myself the blood around your body and the warmth from your skin to know this wasn't true... Just as I can feel the heat in your cheeks now with your embarrassment." Of course, this made it worse even thinking about it.

"You don't know what that does to me, every time I came near you I would watch the blood turn your soft skin into a rose I couldn't touch... it was close to unbearable, as all I wanted was to have you for myself, but I couldn't as you weren't yet mine to have. So, I needed to find out everything. I would have Sophia drill you for any information she could get but you never gave away anything about your past. So, I had to be content with knowing your likes and dislikes." His face fascinated me, and I thought back to all the times I wished I knew things about him. Of course, I didn't have the means like he did.

"I bet face planting into your crotch that day at college didn't help then?" I joked at possibly the most embarrassing moment I'd had with Draven. His eyes slid to me, and I got a knowing grin that on Draven was one of the most handsome sights to see.

"I must confess, you certainly knew how to hit your mark with that one!" I laughed and playfully flicked his bicep.

"Okay, so getting back on track, how did you finally find out?" I asked referring to my real identity.

"After that night you got stabbed, all my fears about you working the VIP came true and I knew I would have to hurt you to protect you. It was the only way and it worked better than I could ever have imagined." His deep eyes looked like the midnight ocean as the memories came back. I placed my hand on his face bringing his eyes to meet mine.

"I understand why, you don't have to torture yourself over it any more, not now I'm here."

"As long as you know I would never put you through that again... *Ever,*" he said forcefully, and the truth in his eyes confirmed this strong statement. I nodded till his frown vanished.

"You see, after that night I vowed I would leave you to live your life, only to watch you from afar. So, if you ever needed my help then I would intervene, but one night it got too much, and then an opportunity presented itself when you called to make an appointment with Doctor Goff..." I frowned at the memory.

"Please don't look at me like that, Keira, I know this was a great violation of your privacy but understand that I had been doing this ever since you arrived." Once again it was like hearing the confession of a personal stalker, one that I was more than happy to have. I couldn't be mad, as I knew that if I'd had the same opportunity, I would have done the very same thing to feed my addiction.

"So, when you told me the dream, I knew what you had done... well thought you had done anyway. So that night I knew after the pills I had given you, there wouldn't be a chance for you to wake up while I was there, but one thing I didn't expect was for you to be talking in your sleep." At this I nearly died with shame!

"Oh no!" I said before burying my head in my palms, but he just laughed as he pulled them from my red face.

"Keira, don't be embarrassed. It brought a lot of comfort to me at a time that I needed it the most." His hands held mine down so that I wouldn't hide from him and I gave up struggling.

"What do you mean?"

"I thought I had pushed you enough to hate me, so when I heard you whisper my name in your sleep in such a loving way, I knew you still held something more for me. I knew I was trying to stop this from happening, but I couldn't help the hope I felt. Of course, you said the name Williams, which was a name I hadn't heard before, so I started my research again."

"But I still don't understand even from that name, how you would have been able…" He cut me off with a mischievous grin.

"I knew where you were from ever since I played doctor the first time. I noticed the sweater you wore and that told me most of what I needed. Your father's name was under the college logo, so that gave me the place and a name." I thought back to that day not realising what I had given away just by wearing my dad's old football sweater.

"So, when I finally had the name Williams, it was the last part of the puzzle I needed. I found out that he had two daughters, one of whom was called Catherine. Of course, when I had your first name then the news about you followed. I cannot express the rage I was in for days when I started to read what happened to you. At first it was unclear… then I found all the news articles starting from when you first went missing right up until they found you. Then I demanded the case file."

"Demanded?" I asked wondering if there was anything this man would be refused.

"Let's just say that I know people in high places due to the nature of what I do, but that is another thing entirely. So once I got the case file, I knew the facts, but because you never gave a statement, which I still don't understand, I didn't yet know the story through your eyes. But it was no matter as I knew what he had done to you and that was enough for me to have his life taken," he said this so matter of fact that I coughed and tried to clear the lump in my throat as his words hung in the air like a gas I couldn't breathe.

"WHAT? You ordered to have him murdered?" I asked in horror!

"Yes of course... what else would you have me do? Keira, I couldn't let him live and breathe the same air as you after what he had done to you!" He looked as if this had been an obvious choice, but I couldn't believe he was talking about murder as if it was nothing but an everyday occurrence. I couldn't help my reaction as I moved away from him, making my body instantly grow cold from the separation.

"Keira, please... he needed to be punished! Do not look badly on me for this... come back to me," he said as his hands came out to me, but I moved out of the way, shifting over to the other side of the bed away from him. I just couldn't understand. I mean, sure I had wished Morgan dead a hundred times over. But that didn't mean when I was faced with it I would have! I had asked Draven to spare his life, which he hadn't done.

"Speak to me," he pleaded.

"Why would you do that? I mean he was sick and in the right place for his sickness! Don't you think that type of thing would be my choice to make? Who made you judge and executor?" I said but his face went stern from my reasons and obviously my question.

"Keira, I know you are good and pure of heart but look what happened. If I hadn't been here, you might have still been a prisoner to that insane parasite! And no, it wasn't just your choice to make! Imagine if roles were in reverse, would you look on kindly if someone had done this to someone you love... *like Libby?* Oh, and in regard to your question, it was God and the Devil themselves that granted me the right," he said, fully making his point, giving me no more reasons to be upset at the thought.

"I know you're right," I whispered regretfully, realising the magnitude of his position. After all, what would I have done to prevent such a thing happening to someone I loved, knowing I had the power to stop the horror before it even began? As soon as the words left my lips his hands flew out to me, sliding me under him, back where I belonged.

The warmth I found made me smile and then my grin felt the heat from his lips. His kiss was long and passionate as if he was sorry in case he had hurt my feelings. However, when his lips left me, I was left wanting as his taste in my mouth had me quickly craving something more. I ran my fingers through the back of his hair as I pulled him back to me, but he stopped above my mouth saying.

"I take it, I am forgiven?" Before giving me a smug smile.

"That depends," I said winking at him, and he caught my full meaning as he laughed, only instead of giving me what I wanted he rolled off me and rested on his side. I did my own version of a growl, which next to him sounded more than lame. But he found it hilarious making the bed shake under his laughter.

"Now that was adorable," he said as he poked me playfully, but I pouted making him say,

"Nope, still adorable!" So I flicked him again, this time on the shoulder and frowned.

"Okay, okay no more adorable but can I go for cute? Alright, I guess not!" he said as my flick turned into a little punch on the arm but considering his muscle, it felt like playfully hitting a brick, so I was surprised he folded so quickly.

"So are you going to continue explaining stuff or keep calling me daft names, like cute?" I was going for stern, but seeing as I couldn't keep the smile from my face, I doubted this was very effective.

"Anything my temptress. So, where was I before you... Umm what is it you say... *wigged out?*" As soon as he said this, he knew another punch was coming his way, so he blocked it by grabbing my fist in his palm before putting it around his back, so I was closer to him.

"So by the time my men got to the hospital it was too late, he had escaped. This news got to me when you left me after our argument in my office on Sunday. I wanted to take you that night, but Sophia convinced me this wasn't a wise move and said that she would take care of it. So she waited for you to get back off your *date,"* he said the word 'date' with bitter venom, and I remembered that day with the guy in the diner who was giving me evil glares…

It had been Draven.

"It wasn't a date!"

"Did he know that? Anyway, I watched your house all night, making sure you were safe, then I waited for you to come to the club. I knew I could keep you safe here, and since Halloween I knew the word was out about you and what you meant to me. So, because of this it would soon start to become dangerous for you to be on your own. That's when I decided to keep you here, even against your will… Of course you know how that went down." Now it was my turn to laugh as I remembered how I had done everything in my power to get away and now I would do the opposite, wanting to remain here in his arms forever.

"Yeah, sorry I was a little difficult."

"A little?" His hand ran up my naked side making me giggle as his fingertips tickled my skin.

"Behave!" I warned as I nestled down into my little nook by his shoulder and neck. I let out a sigh of utter bliss at the thought of what the last few days had brought and how this still didn't seem real. I had been wishing for this so hard that it felt like a dream that I never wanted to wake from.

As I curved into his body it felt as though I had never fit anywhere as well in my life. I knew I belonged here next to him forever, till the end of my time. Then the word time had me thinking, was my one lifetime enough? I knew it wasn't, but I would take it gladly and spend every day loving him with every fibre in my body.

The sound of his heartbeat and the gentle circles he was making on my back were making it difficult to keep my eyes open.

"Good night, my Keira," his voice whispered in my ear, adding to my sleepy state.

But my happy ending wasn't yet in my grasp, as I had thought…

I was just getting ready to fall into a deep world of paradise, as my lids were heavy after the longest night of my life...

When it seemed it wasn't quite over.

Vincent burst through the door making both of us jump with surprise. He looked horrified, and for a powerful Angel who had descended from a mighty bloodline, this was never a good sign.

"Dom, come quickly!" he shouted at him with an urgency that I had never heard Vincent use before.

"Vincent, what is it?" Draven automatically pulled my body closer to him as if I was his first priority.

"It's Takeshi, he has had another vision but, Dom, he is near death from it!" At this, Draven was up and round the bed dressed before I could register his arms leaving me.

"What was the vision?" he asked and Vincent looked back at me with the same worry in his eyes as Draven's.

"It is about the prophecy. Lucius knows about the girl and..." He glanced my way with worry marring his handsome face before he whispered, *"...he has started the hunt."*

This sent a shiver of fear down my spine as I had heard this name before. Lucius was Draven's equal... his *only* equal in power, but more importantly he was his mortal enemy!

"But Dom, there is something else you need to know. Layla has escaped." At this Draven let out a trademark blood-curdling growl, and I shivered as I realised why Draven didn't want to tell me what happened to Layla... she had been here all this time...

Imprisoned!

This was when I realised that my nightmare wasn't yet over. In fact, it was just beginning, as it seemed this was my price for loving Draven, as I started to fully comprehend what Vincent meant...

I was the one that was being hunted!

ABOUT THE AUTHOR

Stephanie Hudson has dreamed of being a writer ever since her obsession with reading books at an early age. What first became a quest to overcome the boundaries set against her in the form of dyslexia has turned into a life's dream. She first started writing in the form of poetry and soon found a taste for horror and romance. Afterlife is her first book in the series of twelve, with the story of Keira and Draven becoming ever more complicated in a world that sets them miles apart.

When not writing, Stephanie enjoys spending time with her loving family and friends, chatting for hours with her biggest fan, her sister Cathy who is utterly obsessed with one gorgeous Dominic Draven. And of course, spending as much time with her supportive partner and personal muse, Blake who is there for her no matter what.

Author's words.

My love and devotion is to all my wonderful fans that keep me going into the wee hours of the night but foremost to my wonderful daughter Ava...who yes, is named after a cool, kick-ass, Demonic bird and my sons, Jack, who is a little hero and Baby Halen, who yes, keeps me up at night but it's okay because he is named after a Guitar legend!

Keep updated with all new release news & more on my website
www.afterlifesaga.com
Never miss out, sign up to the
mailing list at the website.

Also, please feel free to join myself and other Dravenites on my
Facebook group
Afterlife Saga Official Fan
Interact with me and other fans. Can't wait to see you there!

facebook.com/AfterlifeSaga

twitter.com/afterlifesaga

instagram.com/theafterlifesaga

ACKNOWLEDGMENTS

Firstly, I would like to say huge thanks to all the readers out there that picked up Afterlife and especially the ones that took the time to let me know they loved it. You're all brilliant and make my day!

A massive thanks goes to my family and friends for your endless amount of support and for always having faith in me, you really are a force to be reckoned with!

I would like to thank my mum for her commitment to seeing that Afterlife was read the way it always was meant to with her meticulous editing. Also, to my sister who not only read the book about fifteen times but also made sure Afterlife looked the way it was always meant to with her fantastic and sexy front cover. They really are my biggest fans and as my sister often says, "It's easy to Crave the Drave!"

I would also like to say a big shout out to my Dad who loves the saga and has remained a constant strength in my life. The other strength in my life is my fiancée Blake, who has made working each day a pleasure I wake up to. The support he gives me and the saga is immeasurable and mirrors my own enthusiasm when giving life to my stories. He is my anchor in the storm that is my imagination and keeps me floating along the waves of discovery.

I love you my rock.

I would also like to thank bands like 30 Seconds To Mars, Shinedown, Foo fighters, Kings of Leon, Coldplay and so many others that helped me write the book of my dreams and inspired every word. If I was ever to pick an Afterlife theme song it would be the "Sound of Madness" by Shinedown which I listened to for hours on end during the writing of the "Battle" in the last couple of chapters.

Also by Stephanie Hudson

Afterlife Saga

Afterlife

The Two Kings

The Triple Goddess

The Quarter Moon

The Pentagram Child /Part 1

The Pentagram Child /Part 2

The Cult of the Hexad

Sacrifice of the Septimus /Part 1

Sacrifice of the Septimus /Part 2

Blood of the Infinity War

Happy Ever Afterlife /Part 1

Happy Ever Afterlife / Part 2

The Forbidden Chapters

*

Transfusion Saga

Transfusion

Venom of God

Blood of Kings

Rise of Ashes

Map of Sorrows

Tree of Souls

Kingdoms of Hell

Eyes of Crimson

Roots of Rage

Heart of Darkness

OTHER WORKS FROM HUDSON INDIE INK